The End of Gods

A Welcome to the Underworld Novel

Book 4

Con Template

Also by Con Template:

Welcome to the Underworld, Book 1
The Fall of Gods, Book 2
The War of Gods, Book 3
The End of Gods, Book 4

Cover Photo by: C.U. Con Template

Cover Illustration Design by: Dorothy Duong

Dedicated to *You*:

You who have been with TaeRi since the very beginning—even before you knew their names.

You who walked alongside TaeRi in their long journey and watched as they evolved into the couple they had become.

You who laughed, cried, and went through the obstacles of life with them as they grew up before your very eyes.

This entire story is dedicated to you, my Welcome to the Underworld reader, who has been *unconditionally* there for TaeRi from the very beginning—when they first sought Paris—*to the very end*, when they finally found Paris . . .

ACKNOWLEDGEMENTS

Firstly, this book is dedicated to my uncle Anthony, who passed away on February 2015. My uncle was like a second father to me and his sudden passing has devastated our family. To my beloved Uncle Anthony: I love you so much, and I will miss you everyday. Thank you for being there for everyone who needed you and for inspiring all of us. We will miss your sarcasm, your laughter, and most of all, we will miss your kind and generous heart. Thank you for being such an amazing uncle. We love you—always and forever.

As always, none of this would be possible without the love and support from my beautiful parents. Thank you to my incredible mother and father for always spoiling me with so much love and for enriching my life with so much laughter. Thank you to my sister for being an all around awesome human being and for being my version of "The Secret". You are a gift to have in my life. Thank you for being my sister! A big chunk of my gratitude also goes to Hoff-Hoff, Snyderman, Forever Young, Chief Little Fingers, and Waddup G for being my rocks during some of the most difficult times in my life. You guys rock, and you already know it. I want to also give thanks to Trinh, Fey, and Van for being such amazing friends. Brandon, Dearian, and Tiana: The three of you know why you're here. I love you all so much. Kevin N., I have not forgotten about you, little cousin. I miss you everyday and I hope that we can all reunite for Thanksgiving dinners soon. This book is for you as well. I love you with all my heart. Please stay safe, stay strong, and come home soon.

A massive "Thank You" is owed to my beloved beta readers: Jocelyn H., Anita Law, Anna Chanthakhoun, Annie Park, Ghetty Hilaire, Jamie Lee, My-Trinh Nguyen, Vivian T. Hoang, Yanny Zhang, Maria L. Loo, Joules, Tiffany H., Cindy Thi Cao, Shirley L., Theresa, Grace Suh, Liliane Wong, and Sandra. Thank you so much again for being so fun to work it and for always being so amazing to me and my beloved story! You're all so wonderful!

Thirdly, thank you to my graphic artist, Dorothy Duong. I can't believe we've reached the final book. As I said before, there will never be enough words to summarize the love and appreciation I have for you. Thank you for blessing Welcome to the Underworld with your talent and thank you for always inspiring me. You are an amazing graphic artist and an absolutely incredible friend. It's been an honor "kicking" all those ducks with you. Red velvet cupcakes again, Thy. You are the best!

Last, but never least, all my gratitude goes to my once-in-a-lifetime readers. Thank you for spoiling me and my stories with so much love and support. I could've never come this far without all of you. Whether you've been there from the beginning or have just started this adventure—thank you for joining me on this journey to "find Paris" all the same. Most importantly, thank you for allowing me to "con" your realities. You've been nothing but worth it.

Until Paris Fades,

Con

CONTENTS

Acknowledgments

0	The Beginning of Gods	6
1	The Lord of the Underworld	27
2	The Return of the Queen	44
3	The War Clause	58
4	'Till Death Do Us Part	70
5	The Rumblings of War	91
6	The Seduction of Gods	105
7	The Meeting of Gods	117
8	Flying Gods	124
9	Game of Preys	135
10	Reunion	142
11	Kwon Ho Young	158
12	The Queen's Forbidden Fruit	169
13	Intoxicated Gods	189
14	Home	197
15	Of Gods and Humans	208
16	The Lighthouse	217
17	Further South	229
18	Only Yoori	235
19	The Temptation of Gods	243
20	The Battle of Gods	252
21	War of the Underworlds	266
22	Royals Without a Throne	279
23	Every Stubborn Inch of It	286
24	Welcome to My Underworld	294
25	Perfection	297
26	I found Paris	317
27	Wherever You Go, I'll Follow	332
28	Two Steps from the Underworld	346
29	The Stadium	355
30	Kingdom of the Fallen Gods	367
31	The Darkest Hour	390
32	The End of Gods	400
33	You're Worth All of It	426
Epilogue	Until Paris Fades	446

"Once you're in, the only exit is death."

00: The Beginning of Gods

"Uncle Ju Won, what will we do when I come live with you?"

Holding her uncle's hand on the patio, ten-year-old An Soo Jin could feel her small body shake as her little pink princess dress danced along with the cold wind. The view of the infinity pool spilling into the night's horizon filled her vision, rendering her prisoner to its beauty. Soo Jin watched in awe as the twinkling city glowed like diamonds in the distant horizon, happily illuminating itself in the cold night.

Though every fiber of her body was urging her to return to the masquerade ball where it was warm, little Soo Jin was stubborn. She wanted desperately to talk to her uncle before the evening came to an end. Her father had told her weeks before that she was moving in with her Uncle Ju Won. Now that the deadline was fast approaching, Soo Jin wanted to find out what the fuss was all about. She wanted to understand why it was so important for her to live with him.

Soo Jin knew that if she wanted her answer, then this was the moment to ask. Her Uncle Ju Won was a busy man. She had to take advantage of this rare stolen moment with him.

Seo Ju Won smiled, slowly assuaging her curiosity as he took his eyes off the panoramic view.

"I will teach you everything I know," he enlightened, staring down at her like he would his own daughter. His eyes held love and adoration for the young girl. As she peered up at him with innocent brown eyes, Ju Won went on, pride pouring from his voice. "I will do everything in my power to make you the most infamous God this world will ever know, and after that feat is accomplished, you will be the one to carry on your family's legacy, my legacy, and the Underworld's legacy."

Soo Jin bunched her brows in confusion. There was so much in his answer that she didn't understand, the principal one being what he wanted to turn her into.

"God?" she voiced in perplexity. The concept didn't make sense to her. How could humans become Gods?

Ju Won nodded, releasing his hold on her hand. He bent his knees and squatted down in front of her. When his eyes were completely leveled with hers, he inclined his head towards the world inside his palatial mansion. At this prompt, Soo Jin followed his gaze and stared into the ballroom as well.

Ballroom music swayed in and out of the seven open windows surrounding the mansion on the mountain. All around her were people dressed in tuxedos and beautiful dresses. They were dancing along with the ballroom music, looking so regal that she could not help but feel like she was in a castle with royalty rather than at a simple party. To Soo Jin, there were no other groups more regal than the group of people in that very room. Even at that age, she was already aware of the power, influence, and wealth each individual possessed. Even at that young age, she admired them.

"In there are some of the most powerful people you will ever know," Ju Won whispered, sharing in her wonderment. Her eyes continued to admire the world within the ballroom as he spoke. "They are the pride of our elite world; they are the Royals of our world." He turned back to her, his determined gaze meeting hers. "Would it not be amazing to have them kneel before you, Soo Jin?"

Bewilderment overcame her at his odd inquiry. "Why me?"

Why would they kneel before her? What was so special about her?

Something stirred in Ju Won's once prideful eyes. The stern power that normally inhabited his gaze subdued subtly. It gradually became replaced with an emotion that mirrored sadness—regret.

"Did you know that I had a daughter?" he finally asked.

Soo Jin shook her head, surprised by this new information. He had never mentioned his daughter.

"She would've been eighteen this year," he told her quietly, his voice softer than she had ever heard it.

"What happened to her?" Soo Jin asked, curious as to why she had never met or heard of her uncle's daughter before.

The light in his eyes dimmed. Ju Won inhaled deeply, taking a moment to collect his own composure. He casted a quick glance into the distance before returning his attention to her. With heavy sadness in his voice, he said, "She died from cancer eight years ago."

Comprehension found its way into Soo Jin's blossoming eyes. "Is that who this party is for? Her?"

Ju Won gave a sad, confirming smile. "If Hye Sun was here, then she would've made her appearance in this world as a God. If she was alive, then tonight would've been the night where she would grace this world with her presence and be known as the Queen of the Underworld."

Now there was another term she didn't understand. "Queen of the Underworld?"

Her uncle nodded, cupping a hand over her right cheek with eagerness. The melancholy in his eyes morphed into resolve. Despite the tragedy of losing his daughter, he had found hope in the prospect of turning someone else he loved into a God. *"That's* what I'm going to turn you into, Soo Jin. I'm going to give you everything I could never give Hye Sun. I am going to train you to be a Queen, and in turn, you will rule over those people in there and be their God." He regarded the world before them again, relentless determination overpowering his face. "Don't you want to be the crown jewel of the world in there, Soo Jin? Don't you want to rule over the Kings and Queens in there and become an immortal legend in our world?"

Soo Jin was still confused with everything that he was telling her. "How will I become a God?"

At her question, Ju Won's once enthusiastic visage faltered slightly. Grimness darkened his features. As this occurred, the skies above were faltering with their tranquility as well. Soft rumbles disturbed the skies, indicating to those below that an unstoppable storm was about to commence.

"You will go through one of the most difficult ordeals anyone could ever dream of going through. Once you say yes, you're in it for life. There will be days where you will be in so much pain that breathing will feel like a burden rather than a blessing. There will be days where you'll wish you had chosen another life, and there will be days where you will pray to God for death." His eyes grew sterner, his features multiplying in solemnity. "The road will be agonizingly difficult, and you won't be able to escape from it. Once you're in, I will not let you quit. If you quit, then I will punish you for your weakness."

Soo Jin laughed, not even taking anything her uncle was telling her to heart. She was already so confused with everything else he was conveying to her. His last line about punishing her was too comical for her; it was simply too silly for her to take seriously.

"How will you punish me, uncle?" she inquired with a sheepish and innocent smile. "I've never even seen you mad at me."

Ju Won smiled sadly. He made an effort to soften his features. It was clear that he wanted to enlighten her, but he did not want to scare her.

"I don't want to punish you; I don't ever want to punish you," he assured her, his eyes genuine with confliction. "But this world that you're born into, it is different from the rest. It is a very powerful world, and a very strict one at that. I have the responsibility as an Advisor of this world to make sure that the future leaders of our society are the best leaders this world could have. I love you, but I am bound by the laws of this world—by my responsibility as an Advisor." He swallowed tightly, tilting his head while telling her something that broke his heart to share. "You will not get any special treatment, Soo Jin. If you show weakness—if you make the unforgivable mistake and show weakness to the entire Underworld—then I will show you the consequences of your weakness. You will not be forgiven, and you will be punished severely for your oversights."

For the first time in her life, ten-year-old Soo Jin felt pure fear slither through her body. She may not have been afraid of her uncle, but she was terrified of being punished by the world that he described. It seemed cruel and unforgiving. Her uncle looked so serious that even if a part of her still didn't believe he had the heart to punish her, there was a bigger part that was now apprehensive of that belief.

"I . . . I don't want to get punished," she said fearfully, truly meaning it.

He smiled, nodding his head. She gave him the exact answer he wanted.

"I know you don't, Soo Jin. I know you don't," he said vehemently, calming her with a reassuring voice. "All you have to do is train well, work hard, never give up, and keep your eyes on the prize, then you will be fine. Never disobey me, never disobey what the Underworld wants from you, and never disobey our bylaws. If you adhere to all of that, then you will never get punished. You will only be rewarded."

He turned towards his ballroom as a still-nervous Soo Jin nodded her head, feeling unease with the whole conversation.

"What is . . ." he prompted, his eyes scanning through the mansion.

Soo Jin's gaze followed his lead and trailed into the decadent ballroom. Her eyes wandered over the room before something arrested her complete attention. Her eyes zeroed in on her other uncle, Shin Dong Min. Her attention was not arrested because of her Uncle Dong Min; it was captivated because of *whom* her uncle was speaking to.

When she rested her eyes on the one her Uncle Dong Min was interacting with, Soo Jin felt an emotion she couldn't decipher surge through her.

Laughing merrily, Dong Min squatted down and hugged the young boy who simply fascinated Soo Jin.

Dressed in a black tuxedo, this boy was tall for his age, utterly striking, and he evoked nothing but attraction from Soo Jin (and she imagined the rest of the girls her age). For the first time in her young life, little Soo Jin could feel her heart race while butterflies began to flutter in her tummy. Suddenly, the conversation she had with her Uncle Ju Won seemed insignificant when vying for her attention with the hunky boy.

Oh my God, she thought dreamily, never before seeing someone who captured her attention as much as this cutie in front of her. In a matter of seconds, the fear she felt vacated. This handsome creature eclipsed all of her other thoughts. *He's so cute . . .*

Gazing unblinkingly at the boy as he spoke to Uncle Dong Min, a dazed Soo Jin could scarcely hear her Uncle Ju Won's voice as he finished the rest of his question, ". . . that saying your dad always lives by? The one he uses whenever he needs to remind himself that to get into a position of power, some actions are unavoidable?"

"'The best are never distracted,'" Soo Jin answered distractedly, her eyes glued on the cutie.

Ju Won smiled, his eyes settling on Soo Jin's father. The King of Scorpions stood in the center of the ballroom, laughing boisterously while interacting with his allies from Japan's Underworld. "Your father is like a younger brother to me. He's one of the best Kings I've ever had the pleasure of meeting. Learn from him, learn from me, and this world will fall to its knees for you."

Soo Jin was no longer listening to Ju Won. She was too preoccupied with admiring her newfound crush. As her response to Ju Won, she merely nodded distractedly, finding it hard to keep that dazed-like smile from forming on her lips when the boy started to laugh, his smile and laughter warming her heart.

Finally catching on to her distracted state, Ju Won chuckled and attempted to follow her line of sight. "What has gotten the Princess of Scorpions so smitten?" he teased. "Did a boy catch your eyes?"

"No!" Soo Jin answered immediately. She snapped out of her staring state. Her face was bright red. "I—I was just staring at a pretty dress."

Ju Won nodded, not pushing the matter any further. Soft sprinkles began to descend from the sky, reminding him that he had a party to get back to.

"I think I've taken up too much of your time, Soo Jin," he said, straightening his black suit after he stood up. "What we spoke about . . . we'll finish all of that later. For now, go run around and have lots of fun. Enjoy the rest of your night."

"Thank you, uncle," Soo Jin bid happily, beaming while she hugged him. Though she enjoyed being around him, she didn't enjoy being confused. More importantly, she wanted to distract herself with someone else who made her heart race faster than a runaway train. "Bye!"

With the determination of a hungry little mouse, an eager Soo Jin disappeared into the crowded ballroom, scampering through the sea of beautifully dressed people in hopes of being closer to the boy who had stolen her heart. She was beyond excited. She had no idea what she wanted to do. All she knew was that she wanted to keep staring at him. Perhaps she would even talk to him if she were brave enough!

Soo Jin was on the verge of getting close to him when someone grabbed her wrist.

"Lil sis, where have you been? I've been looking for you."

Her older brother, An Young Jae, who wore a black tuxedo and had his dark hair slicked back, was all smiles as he appeared before her and pulled Soo

Jin with him. He steered her in the opposite direction of where she wanted to venture off to find her crush.

"Why are you looking for me?" she squeaked out under the ballroom music, upset that her brother had foiled her chances of hanging out with her crush.

"I want to practice dancing, and you're going to practice with me."

"Me?" she cried, outraged by this impromptu development. She groaned and shook her head. She wouldn't have any of it. "But I don't want to! I want to dance with someone else!"

"You don't want to dance with me?" he asked, feigning hurt. "Well, too bad! You're going to!"

"Oppa!" she screamed as her older brother, who gave no concern to what she wanted, tugged at her arm and dragged her through the regal crowd that moved like waves in the ocean. "Oppa! No, no, no!" she repeatedly shouted. "I don't want to dance with you! You're so weird! I want to dance with that cute boy I saw!"

Soo Jin looked around vividly, searching for the cute boy. Her heart fluttered when she spotted him in the corner with a teacup in hand. He was so handsome. She wanted to run after him and talk to him, but her stupid big brother wouldn't stop dragging her away from the cutie.

"Come on, you dumb-dumb!" Young Jae shouted. He continued to tug her into the middle of the dancing crowd. "I need to practice so I can dance with my future wifey! After that, you can go find your future husband and dance with him."

"Why me?" Soo Jin whined petulantly. "Why do I have to dance with you?"

"Because you're my baby sister. That's what siblings do for each other!"

"Do what?"

"Have each other's back!" Young Jae preached like a shepherd on a mission. "I got yours and you got mine!" He laughed, pinching his baby sister's nose who, despite her own bitterness, would do this stupid favor and dance with him. He was, after all, her brother and she loved him. "You got my back right, lil sis?"

Soo Jin groaned, wanting to face-palm herself as they started to move cohesively with the music. "Okay, but only for a little bit. Then I'm going to go hang out with someone else."

Her brother laughed, not even bothering to tease his baby sister about her newfound crush. "Deal."

Though anyone else would have been relieved that her older brother wasn't teasing her about her crush, Soo Jin didn't feel that same relief. There was something off about her brother tonight. She gazed at him warily, her eyes forming into suspicious slits. In that instant, another thought came to her mind.

11

"Why am I *really* dancing with you?" she questioned at once.

"Because I have a question for you. I want to ask it without looking suspicious," Young Jae admitted, confirming her suspicions that her older brother had something more up his sleeve than simply wanting to practice dancing with his baby sister.

Anxious to expedite this "dance session" so that she could go hang out with the cutie, Soo Jin immediately asked, "What is it?"

He pointed over her shoulder. "You see that guy over there?"

Soo Jin followed his inconspicuous cue and attempted to trail after his gaze.

"Who?" she asked when she wasn't able to pinpoint who he was pointing out.

"That kid standing over there. He's talking with those Advisors in the corner," he said again, jerking his head to the right to cue her in the direction he wanted her to stare at. "Doesn't he sort of look like me?"

Soo Jin carelessly looked in the direction he pointed and spotted the kid her older brother was talking about. He wore a black tuxedo and had a buzz-cut. It was hard to miss him because in a crowd of formidable looking Advisors, he was the only kid in the area.

Soo Jin attempted to squint her eyes to make out his facial features in the distance. She failed horribly as the dimness of the ballroom did not aid in her endeavors. It also did not help that the boy was too far away. Moreover, she was too distracted with wanting to do other things. She didn't really care enough to see if the guy looked like her brother or not.

She couldn't see him too clearly, but Soo Jin was clever enough to deduce that if her brother came to ask her if she saw a resemblance, then it obviously meant that her older brother saw some similarities. Fully aware that being agreeable would be her ticket out of there, Soo Jin feigned concurrence.

"Yeah, a little bit."

Young Jae nodded approvingly, relieved that someone else acknowledged the resemblance. An expression of uneasiness enveloped his face when something unsettling came to mind.

"I asked dad, and he says that the kid doesn't look like me at all. He seemed annoyed that I was asking, but it's true, isn't it? The kid does look a bit like me." He shook his head, not comprehending his father's bizarre behavior. "Why would dad get annoyed with me for asking?"

"Daddy is looking for you, by the way," Soo Jin interrupted his thoughts, not even bothering to listen to whatever her older brother was rambling about. She recalled her father asking her to help find Young Jae before she became distracted with Uncle Ju Won.

Maybe this will get him to leave me alone, she thought naughtily, staring at Young Jae as his expression changed.

Her words caught her brother's attention. "Why?"

"Uncle Hayashi and Uncle Fukuji are here."

His eyes bloomed in exhilaration. "My Advisors are here?"

Young Jae laughed, putting thoughts about his lookalike aside. He loved his Advisors from Japan. Young Jae would never miss a chance to greet them if they were in the same vicinity.

"I have to go see them," he said expectantly, pulling himself away from her when the prospect of hanging out with his favorite uncles came to mind. "Thanks for the dance, little one. Later!"

Finally! Soo Jin exclaimed in her mind, pleased with herself that she had gotten rid of her brother.

Anxious to continue her pursuit before she was interrupted again, the determined little girl fought her way through the crowd and commenced the search for her hunk. To her dismay, this particular search was becoming more arduous. The lights had dimmed substantially, and there were a greater number of people on the dance floor now. Everywhere she turned, she was pushed from side to side, making it difficult for her to spot him. He was no longer in the place where she first saw him and with the happy chattering, lively music, and affluent people in masks everywhere, Soo Jin was disoriented with the pandemonium. Where was he?

A dejected Soo Jin was ready to give up on her quest when she reached the other side of the ballroom and felt her world pause in enthrallment.

Standing at the further end in a more secluded part of the ballroom, there her crush was, pouring another cup of tea while the world around her began to fade into the background.

Finally, Soo Jin thought in relief. She debated on whether or not she should run to the corner and hide so that she could stare at him from afar. However, a smaller and braver part of her urged her to go talk to him. *You don't meet someone like him every night,* that squeaky ten-year-old voice encouraged, giving Soo Jin the bravery she needed to disregard her shyness and approach him.

After fixing her dress so that she wouldn't appear unkempt, Soo Jin did her best to fight through her nervousness. She took one step forward, finally drawing closer to the one who had gotten her so smitten all night.

Here goes nothing . . .

"Hi . . ." Soo Jin timidly greeted, stepping close to the table where the boy was standing, drinking from his teacup.

At the call of her soft greeting, the boy turned. His captivating brown eyes settled on her with inquisitiveness, and Soo Jin felt her breath hitch. She took in his perfectly sculpted face, his short dark hair, his smooth skin, and the charisma that emanated effortlessly from him. He was even more handsome up close.

His curious eyes scanned her up and down, his gaze taking inventory of the pink dress she wore, her pink shoes, her curled black hair, and then her face. There was an air of guardedness to him. He was looking at her with a mixture of curiosity and suspicion—curiosity as to her identity and suspicion as to her motives for talking to him.

At the sight of this guardedness, Soo Jin offered him a sheepish smile, wordlessly telling him that she came in peace and that she wanted to be friends.

As if that sheepish smile from Soo Jin had melted the caginess he had, the once serious expression on his striking face thawed. He parted his lips and tentatively returned the greeting. "Hi."

So far so good, Soo Jin thought optimistically. Her face brightened with hope. Their relationship was already making progress. Unable to control her nervousness of being around someone as good-looking as him, Soo Jin unknowingly found herself swaying from side to side, her legs kicking air while she continued to talk to the boy.

"What are you drinking?" she initiated, attempting to appear super shy as she moved closer to him.

"Tea," he answered, his eyes inspecting her with interest, "but it's disgusting." His voice maintained its dry neutrality. He was still trying to figure out her motives for approaching him.

"Oh, okay." Soo Jin nodded and hoped that he would continue the conversation. She was disappointed when an awkward silence befell them. He still said nothing; he simply stared at her with his unreadable expression. It was as though he expected her to entertain him because she approached him first.

"So . . ." she initiated again, uncomfortable with the silence deluging over them. She was determined to get to know this cutie. It did not matter how hard he was making it for her. She had to persevere and steal his heart! They might well be on the road to being boyfriend and girlfriend if it all worked out, and she refused to give up. Hopeful with the prospect of that blossoming relationship, her mood perked up. She knew what to ask to move their relationship to a more friendly level. "What's your name?"

He didn't say anything. He merely took another moment to tilt his head and silently observe her like she was a new species of zoo animal he had come across. He was quiet for another lingering second before Soo Jin urged him to answer her with another one of her sheepish smiles.

Peering at her with calculating and sly eyes, he cleared his throat and casually said, "Boss."

"What?" Soo Jin's composure disintegrated at the oddball answer from the cutie. She stopped swaying from side to side and stopped kicking air. She gaped at him in shock. Soo Jin knew it was complete bullshit. No one in their right mind, especially in the Underworld, would call their kid that name.

"What?" he asked, unperturbed by her outraged response. Though his voice was untroubled, his expression changed. There was now a poorly hidden expression of amusement on his face. It was evident he was proud of himself for breaking through the "I'm-a-nice-shy-and-soft-spoken-girl" act that Soo Jin was fostering. It was obvious that he found entertainment in seeing her for the sassy girl that she was. He hid a smile while he continued his efforts to provoke Soo Jin to show her true colors. "My dad's bodyguards call him 'Boss' and I want to be called that too, so I'm telling you my name is Boss."

Soo Jin gaped at him like he was the strangest person she had ever met. Then, she began to shake her head judgmentally. She was utterly disappointed. It would make sense that the beautiful boy she was crushing on would wind up to be dumb and strange. Why couldn't he be a gorgeous genius?

"Well," she replied, unable to conceal the meanness in her judgmental voice. "My daddy calls me 'Princess', but you don't see me introducing myself as 'Princess', do you?"

"Yeah," the hunky one agreed, inspecting her up and down. "You look more like a maid anyway—like someone's assistant or something."

Two pink circles formed on Soo Jin's cheeks. "An *assistant*?"

She was beside herself. And to think she thought this mean boy was cute!

Biting her lips to keep from cursing at him, Soo Jin felt her eyes twitch in anger. She was feigning niceness when she first met him because she wanted to impress him. However, everything had shot to hell because he brought the worst out of her. And unfortunately for him, the worst out of Soo Jin was a spoiled little brat who wasn't polite to anyone who made fun of her.

Unable to resist some form of retaliation, her small hand raised up and with much resentment, she bestowed him with the middle finger that did all the cursing for her.

The hunky one frowned. "Wow, you're a little brat, aren't you?"

"You were the one being a snob first," she retorted, bringing her hand down. Her face was molded into a scowl. So much for finding her future hubby in this guy. He was such a jerk! No longer keen on being around the disappointment that was her failed relationship (or could-have-been relationship), Soo Jin let out a scoff and turned away from him. She didn't have time for this. If he didn't plan on being nice, then she would return the favor. "Whatever. Peace out, *jerk-face.*"

"Okay, no, I'm just kidding. I'm just kidding!" he swiftly amended, wrapping his hand over her wrist when he saw that she was leaving. The hunk had seemingly found himself interested in little Soo Jin. He wasn't about to let his newfound distraction get away. "I wasn't serious about you being someone's maid. You look too cute to be someone's maid."

Soo Jin wasn't having any of it. She knew he was lying about her being cute. This made her angrier. "No! Let me go, you liar!"

"Okay, okay," he appeased, irritated and overwhelmed by her. His demeanor showed that he wasn't the type of boy who compromised with anyone too easily. Despite this, he was willing to negotiate with her. "How about this, how about this," he proposed quickly, trying to calm her overdramatic tantrum. "I'll call you Princess, and you can call me Boss. Can we do that?"

This caught Soo Jin's attention. She had always wanted to be called Princess by someone other than her dad, and being called Princess by this cute boy would fulfill that desire. She glanced at him, her mind churning with what she should do.

He was quiet, staring at her expectantly.

Despite the arrogance streaming out of him, it did look like he was genuinely apologetic. It wouldn't hurt to forgive him, right? She regarded him with sneaky eyes. Her face lit up when she deduced that he was willing to do anything to make her stay. That thought in mind, it wouldn't hurt if she—

"Say Princess is better than Boss," she ordered suddenly, wanting to punish him for upsetting her.

Mystification stole his visage. "*What?*"

He was confounded. She knew the guy was prideful and snobby. He'd rather pound his head against the wall than admit someone was better than him. This was why she insisted on him saying that. She wasn't going to let him get away with calling her an assistant. She planned on making him eat his words.

"Say it," Soo Jin commanded firmly, her voice unbending. When he refused, she proceeded to shove him as an added threat that she would leave if he didn't. "Say it!"

"Okay!" he conceded, exasperation marked all over his face. "Princess is better than Boss! Are you happy now, you little brat?"

Soo Jin nodded happily, pleased that he was letting her win. Though she was annoyed with him and his crass personality, she had to admit that there was a certain charm about him that she really liked. He was cute and despite his jerkiness, she still wanted to hang out with him. There was something about his personality that completely complemented hers.

"Lift your dress up," he ordered, snapping her out of her reverie.

Soo Jin's eyes widened like saucers. "Huh?"

The boy rolled his eyes at her reaction.

"Oh, come here, smart one," he muttered softly, pulling her with him. He guided her hands to the sides of her dress and showed her what he meant when he lifted the first layer of fabric on her multi-layered dress.

"I'm bored," he said, motioning for her to hold the top fabric of her dress up, "and you're going to help get rid of my boredom."

"By doing what?" she squeaked out, watching in amazement as he began to gather an assortment of tea packages, cups, and sugars. He started to deposit them all onto the top layer of the fabric she was stupidly holding up.

Soo Jin was mystified. She had planned on telling him that she wasn't going to help him carry all this stuff like she was his lowly assistant. However, when he suddenly cupped her face and stared into her eyes, Soo Jin felt those strong convictions fade away.

"I want to hang out with you, but I have to hide so we have to go somewhere else, okay?" he whispered, eliciting another round of butterflies in Soo Jin's tummy at the feel of his touch.

She melted like butter on hot toast. *He's so hot!*

"So in a bit," he continued, "we're going to run really fast and not have anyone spot us, okay? Are you with me?"

Soo Jin nodded vehemently. This guy was as strange as strange could be, but she couldn't deny that she was enthralled with him and his peculiar ways. If he had to hide—and if she could only hang out with him if she hid too— then she would gladly hide with him.

"Okay," he said, bringing his hands down. He turned to retrieve two huge teapots from the table. He smiled at her and motioned his head for the escape plan to commence. "Let's disappear."

With shifty eyes, Soo Jin and the boy poked their heads out from around the corner. They stared at the swarm of people occupying the ballroom and with the speed of two little cheetahs, made their flight through the distracted masquerade crowd.

Huffing and puffing, they swept across the room, their faces shrouded with determination. They skidded past little Lee Ji Hoon as his father and Shin Jung Min were introducing him to other Advisors in the 2nd layer. They ran past Ju Won as he spoke to Soo Jin's father. They flew past the King of Serpents and his wife as they spoke to Shin Dong Min, and they dashed past Young Jae as he introduced himself to Kwon Ho Young.

All around them, their world continued to move forward, unaware that the two ten-year-olds were scampering away, slowly disappearing into their own world.

"Hurry up, *Princess!*" the hunky one coaxed from behind Soo Jin. He struggled to maintain the steadiness of the teapots after they made a turn for the outdoor patio.

"I'm trying!" she cried, finding difficulty with balancing all the cargo on the fabric of her dress. As they bounced towards the doors that led out to the outside world, Soo Jin's eyes broadened when she observed that the heavens had opened up, bringing forth rain that was splashing every which way.

"Hey!" Soo Jin announced, stopping before she reached the outside patio. She peered up at the downpour of rain in amazement. "Hey *Boss*! It's raining outside!"

"Aw, damn it!"

Stopping beside Soo Jin, the hunky one struggled to stabilize the two teapots he was holding. He followed her gaze and stared up at the rain falling from the bejeweled night sky above. Disappointment marred his young face. When it appeared as if he was ready to curse the fates, his once dejected eyes illumed with life after he spotted something in the corner of the patio.

Soo Jin followed his line of sight. Her eyes enlarged when they settled on an enormous black table that sat on the marble floor in the distance. Albeit rain was pitter-pattering on the surface, the world beneath it remained dry and completely sheltered from the rain.

The hunky one smiled, turning back to her. At that moment, Soo Jin knew that he had an alternative plan, which would allow them to stay outside.

"Do you want to go back inside," he asked her, the tone of his voice indicating an awareness of what her answer would be, "or do you still want to hang out with me?"

"I want to hang out with you . . . only because I want to see what we're going to do with all of this," Soo Jin replied easily, deducing from the gleam in his eyes that sitting underneath the table was the alternative plan to protect themselves from the rain. Under normal circumstances, she would not bother to head outside in this rain. Nevertheless, she had already come this far with him. She wasn't going to leave, not when all the fun was about to begin.

With a mischievous smile to one another and a final nod of confirmation, the two children sprinted across the damp patio, their small shoes clacking over the opulent marble floor of Ju Won's mansion. Soo Jin was still holding the top fabric of her dress up, fighting to stabilize the supplies they looted from the masquerade ball. Behind her, the hunky one was still trying to balance the two huge teapots to keep them from spilling all around him. Splashes of rain kissed their heads and ran down their bodies. Although they were getting damp, the rain couldn't soak them fast enough as they ran like there was no tomorrow.

Both expelled an air of relief when they finally reached the table. They wasted no time and began to work together to deposit their stolen treasures underneath it. After that was done, the hunky one slid underneath the table to shift items away in order to make room for Soo Jin. Once he was fully situated, he immediately reached his hand out, helping Soo Jin slide under their rain shelter. With self-satisfied grins that they had outsmarted the weather, they made themselves comfortable underneath their newfound sanctuary. The two ten-year-olds sat with their legs crossed, their backs against the wall, and their faces shrouded with excitement. After a breath, they began to check out their stolen goods while the rain fell melodically around them.

"What are we doing with all of this?" Soo Jin asked as she moved all the various tea packages to one corner and the sugars to the opposite corner.

"I want to find a tea I like, so I'm taste-testing all of it."

"Oh! Is that why you had a teacup all night?"

He looked at her bizarrely, clearly wondering how she knew he was holding a teacup the whole time. Soo Jin, much to her own horror, gave him a strange look as well. She belatedly realized that she had unknowingly admitted that she had been stalking him throughout the night. Even though he was slightly perturbed by her eccentricity, the boy didn't delve deeper into how Soo Jin knew he had a teacup with him the entire night.

Instead, he casually said, "Since you helped me carry all this stuff here, you can help me decide what tastes good and what can be my new favorite tea."

Soo Jin grinned in delight. She nodded, both grateful that he didn't delve into that embarrassing topic and grateful that he wanted her to do this tasting with him. She had never drank tea before and doubted she would like it, but who cared? She had never hid underneath a table during a rainstorm with a cute boy before either!

"Okay."

Soo Jin began to take each tea flavor out of its respective can. Beside her, the hunky one carefully poured hot water from the teapot into one of the many cups they looted. Once each flavor of the chosen tea leaves was placed into its own cup, Soo Jin and the boy pressed their backs closer against the wall, stared admiringly at Ju Won's rain-soaked garden, and enjoyed their taste-testing.

"Why are you hiding?" Soo Jin asked him after they sipped three different flavors that they didn't like. Her face twitched in aversion after tasting the most recent tea. She quickly handed the cup to the boy to taste-test.

Although the drumming of the rain had picked up in intensity during their time outside, the rhythmic drumming became something like a lullaby to their ears. It did well to drown out the crowd within the palatial mansion and the existence of the lively world around them. All that existed in their serene world was the rain, the breathtaking view of the vista before them, the teas, and each other.

Grabbing the cup she handed him, the boy brought the teacup to his lips, tasted the tea, and scrunched up his face in immediate distaste. He dumped the tea out of the cup before answering her. "Because my dad is going to be looking for me soon."

Soo Jin slanted her head in curiosity. "Do you not like your dad?"

"No, I like him. I like him a lot," he assured, handing her another flavor to try out. "It's just . . . it's just that I'm going to miss my family."

A part of her heart ached at the depression in his voice. Grabbing the cup, but not yet drinking from it, she probed him for more information. "What do you mean?"

There was a brief expression of despondency on his face. He took a second to bite his lips before answering her.

"Tonight is my last night here," he told her while motioning for her to drink from the teacup. "In a bit, I'll be leaving."

Aware that drinking quickly from the cup would merit the conversation to flow faster, Soo Jin swiftly taste-tested the new flavor. She handed the cup back to him while asking, "Where are you going?"

It was silly, but she could feel a sinking sensation manifest inside her at the thought of him leaving her.

He grabbed the teacup from her and sighed. His voice became the melody that harmonized with the rain. "My dad said that because I'm growing up, I have to be trained to be a man. He's going to send me to visit his friends from all over the world. He said that they will teach me the ways of the world, turn me into a man, and that when I'm ready, I'll come back and become trained on how to be better than a man. Then I'll be able to rule over this world as a God amongst men."

Soo Jin raised her brows. Astonishment heaved through her when she registered that he had been given the same pep talk that Uncle Ju Won had given her. Though the words differed, the meaning was the same. It amazed her to discover that there was someone else going through the exact same thing. Along with that astonishment came jealousy. She was envious that he would get to travel the world while she had to stay in Korea and be trained here. She was jealous of him, but that emotion was fleeting when she took inventory of the apprehension in his demeanor as he drank his tea. He looked brave—a trait she imagined he would retain as he grew to become a man—but she sensed his trepidation all the same.

Unable to help herself, she asked, "Are you scared?"

He appraised her, his features surprised that she caught the emotion he didn't physically show. There was an edge of guardedness in his eyes that told her he didn't plan on answering her. Yet, as he stared deeper into her big brown eyes, his expression softened and the walls he held up came down. He slowly nodded, the weight of the world seemingly resting on his shoulders.

"When my older brother came back to visit during his first year of training, he was different. I mean, he's still the same. He's still nice, he still protects me, and I still love him . . . but he changed. He had bruises all over his face, he was limping, and he looked tired and sad all the time."

Soo Jin's own memory flashed before her eyes. She remembered Young Jae and how physically torn up he was after his first year of training. It was so bad that he had some facial surgeries for the serious injuries.

The boy went on, taking a sip from the teacup. "I don't want to train, but if I have to so that no one hurts my family, so that I can protect my family like my dad protects us, then I'll do it. I'm not scared of getting hurt; I'm scared of becoming different. I like who I am right now; I'm really happy right now. I don't want to change." He smiled apprehensively, handing her another teacup before he deposited some tea leaves into the pot between them. "My dad said that my brother was like that too—that he was afraid. He said it's only normal that I'm afraid because it means I'm human. He said that anyone who trains to become better than human would be afraid and hate what they're going through. But he also told me that all of it would be worth it. He said that once the training was over, nothing but great things will come to our family. Nothing but great things will come to me—that once I was done, everyone would kneel before me."

"That's what they say to me too," Soo Jin finally shared, her fingers nervously playing with the various teacups filled with remnants of flavors they didn't like.

The boy turned to her, his face rife with confusion. He arched an inquisitive brow. "What do you mean they say that to you too?"

"I'm leaving too," she answered quietly, purposely being vague because she didn't want to tell him that she was staying in Korea instead of being cool and traveling the world like him. They were being "trained" to be better than humans, but even then, Soo Jin knew her training was going to be much different from his. "But I'm leaving tomorrow, not tonight like you."

Interest teemed in his gaze. Now it was his turn to ask all the questions. "Where are you going?"

"Away," she answered elusively. It occurred to her how afraid she was. She didn't grasp how scary all of this was until he mentioned *his* fears. Soo Jin didn't want to change either. She liked who she was right now. "To learn how to fight, to protect my family, to have great things come to me, and to have people kneel before me."

His face was veiled with disbelief after he processed what she was telling him. "But you're a girl."

Even though that statement could have easily been taken wrong, Soo Jin knew he wasn't insulting her in a derogatory way. He was simply stating his shock.

"I'm going to be a special girl," she merely told him, not knowing herself why, out of all the possible Underworld heirs, her Uncle Ju Won chose her to live with him and train with him. As Soo Jin became distracted, she mindlessly stuck another type of tea leaf into the teapot, unaware that the boy had already added something in. "I think I might live forever if I work hard and train right."

The boy was ready to nod in understanding at the last of her words. He was about to say some comforting words after hearing the sadness in her small voice. He was about to do all those nice things, yet, when he heard her close the lid over the ceramic teapot, all those good intentions obliterated. It occurred to him that she had unknowingly placed random tea leaves into the teapot that he already placed his own tea leaves into.

"What are you putting into the teapot?!" he shouted, causing Soo Jin to jump in surprise, completely knocking her out of her solemn thoughts.

As quick as they were to open up to each other about their fears, the two children were also quick to be distracted when their hotheaded personalities came into play.

Pissed off at him for scaring her, her eyes burned with rage. Her fear of training to become a God was long gone. All that existed was her bitterness towards him.

"Don't yell at me!" she cried back, not even processing that she was adding some other random stuff into his tea until it was too late. Though she should've paid attention, the jerk didn't have to react so dramatically. Annoyed, she threw the remainder of the random tea leaves into the pot just to piss him off some more. "What's so special about your teapot that I can't add things into it? I helped carry all of this here, didn't I?"

"Those were our last tea flavors, smart one," he argued back, outraged with her behavior. "We haven't enjoyed any of the tea. Now you've ruined our chance of enjoying these last two. Good going." To dramatically make his point, he threw a touch of German rock cane sugar into the teapot as well. It was like he was saying, "*Since you already screwed up the tea, I might as well screw it up some more.*"

"I hope you enjoy this last tea because we have no more to taste-test after this mutant one."

"Do your worst," Soo Jin retorted bravely, lining up two teacups beside the teapot that was now immersed with mutant tea. Though she was nervous to drink this tea mix, she wasn't about to chicken out. She participated in helping pollute it; it was only right that she learned how badly it had been messed up. "But if it tastes bad, it's because *you* added that weird sugar cube thingy."

The boy rolled his eyes at her shady attempt to take the accountability off herself. With no more delay, he began to pour the contents of the teapot into the teacups. When the tea filled to the brims, they picked up their respective cups. They gazed nervously at one another, and with much hesitation, as if whispering prayers to not die after drinking this tea mix, each took a sip and then . . . something *heavenly* happened.

All the synapses in Soo Jin's brain sparked up as the taste of this blissful tea graced her tongue and swam down her throat. Her eyes illumed as the most delicious thing she had ever tasted lit up every part of her body. She eagerly gazed up and saw that the hunky one had the same reaction. Staring dumbfounded at the teacup, he smiled incredulously at her. Their smiles confirmed it all: this mutant tea was the most delicious thing they had ever tasted. It tasted like heaven.

Already getting over their nonsensical bickering, the two children were now lost in a peaceful state as they quietly drank from their teacups and stared out into the beautiful, panoramic view. There was a companionable silence that surrounded them in the hushed ambiance. Although Soo Jin hadn't known this boy for that long, she couldn't deny the connection she had with him. They knew when to be serious with one another, they knew when to honestly share their feelings with one another, and they knew how to distract one another from the dark possibilities of their scary futures.

"If you had a choice and you could go anywhere," the boy suddenly prompted, still gazing at the majestic garden and the twinkling city behind it, "where would you go?"

Soo Jin shrugged, her eyes roaming over their pretty surroundings. She truly didn't know the answer to that question.

"I don't know." She took a sip from her teacup, transferred her eyes from the rain-drenched world, and focused her sole attention on him. "How about you?"

The coffee brown eyes she loved so much held her prisoner for a brief moment. "I don't know either." Another breath of silence suspended above them before he thoughtfully added, "My parents just came back from Paris though."

Soo Jin canted her head in interest. She had never heard of "Paris" before. "Where's that?"

"In France."

"Why did they go to Paris?" she asked, knowing deep in her heart there was a reason why he brought Paris up. "What's so special about it?"

The boy smiled, taking note of the interest in her eyes. Quenching her curiosity, he took it upon himself to enlighten her about the significance of Paris.

"My dad says that Paris is the city of love. If you want to win a woman's heart, then you have to take her to Paris—you have to *show* her Paris." His smile grew slightly wider as he thought about the future when he might be able to travel there. "I might go there when I'm older, when I have a girl I want to take."

"That sounds nice," Soo Jin commented whimsically, locking her gaze with his.

She didn't know what Paris was or what it looked like, but she imagined it must be nice if it could help a guy steal a girl's heart. She also imagined it must be nice if the simple conversation about it warmed her insides and lifted her spirits. She wanted to go. She wanted to see Paris.

"Yeah, it would be nice," he responded, finding it hard to take his eyes off of her just as she found it hard to take hers off of him.

Although the insistent tapping of rain had decreased in volume, the residual water continued to drip from all four corners of the table. The remnants of water on the marble floor were threatening to pile up and move towards the area in which the children were sitting. Despite the fact that Soo Jin knew all too well that the world was trying to divert them from their stolen moment together, she couldn't help but tempt the fates and sit there a little while longer with this fascinating boy. She could get her dress a little wet. This nice, safe feeling was too special. She had never felt this way before. She wanted it to last for as long as possible.

A gust of cold air moved between them before he parted his lips and asked the question he should've asked her when they first met. "So, what's your name—?"

Before he could finish his question, the melodic chiming of midnight emitted from Ju Won's clock. The sound drifted from inside the mansion and coursed into their ears, effectively snapping the children out of their dream world. It was soft in sound, but powerful enough in decibels to indicate to Soo Jin and the boy that it was time to part ways. *Their borrowed time with one another was over.*

"I have to go," he told her, a tinge of regret touching his eyes that he couldn't hang out longer. While it was evident that he'd rather spend more time with her, the young boy didn't appear to be the type who would neglect his responsibilities to his family—or to his father's plans for him. He allowed himself to be distracted momentarily, but never entirely.

Soo Jin nodded, already sliding out from beneath the table. "Yeah, I should go too."

Her dad always took her and her brother home early during any Underworld events. Midnight was typically the time when he would begin to look for them. She imagined that since the big day that she was to move in with her Uncle Ju Won had arrived, her dad must have been looking for her to take her home. Much like the boy beside her, Soo Jin wasn't the type of child who neglected her responsibilities, especially ones pertaining to her future.

Straightening up beside the table while still holding their respective teacups, Soo Jin and the boy could feel the soft sprinkles of rain dust over them, embellishing their heads and clothes. It was raining, but it was not raining hard enough that they felt that they had to find shelter right away. If anything, Soo Jin enjoyed standing out in the rain with him. It felt nice.

"Well, thanks for saying hi," the boy told her, staring briefly at his teacup before returning his gaze to her. It was clear he didn't enjoy bidding farewell to her. "I was really bored for a while, so I'm glad I kinda had fun with you."

She laughed, glad that he wasn't being overly mushy. It allowed her to thank him without becoming a cheesy fangirl. "Thanks for being mean. It gave me a chance to be myself."

Swallowing tightly, the boy forced a smile to form on his lips while he did something that he obviously didn't want to do: he began to make the move to leave. "Maybe I'll see you around."

She nodded, forcing herself to smile as well. Then, Soo Jin did something she didn't want to do either: she mirrored his efforts and began to distance herself from him.

"Maybe," she replied as they moved further and further away from one another.

She moved into the direction of the east wing, where she was sure her father would be, and the boy moved into the direction of the west wing, towards the direction of the exit and where she was sure his family awaited him.

"Good luck," she added as her small feet stepped across the puddle on the marble floor.

She hadn't forgotten what he was leaving to train for, and she truly wished him luck. She hoped that his wish would come true and that he wouldn't change too much after being trained. She also really liked the person he was right now.

"You too," he replied softly, his pace slow and hesitant.

Sighing to himself, the boy gave her a final wave. With much effort, he then turned on his heels and began to swiftly walk away, his head turning back every now and then to watch Soo Jin depart to the opposite wing.

He did not know then how much his and her life would change after that night. They had no idea then that the memory of briefly meeting each other would fade away in their subconscious as the shadows of the Underworld took over and plagued their reality. They had no idea that the innocence little Soo Jin possessed would be tainted as she became the first revered Queen in the Underworld—that the innocence the boy once possessed would fade away as he became one of the greatest Kings in the Underworld.

Casting one final glance at him as he disappeared into the other entrance of the ballroom, Soo Jin could feel the weight of the teacup tremble in her small hand.

Maybe, she thought before she disappeared into the ballroom and immersed herself in a crowd of people who would end up kneeling before her in the distant future. *Maybe someday it will all work out*, she reasoned, spending her last night as an innocent ten-year-old girl before she became the most powerful Queen in the Underworld.

Maybe someday, it'll all work out, and I'll meet him again.

"You can run..."

01: The Lord of the Underworld

Present Day

In every Kingdom, every government entity, and every exclusive society, there are Advisors chosen to uphold the mentorship of great leaders. They are entrusted to help these great leaders adhere to the principles of their world and garner the undisputed respect of the very people these great leaders are meant to govern.

In the Korean Underworld, this revered group of Advisors are known notoriously as Shin Dong Min, Shin Jung Min, and finally, the eldest and most high-ranking Advisor of all—Seo Ju Won.

There were few in the past who had ever held as much influence as Seo Ju Won and few in the future who would ever acquire as much power as the one they called, "The Creator of Legends". Having once been a revered King in the 3rd layer, a formidable business tycoon in the 1st, and finally being the most celebrated Advisor the 2nd layer had ever known, Ju Won was the epitome of an Underworld legend. In short, because he was the chosen Advisor for the Underworld, his support was considered infallible to any King who wished to swing the pendulum of power in his direction.

Seo Ju Won's support wasn't absolute in a society where the powerful stood beside each other in great numbers, but because the majority respected his judgment immensely, his decisions were rarely questioned. They trusted that in the end, the eldest Advisor would always ensure the harmonious wellbeing of the Underworld as a whole.

This was the reason why, as the King of Serpents and the King of Skulls made their way through the palatial castle that housed the unforgettable 65th birthday party for the legend himself, Ju Won's birthday was the most crucial event of the year. It wasn't the simple fact that the Underworld was celebrating the marking of another healthy year for this revered legend, but it was because this revered legend, who had been entrusted by the majority of the Underworld to mentor a great leader, was about to anoint the new heir to his empire, and in turn, subtly let the entire Underworld know who would be his pick to be the first true Lord of the Underworld.

And what an epic decision that would be.

The fight between the two Kings, if the Underworld society had anything to say about it, had been one of the most historic battles this world had ever seen. There had never been Kings who were younger, more skilled, or more ruthless than the two reigning Kings. The battle had been long and hard, and no one but the two young Kings could've been more relieved that the waiting period was over.

No one could have looked more anxious than Kwon Tae Hyun, who not only appeared as if he was ready to conquer the world, but in certain vantage points, as he swept across the massive room, speaking to his peers, associates, and mentors with his younger sister by his side, it also appeared as if the great King was distracted with something else. Some would even dare say that he was upset and troubled over *someone*.

This small disturbance in the otherwise perfect demeanor of the great King was only completely extricated when he latched on to his baby sister's arm and pulled her away from the influential crowd in annoyance.

Kwon Hae Jin's face was cloaked with the utmost rage.

Since his arrival at the party, Hae Jin had been following him like a condemning shadow, whispering curses of revulsion towards him and finally garnering his undisputed (and aggravated) attention when she threatened to make a scene in front of everyone if he didn't cease ignoring her.

Never one to risk compromising his coveted throne—*especially* when he was so close to acquiring it—Tae Hyun, with an artificial smile plastered on his face, bid goodbye to his high-ranking mentors and heeded his sister's verbal threat. He didn't look happy to do it, but he heeded it nonetheless.

"How could you do this?" Hae Jin chastised, fighting against his strong grip. Her white pumps shuffled onto the gold tiles while she walked with him. "What the fuck is wrong with you?"

The rotunda shaped room they stood in, along with more than a thousand of the Underworld's most revered elites, was the grandest and largest room in Ju Won's extravagant estate. Everything that graced the interior of the room was first-rate and top of the line.

The room was adorned with gold-toned marble tiles that had intricate, crème-toned patterns running through the ground floor. Gold plated pillars supported the six-story-high ballroom and hugged across the majestic space. A decadent, diamond-like chandelier hung from the high ceilings, illuminating the world below. Behind the chandelier, the glass ceiling held the beauty of the dark skies and the peaceful night stars in its hands. The celebratory music from the grand piano filtered in and out of the six-story-high windows that wrapped around the rounded ballroom, showcasing the vibrant city surrounding it.

Power and prestige rippled amongst the ocean of professionally dressed men and women gathered on the ground floor. Whether it was on the grand gold staircase or the various balconies that surrounded the rotunda ball, everywhere guests turned, they would be greeted with the sight of the most powerful figures in the country.

It was truly an event fit for royalty, especially with the three sets of thrones residing in the already decadent ballroom. The thrones were there to follow the old traditions of the Underworld, a respectful seating arrangement for the eldest Advisor and the Kings of the 3rd layer.

Placed purposely on a red, carpeted platform with five steps of stairs leading up to it, a magnificent gold throne for the eldest Advisor claimed one side of the rotunda room while the King of Skulls' seat sat in another section of the room. This grand seating arrangement was finished off with the King of Serpents' seat being placed in the further section of the room, adjacent to the King of Skulls' and parallel to Ju Won's seat. In the final corner of the room laid a large podium that had the backdrop of the city behind it. It was the stage where Ju Won would make the speech everyone had waited years to hear.

At the moment, all the seats, which resonated supremacy and prestige, were empty as the Advisors and Lee Ji Hoon were busy conversing with the rest of the Underworld populace in attendance, and Kwon Tae Hyun was preoccupied with speaking to his little sister.

With his hand still on her arm, he continued to steer her with him until they reached a large pillar. They stood behind it, hidden under the shadows and veiled by the music that waltzed around the busy ballroom.

"Hae Jin, stop it," Tae Hyun reprimanded firmly, pulling her closer to the red and gold drapes that hung down from the high windows like a waterfall.

He averted his eyes from her and took a moment to scan their surroundings to make sure that no one was staring in their direction. When he concluded that the coast was clear with the ground floor, he gazed up at the dark ceilings where the balconies sat above them. He assessed the darker, canvassed areas where he knew Ju Won's many snipers were hidden in the shadowy corners of the ceiling. When it was palpable on his expression that, at the moment, no one could eavesdrop on them, he turned back to his sister.

"Keep your voice down."

Fuming, Hae Jin, dressed in a black knee-length, formal business dress that had a white suit jacket layering over it, ripped her arm out of his grasp.

"I went to her for you," she continued to say, disregarding his command to keep her voice down. "When she should've never forgiven you for the crap you pulled because she resembled An Soo Jin!"

A muscle tightened in Tae Hyun's jaw, but Hae Jin paid no mind to it, for she didn't realize she was never privy to the truth that her brother's ex-girlfriend, Choi Yoori, was actually the revered Queen of the Underworld, who somehow acquired amnesia three years ago. She did not simply resemble An Soo Jin; she *was* An Soo Jin.

Oblivious to this and blinded by rage, she went on. "I went to find her at the library. I told her how much you cared about her and how much she meant to you. I went to her for you and pleaded with her to forgive you because you were hurting. She came back to you under the belief that she meant something to you, and you do this? You kicked her out of the country? Are you *fucking* serious?"

"You don't know what happened, so stay out of this," he snapped, furious that she had to remind him of his *ex*-girlfriend.

"Did she get too emotional for you, big brother?" Hae Jin accused. Pain drenched her angry voice as she stared up at her brother with reproachful eyes. "God knows what had happened to her to make her so frail and miserable! You, her, and everyone else seems intent on keeping everything from me and Chae Young. You never tell me about the bruises on her body, you never tell me why her eyes are swollen from tears, and you never tell me why it looked like her soul had been broken." Sparkles of liquid marred her eyes while reserved pain filled Tae Hyun's. "But despite not knowing what happened, I know she's been going through hell. What happened, oppa? What the hell happened that made you force her to leave the country? What did she do to have you treat her so horribly?"

"I'm *not* discussing this with you," Tae Hyun replied decisively, set on not divulging that the woman his little sister loved so much was the one who killed their mother. "Not now and not ever. How I break up with my girlfriend is none of your concern."

"And you kicked Kang Min and Jae Won out too?" she asked, her voice breaking apart. If it was possible, there was more agony in her eyes. "How could you?"

"It's been done." Although he stated this with finality, there was a trace of regret in his eyes when he was not only reminded of his ex-girlfriend, but also the two gang members whom he had formed close bonds with as well. "The three of them are probably long gone by now. We will never see them again. What happens now doesn't change anything—"

"Sir?" a voice suddenly interrupted from the side, drawing the siblings out of their private conversation.

Tae Hyun turned and caught sight of an elderly man dressed in a black suit. He was one of Ju Won's workers. It was evident in the man's anxious demeanor that he had been searching all around the ball for Tae Hyun.

"Sir," he repeated respectfully, bowing to Tae Hyun. "The toast is about to begin."

"I'll be there soon. Thank you," Tae Hyun dismissed with a warm smile.

As the man gave a parting bow and left them, Tae Hyun spared one last glance in his sister's direction.

"You have no one now," Hae Jin whispered tightly, aware that she had lost the moment she needed with her brother to convince him that not only was he wrong, but that he also had to reconcile the situation and bring everyone back together. It was apparent in her hopeless expression that she knew their moment had passed and that he was desperately latching on to something else to fill the new void in his life.

"I have my throne," he told her, his face clearing out any evidence of weakness or distraction. With his hands in his pockets and the illumination of the chandelier running over the perfect features of his face, the King of Serpents was as striking as ever. "And soon, I'll have the world."

Walking away from her, Tae Hyun glided over the grand staircase that led to the upstairs quarter of the ballroom. When the soles of his leather shoes made contact with the red carpet, he greeted a couple of mentors and approached the rows of balconies that overlooked the entire first floor of the rotunda ball. He stepped onto the center balcony and made himself comfortable there.

His eyes wandered to the ground floor where the happy chattering of the Underworld populace and the clinking of champagne glasses rose up to where he stood. Ju Won stood in a circle, conversing with Jung Min, Dong Min, and various 1st layer crime lords. Ju Won was all smiles as his laughter intermixed with the music moving over the room. Tae Hyun involuntarily shifted his attention to the northern corner of the surrounding balconies. He sighted Lee Ji Hoon, dressed in an expensive tuxedo, standing on a private balcony of his own. His face was veiled with supremacy as he took a furtive step forward and held his champagne glass high in the air. It only took a second for Ji Hoon to stand there before a wave of silence claimed the lips of those in the ballroom.

Despite the aversion he harbored for Ji Hoon, Tae Hyun, like the rest of the Underworld surrounding him, was quiet as the music from the piano died down. Soon after, the lights dimmed slightly while a subtle spotlight hung over the King of Skulls.

Ji Hoon began to speak, confidence and pride teeming in his voice. "When asked about the three men I admire most, my answer has always been consistent. It has always been my father, my Advisor, and the eldest Advisor, Seo Ju Won. I have never wavered from those three names, and I'm sure the third name is a name that no one in this room has wavered from either."

Ji Hoon smiled, looking down at Ju Won and Jung Min, both of whom were beaming up at him.

"Uncle," Ji Hoon began respectfully to Ju Won, extending his champagne glass in the air, "never in my life have I met a man who has as much experience, virtue, and knowledge as you. You have left such a big footprint in our world, and I doubt any other Advisor coming after you would ever be able to fill your shoes. I am grateful to be one of your advisees and even more grateful that you are considering me as an heir. In forty years, if I could be half the man you are today, then I'd consider that my biggest honor. Happy 65th birthday. Here's to a wonderful year."

An explosion of applause erupted from all around the room after the conclusion of Ji Hoon's speech. Ju Won and Jung Min raised their glasses and nodded approvingly at Ji Hoon. Beside them, Dong Min lackadaisically lifted his glass, his expression clearly unimpressed with Ji Hoon's toast. A few lingering cheers from Skulls gang members continued to echo from below until Tae Hyun grabbed a champagne glass off a waiter's platter and took two steps forward. He stood in front of the gold railing of the balcony and looked below.

As if sensing his presence, the room fell silent in some sort of quiet awe. All eyes gradually landed on him. The silent change in reverence from Ji Hoon to Tae Hyun was very subtle, but very noticeable. Tae Hyun not only held everyone's unyielding attention with his mere presence, but the natural magnetism that resonated from him also demanded their immense interest.

"Our world is a society unlike any other," Tae Hyun began diplomatically, poise and power exuding effortlessly from him. "Standing in this room right now is the most eclectic and powerful group of individuals this country has and will ever know."

His deep brown eyes roamed around the room as a ghost of a smile tilted on his lips.

"I am honored to be born into the Serpents' bloodline, but so much more honored to be taken under the wings of great business, political, media, and economic leaders who have mentored and trained me to be the man that I have become." His eyes found Dong Min's, who was staring up at Tae Hyun like a proud father would at his son. "I am especially honored by Shin Dong Min, who has not only taken me under his wings since my inception into the 1st layer, but has also become like a second father to me all these years." He gave his Advisor a genuine and appreciative nod. "I know that I'm not the easiest advisee to deal with, but please know that I will never forget your undying support, all those times when you stuck by me when I couldn't see past the fog. I will forever be grateful for it. It's been such a great honor."

Dong Min inclined his head, lifting his champagne glass higher. Warmness filled his eyes as he silently said, "It was my honor as well."

With a deep inhalation, Tae Hyun averted his focus to the one who had the power to change his future. Albeit the kindliness in Tae Hyun's eyes dissipated slightly, he made sure the warmth was still solidified on his handsome face while he spoke to the one who was the reason for this event.

"With all these thanks, I think I speak for each and every one of us here when I express my gratitude to the eldest Advisor. He has helped uphold the bylaws of our society and kept our world as pure as the day it began. Over the past few decades, he has been a staple in our world, mentoring the best of the best while safeguarding the values that we hold dear."

He raised his champagne glass an inch higher and inclined his head at Ju Won.

"Uncle," Tae Hyun began, noting from his peripherals that Ji Hoon was seething with aggravation. Tae Hyun was not only overshadowing Ji Hoon in terms of holding the interest of the Underworld populace, but he was also holding the undivided attention of Ju Won himself. "In a room filled with prominent leaders and fearless soldiers, I am humbled to be in your presence. You have taught me so much in the ways of our world. I couldn't have learned it better from anyone else. If my father and mother were here, then I'd stand before them a proud man because I have everything a great King could dream of."

In that split second, a pained emotion gave way in Tae Hyun's eyes. It was as though he was thinking about a particular person who took his heart with her earlier in the night. He swallowed tightly, disregarding this fleeting pain to finish his speech. He no longer had time to be a man; he had to be a God.

"And I have you to thank for that. Sixty-five years and you're still a living legend. Thank you for your patience, your service, and your dedication. Happy birthday. Here's to sixty-five more years of greatness."

An eruption of cheers and applause rumbled throughout the rotunda ball. Below, Ju Won laughed proudly after Tae Hyun's toast and cheered with the rest of the Underworld. In a synchronized movement, champagne glasses were raised in the air like torches. The entire room toasted to the two Underworld Kings.

While drinking from his champagne glass, Tae Hyun looked over to Ji Hoon. The King of Skulls was staring back at him with daggers in his eyes. Tae Hyun bestowed him with the same hateful gaze. Ji Hoon's simple existence offended him, and Tae Hyun did not trouble himself to hide that fact. He was holding on to his champagne glass with such vigor that he had to use opposing strength to keep from breaking the feeble glass. The heated glares lasted for a long minute before they became swept away.

Unaware of the hate spewing from the two Kings, the rest of the Underworld attendees gathered around each of them, congratulating them for their well-spoken and equally powerful speeches. Throughout the next hour and a half, they were in the company of Underworld associates as they ventured down the staircase and mingled with everyone in attendance. The mundaneness of this event was only broken when they were face-to-face with the celebrated Advisor himself.

Ju Won was the epitome of an elated host when he motioned for them to convene with him in the center of the packed ballroom. An unhappy expression settled over the two Kings' faces when they realized they had to be in close proximity to one another. Though they were unhappy, they did not allow their emotions to dissuade them from heeding the eldest Advisor's request.

"Any Advisor would be honored to have two great Kings give such wonderful toasts," said Ju Won with a warm chuckle, the champagne in his glass swaying in merriment.

"The honor is ours," Tae Hyun replied, purposely ignoring Ji Hoon while he kept his attention on Ju Won.

"How is your birthday so far, uncle?" Ji Hoon asked cordially, taking a sip from his champagne glass. He also made it a point to ignore Tae Hyun. Up close, one could see the dim bruises on Ji Hoon's face, the aftereffect of his confrontation with Yoori. She had found out that he was the one who orchestrated Lee Chae Young's rape, and she was unforgiving with his punishment. Though it was scarcely visible, one could also see the scar on his head where she broke an alcohol bottle. The sight of these maladies brought a satisfied smile to Tae Hyun's face.

"Very nice," Ju Won replied with a passive-aggressive grin that hid his true and unfiltered feelings. The shadows darkened his eyes when he was reminded of something disconcerting. "Of course, it would have been nice if my niece was here. However, because she was framed for something she didn't do," —he eyed Ji Hoon, who swallowed uncomfortably at the words, before looking at Tae Hyun— "and punished unfairly for it, she will be in the hospital for a few more weeks."

Albeit Tae Hyun didn't form a reaction on his face, it was palpable in his eyes that he harbored a tremendous amount of regret for what happened to Jin Ae.

"I'm sorry again," he whispered, his apology genuine. "Whatever I can do to help accommodate her in the hospital, let me know, and I'll take care of it.

A tinge of warmth enveloped Ju Won's normally impassive eyes. "You've already made up for it the past two weeks, Tae Hyun," he said approvingly. There was a pause before he added, "Have you done what we spoke about?"

Tae Hyun's usually unruffled demeanor subsided faintly. "It's over," he answered, nodding in confirmation. "I ended it tonight."

"What have you done these past two weeks?" Ji Hoon interjected instantly. Unhappiness outlined his features at the thought of Tae Hyun being under Ju Won's good graces again.

Tae Hyun disregarded Ji Hoon like he was a pest that wasn't worth his attention. Instead, it was a pleased Ju Won who answered Ji Hoon.

"After much stubbornness, Tae Hyun placed his pride aside, came to my estate, and was personally trained by me these past two weeks."

A forced smile appeared on Tae Hyun's lips.

For the past couple of months, it was a secret bid that Ju Won offered Tae Hyun to train him and officially take him on as an advisee. At the offset, Tae Hyun resisted, not because he felt Ju Won's combat skills were useless—on the contrary, learning anything from the revered crime lord would help any fighter vastly—but because he knew being "officially" trained under Ju Won would essentially place Tae Hyun under his debt. Tae Hyun had never been one to voluntarily place himself under anyone's debt, least of all Ju Won's. Nevertheless, as Dong Min advised, being trained under Ju Won for two weeks was the only way to obtain his forgiveness and maintain his favor for Tae Hyun to be a contender for the Lord of the Underworld throne. After Tae Hyun allowed Yoori to beat Ju Won's niece to the brink of death, the King of Serpents had to bite his tongue, put on a happy face, and endure training with Ju Won.

"Oh," Ji Hoon said, nodding a bit too pompously. "You were trained right after I was trained."

Tae Hyun's eyes snapped up towards Ji Hoon. He hadn't anticipated Ju Won to train Ji Hoon as well. The fact that he and Ji Hoon were trained under the same mentor, even if it was only for two weeks, pissed him off greatly. He made no effort to hide his distaste.

"Ju Won trained you two weeks prior to me?"

Ji Hoon chuckled, drinking pretentiously from his champagne glass. "It seems that way, doesn't it?" He paused to swallow his drink before his thoughts reverted back to the earlier part of the conversation. "And what exactly did Tae Hyun put an end to tonight?"

"Something that you should've ended three years ago when I spoke to you," Ju Won reprimanded swiftly, his voice cool. His eyes softened on Ji Hoon, whose jaw tightened in anger at the chastisement. "But you made up for it when you accepted the training, *among other things*."

Vigilance entered Tae Hyun when the puzzle pieces started to click together. "*How* had Ji Hoon made up his worth in the past two weeks? What other things are you talking about?"

When Tae Hyun assessed the silence that emitted from Ju Won and the smile on Ji Hoon's face, his ability to read people came into great use.

"Your condition for Ji Hoon to garner your favor was for him to do everything in his power to tear Yoori and I apart." His words came out instinctively, but there was conviction behind his statement. If the fire brimming in his eyes was any indication, it was clear that he was using his entire strength to not punch Ju Won and his nemesis at that very second. He looked beyond pissed.

"Where do you get your ideas, Tae Hyun?" Ju Won asked in bewilderment.

However authentic Ju Won appeared in manufacturing confusion, Tae Hyun wasn't fooled.

"Listen," Tae Hyun started inflexibly, moving closer to Ju Won. Tae Hyun towered over the Advisor, the build of the muscles hidden under his tuxedo overpowering Ju Won's 5'7" frame—as well as almost every other individual in the rotunda room. There was a fatal air in the way Tae Hyun spoke to Ju Won. He was no longer composed; he was simply furious. "I didn't get this far because of my looks, which may I add," —he glanced over to Ji Hoon to just piss him off— "outranks this bastard's here a million times over."

Ji Hoon cursed indignantly while Tae Hyun firmly went on.

"But it's because I have the best instincts. I have an uncanny ability to read people. There are few who could lie to me and even fewer who could lie to me and get away with it." His eyes became severe as his gaze bore into Ju Won's. "Don't play me for a fool. I may have respect for you, but that doesn't mean you're above me. My authority far exceeds yours. Do not make the mistake of thinking that my reverence for you means that I'm afraid of you. I'm not afraid of you. I'm merely respectful around you because I understand that this world has high regards for you. I share in that regard—though it may waver quite often. But if you continue to insult me, I'll treat you like any other subordinate and make you kneel in front of me before I kill you with my bare hands. Do we have an understanding?"

Although Tae Hyun spoke in an even, diplomatic tone, it was clear in the uncomfortable shifting of Ju Won's stance that he was afraid of Tae Hyun. The King of Serpents was a feared Underworld King for a reason, and even Ju Won had to acknowledge that.

The Advisor sighed seconds later, straightening the jacket of his tuxedo. He took a gulp from his champagne glass to silently soothe his nerves. When he regained his composure, he said, "Ji Hoon's method of going about what I asked him to do was problematic, but it got the job done nonetheless."

A muscle worked in Tae Hyun's strong jaw. He looked like an angry lion that was prepared to kill everyone in this room to satiate his fury. "So, you've been having some fun, interfering with the lives of the people you call your Kings, right, Ju Won? My love life being the forerunner?"

Insulted, Ju Won's eyes grew severe as well.

"This society has entrusted me to mold the first true Lord for our world, and you think I give a damn about whom you or Ji Hoon sleep with?" His spine straightened with pride as he plowed on, looking between Tae Hyun and Ji Hoon. "You can have a thousand girls kneeling at your feet, and I wouldn't give a damn. But as every disastrous story goes, the downfall of great Kings will *always* be the woman they keep in their company." He eyed Tae Hyun. "You, yourself, have said that our world is a society unlike any other. Do you think our people would give up their lives for a King who cared more about the wellbeing of his woman than the society as a whole? Do you think the Kings and Queens here are willing to be governed by anyone who is less than a God?"

He breathed deeply, his eyes swiveling from Tae Hyun and to Ji Hoon. Both were quiet as he surged on. "Both of you are great Kings, but do you think you'd be able to take our world to great heights if there's a woman wearing you down, making you vulnerable to human emotions?" He looked at Ji Hoon. "An Soo Jin was that woman for you." He faced Tae Hyun. "And Choi Yoori was that woman for you."

He sighed, seeing the dawning lights of realization that filtered into both of their eyes. It had always been an age-old warning for any leader in the Underworld to be vigilant about the person they wanted their significant other to be. Love is considered flexible—power isn't. A lover should never supersede the quest for power, the very thing their enigmatic and powerful world was built upon. If it did, then the Underworld population would be ready to tear that leader down and appoint another great leader to take his place.

"Love blinds even the best of Kings, and at this point in your lives, you have no time to be tied down." He gazed directly at Tae Hyun, who was still fuming in silence. "I arranged for Ji Hoon to break you two up because she was unhealthy for our world. I saw what she was doing to you. I saw how human she made you, how much kinder and more irrational you've become since meeting her. I arranged for you to personally kick her out of the country because I know that despite my advice, you would never kill her and you would kill anyone who dared to touch her. I know that you believe I take enjoyment in pitting people against one another. Trust me when I say that I don't have time for games. I'm doing all of this with the best intentions, not only as your Advisor, but also as the eldest Advisor in this world. I trust that I have two potential Lords standing next to me, and I offer no apologies for trying to keep the best and most skilled contender to be a revered Lord for my world. With all that said, I'm happy that both of you have severed ties with her and are done with her." He regarded them, his fierce eyes scrutinizing them. "You are both done with her, *right*?"

"I'm a competitive guy," Ji Hoon stated haughtily, his eyes on Tae Hyun. "As long as Kwon Tae Hyun doesn't prance around with my sloppy seconds, then I'm good. Choi Yoori evokes no emotional attachment from me." He spared a glance at the crowd of girls staring in their direction, admiring both him and Tae Hyun. "I have my options of whores who are ready to kneel before me."

Ju Won grinned at Ji Hoon's words before turning to Tae Hyun. "And yourself, Tae Hyun?"

Tae Hyun smirked dryly, staring into Ju Won's eyes with dark conviction. "Choi Yoori is dead to me. I gave her the chance to live and have already told her that if I see her again, I'm bypassing the courtesies and I'll do what's necessary to protect my throne. She evokes no more emotional attachment from me, nor does she continue to hold my interest. She was merely a mistake that I should've gotten rid of sooner. It was my pleasure to kick her out of this country."

Ju Won grinned widely while Ji Hoon scoffed disbelievingly. Before either Ju Won or Ji Hoon could respond to Tae Hyun's words, a man dressed in a grey suit promptly interrupted them.

"Sir," Ju Won's right-hand man said tentatively, nervously handing him a silver cellphone, "you have a phone call."

"Can't you see that I'm busy?" he snapped. Ju Won wasn't a crime lord who appreciated being interrupted, especially when he was in the middle of a conversation with the Kings of the Underworld.

"It's the King of Scorpions," his right-hand man replied timidly, holding the phone out. His body shifted uncomfortably under his suit. Despite his trepidation, he stood in his stance. He was aware that Ju Won hated being interrupted, but he was also aware that the eldest Advisor would not ignore a phone call from the elusive King of Scorpions.

Vigilance met the eyes of Tae Hyun and Ji Hoon. Both alertly tensed up while Ju Won stared at the phone for a few lingering moments. After a few breaths, he grabbed the phone, motioned for his right-hand man to leave them, and put the phone on speaker.

"Young Jae?" Ju Won asked carefully, his voice tightly guarded.

The crowd around them chattered happily in the background as the celebratory music continued to grace the air. They were all blissfully unaware of the tense phone call that was about to take place.

A soft chuckle resonated from the receiver. Soon after, the familiar voice sauntered out. "It's good to hear your voice again, uncle. It's been a while."

Ju Won closed his eyes in aggravation when it was confirmed that it was indeed the King of Scorpions on the phone. Tae Hyun shared this aversion while Ji Hoon simply held a mask of curiosity on his face.

Unwilling to lose his composure, though it was blatant that Young Jae was Ju Won's least favorite person, Ju Won continued to diplomatically speak into the phone.

"Young Jae, your presence would've been appreciated here," he said with forced warmth, concealing the hatred he harbored for Young Jae. "You've been out of our world for quite some time. I would've appreciated a little reunion of the Titans here."

"I would be there, but some . . ." A pause lingered for a few pregnant seconds before he said, "*favorable* things are occurring in Japan, and it requires my presence. I'm sorry that I can't be there for your party. I'm even more apologetic that I can't be there to see which of my fellow Kings would become your crowned heir." He laughed again and casually added, "They *are* standing beside you, aren't they?"

A jolt of surprise coursed through the three at his statement.

The edge of Tae Hyun's lips lifted into a smirk. He stared lethally at the phone. "You can see us, Young Jae?"

Young Jae chuckled as Ji Hoon and Ju Won's eyes roamed around the crowded rotunda room for signs of the King of Scorpions. While their eyes scoured the room, Tae Hyun kept his eyes solidified on the phone. He knew that Young Jae wasn't in attendance tonight.

"Tae Hyun," Young Jae greeted as if he was a long lost friend. "Some of my associates are in attendance. They are giving me a live feed about what's happening over there. I was told that you and Ji Hoon made some impressive speeches—congratulations on that. It is a rarity to impress anyone in our world." Tae Hyun and Ji Hoon did not bother to express their thanks to him, and Young Jae did not wait for it. He brought everyone back on to another topic of conversation. "In any case, I apologize for not being able to see you again, uncle, especially when I made an appearance for the masquerade ball a few weeks ago and ran into Tae Hyun and Ji Hoon."

Much to his own dismay, Ju Won's eyes enlarged at this revelation.

He looked at Tae Hyun and Ji Hoon. Both were staring at him without an apology in their eyes for withholding this information from him.

He veered his attention back to Young Jae. Although his hardened expression betrayed his emotions, Ju Won kept his voice even. "You were in Korea?"

"Very recently," Young Jae confirmed haughtily, undoubtedly aware that it was pissing Ju Won off that he didn't realize Young Jae crashed a party that *he* threw. "I was there for a couple of days, had a small errand to run, but unfortunately, it was veered off by the King of Serpents. Regardless, I'm in the process of working things out now. This reminds me . . . why isn't my baby sister there?"

"Apparently she's on the run, Young Jae," Ji Hoon shared blithely. His eyes teemed with amusement as he gazed at Tae Hyun. "Tae Hyun wasn't particularly fond of the fact that she killed his mother."

Young Jae let out an amused laugh. "Of course he wouldn't be."

While Ju Won's face displayed alarm at this information, Tae Hyun looked livid. Anger shot through his eyes when Young Jae's taunting laughter rolled over him.

Tae Hyun looked at Ji Hoon with elevated hatred. "You were working with Young Jae?"

Young Jae answered in Ji Hoon's place.

"Ji Hoon and I may not see eye-to-eye on a lot of things, but we have always been the types to put things aside and work together towards a similar goal. I didn't want you with my sister, and he didn't want you with my sister, so we worked it out." Another pause came before a woman's voice was heard murmuring in the background. Young Jae's voice came through again. "In any case, it's great to hear that everyone is having a wonderful time. My wife and I have meetings to attend now. I'm glad I got to catch up with all of you before I make my return to Korea. Happy birthday, uncle. I look forward to seeing you soon."

Click.

The fury that spilled out of Ju Won was transparent, especially when the phone shattered against the expensive tiles. Though there was steam coming out of his ears, he made sure to keep what was left of his cool while addressing his advisees.

"Both of you didn't think it was necessary to tell me he was at my party?" Ju Won asked through gritted teeth.

"Slipped my mind," Tae Hyun provided, unwilling to apologize. Using this moment as his leeway, he added, "You hate him, I hate him. Make the right choice tonight, give me that throne, and I'll kill him for you."

Interest lit Ju Won's eyes at the proposition.

Ji Hoon swallowed tightly, shifting closer to Ju Won. He did not hesitate to make his own proposition. "I may have gone to Young Jae briefly to gather suitable information to break them up, but I assure you he doesn't have any loyalty from me. Give me the throne, and I'll be happy to give you his head on a silver platter."

Ju Won's mouth curved into a calculating smile. He openly considered their promises. "I'll consider everything," he said, his fury subsiding substantially. "Thank you both for your attendance. I'm sorry to one of you that it's not going to work out tonight. Now please go enjoy the night while I try to forget about the bloodsucking bastard who has raised my blood pressure with his simple existence."

Kicking the broken cellphone as he walked away, an irate Ju Won immediately found Jung Min and Dong Min, leaving Tae Hyun and Ji Hoon alone in his wake.

If the atmosphere was tense before with Ju Won as the buffer between the two of them, then the tension was multiplied a million times over as the two Kings stood parallel to one another. Both were staring quietly at each other, neither saying anything for a long time.

It was Tae Hyun who decided to finally break the silence. "Young Jae was the one who told you about Soo Jin killing my mother?"

Always to the point. That was always Tae Hyun's personality.

"He confirmed it," Ji Hoon clarified with no hint of remorse or shame. "Soo Jin had bragged about it once, but I didn't take her seriously. Yet, when Ju Won requested that I do him this favor and when it was clear that I couldn't sway Yoori with my own charms, I decided to play another piece on the chess board."

"You weren't afraid that I'd kill her after finding out?" Tae Hyun asked disbelievingly, his eyes still wondering how much this girl meant to Ji Hoon — if she even meant anything other than a possession to him.

"Why didn't you?" Ji Hoon asked instead, genuinely curious.

Unable — or unwilling — to answer it himself, Tae Hyun allowed the silence from his lips to answer for him.

Ji Hoon laughed sardonically, shaking his head at Tae Hyun. "Of course, how could you kill your innocent Yoori when it was the bitch Soo Jin who caused all this chaos?" Ji Hoon mocked with amusement, feeding on the fact that Tae Hyun was visibly upset over the loss of the one who stole his heart.

Ji Hoon, much like Tae Hyun, was a cunning and observant King. He knew what buttons to push in order to force his enemies over the edge.

"And to answer your question," Ji Hoon said tauntingly. "I trusted that you wouldn't kill Yoori. Even if I was wrong and you did, then it would've been no harm to me because it would only mean that in the end, you would never get to have her just like I didn't get to have her." Ji Hoon laughed with hilarity at the livid gaze on Tae Hyun's face. He dramatically peered up at the dark sky swimming over the glass ceiling. He feigned a despondent sigh. "Poor thing. She must be crying her eyes out. Maybe after this, I should find her again and — "

Bam!

Ji Hoon didn't see it coming.

The punch that Tae Hyun threw was as quick as a lightning bolt, and the strength he imparted was a force to be reckoned with as his iron-like fist rammed into Ji Hoon's nose.

Blindsided by the sudden attack, Ji Hoon was left reeling when Tae Hyun, who wasn't satisfied with a mere punch, drew his left leg high in the air, stopped above the apex of Ji Hoon's head, and then with supreme strength, drew his leg downward and executed a powerful axe kick down on Ji Hoon's face.

Boom!

"Augh!"

Ji Hoon was left stumbling into the crowd. Sounds of drinks being spilled and screams emitted at the sudden cargo falling onto them. Ji Hoon's nose was already bleeding from Tae Hyun's punch, but with the added blow of Tae Hyun's merciless kick, what was left of Ji Hoon's nose was ruined as blood poured like a waterfall from his nostrils. It also didn't help the situation when the drink he was holding spilled on him as he fell to the floor. His face was utterly drenched with champagne and blood.

"Damn, did you see the fist and axe kick boss executed?" a couple of Serpents announced to one another while they watched the scene from the balconies.

"He didn't even see his fist coming!" cried a 1st layer heir to his friends. He craned his neck, laughing with his fellow heirs as they enjoyed the scene before them.

"Oh shit! Did that just really happen? I thought they were going to fight when this night ended?"

"Crap! I missed it!"

All around, the commotion from the audience surrounded them. Everyone was surprised by the unexpected violence from the typically composed King of Serpents.

The fire raging in Ji Hoon's eyes came from the depths of hell. He glared at Tae Hyun, his fury growing by the second. "You fucking—"

Unafraid of the anger he elicited, Tae Hyun inclined his head challengingly as if saying, *"Talk about Yoori again, and I'll break every bone in your face."*

"Tae Hyun! What the fuck did you just do?!" Jung Min shouted, staring from the side in horror. He pushed past the crowd and ran over to his newly assaulted advisee in disbelief.

Behind him, Dong Min, along with several other Advisors, stifled chuckles of pure amusement.

"Bad reflexes," Tae Hyun replied innocently, unabashed by the stares he garnered from the attendees.

Hiding a satisfied smile, he sighed before shaking his punching hand off and grabbing a champagne glass off the silver platter held by a passing waiter.

Tae Hyun smirked mockingly, raising his glass towards Ji Hoon, who was spitting out a thousand curses. He tried to push past his Advisor and his Skulls, all of whom were trying to help tend to his wounds, and charge at Tae Hyun. He wanted to bestow him with a nose-breaking assault of his own. His Advisor kept him at bay, telling him that he had to clean himself up instead of making matters worse.

"It was nice talking to you," Tae Hyun said nonchalantly, smirking one last time at Ji Hoon. He turned on his heels and casually walked away from the scene as if nothing took place.

"If Yoori was here, you wouldn't have exploded like that," Hae Jin whispered coolly, veering through the crowd and walking alongside him. She glanced over her shoulder and saw a dozen people, girls included, fighting to help tend to Ji Hoon's wound. She grinned to herself. She kept her pace with her brother while laughing at the hilarity of the scene. "But boundaries of politics aside, it's nice to see you show that bastard who the Alpha King is. How did that feel?"

"Satisfying," Tae Hyun answered contently, drinking from his champagne glass. "Like I just wiped shit off the soles of my shoes."

"At least you did one thing right tonight," said Hae Jin as they strolled through the crowd.

Smiling at her approving words, Tae Hyun held his little sister close to him for the next hour as they socialized with the powerful elites of Korea and thoroughly ignored the violent tension that had infiltrated the room.

"And if Yoori was here," he added to his sister, unknowing to himself that he was not only speaking freely about his ex-girlfriend with warmth in his eyes, but he was also unknowingly predicting a potential event that was likely to occur in the near future, "she'd slap the shit out of him."

"You can hide..."

02: The Return of the Queen

The evening was quite peaceful as it lingered on.

Ji Hoon had retreated to the back room with some of his Skulls and a couple of 1st layer Princesses, all of whom were more than willing to help nurse his wounds. Meanwhile, Tae Hyun had traveled up and down the grand staircase to converse with his Underworld associates. Despite the attention of some young ladies who were intent on flirting with him, Tae Hyun paid no mind to them as he walked around, ignoring their advances as though he was a taken man.

It wasn't until near the end, when he noticed a familiar heavenly aroma from the bar, did he finally show some strain in his normally composed face. He recognized the scent as the heavenly tea that he and a certain girl loved so much.

Looking around the rotunda ball that was filled with people who revered him like a God, Tae Hyun couldn't have looked lonelier as he drank the last of his champagne, gave up on the wearisome duties of conversing with people, and ordered a cup of the famous Underworld tea. He quietly walked up the steps leading to the platform and sat down on his throne. Around him, the party continued animatedly. The lights were dimmed, and the area he was sitting in was considerably dark. Few could see him, and no one was looking in his direction in that suspended moment in time.

The brief concealment liberated him, for he was lost.

Lost while drinking his tea, lost while touching his lips, and lost while his thoughts took over his reality. He was on the verge of being completely adrift when the party finally reached its climax. The moment everyone had been waiting for had finally come to fruition.

"Ladies and gentlemen, may we have your attention, please?"

The volume in the rotunda ball began to die down under the microphone-enhanced voice of Shin Jung Min. Once he garnered the attention of the room, he handed the microphone to his brother. Dong Min was standing beside him on the same platform, facing the entire Underworld in attendance. Behind them, the speckles of the city night glowed like a picturesque mural in the backdrop.

"Please gather around because I think this will be a moment in time that we all want to treasure," Dong Min said proudly, smiling at the crowd.

Everyone murmured in excitement and agreement. They all knew what was about to take place.

While Tae Hyun was already in his seat, Ji Hoon had emerged from the back room, completely washed up. Even if it was clear that his nose was killing him, the King of Skulls was intent on sitting through the ceremony—something he did with angry pride after he sat down on his throne and looked up at the stage ahead of him.

With his seat still empty, Ju Won stood proudly on the platform with the Shin brothers. All eyes were focused on the stage as the lights dimmed almost completely. The spotlight was firmly focused on Ju Won, who was accepting the microphone from Dong Min. He thanked the brothers for their help before they took their places on either side of him. Albeit the Shin brothers had become respected crime lords in their own rights, when in the presence of Ju Won, they would always be his loyal soldiers.

An undulation of cheers and applauses rang through the colossal estate once Ju Won took the stage.

"You're all very kind," Ju Won voiced humbly, nodding at all the applause. He motioned his hand up, wordlessly asking for silence as he continued to deliver his speech. "As we all know, the reason for this big celebration is not only to celebrate my humble birth, but to also celebrate the birth of someone else: the new heir to my throne and quite possibly the new Lord of our world."

The room grew silent with anticipation.

The moment everyone had been waiting for had arrived, and they were all giving Ju Won their undivided attention—all except the King of Serpents, who was merely staring off into space, utterly lost in his own thoughts as Ju Won continued to make the speech that others had spent years waiting for.

"The decision between our two Kings has been a difficult one for me—as I'm sure it's been for the rest of our world seeing as that the distribution of power for our two Kings has been about the same." His lips stretched into a prideful smile. "But all of that will change tonight. In announcing my new heir, I am in high hopes that because of my years of service for our society, the entire Underworld will heed my support, trust my judgment, and support this chosen King as the new Lord of our world. I only want the best for our society, and I trust that this King will be a force to be reckoned with in the outside world. I trust my future in his hands, and I trust our entire livelihood under his governance."

Ju Won's smile grew wider as the eagerness in the room intensified.

"Without further ado," he said, staring directly at Tae Hyun, who wasn't even paying attention to the speech. "I'm pleased to announce the heir to my throne—"

BOOM!

Sounds of the doors blasting open stole everyone's attention.

In a fleeting second, the room collapsed into silence as several things happened at once.

Ju Won had ceased with his speech.

Breaths hilted in the chests of the Underworld populace while all eyes averted from Ju Won and landed on the opened, two-story-high doorway. The stream of light from the hallway filtered into the entrance area of the rotunda room, acting as the awaiting carpet for the attendees to come.

As this took place, Ji Hoon had instinctively angled his head towards the noise. Behind Ju Won, Dong Min and Jung Min's eyes had grown perplexed at the sudden interruption. And Tae Hyun, who wasn't even paying attention to the speech, was dragged out of his stupor when the intenseness of the noise garnered his attention.

He lifted his head up and casted his eyes over to the entrance of the door that was half a ballroom away from him. Hae Jin, who was standing near the stairs that led up to his throne, stared up as well. Although Tae Hyun's seat was closest to the entrance, that did not mean he had the best vantage point to see everything clearly. On the contrary, he was the one who had the worst possible angle. Still sitting calmly in his seat and refusing to crane his neck out like everyone else in the room, Tae Hyun stared at the doors that were held ajar. Curiosity glowed in his reserved eyes.

The silent, yet powerful, ambiance taunted the anticipatory air until—

"Augh!"

Sounds of groaning echoed in the dark halls before five of Ju Won's bodyguards tumbled into the rotunda room. Their faces were utterly smashed in, their guttural breathing indicating that they were on the brink of blacking out. Albeit shadows veiled them, one could clearly see the torrent of blood dripping from their jaws.

Ju Won's eyes expanded at the sight of this. The rest of the Underworld shared this reaction. In that collective and vigilant stillness, sounds of people cocking their guns vibrated throughout the room. An Underworld event was never the place for anyone to disturb the peace. As the unspoken bylaws went, any undue interruption during an Underworld event was punishable by death. The Royals in attendance were known to be vicious and utterly unforgiving. All had arrogant personalities and hated having their night interrupted. For anyone who dared to piss them off, especially with more than a thousand of them gathered together, there would be absolute hell to pay—hell in the form of a painful, torturous, and slow death.

"Augh . . ."

As if foreseeing the arrival of the one who attacked them, the groaning bodyguards began to crawl away from the door. A second later, the flickering light surrounding the doorstep suddenly darkened when a pair of black boots stepped into the light. The silhouette of the new attendee appeared at the doorway.

If it was possible, the anticipation in the room amplified. And if it was even more possible, the prestige and power in the air was multiplied fifty times over with this dark silhouette's presence.

The Underworld populace should have started shooting, but there was a certain enchantment this uninvited guest had over them. Rather than shooting the intruder, they allowed her presence to arrest their attention.

The King of Serpents was not immune to this intruder's magnetism. His unyielding interest was all hers, which was surprising given that he rarely gifted his undivided attention to anyone. He furrowed his brows and inclined his head at the dark silhouette. All he could make out was a shadowy figure. Regardless of the fact that he couldn't see the individual's face, he couldn't take his eyes off her as she sauntered haughtily into the ballroom.

The intruder was dressed in a pair of simple black jeans, boots, and a black hoodie. In the background, two bodyguards trailed three paces behind her, their faces obscured by shadows. The further she advanced into the room, the clearer it became to her spellbound audience that it was indeed a woman who captivated their attention. The young woman was ordinarily dressed, but the extraordinary air that exuded from her was undeniable. It was the only reason why the ruthless Underworld crowd had yet to open fire on her.

Marching into the room like she owned the world, she carelessly stepped over the backs of the men she assaulted. Though her facial features were not yet visible, the familiarity that many felt from her was what mesmerized the room. Those on the ground floor instinctively stepped out of the way, allowing her a pathway from the entrance towards the center of the room.

As the audience tracked her every movement, they could see her silhouette turn to face Ju Won, whose eyes became even more massive when he realized *who* he was staring at. She approached the residual lights from the podium, and they could vaguely see her smirk. When she looked over to the King of Skulls, who stood up and stared at the dark figure like she was a figment of his imagination, the Underworld populace could see the smirk grow on her face. The King of Skulls' eyes were filled with incredulity. He could not believe any of this was really happening. However shocked he was, his reaction was nothing compared to the King of Serpents' reaction. Shock filled

Tae Hyun's gaze after the young woman stepped into the trail of light that led up to Ju Won's throne.

Without warning, she stopped midway. While she paused in her stance, her two right-hand men, Kang Min and Jae Won, continued to walk ahead, each taking their places on either side of the steps leading up to Ju Won's seat.

Then finally, as the atmosphere in the room became intolerable, the intruder slowly spun on her heels, allowing the warmth of the light to illuminate on her porcelain skin. The light washed over her features, gradually revealing her face to the spellbound crowd.

A tidal wave of gasps permeated the room when they realized who they were in the presence of.

It was not just a woman; it was a God—an immortal legend in their world.

"Oh my God . . ."

"Is that—?"

"But she died!"

"It can't be . . ."

"The Queen is back."

The Queen's exhilarated brown eyes ran over the disbelieving gazes of those who stood on the balcony. Her focus lowered to the stunned attendees who stood on the staircases and streamed down to all the ones on the ground floor. The sensuous curve of a wicked smile appeared on her beautiful face as she bathed in the spotlight. Then, with tactical deliberation, she straightened her stance to an angle where she was standing parallel from the one who had yet to see the full features of her face and the one who mattered the most.

While standing half a ballroom away from him, she allowed her emotionless eyes to land on the King of Serpents. His hands were gripping at the golden armrests of his throne, and he looked like he was watching her with bated breath.

At that frozen moment in time, the world around them receded. All that existed was the emotionless gaze An Soo Jin held on him, and the faint daze-like gaze Kwon Tae Hyun held on her.

His stupefied eyes took in the black hoodie she wore, the dark jeans, the boots, and the bodyguards who stood beside her. Then, at long last, his eyes returned to her cold ones. The daze in his eyes became replaced with a look of unquestionable desolation. A heavy breath escaped from his lungs. His strained expression and the tense tightening of his jaw conveyed that the great King had just realized that this was the girl he prayed he would never come across again. And if his expression was any indication, then it was clear that he no longer recognized her as the innocent girl he left. He viewed her as the heartless, legendary Queen who had just made her return to the Underworld.

He knew she was no longer his ex-lover.

She was now his enemy—and a powerful one at that.

Acutely aware of what was running through his mind, Soo Jin grinned cruelly at him. Her silent eyes promised him that she had nothing but ill intentions with her return. Her homecoming brought back a reckoning, and he was going to be the principal target of her war.

A million different emotions rippled in his eyes. Yet, after swallowing tightly, Tae Hyun did not release any sign of emotions and pressed his back against his chair, becoming resolute about something. An abrupt coldness teemed in the contents of his eyes. It was evident that he had not only pushed back his human emotions, but he also remembered clearly that this was the woman who killed his mother. The anger became strongly prominent on his facial features. They continued to remain that way as he averted his gaze from her, no longer deeming her worthy of his attention.

At the sight of this, Soo Jin merely laughed to herself. She inclined her head to silently say, *"I'm not even close to being done with you,"* and turned on her heels to continue with her night.

With a purposeful look, she continued to tread across the massive ballroom, the deafening silence burning into the eardrums of those in attendance. The soles of her boots met the five steps that led up to Ju Won's majestic throne. She glided up the steps like it was her preordained birthright and stopped in front of the throne that seemingly beckoned for her to grace it with her presence.

Oh, yes . . .

She traced her fingers over the beloved chair that belonged to Ju Won— the very throne she had her eyes on for over a decade now. Soo Jin inhaled with delight and spun around to face her more than captive audience. She helped herself onto Ju Won's seat, effortlessly exuding a formidable air that was only shared by the two Underworld Kings who sat on their respective thrones.

With no fear or inhibitions, she arrogantly lifted one bent leg up and rested an arm on it. She leisurely allowed her other leg to hang free from the throne, swaying it back and forth as her eyes measured the room.

Although she could no longer see the King of Serpents at the opposite end of the ballroom, she could clearly see the King of Skulls from the illumination of the moonlit rays behind him. When their gazes crossed, she favored him with an alluring smile before she allowed the wonder of the scene to cascade over her. *How she had missed this world and all the power that came with it . . .* From the corner of her eyes, she could see Ju Won seethe with anger at her complete show of disrespect. She laughed to herself. She couldn't care less about his resentment. She was too delighted to return to her rightful station in life. This was where she belonged; this was what she was born to do. She was born to rule over this world.

She leaned against the gold frame of the throne and kept her deep brown eyes on the crowd in front of her. In doing so, An Soo Jin couldn't have looked more powerful as she continued to hold her captive Underworld audience in the palms of her hands.

Seconds later, after what felt like an eternity, she finally decided to gift her influential world with her long awaited greeting.

"It's been . . . *a very long time*," she spoke lazily, her eyes half-closed. She continued to rest her head against the throne like it was a bed specifically made for her. Her voice undulated throughout the massive ballroom, sending chills up everyone's spines. "When I left this world three years ago, I could've never anticipated how much this world would change." She smiled, looking over to Ji Hoon. He was beaming in happiness at her favorable attention on him. "I could've never anticipated that out of the four top gangs, it would only be the Serpents and the Skulls who would remain, and I most certainly couldn't have anticipated taking a three-year break when all this change was taking place."

She sighed, pressing her hands against the armrests of the throne to lift herself up. She took two strides towards the edge of the platform to ensure that she was visible to everyone. Up above, she could see the crowd on the balconies lean their arms over the railing, moving themselves along to get a better view of her. She could see 1st layer crime lords, most of whom she knew all too well, smile to themselves. They sipped from their champagne glasses, murmuring to themselves that they should've known she wasn't dead. She could see everyone's elevated interest with her and what a powerful figure she still was in this world.

There was no way around it.

An Soo Jin captivated and fascinated the entirety of the Underworld. She commanded their fascination three years ago, and she continued to captivate them now.

"For those who don't know, let me introduce myself," she launched, her focus moving over the thousands of eyes that were glued on her. "My name is An Soo Jin. I have many nicknames in this world. I am known as the Princess of Scorpions, the Enforcer of the Scorpions, the Heartless Bitch of the Underworld, and of course, the Queen of the Underworld." She continued with her purposeful speech, her voice becoming stronger with every word. "Those who know me already know of the legends that surround me, and those who don't will never forget me after tonight. I may have died a Queen, but I'm returning as a God. I came here for a special purpose, and I, along with all of you, will not be leaving until I get what I want."

She was well aware that this threat did not sit well with the alpha males and the alpha females of her world. Despite this knowledge, she didn't give a flying fuck what sat well with them. Her throne was slipping out of her grasp, and she had to rectify this situation.

She turned to Ju Won, knowing that if anyone could fix this situation, it was him.

"Uncle," she began respectfully, well aware that she was not on his good side. She had already infuriated him after disappearing for three years and concurrently pissed him off for sitting on his throne. She knew he was livid, but like all masterful charmers, she was unwilling to let all of that deter her from trying to get on to his good graces. "I understand that this is the eleventh hour, but you should know that I'm here especially for you, for that beloved anointment of yours that seemed to have taken this world by storm. I'm here to reclaim what was rightfully mine." Her eyes teemed with rightful determination. "I want my throne."

"Who is she?!" a voice suddenly roared from the back.

A big muscular man, who was dressed in a dark gray suit, appeared at the center of the room. His face was shrouded with outrage. He walked out further while some of his gang members attempted to pull him back. Regardless of their efforts, he easily thrust his arms away from their grasp and continued to stride through the ballroom like the pompous idiot he was. It was clear that he was a small-time gang leader in the Underworld—a novice who didn't know that it was a grave mistake to interrupt the Queen of the Underworld while the stage was still hers.

Annoyance glinted in her eyes while her nose flared. Akin to watching a stupid child throw a tantrum in front of her, she quietly placed her hands on her hips and listened to the imbecile as he bantered on.

"How dare you walk in here like you own the place and demand to be considered as an heir—to be considered as our Lord when you have no gang or power of your own? Who the hell knows what you've been doing all these years?" He scoffed to himself. "Probably hiding out for all we know. We all know that the rumors about you are nothing but exaggerations, so don't come in here and disrespect the two Kings who have actually *earned* the respect and power from our society."

The infuriation in Soo Jin's expression was palpable as Ju Won stole her attention.

"He has a point, Soo Jin," he said while her eyes remained on the imbecile who interrupted her. "You've wasted three whole years. Your time has passed. I no longer have time to deal with you."

"Three years were *stolen* from me," she snapped, anger lining her fiery brown eyes. She turned to Ju Won. "*You* knew of my plans!" she gritted out. "It was foolproof . . . until I was betrayed." The image of Anna came into her mind, and she pushed past it for the time being. She would deal with that backstabbing bitch later. For now, she had more pressing matters to take care of. She swallowed tightly, speaking in the respectful tone she knew would be her ticket to getting her way tonight. "But I'm here to make things right. It may have been three years, but you" — she looked around the room— "and everyone here, aside from that stupid imbecile right there" —the man scowled when she said this— "wouldn't dare to question my rightful station in life . . . or my power."

"You need to hold power over a gang, Soo Jin," Dong Min finally interjected, his expression more gentle on her than the cold stare she was receiving from Ju Won. "Not just hold reverence over a society."

"The Skulls and the Serpents are the two biggest gangs right now," Jung Min answered as well, folding his arms together. His stare on her was expectant, borderline proud that she had finally made her return—regardless of how late it was. "We raised you better than this. We raised you to know that a King—or Queen—is only as powerful as their gang."

Soo Jin expelled a dry laugh at the stupidity of the situation she was in.

It took all of her control to not raise her voice to a high falsetto tone and mock them. Her propensity to be a troublemaker aside, she understood that this wasn't a savage society; this was a heavily domineering and political one. She was in the presence of people who were Royals in their stations in life and becoming too pompous and rude was out of the question—no matter how much her fighting skills and her ruthlessness may supersede others.

"So, all I need to do is form a gang of my own?" Soo Jin asked sweetly, keeping her emotions intact.

She didn't wait for a response.

After she asked this, she eyed the bastard who dared to question her.

With blades of sharp daggers morphing in her cold eyes, she simply said, "Then kneel."

"Excuse me?" he asked in outrage. He laughed to himself. "You have no control over—"

Swish!

The words lodged in his throat when Soo Jin, with predator-like swiftness, whipped a small knife from her pocket and threw it at him. The blade of the knife entered through his forehead like a perfectly angled bullet, finishing off when the sharp tip of the knife peeked out from the back of his head. With his eyes wide opened, his lifeless body crumpled to the floor as Soo Jin tilted her head with amusement.

There were no whispers or murmurs of amazement, nor were there gasps of horror over what had transpired. Her world was all but too used to seeing death displayed in front of them. And as for being surprised, it was clear that the entire crowd, apart from the dead imbecile, had anticipated that the man was living on borrowed time after he rudely interrupted An Soo Jin mid-speech.

"I wasn't talking to you," Soo Jin told his corpse with flippancy. Her hardened eyes rested on the twenty men standing in the corner—the ones who were the dead idiot's gang members. "I was talking to them."

Shaking in their stance while they eyed their boss's dead body, all it took was for the Queen to say "kneel" again before twenty pairs of legs hit the floor and kneeled before her like she was a revered deity.

Soo Jin smirked, looking all across the room with challenging eyes. "Anyone else who objects to my presence and me reclaiming my rightful throne?" she asked, knowing that no one would say anything. "If you have any issues, I could have the same discussion with you."

She was a walking dichotomy, and she knew it. She very well knew that people had described her as a devil with the face of an angel. She knew how contradicting she looked as she stood there, completely underdressed in a black hoodie that clearly belong to a man and black jeans and boots that unquestioningly belonged to a more innocent Princess—one who would never kill a man for simply disrespecting her.

The hushed silence was her answer when she saw the entertained smiles on the faces of the crowd around her. Based on how some of the 1st layer heirs on the balconies were staring at her with desire in their eyes and how some of the 1st layer heiresses were gazing at her with idolizing eyes, Soo Jin knew she was more than making their night. Her return brought forth a fabled legend that was so widespread around her world that even those outside her society had heard of her. The Queen that everyone once thought was dead . . . was back. It didn't take a rocket scientist to decipher that the elders in the Underworld and the future of the Underworld were extremely pleased with this turn of events. They lived for historic nights, and this night was proving to be the most historic of all.

Marveling in a similar state, she looked at Ju Won, whose face had already softened after bearing witness to what she did and the power she easily displayed. "I have a gang now."

"Don't insult us, An Soo Jin," a familiar male voice boomed from the opposite corner of the room.

Something in her gut clenched at the condescending voice. Even though she was surprised with who it was that spoke, she was also pleased with the prospect of such a comment.

With an amused smile on her face, she lifted her hand up and motioned a wave with it, a silent command for the attendees blocking her view to move aside.

Like parting waters, they adhered to the silent command, giving Soo Jin an unobstructed view of the King of Serpents.

He was still sitting in his seat, looking as powerful and indomitable as ever. His eyes—cold and unfeeling like hers—were glued on her. She could see his nine Cobras standing on the ground floor beside him, and she could see the hatred in their eyes.

"Insult you?" she asked carefully, scrutinizing the demeanor Kwon Tae Hyun wore. Even though she *was* insulting him, she refused to gracefully accept him calling her out. A cruel laughter echoed into the ballroom as she regarded him with hateful fire in her eyes. "I haven't even *begun* to insult you."

"Your twenty-something gang members are a joke compared to the real players in the game," he went on, deliberately ignoring her last comment. "You're not only wasting the Underworld's time, but I would daresay you're wasting my time as well. You left this world three years ago for a reason, and I promise you will leave it again tonight. This isn't three years prior. You may have reverence, but you do not have an Underworld army to govern. Go home, Princess. This is no longer your world, and as long as I'm in it, it won't ever be your world again."

"Then we can arrange for you to be out of it," she retorted quickly.

"If you can even touch me that is," he countered just as quickly.

She didn't like the condescending tone he used with her, and she most definitely didn't like that when she spoke to him, she was also feeling a bit affected and intimidated by the sternness he radiated. Kwon Tae Hyun was a natural born leader who had the charms of a politician and an untouchable quality that made him a great King. The aura of his power could supersede many, and when one was around him, they could not deny his overwhelming presence. The fact that he was an alpha male by nature was also a problem. His promise of protection was a godsend, and his opposition was hell on earth.

By how things were going, she knew he merely viewed her as an opposition. This alone sparked the competitive fuel in her veins. It definitely helped that she was an alpha female by nature, and it helped even more that his prevailing personality didn't frighten her. All it did was remind her of the epic fight to come. It was a fight that she could not wait to wage against him.

She smirked, not even deigning to reply to him, for she knew it pissed off the prideful one whenever he was ignored. She could hear Tae Hyun's scowl of anger from across the room for her complete disregard of him. She maintained her air of indifference and turned back to the Advisors. She had other things to resolve before she dealt with the favored King.

"Uncle," she started cordially, staring directly at Ju Won, "please reconsider—"

"I have mixed feelings about you, Soo Jin," Ju Won admitted, his face cool with aloofness. "I spent three long years feeling disgraced by you because I thought you actually felt remorse and committed suicide. But now that you're here, I can't help but feel intrigued." He grinned, his eyes roaming around the room at all the people in attendance. "But in matters like this, it is not my place to decide if you should become a contender."

Soo Jin furrowed her brows in confusion before someone spoke in Ju Won's place.

"You're in a precarious position right now, Soo Jin, for it is not the Advisors who decide your future in this world," a Corporate Crime Lord from the balconies shared as he held his champagne glass in hand. She immediately recognized him as Choi Min Hyuk, the owner of the various conglomerates around the world. He was one of the, if not the most powerful and respected, Corporate Crime Lord in the 1st layer. To add insult to injury, he was also one of Tae Hyun's mentors.

Ju Won nodded, staying quiet as Choi Min Hyuk continued to speak. "The three elder Advisors are the mentors, but apart from working together to choose an heir for their empires, their powers have never been absolute. They may choose their heirs, but it is the majority of the Underworld who ultimately decides who their Lord should be. We consider the eldest Advisor's decision as a supplement to our end decision—nothing more, nothing less. With that said, they do not hold vetoing or approving power in terms of who gets to be a contender for the throne. The choice resides in the Kings and the rest of the Underworld. Three years ago, we all agreed on two competing Kings. The King of Serpents and the King of Skulls had already been crowned the contenders. Your sudden appearance, although very fascinating and intriguing to me, does not surpass the traditions of this world. One King has already opposed you joining the ranks—"

"—I want her as a contender," Ji Hoon interrupted, staring directly at Soo Jin, who smiled as she kept her eyes on Min Hyuk.

"I believe that equals out the vote of the Kings," she replied blithely, more than elated with Ji Hoon's overt support.

Min Hyuk did not get a chance to respond when a woman standing on the adjacent balcony, a woman she recognized as an Advisor for the 2nd layer and a Ji Hoon supporter, said, "Make your speech then. Tell us exactly why we should kneel before you. Afterwards, we'll all decide as a society about what course to take."

Soo Jin nodded and complied, not because she was afraid of them, but because she respected them. Her society was a tough world to infiltrate and an even tougher world to impress. One had to be born into it, be raised within it, and be willing to die in it to make any sort of impact. She was born to rule, but she still had to fight for power. She still had to remind everyone why she was better than them.

"You've all heard of me, remembered me, or dreamed of meeting me," she began powerfully, her voice resonating across the enormous room. "I am the very embodiment of greatness. I was born with the prestigious Japanese and Korean Underworld blood pumping in my veins. I was raised to be powerful in this world, to be the pride of this world, and to rule over this world. If I wanted to, I could kill over five hundred of you in the span of an hour without even breaking a sweat. If I wanted to, I could outsmart and outwit each and every one of you without thinking about it. I could do whatever I want because I was trained to be above the rest—I was trained to be your God."

She made sure to pause and allow them to soak in her words before continuing with unmatched authority.

"Will you really forgo what the future may hold because of a few minor problems that I could easily solve in a few days? I don't have an official gang right now, but I could easily form one. All I ask for right now is your trust in my capabilities, the things I can bring, and the greatness that you all know have always awaited me. I am a walking and breathing legend. I am the only one who has captivated this world and the world outside ours with such allure, that I can't help but wonder if seventy-percent of your recruits didn't join out of fascination about me and the world that raised me." Her eyes grew firmer, more determined. "Give me back the throne that has been rightfully mine the moment I took my breath in this world. Give me a chance to retrieve the throne that was stolen from me three years ago. Give me what I want, and I'll bring you an epic era that you will never forget."

She knew her speech worked. She knew it was effective when a profound silence collapsed over the room after she was done speaking. She smiled inwardly, pleased with this response. It was only a matter of time before she got what she wanted tonight.

"Please leave for the time being," Ju Won told her softly, a crafty light playing off in his eyes when he realized what he could do with this historic moment. The wickedness in his eyes didn't sit well with Soo Jin, but she didn't have time to try and figure it out. "We have things to discuss, and there's no need for the two Kings and our Queen to be in the room when we discuss it."

"Of course," said Soo Jin, already anticipating having to leave the room as they held their discussion.

Bowing slightly, she raced down the steps and motioned for Jae Won and Kang Min to stay where they were. Then, she made sure her wicked eyes were trained on Tae Hyun's, who was watching her every move with a cold expression on his face. She bestowed him with a devious smile before veering her attention to Ji Hoon.

Watch this, Kwon Tae Hyun, she thought cruelly.

She smiled seductively and extended a hand out to Ji Hoon.

"Hi babe," she whispered to him after he raced down from his seat and enveloped her in an embrace.

"God, I've missed you, baby," Ji Hoon murmured against her neck, holding her close to him before he hovered his lips over her, reveling in the feel of her being close to him. "It's been hell without you."

"I've missed you too," she cooed before she wrapped her arms around his neck, closed her eyes, and brought him down for a kiss that was long overdue between them.

She kissed him for a few long breaths, angling herself into a methodical direction. She kissed Ji Hoon with more deliberation, her cruel eyes fixing on Tae Hyun. She noted that Tae Hyun was doing his best to not look their way— he was employing everything in his power to not rush over from his seat and tear Ji Hoon apart for even touching her. She knew this scene was a painful one for the King of Serpents, which was why she so callously displayed it in front of him.

After a long moment she pulled out of the kiss, stared up admiringly at Ji Hoon, and tugged at his hand, leading him towards the door where an adjoining room laid. She kicked the door closed with her foot, catching one last peripheral glance of Tae Hyun rising from his seat and storming out of the opposite doors, away from the room she and Ji Hoon were in and away from the privacy she wanted herself and Ji Hoon to have.

They still had unfinished business to tend to, and she intended to take care of it without delay.

"And you can fight all you want..."

03: The War Clause

"I thought Tae Hyun kicked you out of the country," Ji Hoon murmured in a perplexed state of mind. As they continued to stumble into the adjoining room, he embraced her with an iron-grip and continuously molded his lips with hers.

"I got the trigger I needed to come out," Soo Jin explained, panting for little bouts of air. Their mixed breaths continued to mingle as she affectionately pressed her body against his. As the tempo of their kiss leisurely came to a halt, she steadily withdrew her lips and moved her fingers through his hair, feeling the silky texture between her fingers. She gazed at him warmly and suddenly asked, "Have you really?"

"What?" He tilted his head to the side in confusion. He didn't understand her question.

"Missed me? Have you really missed me?"

"Yes, of course," he uttered, thunderstruck by her query. "Why would you ask that?"

A chilling air settled over them. Soon, the warmth from her eyes abruptly dissipated. While the rest of the Underworld was discussing her future, she might as well resolve some of the issues with her "boyfriend" too.

"You've been having so much fun these past three years, haven't you, Ji Hoon?" Soo Jin casually observed. Her voice encompassed all the vile feelings she was harboring. It was low, concentrated, and lethal. "Sleeping around with your many playmates when you told me for years that no one would be able to catch your eye after me." The vacant stare slowly morphed into a dangerous glint, and Ji Hoon grew more and more wary of the impending confrontation. "But you know what pisses me off *more*? The simple fact that you didn't even try to help me regain my memories when you saw me again as Yoori."

With Soo Jin's evident animosity, the hope and jubilance in Ji Hoon's eyes instantly vanished. He realized now that this reunion wasn't going to be as heartwarming as he anticipated. In fact, it was painstakingly clear that it was going to be the polar opposite.

"I didn't want you to go through with your original plan," he justified in hopes of vindicating himself.

"No," she rebutted, dismissing all his bullshit excuses. After unwrapping her arms from around his neck and pulling out of their embrace, she stepped away from him calmly—too calmly. "You didn't want me to regain my memories because you preferred my body and not the killer impulse that came with it. I was your pretty little trophy, and my memories or wellbeing didn't matter to you." She smirked dryly, shaking her head at him in great pity. "But of course, since our dear Yoori couldn't care less for you, you decided it was finally time to have your trophy emerge by sending *eleven men* to rape an innocent girl, and thus, provoking my anger. And, oh yeah, choking my neck against a wall and slapping the hell out of me when my counterpart didn't give you what you wanted."

Even though her voice was serene, her eyes were fuming with toxic fire.

"I hit Yoori, *not you*," Ji Hoon defended as if he were the victim in this scenario. Aggravated by Soo Jin's belittlement, his voice escalated to the same level of anger as Soo Jin's. "I sent men to rape Chae Young, *not you*. All of this happened *because* of you. You just had to go through with that stupid plan of yours when I told you not to. Do you know what it was like for me to go through three years of hell by myself when I once had the best woman by my side? It also didn't help that your precious human counterpart had to get into bed with my greatest enemy."

Soo Jin smirked, her patience wearing thin with Ji Hoon. The next words out of her mouth throbbed with restrained fury. It brewed with a storm that would annihilate Ji Hoon if she liberated it.

"The fact that you're breathing is a miracle. If I hadn't taken into consideration all those times where you helped me and stuck with me through my 'stupid plan', then I wouldn't even have cared about keeping you alive. Regardless of how tempted I am to skin you alive, I owe you for your help, and I'm returning the favor. But believe me, one of the blessings of being Yoori was seeing your true colors. I will never forget when you didn't even give a fuck about my well-being and told Tae Hyun that I killed his mother." Her breathing became harsher. She was absolutely livid with the remembrance of Tae Hyun confronting her about his mother's death. "Kwon Tae Hyun is a *fucking* King in this world. Under oath, he is required to put the loyalty for his family and his gang above anything else. He is required to *exterminate* anyone who dares to hurt his family, and you didn't put my fucking *safety* over your petty jealousy?"

She did not permit him to speak when he tried to chime in.

"It was pure luck that he showed me mercy because of his feelings for my stupid human counterpart, and it was pure luck that your idiocy didn't get me killed. I'll never forget that—among other things. Having said that, it looks like we're not going to work out anymore."

Unable to believe the words ringing in his ears, Ji Hoon's calm composition deteriorated. His eyes rounded incredulously. "Are you breaking up with me?" he asked heatedly, his voice laced with outrage. "After I gave you my support in there while Tae Hyun opposed you? Do you think they'd even be considering you as a Lord if I hadn't given my approval?"

"Yes," she responded flippantly. Her voice teemed with artificial sweetness. "Thank you for your support. It was much appreciated." She then tilted her head out of curiosity. "By the way, what happened to your nose? Did Kwon Tae Hyun kick the shit out of you?"

He didn't say anything and merely looked away from her.

Ji Hoon was unable to maintain his poise when—

Bam!

Without notice, Soo Jin whipped her hand in the air and slapped the shit out of him with the back of her hand. The sound of flesh hitting flesh resonated into the air. A red handprint formed on Ji Hoon's handsome, but completely fucked up, face.

Fire raged in his eyes. He muttered a spiteful curse, glaring at her with the utmost hatred. He was no longer infatuated with her; he was simply infuriated with her. "What the fuck are you doing—?"

"*That* was for slapping me in your bar the other night," she told him unapologetically. "And believe me, if you so much as go near Lee Chae Young, I will bypass the debt I owe you, and I will cut you into a million pieces before I feed you to the dogs. Do you understand me? Now if you'll excuse me, I have an Underworld meeting to attend."

"Don't you fucking betray me like this, Soo Jin!" Ji Hoon bellowed, following after her. He pushed the doors open and marched back into the ballroom where everyone awaited them. "After all I've done for you, don't you fucking walk away from me like this!"

The entire Underworld didn't miss Ji Hoon's resentful shouts, nor did they miss the red hand mark on his cheek as Soo Jin openly ignored him and sat back down on her seat. Once Ji Hoon realized the attention of the Underworld was on him and how pathetic and deranged he looked, he quelled his fury and went back to his own seat with quiet rage.

After Soo Jin was settled on her throne, she cast a glance over to Tae Hyun, who looked like he had been holding his breath the entire time she was in the room with Ji Hoon. To her amusement, he exhaled a small air of relief when it was clear that she had kicked Ji Hoon to the curb. Soo Jin smirked.

Figures that he still saw—if only remotely—a fraction of his Princess when he looked at her. Soo Jin laughed to herself, ready to use it against him in the very near future. Until then, she had another matter to tend to.

"Give me good news," Soo Jin prompted loftily. She lifted one bent knee up on the throne and sat comfortably, ignoring the quiet stream of curses coming from Ji Hoon's corner.

Ji Hoon was never good with rejections, and his display of anger made it obvious. This night was clearly not in his favor.

Ju Won grinned from the podium, looking directly at Soo Jin. There was a wickedness to his smile that caused ice-cold chills to form on her skin. "What would you do for the throne, An Soo Jin?"

"Anything," she answered swiftly, meaning it wholeheartedly.

She then shifted uncomfortably. There was a change in the air that she couldn't decode. It was as if the anticipation in the room had grown . . . higher. She looked at the crowd curiously. What the hell did they talk about when she was in the next room with Ji Hoon?

Ju Won nodded proudly, pleased with her response. He had taught her to ruthlessly seek power, and he was thrilled that she was displaying such determination tonight.

"I have spoken to the other elders in the Underworld about what has taken place tonight, what has happened these past three years, and what we want to add—in terms of a little twist—for this anointment."

Soo Jin, Tae Hyun, and Ji Hoon's ears piqued in interest as he continued.

"This Underworld has become too much about the politics and not enough about the savagery that this society was born upon. After much deliberation and agreement from the majority in this room, we decided to uphold one of our old values and keep it solely at two contenders."

Soo Jin was about to swallow in anger until Ju Won turned apologetically to Ji Hoon and said, "Unfortunately, we have decided because An Soo Jin— under your support—has joined the ranks, then someone has to be cut. I regret to inform you, Ji Hoon, that it has been agreed upon that you will no longer be a contender for the Underworld throne."

"*What?*" Ji Hoon roared in disbelief, propelling himself from his chair in anger.

Tae Hyun's eyes grew wide in outrage as well. The last thing he wanted was for Soo Jin to be his sole opponent.

Soo Jin, on the other hand, was thrilled.

This was *definitely* not Ji Hoon's night.

"Ju Won," Jung Min began, looking troubled. It was evident from his demeanor that he had spent the majority of his time trying to convince Ju Won and the rest of the Underworld to not eliminate his beloved advisee.

For some reason, Dong Min didn't look as happy as he should have been either. She couldn't understand why he was not beaming with happiness. Was he upset because he was trying to help Tae Hyun keep her out of the ranks and lost, or was he upset about something else?

"Ju Won, you fucking bastard!" Ji Hoon lashed out with blinding rage. "After all these years, you throw me aside like this?"

"I'm sorry, my child," Ju Won placated, looking genuinely apologetic. "The decision was out of my hands. This outcome was based solely upon that of the other Royals in the Underworld. In terms of competition, you are a great King, but you knew from the get-go that you were the contender for Tae Hyun's throne. Soo Jin had always been the favorite three years ago, and now with her return, she has reclaimed the spot you once had."

This explanation did not sit well with the Skulls.

"You're all idiots!" they started to scream out.

"This is an outrage!"

"—A big mistake!"

"We don't have time for this!" a high-powered politician—a mentor who had always supported Soo Jin—shouted from the furthest end of the balconies in annoyance.

All around him, the rest of the Underworld populace casually hung their arms over the railing of the balconies to showcase their glinting guns. When outside of Underworld gatherings, the powers of the 3rd layer Kings are unsurpassed. However, when in the presence of a gathered society, it was an unspoken law that everyone abided with the peace and left the bloodshed outside. This was what set the Underworld apart from all other crime worlds. They not only prevailed with strength, but also with bylaws, respect, and high standards of composure. The members of the Underworld did not allow themselves to embarrassingly stoop down to the level of stereotypical parasites who shoot at one another for the sake of shooting at one another. Nevertheless, if provoked with disorder or violence, then all was fair in their books. They may have been politicians by design, but they were ruthless by nature.

"It has already been decided that the King of Serpents and the returning Queen will be the two contenders," he went on, earning the concurrence from the rest of the Royals beside him. "No amount of bitching will change it. If you're unhappy with the decision, then you can try to bring war upon us right now. Either do that or simply get over it."

"It should be me and Ji Hoon," Tae Hyun contended from his seat, shaking from his own restrained fury. He was barely able to conceal the indignation in his voice. "It has always been the Kings' decision, and I never agreed for her to be a part of this."

"Tae Hyun," Min Hyuk said sternly, looking down at him with cool eyes. "This isn't a tea party, son. We try to accommodate your wishes because you're the Kings of this layer, but that doesn't mean your power is absolute— not unless you become the Lord. We only want the best to compete, and the best are you and An Soo Jin. Having Ji Hoon in the mix, especially with our next condition, will not make sense."

Before Tae Hyun could even argue his point, the future of the Underworld was set in stone with Ji Hoon's next set of actions.

"Fuck this," Ji Hoon snapped, looking down at his gang members and furiously flying down the steps.

Even from across the room, Soo Jin could hear Tae Hyun curse under his breath as he watched Ji Hoon completely lose his cool.

"Send out the word!" Ji Hoon bellowed out. From all corners, hundreds upon hundreds of Skulls started to withdraw from the crowd and follow his departure. "I want the Skulls to decapitate every Serpent they come across and any gang member under An Soo Jin's rule. We'll see how much power they'll both have over me after that." He then glared murderously at Ju Won. "And give the green light: before the month is over, I want the eldest Advisor's head."

He scrutinized the room with hate shooting from his eyes. For the first time, he shed his calm exterior and freed the ruthlessness that had always possessed him.

"You think I'm going to lie back and allow you to screw me over? Think again. This throne has and will always be mine. Trust me when I say that, with or without your support, I'll become the new Lord of this world, and I'll eradicate anyone who threatens me. So please, everyone who helped make the decision to kick me out of the ranks tonight, I hope you sleep well because once I become the Lord—you're all dead."

Jung Min shook his head in dissatisfaction at Ji Hoon's thoughtless actions. He and the entire Underworld watched disapprovingly as the King of Skulls made his grand exit from the ballroom.

Not allowing Ji Hoon's outburst to deter him, Ju Won persevered with his speech. He gazed at Soo Jin with resolve in his eyes.

"Sitting in the room right now is the King, who is beloved and feared by the majority of the Underworld. He is the mountain that stands in your way."

Soo Jin smiled, staring directly at Tae Hyun, whose icy gaze met hers.

"Tae Hyun," Ju Won spoke firmly.

In the background, the entire Underworld populace began to put their guns away. With hushed silence, they all listened to the announcement.

"The moment you stepped foot into our world, it was decided amongst the Advisors in the 2nd layer and the Corporate Crime Lords in the 1st layer that you would be the crowned Lord. This was your throne to lose, and Ji Hoon was merely the one to take it from you if you couldn't hold on to it. But now that we have the Queen herself reclaiming her shot at the throne, I think I speak for everyone here when I say that between the two of you, you truly are the Gods of our world. With that said, there will be no more choosing of heirs."

Tae Hyun and Soo Jin straightened in their seats, their shoulders stiffening uneasily.

They knew that things were about to get more . . . *stringent*.

"It was a privilege to see the battle, no matter how constricted, between the King of Serpents and the King of Skulls, but my biggest honor in life came when Soo Jin made her return. Now, it feels like the stage is complete." He beamed, pleased that the stars had aligned and he was finally gifted with the most perfect birthday present of his life. "Kwon Tae Hyun, An Soo Jin . . ." He paused a moment for the whole Underworld to listen attentively. "When you two were out of the room, I took it upon myself to share your story."

A sinkhole materialized in Soo Jin's stomach. She imagined the same thing had happened to Tae Hyun as the blood drained from his face. It was then that Soo Jin understood why Dong Min looked so crestfallen. He didn't care about Ji Hoon being taken out of the ranks. He was unhappy because Ju Won had exploited the fact that she, or Yoori to be exact, used to have a relationship with Tae Hyun. With the cruelty that Ju Won possessed, she was sure he made their story appear like a show to the rest of the Underworld—a form of entertainment for them in which this love story would end with one of them killing the other.

Ju Won observed Tae Hyun, who was silently seething while he listened to the Advisor. He understood all too clearly why Dong Min greatly opposed him being with Yoori. It wasn't because Dong Min was trying to align himself with Ju Won's wishes or because he was loyal to the eldest Advisor; no, it was because Dong Min had long been anticipating that one day, Ju Won would realize the gem he was sitting on and he would exploit them, just as he was doing right now.

"I told them about who had been distracting our King these past couple of months, and I told them who stole your heart." He looked at Soo Jin, who was silently fuming at the thought of the entire Underworld being privy to her private affairs. "I told them about your amnesia, the moment you reappeared in our world months ago, the fact that you were the one who accompanied our King of Serpents to the masquerade ball, and that you had your heart—or your counterpart's heart—stolen by the King himself."

Soo Jin could distinguish a mixture of two different emotions in the crowd. The minority were shaking their heads in disbelief at Ju Won's cruelty while the majority were breathing in excitement and eagerly anticipating his next words.

Ju Won forged on. He was the most excited of all. "Your story has become a legend in this world. It has fascinated us so much that we wanted to see how much more epic both of you can make it. We decided that we're going to add a very fair twist to it . . . we will do as every potential Lord has done in the past." He eyed Soo Jin cold-heartedly. "An Soo Jin, give us Kwon Tae Hyun's head, and this world will kneel before you."

He then turned to Tae Hyun.

"Kwon Tae Hyun, be the powerful King we know you can be, give us An Soo Jin's head, and we'll give you this world."

He divided his attention between the most revered King and Queen of the Underworld.

"We know of the relationship the two of you shared, but it seems to have been confirmed that both of you have gotten over one another. Your final task in proving your capabilities to be an Underworld Lord will come into existence in a month's time. Once you've gathered your entire army and train as you need to be trained, we will all meet at a chosen location. You will then give us the once-in-a-lifetime-duel that will set off a legendary era for the new Lord of our world. You will not only prove to us that you are the best physically, but that you are also ruthless enough to lead us. And what better way to show us how dedicated you are to this throne than killing the one you used to love?"

Ju Won sadistically grinned at both Tae Hyun and Soo Jin.

"What do you say? Right here, right now, in front of the entire Underworld's elites, are we in agreement? Will you give us the most historic fight of the century?"

Soo Jin couldn't decipher what the King across from her was thinking.

Kwon Tae Hyun was a master when it came to hiding his true emotions. True to form, at the moment, the impassiveness on his cold face was a tough exterior for her to read. She felt his gaze rest on hers. He was attempting to read her emotions as well. When neither could decipher the other's thoughts, they merely stared at each other for another hostile moment before the ruthlessness of their world caught up to them.

Without any further hesitation, they both sternly declared, "Done."

Not deigning to spare another glance in her direction, Tae Hyun expelled a lethargic sigh, looked at the audience before him, and apathetically announced, "An Soo Jin would never walk into an Underworld meeting without an army of her own—at least not without a plan to obtain one."

He regarded her, and Soo Jin smirked, recognizing that he had figured out what she was doing. She also understood *why* he was so intent on not letting her join in the ranks to become a fellow contender. He already suspected that she had come here with a plan.

"In her quest to 'reclaim' her throne, she has not only proven to the entire Underworld how powerful she is as an individual, but also proved to any doubtful, future gang members of hers that she is going to be the perfect Queen to resurrect them and lead them after five years of extinction." He regarded her with growing boredom. "Time is money, Soo Jin. Hurry up and form your gang so we can get on with the night."

For the first time that night, Soo Jin laughed in exhilaration.

Oh, she was impressed. This was most certainly the worthy opponent that she spent her entire life dreaming that she would conquer one day.

"You are truly the best match I could ever hope for," she said before suddenly whipping out the jade knife from her jacket.

Whish!

Without missing a beat, she threw it across the room. It soared through the air at lightning speed, nearly piercing into Tae Hyun's forehead. He skillfully kicked the knife away before it hit him. The flying knife retracted to the side and dove straight for the podium where Ju Won stood. In a swift and fluid motion, the knife buried itself into the microphone that Ju Won held, centimeters away from the Advisor's heart.

Tae Hyun was pissed. Soo Jin wasn't sure what he was more pissed off about: the fact that she tried to bury the knife into his head or the fact that he missed and buried the knife into the microphone instead of Ju Won's black heart.

Her face morphed into an enormous grin. She was sure he was pissed because he missed Ju Won's heart.

As gasps and Ju Won's stream of spiteful curses filled the room, Soo Jin stood up from her throne and sighed. She commenced with the procedure to invoke the army that awaited her from the moment she walked into the ballroom.

"On the left side of the Siberian Tigers' estate, buried deep in the ground under the red roses, what you're looking for, you'll find it there . . ."

She allowed a moment's pause for the sound of her voice to resonate across the ballroom before she continued.

"Three years ago, nine Cobras were scarred on the left side of their cheeks with the number '57'. The person who did that was me, and the person who has the jade knife is me. From what transpired here, you know of the reverence I hold over this world and the power I would bring to you if you returned to your roots and allowed me to resurrect you."

She smiled, inhaling proudly.

"I hereby call upon the oath you swore to the gang when you were initiated, and as your new leader, I command your loyalty and your undying allegiance."

She looked all around.

"Siberian Tigers," she said loudly and clearly. "*Down.*"

At her command, a multitude of events occurred at once: twenty-eight snipers, all dressed in black with sturdy black ropes attached to their harnesses, fell from the dome shaped ceiling. Behind them, countless men and women jumped from the balconies and staircases they were on, while a collected wave of people throughout the ballroom trudged forward. With one command, the resurrection of a once extinct gang transpired as they fell to the floor on one knee. Over three hundred of those in attendance bowed before her. They were all the former elites of the Siberian Tigers, and they were all offering themselves to serve under her reign as their new leader.

Soo Jin nodded approvingly before measuring the crowd again.

This time her eyes were warmer and gentler.

"Before I left you, I told you that once the time comes, I'd retrieve you and would never forget your loyalty. The time has come, and I want all of you back. With that said, step forward."

In a move that warmed Soo Jin's heart, about two dozen of her loyal Scorpions, the ones she commanded to infiltrate other gangs or form their own gangs, stepped forward. Her smile grew wider when she realized how much they had grown over the past three years. She hardly recognized them. Some had become leaders of successful, smaller gangs, while others had become high-ranking members in other established gangs.

With their appearance, murmurs of shock and bewilderment echoed through the ballroom. Displaying apathy to all the curses from the infiltrated gangs, they all stood proudly before her. As they prepared to fall to one knee before her, she held her hand up and motioned for them to stop.

"You will *never* kneel before me or anyone else again," she proclaimed, smiling as her eyes scanned the room. Pride surged through her veins at the sight of her new soldiers. Once the news of the Siberian Tigers' resurrection circulated, her army would expand exponentially.

Gesturing for them to stand, she sighed and sat back down in the comforts of her throne.

"Siberian Tigers," she commanded loftily. "Spread the word. Find your brothers and sisters and bring them before me." She glanced at Tae Hyun. "This world has been too damn peaceful for my taste, and I'm hungry for a war."

With a respectful bow, over three hundred Siberian Tigers dispersed from the ballroom, ready to call forth the rest of the Siberian Tigers, who had been scattered throughout different regions of the country, and ready to recruit an army for their new Queen.

Soo Jin smirked smugly at the expressions of the various people in attendance. They were all staring at her in awe. In a matter of seconds, she went from having no soldiers to acquiring an army that would rock this world to its core.

Feeling satisfied with herself, she leaned her head against the chair. Now that she was done with one task, there was another bullet point to check off. Her vigilant eyes trailed up to the balcony in the far right-hand corner. She spotted a blonde Asian man—the one she knew was present as soon as she walked in.

"P.C., Jae Hyuk, Mike, Izzy, and Jess," she greeted with a lethal, unforgiving tone. She watched carefully as P.C. and a few scattered men and women in the room shifted uncomfortably, bewildered that she knew they were there the entire time. "Tell my brother that I haven't forgotten about him—or his wife." Although her voice was calm, her eyes promised retribution. "Please send my regards and let him know that I'm dying to see him again. It has been too long, and there is unfinished business that I have to take care of."

"With that said," Tae Hyun began, never taking his eyes off Soo Jin. It was clearly evident he was tired of being around the rest of the Underworld.

"—The party ends now," Soo Jin finished for him. Her eyes never left his as she whipped out her two gold guns and made sure they were in plain sight. "I want to be alone with the celebrated King."

Before any protests could come about, Tae Hyun said, "Mina, Ace."

At his call, both instantly handed Tae Hyun his two silver guns.

Scanning the audience again, he impatiently said, "This is the last time we're saying this. I've been composed for long enough. If the Queen and I want to be alone, then our wishes will supersede any event tonight, which has already died. Again, with all that said, leave *now* before things get . . . messy."

Since "the war" was to take place in a month's time, Ju Won was hesitant to leave the revered King and Queen alone in the same room. He was afraid they would kill each other before the designated moment. Nevertheless, despite Ju Won's opposition, he bit his tongue.

Then, in a show that had never been seen, the Advisors and the entire Underworld heeded their King and Queen's stringent commands. They bowed slightly as a show of their respect, and in an instant, sounds of chattering were ringing in the air. The Underworld populace began to file out of the various exits, each throwing back lingering looks onto Soo Jin and Tae Hyun. They were all wishing that they could stay and enjoy the official confrontation between the two Gods.

They were aware that, despite the bylaws of their world and the agreement Soo Jin and Tae Hyun made, An Soo Jin and Kwon Tae Hyun were the type of King and Queen who followed their own laws and none others. They not only dictated their own laws, but if they chose to, could also initiate their own private wars.

And if the icy, merciless looks the King and Queen gave one another were any indication, then blood was definitely going to be spilled tonight.

Their own private war had already started.

"But the inescapable truth is that your blood belongs to this world."

04: 'Till Death Do Us Part

If there was ever another moment in her life where she felt so jubilant, Soo Jin wasn't sure. The exhilaration that whipped through her was unrivaled by anything she had ever felt as she observed Tae Hyun. He was staring at her with such cold reserve that she wondered if he was feeling anything at all.

No longer finding the peace acceptable, Soo Jin decided it was due time to break the silence and get the night moving.

"Isn't it funny," she began in a flippant tone, "how even in a room filled with people who have made the biggest impact on my life, the only one I've been dying to see is you?"

Although he did not say anything, she knew he was listening to her every word.

Encouraged by the excitement streaming inside her, she continued to speak; the competitive fighter in her was thrilled to have finally met the one who made such an impression on her life.

"I spent my entire life training to meet you, Tae Hyun, even before I knew your name or knew of your existence." She laughed, taking her eyes off of him while playing with one of her gold guns. "Other girls spend their entire lives wishing for their Prince Charming to come and sweep them off their feet. For me, all I prayed for was to meet someone as great as me—someone who was just as legendary and would give me the fight of my life. All that blood I shed, all those times the Advisors buried me alive in a coffin, all those times I nearly had my neck ripped off, all those times I laid in a pool of my own blood thinking that I was seconds away from death . . . I fought to breathe, to continue to live so I could finally meet you—the one person who had always given me such a purpose in life."

"Should I be honored that I'm the one you've waited your entire life to kill?"

She didn't miss his antagonism towards her. She shrugged, eyeing the gold guns that sat peacefully on the small counters that flanked either side of her throne. "I rarely think highly of anyone, so yes, I think you should take it as a huge honor."

"How did you regain your memories?" he asked instead, getting right to the point. She knew all too well that he had been dying to ask her this as soon as she walked in. "Did it happen as soon as I walked out?"

She shrugged again, purposely trying to enrage him by being flippant. "Why wouldn't you assume that I remembered everything all along?" A cruel smirk lifted on her lips. "That I was merely playing you and that there was never a 'Yoori' to begin with."

When she saw a muscle loosen in his jaw at the reminder of her counterpart, Soo Jin jumped on that weakness with the brutality of a predator.

"I should thank you, Tae Hyun," she launched, uninterested with perpetuating the lie that Yoori never existed. "Choi Yoori, as weak and as *human* as she may have been, was truly a force to be reckoned with in matters pertaining to you. God, the girl just kept holding and holding on until you . . . so *cruelly* . . . walked out of her life and pretty much kicked her to the curb." Soo Jin shook her head at him, fully aware of the pain she was inflicting upon him. "What happened, Tae Hyun? I wouldn't take you for someone who would trust Ji Hoon's words, yet you believed what he said and kicked your beloved girlfriend out? Has hell frozen over, or is there a tidbit about your mother's death that stuck out in your mind enough to convince you that I actually killed her?"

He swallowed tightly, speaking through bottled emotions that he was unwilling to reveal to her. "It was never divulged to the public that my mother died because she slit her wrists with the jagged edges of broken bottles. How my mother died should not have gone beyond my family's knowledge. When I came home and inspected the bathroom, I knew something was off. Everyone thought it was a suicide. I shared my suspicions with my brother, but he told me that it was merely grief on my part. Despite this, I double-checked it anyway. Ji Hoon and Young Jae couldn't have been there that night because their whereabouts were confirmed by the mentors they were with. There were few individuals who could bypass Serpents' security and my Cobras, no less, unless they were highly skilled."

He regarded her with impassive eyes. "I didn't consider you as an option then because you never crossed my mind. I know the truth now. You were there, Soo Jin. You were there with my mother in that bathroom. You were the one who bypassed our security, you were the one who broke those bottles, and you were the one who helped her along."

A proud smile curved on Soo Jin's lips. Her bored eyes ran over the unfathomable pain that crossed Tae Hyun's face when he acknowledged this truth.

"You are truly one of a kind, Kwon Tae Hyun," Soo Jin said with genuine marvel. He never ceased to amaze her. She had high hopes for him, and he did not disappoint her. "You are truly the most gifted opponent I could ever ask for."

She tossed her gun from one hand to the other as if she were playing with a child's toy. "I see now how you've managed to acquire so much of Ju Won's reverence in three short years. That menacing old man is rarely ever impressed with anyone, but I can see why you've become such a favorite of his and the majority of our Underworld populace."

She then nodded, feeling as though she should respect him enough to tell him what he needed to know.

"Young Jae told me that in order to be second in command of the Scorpions, I had to kill someone of high status. As my fellow second born heir, it was supposed to be you who I killed that night. Yet, because you were out of the country, you weren't an option." She tilted her head as she stared admiringly at her gun. "But then Young Jae told me that he wanted me to kill your mother because he wanted to break Ho Young. I followed his command because I wanted to be the enforcer for the Scorpions. Additionally, because of my own devious ways, I assumed that after your mother died, Ho Young would break even more if he thought his mother had committed suicide as opposed to being murdered." Her emotionless eyes locked with his. "You were right all along, Tae Hyun. Ji Hoon didn't lie, my brother didn't lie, and you didn't leave the love of your life for the wrong reason. It was me. It has always been me."

The anger in him was potent—she could feel it. By now, she could see him gripping irately at his armrest. Slowly, but surely, he was losing it.

To his credit, he did a valiant job of maintaining his composure when he asked her another question. "How much of the past three years do you remember?"

Soo Jin laughed. She knew he was thinking about Choi Yoori when he asked this. The thought of Choi Yoori pissed her off, and she used that anger as her fuel to push the buttons that she knew could only be aggravated whenever his beloved Princess was mentioned.

"I remember everything," she told him uncaringly. "I remember the first meeting in the diner, I remember the handcuffs, I remember the park with the swings, I remember the lake house, I remember the Winter Wonderland, and I remember that elusive city . . . ."

This was where her eyes grew colder.

"I remember everything, but I merely remember it like it was a dream. There's no sentimental value attached to it for me because it was, after all, Yoori's life and not mine." She feigned a pout for Tae Hyun, who she knew was feeling every bit of pain she wanted him to experience. "If you asked that question because you wanted to see if your Yoori is still here, somehow 'buried' within me, then I'm sorry to disappoint you. Your Princess is gone. She was gone the moment you left her; she was gone the moment I came back."

When she saw Tae Hyun do that painful swallowing he did every time a piece of his heart broke, Soo Jin decided it was time to move on.

"Do you know why I'm here right now?" she inquired, placing her gun aside while she pulled herself up from her seat.

In a fluid motion, she treaded down the steps. She walked on the marble tiles, stretching her arms out like she was preparing for an intense workout.

"Yoori wanted to give you your revenge," she told Tae Hyun, who was still sitting in his throne, his hand clenching onto the armrest while his back was resting against his chair.

In spite of his calm demeanor, the raging fire in his eyes followed her like a shadow as she slowly made her way down the ballroom. She forged on, her voice taunting him. "She wanted to make things easier for you because she understood how much you despised me and wanted to kill me. She knew you would never be able to do it if she were still 'here', so she took care of it herself and pretty much let me out."

A spark of shock flashed across his face at this revelation. "Yoori *voluntarily* let you out?"

"Fight me now, Tae Hyun," she coerced, sensing his hesitation even though he was plagued with the duty to avenge his mother.

Tae Hyun was a man who could be a bit too honorable for his own good, but honor wasn't what she needed from him. All she needed was for him to satiate her need for a good battle after three years of peace.

"I can't wait a month from now to face you. I've been dying to meet you since I scarred your Cobras three years ago. I daresay that I've even lived for this moment. So screw any promises you made to Yoori. We both know that Yoori and I are as different as night and day. I don't give a fuck that you promised her you wouldn't fight me for the throne, or that you'd let me kill you if I wanted to, or that you'd always protect her. I don't need those promises—they mean nothing to me. The only thing I want from you is my battle. Show me what you have in store for me a month from now; show me the God I've been waiting all my life to fight."

When he didn't budge and then had the audacity to turn away from her, she lost it and grew angry as she neared the center of the room.

"Don't force me to bring Hae Jin into this," she warned.

Triggering the wrath that she knew would push him over the edge, Soo Jin continued to pick at the wound. She was willing to use anything to coerce him to fight her.

"You wouldn't touch her," he stated, gazing at her unblinkingly. His voice was stern, yet there was no conviction in them.

Tae Hyun might have had a soft spot for his precious girlfriend, but he had no soft spot for her. He was realistic about his knowledge of what she was capable of. He was fully aware of everything she had done in the past, and Soo Jin was intent on showing him how far she was willing to go to get what she wanted.

"No, I wouldn't touch her," she placated before tilting her head mockingly. "I'm sure it would be more poetic if Kang Min was the one who touched her. Or perhaps, it would be even more poetic if he ripped her heart out—*literally*—"

Bam!

He was there before Soo Jin could even anticipate it.

Seething, Tae Hyun had already thrown his tuxedo jacket off, ran towards her like a speeding bullet, and wrapped a hand around her neck. He lifted her off the ground, pinning her against the gold pillar across the room before she could even blink.

Astonishment echoed through her.

Soo Jin could not fathom how Tae Hyun did all of that with such alacrity. All she knew was that she couldn't keep the excitement from pumping in her veins. *This* was what she wanted . . . for Tae Hyun to be pushed over the edge.

As she felt air tread under her feet, Soo Jin did her best to regulate her triumphant smirk. She knew all too well that she only had to threaten the people he loved to provoke him.

Biting back a smile, she tried to breathe past the pain of not having enough air in her lungs and the pain surrounding her neck from his ironclad grasp. She stared at the fire brimming in Tae Hyun's eyes. She was pleased to finally begin to see the God she had wanted to come out.

"I didn't get the typical training that every heir gets, An Soo Jin," he warned her through clenched teeth. The inferno in his eyes intensified. "You were trained specifically by the Advisors, Ji Hoon was trained in Korea, Young Jae was trained in Japan, and my brother was trained in China . . . but I'm the wildcard in this mix. I've had mentors from all over the world, and I'm the best out of this group." He leaned in closer, giving her a whiff of his enthralling cologne and the potent fury exuding from him. "You don't know what I'm capable of, and you shouldn't try to learn."

"I know how skilled you are," she whispered. "I fought your Cobras—"

"Then you should know that every master is a hundred times better than the students they teach," he countered. "You didn't even see me coming a second ago; you won't be able to beat me. Stop forcing my hand, stop provoking me, and just stay away from my sister."

Even with all the anger he displayed, the bunching of all the muscles across his body told her that he was only using a minute portion of his physical capacity—he was holding back on her. If he wanted to, he could've choked her to death or ripped her neck off before she could process what had happened. He was still treating her like a fragile china doll that he was afraid to break.

She had to change that.

"What are you going to do now?" Her voice was soft, smooth, and rolling with mockery. "Will I be free to go if I promise to leave your sister alone? Will I be forgiven for what I did to your poor mother?"

He applied a bit more pressure around her throat, further constricting the limited air that was reaching her lungs.

Soo Jin saw that she was close to forcing him over the brink of sanity, and she loved every second of it. This was the way it should be. A God should never be controlled. He should be liberated; he should be free to exhibit his true powers.

"Every fiber in my body is telling me to kill you right now for what you did to my mother and all the trouble you've caused in my life," he said with conviction.

He appraised her, a thousand different emotions plaguing his eyes. Just when she thought he would apply more pressure, she felt him loosen his grip while carefully allowing her feet to touch the ground. She knew that there would be no marks around her neck nor would she have trouble breathing tonight. The King of Serpents was too careful with her, even when he seemed ready to kill her. He freed her neck from his grip and simply shook his head at her.

"You will never beat me. I'm not fighting you, Soo Jin," he dismissed, turning around and walking away from her. "Just stay away from me and stay out of my life."

"Kwon Tae *Hyunnnnn*," Soo Jin uttered in a singsong voice, watching him proceed to his chair to retrieve his guns. She began to retreat backwards towards her own throne. "Are you really going to turn your back on me now?"

He refused to say anything to her. The only sound that emitted from him was the aggravated stomping of his feet.

Anticipation, exhilaration, and fury were biting through Soo Jin's nerves as she watched him move further and further away from her.

She smirked to herself.

There was no way in hell she was letting him leave.

Ascending up the stairs at the quickest of pace, Soo Jin effortlessly jumped onto the cushion of her throne and stood up straight. She extended her hands out and formed a grip over the two pointed gold spindles that were sticking out of the throne as embellishments. She rapidly pulled the gold handles out, revealing two one-inch blade swords that shimmered once released from the golden throne.

"You should know," she began under her breath, "that I don't do well with rejection."

As if feeling her near presence, Tae Hyun's eyes enlarged once he reached his throne.

Swish!

He leaned backwards, ducking just in time before the sharp blade of a sword could slice off his neck. His instincts coming to life, Tae Hyun swiveled around his chair. He wrapped a hand around one of the gold embellishments and whipped out a sword of his own. With quick reflexes, he was able to position the sword just inches above his face. In that same second, Soo Jin's double swords came down upon it, its blades hungry for his skin.

The earsplitting shrill of metal hitting metal resounded through the air as Soo Jin, who was clearly elated that Tae Hyun had also been aware of the weapons that Ju Won hid in the thrones, wielded her swords with ease. She swung each sword to the side in an attempt to slice into either one of his hips.

As if already anticipating her move, Tae Hyun swiftly blocked one of Soo Jin's arms with his free forearm and blocked her other sword with his own, successfully deflecting both swords away from him. In a rapid move to defend himself, Tae Hyun was able to disentangle her blocked arms from his and use that split second to elbow her hard in the stomach, leaving her to tumble towards the steps leading up to the platform.

"Now that's more like it," Soo Jin said approvingly, walking backwards into the center of the rotunda. While doing so, she twirled each sword in her hands with ease. No longer having use for the weapons that were merely disguised as a way to provoke her hardheaded opponent, she threw them both aside, accurately burying the blades into the gold pillars on either side of the ballroom.

"I was getting bored of you, King of Serpents. I've been anticipating this match for a while. You're not going to disappoint me now, are you?"

He panted to himself as he watched her. He clearly did not anticipate that Soo Jin would provoke him to this degree.

Unfazed by his reaction, Soo Jin mumbled to herself as she stared around the elegantly decorated room. Dissatisfaction hung over her. Something had to be done about this room . . .

"Now to set the stage," she announced, pulling out her two gold guns from her pockets.

Tae Hyun smirked, his handsome face mocking. He tilted his head at her. "You're bringing toys into this duel now?"

Soo Jin laughed, shaking her head.

Authentic fighters rarely employed the use of guns when they wanted a real battle to see who was more skilled. She had too high of standards for the King of Serpents than to resort to using guns.

"Guns would be an insult to the type of fight I want to have with you," she replied. "I'm simply trying to set the mood for tonight."

Before giving him time to decipher what she was up to, Soo Jin, unable to withstand the elation streaming through her like an electrical current, lifted her guns up in the air and started shooting upwards towards the glass dome ceiling above them.

The entire time as she did this, Tae Hyun watched her in raw fascination.
Boom!

A myriad of sharp shards of glass started tinkling down like crystals as she ran through the room, shooting upwards nonstop before having to reload another round of bullets into the guns. Once fully loaded, she started firing another round before jumping onto her platform and pointing both guns at the grand chandelier hanging above them. She shot at it and effectively extinguished all the lights around them, leaving only the feeling of the cold air and the natural moonlight to stream into the now dark, quiet, and hazardous ballroom.

"You've thought this confrontation out thoroughly, haven't you?" Tae Hyun asked mindlessly, gazing up at her handiwork.

The glass ceiling was completely destroyed, and if one wasn't careful underneath it, then it was quite possible that a couple pieces of loose glass would fall from the heavens and stab the hell out of one's head. Below, the marble tiles were littered with shards of glass that glimmered under the moonlight.

It was the perfect stage for a fight.

Soo Jin released a satisfied sigh. "I actually envisioned that my historic battle with you would take place on the roof of a high-rise building in the center of the business district. We'd be surrounded by the entire Underworld, who would watch the entire affair in the various buildings that wrapped around the roof. In this scenario, we'd fight under the heavens, amongst the Gods."

She began to walk down the stairs, her boots stepping over the assortment of glass that was still twinkling under the night's sky.

"This is why tonight will merely be a warm-up for us to better introduce ourselves to one another." She pursed out a thoughtful lip. "Of course, if I accidentally kill you, I won't cry about it either. It would just suck for the

Underworld citizens because I think they're dying to watch the fight of the century."

"You're playing with fire, An Soo Jin," Tae Hyun admonished darkly, walking down the stairs with his sword outstretched in his right hand. He tossed it aside as he approached her. The sword fell with a loud clink when he reached her. "I keep giving you chances after chances to leave unharmed. Considering how much anger I harbor for you, you should be counting your blessings that I'm giving you this much allowance. But, like a fool, you keep on pushing me and pushing me. Do you really want to force my hand like this?"

"I can be pretty convincing," she amended coolly, bouncing in her stance. She loved fighting with guns, swords, or any other types of weapons, but for their first match, she was all too excited to fight fist-to-fist. There was no better way to assess an opponent's skill than through hand-to-hand combat. "Let's play."

With no further warning, she rocketed towards him, more than ready to start the night off.

Extending her leg out, she bestowed a reverse roundhouse kick to his face. It was an attack that left Tae Hyun momentarily disoriented. With eagerness, she finished the attack by planting her palms on the marble tiles (and ignoring the sharp shards of glass eating at her palms) and performed a low reverse roundhouse kick on the floor that had Tae Hyun falling off balance, his back meeting the glass-covered tiles with a big thud.

"Augh!"

He let out a tortured groan as the pieces of glass etched themselves into his shirt and stabbed into the flesh of his back. Blood started to seep through his expensive white shirt.

Smirking, she seized the opportunity for another attack. She had planned on giving him a swift kick to the face for good measure, but sadly for her, this time around, Tae Hyun wasn't letting her get away with hitting him so easily.

"I don't think so," he muttered before pushing himself up. He propelled himself to his feet and caught her leg before she could get a side kick in.

"Ugh!" Soo Jin groaned in frustration.

Competitive blood—as well as her prideful killer instincts—pumped within her veins, causing her to go from zero to a hundred miles per hour. She went crazy performing all the various types of attack moves under the moon, only to have him successfully hinder them every which way by constantly moving his body, keeping his hands opened, and holding his arms stretched out at an oblique angle.

Soo Jin growled under her breath.

It enraged her that he wasn't fighting back. Soo Jin used the boney tip of her elbow and swept it across Tae Hyun's cheek, fury mounting inside her. Once the attack connected, she slashed another elbow bone across the left side of his face. The assault left him to tumble backwards as blood started pouring from his mouth. He fell, but not before attacking with a spinning back kick to her chest that had Soo Jin gasping painfully for air.

"Ugh!"

She spun momentarily in the air and collapsed onto the glass-strewn ground at the same time as Tae Hyun.

Boom!

Two loud, rumbling thuds echoed into the night as both muttered curses at the shards of glass that were burrowing into their skin.

"Motherfucker," Soo Jin growled, groaning at the small pieces of glass that made it inside her flesh. In the past, having broken glass litter the floor was one of her favorite accessories for a battleground. She realized now that she only appreciated it because she rarely, if ever, fell to the ground when she fought an opponent. But now, with Tae Hyun giving her a run for her money and throwing her every which way, she was seriously regretting shooting up the dome ceiling. The hungry shards of glass didn't discriminate in terms of whose skin it ate, and she was realizing it all too clearly as she felt them inside her own body.

Soon, her resentment for the glass was overshadowed when she saw Tae Hyun rise up from the corner of her eyes.

No!

A gush of adrenaline entered her body. Refusing to give him the upper hand, she bolted back towards him. Soo Jin extended her legs out inches before she met him and purposely slid on the tiles. As she slid on the left side of her body, she felt every bit of the pieces of glass that attached themselves to her hoodie and ran into her skin. She fought through the pain, her only focus being Tae Hyun. Once she reached him, she skillfully spun herself up in a diagonal motion in mid-air and kicked him across the jaw with her right leg.

Bam!

His teeth brutally clacked together from the intensity of the kick. He tumbled backward, struggling to maintain his equilibrium while panting for air.

She took advantage of his disorientation and ran over to him with the intent of getting another bone-cracking kick in. She was sorely disappointed when he caught her leg in mid-air, twisted her body up, and then kicked her in the stomach, leaving her to fly into the flight of stairs that led up the upstairs quarter.

Boom!

She groaned at the spikes of pain that materialized in her back after her collision with the hard edges of the stairs. She could've also sworn she felt every nerve in her body vibrate in agony. That was the thing about fighting: people had this unrealistic notion that skilled fighters no longer felt pain when they fought, which was completely false. One may have had a slightly higher tolerance for pain, but it was still an agonizing experience. Unfortunately for Soo Jin, what was beginning to piss her off more was that despite the pain, she knew that none of this fighting even equated to the type of battle she knew Tae Hyun was capable of.

"You're going easy on me, aren't you, King of Serpents?" she sneered, shaking off the shards of glass that were stuck in her hands. She gripped onto the railing and pulled herself up, her eyes staring at him without deviation.

Even through the insurmountable pain, she recognized that this battle could be worse. She noted the tenseness in the muscles hidden underneath the affluent clothes he was wearing. He was holding his power back so much that she wondered if he was hurting himself in the process. It was clear that he was constraining his own strength to keep himself from instinctively hurting her.

"You really don't get it, do you?" he whispered, stepping onto the stairs. "I'm not even fighting you right now. This is merely self-defense."

She grimaced, having enough of this bullshit.

She wasn't going to walk around eggshells with him any longer.

She was going to exploit his pain.

"What a disappointment you're becoming to me, Tae Hyun," she taunted, breathing painfully as she hung her hands over the railing, "kinda like what a disappointment you were to your girlfriend."

At long last, the last vestige of Tae Hyun's armor cracked at the mention of the one who stole his heart.

"Do *not* bring her up," Tae Hyun snapped, inhaling with difficulty as he took another step.

Soo Jin knew that Tae Hyun didn't like her. In fact, he *hated* her. She knew he hated her for the sole reason that the woman he loved was no longer with him because of her. She knew this, and she was prepared to provoke him with this knowledge.

"How terrible it must be for you," she plowed on mockingly, laughing with hilarity at him, "to realize that just moments prior, you were kissing the love of your life, *forcing* her to leave the country so you could spare her life. Yet, here she stands . . . no longer the feeble bitch you left, but now the self-serving bitch you want to kill."

"That's enough, Soo Jin!" he screamed, getting angrier with every mocking second.

Soo Jin was having too much fun to stop. "Make me stop, King of Serpents!"

Using this moment of distraction, Soo Jin jumped off the stairs and punched him clear across his face, triggering him to take a couple of involuntary steps up the stairs. His teeth snapped together, and she was ready to deliver another punch when he caught her wrist and nearly twisted her hand back. In lieu of using his momentum to break it, Tae Hyun instead rose up and elbowed her across the chest, causing her bones to vibrate before she hit the stairs, her temple colliding against the gold railings.

Yes! That's more like it! The competitive part of her screamed in joy when she hit the floor, her body starting to feel the full effects of Tae Hyun's strength.

Finally.

Finally they were fighting like Gods instead of mere humans.

As blood seeped from her lips, Soo Jin decided to break the human in Tae Hyun and release the violent killer within him.

"Do you know how I killed your mother?" she jeered before running down to him while they were still on the stairs. With easy agility, she ducked to the ground and spun her leg on the steps to steal the ground beneath his feet. As he plunged down, she proceeded to kick him in the face, causing the back of his head to slam against the wall just before he fell and banged the side of his head against the stairs.

Soo Jin let out a cruel laugh.

She used this sublime moment to her advantage and kneed him in the jaw. She followed that by punching him across the face in three consecutive motions before she kicked his face and buried the sole of her boot into his neck.

"Don't you wanna know how I ended her life?"

"Shut up!" he snarled, grabbing a railing and pulling himself up. As he did so, he kicked her across the stomach before she was able to land another attack. The force sent her flying up towards the remainder of the stairs and slamming into a granite column that decorated the upstairs quarter of the ballroom.

Although pain throbbed like piercing knives in her body, she didn't care. He was losing it . . .

And she was loving it.

Soo Jin laughed, enjoying this moment more than she could ever imagine.

She had to push him more.

"She was drinking in her room!" she stated loudly, reveling in the sound of his screams for her to shut the hell up.

Her heart pumped ecstatically at the loss of his control.

She rose to her feet and effortlessly jumped onto the connected balcony railings that blocked the upstairs quarter from the wide-open space leading to the ground floor. She proceeded to walk backwards on the two-inch gold railing with ease. She smiled in anticipation while she watched Tae Hyun glide up the stairs like the fighter that he was.

She continued to taunt him in a singsong voice. "She was drinking like the miserable bitch that she was before I snuck in and found her all alone, ready to be tortured by me . . ."

Soo Jin crouched down, still smiling as Tae Hyun jumped smoothly onto that same railing. He walked on the thin rail like the skilled predator he had always been. He, like her, was able to easily balance himself on the railing, walking on it with such ease that they both made it appear as if they were gallivanting on the ground floor instead of on a railing that had a three-story fall beneath it.

She continued to taunt him, loving it more and more that she was coaxing the God out of him.

"This was just a while before that perverted brother of yours—the one that you killed, by the way—snuck into his thirteen-year-old sister's room and had his fun *raping* her."

"*Don't*," Tae Hyun warned, breathing so violently that she could see the humanity disperse from his furious eyes. All she saw was a God who had been pushed to his limits; all she saw was a God who was now ready to kill. "My patience with you is fading. If you don't shut up right now, I won't hold back any longer."

Unfazed by his warning, for she was waiting for him to explode, she plowed on. The adrenaline pumping through her was too addicting to stop.

"I taped your mother's mouth, dragged her by the locks of her hair, and brought her into the bathroom where I helped her out by breaking the alcohol bottles that were already littered around her room . . ."

"*SOO JIN!*" he roared, leaping towards her at once. Then, much to her delight, he began to fight her on the railing.

Each punch he threw, she blocked with ease. In the same degree, each punch she threw, he blocked with proficiency. Punch after punch, kick after kick, and head-butt after head-butt, their bones vibrated in pain at the excruciating violence inflicted upon them. In spite of this trauma, neither Tae Hyun nor Soo Jin yielded from the volatile situation they were fighting in.

"She cried, you know?" she told him, grinning callously while tilting her head after he held her arms, pulled her to him, and growled at her to stop talking. Agony appeared in his eyes, and she continued to stab the words into him, wanting every word to not only hurt him, but also infuriate him.

"She begged me to spare her life. But you know how killers in the Underworld are. We don't react to people who plead like dogs. I turned on the water in the tub, lifted her wrists, and began to *drag* the broken glass bottle across her wrist for her. I watched as her flesh ripped apart, as her veins were sliced, and then just sat there . . . holding her neck against the wall. I allowed her to watch as the blood seeped out of her—as the life escaped her eyes. And then when I was done, I left her there to rot like the worthless person that she was."

And this was where he lost it.

An unforgiving inferno claimed his eyes and he lost all sense of control.

Pulling herself out of his grasp, Soo Jin took her final steps backward in satisfaction of finally breaking him. In a swift movement, she ran back towards him and allowed her body to fall forward a foot from reaching him. She gripped onto the railing and swept her legs in the air. When her legs connected with his body, it threw him off balance and left him to fall off the railing.

Tae Hyun's body was primed to plummet to the world beneath them before, with the agility of an animal, he averted to the side to hold onto the railing in mid-air. He used it as an anchor to keep from falling to his demise, and then, with unparalleled strength, he lifted his legs up, swung his body backward, and found an unsuspecting Soo Jin. She was barely able to let out a gasp when he locked his legs around her neck in a tight knot and then swung his body forward, knocking her off her feet and throwing her over the railing.

"Ahhhhh!"

She dove through the air, plummeting towards the ground before she felt the back of her body slam violently into the gold pillar behind her. Every nerve in her body screamed at the earth-shattering impact.

"Augh!"

Groaning, Soo Jin was still conscious enough in midair; she knew she had to do everything in her power to alleviate the impact of the fall. She bent her legs slightly in preparation for the extreme collision ahead.

Boom!

The soles of her shoes met the ground with a loud crash, triggering pain to jolt up her body before she quickly rolled to the side to ease the momentum (and the pain) of her fall. The fact that it felt like a million different shards of glass were buried in her body did not help matters either. She wasn't entirely sure if it was pain from the fall, pain from the glasses slicing into her skin, or a combination of both. All she knew was that she could barely focus on her surroundings. The throbbing ache in her body was all consuming.

She was so overcome by the blinding ache that she didn't even register that Tae Hyun was already on the ground floor with her. It wasn't until she heard the sound of his shoes stepping over the various pieces of glass was she aware of his presence. Her observations came too late. A pair of strong hands grabbed a fistful of her black hoodie, raising her body into a sitting position with a pillar behind her. Soo Jin gasped when she felt the blade of a sword against her neck.

She looked past the excruciating pain she was experiencing and stared into his wrathful eyes.

She was no longer in the company of a King, but a God.

Perfect.

"Do it," she urged him, feeling the sharp blade flirt with the skin of her neck.

She searched his eyes, wishing with all her might that he'd just do the deed. She wanted him angry like this, she wanted to break him, she wanted him to not go easy on her—she wanted to make a God out of him.

"Do it, King of Serpents," she advised tauntingly. "This is your only chance. Once you let this moment pass, you'll never get it back again. You'll never be able to kill me again, and you'll never be able to avenge your mother or your precious personal assistant."

Mentioning his mother was the perfect tactic, for she saw the bloodlust in his eyes. On the other hand, her ultimate mistake was using the nickname that belonged to the one who continued to own his heart and his humanity. Slowly, the bloodlust began to deteriorate from his gaze. In place of that rage, all she saw were eyes teemed with pain. Tae Hyun began to stare at her with a longing that she couldn't describe.

Clank.

Then, it was the sound of the sword dropping to the floor that heightened the beating of Soo Jin's own heart.

She watched as his eyes slowly ran over the blood seeping from her mouth, the blood on her skin, and the shards of glass all over her body. He returned his focus to her face and stared at all the maladies present. His quiet eyes returned to hers. In that instant, a heart wrenching expression came over his face. It was clear that he had finally processed what he had done: he had just hurt the woman he loved more than anything else in the world.

"*Yoori* . . ." she heard him say to her. He breathed in painfully, raised a hand up, and gently cupped her right cheek.

He was staring at her with so much love that she felt hypnotized by him.

"I'm sorry," he started to whisper, kissing over the bruises on her face, the cuts near her lips, and every part of her face with so much adoration that she was just lost in it.

Something odd happened to Soo Jin at that instant. As he expressed his apologies for hurting her, for fighting her, Soo Jin just felt . . . out of place.

She couldn't control the warm butterflies that escaped into her stomach at his gentle touch, at the way those captivating eyes held hers. She couldn't control the warmth that overcame her as he showered her with affection. The way his lips—his damn gorgeous lips—moved over her skin just felt so nice. She no longer felt pain. All she felt was distraction.

She peered up at him, somehow unable to rip her gaze from his when she realized that the maladies on his face were bringing some sort of pain to her as well. The fact that he couldn't prompt himself to kill her, even though he believed she was his mother's killer, was also doing some strange things to her sensibility.

She tried to shake off these peculiar thoughts.

It was probably the pain, she placated after she processed what was actually happening—that Tae Hyun, despite all her efforts to piss him off, wasn't going to even attempt to kill her.

Are you kidding me?

Frowning at him and the thought of herself becoming weakened by his charms, Soo Jin decided it was due time to end things for the night. She wanted to incite the legendary fighter—the epic God—to come out of him; she did not need to be mesmerized by the handsome King in the process.

"You're such a disappointment right now," she complained, pushing him away in bitterness.

It wasn't like she had planned on killing him or allowing him to kill her tonight. She simply wanted a prelude to the fun that was to come at their actual battle in front of the Underworld. It was an understatement to say that this anticlimactic fight had ruined her mood.

"You! You're the once-in-a-lifetime fight I've been waiting for?!" she shouted, standing up in disbelief. After years of training, years of pain, years of hell . . . her one true match was someone who wanted to kiss her wounds after a good fight? She stared at him with incredulity when he stood up to face her. "You're really not going to kill me?"

He gaped at her with his own expression of disbelief.

"Does it look like I can?!" he asked in aggravation. His eyes widened disbelievingly at her naïve inquiry. "You think I didn't know that you were saying all that stuff to push me over the edge? Do you think it's easy for me to stand here conflicted when the simple thing to do would be to kill you for murdering my mother?" He tightened his jaw in frustration. "But I can't kill you. I'm more willing to slice my own neck off before I even touch you with that sword."

She shook her head, determined to not allow his words to soften any emotions within her. She was getting more and more frustrated by the second and she didn't know why.

"You're a piece of work, King of Serpents," she said through clenched teeth. She allowed a moment's pause before adding, "So, what now? Am I supposed to jump into your arms and be touched that you couldn't kill me because you still see your beloved Choi Yoori in me?"

She scoffed at his expectant silence. His lack of response only served to vindicate her beliefs that he still saw her as Yoori.

"Get your act together, Tae Hyun," she advised, feeling her heart rate increase. "Your Princess is dead and will never come back. This is just a warm-up. In our next fight, I'm killing you, and I won't be going easy on you."

"Will you really?" he asked, skepticism present in his voice.

Soo Jin felt the air escape her already pained lungs at the absurdity of the question. "Why the hell wouldn't I be able to?"

He smirked, taking a step forward to meet her. He looked completely fucked up—just like her—but goddamn, he continued to look hot as hell with blood and shards of glass stuck to his body.

"There were exactly nineteen times where you could've killed me tonight. I knew you were going easy on me as well. Why didn't you kill me and get it over with? I'm sure that beloved throne would be all yours if you finished the deed. So, why didn't you?"

It took all her control to not breathe in the cologne that was becoming a favorite aroma of hers. She looked up at him with unrelenting conviction. "I'm saving everything for our big fight. I just wanted to get a sneak preview of what I was up against. Apparently, I didn't get much because you were holding back. Regardless, I saw enough. At least I know how hard I had to push to piss you off."

She laughed dryly, finding amusement in how he was gazing at her. He was looking at her in brooding silence, indicating that he was in deep contemplation about something.

Then, he did something she didn't expect.

Pushing against the sword with the leather of his black shoe, he kicked it up to her.

Soo Jin caught it with easy grace, yet the expression on her face was anything but graceful. "What are you doing?"

"Go ahead," he dared. He took another step closer with his arms outstretched. "I'm all yours."

"Don't insult me," she spat. "I was waiting for a momentous battle that will leave a mark on history, not for you to drop down and play dead for me."

She threw away the sword, silently hating herself for conjuring up other distracting images when he said, "I'm all yours." What was happening to her?

Why was she feeling so out of it? She attempted to shake herself back to logicality.

"Don't make the mistake of thinking that just because my counterpart was with you when I had amnesia that I hold any residual feelings for you, Tae Hyun," she admonished, knowing all too well why he was behaving this way towards her. "You're nothing to me but an obstacle I have to climb in order to claim my immortality over this world. When the time comes, trust me when I say that I'll kill you. With all that said, I hope you prepare yourself well because when we meet again for our battle, I hope you won't go easy on me like you did tonight. I sure as hell don't plan on holding back with you." She began to walk away. "Now if you'll excuse me, I have a war to prepare for. Thanks for a disappointing night."

"An Soo Jin," Tae Hyun voiced, stopping her in her tracks.

Every part of her mind advised her to not listen to him and to continue to walk away. Unfortunately, her body, which seemed to have a mind of its own and was somehow conditioned to *want* Kwon Tae Hyun to stay beside her, stopped for him as soon as he called out to her.

Soo Jin expelled a weary breath.

Knowing very well that she was dealing with the residual feelings of Choi Yoori's, she made a mental note to figure out how to deal with this conflict later.

She turned and eyed him tiredly. "What now?"

"You should know that in this world, there are few people who can lie to me and even fewer people who can lie to me and get away with it." There was a look of conviction on his face, one filled with a determination she couldn't understand. "There are some I can read as soon as I meet them, but on rare occasions, there are others . . . others who are exceptional, skilled, and cunning like yourself. With those types of people, I have to be around them long enough to understand how they speak, how their bodies react to certain emotions, and what they do when they are bluffing."

She canted her head questioningly. "What are you getting at?"

"What was my mother wearing the night you killed her?"

Soo Jin lifted her brows in amusement. Although she deduced what he was trying to do, she humored him anyway. "A crème colored blouse and black pants." She let out a dry laugh. "You're *that* desperate that you actually want to put me through a lie detector to see if I really killed your mother?"

"*How* did you kill her?" he asked swiftly, ignoring her remark. His eyes were now undecipherable.

Her eyes became equally stagnant and unreadable. "Like I told you . . . with the jagged edges of the alcohol bottle. I slit her wrists."

"Both?"

"Yes.

"In that case, which wrist did she have a butterfly tattoo?"

Another laugh escaped Soo Jin's mouth. "It's been years. Why would I remember such useless details?"

"Because killing someone of her status would give you bragging rights. You would never forget the details."

Soo Jin fell silent at his correct statement.

She lowered her eyes to the glass-covered tiles and replayed the contents of that night in her mind. When the memories played through her mind like a movie, she lifted her eyes and confidently said, "The right."

The sternness of his eyes soon faded. Tae Hyun was quiet as he inhaled a painful breath at her correct answer.

Soo Jin smiled, giving him the "I've-been-telling-you-the-truth-all-along" look. It was a look filled with pity for his failed efforts to prove that she didn't kill his mother. She was prepared to make her exit when his next words washed over her and froze her blood.

"I'm winning you back."

A multitude of emotions deluged through her as she turned to him in bewilderment. "What did you just say?"

"I'm winning you back," he repeated resolutely, his eyes never leaving hers. "I want you back, and I've decided now that I'm *getting* you back."

"What the hell are you talking about?" she laughed, confused.

"You confirmed that my mother had a tattoo on her right wrist instead of her left wrist."

She scoffed disbelievingly. "So I forgot which wrist it was and that instantly frees me? Man, Tae Hyun, you are just so desperate to forgive the lookalike of your girlfriend's, aren't you?"

Soo Jin wanted to tell him how stupid he was, how ridiculous he was until Tae Hyun vocalized his next words.

"My mother didn't have tattoos."

It was then, as An Soo Jin felt fear escalate in her heart, did she realize how cunning Kwon Tae Hyun was. She was a skilled liar, but it seemed that the King of Serpents was equally as skilled when it came to figuring out liars—that, or he was just really good at tricking people into telling him the truth.

"It was a trick question," she said finally, never ceasing to be impressed with the genius that was the King in front of her.

"You never killed my mother," he said knowingly, staring at her with newfound knowledge in his eyes. "You were there, but you weren't the one who killed her."

She stayed quiet.

"What happened that night, Soo Jin?"

She kept her mouth shut, unwilling to answer his question.

When it was blatant to him that he wasn't going to get anything out of her, he continued on. "Would you really force Kang Min to kill Hae Jin? Do you really have the heart to hurt her?"

For the first time since her return, Soo Jin's eyes softened.

"No one will ever touch her or Chae Young again if I can help it," she confessed. She looked away for a brief moment. "But make no mistake about it, Tae Hyun. I *will* be the one to kill you. I've waited my entire life to meet you, and I'm not letting this historic moment pass me by. I know what you're trying to do, that you're trying to use me to replace Yoori. I won't let that happen. I'm here and your Choi Yoori is dead . . . long gone from the moment you left her. Get your head out of the clouds and face me like the person I am to you—your enemy, and the one who will kill you for the most coveted throne. Don't make the mistake of becoming human for me, Tae Hyun, because you'll only pathetically die as one."

He smiled, taking several steps closer to her. When he was finally right across from her, he held her gaze with determination.

"I've waited my entire life for you, Soo Jin," he whispered, his eyes searching hers. "Long before I even knew what I wanted, long before I knew of your name, and long before I knew of your existence. I let go of the love of my life because of all the lies you spread, and I put myself through hell because *I* was the one who left her and broke her when all I wanted to do was run back to her, hold her in my arms, and kiss her until the world faded around us." His eyes grew stern. "But mark my words tonight: I'm winning her back. There will be no more ifs, ands, or buts. Against your wishes, against your ironclad resolution, and against your will—I'm breaking through that ruthless exterior of yours, and I'm winning her back. And trust me when that life-changing moment happens, I'm never letting her or *you* go again."

"You know you're in for one hell of a war then?"

"I do."

"Promises can be broken," she reminded him, not knowing herself why she was bringing that up.

Every promise he made to Choi Yoori broke. Why would his promises mean anything now?

He didn't say anything in reply. He merely nodded and brought a finger up, running it over her cheek with such lazy grace that she was tempted to close her eyes and enjoy it. She realized then that she was going to enter the most epic battle of her life—in more ways than one.

His scent, his presence, and the allure of his confident soul enraptured her. Soo Jin was so conflicted; she resented herself for not being able to control her emotions around him, especially when he stood in such close proximity to her and especially when she could feel his warmth and his love.

She didn't fight his touch, though she knew she should've. She didn't fight him when he cupped a hand over her cheek, she didn't push him away when he whispered words that had her heart galloping against her better wishes, and she didn't put an end to him when she knew he was going to make this the biggest battle of her life.

"Before these next four weeks are over," he whispered, his warm breath caressing her ear, "I'll do everything in my power to win you back. And that isn't a promise—it's a vow."

"I'll kill you before I let you win me back," she retorted, meaning every word of it.

And with an alluring smile that promised the adherence of his vow to her, he extracted his hand away, took a step back, and walked past her. He only deigned to stop long enough to express words that had her heart racing in dread, fear, and anticipation, for it marked the commencement of a form of war she never wanted to get into with anyone, especially not with someone like Kwon Tae Hyun, who had the indisputable power to make her a God . . . and the indisputable power to make her human again.

"I guess it's time to start our war then," he began with finality before quietly adding, "'Till death do us part, Princess."

"No matter where you go, we will find you."

05: The Rumblings of War

In the dead of the night, the world was nothing but a hushed and vacant lot. A raging storm had rolled over the country, bringing with it a tsunami of rain and hail. The weather experts had predicted that this would be the most dreadful and callous storm of the year. They had no idea how right they were.

Situated in three different points of South Korea, two of the most dominant crime lords and nine of the most powerful assassins in the Underworld resided on three different roofs. Their prideful eyes roamed over the army that had assembled before them.

On one side of the country, dressed in a black coat and equally dark pants, Lee Ji Hoon stood atop his four-story Skulls' estate. His ruthless eyes overlooked the hundreds upon hundreds of Skulls that had gathered on his rain-dampened land. All were kneeling before him, showering him with the utmost respect.

On the opposite side of the country, at another great King's domain, the King of Serpents' infamous Cobras stood in a sequential line at the apex of the four-story Serpents' estate. All stood on the roof, dressed in black from head to toe. Their eyes moved over the masses of Serpents who were kneeling before them, listening to them while they acted as conduits for their King's spoken words.

"Serpents," Ace, the leader of the Cobras and Tae Hyun's right-hand man, began with pride booming in his voice. "After all our training, all our hard work, and all our blood, sweat, and tears . . . the moment has finally come . . ."

"—Ju Won's birthday has finally come and gone, and the pact prohibiting us from shedding blood is no longer valid," Ji Hoon began on the other side of the country, his eyes pulsing with rage. He had enough with a diplomatic and peaceful Underworld. He was ready to shed blood.

"It's finally time to shake this world up," said Mina, the other leader of the Cobras. Above her, more rain clouds appeared as the storm worsened around them.

"Before the night is over . . ." said Ji Hoon, his fists curling at either side of him.

"Fifty dead Skulls are to be floating across all the rivers of this country," Ace commanded fiercely.

"—I want the beheaded bodies of the Serpents and the Siberian Tigers to pile up in the business district," said Ji Hoon, evoking his gangs' tradition of starting a war.

A subtle change was present in Ace and Mina's eyes as they gave out another set of orders that their King had given them.

"Kill them quickly," they added. "Don't torture them and don't drag anything out. Make sure they die a quick death."

"Kill them slowly," said Ji Hoon, his voice cold. "I want them to feel every drop of pain."

"Start our war," Mina ordered. "Make it memorable."

An eruption of cheers resonated from the estate until Mina, who didn't look so satisfied, stared at the rest of her Cobras. They all nodded at her to give their King's final order of the night.

"But remember not to touch any Siberian Tigers, and if any one of you touches An Soo Jin, then boss and the nine of us will have you floating in the Han River before you could even begin to regret it."

And finally, at the final point in the country, standing atop the roof of one of Seoul's tallest buildings in the business district, the Queen of the Underworld stood inches away from the edge with prestige, power, and superiority emanating from her.

She was dressed in a white, long-sleeved suit jacket complemented by white tailored shorts. The short fabric stopped at her thighs, showing off her stunning legs. Kang Min and Jae Won stood behind her; both were dressed in black trench coats that reached the knees of their dark slacks. In this scene, they only served to make Soo Jin look more powerful.

With her hands wrapped behind her back, her gold chandelier earrings and the curls of her black hair dancing in the wind, Soo Jin wore a satisfied smirk on her face. The silhouettes of the city lights flickering across from her reflected in her powerful eyes. Her focus then shifted to the buildings standing parallel and adjacent to hers.

All around, countless lost Siberian Tigers stood on the roofs of the surrounding buildings. They had all convened after hearing whispers that the Queen of the Underworld had not only resurfaced in their world, but that she was also their new gang leader—the newly crowned Queen of Siberian Tigers.

Needless to say, excitement and anticipation radiated from them as their focus locked on their beautiful Queen.

"Good evening," she greeted, her soothing voice traveling into the misty air and streaming into the phones both Kang Min and Jae Won held in their grasps. As she spoke, her voice was concurrently transmitted into the speakers of the phones that her former Scorpions held in their own hands. The sound of her voice traveled into the ears of the Siberian Tigers in attendance, and in a synchronized wave, an amazing show of respect was bequeathed to her as the Siberian Tigers fell on one knee and kneeled before her.

What a beautiful sight, thought Soo Jin.

She grinned, feeling every ounce of their respect, devotion, and undying loyalty. She could feel it in the air around them. They were utterly grateful to be reunited with their fellow Siberian Tigers. She could also sense how proud they felt to be surrounded by the Scorpions' finest gang members and the Queen herself. It was an unlikely union, but a powerful and historic union nonetheless. It brought nothing but pride to Soo Jin and her newly extended family.

Extracting a hand from behind her back, Soo Jin silently gestured for them to rise.

Soon after, she began to speak into the night. "It is an honor to finally stand here before you," she said while they rose to their feet. "I know that the wait has been extensive and tedious. It has been roughly three years for some of us, and five longer years for all of you. The years have been long and strenuous, but the waiting period ends now." Cruelty appeared as the sole emotion on her face. "I want to come back with a vengeance; I want this world to be shaken up by its horns; I want the blood of my enemies to stream like water in this fair city, and I want to obliterate them—to conquer them."

She smiled, gazing at her soldiers as she felt their hearts beat in anticipation.

"Siberian Tigers," she launched with pride, "do you want to be legends?"

Cheers resonated from them.

"Do you want to shake this world up?"

The cheers grew louder.

"Do you want the world to kneel before you?"

The cheers built up so much that it began to rival the thunderstorm resounding overhead.

Soo Jin beamed, feeling the torrent of violent wind eat at their skins. "Then before the night is over, I want you to go after the Scorpions, Skulls, and the Serpents." Her voice grew stern when the image of a certain King came to her mind. "But remember, no one touches Kwon Tae Hyun. His head belongs to me and only me." Her sadistic smile enlarged. "Now go. Start your war, and before the night is over, I want you to bring me fifty-seven live captives so we can introduce them to the once-extinct Siberian Tigers."

93

Cheers rivaled the skies as countless Siberian Tigers bowed before their Queen and heeded her command.

With a breathy sigh, Soo Jin turned to Kang Min and Jae Won. She retreated from the roof and took shelter in the high-rise building, biding her time until her Siberian Tigers returned later that night with their live captives.

"This world is not ready for an Underworld war," she said with amusement, feeling her two gold guns grow heavy behind her back. She let out a laugh as she waited for her captives to come. "But oh well."

■ ■ ■

Pandemonium was the only word to describe the city of Seoul when the light of dawn speared through the rain dampened clouds the next morning. The city may have been flooded with excess water from the storm, but the aftershock it awoke to was not from Mother Nature's scorn; it was the aftereffects of human nature's brutality.

". . . In all my years as a reporter, I have never seen anything like this."

A slender news anchorman wearing thick gold glasses and a brown coat spoke into the camera as his microphone shook in his hands. The lens of the camera zoomed into the scene above him, focusing on the images of the fifty-seven dead bodies suspended above the city. The fresh corpses were hung on long, sturdy ropes that wrapped all around the high-rise buildings in the business district.

Countless news vans lined the streets, their terrified cameras capturing the horror above them.

"Fifty-seven people were brutally murdered last night. Their eyes were gouged out while the number '57' was carved onto the left side of their cheeks. The dead bodies were ruthlessly hung by ropes across the buildings of the business district."

Soon after, the cameras focused on several buildings where body bags were being wheeled out.

"Fifty-nine dead bodies with their heads cut off were found piled on top of one another in seven buildings throughout the city. On their cheeks were the carved depictions of skulls . . ."

Then, another news channel played the video reel of divers pulling out dead bodies from the waters.

"Fifty corpses were found floating in the Han River with the depiction of a snake carved on their necks . . ."

Chaos.

The entire world was in chaos as they tried to make sense of this unbelievable nightmare.

"The authorities have yet to make a statement about who they think may be responsible for a massacre of this magnitude," said a female college student, speaking into the camera and recording a video that she and her production crew planned to post on their independent conspiracy website. She held her microphone higher, looking more solemn as she pointed at the dead bodies hanging in the distance. "However, many are saying that it doesn't appear to be the doing of a small-time street gang. The culprits were able to bypass security, law enforcements, block traffic, and essentially kill hundreds of people in one night without a single witness. Some users on our website are even going as far as theorizing that the people behind these massacres aren't actually gang members, but leaders of a secret society rumored to not only control the inner workings of government affairs, but also the business and economic affairs of their respective countries. There are a lot of speculations about who may be behind this, but as of right now, nothing is set in stone. The only real detail we know is that it is advised for everyone to be conscious of their surroundings, especially at night. We'll keep you updated on this matter when the authorities give their official statement in just a few hours . . ."

Days after the media frenzy died down, An Soo Jin couldn't have looked more aloof and carefree as she sauntered down the busy sidewalk of the business district.

With her black pumps gliding on the concrete with womanly grace and the curls of her hair bouncing vibrantly under the appreciation of the afternoon sun, Soo Jin easily attracted admiring stares from businessmen and women alike. They simply couldn't keep their fascinated gazes off of her. Her purple silk blouse, which was accentuated with a black pencil skirt that hugged her lower body in all the right ways, was more than catching everyone's undivided attention. Imparting them with one of her breathtaking smiles, the Queen of Siberian Tigers radiated nothing short of beauty as she maneuvered her way through the congested sidewalk.

Soo Jin eyed her Siberian Tigers, many of whom were scattered all around the business district, going back to their daily lives and pretending to be ordinary businessmen and women, police officers, investigators, and news reporters. She gave them a subtle nod, to which they gave her a slight bow as a show of respect and hurried about their day.

Ah yes, after three years of inactivity and after devoting so much time to resurrecting her entire gang, she was thrilled to finally get some time away from her busy schedule. Commencing epic wars that had shaken the entire country aside, one of the revered Queen's passions in life was dealing with the business aspect of the Underworld—or more specifically, enjoying her day job like the rest of her world.

Businesses, investments, negotiations, alliances, and profits.

The layers in her world were like an interrelated pyramid. Entry into the secret society was exclusive and rising up the ranks was even more inconceivable. Nevertheless, for the few who were able to survive the training and were cunning enough to barter through the brutality of this world, the rewards at the top of the food chain were magnificent. Her day job consisted of negotiating deals and services with the Corporate Crime Lords of the 1st layer, getting advice in future investments, and starting up her own companies. She loved it. She loved doing all of that just as she loved a good combat.

After three years of absence from this wonderful world, it was an understatement to say that she was exhilarated to be back.

The day was almost over. She had spent most of the day reuniting with old mentors, and she was ready to call it a night—that was until she caught sight of an Advisor inside the lobby of a high-rise building. He was conversing with two younger business associates. Unable to contain the elatedness inside her—as he had always been one of her favorite mentors while growing up—Soo Jin placed all apprehensiveness aside and walked into the busy lobby.

"Uncle Dong Min," Soo Jin greeted with a smile. She stopped a pace behind him, waiting as he turned around to face her. All around them, people in the building were waving their goodbyes and leaving for the evening.

"Soo Jin," he greeted back, turning away from the two young men he was speaking to. He wore a surprised expression, the kindness from his face accentuated by the brown knitted sweater and brown pants he wore.

There was subtle warmth in his eyes that told Soo Jin he was happy to see her. The subtle warmth was a complete contradiction to his actions towards her only weeks prior. She hadn't forgotten how distant he was when she was 'Yoori'. Regardless, she understood now that despite his adoration towards her, his main priority was Tae Hyun and eradicating any threat that endangered his advisee's station in life. In this case, it was getting rid of a pathetic and weak human girl who was a walking death trap for the King himself. She understood that he distanced himself from Yoori simply because he had to and took no offense to it.

She swallowed uncomfortably, pushing the thoughts of Yoori and Tae Hyun aside. Nothing good could come out of it if she allowed those two to plague her thoughts.

Soo Jin kept the smile on her face when speaking to Dong Min. "It's been a while. How are you, uncle?"

She could read the skepticism in his eyes. It had been a while psychologically, but not physically, as he had seen quite a lot of Yoori.

"I'm good," he replied with a tentative smile. He still looked very surprised to see her.

She disregarded the awkwardness and eyed his business associates with a polite smile. Their eyes were firmly set on her as well. Never one to be rude, Dong Min started to introduce the two young men, both of whom were smiling at her with amiable eyes. In that split second, she couldn't help but feel a sense of familiarity to them. There was something oddly familiar about them that she couldn't quite decipher.

"This is—"

"An Soo Jin," one of the tall men, who was dressed in a handsome pinstriped black suit and had spiky brown hair, interrupted Dong Min with a growing smile. He extended his hand out to her, an air of confidence emitting from him. "You've made the most epic comeback I've ever had the pleasure of seeing in the Underworld."

She laughed softly, still ruffled by his presence. What was it about him that felt so familiar to her?

"Do I know you?" Soo Jin asked, uncertainly shaking his hand.

She did not get a chance to ask him for his name when his equally handsome friend, the one who wore a pinstriped gray suit and had short dark hair, extended his hand out and said, "It's an honor to finally meet you. We've heard so much about you—in more ways than one."

Soo Jin canted her head in curiosity.

There was a certain charm to them that continued to remind her of someone she knew. She bit her lip, still feeling puzzled. She gathered, judging by the slightly cocky and charming aura that emanated from them, that they were heirs in the 1st layer. Despite being certain that she had never met them, she could not shake the feeling that she knew *of* them.

"Do the two heirs of the 1st layer have names?" Soo Jin asked cordially, observing that although they were admiring her beauty, both heirs were seemingly very interested in just talking to her and *not* bedding her. Given that the 1st layer heirs were known to be players in their own right, this was an extremely rare occurrence.

They laughed, looking at one another before nodding and murmuring things like, "*Damn, we've been so rude.*"

"Choi Hyun Woo," the first one introduced, flashing her a gorgeous smile that would cause women from all over the world to faint in awe.

"Daniel Lee," the second one introduced, tucking his hands into his pockets in hidden glee. A portion of his lips lifted in an amused smirk that could stop the hearts of women anywhere.

She furrowed her brows at the familiarity of their names. She couldn't put a finger on why they felt so familiar to her until—

"*My best friends,*" a silky and enticing voice answered against her right ear, clearing any fog of confusion that once immersed her mind.

The warm breath acted as a stimulant for her. Its warmth teased the nerves in her ear and sparked a cataclysmic reaction that traveled like a freight train down her body. Her body came alive with desires she couldn't control, and much to her own horror, she knew only one man possessed the natural talent to trigger a reaction of that magnitude from her.

Crap.

Desperate to stay away from him, she wheeled around in haste. She quickly stepped away from the owner of the voice, nearly tripping over Dong Min in the process. Luckily for the Advisor, he was saved from being mowed down by the Queen when an amused Choi Hyun Woo and Daniel Lee pulled him out of the way.

While staring at Tae Hyun's gorgeous and smiling face, she now realized that Dong Min's "business associates" were not mere heirs in the 1st layer. They were the *Princes* of the 1st layer.

It all came together for her.

Choi Hyun Woo was the son of Choi Min Hyuk, the powerful crime lord at Ju Won's birthday party. Daniel Lee was the son of the infamous Lee Sang Min, another powerful 1st layer crime lord who owned the majority of the entertainment and media outlets in Korea. Not to mention, Daniel was also the nephew of the influential politicians who attended Ju Won's party. Hyun Woo and Daniel were both considered the most powerful Princes in the 1st layer, and worst of all, they were also Kwon Tae Hyun's best friends.

"What are you doing here?" Soo Jin asked at once, more shocked to be around Tae Hyun than to have finally met his best friends.

The curves of his tempting lips raised in a teasing smile. His amused eyes took note of her frazzled state.

"Jumping like a scared little kitten," he mused softly, his voice washing over her like hot and delicious honey. "I didn't think the Queen of the Underworld was capable of being spooked."

"What are you doing here?" she asked again, refusing to acknowledge his observation.

She could kill her body for its conditioned reaction to him. Who the hell knew hormones could get the Queen herself like this? Even when she reigned three years ago, she wasn't like this around Ji Hoon—or any man for that matter. But with Kwon Tae Hyun, it was like he was a sexy aphrodisiac created specifically for her. She could control her logicality concerning him— that he was an enemy she was prepared to kill when the time was right—but her body had no such discrimination. It just wanted him—all of his glorious, naked self.

To say the least, the normally composed Soo Jin was appalled with her abnormal behavior. After the fight with him, she had reasoned that she was off her game because she had just returned after three years of amnesia. It was clear now that feeling disjointed was only relevant when in the presence of her biggest enemy—and apparently her body's biggest aphrodisiac.

"You're in the business district," he replied smoothly. He did not deign to spare a look at his Advisor or his best friends. His attention was wholly and solely focused on her. "This is my playground."

"Why are you here?" she asked again, recognizing that she sounded like a broken record.

"Business. You?"

"Business," she replied just as simply.

She abruptly decided that it was time to leave him and the ridiculous state she was finding herself in. After three years of being a "normal" girl, Soo Jin was dreadfully embarrassed that she didn't have more control over her own body. She was so immersed with his presence that she didn't even realize his baby sister was standing next to him. It wasn't until Hae Jin moved slightly beside him did Soo Jin notice her.

Hae Jin's pretty eyes brightened when Soo Jin finally made eye contact with her.

A little too excited, Hae Jin parted her lips and elatedly said, "Hi Yoo—!"

"It's *Soo Jin*," she snapped without thinking.

Soo Jin instantly regretted speaking so brusquely when Hae Jin clamped her mouth down in shock, thrown by her authoritative voice.

Hae Jin swallowed convulsively, doing her best to maintain the smile that was fading from her face. As she nodded apologetically to Soo Jin, Tae Hyun placed a hand on his sister's shoulder, his eyes seemingly saying things to Hae Jin that Soo Jin couldn't read. Whatever it was he wordlessly said to her, it made Hae Jin feel better. She was once again staring at Soo Jin with a hint of warmth in her eyes. It was the same warm look she always gave to Yoori whenever she was around her.

Soo Jin's throat grew dry at the reminder of her human counterpart. She would not allow the memory of Choi Yoori to ruin her day.

"Well, I should go now," she said with finality, composure still laced in her serene voice. No matter how flustered she was, she refused to show these people how much they fazed her.

"You know, out of the three of us, Tae Hyun has always been the chick magnet. It's pretty rare to not see a woman fawn all over him when he gives her his attention. Though I must admit that it's pretty entertaining to watch his ex-girlfriend jump around like a scared kitten at his near presence."

"His presence has no effect on me," Soo Jin bit out at Daniel, secretly horrified that others could see that his presence not only had an effect on her, but it also intimidated the hell out of her.

"The Queen of the Underworld gets amnesia and becomes someone else, only to fall in love with her future enemy. After regaining her memories, the King is still pining for the Queen who wants nothing but war from him," Hyun Woo mused to himself, already lost in his own set of thoughts. He shot Daniel with a curious look. "Doesn't that sound like a good TV drama to create?"

"I should pitch it to my father," Daniel agreed fervently. "I'm sure we can make something work out."

Soo Jin understood now why they made her so uneasy when she first met them. It was because they were almost exactly like Tae Hyun. They were blunt, witty, sarcastic, and had the charisma to make the entire world fall to their feet.

"Don't you trust fund babies have meetings to get to?" Tae Hyun interrupted firmly, his eyes still heavily invested on Soo Jin, who was staring at him with unconcealed malice.

"We actually have dinner plans," Hyun Woo answered, laughing with Daniel when it was all too clear to them that they were being dismissed. He stepped away from the circle and extended his hand out to Hae Jin. "Come on, little one. Let your brother do what he needs to do."

"Take care of my sister," Tae Hyun said to his best friends as they pulled Hae Jin away from him.

"Don't we always," Daniel answered, playfully tousling Hae Jin's hair when she stood beside them. She murmured words of protest as a little sister would to older brothers who picked on her.

"Tae Hyun," Dong Min started, obviously wanting to knock some sense into Tae Hyun to keep him from trying to seduce Soo Jin.

Before he could say anymore, Hyun Woo and Daniel punctually interrupted him. They placed their arms around him and playfully herded him away from Tae Hyun and Soo Jin, both of whom were still staring unblinkingly at one another.

Soo Jin was still giving him the "if-you-come-near-me-I'll-kill-you" look, and Tae Hyun was giving her the "you're-breathtaking" look.

"Oh, come on, uncle," Daniel placated. "We know you want the best for your favorite advisee, but the King of Serpents can take care of himself around the Queen of the Underworld. You know once he sets his mind on something, it's done and over with. Stop fighting it and just let go."

Defeated by the simple fact that Hyun Woo and Daniel were persuasive charmers themselves, Dong Min expelled an exasperated sigh, and just like that . . . gave up. It was indicative on his face that he knew there was no more he could say or do. Whatever path Tae Hyun chose now, it was his to choose alone.

"Let's go then," Daniel whispered to Hae Jin as Dong Min moved ahead with Hyun Woo. Daniel glanced over his shoulder and gave Tae Hyun an encouraging smile. "Your brother is going to be busy."

With a bright smile on her lips, Hae Jin nodded. Her hopeful eyes landed on Soo Jin, who didn't even dare to make eye contact with her.

"Bye . . . *Soo Jin*," she whispered before making her departure.

Something in Soo Jin's heart gave out when Hae Jin vocalized her birth name. She briefly wondered why it pained her to hear Hae Jin call her by her birth name, but she did not push that thought. Perhaps it was just odd because she was so used to Hae Jin referring to her as "Yoori".

"Bye," Soo Jin replied just as quietly, watching from the corner of her eyes as Hae Jin and Daniel walked out of the building and joined Dong Min and Hyun Woo on the street. Within an instant, they were gone, and Soo Jin was left wondering what had happened to Hae Jin during Ju Won's birthday party. Apart from a small glance of her, she hardly remembered seeing Hae Jin at all.

"Where was she during the party?" Soo Jin asked, finally able to say something else to him. Her chin was inclined, her eyes stern, and her arms were folded across her rapidly rising and falling chest. Although she looked intimidating, she doubted she could evoke any fear from Tae Hyun.

He mirrored her movements by folding his arms over his black suit.

"After you appeared with Kang Min and Jae Won, she was ready to run to you guys. At that time, I didn't know what you were capable of; I didn't know what the brothers were capable of. In case anything went awry, I didn't want her to be there. So I silently ordered a couple of my Serpents to grab her and take her home as a precaution. I wanted to protect her from all of you; I wanted to protect her from bearing witness to things she shouldn't see in case a bloodshed between us occurred."

"Smart choice," Soo Jin replied, feeling relief that Hae Jin wasn't there when she killed the man who questioned her power. She also felt relief that Hae Jin didn't see her making out with Ji Hoon to hurt her brother and relief that Hae Jin didn't see her fighting Tae Hyun. Despite her distant behavior towards Hae Jin now, she did not want Hae Jin to hate her. The last thing she wanted was for Hae Jin to be afraid of her.

"Have you been purposely avoiding me?"

Soo Jin was abruptly tugged out of her thoughts with his ludicrous question.

"Why the hell would I?"

Even though she *had* been avoiding him, she would never admit it to him.

Since their confrontation, she had been disturbed that she couldn't get that butterfly feeling out of her stomach whenever she thought about him.

Being around him made her feel all too human, too much like a young woman instead of a feared Queen. She abhorred the effect he had on her. She wanted to kick herself for being stupid enough to walk into the very building that he was already in. He was probably having a meeting with some trusted alliances, and like a stupid prey, she sauntered into the lion's den and pretty much laid there on a silver platter, conversing with his mentor and friends and unknowingly tempting him to come feast on her.

"Then can we go somewhere private to talk? Alone?"

There was no seductive tone in his voice. Even though it sounded professional and sincere, there was no denying the spark in his eyes. Desire teemed in his gaze. He appraised her appreciatively, openly admiring the outfit she wore and the way her perfect curls were gathered on one side of her shoulder.

"I'm not going anywhere alone with you," she clipped out instinctively.

She had not forgotten what happened after their fight. Her physical wounds had already begun to heal, but the scar he left her—the one where he promised to "win her back"—was still deeply rooted in her mind. She didn't want to deal with this type of war with him, and if she could help it, she wouldn't do anything to encourage it either. Being alone with him was just asking for trouble.

"So you admit it," he noted complacently, knowingly. "You're afraid to be alone with me."

"I admitted no such thing," she snapped, the prideful Queen within her enraged that he dared to voice such a blasphemous thing.

It may have been true that she was hesitant to be around him because no matter how strong she was, Soo Jin also recognized that she was a twenty-four-year-old woman in the presence of a twenty-four-year-old man who had the charms to rival Casanova, the body to challenge Adonis, and the ungodly good looks to rival fallen angels. As her weak counterpart once deemed, Kwon Tae Hyun was made for sex. And unfortunately for Soo Jin, in addition to being a celebrated legend in this world, she was also a young woman who had needs. At the moment, all she wanted was—for lack of better words—to have sex with Kwon Tae Hyun over and over and over again until she died. After that, she wanted to wake up and repeat the process over and over again.

She inhaled a sharp, chastising breath at the thought.

Fucking tempting bastard.

Nope.

There was no way in hell she was going anywhere alone with him.

"I simply don't want to be alone with you," she contended calmly, never one to admit her weakness in front of any man. "I'm not afraid of you. Why would I be afraid of you?"

He shrugged a bit too innocently for her taste. "I don't know. Why would any girl be afraid of being alone with a guy unless she was afraid of the things she might do when no one else was around?"

A wordless curse escaped her lips while her eyes sharpened with daggers.

"Your arrogance is offensive," she commented swiftly.

"And your ignorance is insulting," he contended just as easily before stepping closer to her.

His tall frame towered over hers, reminding her that despite their stations in life—that they were born to be enemies—there was an undeniable chemistry between them. He was a very attractive man, and she was a very attracted woman. She wanted him, and the fact that he was so close only further enticed her.

"What are you apprehensive of, Soo Jin? I only want to talk to you from a King to a Queen." His strong shoulders lifted in a lazy shrug. "But of course, if you want me to speak to you as a man to a woman, then that could easily be arranged too."

Dismayed with his words, an angry Soo Jin was about to tell him to fuck off before he cleverly plowed on.

"We're prospective Lords in the Underworld, Soo Jin, not savages. I know that ambitious body of yours is just waiting to destroy me, but placing your killer instincts aside, how about we act like the civilized and professional business people that we're also trained to be? After all, if you follow the cliché standard and try to fight me every time you see me, then we're no better than the parasitic street gangs our world looks down upon."

Damn, he got her there.

She definitely didn't want to be like the parasites she hated so much. She also knew she couldn't keep avoiding him, at least not when he was standing right there. If she kept on running away, then she knew what that would signify to him. Preys only ran when they were unsure of their capabilities and were afraid of being caught by their hunter.

If she kept playing this cat and mouse game, then it meant that she was running away—it meant that she was the prey. And God help her, that would only further legitimize Tae Hyun as the hunter. She couldn't have that. She could not be hunted when she was a predator herself; she could not allow him to hunt her when he was her biggest rival for the throne. She had to set the precedence early on in their relationship; she had to show him that he was not chasing after a girl—he was chasing after a Queen.

Resolved that she wasn't going to run anymore, Soo Jin kept her chin held high and stared at him challengingly. Although she would not give him the satisfaction of a chase, she would happily give him the beginnings of their war.

"How do you survive with that insatiable arrogance and smart mouth of yours?" she asked, silently crediting him for provoking her into being alone with him. The annoyance of having to be around him aside, she had to give credit where it was due. He was definitely showing her what a formidable King he was.

Tae Hyun chuckled, the vibration of his laughter doing funny things to her stomach. He extended a hand out to her, inclining his head towards the elevator. He obviously had a place in mind for their private meeting together.

"I have a girlfriend who has an equally smart mouth to insult me and keep me in line," he answered affectionately.

Soo Jin caught the underlying message in that statement, but chose to disregard it. She proceeded into the elevator without taking his hand and stood in the corner of the metal box with her arms crossed. She ignored the extreme palpitating of her heart as the doors slid to a close and the elevator began its ascension into the top floors. When Tae Hyun favored her with a breathtaking smile that sent heat to rush to her cheeks, she inwardly prayed for strength.

This private meeting with the charismatic King of the Underworld was not going to be easy, and she prayed she would not come out being his seduced prey when it was over.

"No matter where you hide, we will drag you back."

06: The Seduction of Gods

"Is it a good idea to stay here?" Soo Jin asked minutes later, stepping into a colossal office at the top floor of the high-rise building.

The office was enormous. Its opulent furniture and equipment radiated sophistication and wealth. There was a dashing mahogany desk that was placed in front of the gorgeous panoramic vista of the city. Behind the desk's window, Soo Jin could see the sun's brilliance spear through the cloudy skies. Shifting her gaze from the window, she measured the impressive room once more. The room was massive enough that it could have easily doubled as a grand penthouse. Captivated by the swirls of color on the walls, Soo Jin smirked as she looked at the abstract paintings that adorned the walls. She had to admit that the owner of this office had good taste. When she buys her next building, Soo Jin would definitely take notes from this office space.

She stopped at the center of the room and edgily looked at the door. Although it was closing hour, she didn't feel comfortable staying in someone else's office. How awkward would it be if the owner walked in and found two strangers in his office?

"Why not?" Tae Hyun inquired, closing the door so quietly that she didn't even realize he was standing behind her until a whiff of his alluring cologne reached her nostrils.

"Well, what if the owner comes in?" Soo Jin asked, whipping around and instinctively backing away from him.

With the grace of a tiger, Tae Hyun stalked towards her with ease. "He already has."

"This is *your* office?" Her eyes widened incredulously. As she continued to back away, the palpitations of her heart increased by the second. She surveyed the building, utterly dumbfounded. "This is your company?"

"I may have reign over the 3rd layer, but that doesn't mean I've given up my passion for the 1st layer," he explained coolly. There was a predatory gaze in his deep brown eyes as he spoke to her. It made her so hot that she could scarcely feel the air conditioning in the office. "This company is ran by the executives I've chosen myself and is personally ran by me when I have time. I perform my 3rd and 1st layer businesses in this building. It's essentially my secret hideaway."

"And you told Yoori that your friends could offer her a job when you could've given it to her all along?" The words escaped her lips faster than she could have caught them. A part of her was outraged at this new revelation. It stunned her that he owned a company this entire time. Really? He didn't think it was necessary to share this information?

"Yoori is a prideful, ambitious, and stubborn girl," he replied, smiling to himself in a way that only a boyfriend could when he thought about his girlfriend. His legs continued to inch forward while hers continued to retreat. "She would never work here under the pretenses of getting the job solely because her boyfriend owns the company. On my end, I didn't plan on insulting her by offering it to her. God knows she already hated being my personal assistant. I doubt she would volunteer to work here. She would know that if I were her boss, I'd never let her out of this office."

"Why didn't you tell her who you really were and showed her all of this?" Soo Jin inquired, her vigilant eyes on him like a wolf.

Albeit she was on guard with him, her body was failing to meet the standards of her vigilance. To her horror, it kept playfully pulling her away from him, teasing the man they knew was a skilled hunter and predator.

"All of this is merely a shell," he suavely replied. "She already sees me for who I really am. That's more than anyone else could say in this world."

"Why are we here, King of Serpents?" Soo Jin prompted sternly, quickly recognizing that at the moment, Kwon Tae Hyun had no intention of speaking to her as a King to a Queen, but as a man would to a woman. He was fucking speaking to her as a man would to a woman he wanted to seduce.

"Because I haven't seen you in a couple of days, and I've missed you," he told her without filter, shocking her with his bluntness.

Soon after, he stole her breath when he stalked her to the edge of the mahogany table. His body filled the frigid air between them and pressed against hers. Then, with a sensuous glide, he casually slipped his hands underneath her bare thighs and easily lifted her onto the table. Using her moment of distraction to his advantage, as he had probably anticipated the raging Queen to berate him for his audacity, he gracefully moved into the space between her legs. Arrogantly standing between her legs, his body heat stroked against her bare skin while his enticing eyes held hers.

No one needed to tell Soo Jin what a precarious angle this was. They weren't touching, but the position they were in not only encouraged it, but it also demanded that they mold against each other.

"You're afraid of me," he mused out loud. He raised a free hand and brushed through the long curls of her hair. When he felt her breath teeter, he cupped a cheek with his hand. With lazy strength, he stroked his thumb close to her lips.

"There are exactly eighteen different ways I could kill you right now," she warned, sitting up straight. She attempted to ignore the pleasurable sensations he evoked with his mind-blowing caresses. "If you're smart, then you'd better start backing away."

He expelled a laugh that reverberated throughout the room. It was a rich, deep tone that women dreamed of hearing every morning when they woke up from bed.

"Do you not think I can kill you?" she incited frigidly, her fists curling at her sides. She didn't do well with insults, and she wouldn't tolerate being insulted by him.

"You went easy on me the other night, Soo Jin," he murmured appreciatively, soothing the inferno raging within her with his languid voice. "I've been spoiled. I know I'm in your debt. Of course I know you can kill me."

She stared up at him skeptically and tilted her head to the hand cradling her cheek. She bestowed him with a dangerous smile that only fools would mistake as welcoming. "Then why aren't you backing away?"

"All it takes is one way to kill me," he prompted nonchalantly. Instead of backing away, he leaned forward and laid his hands flat on each side of her. He leveled his eyes with hers, giving her an unobstructed view of all the perfect features of his face. "Why aren't you killing me?"

"Don't mistake my laziness to kill you right now for feelings towards you," she clipped out, unwilling to shift away in fear. She stared at him dead in the eyes, noting that the small space caused their lips to nearly touch. The proximity of those tempting lips elicited nothing but sexual frustration from her. It took all her self-control to keep her traitorous lips from leaning forward and devouring his.

Barely able to contain her own sensuous desires, she frostily said, "You're still my enemy, and I'm just waiting for the day where I can kill you in front of the Underworld. Now, unless you want to get that defined ass of yours kicked, stop invading my space."

He favored her with a dazzling grin. He shook an amused head at her tenacity. "Isn't it funny that although you go by different names, you and Yoori both have the uncanny ability to drive me crazy, tease me to death, and say just the right words to ruin the sensual mood I try to put us in?"

"If that's the case, why aren't you getting up and giving me my space?"

He sighed. Slowly and all but too deliberately, he pressed his forehead against hers. He strategically hovered those dangerous lips of his over hers,

107

teasing her to death, but never kissing her. "I said you ruined the mood. I didn't say you screwed up any endeavors on my part."

This would have been the perfect moment to head-butt him. It would have been the perfect moment to lift her leg up and kick him in the groin. With his guard down, it would have been the perfect moment for her to attack. However, Soo Jin seized none of the moments as she sat there quietly, allowing herself to indulge in his teasing.

Damn.

No man who had this type of power—the power to make a woman's body feel alive with wonder—should ever be allowed out of captivity. He was simply too irresistible, too fantastically sexual, and too dangerous for any woman to try and fight off. If a woman of Soo Jin's caliber was feeling a bit disjointed, then God help all the other women in the world because Kwon Tae Hyun was going to annihilate the entire female species with a simple, sensual smile.

"You're dangerous," she murmured mindlessly. Satisfaction weighed on her lids, begging her to close her eyes so her body could enjoy his tempting endeavors.

"No more than you are to me," he crooned appreciatively.

The feel of his breath on her skin sent chills to stream over Soo Jin's tense body. She quietly cursed to herself. First he made her hot, now chills blanketed over her. This guy was definitely going to give her an aneurysm soon.

"Are you cold, Soo Jin?" he asked seconds later, his fingers running from her kneecap to her thighs. He took stock of the shiver he gave her every time the breath from his lips touched her skin.

"A little bit," she stupidly admitted again, her cheeks flushing with need.

He laughed, resting his eyes on the heels embellishing her feet.

"I'm sure a pair of cute little black Uggs will make it better," he whispered, focusing his attention on her long bare legs before returning to her eyes.

Soo Jin smirked upon being inadvertently reminded that in this conversation, he wasn't the only seductive God in the game.

"Unlike a pair of powerful heels, Uggs do not evoke unrelenting fear from people."

"No," he conceded carelessly, "but I'm sure they'll keep those pretty little feet of yours warm."

Something in her heart dropped. She snapped out of her stupor when she registered why Tae Hyun was referencing the Uggs. She knew who he was referring to when he casually brought the shoes up. The reminder of that person caused a firestorm of rage to brew in her body.

"Don't you feel like you're cheating on her right now?" she bit out, her now icy eyes berating his calm ones.

Intrigue reflected on his face at her accusation. "Is it considered cheating when I want to win my girlfriend back?"

"I was *never* your girlfriend," she corrected, getting angrier and angrier by the second.

Choi Yoori was his girlfriend—not her.

Choi Yoori was the one who was emotionally attached to him—not her.

She was only physically attracted to him. No harm, no foul there.

"And I won't be your girlfriend," she declared with finality. Her stubborn heart meant every word of it. "I don't care what you do. I don't care how hot you are, and I don't care how irresistible you may be—I won't be your girlfriend."

Tae Hyun was silent for a brief second. The shift in his expression told her that even though he had anticipated her blatant hostility towards his advances, it didn't mean it was easier for him to hear the object of his affections speak to him like he was a cursed plague.

"How did Ji Hoon win you?" he asked out of the blue.

For the first time, she saw a tinge of jealousy flicker in his eyes.

"Why?"

"I'm curious," he retorted, aggravation laced in his voice. "I rarely get jealous of him. I find myself a bit envious now because Ji Hoon was the one who got you. Apparently, I'm not doing a very good job because you're already so revolted by me."

Soo Jin clamped her lips shut. Initially, she was unwilling to enlighten him. However, when she saw the seriousness in his eyes and knew very well that he wouldn't let this go, she said, "I became Ji Hoon's girlfriend because I was vengeful, power-hungry, and self-serving. In addition to all that, I was young. I didn't know better. He was delicious eye-candy, he had power, he promised vengeance for my father, and it was all very . . . attractive to me."

She smiled at Tae Hyun, enjoying the jealousy that brimmed out of his eyes. Eager to give him a taste of his own medicine, she decided to employ some teasing of her own.

"Hmm . . ." Murmuring approvingly, her desirous eyes were locked with his curious ones as she slipped her hands underneath the black suit jacket he wore. She immersed herself with the texture of his dark blue dress shirt. She slowly eased the jacket off his shoulders, her fingers pressing tightly against his body. She reveled in the feel of the rippling muscles that tensed beneath the fabric.

"Do you want to know why Ji Hoon is so attached to me?" she whispered softly, confidently.

Her eyes held his while he allowed her fingers to dance against the planes of his body. She dragged her fingers towards the expanse of his muscular chest and began to unbutton the top three buttons, revealing a breathtaking glance of his sculpted chest.

"Because he never had all of me."

There was intrigue in his eyes, a sense of relief that Ji Hoon had only been blessed with kissing her and had never been gifted with anything beyond a kiss. "You're a virgin?"

She supplied a smirk as her answer.

In the two years that Soo Jin was with Ji Hoon, she had never given him her virginity. It wasn't that he revolted her. On the contrary, she was very tempted to have sex with him. It wasn't even that she was using sex as a weapon to keep him in order. The simple reason was that after years of training and killing men who attempted to rape her, she had come to treasure every bit of her virginity and wasn't intent on giving it away so easily. Though she wouldn't openly admit it to herself three years prior, and though Soo Jin had long given up on the fairytale wish for a Prince Charming, she still subconsciously found herself holding out for that one perfect guy.

She evaluated Tae Hyun's reaction. It did not elude her how subtle Tae Hyun was when he pulled her hands off of him and locked them down on the table. He wouldn't let her touch him any further. Like an adept charmer, he knew the skills in making someone weak in the knees—make them break their cold exterior and yearn for you. Much like the sex she withheld from Ji Hoon, Tae Hyun withheld his body from her, only allowing her a sample of the gift she could receive. Although Soo Jin should have found relief in this, she didn't. He was a master of seduction, the very thing that fantasies were made out of. And unfortunately for her, he was well aware of the power he possessed over her. He didn't let her touch him, and worse, he didn't touch her either. He merely stared at her and nearly drove her crazy with his sultry eyes.

She had to rectify this.

She could not allow herself to fall prey to his charms. Being this weak was simply not an option.

"And I plan on being one until I die," she told him coldly, lacing her voice with malice. "Sorry, seductive one, but the throne is more tantalizing to me than you. You can't compete with it."

Offense gripped his eyes. He did not hesitate to combat that statement.

"Can a throne keep you warm at night?" he asked pointedly, his lips drifting just above hers, its curves tempting her own mercilessly. "Can a throne run his lips all over you and worship you the way that pretty little body of yours is meant to be worshipped? Can a throne hold you in his arms and argue with you about the most nonsensical of things while secretly letting you win because all he cares about is making you happy? Can a throne give you phenomenal sex that will always leave you yearning for more? Can a throne give you his heart, what's left of his soul, and kiss you with such adoration that you forget about the world?" He held her chin, staring deep into her eyes while measuring the answer she would give. "Can a throne do all that to you? Can it really rival me?"

"You think you're God's gift to women," she muttered bitterly, wondering how it was possible that a person could be so arrogant.

"No," he contended with effortless charm. "Any other women affected by my charms are casualties. I was gifted to you and only you."

Releasing her hands from his iron grip, he guided her fingers across the surface of his well-built body. He made sure she felt the strength and power that made up his existence.

"This is all yours . . ."

Words from a distant past inundated her mind, whipping her out of any possible stupor Tae Hyun could put her in.

"I'm *not* Yoori," she scowled, sobering up at the reference of her human counterpart. He had given himself to Yoori and only Yoori. She had not forgotten that; she would never move past it. She would be damned if she was anyone's replacement. "I'm not the type of girl who allows anyone to sweep me off my feet, nor am I easily charmed. In saying that, I hope me being around you this long is enough to convince you that I'm not interested in you and that I will be more than happy to kill you. Now, if you'll excuse me . . ."

She hopped off the table in a flash and blatantly ignored the fact that he was standing there, watching her with quiet eyes. She strode away, gathering her bearings and what was left of her logicality. Soo Jin was near the exit when his voice jolted her to a stop.

"I saw the trigger that Yoori watched."

She spun around. "Excuse me?"

Her breath hitched when she saw that he was holding the heart-shaped necklace her father gave her— the very thing that decimated her amnesia and revived her. The pendant was dancing in midair while the silver chain hung listlessly from Tae Hyun's index finger. As he stretched his hand out, his perceptive eyes noted her interest.

"In your haste for your grand entrance the other night, you forgot your USB stick."

Soo Jin berated herself for forgetting something as important as a gift from her father. With her heart racing, she swept across the room and seized the necklace from his offering finger.

A smile broke out on his face—a warm, genuine smile that only the love of his life was ever bequeathed with. "Is it too forward of me to say how human you appeared in that video?"

"Then you watched the end," she prompted tightly, internally horrified that someone else had seen herself in that pathetic state.

This USB stick held the most important moments of her life in its hands. It was the very trigger for everything that had transpired, and she was appalled that, of all people, it was Kwon Tae Hyun who saw its contents. She was embarrassed, she felt threatened, and now she felt all the more vulnerable standing in front of him. It did not matter that she had gathered her bearings before the video ended. The fact was that she still looked pathetically human in that video recording. It enraged her that it must have given Tae Hyun some sort of unrealistic hope that there was a chance for her to be "human" again.

How sorely mistaken he would be to find out that Soo Jin had promised herself that she would never return to that feeble state in her life.

She would *never* be human again.

"I did," he confirmed, the warmth still present in his eyes.

Her heart hammering, Soo Jin knew she had to put the hostility back in the air between them. She didn't need the one opponent she had spent her entire life training to fight to soften up on her.

"Then you know what a big impact I made on you?"

He nodded, a hint of desolation entering his eyes. "You were the one who spread those rumors and brought me back."

"I am the reason for your *entire* life right now," she agreed vehemently, wondering why he was being so civil to her when he knew all this. What would it take to push this guy over the edge? "I'm surprised that you're still pursuing me when I was the reason you came back and killed your brother—when I was the ultimate reason you weren't able to stay in your precious 1st layer with your friends."

"The guilt of killing my own brother resides with me and only me," he responded calmly. "With or without those rumors, I would've found out sooner or later, and the end result would've been the same." He took a second to pause before raising a brow at her. "I didn't realize I made such a big impact on you as well though."

The way he said this left Soo Jin feeling uneasy.

"Then you know that you mean nothing more to me than an obstacle to get my coveted throne?"

"I know where I stand with you," he answered instead. "But all of that aside, there is something I want to speak to you about."

Soo Jin folded her arms and slanted her head. "What is it?"

"The tape of your father's murder," he began seriously. "The one that shows Young Jae working with my brother . . . I need to watch it."

She arched a defensive and skeptical eyebrow. "Why?"

"Because I want to know why my brother was working with yours."

"Why?"

What more could she say? She was a bitch in every sense of the word, and she didn't plan on handing anything over to Tae Hyun unless she felt it was appropriate to. At that instant, it wasn't necessary to give him anything. It wasn't appropriate until he convinced her with his next statement.

"Because it's my life, and I'm tired of being surrounded by secrets that everyone seems to hold from me."

Despite her best efforts to combat his statement, what he said resonated with her. Secrets. Her life was surrounded by them. Secrets of her own, secrets of her unforgiving society, secrets of others' pasts, others' actions, and others' mistakes that she not only had to pay for, but her future also had to pay for. Simply put, she was tired of all the secrets as well.

Just show it to him, her frustrated conscience urged. *Just show it to him and leave. He does too many strange things to us anyway. If we throw him this bone, then he'll leave us alone.*

"It's in here," she said with exasperation, throwing the necklace back at him. She couldn't believe she was giving in.

Although he caught the pendant easily, he did not catch on to the concept the same way. "There was only one video file in here."

"It's hidden," she told him, grinning pompously. She sauntered back and grabbed it from his hand. With teasing amusement, she asked, "Not such a gorgeous genius now, are you?"

The insult and unintentional compliment came out together before she could filter herself. She mentally cursed at herself and tried to remain cool and collected. Uncomfortably gathering her loose curls to one side, she bent forward to stick the USB stick into one of the ports of the computer.

He laughed amiably at her insult, his eyes lingering briefly to her butt just as she straightened up after inserting the USB stick in.

"I suck with technology. I guess that's why I have a thing for geeky computer girls who are talented enough to hide files in a USB stick."

"Was it not part of your training as a 1st layer heir?" she asked caustically, ignoring the unmistakable flirtatious tone in his voice. She turned on the computer and looked up at the 60-inch, flat screen TV hanging on the opposite wall. "Is that the monitor for the computer?"

"Yes," he confirmed as she opened the file. "And yeah, they did train me. I just wasn't good at it."

"Ah yes, you would've been the perfect guy. If only you were skilled at that," she mocked, loving that the guy wasn't perfect and that she whooped his ass in matters pertaining to technology. Soo Jin was competitive like that. In all aspects of her life, she found it a necessity to be the best, and if she weren't, then she would do anything to get rid of anyone who was better than her. Of course, the majority of the people in her enigmatic society shared this character trait as well. Since everyone's arrogance and cockiness went through the roof in her world, she did not feel like a tool for harboring such a competitive mindset.

"I guess I'd have to settle with being stupid and charming," he humored, knowing all too well that Soo Jin was rejoicing in the fact that he was crippled in the technology department.

Soo Jin hid a smile and kept her lips sealed. The bantering would have to end here. Any further playtime with Kwon Tae Hyun was dangerous.

Double-clicking on the second video icon in the folder that just appeared, Soo Jin pivoted around the table and stepped into the center of the room where Tae Hyun stood. Standing beside him, she mirrored his demeanor and folded her arms as well. Soo Jin made sure she was far enough away from him so that he didn't get any ideas that they were chummy. She was only showing him the video because his bastard of an older brother was involved, and she felt like he deserved to watch it. But after the video ended, she would leave him. She did not plan on running into him again until they met for their war in front of the Underworld. By then, any residual feelings, which she knew belonged to her human counterpart, should subside. She would be able to kill him with ease and take the throne that was rightfully hers.

By then, she would officially be a God.

"That's your father?"

His voice jarred her out of her reverie.

She dragged in a pained breath as her eyes landed on the monitor. She felt the strings of her heart tug for the person she saw on the screen. "Yes."

A quiet, companionable silence waltzed between them while they observed the video. Her father was walking out of a warehouse with his men in tow. Watching this video still made her heart clench. Nevertheless, for a reason that she hated to admit, the simple and unexplainable fact that Tae Hyun was standing there, approximately two feet beside her, somehow made the experience less painful this time around.

Tae Hyun remained quiet as he watched, his eyes focusing with intensity on not only her father, but also the entire area the camera lens could catch.

Soo Jin eyed him and instantly saw that something had crossed his face—a knowledge of sorts when the video ended.

"What?"

The look on his face was making her curious.

Without saying anything, Tae Hyun went back to the computer, replayed the video, and returned beside her. His eyes were still locked on the monitor.

"What?" she prompted again, curious with his bizarre behavior.

"Who was recording this?" he inquired. When he asked this, the camera shook at an angle as her father walked out of the warehouse.

"Tony," she answered, reciting what Ju Won told her. "Earlier that day, Hee Jun was planning on executing a small attack on my father. They were planning on recording his moves to anticipate future fights and to determine how Scorpions are trained. But before they could do that, they were unexpectedly interrupted when another attack occurred."

Just as she said this, sounds of sniper shots rang out again, killing her father's men and shooting her father down.

She glanced at Tae Hyun after he returned to his desk and replayed the video again. Only this time, he started the video at the moment when the shots started to fire. Curiously, he did not focus too heavily on the scene where Ho Young and Young Jae shot her father; he simply set up the media player to loop the beginning scene where her father was walking out of the warehouse and ending where he and his men were shot.

Chills continuously chased each other on her body as she watched the dawning light of realization shine brighter in Tae Hyun's eyes.

"Suddenly seeing my father's men getting shot will tell us why Ho Young and Young Jae were working together?" she asked skeptically, still focusing her attention on Tae Hyun. She was getting annoyed that he wouldn't divulge what he was doing. "What is it? Do you think Ju Won lied to me, and Tony wasn't the one recording?"

Then finally, after an extended moment of ignoring her, he decided to enlighten her with his findings.

"Sometimes when we watch recorded videos, we focus too much on the event of what took place and too much on the insignificant things like who was recording. By doing so, we miss important clues altogether." He pointed at the monitor. "From the camera's direction and how far they had to zoom in to get a measly shot of what was happening, it shows that Tony and Hee Jun were pretty far away from the scene. From their angle, you can see there are no buildings closer than theirs. This indicates that the sniper was at least another building behind, if not further, to better conceal themselves. Now if you pay attention to all the shots and how windy it was that day, then you'd see how accurate all the shots were, despite the turbulent weather. The sniper successfully killed the other men with clean, accurate shots. With your father, the sniper shot your father in such a way that would only handicap him, not kill him. The sniper was setting your father up for Young Jae and my brother. He was basically putting your father on a platter for them."

"What are you getting at?" Soo Jin asked, even though in her mind, she knew the chills she was receiving meant that she was heading towards the same conclusion as Tae Hyun.

He faced her with knowledge running through his eyes. "This sniper was *extremely* skilled. It was incredibly windy that day, but he still shot with perfect accuracy." Tae Hyun's voice grew lower, more solemn. "There's only one sniper in our world skilled enough to shoot from that range and with such precision, especially shooting against that type of violent wind that would surely throw others off."

And then the truth slapped her like a whipping tornado.

"Lee Ji Hoon," she whispered, her eyes widening at this revelation. "You're insinuating that Ji Hoon was working with my brother and your brother?" Her head was spinning. The insinuation absolutely made no sense to her. "Why? Why would the three of them work together?"

Tae Hyun sighed incredulously. Everything was finally making sense to him. "*Why* did Young Jae disappear to Japan for three years?"

"My brother grew up and was trained in Japan," she answered him. "He has close ties to the Underworld there."

Tae Hyun nodded. "My brother grew up and was trained in China. He had close ties to the Underworld there as well."

In the road that Tae Hyun was slowly painting for her, Soo Jin finally saw the destination they were headed to.

"Young Jae and Ho Young never wanted Korea's Underworld," she began disbelievingly. "Young Jae wanted to rule over Japan's Underworld, Ho Young wanted China's Underworld, so that meant—"

"In their agreement, Lee Ji Hoon gets Korea's Underworld," Tae Hyun finished for her. His voice held a mixture of amazement and disbelief. "It was a conspiracy. They weren't enemies. The three of them were working together the entire time. They were conspiring with one another to garner control over the three Underworlds."

Soo Jin was still utterly gobsmacked by this revelation.

"*That* was why Ji Hoon never made the effort to get on to Ju Won's good side when I was around, because he knew that he'd have the Underworld regardless. Nevertheless, he wanted to break me, to make me think he cared about me more than the Underworld and that he was willing to sacrifice everything for me. He wanted his coveted throne and his trophy girlfriend."

"Anna wasn't the only one who betrayed you," Tae Hyun provided shrewdly.

"No," Soo Jin conceded. "Anna only knew a bit, but Ji Hoon knew the whole plan. The bitch never realized what I was planning to do to her husband. She only thought I was betraying him; she could've never imagined that I had planned on killing him. It wasn't until Ji Hoon divulged everything to them."

She felt the rage brew like an unstoppable storm inside her.

"*He* was the one who told Young Jae, he was the one who was working with them, he was the one who helped kill my father, and he was the one who betrayed me and ruined everything."

"No matter who protects you, we will annihilate them."

07: The Meeting of Gods

"I'm going to fucking kill that bastard," Soo Jin seethed, gazing at the video of her father's death with an entirely new outlook on what took place.

The more she watched, the more she wanted to rip Ji Hoon apart limb by limb. Fucking bastard. He was right in her grasp the other night, and what did she do? She let him go because she felt that she "owed" him for all his help. In actuality, the fucker was the primary one who screwed her over!

"He's already left the country."

She faced Tae Hyun. He was now sitting calmly on the edge of his desk, his eyes on her. For the first time, their hatred for Ji Hoon matched in intensity.

"*What?*"

"I've been trying to find him for the past few days," Tae Hyun shared as the beginnings of the setting sun began to descend behind him, "to kill him once and for all for what he did to my father. But my Cobras told me he left the country after the war. He hasn't been in Korea for a while."

"Where is he right now?" she inquired, suspecting that Tae Hyun probably knew.

He inclined his head at her. "Where do you think?"

A resurgence of fury flashed through her. After all these revelations, after what had transpired since her return to the Underworld, and after the war's commencement, she knew all too well where Ji Hoon was.

"He went to my brother."

Tae Hyun nodded. He took a slight pause to ponder something before he released a dejected sigh. He abruptly whipped out his phone from his pocket.

"Who are you calling?" Soo Jin asked watchfully, her stern eyes locked on his phone.

"Your brother."

The force of the simple reply nearly had her stumbling in her black pumps. What the hell? Before she could accuse him of anything or ask if he had been working with them all along, he promptly explained himself.

"Young Jae contacted me the day after Ju Won's birthday. He gave me a number to reach him and said that whenever I was ready to talk, I could call him anytime." His shoulders lifted into a shrug. "It seems befitting that I do so right now."

"Why would he give you a means to contact him? What does he want with you?"

"Why do you think?"

Soo Jin inhaled sharply, suspecting that Young Jae gave Tae Hyun a means to contact him because he wanted to work with Tae Hyun—to possibly work out an agreement or form an alliance. Either way, it didn't comfort Soo Jin to know that there was a chance that Tae Hyun and Young Jae were working together.

"Were you planning on calling him and working with him?"

He raised a brow at her, his expression unimpressed with her question. "After my spiel to you about winning you back, you think I'd stoop so low as to work with your brother? If you truly believe that, then you're not the geeky computer genius I labeled you to be."

There was humor in his voice, but she didn't miss the offense in it. Tae Hyun was too prideful to ever consider working with the likes of her brother—or Ji Hoon for that matter—and the accusation was just insulting.

Unwilling to offer an apology, Soo Jin kept her lips sealed while Tae Hyun placed the phone on speaker. Soon, the ringing of the phone infiltrated the office room.

Her brother's voice came on the line after the third ring, and Soo Jin could swear she felt her heart clench and the air around her dissipate. Regardless of how much she hated her brother and wanted to kill him, she couldn't deny the heartache she felt hearing the voice of the person she grew up with and loved. However, she hadn't forgotten that he murdered their father. She hadn't forgotten the promise she made to avenge the Siberian Tigers family, she hadn't forgotten that he was prepared to kill her when she was Yoori, and she definitely hadn't forgotten that she had plans to kill him. Complications of the heart aside, she knew when to get down to business. At the moment, Young Jae was a cancer in her life that needed to be eradicated.

"Tae Hyun," Young Jae's warm voice greeted, acting as a stimulant to the boiling of her already heated blood. After bearing witness to her father's death a moment ago, the fact that he was so carefree infuriated her. "I'm glad you called."

"I'm with your sister," Tae Hyun said swiftly, getting right to the point.

God, the guy is too much of a straight shooter at times, Soo Jin thought with annoyance. She had hoped to eavesdrop on their conversation before she planned on revealing herself. Now, obviously, that plan had been shot to hell.

"I know you are," Young Jae said serenely, shocking both Tae Hyun and Soo Jin with knowledge that he already knew they were together before the phone call. "I was planning on calling both of you. Luckily, you called me just before I could dial you."

Soo Jin smirked, amused that this entire city was seemingly under Young Jae's surveillance. "You still have your spies all over the city, don't you, *oppa*?" Soo Jin said sweetly into the phone.

She laced "oppa" with as much venom as she could. She was positive her brother caught every bit of that venom. After three years apart, it still felt like yesterday that they had last spoken. It still felt like yesterday that she hated his guts.

He elicited a cool, mocking laugh that angered every nerve in her body. "I know enough," he said simply. "I always knew it was only a matter of time before you regained your memories. I still kick myself when I think about the moment you kneeled before me during your amnesia, begging me to spare your life." Soo Jin bit back a curse at the reminder of this, and Young Jae went on. "If only I had killed you, then you wouldn't be such a thorn in my side now."

Ah yes, Young Jae, despite his political correctness at times, was also a straight shooter. The Royals in the Underworld were truly people who hated beating around the bush.

"Ji Hoon is with you, isn't he?" asked Tae Hyun. He, as well as Soo Jin, could sense other presences over the phone.

"And your wife?" added Soo Jin. The words were posed as a question, but they already knew the answer.

Young Jae laughed again, impressed with both Tae Hyun and Soo Jin.

"Yes, they're both here with me," he confirmed. "I was having a . . . *business* meeting with Ji Hoon before you called. This is great, actually. Since we're all in our offices right now, we might as well have a videoconference, don't you think?"

Tae Hyun smirked, eyeing Soo Jin as he had already anticipated that Young Jae would suggest this. "My computer is already on. Just do what you need to do, and we'll be connected."

"Very well."

Click.

Shortly after they hung up, Tae Hyun turned on the videoconference program on his computer and instantly, the monitor changed to a bright, live video of Young Jae. He wore a gray suit and was sitting beside his wife Anna, who wore a flowing black dress. Both were seated behind a long conference desk. In the background stood Ji Hoon, who was wearing a white dress shirt with the sleeves rolled up to his forearms and gray pants. He was leaning against the gargantuan window that looked out to the city life of Tokyo. It was obvious they were in a high-rise building of their own.

"It makes sense that you'd be with your new boyfriend," Ji Hoon stated acidly, looking from Tae Hyun to Soo Jin. His eyes were rippling with rage.

"You worked with Young Jae and Ho Young, helped them kill my father, and betrayed me, you piece of shit. Stop playing the victim," Soo Jin snapped, wishing she could reach into the monitor and kill the backstabbing fucker. "I should've killed you at Ju Won's party when I had the chance."

Soo Jin stood in the middle of the room, her face stern and her arms folded. She was glaring at the monitor like she was about to declare war upon them. In the back, Tae Hyun was seated calmly on the edge of his desk, his legs stretched out and his dress shirt revealing the three missing buttons that Soo Jin had unhooked. With the long sleeves of his shirt pulled up to his forearms, Tae Hyun exuded nothing short of cool elegance as he stared at the monitor.

Unlike Soo Jin, Anna, and Ji Hoon, all of whom were wearing their feelings on their sleeves, Tae Hyun, much like Young Jae, kept his emotions to himself.

Ji Hoon scoffed disbelievingly, looking at her like she had just rattled on and on about the most ridiculous of things.

"Three years of amnesia really fucked up your head, baby. First, you sleep with your biggest enemy, and now you're accusing me of killing your father when it was clear that it was Kwon Ho Young and apparently Young Jae?" He grinned deceptively, glancing at Young Jae. Her brother was smirking without remorse. "Let me guess: Kwon Tae Hyun gave you the idea that I was working with them?"

Tae Hyun laughed with hilarity, not even entertaining Ji Hoon's poor acting skills as merit for him to reply. Soo Jin would've also laughed if she weren't so offended that this pathological liar was still trying to play mind games with her.

"You two are working together now?" Young Jae incited instead, his calm eyes on Tae Hyun. He did not bother to look at Soo Jin, and this had Soo Jin biting her lip in fury.

"No," Soo Jin answered for Tae Hyun, offended that anyone would think that she would collude with Kwon Tae Hyun. Work with the guy she had to kill for her throne? Why would she partner up with him? "We have never worked together, and we will never work together. I don't need to work with anyone to get anything done." Her eyes cooled. "Unlike some people."

"You know what?" Young Jae remarked airily, discounting her comment. He looked around the room and casually changed the subject. "I think this conversation would be more appropriate if all of us convened in one place and spoke—in person."

Soo Jin smirked, amused with this sudden proposal. "You would like a live reunion, brother?"

Tae Hyun folded his arms in interest. His eyes became alight with intrigue. He liked the sound of that. "That actually sounds very fun."

"They will kill you the moment they step foot in the same room as you," Ji Hoon gritted to Young Jae from the back.

Despite her silence, even Anna looked disturbed by her husband's proposal.

"Now, now, Ji Hoon," Young Jae said lightly. "We may have been born humans, but we were raised to be Royals. Regardless of the feelings they harbor for us, I am confident that Soo Jin and Tae Hyun would agree to a momentary ceasefire if we all reunite in one place." He looked directly into the camera lens. "Don't you two think that would be nice? If all of us convened and continued this conversation appropriately?"

"I know just the place in Seoul," said Tae Hyun, his voice not hiding his keenness for an in-person meeting.

Young Jae chuckled, leaning forward with his arms on his knees. "I think it would be more appropriate if the two of you came here."

"You want to continue this meeting in Japan?" Soo Jin let out a disbelieving breath, displeased that this possible meeting would take place on enemy territory instead of her own. "What happened to agreeing to a ceasefire?"

"I'm diplomatic, but I'm not an idiot, Soo Jin. It would be a cold day in hell before I allow you and Tae Hyun to choose the place of our reunion. We'll meet in Japan; we'll meet on neutral grounds."

"I'm sorry, aren't you a shadow Underworld King in Japan?" Tae Hyun stated sarcastically, voicing what Soo Jin was thinking.

Japan was not a neutral ground; it would be a gravesite for Soo Jin and Tae Hyun if they weren't careful.

Young Jae shrugged lackadaisically. "I am, but that doesn't mean that this ground isn't neutral. As the host, I promise you safe passage. As long as you do not break the ceasefire pact, then everything is golden."

"Your promises mean shit," Soo Jin stated spitefully.

"As do yours," Young Jae said just as spitefully to her. A fleeting flicker of anger doused his normally cool visage before he reined his emotions in. He exhaled to regain his composure and added, "I'm giving you my word that as long as you keep your end of the agreement, then no harm will come to you in Japan. What you choose to believe is up to you." He leaned back in his chair, gazing at them with indifferent eyes. "I mean, let's face it, kids. This in-person meeting means more to you than it does to me. You have nothing but questions, and we have nothing but answers. Regardless of our current war, I do not see why we cannot come together to address everything. What fun is a war if you are not appropriately informed of all aspects of your enemies' pasts?"

"Why do you want to see us in-person so badly?" Tae Hyun questioned.

Young Jae grinned coldly. "Regardless of my ill feelings towards both of you, even I have to admit that I am intrigued with the idea of the most powerful crime lords getting together in one venue. I was not able to bear witness to my sister's return to the Underworld—Ju Won was the one who had that honor. Now, I want an honor that supersedes his—I want all four crime lords to come together. I want the King of Scorpions, the King of Skulls, the King of Serpents, and the Queen of Siberian Tigers in the same room where we are simply . . . chatting."

"*Just* chatting?" Tae Hyun questioned again, his voice skeptical.

"Just chatting," Young Jae confirmed before showing them exactly why he was such a powerful King. He may have looked diplomatic, but he was truly a wolf in sheep's clothing. "Our upcoming war will promise bloodshed soon enough. Before we become the Kings and Queens we were raised to be, let us be politicians and enjoy one another's presence. Let's have a reunion before the end comes." He expelled another sigh, not giving them an opportunity to further question him. "I will send the location meeting to you, Tae Hyun. In a day's time, whether you or my sister comes is up to you. It will be of no loss to me, but a bigger loss to you if you do not show up. I plan on bringing hell upon you in the coming weeks. Perhaps during this grace period before your deaths, you should endeavor to uncover all the secrets of your lives before I bury you six-feet under." He cordially inclined his head at the screen, purposely disregarding the look of fury on Soo Jin's face and the look of challenge on Tae Hyun's face. "It's been fun. Ji Hoon and I look forward to meeting you soon. Take care of yourselves."

They then disconnected the call. The 60-inch screen went completely black, revealing only the meager reflection of Soo Jin and Tae Hyun staring at the now dark monitor. Tae Hyun was still sitting on the edge of the desk, and Soo Jin was still standing in the middle of the room; the expressions on their faces were rippling with deep contemplation.

After another stretch of silence, Tae Hyun suddenly said, "So should I pick you up at your place tonight and head out together?"

Soo Jin glowered at him, feeling her defenses rise up. "Excuse me? Who says I will be going with you?"

"I have my own jet," Tae Hyun replied in a matter-of-fact tone. He wasn't the least bit affected by her hostile attitude towards him.

"So do I," quipped Soo Jin.

The beguiling smile on his face remained. With ease, he showed her exactly why he was deemed as one of the smartest Kings in Underworld history. "But Young Jae is sending the location to me."

Soo Jin regarded him with disbelief. "You're blackmailing me into traveling to Japan with you by withholding information on the meeting place?"

Tae Hyun shook his head charismatically, his smile making him appear more innocent than he was. "I'm simply making your life much easier by taking care of all the travel arrangements." He chuckled, closing the distance between them. "Come on, Queen of Siberian Tigers. We're just carpooling. There's no harm in that."

"I don't want to 'carpool' with you."

"That's a shame. It would suck for you to go all the way to Japan and not know where the hell to go for the meeting."

"You should be ashamed of yourself for being this childish."

"I'm actually really proud of myself for being this clever." His grin widened. "Perhaps I *am* the gorgeous genius you coined me to be after all." He chuckled again, moving his lips close to her ear before marching out of the office. "I'll pick you up at your place tonight. I look forward to some bonding time with you. Oh, and pack lightly. If things go according to plan, you won't need much clothing for this trip."

Soo Jin's eyes bloomed as she felt heat infiltrate her cheeks. She whipped around, intent on beating the fuck out of him for eliciting this emotion from her. Luckily for Tae Hyun, he was already halfway across the office, winking at her before he made his exit from the room.

Soo Jin clenched her fists, staring at his disappearing back with heat still cloaked over her. Waging an epic war with him aside, it would be a miracle if they made it to Japan alive. Because, God help her, she was going to throw his ass off the plane if he so much as winked at her.

"You were born into this world . . ."

08: Flying Gods

"So, is this a date?" Jae Won asked softly, staring out into the Siberian Tigers' driveway as they awaited Tae Hyun's arrival.

Soo Jin shot him an annoyed glare. The brisk evening wind brushed past them, mirroring the arctic expression on her face. "I recently declared to the entire Underworld that I would be more than happy to kill him for the throne, and you think I'm going on a date with him?"

Jae Won shrugged, looking at Kang Min dubiously.

"I don't know. He and Yoori were like this." He hooked the joints of his two index fingers together to demonstrate his point. "They were really tight and were like best friends who loved each other. Isn't it normal to ask if you and him are going on a date?"

"Well, we're not," Soo Jin dismissed scornfully, folding her arms and gazing ahead. "This is business. My brother wants to have a face-to-face meeting in Japan and the one he gave the meeting location to is Kwon Tae Hyun. Unfortunately that cunning Serpent made it clear that if I didn't 'carpool' with him, he wasn't going to tell me the location."

"So, he essentially tricked you into being with him for the night, even though you openly told him that you despised him," summarized Kang Min, his voice holding a tinge of admiration for Tae Hyun. He and Jae Won nodded in wonderment. "Very smart."

"You mean sneaky," Soo Jin amended.

"No, he's really smart," said Jae Won, oblivious that Soo Jin needed him to be on her side when it came to talking shit about Tae Hyun.

Soo Jin casted another glare at Jae Won before shaking her head and turning away.

She had updated the brothers that Young Jae had invited her to have a face-to-face meeting with him and Ji Hoon in Japan. Initially, Jae Won and Kang Min were insistent about keeping Soo Jin company in Japan so that she would be safe. However, when she added that Tae Hyun was going with her, they immediately backtracked, telling her that they should keep watch over the

Siberian Tigers in her absence. Though it was obvious that they were very favorable of Tae Hyun being with her, as they knew there was no one better to travel with, she did not probe for explanations for their change of heart. Soo Jin was afraid she already knew why they did not find it unsettling that she was going to be alone with the King of Serpents.

In spite of her newly declared war with the King of Serpents, she recognized that the brothers still harbored a tremendous amount of love and respect for Tae Hyun. She knew why they approved of her traveling with Tae Hyun and why they insisted on keeping her company as they awaited his arrival. They not only trusted him, but they also missed him. Due to their complicated history, she did not expect them to abhor Tae Hyun. The time would come soon enough for them to aid her in bringing forth his demise, but for now, she did not plan to confront the brothers about their attachment to their former King. For the time being, they could continue to be in a "complicated relationship" with Tae Hyun for all she cared.

"He's here. He's here," announced Kang Min, trying to retain his elation when the headlights shone through the imposing iron gates.

The brothers wore black leather jackets and dark pants. Although their dark appearance radiated a sign of menace and peril, their behavior mirrored that of children's.

Beside him, Jae Won excitedly grabbed Soo Jin's luggage and bounced down the stairs, watching the black Jaguar vehicle glide up to the circular driveway they were in.

Soo Jin fought every urge to roll her eyes. It was honestly awkward to watch the brothers behave like children separated from a parental figure after a divorce. Under normal circumstances, she would have dismissed them, as she did not want any witnesses for this embarrassing scene. She had already ordered the rest of the Siberian Tigers to vacate the premises for the time being. She was tempted to order the brothers to do the same. She showed leniency and allowed them to stay because she knew that they had missed hanging out with Tae Hyun. She just wished they wouldn't make the situation so uncomfortable and cringe-worthy for her to watch.

The Jaguar came to a slow stop in front of the quiet estate. With the engine still humming, the driver's door opened and out came the man of the hour.

Tae Hyun wore a business casual attire that consisted of a white dress shirt and black pants. His hair was wet, indicating that he had just showered. His eyes roamed over the brothers and stopped on Soo Jin on the stairs. She was staring down at him with an impassive look on her face. Meeting her gaze, his sinful lips lifted into a breathtaking smile that caused her heart to skip a beat. He appeared refreshed, pumped, and damn well ready for a fun night ahead. To put it simply: he looked delectable, and it scared the shit out of her that she had to be alone with him for the rest of the night.

"Bos—err," Kang Min halted midway, catching himself before he accidentally greeted Tae Hyun with the wrong title. He peered uneasily back at Soo Jin, who was glaring down at him with daggers in her eyes. While holding one of her luggage, trembling in anticipation and fear, he could not have looked more frightful.

Soo Jin exhaled patiently, shaking her head inwardly. Kang Min was normally composed, and it did not please her to see him slip up, especially with her enemy in close proximity.

"Good to see you, Kang Min," Tae Hyun greeted warmly, nodding at Kang Min to alleviate the looming tension that was shrouding over them.

"Good to see you too," Kang Min replied, depositing Soo Jin's luggage in the opened trunk.

Jae Won moved beside Kang Min to place her other luggage into the trunk. While doing so, he immediately greeted Tae Hyun, doing his best to conceal his smile. "Hi."

Tae Hyun laughed, patting them on the shoulders. The awkwardness in the air did not elude him, and he was intent on lightening the atmosphere. "Is she as tough on you guys as she is with me?"

Kang Min and Jae Won released a relieved chuckle. They were ready to embark on a lively conversation when Soo Jin decided to join in on the conversation.

"I am *not* tough on them," she bit out, stomping down the stairs and heading straight towards an amused Tae Hyun. "And for the record, I know they have history with you, but I'm back now. I'm their boss, not you," she clarified. "Don't joke around with them and make this whole thing awkward. I'm only leaving with you tonight because you're blackmailing me with the location of the meeting. Apart from that, we're still enemies, so I'd appreciate it if you stop making things uncomfortable with my right-hand men."

Tae Hyun eyed her incredulously, holding back his laughter. He was dumbfounded by her reaction. "All I did was greet them," he explained with a patient smile. "I didn't ask for their hands in marriage."

Soo Jin opened her mouth to snap back. She halted when she realized that she may have overreacted.

Noting her uncomfortable silence, Tae Hyun gave one final nod to the brothers before vesting his full attention on her. He appraised her black leather jacket, dark pants, and knee-high leather boots.

"I told you to pack lightly and you bring three luggage *and* cover yourself with a leather attire?" He stepped closer to her, the newly applied cologne from his shower wafting into her nose. "What are you trying to do to me, Soo Jin?"

"Nothing," she enunciated, clenching her teeth tightly. Despite her guarded appearance, she was holding her breath to keep from inhaling the intoxicating cologne.

He chuckled, his charismatic laughter echoing into the sprawling estate. "Perhaps it will be more fun for me to unwrap you like a Christmas present on the plane."

"I'll cut off your fingers before you even come near me."

"Um, okay," Jae Won interrupted, clapping his hand together to garner their attention. It was palpable that he and Kang Min were feeling very uncomfortable with this portion of the conversation. It was also clear that he wanted to help Tae Hyun out by diverting Soo Jin's anger. "Perhaps both of you can continue this conversation on the plane ride to Japan?"

"Good idea," Tae Hyun agreed and soon turned to face his car. He strode to open the passenger door for Soo Jin. He inclined his head at her. "Are you ready?"

Soo Jin said nothing. She merely released a breathy sigh and ducked inside the car. She did not want to stand there and lose her composure with him. She simply wanted to get this over with.

"If you need anything, give us a call. We'll be on the first flight out," Kang Min informed Soo Jin.

"Stay safe, boss," added Jae Won. He smiled widely, watching Tae Hyun as he moved to the driver's side. "Please don't kill each other."

Soo Jin scoffed when Tae Hyun got into the car. "Tell me about it."

As Tae Hyun waved goodbye to the brothers and drove off, he turned to Soo Jin with a dashing smile. He was excited to launch a conversation with her until he saw that she had just put her sleek, red Beats headphones on. She blasted the music to full volume, ignoring him as she stared out the window.

Tae Hyun busted out laughing when he realized that she was not going to make this trip easy for him.

"Oh man," he said lightly, gazing at the dark road ahead. "This is definitely going to be an interesting trip."

■ ■ ■

"This is a pretty good pair of headphones."

Soo Jin roused from her sleep when she heard Tae Hyun's voice drift into her ears. She opened her eyes and tilted her head to the side.

After getting on his private jet, she had isolated herself from Tae Hyun by immersing herself with her music. At first, he was eager to converse with her when they got onto the plane. However, when she sat in the furthest seat away from him and continued to place her headphones on her head, Tae Hyun got the hint and left her alone for the majority of the plane ride. For Soo Jin, the ride was so peaceful that she actually dozed off to sleep. Unfortunately for her, Tae Hyun was no longer the patient King who got onto the plane. After traveling for a long period of time, it was evident that he was bored and wanted to be entertained by her.

Tae Hyun was now sitting across from her in the next aisle. He was twisting her headphones around, eyeing it with interest.

"You have the audacity to take off my headphones?" she demanded firmly. The drowsiness shrouding her eyes was instantly replaced with icy ire. If she could shoot lasers out of her eyes, Tae Hyun would have combusted into flames.

Unperturbed by her hardened stare, he displayed an easygoing smile and placed the headphones on the seat beside him. He bestowed his full, appreciative attention on her.

"I was bored and wanted to know what was keeping you so entertained," he explained casually. "Like I said, this is a very good pair of headphones."

"Yes, it is," she concurred dryly, uninterested in embarking on a conversation with him. "Now, give it back."

His impish smile remained. He made no effort to reach for the headphones. "How about you let me entertain you now?"

"How about no?"

"I will not do anything to upset you."

"The fact that you're breathing is already upsetting me."

Tae Hyun laughed, feigning a hurt expression. "You really go for the jugular, don't you?"

"I don't have time to play your little games."

He nodded. "How about this," he compromised, leaning forward with his arms on his knees. "We will land in Japan soon. How about for the remainder of our plane ride here, I give you my word that I will not attempt to seduce you or do anything of that nature. We can just have a simple conversation to keep ourselves entertained until we reach our destination."

Soo Jin folded her arms, overtly showing that she wasn't interested in his proposal. "And if I don't want to talk to you at all?"

"Then you will be entertained by me anyway, and it *will* consist of me using all the charms I have to have fun with you." He expelled an easygoing breath, his handsome face lighting up with charm. "Come on, Soo Jin. Don't disappoint me with all this avoidance crap. I know you're better than this."

Soo Jin released a slow, pondering breath. She bitterly acknowledged that she was better than this. A Princess may be weak enough to play the cat and mouse game with Tae Hyun, but a Queen would stand her ground and challenge him. In this case, despite her reservations with speaking to him, she had to be the Queen she was raised to be.

"Fine," she acquiesced, boldly initiating the conversation to show that she was not afraid of him. She peered out the window. When the city lights of Japan graced her eyes, she knew where to begin. "Do you visit Japan often?"

"Not as much as I would like to," Tae Hyun answered, his expression pleased that she was finally playing nice.

Soo Jin canted her head at his answer. Curiosity gnawed at her. Now that she decided to bite the bullet and converse with him, she might as well quench her curiosity about him.

"Are you as beloved here as you are in Korea?"

Tae Hyun shrugged, not completely understanding her question. "I have a lot of good friends and mentors here if that's what you mean."

"Must be nice," she remarked, her tone slightly resentful.

His brows drew together. "What?"

"To have so many friends while growing up."

A curious glint crept into his eyes. He leaned in closer, his gaze perceiving her in a new light. "Did you not travel often during your training?"

Soo Jin lapsed into silence and averted her attention back to the window. Once a bitter smile adorned her lips, she began to unfold her story.

"Ju Won did not believe that it was important for me to be well-traveled nor did he believe it was important for me to have friends. My only companions were Jae Won and Kang Min and some of my trusted trainees. I did not travel the world. He felt that it was better for me to not be tempted by the weaknesses of the rest of the world. He believed the only things I should know were the throne, the coffin, and my training." She laughed to herself. "I resented him for that until I was formally introduced into the Underworld. I realize now that he did not keep me away from the world to better my training; no, he kept me away because he wanted the rest of the world to revere me. I was not to be anyone's friend or have other mentors. I was to be just that—a God amongst Royals."

Her smile remained as she kept her eyes on the tiny speckles of light outside her window. Feeling like she was in a protective bubble that the rest of the world could not penetrate, she decided to reveal something that she had never disclosed to anyone.

"This is where I will reign next."

Compelled by her words, Tae Hyun's eyes followed her line of vision and glanced at the speckles of light outside. "Next?"

"When Ju Won brought forth the possibility of me becoming the Lord of the Underworld, I did not envision simply ruling over Korea," she explained, staring down at the world beneath her like a true God. "I wanted to be more than that; I wanted to have more power than that. What fun is it to simply rule over one country when I could have the rest of the world to preside over?"

"You want to become the Lord of all the Underworlds," he summed up, looking at her with newfound amazement.

"A true God does not stop in just one country."

Despite the fact that he was fascinated with her plans, Tae Hyun did not hesitate to play the devil's advocate. "Korea loves you, but Japan loves your brother. You may be the crown jewel of our world, but the Underworld in Japan will always favor your brother over you."

Albeit his argument was legitimate, Soo Jin was prepared with her response.

"Our world loves you, yet they are still willing to pit me against you. You are their favored King, the one they truly want to rule over their world. And despite their favoritism for you, they still sacrifice you to me." She turned to him. "Do you know why that is?"

He remained quiet, and she enlightened him.

"Because they favor power more than they favor you. They will never allow their love for you to supersede what our society has been built upon. We are plagued with the never-ending pursuit of power, and the Underworld is only as powerful as the Lord who reigns over it." Her face split into a wide, merciless grin. "My defeat over you will set the precedence for the rest of my reign. Once I kill you, I will go after Ji Hoon, and then I will kill my brother. I will kill anyone who stands in my way because this is not a democracy—this is a dictatorship. Once I stand alone as the sole Lord in our Underworld, then I will expand my reach."

He smiled, nodding at her answer. After a pregnant pause, he revealed, "That was my long-term goal as well."

Soo Jin nodded, unsurprised. The reason she told him was because she knew, at one point or another, he, too, had grand plans like this. This was how the Royal bloodlines of the Underworld were brought up to view the world. They were not raised to simply reside in one country; they were born to do everything in their power to preside over as much of the world as they can.

"What changed?" she inquired instinctively.

"I found something better."

"What could be better than being an untouchable God?"

"Being a snob."

She shot him a chiding glance when his answer scorched her like boiling water. He promised her that he would not use his charms—or anything of that nature—to upset her. As subtle as it was, using the term "snob" constituted as upsetting her.

Tae Hyun smirked at her reproaching stare and perceptively steered the subject on to a more serious note.

"Were you working with my brother?"

She eyed him critically. What the hell kind of question was that? "Excuse me?"

"I've been thinking about it more and more. I don't understand how it was possible that he hid you. Based on your self-recording, it was obvious that you despised him. Unless something happened after you finished your video recording, I can't see you two working together."

"We didn't," she replied tightly, her eyes blinking in rage. She hated Ho Young. She would never work with him in a million years.

"Why do you think my brother hid you?"

Soo Jin pondered the question and expelled a weary breath.

"I don't know," she admitted honestly. "I was openly hostile towards him. Every time I saw him, I wanted to provoke him to fight me so that I could have an excuse to kill him. It baffles my mind to know that he was the one who hid me in Taecin." She shifted slightly, casting a furtive glance to Tae Hyun when an unsettling question popped in her mind. "How long do you think they were working together?"

"You mean our brothers and Ji Hoon?"

Soo Jin nodded.

"It could not have taken place when my father was killed," he answered with certainty.

"You don't think Ho Young had a hand in your father's death?"

Tae Hyun shook his head. "My brother was a sick person, but out of everyone, he loved our father the most. I don't think he could've had a hand in helping to orchestrate our father's death." He continued to gaze out the window. "I think Young Jae was the mastermind behind the alliance. He was the only common link between my brother and Ji Hoon."

After a lapse of silence, he faced her to hear her perspective.

"What do you think happened?"

Soo Jin swallowed tightly, formulating her own assumptions. "I think you are right when you say that my brother was the common link between them. I believe that he befriended them—or at least had some working relationship with them—at some point during their training. As much as I despise my brother, even I have to admit that there's something about him that evokes trust from people. I think he used me as one of the bribes for Ji Hoon to work with him. At that point, I was not giving Ji Hoon the time of day and I'm sure, in addition to promising him sole power over the Korean Underworld, he promised his approval for me to be with Ji Hoon as well."

She blankly stared out the window again.

"I don't know how he managed to convince your brother to work with Ji Hoon though. If what you said is true, then Ho Young would've hated Ji Hoon with a passion. It did not make sense for him to work with Ji Hoon—or my brother for that matter. Among the three, Ho Young was the one with the most power. The fact that you were well on your way to presiding over the 1st layer only meant that even without Young Jae or Ji Hoon's help, he would have still been considered the most powerful King. Having said this, it only means that there is something else that we're missing in this equation—a power that Young Jae held over Ho Young in order to convince him to be part of this conspiracy."

Tae Hyun smirked when the perpetual city lights started to morph into majestic skyscrapers. They have finally reached their destination.

"I guess we'll find out soon enough." Tae Hyun faced her again. This time, he wore a forewarning look on his face. "I want you to know that when we're in Japan, if you try to kill Young Jae or Ji Hoon, I will stop you."

Soo Jin snapped back her head to Tae Hyun's direction, shocked with his declaration. She did not expect the conversation to veer into this direction. Although she found amusement with his statement, she would not tolerate anyone addressing her in such a brazen manner.

"You will have your hands full if you try to stop me." She smirked, laughing to herself. "And who says I'm going after them?"

"I know you."

She laughed out loud again. What a foolish statement for this guy to make. He may have known her human counterpart well, but he knew nothing about her.

"You know nothing about me."

"I know you," he emphasized again. His voice was sterner, more confident. "I was you when Ji Hoon assassinated my father. Just like you, the hatred I had for him was unrivaled by any other. It took me years to rein in my emotions; it took me years to realize that there's a time and place for everything. In this world, we cannot exact revenge based upon whims; we have to do it strategically. We have to get revenge during a war, not a battle."

When he saw the slight doubt on her face, he went on knowingly.

"I've heard about you from my brother, Soo Jin. Although he never went into details, he would always tell me of your hatred for him, your hotheadedness when it came to wanting to provoke a fight with him so that you could kill him. You finding out that Young Jae was behind your father's death may have occurred a little over three years ago, but your amnesia has only recently been cured. Your anger is still fresh—it is still raw. Not to mention, all of this is only exacerbated by the knowledge of Anna and Ji Hoon's betrayal. I know that when we meet them, you will go after all of them—and I can't have that. We're walking onto Young Jae's land—his Kingdom. We are simply there for answers. We cannot be the ones to break the ceasefire."

Soo Jin nodded, thoroughly impressed. He was right on the dot with everything he said. In place of vocalizing her impressiveness with him, she asked, "Do you really think Young Jae will keep his word and grant us safe passage in Japan?"

"I do not trust Young Jae as far as I can throw him. Having said that, I trust his rationalization as a King. He knows there is a time and place for everything. Although I cannot say that he will make sure we come out unscathed from Japan, I can say that he will not kill us. He likes glory too much to kill us in such an underhanded fashion. No. If he tries to kill us, then it will only be when the entire Underworld plays witness to it."

Soo Jin sighed, leisurely leaning back into the comfort of her seat. "You are right when you say that Young Jae will not break his word. As a King, he knows that killing us in front of the Underworld will serve him better. That being said, you forget that Young Jae is not just a King; he is a husband now. You forget that he tried to kill me when I was Yoori—he tried to kill me in a secluded restaurant with no witnesses. Do you know why he did this?"

Tae Hyun remained quiet, allowing her to enlighten him.

"Because he wants to protect his wife," she elucidated. "Glory, as enticing as it is to him, is nothing compared to his wife. He knows how I am. He knows how ruthless I can be, how single-minded I can become when I want someone dead." She gave a sadistic smile. "And he should be afraid because I *will* kill Anna. I will make sure they are in the same room, and when he is watching, I will gut her in front of him."

She laughed in amusement, her callous laughter rolling over the walls of the private jet.

"But have no fear, King of Serpents. I am not going into this meeting with the intention of killing any of them. On the contrary, now that I've thought it over, I quite like the idea of them bearing witness to my crowning as Lord of the Underworld before I end their lives." She gazed at him with feigned reassurance. "The rest of these parasites will know my wrath when the time comes. Trust me when I say that I will bring judgment upon them soon enough, but it will only come after death has knocked on your door. At the moment, my war is with you. Once that's over, I will exact my revenge as I see fit."

Tae Hyun nodded pleasantly, utterly unfazed by her lethal words. "I suppose I am living on borrowed time, aren't I?"

"I would say so," Soo Jin acknowledged.

Tae Hyun chuckled as the plane landed. Despite how morbid the conversation had become, he seemed to be in a better mood. "Then it's only right that I live to the fullest before the end comes."

"Why are you smiling like that?"

He gazed at her with a seductive gleam in his eyes. It was a look that told her of his sensual intentions with her, and it was a look that promised unrivaled pleasure. It was so tantalizing that she could feel her entire body scorch up from his titillating stare alone.

Soo Jin breathed in uneasily, quickly realizing that the harmless King, who promised to not seduce her during their plane ride, was gone. The sinful, utterly enticing predator was back, and he was ready to feast on her.

"Plane ride's over, Soo Jin," he crooned, his voice hot and filled with carnality. "It's time for me to have some fun with you now."

"You lost your soul in this world..."

09: Game of Preys

"You've got to be kidding me," Soo Jin uttered, staring dumbfounded at the travesty before her.

Tae Hyun feigned coyness and closed the door behind them. He followed her gaze around the room. "You don't like the room?"

Soo Jin took one more look at the massive penthouse suite before turning back to him in disbelief. "You put me in the same room as you?" she asked through clenched teeth.

"It's the very best hotel suite," he assured, as if that was her biggest concern.

She narrowed a hard look at him. She was not amused with his attempt at evasion. "You are a King in the Underworld," she enunciated slowly, forebodingly. "You can't afford to reserve two rooms for us?"

His lips edged up in a pleasant smile. "This is my favorite hotel in Japan. There's only one room available here."

"I don't believe you," she stated without missing a beat. She pointed an accusing finger at him. "You bought out the rest of the available rooms to make sure I wouldn't be able to get my own room, didn't you?"

His pleasant smile remained. As opposed to outright lying, he merely said, "I thought it'd be more fun for us to room together."

"You are sorely mistaken."

He expelled a dramatic sigh. With a cool expression on his face, he sauntered over to her with a hotel card key in hand. "We are only preys when we behave like one." He extended the card key to her. His cocky eyes challenged her to take the card. "If you would like to run off to another room, then I will not stop you."

And cement herself as a fearful kitten? She could not have that. Forced to employ every ounce of control at her disposal, she disregarded the card key and begrudgingly picked up her luggage. Soo Jin purposely slammed her shoulder into his as she swept across the hotel suite. She strolled past the living room area and went straight into the bedroom.

"I get the bed," she announced, throwing her luggage on the white, king-sized bed.

Tae Hyun stood at the doorway and watched her in approval. He looked ecstatic with her acceptance of their rooming situation. "I knew you would see it my way."

Soo Jin would not allow him to get the best of her. He wasn't the only one who could play games.

"You will sleep on the right side of the bed," she told him, commencing her own game.

He arched a questioning brow. He eased away from the door and journeyed to his side of the bed. Curiosity marked his features. "I get to share the bed with you?"

"Let's be honest," Soo Jin began shrewdly, unzipping her luggage. "You paid for the suite and made sure there would only be one bed. I'm sure this is what you intended."

"I intended for a lot of things to happen in this room," he whispered seductively. "I just didn't think you'd be this agreeable."

Soo Jin smirked, slipping off her jacket to reveal a black camisole that showed off her toned shoulders.

"You underestimated me," she remarked, leaning forward to unzip her second bag, deliberately giving Tae Hyun a view of her cleavage. "I'm determined to ensure that you learn your most important lesson tonight."

Tae Hyun inhaled deeply, appreciating the view before him. It seemed to take everything he had to avert his focus from her attractive figure. He locked eyes with hers. "What will I learn?"

She reached in and grabbed a pocketknife from her luggage. With the knife in hand, she casually strode over to him.

Fear did not possess Tae Hyun when she reached him. On the contrary, he appeared more excited with her proximity.

Eliciting a soft sigh, Soo Jin playfully moved the tip of the knife up and down his chest. "You will learn that whatever games you plan on playing during this trip, I will be ten times better than you. If you want to play this courting game, then I will play with you." She unbuttoned his shirt with the knife. She felt his breath hitch as her voice became lower, more seductive. "I will make you drool, I will make your heart race, and I will make you want me even more. Most of all, I will make you hate your life because I will never let you have me in the way that you want me. You will be miserable knowing that I will forever be out of your grasp." She presented him with a vicious smile that would cause others to quake in terror. "You will learn the most cardinal lesson on this trip, King of Serpents."

"And what lesson is that?"

"Don't fuck with your Queen."

He chuckled lightly before relieving himself of his shirt. After tossing it to the ground, he reached out and pulled her closer to his naked chest.

"That sounds like a fun game," he murmured favorably, looking turned on rather than fearful. "I will enjoy it very much when I win."

Soo Jin smiled before drawing blood by nicking him on the chest with the knife. When he did not even bat an eye at the pain, she teasingly said, "Here's to a fun trip then."

With that, she tossed the knife aside, walked past him, and proceeded straight onto the balcony. Now that the game had been set, Soo Jin felt the tension melt from her body. She no longer felt constricted; she felt free to interact with him without boundaries. There was no harm because on this trip, she was simply playing a part—a game. What happened in Japan would stay in Japan as far as she was concerned.

Her eyes traveled over the panoramic view. She took in a deep breath, luxuriating in the wind and the sight of the gorgeous city in all its glory. They were on one of the tallest buildings in Tokyo, and the view it offered was like something out of the movies. The twinkling lights of the city soothed her soul, relaxing her more than she had felt since she regained her memories.

Adding to this already beautiful landscape, the favored King himself decided to grace this scenery with his presence.

He came to a slow pause beside her. "Should we consider this our first date?"

She laughed, folding her arms across her chest. The evening wind tumbled around them, roaring with such ferocity that she could scarcely hear the sounds of the world below. She liked that she could not hear anything else. It made her feel like they were in their own secret world.

Letting her guard down slightly, she decided to play this courting game with him.

"I've never been on a date."

His visage illumed with delight. He was thrilled with her answer.

"Then it's my honor to be the first," he said affectionately, jumpstarting the conversation. "Apart from Ji Hoon, have you had other boyfriends?"

Soo Jin smirked to herself. Of course that would be his first question on their "date".

She humored him by not only answering, but also giving him a tidbit to lose sleep over. "Ji Hoon was the first and only official one. Having said that, I did date quite a few Royals for fun."

"The only fun Royals are in the 1st layer," Tae Hyun supplied blithely. His tone indicated that he did not believe she truly dated other Royals for fun. "I know all the heirs in the 1st layer. If you dated any of them, I would've known."

"You have close connections in our Underworld, but not other Underworlds."

His jaw went rigid. He regarded her with surprise in his eyes. "You dated heirs from foreign Underworlds?"

"Yes," she confirmed sweetly, secretly enjoying this part of the conversation. It could not hurt to make him jealous. "Most are actually from Japan. Since we're here, I might stop by to say hi."

He slanted his head at her. His amused eyes searched her knowingly. "Are you trying to make me jealous?"

"It's not my problem if you are."

He laughed to himself, resting against the railing in pleasure. His eyes wandered over the glowing city before them. "Maybe I should stop by to revisit some of the 1st layer Princesses here as well." When she shot him a glare that was cold enough to freeze hell, he grinned charismatically. "Are you jealous?"

"Should I be?"

He shook his head. "I only want you." He leaned close to her. His warm breath tickled her earlobe, sending chills down her body. "And I know you only want me."

Soo Jin scoffed in disbelief. She would normally back away to keep some distance between them. However, for tonight, she did not move. This was a game, and she could not lose.

"Your arrogance is becoming increasingly offensive," she said tightly.

He did not allow her hardened tone to dissuade his flirtatious efforts. "Then you will be in for a fun date because this is just the beginning."

"Why did you downplay who you were when you first met Yoori?" Soo Jin suddenly asked, eager to decode something she had been curious about for a while.

"I told her exactly who I was when we met."

"You told her, but you did not show her." She eyed him questioningly, genuinely interested in his motives. "What was with the whole song and dance with fighting Jae Won in the alley? Or meeting Ji Hoon in a warehouse to fight him? You were raised to be better than that. Why did you behave like a stereotypical gang leader when you are a hundred times better than that?"

The muscles on his bare back flexed as he took a second to lean further on the railing to stare at the moving cars below. Despite how windy it was, there was not a single goose bump on his strong body. In that suspended moment, she was tempted to wrap her arms around him and embrace him from behind. He looked so warm, so inviting that she wanted nothing more than to drown in his sinful heat. Thankfully for her, after a thoughtful pause, he decided to enlighten her and thereby quench her temptations.

"I did not want to scare her," he shared quietly, his voice barely discernible over the roaring wind. He kept his eyes on the cars below. "She was already scared shitless when she found out that she had been blackmailed to become the King of Serpents' personal assistant. I did not want her to be a witness to my killings. She did not have to see that I could rip necks apart with my bare hands." His broad shoulders lifted in a shrug. "Back then, I reasoned that I may have dragged her into the Underworld, but that did not mean I had to let her see everything about our society."

"You started your relationship as any Underworld King would," Soo Jin provided understandably. The understanding in her voice metamorphosed into disappointment. "You seemed to have it all figured out. How did you end up falling so far from your throne?"

He faced her with a soft smile. "You pity me, don't you?"

"Very much so."

"Don't." His smile remained when he pushed himself away from the railing and approached her. "You forget that the throne is mine to lose. If I truly want to fight you for it, then you will not beat me."

"You *should* fight me for it," she coaxed, her eyes imploring him to see reason. How could he not see that they were born to battle one another? How could he not see what a momentous fight that would be?

"I'd rather fight you for something else," he said instead. Unable to stop himself, he reached out and grazed a hand over her cheek. Adulation teemed in the gaze he held on her. "Just say the words and I will have our private plane come. We could go somewhere where no one knows our names. I could take you far away from the Underworld."

Soo Jin could not help but laugh at the absurdity of his proposal.

"I am not a Princess—I am a Queen. I was born to rule, not to run away."

"Yet you run from me," he countered gently, withdrawing his hand from her face. He placed it back on the railing. "You stand here pretending to be unaffected when I can feel your heart racing. What are you afraid of?"

"My demise," Soo Jin admitted simply, honestly. She no longer cared about playing a game. All she wanted to do was instill reason in him. "I've worked my entire life to reach this very moment. The fact that a single person could undo all my sacrifices does not bode well with me." A bitter fire ignited in her eyes. "Do you know why I harbor such hostility for you?"

He leaned his back against the railing. Almost too diplomatically, he said, "Please enlighten me."

"Since my inception into the Underworld, I've had to prove myself. I've had to fight off men who wanted to rape me, I've had to sleep with amputated body parts, I've had to lay in a pool of my own blood, and I've had to endure Ju Won and his sadistic training. I spent the majority of my childhood in Ju Won's mansion, praying that one day, I would complete my training and be free of my living hell." Her eyes elevated with sternness. "Your upbringing may have been difficult, but it was nothing compared to mine. You were loved the second you stepped foot into the 1st layer. Even when you murdered your own brother—an offense that other Royals would get beheaded for—this world did not deem to punish you. If anything, it rallied together to protect you." The animosity amplified in her voice. "I find you to be attractive, King of Serpents, but do not mistake that for love. You may have gotten a girl to fall in love with you, but not a Queen—not someone like me."

"Sounds like you would've gotten along quite well with my past self." He folded his arms across his chest, his eyes never leaving hers. "I was just like you. I did not have plans to stop with Korea. The beauty of my upbringing was that I traveled the world to receive my training. I've met people from all walks of life, and you are right, they love me. Regardless of the difficulty of my training, even I have to admit that I had it easier than many other Royals. Whatever I wanted, I've gotten. This is what I've grown accustomed to; this is what my world has grown accustomed to. Everyone has grown accustomed to expecting the best from me. They've come to expect nothing but legendary things from me."

For the first time that night, resentment started to infiltrate his eyes.

"My only downfall has been you."

Soo Jin paused, thrown by this unexpected statement. Rapt, she stayed quiet and listened attentively as he went on.

"A part of me still wishes that I had never met you. If I had never met you, then I would already be the Lord of this world. If I had never met you, then I would be free of this affliction. If I had never met you, then my life would be unquestionably easy right now."

"It is not too late," Soo Jin supplied swiftly—too swiftly. "The one you met is no longer here."

He smiled at her efforts to persuade him to battle her for the throne.

"I am no longer the same person," he stated as the roaring wind died down. The white noise from the streets below accompanied his voice. "I cannot go back to that cold and empty life, especially not when I gained something so special."

He looked at her, a fierce determination suddenly entering his brown eyes.

"You *will* fall for me again, Soo Jin," he stated, shocking her with the resolve in his voice. "Not only as a woman, but as a Queen as well."

Refusing to reveal that his words had a powerful effect on her, she coldly said, "I will look forward to breaking your heart then."

Tae Hyun was undeterred. If anything, he looked more determined than ever. "Like I said, I look forward to winning."

Her next question tumbled out before she could stop it. "When did you realize that you had fallen for her?"

He chuckled warmly, feigning coyness. "Perhaps one day, I will tell you. However, since this is simply a first date, I will keep it to myself." And with that, he pushed away from the railing and started to walk back inside the suite. "You ready to start the meeting?"

Soo Jin looked at him oddly. When she registered that he was indeed referring to the meeting with her brother and Ji Hoon, she followed him into the living room. "I thought the meeting was tomorrow?"

"Kings and Queens do not wait to be summoned for a meeting, we command it," Tae Hyun answered, taking out a shirt from his luggage and putting it on. "Young Jae set the meeting for tomorrow, but I'm in the mood for it now." He stalked towards the door, opened it, and turned back to her with awaiting eyes. "You ready for a reunion?"

Soo Jin smiled, thrilled with this turn of events. Although conflicted by her relationship with Tae Hyun, she knew clearly where she stood with her brother and Ji Hoon. Tae Hyun would always tempt the human inside her, but Young Jae and Ji Hoon would always incite the wrathful God inside her to come out.

She imagined this was the case for Tae Hyun as well.

She was excited for the Gods inside both of them to materialize.

She no longer wanted to be a conflicted human with him; she wanted to be a God with him.

Grabbing her jacket and heading out with Tae Hyun, she happily said, "I'm dying for it."

"You became a God in this world . . ."

10: Reunion

"This is Young Jae's hotel?" Soo Jin asked, staring up at the towering skyscraper that stood erect before them.

"Yes."

She smirked, folding her arms in knowingness. A soft breeze rustled past them, swaying her hair as she observed the indomitable looking building. "I had forgotten about this place."

Tae Hyun fixed an intrigued gaze on her. Behind him, the city nightlife of Tokyo bustled about, moving with lightning speed. "What do you remember about it?"

"My grandfather was the eldest Advisor in Japan's Underworld," she whispered as an endless sea of people swarmed around them. "When Young Jae was training in Japan, he lived with our grandfather. After he passed away, Young Jae became the sole heir to his empire. I should've known he would have returned to this place."

"It is now a world famous hotel."

"It is filled with the wealthiest tourists from all around the world," she murmured, observing the hotel with great fondness in her eyes. The fondness soon morphed into aversion. "In a public place like this, no one from the Underworld would dare attempt to assassinate him."

Tae Hyun smiled at her. "Isn't it a perfect place to continue with our date?"

Soo Jin flashed him a warm smile, pleased that he brought her here. Regardless of what may transpire between them in the future, at this moment, they were no longer enemies. They were allies in a foreign territory; they were partners with a common goal. There was no better way for two people to bond than to share their hatred for someone else.

"It's the perfect place," she whispered favorably.

Tae Hyun's face illuminated with her genuine approval. Satisfied, he offered his hand to her. "Let's have some fun here then."

Without the slightest hesitation, as she was convinced that all of this was simply a game, she took his hand and entered the hotel lobby with him.

The world stopped spinning the moment they stepped into the five-star hotel. People immediately paused in the middle of their mundane activities when they felt the presence of two revered Gods. Conversations immediately ceased, employees halted in assisting patrons, and children running around stopped to stare. Their spellbound gazes mindlessly followed Tae Hyun and Soo Jin as they strolled into the hotel like the King and Queen of the night. His aura depicted him as a powerful figure who owned the world while her presence felt like the world was created to kneel before her. Although they were mesmerizing by themselves, together, they appeared to be a divine creation.

Despite their unknown identities, all of the people in the room knew there was something utterly extraordinary and powerful about the two. Attracted to their divine status, they simply could not take their eyes off of them.

Gliding through the marble floors of the grand hotel, Tae Hyun and Soo Jin made sure to make eye contact with every security camera before they graced the hotel's restaurant with their presence. They easily walked past the host without confirming their reservations—or lack thereof—and ventured through the room. While doing so, they continued to captivate the attention of everyone in the vicinity.

When they spotted the prime real estate of the restaurant, they leisurely took a seat at the center of the room. In the comforts of their seats, Soo Jin crossed her legs gracefully while Tae Hyun pressed his back against the cushion of the chair and scanned the rest of the restaurant. After being situated, they started to skim through the leather embossed menu.

"Welcome to Maci," a male server greeted over the classical music that adorned the air. He exuded professionalism with his classic black and white attire. His hands were wrapped behind his back as he gazed at them with a hospitable smile. "May I get you something to drink while you look over our selections?"

"We're ready to order," Soo Jin announced cordially, closing the menu as soon as she looked up at him. "I'd like your owner's head on a platter."

Instead of classical music gracing the air, sounds of silver utensils clanking against expensive china plates rang into the room. The world around them collapsed into silence. The shocked couples beside them peered over in astonishment. Even the server's professionalism crumbled as his expression showed he was in a state of perplexity.

His eyebrows drew together in bewilderment. He struggled to maintain his welcoming smile. "My owner?"

"An Young Jae," she simply confirmed.

The server swallowed tightly before vigilantly asking, "And who should I say is requesting it?"

"His sister."

The server's eyes dilated when he realized that he was speaking to his boss's sister. Peering from his peripheral vision, the server furtively peeked at Tae Hyun, fearing who he was as well.

"I'm just her boy-toy," Tae Hyun provided lightly, leaning leisurely in his seat.

"Is that the new name for the most powerful King in Korea right now?"

The sound of the familiar voice caused Soo Jin to stiffen up in fury. She scrutinized the looming figure who towered behind the server and felt that fury escalate. She recognized the voice and physique as the King of Skulls. Matching his dark presence, he dressed himself with an all-black suit ensemble that contrasted his light brown eyes. Much like Tae Hyun and Soo Jin, he also held the attention of the entire room with his magnetic aura.

As the server scurried away, Ji Hoon stepped towards them, grabbed an empty seat from the next table, and placed it at the center of their table.

He beamed, looking between them as if they were old friends. "It's been a while since it's been just the three of us."

"You know," Soo Jin began, finding amusement with Ji Hoon's presence. She originally came for Young Jae, but she didn't mind Ji Hoon's appearance at all. In fact, it was fitting that he wore all black: he came just in time to attend his own funeral. "I just requested Young Jae's head on a platter, but I wouldn't mind ripping your head off as an appetizer."

"You may have some competition there because Young Jae may be your kill, but Lee Ji Hoon will be mine," Tae Hyun offered tactfully. Despite his inflexible words, his persona maintained an air of nonchalance.

His proper tone did not deceive her. From his warning on the plane, she knew if she went after Ji Hoon, Tae Hyun would surely intervene. It was a well-known fact that the King of Serpents wanted to rip the King of Skulls to shreds. He would not tolerate anyone executing Ji Hoon's death for him, not even the Queen he was trying to win back.

Ji Hoon smirked, glaring at Tae Hyun. Albeit he was not interested in fighting with Soo Jin, Tae Hyun was a different story. "Start the war, and I'll end it tonight."

Tae Hyun smiled pleasantly. "You would love that, wouldn't you? For now, we're in Japan for other pertinent things. Rest assured, once everything else is settled, I will not hesitate to finally finish you off."

"Maybe you two should entertain me and fight to the death right now," Soo Jin playfully suggested, folding her arms across her chest. She pressed her back against the cushion of the chair and looked between them. Now that the ban on the bloodshed had been lifted, it would be highly entertaining to watch them fight. She already knew who would win. It was simply a matter of watching it unfold.

Tae Hyun redirected his focus to her. His features were warmer when addressing her. "Who would keep you warm in our hotel bed if I get distracted by this piece of shit?"

Rage dripped into Ji Hoon's eyes. His mask of neutrality cracked upon hearing this. His calm features began to twist in rage. "You're sleeping in the same hotel room?"

"Why would I not sleep with the most powerful King in Korea?" Soo Jin taunted, knowing fairly well that Ji Hoon's Achilles' heel was Tae Hyun—not her. He may have wanted her, but his abhorrence for Tae Hyun overshadowed his desire for her. Realizing that the innuendo of "sleeping" with Tae Hyun only further infuriated him, she continued to taunt his weakness. She would hurt him physically soon enough. For now, hurting him psychologically would be just as fun. "He has the world on its knees, he has everyone in the palm of his hand, and he has the most gorgeous body to boot. Who could resist that?"

"I *am* pretty amazing," Tae Hyun concurred, giving Soo Jin a quick wink. He was aware that she was only saying such complimentary things because she wanted to hurt Ji Hoon. Given that the recipient was someone he despised more than anyone else in the world, he was more than happy to play along.

Catching himself before his mask of composure completely dissipated, Ji Hoon took in a deep breath to calm himself down. Once he was sensible again, he patiently asked, "Aren't you two supposed to battle to the death soon?"

"Soon," Tae Hyun answered. "But not now."

Soo Jin imparted Ji Hoon with a smile that did not reach her icy eyes. "I will kill him soon enough, but unfortunately for you, you will not live long enough to see that."

Ji Hoon laughed to himself. He assessed both of them and shook his head in hilarity. "Don't you two get tired of hating me so much?"

"You killed our fathers," Soo Jin stated bluntly, her own composure dwindling. The longer this bastard sat across from her, the more tempted she became to kill him right then and there.

"They were the casualties of war," Ji Hoon dismissed flippantly. Unlike in the videoconference, he no longer found it necessary to lie. He already knew that no one at this table would believe him. "Think about it. To even be considered as a King in the Underworld, we are mandated to kill someone who holds the same stature in life. Why must you hate me when it is the bylaws of our world that made us who we are?" He smirked. "Plus, you two shouldn't be so quick to judge," he retorted harshly. Looking at Tae Hyun, he asked, "Did you not kill your own brother?" He turned to stare at Soo Jin. "Did you not plan to murder your own brother?"

"Our world is also built on the quest for vengeance," Tae Hyun added, his voice underlined with menacing darkness. He was slowly losing his patience with Ji Hoon. "You went after the wrong King. It does not matter what the bylaws state. The reality is: you killed my father. Because of that, it is only right that I kill you."

"Killing the former King of Serpents may have been for your throne, but what was the purpose of killing my father?" Soo Jin whispered, staring at him with growing animosity.

Ji Hoon's lips lifted into an evasive smile. "Now that is something that your brother has to answer."

"Why are you even in Japan?" Tae Hyun interrogated. He leaned forward and put his arms on the table. He scrutinized Ji Hoon with perceptive eyes. "What are you up to?"

Ji Hoon feigned innocence and shrugged mockingly. "You will have to wait and see."

"You two are early," said another voice from the side, jarring the three Royals from their conversation.

Soo Jin felt her blood boil in her veins when she rested her eyes on the owner of the voice.

An Young Jae.

Soo Jin appraised her brother up and down. Dressed in a dark suit with a white dress shirt and dark slicked back hair, he looked utterly regal. The impeccable aura he emitted was unquestionable, and the respect he commanded from nearly everyone in the room was unmistakable. In short, he emanated everything a King should radiate. In spite of her grievances with him, even she had to admit that he was the quintessence of a Royal.

"It was Tae Hyun's idea," she said brightly, peering at him with a deceptively kind expression. "I couldn't resist having an earlier reunion with my brother."

Young Jae nodded, eyeing all three of them. His eyes then roamed over his restaurant. When it was clear to him that all of his patrons were curiously staring in their direction, he did what any rational owner would do when he feared trouble brewing—he decided to move this conversation somewhere else.

"I am glad the three of you are playing along well. How about we move this to the roof?"

"But we were having such a blast out here," Soo Jin protested lightly, eager to cast a dent in Young Jae's composure. It would be fun to see him lose his cool with so many witnesses.

Young Jae maintained his patient smile. Even though Soo Jin was a skilled instigator, Young Jae grew up with her. It would take much more than a simple protest in his restaurant for him to lose his poise. "The roof may be more appropriate for our private conversation. Nonetheless, if you insist on staying down here, I'm more than happy to oblige."

Impatient, Tae Hyun put an end to this childish shenanigan when Young Jae stepped forward to sit at the table.

"We have an entire country waiting for one of us to be crowned the Lord of their world," he said tightly, causing Young Jae to stop midway. He fixed Soo Jin with a "stop-fucking-around" stare before returning his attention to Young Jae. "We did not travel all the way to Japan to have small talk. If going to the roof will get us the answers we seek, then I think I speak for Soo Jin when I say that we'd be more than happy to change our location."

Soo Jin allowed her silence to act as her concurrence. Tae Hyun was right. They came a long way. They would have to deal with their aversion for one another at a later time. Tonight was simply a night for business—a night for answers.

Young Jae's face split into a wide grin. That was the exact answer he wanted from them.

"Very well." He turned to the woman to his left. Dressed in a black suit, she bowed to Soo Jin and Tae Hyun as Young Jae introduced her. "Please allow Yui to escort you to the roof. I will see you up there soon." He gave a quick nod before eyeing Ji Hoon. "Let's go, Ji Hoon. I have several more people I want to introduce you to before we officially reunite with our fellow Royals."

Ji Hoon smiled pleasantly and rose from his seat. "Of course." His eyes roamed from Soo Jin to Tae Hyun with a tint of craftiness. "See you two in a few minutes."

"You think they're up to something?" Soo Jin asked after they followed Yui into a private elevator and ascended up the building.

Even though the woman was right there, Soo Jin did not trouble herself to lower her voice. If this Yui was an extension of Young Jae's ears, then she wanted him to hear everything. She wanted him to know that she and Tae Hyun were vigilant. If Young Jae tried any unexpected ambush, then they were ready.

"We came too early," Tae Hyun responded in an even tone. He did not share her concern that they were about to be ambushed, but his voice did hold a tinge of concern. "They are not up to something. They are continuing with things as planned."

Her eyebrows drew together. The way he said this made her feel uneasy. "Planned?"

"As Ji Hoon mentioned," Tae Hyun said as the elevators doors slid open and the woman escorted them onto the roof of the building, "we will have to wait to find out."

When they stepped onto the roof, Soo Jin immediately spotted more than a dozen Scorpions. All dressed in black, they silently stood at various parts of the roof like indomitable statues. At the center of the massive roof were two black sofas facing each other and a long brown coffee table in between. Beside the sofas stood four sets of heating lamps to protect them against the cold night.

Soo Jin gazed beyond the roof and took in the breathtaking landscape of Tokyo at night. The flood of wonderful childhood memories that came to her was one she could not control. She remembered running around so carelessly, so freely with her brother here. She remembered playing hide and seek with him while Scorpions surrounded and protected them. Her grandfather had prohibited anyone, other than his family and close friends, from venturing onto this roof. It was to be used as a private sanctuary for his loved ones, and she could see that Young Jae had maintained that tradition. The only difference now was that she was no longer welcomed on this rooftop. Young Jae only made it available to her because she was causing a scene at his restaurant. As a savvy businessman, he did the only thing he could do to prevent her from making a spectacle at his place of business. He did not invite her to this rooftop; he exiled her here.

After she and Tae Hyun sat down on the nearest sofa, they scanned their surroundings.

Displeased with the fact that many Scorpions were blocking her view of the vista, Soo Jin fearlessly said, "Get the fuck out of our sights."

One of the men shot a glare at her. They could not believe she had the audacity to speak to them with such authority. "Who are you to command us?"

"We may be guests in your country, but we are still Royals in every Underworld," Tae Hyun interjected firmly. Steel vibrated in his severe voice. He regarded them in a regal manner that had them shifting uncomfortably. His expression challenged them to test their strength. "Either way, you will adhere to your Queen's will. Whether you leave voluntarily or I throw you over the roof myself, you *will* end up abiding by her wishes all the same."

"What happened to our ceasefire pact?"

On cue, Young Jae appeared at the entrance, walking hand-in-hand with his wife while Ji Hoon trailed behind.

Anna wore a black dress and a white knitted shawl over it. Her white pumps clacked rhythmically across the rooftop as she walked in pace with her husband.

The three approached Tae Hyun and Soo Jin.

"I believe our ceasefire only applies to the four of us," Tae Hyun replied to Young Jae, peering over his shoulder.

"Conversations between four Royals should stay between the four Royals," Soo Jin briskly added, following their movements like a hawk.

She silently gripped on the armrest closest to her when she spotted Anna in the flesh. She dug her long, manicured nails into the leather upholstery, trying to make-believe that it was Anna's neck she was suffocating. One day soon, she would make this ungrateful cockroach pay for her offenses. For tonight, she would substitute this sofa for Anna's neck.

Young Jae nodded his head at his men when they reached the center of the roof. "We'll be fine here. Please go back downstairs."

As his Scorpions obediently filed out, Young Jae took a seat on the opposite sofa with his wife. Beside him, Ji Hoon went to the further end of the sofa and pressed his back against the cushion. Once the last Scorpion vacated the premise, Young Jae began to speak.

"My apologies for this modest meeting. I actually had a grander dinner planned for tomorrow night. I wish you came during the designated time to experience it."

"We couldn't wait," Tae Hyun said simply, giving Young Jae an artificial smile. He glanced at Soo Jin. "I was eager to reunite the Queen with her long lost brother."

With this, Young Jae finally turned to look directly at Soo Jin. He took a moment to stare at her up and down. When he was done with his appraisal, he casually said, "It must have been quite a shock for you to regain your memories after so many years of living as Choi Yoori."

Soo Jin smirked. It made sense that Young Jae would begin this night with such a sour topic. "Quite the contrary, my recovery was an easy one."

"It must be difficult for you to endure this, Tae Hyun," Young Jae empathized quietly, continuing with his plan to fracture their united front. There was no one better to destroy them than Choi Yoori. "I know how deeply you cared for Yoori."

Tae Hyun did not fall for the bait. "You do not need to worry about me."

"How can I not?" Young Jae insisted. "Even when I was with Yoori, I loved her. I could've killed her numerous times when she was with me, but I did not have the heart to." He regarded Soo Jin with pity in his eyes. "To have Yoori leave you with someone like my sister is a tragedy."

"If I wanted your opinion, I would ask for it," Tae Hyun said in dismissive boredom. "We came all the way here from Korea, Young Jae. Let's stop with the bullshit and have the conversation now."

As Young Jae prepared to respond, Soo Jin found herself unable to control her resentment towards Anna. She may have been lashing out her ire on the leather upholstery, but that did not mean she wanted to deal with the traitorous bitch's existence.

"If this is a conversation for Royals," she incited, glaring directly at Anna, who had been avoiding her gaze this entire time, "why is this cockroach here?"

"Watch your mouth, Soo Jin," Young Jae warned gravely, finally shedding his cool demeanor.

"You forget, big brother," Soo Jin reminded coolly, inwardly pleased to see his poise cracking. "I am no longer a Scorpion. I am the Queen of Siberian Tigers. I am no longer below you. If anything, pretty soon, I'll be above you."

"Three years have passed, and you're still the same pompous bitch," Anna muttered in disgust, finally staring Soo Jin in the eyes. If looks could kill, then Soo Jin would have died a million times over under Anna's scorching gaze. Reversely, if Soo Jin's looks could kill, then Ji Hoon, Young Jae, and Anna would have been rotting six feet under already.

"Shut the fuck up, you backstabbing bitch," Soo Jin growled at Anna, unable to regulate her rage. She had never felt angrier. Out of all the people who could betray her, it was the girl whose life she saved. If she hadn't recruited Anna into the Scorpions, then the bitch would have died on the streets years ago. She saved her life, and this was how Anna repaid her? By betraying her? "I had always suspected that you had a thing for my brother, but I didn't think you'd ever go as far as betraying me to get into his bed."

That was when An Young Jae lost the last vestige of his composure.

"You have some fucking nerve calling my wife a backstabbing bitch when you were the one who betrayed me first," Young Jae spat with disgust. Fire erupted in his eyes like a raging inferno. After three years of repressed resentment, he finally released every animosity he harbored for her. "After all I've done for you, giving you the role as second in command and spoiling the fuck out of you, you *still* managed to find time to betray me."

Soo Jin scoffed incredulously. She couldn't believe she was a spectator of this ridiculousness. "You killed our father—the one who raised us, took care of us, and loved us unconditionally. You betrayed—no, murdered—him, and you have the audacity to ask me how could I betray *you*?" The stupidity of the question rendered her speechless for a few seconds. "You betrayed our family, Young Jae. You betrayed our father by colluding with Ji Hoon and Ho Young. Then you betrayed me by having me take the fall for everything you did to that family in the club. You knew the truth all along. You killed them because they had the videotape. I could forgive you for betraying me, for having me take the fall for what happened in the club. But I cannot forgive you for killing my father—*our* father!"

"I killed a piece of shit who was a sorry excuse for a father, but I *never* betrayed you!" Young Jae seethed, his thunderous voice booming across the rooftop. After countless years of wearing a politician's mask, he, at long last, liberated his true sentiments. "You think I don't know that you went to see Ju Won before you found out everything? You think I don't know the type of shit he placed in your head? You and our fucking father are so alike; you let that old bastard plant seeds of doubt in your head, and you listened to his words like he's a God. In truth, he's nothing but a senile piece of shit whose glory days are over. I wanted you to be the one to kill that family because you were my second in command, because I *trusted* you to do it. I thought you would revel in the fact that you could become notorious from that. If I had known you'd be so ungrateful, I would've just had P.C. do it!"

Soo Jin reflected back to her meeting with Ju Won. In retrospect, she felt sick knowing that even then, she took too much of what Ju Won suggested to heart. However, refusing to allow that to cloud her judgment about her brother, she went on. She would have forgiven him for betraying her so all of that was a moot point. The only thing that had ever mattered to her was that he killed their father.

"Why would you kill our father?"

"You were always his chosen one," Young Jae began indignantly. There was no more filter, no more veiling of words. Everything he spoke was a reflection of his true emotions. "The one he had so much pride for, the one he loved more than anything, and the one he was willing to screw his son over for. *I* was the heir, yet because of Ju Won's predictions about your 'legendary' status, he was willing to take *my* gang away from me and give it all to you."

"I told him I didn't want it!" she snapped, recalling the intense conversation she had with her father.

He wanted to take the crown from Young Jae and hand it over to her instead. No matter how much Soo Jin desired power, she told her father that she couldn't do that to her own brother. She could not take what was rightfully his. Once she stood her ground, her father let it go, and she thought that was the end of it. She didn't realize that useless conversation was a discussion that Young Jae was privy to.

She laughed dryly when it hit her that he killed their father because of jealousy—petty jealousy.

"You conspired with Ho Young and Ji Hoon because our father was thinking about giving me the crown?"

"He betrayed me first," Young Jae stated without remorse. "You know that I'm forgiving when it comes to anything else, but not betrayal, and definitely not betrayal from my own family. He wanted to give away the crown that I gave up my soul for? He wanted to give away my glory because a fucking Advisor told him he should?" Young Jae shook his head, pain immersed in his eyes when recalling his father's blatant favoritism. "The bastard had another thing coming. I knew I needed to save my glory—to guarantee it—because I knew that wasn't the end of it. It was only a matter of time before Ju Won screwed with his head more. Ju Won had always despised me because I never revered him like this entire world does, and I knew he wouldn't stop until he screwed me over completely. My own father was too brainwashed from him, and I couldn't have that. So I decided to think outside the box. I realized soon that I needed alliances. I only wanted the Scorpions, and I never once cared about ruling over the Korean Underworld. That was when it all made sense to me. I wanted Japan's Underworld while Ho Young wanted China's Underworld. After that, it seemed simple enough to recruit the one who wanted the Korean Underworld."

He smirked, looking over his shoulder to Ji Hoon, who was still leaning against the sofa with his arms folded.

"You gave Ji Hoon quite a run for his money when you wouldn't fall for his charms," Young Jae continued with slight amusement. Beside him, Ji Hoon's jaw hardened at the reminder of Soo Jin's unwillingness to be wooed by him. "He was getting frustrated that he wasn't winning you over, so I offered him a proposition: an Underworld and a trophy Queen by his side. I knew how you were, how'd you get after our father's death, and how you would be more than happy to accept the power Ji Hoon could offer you to avenge our father."

Soo Jin could feel her veins pop throughout her body. She glared at Ji Hoon with incredulity. "You agreed to be in their alliance and helped kill my father because you wanted to not only win the throne, but also me?"

"We would've never gotten your father right where we needed him if Young Jae hadn't arranged all of that," Ji Hoon shared smugly. There was no remorse present in his voice. He sighed, staring at her with boredom and growing hostility. "You should be flattered that I cared enough to consider you as a big motivator to work with them."

She swallowed furiously, scowling at Ji Hoon with pure hatred. "You told him about my plans after the club event. You were the one who told Young Jae everything."

Ji Hoon's remorseless eyes rolled at her words. He no longer gave a damn about lying or looking good in front of her. "I told you that it was a stupid idea, yet you wouldn't listen to me," Ji Hoon sighed with frustration, recounting what happened. "I told him after you left the car. I couldn't have you fucking up my future and killing one of the instrumental people in my quest to be the Lord of Korea's Underworld."

Soo Jin was ready to lose it and curse the hell out of her backstabber, the person who she couldn't believe she actually thought she loved. Regrettably, before Soo Jin could utter a spiteful word, Young Jae interrupted her.

"Even after he told me, I didn't want to believe it. I didn't believe it until Anna told me about your orders for her and your Scorpions to leave the gang and infiltrate other gangs. And you had the audacity to say it was my indirect order?"

Anna was breathing in anger while Young Jae forged on, staring at Soo Jin with genuine disappointment.

"It's taking all I have right now to not kill you at this moment."

"You should've killed me that night in the alley," Soo Jin whispered, gazing at Young Jae with unblinking eyes. "All of this would've been unnecessary if you had completed the deed." She looked at Ji Hoon. "Ji Hoon would've still been a contender for the Underworld throne." She then looked at Anna. "Anna would not be living on borrowed time . . ." She faced Tae Hyun. "And the favored King here would've never fallen so far from grace."

"I should've killed you the moment you kneeled before me," Young Jae agreed vehemently. "I should've never waited a second longer than that."

"Why didn't you?"

"Because you were my baby sister," Young Jae confessed simply, honestly. "I didn't have the heart to hurt you when you had been nothing but loyal to me. Or so I believed."

There was excruciating pain in his eyes for a fleeting moment before it disappeared.

"I cried that night for you," he went on quietly. "After I had you cut Tony's throat, I knew that I was losing you. I knew I was losing the baby sister I once promised to protect with everything I had. Despite knowing that, I kept hoping that you would never go into that alley—that you would never ask me to meet you there. Even when you were fucking kneeling before me, I kept praying to the fates that you would change your mind and not go through with your plan." He smiled hollowly. "You remember that, don't you? Me asking you numerous times if you were sure?"

She nodded quietly, remembering clearly that he did ask her numerous times if she wanted to do this.

"And you kept saying that you were sure." He laughed to himself. "What a good little actress you were with those tears of yours. If I hadn't known about your plans, I would've thought they were real."

"They were real," she told him, staring into his eyes with the pain that only both of them could understand. "I cried for you, I cried for what we had, I cried for our family, and I cried for being the one to kill you in the future."

Young Jae laughed self-deprecatingly. No matter how conflicted he was, her words acted as the final nail on the coffin. There were no more ifs, ands, or buts. He was resolute on killing her, and he would do everything in his power to do it.

"I would've protected you until the end if you hadn't betrayed me, but what's done is done. I've already cut my ties with you, and you will most certainly pay for everything you've set in motion."

"And you will pay for everything that *you've* set in motion," she replied, sharing in his conviction. She scrutinized all of them with vengeance teeming in her eyes. "All of you will pay."

The atmosphere fell silent until Tae Hyun's voice filtered into the air.

"Did you work with my brother to kill my father?"

He was looking directly at Ji Hoon when he asked this.

Ji Hoon smiled dryly. "No," he replied, not bothering to hide the fact that he hated speaking to Tae Hyun. "I did it all on my own. Ho Young and I rarely spoke during our arrangement of alliances. He was still pissed off at me for killing your father and wanted as few interactions with me as possible. Young Jae was the mediator between the two of us. I didn't care enough to apologize for killing his father, and I didn't care enough to trouble myself with whether or not he was comfortable with the arrangement. All I wanted was my throne, and I imagine it was the same for him."

Soo Jin could feel an exhalation of relief escape from Tae Hyun's lips when it was confirmed that his brother had nothing to do with their father's death.

With the reminder of Ho Young, Soo Jin asked, "Why was Ho Young the one who hid me in Taecin?" She had spent countless hours considering all the different possibilities, but nothing made sense. When he was alive, she made it no secret that she despised Ho Young and wanted to kill him. Out of all people, why did he save her? "How was it possible that it was him?"

Young Jae chuckled, shaking his head to himself.

A long, lingering moment passed before he decided to enlighten Soo Jin and the rest of those in attendance with his earth-tilting answer:

". . . Why wouldn't your own brother try to save you?"

The air stilled in Soo Jin's chest, just as she was sure it stilled in Tae Hyun's chest. She could swear she felt a sledgehammer connect with her gut at this revelation. Although Ji Hoon and Anna also looked stunned with this newly divulged information, it was Soo Jin and Tae Hyun who had the most potent reactions. The blood and color of life drained from their faces as they looked at Young Jae with utter disbelief. Tae Hyun looked like he was about to keel over, and Soo Jin looked like she was about to fall into a black hole.

"*What?*" she uttered disbelievingly, unable to comprehend the stated words.

"Kwon Ho Young is your older brother," Young Jae enunciated, stabbing the truth into her and Tae Hyun's brains, "—my fraternal twin brother."

Her world felt like it was tipping over. She tried to regulate her breathing with shortened breaths. Despite her efforts, her heart wouldn't stop racing, and she continuously felt the rush of horror course through her veins. It didn't help that Tae Hyun also looked as if the world had collapsed all around him.

"Ho Young is not my brother?" Tae Hyun finally breathed out, still looking like he had lost his sense of reality.

"You're lying," Soo Jin said breathlessly. Though she voiced this, in the depths of her heart, she knew all too well that he wasn't lying.

"You think you're the first genius in our family to hide spies in other gangs?" Young Jae asked critically, offended by her statement that he was fabricating all of this. "Our father did that long before you were ever born. He wanted his bloodline to hold power over the Underworld, and it didn't matter to him if his sons were battling each other as enemies instead of brothers. I found out the truth while rifling through dad's files. Once I found out the truth, I knew I was doing the right thing by killing him. He was a ruthless bastard who only favored one child and used his other two children like they were pawns on a chess board." His gaze intensified with resentment. "So I met up with Ho Young and told him everything. We even took a DNA test to prove it. Of course, Ho Young had his own set of demons—one being that he couldn't stop lusting after his 'baby sister' in his Serpents family. He had been doing drugs and drinking nonstop to help take his mind off of her. After finding out, Ho Young couldn't be more pissed that his own father put him through all that hell. Ho Young was like me. He didn't fare well with betrayal. He was more than willing to kill his bastard of a father for abandoning him and putting him through such misery."

Young Jae turned to Tae Hyun.

"But to answer your question specifically, Tae Hyun," he stated, staring into Tae Hyun's stunned eyes, "Ho Young didn't help Ji Hoon kill your father. Initially, Ho Young didn't even want to work with Ji Hoon. He loved your father, your mother, you, and in a fucked-up and sick way—even though he raped her repeatedly—he loved your sister as well." His bitterness for his father continued to pulse in his eyes. "You see, I blame him being sick in the head on our father. In fact, Ho Young blamed him too. Ho Young loved his Serpents family and wasn't willing to work with Ji Hoon in the beginning." Ji Hoon smirked smugly in the background as Young Jae continued to speak. "He wasn't willing until I personally asked him as a brother to help me."

Oh God, Soo Jin thought dreadfully, no longer listening to her brother.

She was too distracted with this explosive revelation.

She had spent countless days wondering to herself why out of everyone, it was her mortal enemy, Kwon Ho Young, who saved her that night and hid her. She couldn't understand why he did it. She didn't understand his actions until now.

My brother. My older brother, she thought, feeling every ounce of her heart clench in unfathomable pain.

She had once believed that finding out that Young Jae was the one behind her father's death was earthshattering, but now, as she processed this newfound revelation, she couldn't help but truly hate her life. Her older brothers were the ones who killed her father. Her father had somehow implanted Ho Young into the Kwon family, probably killing the real Kwon Ho Young as an infant before infiltrating his own son. It also was painful to process that her own brother was dead because she was the one who spread the news to Tae Hyun about Ho Young raping Hae Jin.

Swallowing tightly at the thought of Tae Hyun, she sneaked a furtive glance at him. He was quiet, his solemn eyes staring into a vast space in the city vista. She could only imagine how he felt. He had been through a lot with Ho Young. He grew up and looked up to him as a role model his whole life. Even after killing him, Soo Jin knew that Tae Hyun still loved Ho Young dearly. To find out so casually that the one he grew up with wasn't actually his older brother and that his real brother was more than likely dead must have been ripping Tae Hyun to shreds. Although he was doing a valiant job of concealing his emotions, Soo Jin knew the news must have been devastating for him.

She did not get to delve further into her thoughts about Tae Hyun when Young Jae forged on.

"This was the reason why Ho Young never bothered to hurt you or punish you for all those times you disrespected him. Despite everything, he understood the binds of blood, and he allowed you to live, even after you so stupidly told him that you killed his mother."

"You had Soo Jin kill my mother because you wanted to start breaking Ho Young away from the ties of the Serpents," Tae Hyun said mindlessly at last. Even though both he and Soo Jin knew that she wasn't the one who killed his mother, he did not share this information with Young Jae.

"Ho Young was a very complicated person," Young Jae confirmed, oblivious to the crucial information. "In a sense, he was a wildcard in how he behaved. Ever since he was young, he had a sexual attraction to Hae Jin. To prevent himself from going after her, he decided to completely shut himself out with alcohol and drugs. However, after finding out that she wasn't related to him by blood, he decided to have his fun with her." He regarded Tae Hyun with sympathetic eyes. "But with you, even after finding out that you weren't related to him by blood, he still adored and loved you. The same was true for your mother. And the simple fact was: I couldn't have that. I couldn't have my brother, my main ally, bestow his loyalty to others when they weren't even related to him by blood. That was when I knew I had to have Soo Jin kill your mother—because it was one of the only ways to break him away from the bonds of the Serpents family." He sighed lethargically. "Unfortunately Soo Jin had to brag about it to him, even when it was agreed between us that we would keep it a secret to further break their family."

"He realized what you did," Soo Jin noted thoughtlessly, still trying to absorb everything.

"He was pissed, but Ho Young knew blood was thicker than water. Regardless of how upset he was, he couldn't kill me. Much to my own displeasure, he had this same mentality with our baby sister."

Soo Jin and Tae Hyun lifted their gaze and stared at Young Jae with unblinking eyes.

"What happened that night?" they both asked, the colors continuously draining from their faces.

Determined to unearth every secret about the past before the end came, Young Jae closed his eyes and recounted the story, finally revealing what really happened in the alley that pivotal night.

"It is only fitting that you see your end in it."

11: Kwon Ho Young

Three Years Prior . . .

"I killed her."

"*What?*" Ji Hoon yelled over the other line. "I told you to give her to me when you were done!"

"It's too late," Young Jae lied into the phone. His angry eyes fastened on his sister's immobile, yet still breathing body. He wiped his tears away as the rain continued to hammer over him. "I'm hiding the body now."

"What the fuck, Young Jae?" Ji Hoon was outraged. "You were supposed to give her to me!"

Prior to this night, Young Jae and Ji Hoon had agreed that they would erase Soo Jin's memories when she gave the formula to Young Jae. It was a plan that Ji Hoon concocted because he was still emotionally attached to her. He wanted to spare her life, give her amnesia, and hide her somewhere else because he still cared for her. Although Young Jae had verbally agreed to this pact, he had every intention of breaking it. There was no way in hell he was giving his backstabbing sister to Ji Hoon. He could not risk her regaining her memories and coming after him. He could not risk her ever being a threat to him again.

"Did you really think I was going to give her to you when she wanted to betray and kill me?" Young Jae asked in disbelief. "Get over it, Ji Hoon. We have bigger things to worry about!"

He hung up the phone just as Ji Hoon's curses spilled through the receiver. He didn't have time to deal with Ji Hoon; he had a sister to punish. He bestowed his full attention to the woman at the root of all this. Soo Jin was lying in a puddle of water, rain pouring mercilessly over her body as thunder boomed overhead. In such an anarchic environment, she was the only one who exuded innocence.

Young Jae squared his shoulders, stowing away all the pained emotions that came with seeing his sister in this state. It ripped his soul apart to see her so helpless, so vulnerable. Nevertheless, he rationalized that she deserved it. It would hurt him to torture her, but she had hurt him more by planning his assassination. She started this war and now, he would finish it.

Resolve teeming in his once tear-filled eyes, he bent down and lifted her into his arms. With the rain dripping from their bodies, he began to run off with her. He did not get far when someone appeared out of nowhere and kicked him on the side of his face. Young Jae groaned, his vision darkening for a few seconds as he stumbled backwards. He was barely able to regain his equilibrium when that person snatched his sister's body from him.

"What the fuck are you doing?" Young Jae roared, his eyes enlarging when he saw that it was his fraternal twin brother, Kwon Ho Young, who appeared out of nowhere and stole Soo Jin from his grasp.

Ho Young stood across from Young Jae, holding an unconscious Soo Jin close to his body as he rested his eyes on his brother. His dark suit was drenched from head to toe, indicating to Young Jae that he had been out in the rain for a while. Young Jae feared it might mean Ho Young had overheard everything.

"What were you planning to do to our sister, Young Jae?" Ho Young asked sternly. Even though he posed the question, it was clear that he already knew the answer.

The tears in Young Jae's eyes started to dry. In its place came anger. "Don't look at me like that, Ho Young," he growled, resenting the look of disappointment on his brother's face. Ho Young was the last person who could judge him. "You raped a thirteen-year-old girl as soon as you found out that she was no longer your sister. You have no right to act pious with me."

Ho Young smirked, showing no remorse. "What I do to that girl is my own personal business. I spent years torturing myself because I thought she was my sister. I made up for lost time, and I don't need you to get into my business. With that said, you're not hurting our sister, Young Jae."

"She knows everything!" Young Jae screamed, losing the last vestige of his control. "She knows what we did, and she was planning on betraying me— killing me after all that I've done for her! That ungrateful bitch would've never gotten this far in life if it weren't for me. I spoiled her. I gave her everything, and now she does this? She betrays me for our bastard of a father and for the throne?" He laughed to himself, his anger manifesting into unforgiving fury. Every sentence he spoke reminded him of how much he despised her. He had given her everything, and she *still* had the heart to betray him. That bitch had another thing coming. "She's going to die of torture before I let her off so easily."

"Give her amnesia then," Ho Young suggested, unwilling to permit Young Jae to hurt Soo Jin.

"Ji Hoon's formula will not work," Young Jae spat out at once. "I know it won't."

"I know underground doctors who can make it work and it will be permanent."

"I don't want any other alternative!" Young Jae snapped, finally releasing all his pent-up resentment. "All I want is for her to wake up again so I can torture her!"

"This world has fucked her up," Ho Young contested with conviction. He gazed down at her, watching as the rain cascaded down her pale face. "Let's give her the life she wants—one that's far away from here."

"She was acting!" Young Jae was incensed that Ho Young couldn't see beyond her mask of lies. "She didn't mean any of it!"

"Maybe she was acting with you, but you can't ignore the yearning in her voice. She wants this—she wants another life."

"Ho Young," Young Jae growled with finality. He would no longer endure this. One sibling had already betrayed him; he would not tolerate disloyalty from another. At the going rate, he was willing to kill Ho Young if he continued to go against his wishes. "Give her to me."

Instead of obliging with Young Jae's wishes, Ho Young shook his head. He slowly readjusted his grasp on her so that her legs were on the ground while he held one arm around her. As her immobile body leaned on him, he withdrew something from his back pocket.

"I'm sorry, brother," Ho Young whispered, pointing his black gun at Young Jae.

Young Jae stood frozen, utterly stunned with the scene before him. He stayed rooted in his position because he could see that Ho Young was not bluffing. Ho Young was resolved on keeping Soo Jin alive and if Young Jae so much as made a move to snatch her away, then he would not hesitate to shoot.

Slowly, Ho Young, with Soo Jin in tow, began to back away towards the car he had parked on the street. Young Jae watched carefully, his eyes assessing for any opportunity to attack Ho Young. If he had brought his own gun, he would've shot Ho Young already. Regrettably, he hadn't, and he was afraid that Ho Young was aware of this fact.

To his horror, before he could conjure up a plan of attack, Soo Jin was already in the car.

"Ho Young, don't do this!" Young Jae shouted, peeling away from his rooted position.

He was no longer afraid of getting shot; he was more afraid of losing the perfect opportunity to kill his sister. He knew how this would all play out. No matter how far away Ho Young hid her, one day, she would return and come after him again. She would not rest until he was dead, which meant that in turn, Young Jae would not be able to rest until *she* was dead.

Ho Young shot Young Jae an apologetic look as he opened the driver's door. "I know you want her dead, but I can't have you kill our sister, Young Jae. I'm sorry, but trust me. You will never see her again."

"Ho Young!"

And just like that, Ho Young escaped into his car, started the engine, and drove off into the night, taking Soo Jin far away from Young Jae and far away from the Underworld.

■ ■ ■

Young Jae sighed, lifting his eyelids to meet Soo Jin and Tae Hyun's.

"Ho Young's sudden death and Tae Hyun's rise to power was what turned the whole plan upside down. The dynamic was compromised when Tae Hyun was crowned the King of Serpents." He looked Tae Hyun over with amusement. "You simply had too much support, and it did not help that Ji Hoon and I lost an ally. Because of all these unexpected dents in our plan, my gang and I left to Japan in order to do damage control. I no longer had Ho Young's support, and Ji Hoon no longer had supreme control over the Korean Underworld. Our alliance was at a standstill until our Queen of the Underworld made her return." He grinned tauntingly, briefly casting his attention to Soo Jin. "Since I've acquired all the power I needed to become a contender for the throne in Japan's Underworld, I would say that she arrived at the perfect time."

Young Jae gazed at Tae Hyun with the promise of partnership and camaraderie in his expression. "An Jae Sook started this mess. He not only pitted his two sons against one another, but he was also the reason why my mother died. She was sick with depression because she wanted my twin brother back and wanted to keep her baby daughter from joining the Underworld. She told him this, but my father, being the piece of shit that he was, did not heed any of it. She died from heartache, and he was left to use his children as pawns in his sick game. *He* was the reason why your real brother— your blood brother—died when he was a baby. Jae Sook killed him after he switched the babies." His laughter rolled over the roof when he evaluated the two Royals sitting across from him. "And now you're helping the daughter who is looking to avenge him? To bring justice to his death when he doesn't deserve any?"

His persuasive eyes tried to reason with Tae Hyun's dazed ones.

"Join us, Tae Hyun," he advised gently. "Ho Young may not have been your actual brother, but he loved you like you were his brother—even after he found out the truth. He still thought highly of you, still loved you, and spoiled you like you were his little brother. Finish what he couldn't finish; join us and join our alliance. You can have the Korean Underworld, I'll take Japan's, and we'll give Ji Hoon China's Underworld." Though Ji Hoon was bitter, he kept quiet while Young Jae went on. "The only one who stands in our way is An Soo Jin; she is the only one who stands in the way of your throne. She's the cause of all these problems between us. Work with us, Tae Hyun. Kill her, save yourself from this unnecessary war, and let's make history together."

He glanced over to Soo Jin. His expression did not conceal his disgust for her. "An Soo Jin is a ruthless woman. Do you think she would choose you over the throne? No, she will choose her throne and kill you in a heartbeat. Ju Won taught her to be self-serving and in the end, if you choose her, then she will be your death sentence—as well as your executioner. Get rid of her and you will be our ally. Together, the three of us can be an unstoppable force in this society."

"He's right," Soo Jin agreed from the side.

At her words, Tae Hyun turned his surprised gaze to her.

Her eyes on him were cold, challenging, and deadly.

"I have no emotional attachment towards you," she forged on emotionlessly. "I don't care about you. The only reason why you're still here is because I'm waiting for that historic day where I can kill you in front of our world. It doesn't matter what road you take because in the end, I will be your executioner. I will make a show of your death because that's all you are to me: a sacrificial prize—a gift to myself before I become an actual God in this world."

Soo Jin was already set on this. After all that had transpired today, she was still committed on killing Tae Hyun. She was going after the throne because despite everything, the love and desire she had for power would always override anything else in her life.

"Words spoken by the heartless bitch herself," Anna breathed out in revulsion. She scrutinized Tae Hyun, who was gazing quietly at Soo Jin. "I grew up with Soo Jin, Tae Hyun. I know how she is. She has always been coldblooded. Nothing but power satisfies her. She will use your weakness against you, betray you, and destroy you. I know that you're infatuated with her, but when it's all said and done, will she really be worth all of that? Will she really be worth your inevitable death?"

With his eyes fixed on Soo Jin, Tae Hyun did not miss a beat.

"She's worth every stubborn inch of it."

Soo Jin felt the pit of dread manifest in her stomach at his unfiltered and resolute response.

Fool, she thought with disappointment. *You're nothing but a fool.*

As Soo Jin shook her head in disbelief, Tae Hyun turned his attention to Anna. "I hope you enjoy the remainder of the days you have left with your husband because his days in this world are limited." He locked his resolute gaze with Young Jae. "I'm not working with you—not now and not ever."

A wide grin outlined Ji Hoon's mouth. He was relieved that Tae Hyun had stupidly declined Young Jae's proposition. He did not want to work with Tae Hyun and was thrilled by their ongoing war. To the left of him, Young Jae's cool composure faded as his eyes grew severe with unrelenting fire.

"Very well then," Young Jae said with finality. He rose from his seat and nodded cordially at them. "May your end be more merciful than your fall. Let's hope she gets to you before we do because trust me when I say that Ji Hoon and I will not be gracious killers."

He presented them with a slow, wicked smile that only the devil himself could bequeath. He was done being a politician. It was time to bring forth hell.

"We will see the both of you again soon. Until then, enjoy the remainder of your days."

With that, he bid goodbye to them and departed from the roof with Anna and Ji Hoon by his side.

For the longest time, all Soo Jin and Tae Hyun could do was sit there in total silence.

Soo Jin couldn't think; she was too traumatized with everything and she was pissed off with Tae Hyun.

What a stupid fool, she thought as his words echoed in her mind.

She turned to him, ready to berate him for his foolishness when he spoke first.

"Tell me what happened between you and my mother that night."

"No," she rejected at once. Who did he think he was telling her what to do? Why on earth would she talk about his mother at a time like this?

"An Soo Jin," he began sternly, locking her stubborn gaze with his own.

There were so many pained emotions in his eyes that Soo Jin felt like someone had knifed her heart. Despite how unaffected she wanted to appear, she could not deny that seeing his hurt pained her. She remained quiet as his soft, melancholic voice filtered into the night.

"All the secrets pertaining to my family have been spilled except the last one concerning her." His eyes searched hers, imploring her to finally give in. "Tell me. Let's unearth all the secrets so we can move on with our lives. I'm sick and tired of always being consumed with the shadows of the past. Do me a favor and tell me. Don't let me go through this again."

Soo Jin considered not telling him, but the agony in his eyes was too much for her to bear. Against her better judgment, she decided it was time to reveal the truth.

"No one killed her," she admitted quietly. Unable to retain eye contact with him, she averted her gaze to the city lights. "Your mother committed suicide."

Tae Hyun regarded her with the utmost curiosity. He had a plethora of questions. "What happened when you were there?"

Soo Jin took in a lungful of air, getting lost in the panoramic view while recounting emotions she didn't want to feel. Her memories played out like a movie in the backdrop of her mind.

"Nothing shocking, nothing mind-blowing, nothing that turns this world upside down," she told him truthfully, remembering everything vividly. "I snuck in, I brought her to the bathroom, I couldn't kill her, and then I left. No one was there with your mother. She killed herself. There's no twist to it; it was just her."

In a world so callous, brutal, and unforgiving, the truth was that Tae Hyun's mother died because she had committed suicide. It was nothing more, nothing less.

Tae Hyun exhaled sharply, staring at her with soft eyes. "Why didn't you kill my mother?"

"Because she was already dead after your father's death," she answered, recalling how broken his mother was when she found her. "She was breathing physically, but her soul was long dead after your father passed."

"I remember how she was," he whispered, finally making peace with himself that the truth had been in front of him this whole time. His mother truly did kill herself because she wasn't strong enough to go on after his father's death.

"When I saw her that night, she begged me to kill her, to end her life because she had planned on doing it anyway. But for some reason I couldn't do it, so I left her. When I went home, the next day it was all over the news that she died. I knew then that she committed suicide after I left. Young Jae knew I was there. And because I wanted to be his second in command, I took credit for it. I suggested to him that it should be a secret only because I didn't want to mess with the truth."

"Why didn't you kill my mother, Soo Jin?" he asked again, suspecting that there was more to what Soo Jin was saying.

Her stomach clenched as she replayed the simple, but memorable, conversation she had with his mother.

"She was nice," she uttered, meaning every bit of it. "She was really nice, and I didn't want to kill her." Soo Jin was quiet for another long moment before she looked him dead in the eyes and said, "Why would you do this to yourself, Tae Hyun? Why would you want to fall in love in this world? Love is a disease—it makes you interdependent, it makes you weak. How can you be dependent upon someone else for your happiness when life is so fleeting in our world? You have to know that the only thing that awaits you if you choose this road is misery. Are you completely out of your mind?"

"Humans are greedy," he replied simply, not apologizing for his feelings.

She laughed mockingly and rose to her feet. She stared down at him with reproachful eyes. His stubbornness made her angrier and angrier by the second. Why couldn't he see things as she did?

"Do you see how ridiculous you're being? How silly it is for you to chase after me when you know that our fate in this world was set the moment we were born? We have always been enemies. It couldn't be more evident with everything my father did to your family and the battle that awaits us in the future. We can't change our lives and we can't escape fate."

"Are you done talking?" he asked impatiently, standing up and stepping closer to her.

"No, I'm not done talking, you idiot!" she snapped against her better control. She had lost it. "You're being a stupid snob, and I'm trying to knock some sense into you!"

"And you're being a fucking annoying brat!" he shouted back. "Do you realize that every excuse you gave has nothing to do with us, but everything to do with the world we live in?"

"It factors in!"

"It's annoying me!" he retorted, breathing sharply. "I'm sick of all these revelations that do nothing but ruin my present and my future. I'm so fucking numb from this world. I'm so fucking numb from losing my parents. I'm so fucking numb from losing a brother who wasn't actually my brother, but I loved him like my brother nonetheless. I'm so fucking numb from everything."

He swallowed tightly, the resolve illuminating his eyes.

"Everything makes me numb . . . except for you." He extended his hands out, his palms cradling her cheeks with adoration. "You're the only thing that matters. Nothing else matters and nothing else will ever matter."

Soo Jin laughed dryly. With effort, she pulled herself from his grasp. She backed away from him, staring at him with pity in her eyes.

"Do you remember that night at the supermarket with Yoori? When you guys slipped?" she asked, reliving memories she didn't want to relive. The only reason she did was because it was her last ditch effort to help keep her opponent a God. She wanted to save him from himself—she wanted to save him from her. "Later that night, you told her about the two things conflicting you and how you had to choose between them. You ultimately chose choice number one and you asked her to remind you every now and then that 'to get into a position of power . . . some actions are unavoidable.'"

Her eyes grew severe, urging Tae Hyun to see the light.

"You look distracted, Tae Hyun," she told him flatly, "*heavily so*. I want to remind you that in order to get into a position of power—to become the Lord of our world—some actions will always be unavoidable. One of those actions is forsaking the idea that I'll fall in love with you. All I want is a battle with you, the glory of defeating another God in this world, and my throne. I don't want to love, I don't want to be human, and I don't want you—not now, not ever. Get that through your stubborn head and start being the intelligent King you were raised to be. You're acting like a fool right now."

She had hoped her pearls of wisdom would be the rationale he needed to knock some sense into him. To her greater disappointment, the nostalgia that seeped into Tae Hyun's eyes when she brought up the past made her regret bringing it up in the first place.

"Do you remember when I asked you for advice about what to do? Which choice to choose? Do you remember what you said?"

Although she said nothing, she did remember.

"You said, 'Just follow your instinct. Whatever you want more, I'm sure your instincts will go after that in the end.'" He expelled an agonized breath and smiled. It was a smile filled with faith and gleamed with hope. "Today, I met with my Advisor, my best friends, and my little sister. During our meeting, I told them that this world means nothing to me. I told them, 'fuck the bylaws of our world, fuck anyone who stands in my way, and fuck the fear of death and misery because from this moment forth, I'm following my instincts and I'm not letting anything or anyone deter me.'"

Soo Jin scoffed to herself, already walking away. "You're hopeless, aren't you? Why am I still here?" She set off for the awaiting elevator. She was not going to be a participant in this shit show. "I can't be around this! This is your death sentence, buddy. Whatever you want, it's up to you. You'll simply make it easier for me to kill you when the time comes. *Bye*."

"An Soo Jin."

He came to her so quickly that she couldn't even think.

One second she was power walking towards the elevator and the next, she was whipped around and lifted up from the floor. On instinct, her legs curled around Tae Hyun's hips while her arms wrapped around his neck. When his enticing lips pressed against hers, an explosion of fire penetrated her soul. Unable to contain her own womanly desires—even though she knew it was so damn wrong of her to give in—she parted her treacherous lips and allowed herself to fade away with him.

In that instant, all the pain they felt ceased to exist. The only thing that mattered was the scorching kiss that seemingly erased all the troubles out of Soo Jin's life. All that she was left with was the gift of life.

There may have been witnesses to her lapse in judgment as Tae Hyun easily pressed his body against hers, but she didn't care. There may have been eavesdroppers who might hear her whimpers while he moved them across the empty roof, but it didn't matter.

All that mattered was Tae Hyun.

He kissed her with possessive, male dominance that spoke of incomparability—a promise that no other man alive would ever be able to claim her and drive her over the edge like him. He held a hand out, his palm holding her face to his while his other hand wrapped around her small waist, silently promising her safety if she gave herself to him.

Soo Jin let out a needy whimper. She was utterly immersed in him. She couldn't stop kissing him and couldn't stop her hands from grabbing the edges of his shirt. She ripped it apart with ease, sending buttons flying everywhere. Exploding with need, she flattened her hands over his sculpted chest, silently declaring her claim over him.

The Queen was so deliriously lost in kissing this gorgeous creature that she didn't even process that she was already in the elevator until Tae Hyun pulled his decadent lips away from her. With an exhale of a lustful breath, he carefully deposited her legs back onto the ground. He imparted one final, heart-stopping kiss on the cheek before he backed away from her, his tantalizing abs peeking seductively through the rip in his shirt.

Pressing the lobby button on the elevator, he retreated backwards from the elevator, holding her undivided gaze with his.

His eyes were filled with lust not yet sated, but satisfied for the time being. Then, those tempting lips of his rose into a charming smirk, triggering her to gasp for air. She belatedly realized what had transpired.

Her eyes enlarged from shock.

Holy fucking shit.

What did she just do?

With her chest rising and falling, she fell back against the elevator wall. Her worst nightmare had come true: she had not only unknowingly encouraged Kwon Tae Hyun to chase her, but she had also intimated to him that she was an easier catch than she had let on.

She swallowed uneasily, doing a terrible job of regulating her rapid breathing.

Despite the fact that she felt numb and dead from Young Jae's horrible revelation, she had never felt more alive from Tae Hyun's kiss. She clenched her fists, cursing the joke that was her life. What a terrible thing it was for a God to feel alive. Feeling alive only meant that you were human, and Soo Jin knew all too well the debt that fallen Underworld Gods must pay when they become human again.

And, God help her, she thought, she would do everything in her power to evade Tae Hyun until their epic battle. Being around him was no longer acceptable. She did not like the things he did to her and she most certainly did not like the emotions he elicited. No single man should ever be able to hold such power over the Queen of the Underworld.

Don't fall, she told herself, hardening her emotions as the coldness returned to her eyes. *Don't fall for him. You know the debt that all fallen Gods pay. No man will ever be worth it. No one will ever be worth your demise.*

"An Soo Jin . . ." Tae Hyun called out, his melodic voice dispersing over her like soft rose petals. He couldn't appear more beautiful standing there like a sin for her desires. He also couldn't have looked more dangerous, like the angel of death coming for what was left of her soul.

The elevator door started closing as he smiled warmly, his deep brown eyes staring at hers with love. Then, as if reading her rampant train of thoughts, he imparted words of assurance that would inevitably lead the revered Queen to label him as a threat to her existence, ignore him like the plague, and avoid him at all costs for the days to follow.

"I promise it'll all be worth it. Every splendid, euphoric, and magical moment of it will be *worth it*."

"Love is every God's worst nightmare..."

12: The Queen's Forbidden Fruit

With a blindfold covering her eyes, Soo Jin took a slow and deliberate step into the arena of her estate. The breeze from the air conditioner stirred around her, following her as her boots echoed across the tiles. Soo Jin tilted her head and carefully listened to the sound of those breathing around her. Although she could not see them, she knew that they were everywhere . . .

After leaving Tae Hyun in Japan and taking a private plane back to Seoul, Soo Jin had been unable to categorize her disjointed thoughts. She could not stop thinking about the mind-blowing kiss they shared or the emotions he elicited from her. She could not deny how his very existence affected her. This type of affliction was a foreign one for her. She was not the type of person who could be easily disconcerted. She was raised to possess power over every aspect of her emotions and to be a master at keeping her feelings controlled.

But Kwon Tae Hyun was something else.

He wasn't the best of them, and he wasn't the worst of them; he was simply the most dangerous one of all.

He was the one who captivated the Queen in her with his impressive fighting abilities and cunning mind. He was also the one who captivated her human self. Though "Yoori" was long dead, Soo Jin was smart enough to deduce that the death of a counterpart—who owned her body for a good three years—did not mean that the residual feelings that counterpart felt died as well. In matters pertaining to sexual frustration, Soo Jin could not deny the desire she felt for the King of Serpents whenever he was in close proximity. The simple truth was that he was a threat to her entire existence. This was why, for the days following their trip to Japan, she opted to avoid him until she had better control of her own body.

In addition to avoiding Tae Hyun, Soo Jin was also preoccupied with thoughts about her family. She felt her heart ache at the reminder of Ho Young and Young Jae, and then she felt her heart clench in agony at the thought of her father. The very scene of the three of them together one last time—right before her brothers killed her father—haunted her.

169

Only in my world, Soo Jin thought with immeasurable sadness, wishing to herself that she was stronger than this pain.

She exhaled tightly and stowed those dreadful thoughts away. The only purpose they served was to bring her down and make her weak—the very human aspect she promised herself long ago that she would never fall victim to again. She no longer had time to be weak. She had to get stronger; she had to become more powerful. And the only way to do that was to train her mind, body, and what was left of her soul.

For the days that followed, Soo Jin made up for lost time by training every minute of everyday to prepare for the biggest fight of her life. The scheduled war with Tae Hyun was now a mere week away. Every single day, Soo Jin could be found on the grounds of her Siberian Tigers' estate, wielding swords with precision, shooting guns with accuracy, and knocking her Siberian Tigers to the ground with unrivaled ease.

While Soo Jin was training herself, she was also training her Siberian Tigers. It was said that one night of training with the Underworld Queen would lengthen a gang member's life for a month, for the skills and wisdom they acquired from her was invaluable. The Queen, no matter how young in age, petite in stature, and cruel in nature, was a skilled mentor. She did not believe in raising soldiers; she believed in raising future Kings and Queens. This was why more than three hundred of her Siberian Tigers were in attendance at the arena. Lips sealed shut, they watched in rapt silence as their Queen fought with twenty-eight of their brothers and sisters.

With the darkness from the blindfold encasing her eyes, all Soo Jin could use was her other four senses—primarily her hearing—to determine the location of the twenty-eight Siberian Tigers training with her.

She took inventory of all the sounds around her. She calculated the proximity of their breathing, assessed the sounds of ruffling, and after she sensed the fear that emitted from them, the positions of all twenty-eight Siberian Tigers became clear in her cloaked eyes.

Boom!

"Ugh!"

"Ah!"

The first three spin kicks, four elbow-punch combo, and five axe kicks was what sent her Siberian Tigers flying throughout the room in pain. The next seven sweeping leg kicks and thirteen bone-vibrating punches set forth a productive night of training that she knew would successfully educate the ones around her. While fighting with the Siberian Tigers on the ground floor, Soo Jin shouted out coaching instructions to those sitting in the stands. She did all this while the blindfold continued to encase her eyes; it didn't deter her ability to conquer her twenty-eight opponents.

"I promise it'll be worth it . . ."

His cursed words haunted her mind as she dismissed all of the Siberian Tigers from the arena. *His* blasphemous words continued to occupy her thoughts as she jumped on the balls of her feet and kicked, punched, and demolished a punching bag with all the aggravation that she had. There was a plethora of emotions that she couldn't compartmentalize. To worsen her already fragmented state, she also felt handicapped with a certain dissatisfaction that had plagued her since she regained her memories. She did not understand what the malady was. She just felt utterly incomplete; she felt numb to everything around her.

To some degree, Soo Jin would even daresay that she was quite bored with her life.

After her historic homecoming, life had become something of a drag. The casualties from the war she instigated no longer entertained her, the reverence she received from her society no longer fazed her, and the fact that she was close to getting everything she wanted in life no longer excited her. The only thing that kept her going was the thought of getting crowned as the ultimate God in her world and finally sitting on that coveted throne—that and something else . . .

Slipping her red bathrobe on after an invigorating shower, Soo Jin sat quietly on her couch. She drank her favorite heavenly tea and stared in a daze at the fireplace. It crackled peacefully, illuminating the dark room and acting as music to her ears.

Soo Jin drew in a deep breath, taking another sip from her red teacup. She could feel the beginnings of a headache commence in her head, yet the prominent thing on her mind was a memory she didn't want to recount. Her index finger mindlessly grazed her lips. The image of Kwon Tae Hyun—all hot and dominating—as he kissed her like the world was ending rushed through her like a typhoon. It brought forth emotions that were so powerful that it shocked her back to life. The very remembrance of her hands savoring the feel of his hard chest livened the more numb part of her heart. The thought of him was simple, yet the reasoning of *why* he evoked such a potent reaction from her was mindboggling.

What a temptation . . .

Soo Jin bitterly concluded that three years of inactivity in her own body had definitely fucked her up. She resented that she felt more like a stranger in her own body than the owner. How was it possible that she could have so little control over her own state of mind? She tried to condition herself to despise Tae Hyun, to feel aversion every time she thought about him. Sadly for her, every time she thought of him, all she could feel was warmth and longing. He had too much power over her, and it did not sit well with her. No one in this world should possess such power over another human being.

Before her thoughts could lengthen, the sound of impending footsteps jolted her out of her reverie. Her gaze averted from the fireplace. She locked eyes with the ones who would never fail to make her smile with their presence.

"Hi boss," Kang Min greeted quietly, treading into the living room with a black beanie, a zipped up jacket, and jeans. Despondency marked his features as he smiled softly at her.

"It's been a while, boss," Jae Won remarked, walking in with a pair of black jeans and a brown zipped up jacket. His face was pale while his lips quivered from the wintry weather he walked in from.

Soo Jin's once heavy heart lifted. With one leg crossed over her knee, her bare feet kicked out elatedly at the sight of them.

"Hey kids," she greeted with the endearment she had given them since they were young. Even though they were anything but kids, Soo Jin couldn't break the habit. They would always be like her little brothers.

She smiled widely at them.

Since her return from Japan, she had not had the opportunity to converse very frequently with the brothers. They had all been extremely busy with resurrecting a once extinct gang. The brothers hadn't had time to chitchat with her like three years ago or like when she used to be Choi Yoo—

No.

Soo Jin shoved back the thoughts of that unpleasant name. She further took her mind off of it by gesturing for the brothers to follow her into the kitchen. While they fixed themselves evening snacks, she nonchalantly informed them that she wanted the Siberian Tigers to not only actively kill Skulls and Scorpions, but that she also wanted them to start going after more Serpents.

Although the brothers' solemn reactions did not elude her, she respectfully ignored them. She recognized their conflictions whenever the Serpents were involved, and she, quite frankly, did not want to trouble herself with their dilemma. It was imperative that she turned the Siberian Tigers into the most powerful gang in the Underworld. She could only do that by fracturing Tae Hyun's precious army. Regardless of how charming he was, Soo Jin would never forget that Kwon Tae Hyun was a threat to her entire existence. His simple existence was the single roadblock in her quest for the throne. For that, his legacy had to be destroyed; he had to be eliminated.

She drank the last of her tea after they returned to the living room. She abruptly found that she could not take her eyes off the brothers. More specifically, she could not take her eyes off the dark circles under their eyes. An unsettling feeling besieged her.

Before registering what she was doing, Soo Jin said, "I know we haven't been able to talk much, but I just wanted to thank you for everything—especially for things pertaining to Yoori."

Sitting on the sofa adjacent to hers, they looked up at Soo Jin in surprise. Their widened eyes indicated that they were shocked. They did not anticipate that she would bring up the topic she had been working so hard to evade.

Soo Jin did not know herself why she was suddenly treading on this topic. Perhaps it was because she finally saw the physical maladies on the brothers' faces—a clear result of being troubled and conflicted with her return. Her homecoming brought back a war, and they were ultimately caught in the crossfire.

Having garnered their attention and feeling a bit uncomfortable with what she was about to vocalize, she struggled to go on. It may have been her prerogative to avoid this topic, but it was their right to get closure on it.

"I know how loyal you were to Yoori. I'm also fully aware of how well both of you took care of her. Thank you for that."

"It was our honor, boss," Kang Min replied warmly.

Beside him, Jae Won nodded in response. Their eyes were beaming. After weeks of avoiding this subject, they were relieved that she finally opened this topic for them to venture on.

And now that she had paved the road for them, it was time for her to quench her own curiosity.

"Do you guys miss her?"

The brothers had never lied to her. They respected her too much to do so. When she asked them that question—and all she received from them was silence as they averted their gazes from her in guilt—she knew their answer.

Yes, they missed Choi Yoori.

Soo Jin tried to swallow past the pit of jealousy. It brewed in her stomach, bubbling about like volcanic lava. She inhaled sharply, keeping a smile of nonchalance plastered on her face.

She swiveled her eyes to Jae Won.

Now all she wanted to do was change the subject away from this painful topic.

"Earlier today, you said there was something you wanted to ask me. What is it?"

"Is it possible for me to have the day off tomorrow?" Jae Won inquired tentatively, guilt still visible in his eyes. He had missed Yoori, but he did not want to offend Soo Jin with this truth. The fact that he was not as elated with his boss's return tormented his conscience.

"Yeah," Soo Jin approved, smiling at him to appease his guilt. She angled her head in curiosity. "What's the occasion?"

"Tomorrow is Chae Young's birthday,"—something leapt in Soo Jin's heart at this— "and I plan on helping out at the diner before we take her to dinner." He swallowed uncomfortably. "There's something else about that as well."

"What?" Soo Jin asked, her insides clenching when she registered that it was her—or Yoori's—best friend's birthday tomorrow.

"Hae Jin will be there," Jae Won said in a low tone.

Kang Min, who was staring off in a daze, looked at Jae Won in surprise. The numbness in his demeanor vacated as soon as he heard Hae Jin's name.

"I don't know if that's appropriate or not," continued Jae Won, eyeing both Soo Jin and Kang Min with apprehension, "seeing as the Underworld is at war."

"I'm at war with her brother, not her," Soo Jin answered swiftly, genuinely meaning it. She would never prohibit the brothers from speaking to Chae Young or Hae Jin. "You two can socialize with her. It doesn't matter to me."

Jae Won divided a hopeful look between them. "Do you both want to come?"

"No," said Soo Jin.

"It's best that I don't go," Kang Min stated half a second later.

Soo Jin straightened in her seat. Thrown off by Kang Min's answer, she turned to him. "Why aren't you going?"

Kang Min offered her a sullen smile. Desolation gripped his eyes as he thought about his ex-girlfriend. "We're no longer together. After abandoning the gang that took me in and betraying them, I don't deserve to be around her."

His unfiltered answer left Soo Jin and Jae Won whirling. Knowing that Kang Min had already thought this decision through, Soo Jin said no more on the matter. This conversation had already taken a turn for the worse. She no longer wanted to kindle that unsettling fire with further questions.

"You're really not coming?" Jae Won asked as they bid their goodbyes for the evening. His expression was hopeful that she would change her mind. "I'm sure Chae Young would be happy to see you. She thinks that you no longer want to be friends with her because you've regained all your memories. If you show up, it'll really make her night."

"I'm not interested," Soo Jin lied easily. Under normal circumstances, she would have been furious that Jae Won divulged Underworld business to an outsider. Last she knew, Chae Young had no idea Choi Yoori was actually An Soo Jin. It was clear that Jae Won had updated her on the truth of the situation. For any other Siberian Tiger, this infraction was punishable by several nights in a sealed coffin. However, because it was Chae Young, she did not dwell on

Jae Won's infraction. With a mask of nonchalance still solidified on her face, she simply shook her head. "Go and have fun. I have plans anyway."

"Boss," Kang Min began after his brother walked out.

"Hmm?"

"This may be too forward of me," he continued, his pale eyes holding hers, "but do you miss Yoori?"

The simple question hit her like a ton of bricks. Akin to a wall materializing inside her heart, she hardened her emotions and stared at Kang Min with cold, inflexible eyes. She did not like his question, and she damn well expressed that in her sharp gaze.

"If Yoori was here right now, then I wouldn't be here," she answered through gritted teeth. "*You* answer the question. Would I miss her?"

Kang Min measured the resolve in her icy eyes. For a brief moment, she feared that he could read the vulnerability through her masked face. To her relief, he did not answer her question. With a respectful incline of the head, he merely ended the conversation by saying, "Have a good night, boss."

Click.

No one could have prepared Soo Jin for the torrent of loneliness that spread over her as soon as Kang Min closed the door. She looked around the massive living room. The fading embers of the dying fire made her feel a hundred times lonelier than she did earlier in the night. She debated on going outside to kill a few dozen Serpents. She wanted to harden these stupid human emotions that were scorching through her and weakening her. Soo Jin vetoed that idea as quickly as it materialized. She was exhausted from all the training, and her body strength was completely spent. All she wanted at that moment was to rest and to forget about her bleak reality.

Although she had intended to go to bed, her body had a mind of its own as it guided her to the walk-in closet. Before she could process what was happening, her knees dropped to the floor. Kneeling in front of a small white dresser, she slid the last drawer out, pilfered through it, and with much effort, pulled a black garment out of it.

She bit her lips, breathing in a lungful of anticipatory air.

With her back pressed against the closet wall, she quietly held the innocuous black hoodie in her hands. She brought her fingers up and grazed the hoodie carefully. She found herself shaking as the simple garment brought forth a wave of feelings and memories that never belonged to her, yet she allowed to filter into her mind. The numbness she felt was killing her, and the only thing to ease it was this hoodie.

Fully aware of how pathetic she looked, Soo Jin sat hidden in the closet for the remainder of the night. She closed her eyes, allowed all logic to fade away and gripped the hoodie to her chest. She listened to the quiet thumping of her heart. She could feel her heart yearn for a life that never belonged to her—another reality that felt like a dream.

This pain was a debt that she had to pay—a sacrifice that she had to offer.

No one said the road to being a God was easy, and this final phase of killing the last shred of her humanity was going to be the most difficult of all.

■ ■ ■

"Mr. Lee! This place is packed tonight!" Hae Jin cried the next evening. She ran around the diner, taking orders from customers before they closed up early and went out for Chae Young's birthday dinner.

Mr. Lee chuckled, his chubby hands holding plates upon plates of food for his customers. "It's like they know we're planning on closing up early," he told her warmly. He skidded past her in haste, his little white apron dancing over his brown sweater and pants. "Thank you for helping out."

"No problem!" Hae Jin replied with a bright smile. Her black halter dress moved gracefully as she went to another table to ask if they needed anything else.

"Whoa! Watch it, Pops!" Jae Won shouted from the other end of the diner. Instinctively, he bent his body backwards and tipped his head before Mr. Lee's dishes slammed into his face. Had he not moved in time, the food would have spilled all over his black jacket and jeans.

"Ho, ho! Sorry, son. But nice reflexes!" Mr. Lee chortled in apology, thoroughly impressed with Jae Won's reflexes. He couldn't have known, as Jae Won and Chae Young decided it was best to not divulge this to him, that Jae Won was one of the highest-ranking members of a powerful Underworld gang—hence his impressive reflexes. "I wouldn't want to hurt my best waiter."

"Yeah, slave labor, you mean," Jae Won humored with a laugh. Shaking his head humorously, he brought the dirty dishes to the back.

"How was therapy today?" Hae Jin asked Chae Young moments later.

While all the patrons were happily enjoying their dinner, Hae Jin stood beside Chae Young as they took their breaks. Their eyes scanned over the packed diner. After these last sets of patrons left, they could finally close up and leave for Chae Young's birthday dinner.

"It was good," Chae Young answered with a bright smile. Unable to help herself, she extended her hand and wrapped her arm around Hae Jin, smothering her with a sisterly half-hug embrace. "Thanks for coming and helping out tonight, babe. My dad and I would've died if it was just the two of us."

Hae Jin laughed, waving a hand and quietly saying, "It was nothing."

"Have you spoken to Kang Min since . . .?"

Chae Young's question trailed into the abyss once she saw Hae Jin's smile wane.

With her positive air wilting at the reminder of Kang Min, Hae Jin shook her head. "He hasn't returned my calls."

Chae Young sighed sympathetically. Her voice mirrored the pain in Hae Jin's. "Have you spoken to Jae Won about it? It's so unlike Kang Min to act like this. The guy's crazy about you."

Hae Jin shrugged. "I don't know. Jae Won's been busy helping your dad with the diner. I didn't want to bug him about it. Plus, Kang Min's a big boy. If he wants to see or talk to me, he knows how to reach me."

"Yeah, but still," Chae Young said bitterly, upset with Kang Min for behaving this way. Her eyes perused the room. When she caught sight of Jae Won, she knew what to do. She unhooked herself from Hae Jin and approached him. "Hey hun."

Jae Won stopped in mid-pace after walking out of the kitchen. He beamed at her and took a couple of steps closer to the counter. He placed his hands atop the counter as leverage and leaned forward to talk to his girlfriend. "What's up, hun?"

"Do you know if Kang Min or Yoori are coming tonight?" Her voice was hopeful; it matched the hopeful expression on Hae Jin's face.

Jae Won did his best to conceal his solemn expression. He shook his head. "They're a bit busy right now. They won't be coming."

The despondency on the girls' faces was clear. They tried to keep their smiles intact.

Unsettled that he had singlehandedly dampened their spirits, Jae Won hastily added, "For what it's worth, I think they really wanted to be here." He released a weary sigh. "It's just . . . things are complicated. It's not like it used to be—"

"Chae Young!" Mr. Lee interjected happily, trotting up from the side and startling Jae Won. "Look who finally came back after quitting so suddenly!"

Chae Young, Hae Jin, and Jae Won's eyes broadened when they saw who it was.

Stepping out from behind Mr. Lee, Soo Jin presented them with a warm, beautiful smile. The white jacket she wore brought out the pink in her cheeks, while the black jeans and Uggs she wore enhanced the silky hue of her long black hair.

"Hi everyone," Soo Jin greeted. Her eyes ran from Jae Won, to Chae Young, and then to Hae Jin; they all wore shocked but excited expressions. Her smile lengthened when she held up a blue Tiffany & Co. bag in her hand.

"I won't be able to stay long. I just wanted to stop by and give the birthday girl her gift."

"Wait," Mr. Lee said after hearing this news. "Why can't you come to dinner with us? We haven't seen you around in a while, Yoori."

Soo Jin feigned a pout at the usual tone Mr. Lee used with her—or Yoori—whenever she was late for work or argued with customers. She wouldn't normally respond to being called "Yoori", but because Mr. Lee was blissfully unaware of her stature as the Queen of the Underworld, she decided it was best to play along. She added a tinge of regret to her warm smile. "I've been really busy. It took a lot of effort to push my schedule back to come tonight."

That was a complete lie. It did not take effort to push her schedule back. It did, however, take effort to succumb to her human emotions and stop by the diner. Because when it was all said and done, hating the reminder of Yoori aside, she really missed Chae Young. Chae Young was her first real friend, and Soo Jin loved her dearly. She couldn't push her friend away, especially not on her birthday.

It will be the last time I see her, Soo Jin reasoned once she gave herself the concession of seeing Chae Young. She would see Chae Young and catch a glimpse of Hae Jin one final time before she cut them out of her life. She knew the weakness of her attachment to them was a problem, and Soo Jin was more than willing to reconcile that matter. But, for tonight, she simply wanted to be normal before she completely immersed herself with the darkness that was the Underworld. She had the rest of her life to be a God. It could not hurt to be human for a small part of this night.

"Well, let's give them their alone time then, yeah?" Hae Jin uttered. Even though it was clear that she wanted to stay and talk to both girls, she respected the fact that Soo Jin may not want any interaction with her. Being the sweet person that she was, she put her needs aside and put Soo Jin's first.

It was an act that grated Soo Jin's insides. Hae Jin could have never known that Soo Jin's purpose for coming here was to catch a final glance of her as well. She wanted Hae Jin to stay, but given everything that had transpired, this was not something she could voice.

Mr. Lee and Jae Won followed Hae Jin's lead as they left Chae Young and Soo Jin alone.

Chae Young did not wait a second longer to greet Soo Jin. She ran to her, happiness beaming out of her like the rays of the sun.

"Ahh! Yoori, Yoori, Yoori!" she squealed ecstatically, pulling a laughing Soo Jin into an embrace. The fabric of their jackets clashed as Chae Young bounced up and down. "I thought you weren't coming! I—" Chae Young stopped when she realized something. "Um, I can call you Yoori, right?"

"Yeah, it's completely fine. Don't worry about it!" Soo Jin appeased her worries, honestly not minding when it came to Chae Young.

Her heart warmed from merely being around Chae Young. She could not stop smiling as she looked at her. Since this was possibly the last moment she would ever see Chae Young, she wanted to treasure every bit of it.

"Look what I brought," Soo Jin shared, handing the blue gift bag to Chae Young. "Happy Birthday."

Chae Young grinned, accepting the birthday gift and thanking her. Once she placed the gift bag on the counter, she faced Soo Jin with a frown. "Why can't you come to dinner? I miss you."

Soo Jin's heart dropped. Outwardly, she forced the smile to stay on her face. A part of her wanted to go. Nevertheless, a bigger part of her knew it was a bad idea. Seeing Yoori's best friend for a brief moment was already a bad idea. Going out to dinner and encouraging the human emotions she was trying to eradicate was plain reckless. No, she would not go to dinner with everyone. She could not be that reckless.

"I'm really busy," she lied with ease, "but I had to stop by to see you before things get crazier."

Chae Young nodded sadly. She was smart enough to deduce that Soo Jin was lying, but also perceptive enough to not force the issue. She would take what she could get from Soo Jin.

"You know," she launched, reaching out and holding Soo Jin's hand with hers, "when Jae Won told me that you remembered everything and that you were actually the Queen of the Underworld again, I kind of envisioned you being snobbier, meaner, and bitchier." She laughed, gazing at Soo Jin in the same way she would look at Yoori. There was nothing but love in her eyes. "It's kind of weird, but I don't think you've changed at all."

Soo Jin maintained her warm smile, refusing to allow Chae Young to see how much she disagreed with her observation.

Chae Young did not know how much she had changed—that before stopping by the diner, she had singlehandedly amputated, tortured, and killed seventeen Skulls and Scorpions. Chae Young would never know, and for this, Soo Jin was grateful. Everyone in the Underworld knew what a ruthless person she was—it was nice to know that someone she cared about did not know what a monster she truly was.

Eager to veer the spotlight away from her, Soo Jin tilted her head and said, "How are you doing?"

She had not forgotten that eleven men raped Chae Young. She had also not forgotten the guilt and pain that ran through Yoori—and ultimately her—after the horrendous event. The simple fact that this amazing young woman was standing before her, smiling and staying so strong, amazed Soo Jin to no end.

"Good," Chae Young answered. As she spoke, the only thought in Soo Jin's mind was how much she was going to torture Ji Hoon for putting this kindhearted girl through such hell. "Been going to therapy . . . my dad and Jae Won are always there for me . . . Hae Jin constantly stops by to check up on me, hang out, and do normal girl stuff." A spark of melancholy inhabited Chae Young's eyes at the mention of Hae Jin. She looked over to Hae Jin, who was refilling water into a customer's glass. "She doesn't think that you like her very much now that you've regained your memories. I told her she was being silly. Maybe you should go say hi to settle her nerves?"

Soo Jin's focus momentarily shifted to Hae Jin. "It's probably best if I don't talk to her anymore. I don't know if you know, but her brother and I aren't exactly best friends in this world."

Enemies, she wanted to correct out loud. In this world, he was the only one who stood in the way of her throne and endless power.

"You really have no more feelings towards him?"

Soo Jin shook her head swiftly. Though the very nerves in her body were disagreeing with her actions, she said, "He means nothing to me."

Chae Young swallowed quietly, accepting her answer.

Soo Jin wasn't certain if Chae Young believed her, but it did not matter. In that moment, something more distressing occurred. As if knowing that the only reason why Soo Jin appeared tonight was to see her for one last time, Chae Young started to gaze at her with sadness in her eyes.

"It's been . . . it's been a long time since this sweet girl named Yoori bounced into this diner and harassed my dad for a job."

The simple sentence ripped a wound in Soo Jin's heart. Though her face was composed, Soo Jin knew that the end had come. She could no longer stay. She had to leave and permanently say goodbye to this type of life—a life that would always belong to Yoori, a life that would always be a dream.

"I want you to know how much I admire and love you," she began as Chae Young's eyes widened at the words she was saying. Soo Jin could not stop herself. If this was truly their last moment together, then she had to leave by telling Chae Young how much she admired her.

"You don't know how to fight, you don't wield swords with ease, and you don't shoot guns with precision, but in all my years in this world, I've never met someone stronger than you. You have been through hell, and yet you still stand here, smiling, moving on with your life, and being an inspiration to any other women alive. You're pretty much stronger and more resilient than any Advisor or crime lord I know—and God help me, I know a lot. I'm truly in awe of you, and I'm grateful to have you as a friend. If I could be half the woman you are, then that would be the most amazing feat a ruthless person like me could hope to attain."

Tears started to mist Chae Young's eyes. She inclined her head in confusion.

"What the hell was that?" she asked, her voice breaking slightly. She was deeply touched. "Where'd that come from? Why the hell are you calling yourself ruthless and saying all of that stuff?"

Soo Jin shrugged, her heart thumping wildly. It was time to leave. "I don't know . . . If I don't see you again, I just wanted you to know how amazing you are."

"You loser-face," Chae Young commented, clearing her throat to stop the impending tears. Always the cunning and smart one, she tried to use this to her advantage and guilt Soo Jin into staying. "How could you make me cry on my own birthday? Now you have to stay and make me stop crying."

Soo Jin laughed, finding this to be a lot harder than it was supposed to be. "Don't cry, you big baby." She playfully pushed Chae Young to ease the tension. "Are you trying to make me look bad before I leave? Everyone already thinks I'm the world's biggest bitch, and now you cry while I talk to you?"

Chae Young breathed in deeply. "You're right, you're right." She brought a hand up and waved it with a cheeky smile. "Stay? Please?" she whispered. She took in a deep breath and added, "I really don't want you to leave."

Soo Jin smiled sadly and was about to turn around to leave when the door dinged open, indicating that another customer had walked in.

"Hey son!" Mr. Lee's voice greeted happily, evidently knowing this customer very well.

"Hi uncle," the new customer greeted. "How are you?"

Soo Jin's world froze as her traitorous heart thumped uncontrollably. It recognized the sound of the familiar voice it loved so much. Her once bleak reality exploded with color. There was only one person on earth who held the power to rock her world to its core.

She was afraid to turn around.

"Hi oppa," said Hae Jin's surprised voice. It was clear she didn't expect to see him tonight.

"Hi little sis," the voice greeted back, coming closer to Soo Jin.

No, it couldn't be . . .

Seconds later, as a big smile danced across Chae Young's lips, Soo Jin knew what she dreaded most had come to fruition.

"Yoori!" Mr. Lee called, confirming her worst fear, "Your boyfriend is here."

"Hey babe."

Crap, Soo Jin thought hatefully, too stunned to face him. Perhaps if she ignored him, he would disappear.

Although she could not see him, she could feel the sexy bastard smile as his cologne assailed her nostrils, reminding her of what took place the last time she was with him—reminding her of how much she wanted him.

"Hi Tae Hyun," Chae Young greeted with a bright face. She eagerly circled around a frozen Soo Jin to hug him.

"Hey birthday girl," Tae Hyun replied warmly, embracing Chae Young while eyeing Soo Jin, who refused to make eye contact with him. "Are you having a good one?"

"Yes," said Chae Young, thrilled with his unannounced appearance. "I got a really good birthday present with Yoori's sudden appearance." She cast a glance at Soo Jin before smiling at him. "She hasn't changed."

He smiled and nodded. This wasn't a revelation to him. "No, she hasn't."

Soo Jin was no longer paying attention. Her mind was too preoccupied with conjuring up a stealthy exit plan that didn't involve the King of Serpents following her. She did not need another one of his epic "goodbye" kisses. She had been through too much in one night. The last thing she needed was for him to rock her already disjointed world. They were a few days away from their historic battle and she wanted to avoid him until then. She had hoped that by then, she would finally rid herself of all her human emotions and become the ruthless God she was raised to be.

"Does this mean you two will be going out to dinner?" Mr. Lee asked, hopeful that Tae Hyun's appearance meant they would be able to join the group for dinner.

"No," Soo Jin replied swiftly, finally turning around. Now that Kwon Tae Hyun was here, there was no way in hell she was going to dinner.

Afraid that one peek at Tae Hyun would lessen her resolve, Soo Jin made sure to avoid eye contact with him as she bowed apologetically to Mr. Lee. "I'm actually leaving right now."

"Yeah," Tae Hyun agreed from the back. He further boiled Soo Jin's frantic blood when he added, "I just wanted to stop by and check up on my sister, but I'll be leaving with Yoori as well."

"I hate you, don't follow me," Soo Jin wanted to shout at him. She resisted the urge. The last thing she needed to do was make a scene, especially when the easiest solution was to leave.

Soo Jin gave Mr. Lee a meek smile and quickly headed for the door.

"Tae Hyun," Chae Young called when Tae Hyun was about to follow Soo Jin out. "Can you come to the back with me for a second? I have something I need to give you."

He looked at her apologetically.

"Can I get it later?" he whispered. His eyes lingered on Soo Jin, who was walking at a swift pace. She showed no signs of slowing down.

Chae Young smiled at him softly. Her eyes assured him that she would not delay him unless it was important. "I think this gift will mean a lot to you."

Acknowledging that Chae Young would not insist unless it was important, he nodded slowly. Taking his lingering eyes off Soo Jin, he speedily followed Chae Young to the back of the diner.

Soo Jin thanked the fates for distracting Tae Hyun for her. She gathered her bearings and waved goodbye to Jae Won and Mr. Lee. She was a step away from walking out of the diner before she spotted Hae Jin in the corner.

Her heart thumped softly.

Oh, screw it.

Against her better wishes, Soo Jin ran over to Hae Jin and gave her a bear hug that only a big sister could give to her little sister. After that, she raced out of the diner, leaving a shell-shocked Hae Jin behind.

"Shit. Shit. Shit," she muttered when she burst out of the diner like a bat out of hell.

The frostiness of the night attacked her skin as she power walked to her Lamborghini. She silently cursed herself for parking so far. She parked further away from the diner because she was afraid Mr. Lee would see the car and start asking her a million questions about how she could afford such an expensive vehicle. It was an interrogation that she did not want to be inundated with. She was initially proud of herself for coming up with such an ingenious plan. Now, as she continued to make her escape, she was beginning to regret the distance. The knowledge that Kwon Tae Hyun was in the vicinity unsettled her greatly. She had to hurry. He would catch up to her soon if she did not leave the premises now.

She was near her car and was almost home free when—

"Damn it," said a voice from behind her. "Were you a cheetah in another life or something?"

"Augh!" Soo Jin growled out loud, infuriated that Tae Hyun was an equally fast cheetah. She knew she should have run, but she had too much pride. Although Choi Yoori ran often, Soo Jin refused for that to be her legacy as well. The most An Soo Jin did was power walk; she did not run from threats.

She turned around as he appeared out of the darkness and stepped into the light cast by the orange streetlight hanging over them. The corner of the street they were in was empty due to the cold. The only sounds that could be heard were the sirens in the distance, the muffled music from a nearby restaurant, and Tae Hyun's soft panting.

Soo Jin looked at him up and down and immediately wished that she hadn't. Even under the limited lighting, he was candy for her eyes. He opted for an all black attire tonight. The sleeves of his button-up shirt were rolled up to his forearms, and a few of the buttons were left undone, revealing a peek of his muscled chest. His face was flushed with color from chasing after her, and he looked devastatingly handsome.

Once he deduced that she wasn't going to run away any longer, he bent forward slightly and rested his hands on his knees.

"What the hell, woman?" he complained breathlessly. He struggled to catch his breath. "You act like I'm some sparkling vampire out to get your blood or something. What are you running away from?"

"Go to hell," she snapped. She was furious that this hot bastard was making her feel so pathetic in her own skin. When would this madness end? When would she finally regain her senses and become the ruthless Queen she once was?

"I swear I've never been abused this much by a girl," he said with amusement, taking no offense to her unfiltered aggression. He stood tall after finally regaining his normal state of breathing. His warm eyes held her angry ones. "You're really not happy to see me?"

Well, that was a stupid question.

"Why would I be?" she asked coldly, folding her arms in annoyance.

He smirked, taking note of the icy tone in her voice and the hostility of her body language. "I don't know. Unless I dreamed it up . . . then I have to say that you gave me one hell of a kiss the other day. I thought you'd be jumping into my arms the next time you ran into me—not run away from me like I'm a walking plague."

She glared at him. Her blood simmered at the very reminder of her one moment of weakness.

"That wasn't a kiss, Kwon Tae Hyun," she corrected swiftly. "That was an attack on your part."

"An attack?" The amusement left his face. In its place came an affronted expression. He didn't like her denial. "Oh, I see," he stated with mild sarcasm. "So ripping my favorite shirt off and running your fingers over my chest was your act of defense?"

Soo Jin opened her mouth with the intention of firing a clever comeback. When nothing but embarrassment enflamed her cheeks, she closed her mouth in silence.

"What do you want from me?" she asked seconds later, doing her best to retain any semblance of dignity she had left. "Do you want a sequel to that kiss? If so, then I'm not in the mood, and I'm not giving it to you."

"It's a nice night," he placated, taking an assertive step forward. A heartbreakingly gorgeous smile graced his lips when he added, "we should go out."

"I'm busy," she rejected at once.

"With?"

"I just am."

"Come on," he coaxed with a laugh. "You and I both know the flexibility that comes with our 'jobs'."

Soo Jin smirked. She feigned deliberation with the tilt of her head and slowly said, "*No*." When he laughed in disbelief, Soo Jin added, "You're only doing this because of that stupid pride of yours."

Tae Hyun canted his head in curiosity. He gazed at her with dubious interest. "You care to elaborate on that?"

"About three weeks ago, you said that before the month is over, you'd win me back. Well, we're a week away from fighting each other to the death, and you haven't won me back yet. You're on a timeline right now. This is why you're following me like a stalker. You haven't been able to successfully woo me, and now you're at the end of your rope. Your time is running out. This is your last ditch effort." Her face held a resolve that appeared inflexible. "I won't be part of your game, King of Serpents; I won't have my time wasted."

His amused smirk widened when he took three powerful strides closer to her. He effortlessly filled the air between them with his enthralling presence.

"You think I needed every day of those three weeks to woo you?" he asked with light hilarity. "Is that why you've been avoiding me? Because you think I needed to catch you at every moment, run after you every minute, and court you every second to win you back?"

His warm laughter rolled over the darkness of the night. When it died down, he gazed at her with a seductive look that made her feel hot all over.

"I only need one night with you, Soo Jin," he told her gently and confidently. "Not to woo you, not to chase you, not to court you, and definitely not to save my pride because my 'time is running out'. When I told you that I'd win you back before our historic battle, I meant that I had planned on spending one quality night with you." He shrugged lightly. "I knew you'd spend the remaining weeks avoiding me. I was not foolish enough to think I had the luxury of all four weeks to pursue you."

"One night, huh?" she repeated after him. "Pretty cocky, don't you think?"

"Hopeful," he corrected with humble eyes. "Pretty hopeful of me." His gaze searched hers. "So, what do you say? One night? Just tonight." He looked around appreciatively. "It's such a beautiful night. You don't want to stay cooped up inside, especially when our friends are having dinner with each other anyway."

"Why didn't you go eat with them?" she asked instinctively.

"Because I knew you'd come for Chae Young and my sister. I knew you would come visit them and that you weren't going to stay. I knew this, and I wanted to spend time with you." He smiled at her. "What do you say, Soo Jin?"

185

She was tempted to agree, but she knew better. She would not give Tae Hyun any opportunity to weaken her already fragile resolve. She turned away from him and began to walk to the driver's side of her car.

"No," she said simply.

To her surprise, he nodded. He tucked his hands into the pockets of his black pants in acceptance of her answer. Without so much as a disappointed expression, he began to walk away from her.

"Damn, you're boring," she heard him murmur. "Definitely nothing compared to Yoori."

Soo Jin instantaneously stopped in her tracks. A jolt of jealousy rang through her. She narrowed her eyes on his departing body.

"*What* did you just say?" she gritted through her teeth.

He wore a sly and unapologetic smirk when he turned around. "You heard me."

She had every urge to get into the car and run him over for comparing her to Choi Yoori. Of course, running the guy over would suck for her reputation because she was supposed to officially kill him during their epic battle. What would running him over do? Instead of being a revered Lord in this world, she would be known as the homicidal bitch who ran over the great Underworld King with a car—a goddamned car instead of killing him during a larger-than-life battle.

Damn.

Petty anger aside, Soo Jin wasn't willing to let Kwon Tae Hyun die such a measly death.

"What happened to being a charmer, Kwon Tae Hyun?" she inquired tightly, her angry gaze burying knives into his.

"There's more to me than my charms, you know that," he replied, approaching her with such male grace that she wondered if there was anything he did physically that she did not like.

He grinned once he reached her, his eyes speaking highly of his adoration for her.

Soo Jin held in a laugh of remembrance. She recalled from distant memories about Tae Hyun's *other* charms—those that left one's blood boiling like acid.

"Yes, I do recall your sarcasm, your temperament, and the invariable fact that you picked on my counterpart constantly. Not always your best side, right, King of Serpents?"

It was a lie. His charms aside, she found every other aspect of him fascinating as well.

"I was hoping that if any woman would accept me for who I am, it would be you."

The sweet smile on her face was canceled out by her acidic reply. "Bite me."

Tae Hyun's lips curled in an alluring smile that basically said, *"I'll take you up on that offer later."*

Instead of vocalizing this, he politely said, "I want to challenge you."

While Soo Jin's eyes widened suspiciously, her ears perked up in interest. She folded her arms over her chest once more and evaluated him with curiosity. "Come again?"

"Our relationship has become a bit bland. Since you're more prone to avoiding me, being angry at me, and avoiding me some more after that . . . amazing . . . kiss the other night."

Soo Jin did her best to keep her eyes away from his lips while he forged on.

"Having said that, I decided that we should have a mini-challenge tonight to settle things."

As if knowing that this was the only thing he could do to get her where he wanted her, he said, "If you win, I'll leave you alone, and I'll do whatever you want in matters pertaining to the throne. If you want me to give it up to you, I'll do so willingly. However, you should know that I've been ready to hand it over to you for quite some time now—"

"What if I want you to actually fight me?" she interrupted, intrigued with this challenge. "What if I want you to use all the strength at your disposal to give me the epic fight I've been yearning for?"

"You can have whatever terms you like."

She scoffed at the fact that he did not seem to care what her terms were. As he was sure he'd win anyway, her terms did not matter.

"You're awfully arrogant that you'll win," she observed critically.

He shrugged loftily. "People mistake my confidence for arrogance. Granted I walk the fine line, I'm actually just confident. I believe in my abilities, and I'm very good at making others believe in them too." He looked at her, his eyes filled with challenge. "I heard the great Queen never backs down from a proposed challenge, but if you're afraid of losing to me . . ."

"When I win," she interrupted, refusing to back down from a proposed challenge, "you will leave me alone until the day of our official fight. And on that day, I want you to fight me with all that you have—you will hold nothing back. I don't want a flippant victory; I want to win fair and square, and I want to win during a legendary fight where the Underworld sees me as the God that I am."

"No problem," he agreed without hesitation. He did not seem the least bit concerned that he would lose.

"What are your conditions?" she asked, though deep down, she already knew what he wanted from her.

He favored her with a wolfishly seductive smile that had her swallowing uncomfortably for a moment.

"When I win," he told her, his voice lowering into a tone that could only be described as the sexiest thing she had ever heard. "I'll let you know."

"Okay," she responded. She instinctively pulled herself away to keep from pouncing on him. With her game face on, she asked, "What are you challenging me to?"

"... every God's death sentence."

13: Intoxicated Gods

This cannot be happening . . .

Soo Jin stared dumbfounded at the scene before her. Never in her wildest dreams would she have anticipated this. When she accepted this challenge from Tae Hyun, she truly believed she was either going to get her ass handed to her or she was going to kick some ass. The prospect of such an epic challenge disintegrated as she stood on the grass with one leg pointed out. She shook her head and folded her arms in disappointment.

She thought her eyes were playing tricks on her when he brought her to a grocery store and proceeded to clear out the entire alcohol aisle. She was certain she was losing her mind when she walked with him holding bags upon bags of heavy alcohol bottles. She was positive she had gone over the edge when Kwon Tae Hyun sat his defined ass onto the grass and started withdrawing the bottles from their bags.

Her eyes followed the clinking noises of glass hitting glass. Tae Hyun, comfortably seated with his legs crossed, organized bottles of all shapes and sizes around him. Directly in front of him sat ten shot glasses. He started to fill the shot glasses with a mixture of Southern Comfort and Grey Goose vodka— her two favorite drinks. The flickering pond rippled behind him, twinkling under the admiration of the moon. Had it not been for the excessive presence of hard liquor, it would have looked like he was preparing for a picnic rather than a wild fraternity party.

Flabbergasted, Soo Jin surveyed her environment to allow the peculiar scene to sink in. They were in *Mint Park*, a park that reminded her of a past she wanted to forget, but unfortunately, brought back the memory of an animal she hoped she wouldn't run into again. She veered her attention back to Tae Hyun. After another minute of staring at him in disbelief, she finally accepted that the stupidity of this scene was definitely her reality.

Her eyes morphed into indignation. This was not the challenge she had anticipated.

As if feeling her peeved eyes on him, Tae Hyun peered up at her.

"What, smart one?" he prompted with teasing charm. His striking face lit up under the kiss of the moon and stars. He flashed her a smile that was hot enough to melt glacial ice. He filled the last shot glass with a round of Southern Comfort. "Did you think I was going to physically fight you?"

"You lunatic!" she sputtered out, abhorred with the scene before her. She could no longer contain her outrage. "I thought we were going to duel with kendo sticks, katanas, guns, pool sticks, or even chop-sticks! You brought us here to do *this*?"

How? How was it possible that this was the King she had been dying to meet her whole life? How was it possible that the God of all Gods was nonchalantly sitting on the ground, pouring drinks for her instead of fighting her to the death?

"This is so anticlimactic," she whispered under her breath. She was tempted to shove him into the pond to appease her rage. She promptly resisted the urge. Knowing the guy, he would probably use his animal reflexes to grab her and haul her in with him.

"We could easily arrange a nude wrestling match. I could give you that climax you want," Tae Hyun replied almost too innocently. He favored her with a wink that nearly left the horny twenty-four-year-old girl in her to faint in shock.

Soo Jin diffused those thoughts before they could conjure any side effects. Maintaining her poise, she simply bestowed him with an unimpressed look.

The King before her laughed to himself.

"You've already agreed to the terms, Soo Jin. You can't back out." His crafty eyes scrutinized her for apprehension. "You're not afraid of losing, are you?"

"I'm afraid of nothing," Soo Jin answered swiftly.

It was a lie.

The challenge was ridiculous, yes, but it wasn't an easy one.

With fighting, she could at least use her strength and power to knock him out. She would be able to do so without anything inhibiting her logic. The truth was: alcohol, Kwon Tae Hyun, and An Soo Jin should not mix. This combination would not only spell disaster for her self-control, but it would also pave the road for Tae Hyun's advances. She knew this, and she was damn sure Tae Hyun knew it too. This was why he opted to have this "challenge" as opposed to any other challenge. What better way to court someone than to get them drunk?

"This is ridiculous," she grumbled, hopeful that she could convince him to challenge her on something else. "How are we going to compete? Are we just going to drink?"

"We'll do as the frat kids do," he answered, his tone of voice affirming that they weren't going to do anything else. "Whoever gets drunk first is the loser. Plain and simple."

Soo Jin was all set to complain about the childishness of the challenge. Any gripes she wanted to articulate dissolved after he handed her the first shot glass of the night.

"For tonight, let's forget about our problems," he started, staring at her with poignant emotions she couldn't decipher. Even though he knew she was pissed off about the challenge, he did not want her to go into it hating the game entirely. He wanted her to enjoy it as well. "Let's forget about our fucked up pasts and our screwed up futures. Just be my distraction tonight, and I'll be yours."

The memory of her sitting alone in her closet, pathetically hugging his hoodie the night prior materialized into her mind. It reminded her that she had nothing but an empty estate to go home to and an empty arena to seek solace in. The loneliness that threatened to overtake her receded as she stared into his eyes.

Sighing, she finally gave in to a temptation she knew she should never give in to. Soo Jin grabbed the shot glass, took a swig of it, and sat down across from him.

As she crossed her legs and handed him the empty shot glass for a refill, he rewarded her with a dazzling smile.

"Let the games begin," he whispered favorably.

■ ■ ■

"Damn cheater. Did you even drink that?" Soo Jin asked several hours later, eyeing him with open suspiciousness.

"Of course I did," Tae Hyun retorted defensively. He discarded another empty alcohol bottle into the big pile beside them to show his point. "Just because I'm still awake doesn't mean I'm cheating."

"Surrender, you loser," Soo Jin immaturely urged, downing another swig of Grey Goose. Her face was utterly flushed.

It had been hours since they started the drinking game. Despite her best efforts to maintain control, she was slowly losing her inhibitions. After the vast amount of alcohol she consumed, she was definitely feeling freer as she drank with Tae Hyun. The change in her normally controlled disposition was visible to her drinking buddy.

"Soo Jin," Tae Hyun prompted. His perceptive eyes took note of the evolution of her personality from the beginning of the night up until that moment. "Are you getting drunk?"

"Of course not," she borderline slurred. She was more relaxed, but she definitely wasn't drunk. Would a drunk person be as coherent as her? Would a drunk person still be aware of the hostility she harbored for Tae Hyun, even when he was throwing his disarming charm her way?

"Because it's okay to be," he coaxed melodically. "I wouldn't think less of you."

Soo Jin glared. His attempt to lure out a victory for himself did not amuse her.

He chuckled at the evil eye she presented him and poured them another round of shots.

As Soo Jin held the shot glass in her hand and took another heavenly swig of Southern Comfort, she was suddenly reminded of something that had been bothering her.

She narrowed her eyes on him. "I have a question for you."

"What?" he asked, taking two simultaneous shots.

A big puff of cold wind stampeded through the park, momentarily grazing over their skin and tossing leaves about.

Tucking her windblown bangs behind her ears, Soo Jin's eyes rippled with annoyance. "Where the hell do you get off taking credit for a tea mixture that *I* created?"

No beating around the bushes, no walking on eggshells.

The drunken war was on.

Tae Hyun arched an affronted brow. "*Your* tea?"

"Yes, my tea—that heavenly tea!" she cried a bit too passionately. Her big brown eyes were wide with accusation. "You plagiarized my invention!"

He gawked at her like antennas had sprouted from her head. He eyed her accusingly. "Are you drunk?"

"Why do you keep asking me that?"

"Because you're out of your mind, woman," he berated. He was not fond of anyone—not even a girl he was trying to charm the pants off of—accusing him of plagiarizing someone else's tea concoction. "Where do you get off taking credit for something *I* created?"

"Prove it," Soo Jin snapped. She was beside herself that he was lying.

"Prove what?"

"That you made it."

"Do I look like an all powerful, supernatural entity to you?" he asked sarcastically, using a tone that only Kwon Tae Hyun could employ without appearing like a total jerk. "How am I supposed to prove I created it? I was screwing around with the mixes when I was a kid. I didn't get a patent on it."

"So was I," Soo Jin replied. "So. Was. I."

He stared at her in silence. He did not know how to react to her nonsensical retort.

Soo Jin went quiet. She did not know why the hell she said it either.

The blank look on Tae Hyun's face would have been comical if Soo Jin was not on its receiving end.

"You're so amazingly drunk, it's not even funny," he said moments later, shifting all the shot glasses away from her.

"Nice try, pretty boy," she retaliated, snatching all the shot glasses and returning them to their rightful place—beside her. She lifted a shot glass to drink. "I'm not drunk."

A wide smile split Tae Hyun's face before his eyes noticed the bruise on her arm. Humor fled his expression while his visage lit up with concern. It was like someone had doused him with ice-cold water.

"Who touched you?" he asked tightly. His jaw tightened gravely. There was no mistaking the protectiveness he harbored for her, even if she was more than capable of taking care of herself.

"No one," Soo Jin answered swiftly, staring at the bruise for a second. She shrugged it off. "I've been training."

"Why?"

Soo Jin laughed to herself. The answer was already ridiculous in her mind. She was not eager to vocally share it. Nevertheless, given that she was feeling freer tonight, she reasoned there was no harm in sharing the silly truth.

"Because Yoori was lazy and didn't work out. In three years, she destroyed the muscle and stamina I gained in my ten years of training. I can't run without panting now. It's embarrassing to say the least." Her eyes then metamorphosed into poisonous slits. "This is all your fault."

Tae Hyun smiled with genuine confusion. Comfortably perching his hands behind his back, he asked, "What did I do, my lovely accuser?"

"She ate a lot more when she was with you."

He choked back a laugh. He nodded as if in concurrence and patted his stomach. There was no fat, just solid muscle when he tapped on it.

"Yes," he concurred blithely. "We're fat pigs to say the least."

She had no idea if he was trying to subtly seduce her by bringing attention to the abs that she worshipped so much. Perhaps it was an innocent action or perhaps it wasn't. Regardless, it took all of Soo Jin's willpower to not lick her lips and stare at the seductive area.

She was doing a valiant job of staring at the pond behind him when a sudden sound infiltrated her ears. Her eyes bloomed in watchfulness. Soo Jin snapped her head around the park.

She turned back to Tae Hyun, who was staring at her blankly.

"Did you hear that?" she hissed quietly.

He tilted his head in curiosity. There was a tint of unease in his eyes when he processed her reaction. It was clear that her bizarre behavior was disconcerting him. "Hear what?"

"No, seriously," Soo Jin insisted earnestly. Her eyes vigilantly surveyed the quiet and dark park. "I know you heard it too."

"Wait, what the hell are you talking about?" he asked, his eyes sharing in the alertness. "Hear what? Is someone else here?"

"No! Shhhh!" she shushed in her now drunken state. "Just listen!"

Tae Hyun examined the park.

Wind was blowing the leaves of trees, running over the grass, and howling over the quiet pond, yet no other sound accompanied it.

He faced her again. This time, the watchfulness of his eyes was set on her, not the supposed noise in the park. He evaluated the paleness of her face and how outrageous she sounded.

"How many fingers am I holding up?" he asked a second later, holding up three fingers.

He clearly thought she had gone bonkers.

"Oh, give me a break, you dumb Snob!" she dismissed, holding up three fingers of her own. "Read between the lines, and stop lying to me. You're trying to make me look crazy. You know you heard a duck!"

Tae Hyun choked back a round of laughter before taking a shot to ease his nerves.

"First of all," he launched, finding amusement in her anxiety, "I really didn't hear anything. Secondly, I knew Yoori wasn't fond of ducks, but I didn't realize that the dislike transcended to you too." He stopped for a moment's pause before saying, "Do you have your gun?"

Soo Jin's eyes expanded further. She could feel the effects of the alcohol in her system. "You must be drunk if you want to shoot a duck," she concluded prematurely. A wave of exhilaration coursed over her. The existence of the duck in question faded from her thoughts. Another prevailing realization entered her mind. "This means I win. You have to leave me alone and use all your strength to fight me to the death in five days."

Tae Hyun shook his head, holding up a single index finger to rain on her parade.

"Nice try, Brat. Although I'm amused with your belief that we have a duck around us, I insist you're very drunk. With that said, I've thought of a nice tie-breaker so we can end this challenge and get on to the more . . . exciting . . . parts of the night."

"So, we're going to shoot each other?" she asked with hope. She surveyed the area. There were so many trees around them that it acted as the perfect camouflage. They could shoot as if they were playing laser tag—only with actual guns.

He gave her an unimpressed look. "As flattered as I am about your excitement to shoot me, I actually have another thing planned . . ."

"I must say, you're quite the tease, Tae Hyun," Soo Jin murmured moments later, holding her gun in amusement. She observed the ten empty alcohol bottles that Tae Hyun had placed in the far distance. They were all lined up, waiting for them across the park's pond like targets for a firing squad.

"Ten bottles," Tae Hyun launched, standing close behind her as he stated the terms, "and we'll alternate shooting." He whipped out one of his silver guns. "Whoever hits the most targets wins. Sounds fair?"

Soo Jin smirked.

Boom!

Without warning, she aimed her gun and obliterated the first alcohol bottle. As the gunshot boom died in the air, she regarded Tae Hyun with challenge in her eyes.

"Don't fuck up," she told him, eager to pilfer his concentration.

Unfazed by her efforts to sabotage him, Tae Hyun simply favored her with a smile before he fired his gun. The bullet sprang out with precision, annihilating the alcohol bottle beside Soo Jin's demolished one.

He gazed back at her, the smile still solidified on his beautiful face. "Good luck."

For the next few minutes, they took turns firing their guns until there were only two bottles left.

"Don't screw up," Tae Hyun whispered into Soo Jin's ear as she aimed at her final bottle.

She laughed, knowing that they would probably have to put out more alcohol bottles if she got this one and if Tae Hyun got his last bottle.

Fixing her aim as the wind came at full force, Soo Jin was prepared to pull the trigger when—

Quaaack!

"Holy fuck!"

Thunderstruck by the devilish duck's scream, Soo Jin instinctively pulled the trigger of her gun. The bullet was unleashed, unsteadily shooting at the alcohol bottle. The bullet missed the glass bottle by an inch and flew into a tree trunk instead.

Quack. Quack.

A chubby white duck, which looked suspiciously similar to the one her human counterpart had kicked in this very park, emerged from the darkness. It shook its feathery butt as it trotted onto the scene, circling Soo Jin as though to taunt her.

She stared angrily at it, abhorred that this stupid feathery creature had ruined everything.

Quack. Quack.

Its little webbed feet stepped over her Uggs. If she didn't know better, she would have said that it was wordlessly urging her to kick it. Beside her, Tae Hyun smiled adoringly at the duck, loving how pissed off it was making Soo Jin.

She restrained herself from kicking the stupid duck and sending it flying to the moon. Yoori had no control, but Soo Jin would remain civilized—at least in front of the King she was scheduled to battle. She lightly nudged the duck away with her shoe. She struggled to maintain her poise in the face of this embarrassing scene.

Quack. Quack.

"You seriously didn't hear it?" she asked, watching as the duck changed course. It began to waddle around Tae Hyun and trot over his leather shoes instead.

Tae Hyun shook his head, his smiling eyes trailing after the playful animal. "We both have different strengths. My sense of hearing is not as developed as yours."

He chuckled lightly, gently herding the duck into the pond with his shoe. Once the duck was safely swimming in the water, Tae Hyun got back to business. He assumed his position in front of the pond, fixed his aim on the final alcohol bottles, and prepared to eject his last remaining bullets.

Soo Jin's heart raced as she stood behind him. She peered at the bottles and nervously looked back at Tae Hyun. It horrified her that she was reduced to this vulnerable position. She hated that she had no control over her own fate.

"You're going to miss," she told him, expelling her last effort to stay alive in this game.

In lieu of retorting, he merely raised a hand up and began to caress her cheek. Tae Hyun never once wavered his gaze from hers as he began to shoot at the remaining alcohol bottles with accuracy, thereby sealing his fate as the champion of their game.

With all the glass bottles destroyed, his tempting lips curved into a slow and seductive smile. He was more than happy to share the specifics of her fate now that he had won.

"You're going home with me for a week, Princess."

"It is the one human aspect that is strong enough to break Gods..."

14: Home

"Go home with you for a week?" Soo Jin breathed out. She gaped at him with wide eyes. She did not make an effort to conceal her incredulity. "Are you that drunk?"

"Even if I'm drunk out of my mind," Tae Hyun said with effortless charm, "you're the one who has to abide by my wishes."

He eyed the demolished alcohol bottles in the distance. A satisfied look came over his face before he took out his phone. It took one ring for the recipient on the other line to answer his call.

"Yes, boss?"

"Come to Mint Park," Tae Hyun commanded without preamble. "I want the area around the pond to be cleaned up within an hour."

"No problem, boss."

"Thank you." As he hung up, Tae Hyun turned back to Soo Jin with an expectant smile. He was ready to move this interaction to the next stage. "Shall we?"

Soo Jin did not move an inch. Defiance burned in her eyes, strengthening the already rigid expression on her face. "I'm not going anywhere with you."

"Twelve of my Serpents are on their way here as we speak," he shared in a matter-of-fact tone. His pleasant demeanor remained as he spoke to her. "They are my most prompt men, the very best to call whenever I need something done under a time constraint. They will be here within two minutes. Would you like them to witness us together? To be privy to the fact that you lost a challenge to me?"

Soo Jin muttered a curse. Her defiance bled away as she mulled over her dilemma. He got her there. She may have dreaded prolonging her alone time with him, but she dreaded having witnesses to her embarrassing state even more.

Accepting her silence as her confirmation, he wrapped his hand with hers and guided her out of the park. Soo Jin had assumed that they would be taking their cars home. When he walked past the Jaguar and the Lamborghini, a swarm of confusion bombarded her mind.

"What are you doing?"

"We're too drunk to drive," he answered, looking both ways before crossing the street with Soo Jin in tow.

Soo Jin nearly tripped over the curb when they reached the other side of the street. "You're serious?"

"Come on, Soo Jin," he cajoled in a patient voice. His hand tightened its affectionate hold on hers. "Be a team player."

"Isn't your apartment within walking distance from here?" she inquired with growing confusion. She peered over her shoulder to assess the path they should be on. The wind whipped her hair when she turned back to face him. "Why are we walking in the opposite direction?"

He pursed his lips blithely. His focus remained on the dimly lit path ahead. Apart from the cars and bikes parked on the street, they were the only two in the immediate vicinity. "Who says we're going to my apartment?"

Panic set off inside her. Her eyes broadened like baseballs. "Where the hell are you planning on taking me for a week then?"

"You will find out when we get there," he said coyly, glancing further ahead. After he spotted the headlights of a cab, he stepped into the street. "In the meantime, since we've both been drinking, I don't think it's a good idea to drive. At least not until morning."

"I'm perfectly fine," retorted Soo Jin, refusing to admit that she was intoxicated.

Tae Hyun chuckled and raised his hand to hail the cab.

"Friends don't let friends drive drunk," he whispered adoringly.

Soo Jin ignored the familiarity of that saying as the cab came to a slow pause beside them.

"This is the strangest night of my life," she grumbled under her breath, unable to grasp the strange turn of events. She felt like she was ending a date night with Tae Hyun rather than a challenging battle. First she got drunk with him, and now he was hailing a cab for her? What was next? Were they going to kiss goodnight and meet up for a coffee date tomorrow?

"Go home and get some rest, Soo Jin," Tae Hyun urged, leaning in to press his forehead against hers. When it looked like he was tempted to give her a goodnight kiss, he controlled himself. Instead, he moved backward to open the cab door for her. "I'll meet you back here tomorrow morning," he finished with a sense of longing in his voice. "We can jumpstart our fun then."

"I'm not going anywhere with you," she snarled, refusing to get into the cab.

He laughed and placed his hand over the opened cab door. He leaned in, causing Soo Jin to catch her breath. She wondered if he could hear her heart pounding as he whispered into her ear.

"If I don't see you here tomorrow morning, I will go to the Siberian Tigers' estate and pick you up myself. You may choose your poison. Either you meet me back here and maintain your privacy or I show up at your home and flaunt my relationship with you in front of your soldiers."

Soo Jin shot him a look that was rife with venom. Being attracted to him aside, she felt this unbearable need to beat the shit out of him. There were few people in the world who could beat her—much less outwit her. Unfortunately for Soo Jin, she had met her match. She had not only lost the challenge, but the favored King had also outwitted her. This was not her night. She might as well end it by getting as far away from him as possible.

"You have no idea how much I want to skull-bash you right now," she stated bluntly, pushing past him and getting into the cab.

His playful laughter trailed after her hostile words. "I will make sure you have a wonderful week, Soo Jin." He flashed her a heart-stopping smile that promised nothing but fun times. He waved goodbye as the cab took off. "See you tomorrow, Princess."

■ ■ ■

Soo Jin could not sleep a wink when she got home. At the offset, she debated about whether or not she should meet him. Given that the last thing she wanted was for him to make a scene in front of her Siberian Tigers—and thereby undermine her authority as their Queen—she chose to meet him back at the park the following morning. Now that the alcohol was out of their systems, she hoped she could knock some sense into him.

She waited on the sidewalk with a blue carry-on bag on the ground near her boots. She stood across from Mint Park with her arms folded and her eyes locked on the joggers sprinting through the park. After having the park to herself, it felt odd to see other people occupying the very spot where she had a drinking and shooting contest. What transpired the night before felt like a dream. She wondered how she allowed herself to get roped into this situation. Did she lose because of luck, because of the alcohol, or because of something else?

The sound of an oncoming car assailed her senses, steering her out of her reverie.

She glanced in the direction of the sound and nearly did a double take. Her chest tightened when she saw the black Mercedes convertible—the very car that Yoori and Tae Hyun adored like no other—drive up to the curb. It was like a ghost was approaching her.

Soo Jin released a breath, mentally shaking herself out of her stupor. She could not allow herself to be distracted. She had to convince a certain King that it was a very bad idea for them to spend a whole week together. She did away with the host of unsettling emotions and tentatively approached the car.

Tae Hyun, who was wearing a gray leather jacket and black pants, got out of the car as she reached it. He approached her with a beaming expression.

"I'm glad you made it."

She appraised his appearance and immediately resented him. He really was a gorgeous bastard. He looked far too handsome for a guy who drank too much the night prior. There she was, feeling like shit from a hangover that was splitting her head. He, on the other hand, could not look more easygoing. She doubted he knew what a hangover was. Was there anything he wasn't blessed with in this life?

Oblivious to her morning resentment, he helped pick up her bag and opened the door for her.

"We can't do this," Soo Jin declared at once, refusing to get in.

His patient smile remained.

"We're the King and Queen of this world," he coaxed gently. "We can do anything we want."

"I was hoping you'd be more clearheaded today."

"I am," he stated confidently. "I've never been more excited to go somewhere." He cocked his head and observed her with a tread of disappointment in his expression. "Are you backing out on your word?"

"I—"

"Because I'd be disappointed if you were," he interjected, a frown troubling his handsome face. "You lost fair and square. It'd be fucked up if you went back on your word, especially since I got up really early when I could've been sleeping in."

"Oh God, you're so dramatic," Soo Jin groaned, relenting and finally getting in the car. It was clear that she was not going to win this argument. He was no longer intoxicated with alcohol, but he was still intoxicated by her. There was no way he was going to let her persuade him out of this.

He optimistically closed the door behind her. "We're going to have fun. I promise."

"Where are we going?" she asked after he settled into the driver's seat.

"Away from the Underworld," he said simply, pulling away from the curb.

"This is insane," Soo Jin complained. Although it would be close to impossible to convince him to cancel this trip, she had to at least try. She twisted to the side to face him. Beside her, the city around them morphed into

---

a line of blurs as the car picked up speed. "I can't stay with you for a week. I have mentors to meet, soldiers to train, and a throne to prepare for!"

"You are the Queen of the Underworld," he reminded nonchalantly, turning up the heat in the car. "The mentors will understand if you're too busy to meet with them, your soldiers can train themselves, and as far as preparing for the throne . . ." He bequeathed her with a seductive smile. "I am the one you're battling. Spending the week with me can only be used for your advantage."

"Or yours."

His smiling expression did not sympathize with her grievances. If anything, it amused him to no end that she was voicing any grievances at all. "You lost, An Soo Jin. Fair and square."

"Won't your people wonder where you are?"

"They will think I'm training, just like your people will think you're doing."

"Are you trying to destroy my reputation a week before I become crowned?" she blurted out disbelievingly. "What will the Underworld think of me when they learn that I spent a week with my opponent?" She glowered at him. "Even if I win, they will think it's because you're giving it to me."

"That's why we're leaving this city," Tae Hyun provided coolly. He swatted her concerns away like he would a fly. "No one else from the Underworld will be at the place I'm taking us. The only ones who will exist there are you and me."

She muttered a curse and briefly rubbed her temples in frustration. She could not understand his motives. What did he realistically hope to gain from this week?

"Why are you doing this?" she voiced in a defeated tone.

"Because I won," was his simple reply.

She swayed an agitated head from side to side. She faced the window as the world passed by. "I can't believe this is happening to me."

Ignoring her grumpiness, Tae Hyun happily steered them into a new topic of conversation. "Now, let's set some ground rules."

Soo Jin was not amused. She folded her arms across her chest and glowered at him from the side of her eyes. "You want to have ground rules?"

"I think it's nice to be on the same page."

"What are your ground rules?" she humored through gritted teeth.

"I only have three," he provided warmly. He cleared his throat and shared his first ground rule. "The first is that you will not run away."

Soo Jin made a rude noise. "Do I look like a scared little mouse to you?"

He shrugged pleasantly. "I just wanted to put it out there."

"What is the second ground rule?"

"You will go along with anything I want."

She smirked scathingly. She was certain that was the ground rule she would have the most trouble enduring. "And the third?"

"You will keep an open mind," he whispered.

Soo Jin raised a piqued brow. The third ground rule was interesting. Sans the first two rules, this seemed pretty easy. "That's all?"

"That's it."

Soo Jin smiled to herself. She cast a brief glance out the window and decided it was more amusing to be difficult than to be compliant. "What makes you think I'd follow any of those rules?"

"Because if I had lost, I would've abided by your request and left you alone," he assured her at once. There was a finality to his voice that told her he meant what he said. "No matter how difficult it would've been for me, I would've never come near you again."

"This is your dying wish?" she whispered, turning around to face him again. He could have stipulated any condition after he won the bet. He could have stipulated that she give the throne to him right then and there. He could have stipulated that she give up her army. He could have easily stipulated anything else to get him one step closer to the throne, and he wasted it all with this trip? He wasted it all to spend time with her? The extent of his hardheadedness astounded her. "To spend your last week with me?"

He did not miss a beat. "Yes."

She wished he did not answer so quickly. His certainty made her feel things that she should not feel, especially for a Queen who was about to inherit the Underworld throne. She wanted to feel cold and detached, yet what he elicited was the polar opposite. When she was with him, all she felt was warmth and security. She felt love, and this was an emotion she did not want to be beleaguered with. She was scheduled to go to war with him in a matter of days. The last thing she should feel for him was any form of affection.

She expelled an exhausted breath. This was going to be a difficult week for her to endure. "Why must you make the road to my immortality so complicated?"

He chuckled before leaning back in his seat. "What fun is it to attain things easily?" Aware of her reticence to be alone with him, he reached out and grazed a hand over her cheek.

"I've missed you," he said without filter, without an ounce of hesitation. There was no doubting the genuineness of his words or the aching tone in his voice.

She said nothing back.

Although her heart raced at his words, she did not allow her features to betray her emotions. She remained stoic, cold. He would never know her true feelings if she could help it.

"There is not a single day that passes where I do not think about you," he persevered quietly.

Soo Jin could feel his poignant eyes on her. The sadness that rippled in that declaration ruptured her sensibilities. She did not doubt the verity of his words. However, for the health of her future, she could not react to it.

She continued to say nothing, for it was better to let it roll off her than to address it.

He smiled in understanding at her silence. Determined to make her feel more comfortable, he casually moved her bangs from her face and said, "I hear that you've been training hard for our battle."

"Something you should be doing as well," she finally spoke, locking eyes with him. She wished he would understand how difficult he was making this situation. Why was he chasing after a dream that would never come to fruition? It was their destiny to battle one another for the throne, not to fall in love and fade away from the rest of the world.

He quietly laughed to himself. "I feel like I've been preparing for a battle, but it may not be the one you're training for." He sighed, turning his attention back to the road. "Go to sleep."

"Excuse me?"

"You must be exhausted," he stated lightly. "Go to sleep."

Even though fatigue was riding her, she did not feel it was necessary to sleep. "I'm okay."

"It will take us a while to get there. You should rest," he insisted. He regarded her with warm eyes. "You do not have to be a Queen this week, Soo Jin. You do not have to be alert, you do not have to be a God, and you do not have to make plans to rule the world." He looked at the cars around them. "You can simply exist as the rest of us humans here."

"You are not one of them," she corrected without delay.

"For this week, we are." He laughed. "Did you forget about the second ground rule already?" He locked his gaze with hers. "Please get some sleep. I want you well rested."

She recalled the second ground rule that she agreed to: that she would abide by anything he wished. It was such a simple request that it was not worth fighting him on it. Since her homecoming, she had been getting little to no sleep. It could not hurt to close her eyes and rest for a few hours.

With that thought, she laid back and permitted herself to fall into a peaceful slumber.

The sense of security that overcame her was unlike anything she had ever experienced—at least as An Soo Jin. In that dreamlike moment, she no longer felt like she had to be a Queen amongst Gods; she no longer felt like she had to oversee an entire society to ensure their compliance. In that suspended moment, she was a normal girl in a car with the person she trusted most.

Nothing in this world could touch her because he was there. Nothing in this world could hurt her because he would never allow it. Nothing in this world mattered because wherever he was taking her, she knew she would be safe . . .

Soo Jin awoke to the feel of the wind grazing over her face.

She opened her eyes and felt an onslaught of warmth run through her when she realized the roof of the car was down.

Then, she froze in her position.

Soo Jin could not believe what she was seeing at first. She truly believed she was dreaming. She rubbed her eyes to ease her vision from what she thought was a web of dreams. As she continued to stare at the masterpiece before her, she realized that this was not a dream. This was reality.

The lake before her was just as she remembered from Yoori's memory. It was as beautiful as the last time she set eyes on it. The warm sun hovered above, shining over the surface of the water and reflecting over it like diamonds. Her eyes shifted from the lake to the surrounding landscape. The windy and deserted road they were on brought them into the heart of the mountains. Soo Jin could not help but be in awe of everything. The trees, the acres of green grass, and the sanctity of this stunning scenery left her spellbound.

The wickedness of the world did not appear to touch this place. It was pure, completely free of evil. Nothing about this magical place had changed.

Nothing had changed except her.

She heard ducks quacking in the distance and did her best to not pay attention to them.

Soo Jin drew in a fearful breath. She was positively unnerved with where she found herself. She prayed that she would survive this place.

"Why this place?" she uttered over the roaring wind.

Tae Hyun rested his soft eyes on her. With the backdrop of the majestic lake behind him, he looked like he belonged in a dream. "You really don't know why?"

She knew very well why he brought her here. This was where his relationship with Yoori progressed into something more than a "boss and assistant" relationship. This was where they first kissed—where they realized they had fallen for one another.

"It's as beautiful as I remember," she commented, fearing everything this place represented. At least in the Underworld, she had her society to remind her why she had to be a God amongst humans. In this lake house community, she had nothing but the memories of a life a God should never seek.

It went without saying that she was out of her league here.

Soo Jin could scarcely get out of the car when he parked in front of the lake house. Despite the wonderful memories, this was the last place she needed to be. Gathering all her bearings—as she did not want to appear too affected in front of Tae Hyun—she pushed the door open and stepped out. With her bag in hand, she followed Tae Hyun as they entered the house.

It felt like she had stepped through a time machine.

Her gaze charted the lake house with quiet awe. From the corner of her eyes, she sighted the unopened alcohol bottles that Yoori and Tae Hyun had left behind on their last trip. She could see the unmade blanket on the sofa that Yoori used, and she could even see the chair that Yoori angled in front of the floor-to-ceiling window so she could admire the lake. Everything was just as Yoori and Tae Hyun had left it, and she had never felt more like a stranger. This sanctuary belonged to Yoori and Tae Hyun, not Soo Jin and Tae Hyun. It could not be more abundantly clear than at that very moment.

Tae Hyun held a hand out, guiding her out of her reverie. "Let's go."

Soo Jin threw him an inquisitive look. "Where?"

He angled his head lightly. A mischievous sheen illumed in his eyes. "You were such a good sport in the car. Did you forget the second condition already?"

She snorted rudely.

These "ground rules" were going to be the death of her.

With nothing more to say, she begrudgingly took his hand and followed him up the glass stairs.

They entered a bedroom that could double as a penthouse suite. The bedroom had its own balcony and an uncompromised view of the lake in all its glory. It made the last room her human counterpart stayed in look like a closet space. It did not take her long to deduce that this was Tae Hyun's master bedroom. Unlike the last trip, she would not be getting her own room. She would be sharing with the irresistible bastard himself.

"Looking to finish what you started in Japan?" she asked bitterly, staring at the king-sized bed that was seemingly beckoning them towards it.

A smirk edged his lips. With the refinement of a tiger, he began to walk toward her with such predatory grace that she found herself reflexively taking several steps back to avoid him.

"Just because I won the challenge does not mean that you can't have fun as well," he murmured, strategically herding them towards the bed. He relieved the bag from her grasp after she hit the mattress with the back of her legs. His silky voice came over her, easily entrancing her as he spoke. "You like the right side, don't you?"

She said nothing. She merely looked up at him, feeling utterly hypnotized by his enticing eyes.

The smirk continued to adorn his lips as he wrapped his thumb and index finger over the zipper of her jacket. Slowly and deliberately, he unzipped her jacket, revealing the black camisole tank top beneath it. Never taking his eyes off of hers, he gently slipped the jacket away from her and tossed it to the ground beneath their feet.

"Get on the bed," he commanded. Though his expression remained cool and collected, it was his voice that throbbed with carnal need.

The entranced woman in her was eager to adhere to his command. It was the Queen in her that convinced her to stay where she was.

She regarded him with combative eyes. "Is that a request or are you invoking your second ground rule?"

"Get on the bed," Tae Hyun repeated, staring at her with adoring eyes. He pressed his muscled physique against hers, letting her feel exactly how hot his body was. "*Please*," he added, falsely making her believe he was more innocent than he was.

Overwhelmed with the sexual magnetism that was radiating from him, she did as he commanded and cautiously got onto the bed. To her surprise, instead of joining her in bed, he reached for her boots and pulled them off. He leaned over the mattress to pull the white comforter over her. When he brought the comforter to the area around her neck, he leaned forward to ensure that the pillows were angled at the perfect height for her neck.

Bewilderment clawed at her. "What are you doing?"

"I promised you a wonderful week, Soo Jin," he crooned against her lips, taking his sweet time to readjust the pillows around her. She was so enthralled by his actions that she could hardly focus on anything else. "But before that, try to get enough sleep. I'll come back for you later."

Click.

Something cold encircled her wrist, snapping her out of her stupor. Soo Jin peered up. A round, silver metal imprisoned her wrist, winking at her in the wake of the afternoon sun. It took her half a second later to register that she had been handcuffed to the bedpost.

What the fuck?

A raging inferno flared in her eyes. Was this guy out of his mind? Who did he think he was handcuffing her to a bed?

"What the hell do you think you're doing?"

"Making sure I see you later this evening."

She was livid. "What happened to trusting me to abide by your rules?"

He graced the room with an amused laugh. "I'm smitten with you, but I'm not stupid, Soo Jin. I know your game by now. At the first sign of trouble, you will cut your losses and make your escape. I can't chance that." He smirked, dividing his attention between her and the handcuffs. "Plus, I clearly recall having this misery bestowed to me. I've been meaning to get revenge. I can't pass up that chance."

"I wasn't the one who handcuffed you to the bed," she corrected irately.

He showed no signs of changing his mind.

"Get your rest, baby," he advised, running his fingers through her hair before backing away from the bed. "We'll start all the fun later tonight."

Brief confusion fractured the anger mounting inside her. Puzzled, she furrowed her brows. "You're not staying?"

Tae Hyun chuckled as he began towards the door. He tossed his leather jacket to the floor and then pulled his black shirt off.

Despite her grievances with him, she felt her eyes roam over his perfectly sculpted body. He seemed to have gotten more ripped since she last saw him. There was more definition to his tempting physique, more muscles that left her feeling hot all over and threatened to shoot her control to hell. She could barely hide her appreciative sigh as she watched this flawless creature make his way to the door.

"You look like a delectable offering lying there, handcuffed on the bed. If I stay, I doubt I'll let you get any sleep." He gave her a wink before he departed into the hall. "See you soon, my Queen."

Soo Jin shook her head after he disappeared out of sight. She peered up at the handcuffs, stared at her reflection in one of the windows, and groaned in misery. She truly wished that she had won the challenge. Now that she was at his mercy, she feared what he could do to her. He was already a force to be reckoned with when she attempted to avoid him all these weeks; she was terrified of what a week of being with him would do to her.

She peered up at the handcuffs and did her best to ignore the reminiscent feeling that came with it.

"Do not let him distract you," she whispered to herself, determined to preserve her control.

She could not allow Kwon Tae Hyun to redirect her focus on this trip; she could not allow him to compromise everything she had worked her entire life for.

"Stay strong," she desperately went on before she closed her eyes and slowly fell asleep. "Please stay strong."

"... and make them human again."

15: Of Gods and Humans

The slumber that Soo Jin awoke from felt like a dream in itself.

She could feel the sun's warm rays bask over her, rousing her into waking up. Everywhere she moved on the bed, she felt nothing but comfort. The soft quacking of ducks swimming over the water filtered into her senses, acting like music to her ears. Even the gentle warm breeze that streamed around the room felt like an extra comforter for her slumber. She did not want to open her eyes, but what was a well-rested Queen to do when she had all the sleep she needed?

Soo Jin opened her eyes. A smile crossed her lips when the beauty of the room reflected the exquisiteness of her dreamlike state. She nuzzled into her pillow like a lazy cat, relaxing in that big bed while staring out the enormous windows. The beginnings of the sunset had just penetrated the heavens. The vibrant hues of orange, purple, and pink swirled over the canvas of the sky. The stunning scene above was captured in the reflection of the lake beneath.

It continued to astound her that such a beautiful place existed in the world. It amazed her that she had somehow found her way back. The only thing missing from this perfect picture was the host who brought her.

Soo Jin examined her wrist and found that she was no longer handcuffed to the bed. She also observed that the windows had been cracked open, permitting the warm breeze and the melodic sounds of nature to accompany her. She was certain the windows were closed before, which meant Tae Hyun had returned sometime during her sleep to "tuck her in".

She peered into the quiet hall.

Where was he?

Ignoring the plea of her body to stay in the cozy bed, Soo Jin arose, put on her leather jacket, and walked barefoot down the hall. She inspected every inch of the lake house in an effort to find him. When it was clear that her host was not inside the house, she took her search outside.

The happiness that entered her when she set eyes on him frightened her.

Tae Hyun sat on the grass in front of the sunset-glittering lake. His head was tilted back as he gazed up at the heavenly skies. His bare upper body glowed underneath the favoritism of the setting sun. There were droplets of water covering his body, indicating that he had just went for a swim. The droplets of water clung lovingly to his flawless physique, enjoying every inch of him before they melded with his black shorts and dripped onto the grass. In this breathtaking scene, he was most certainly the showstopper.

Soo Jin briefly averted her eyes and mentally chastised herself. She wished he did not possess this type of power over her. She wished he did not mesmerize her to this degree.

"Get a hold of yourself," she whispered before returning her attention to him.

After drawing in a deep breath to regain control, Soo Jin cleared the distance and sat beside him.

Her heart stuttered to a stop when he shifted his gaze from the sky. The smile he rewarded her with was something that dreams were made of. She may have been revered by an entire Underworld society, but their reverence was nothing compared to Kwon Tae Hyun's adoration. As a Queen, she had the Underworld in the palm of her hand, but as Tae Hyun's object of affection, she felt like she had the whole world on its knees. In that heart-stopping second, it was not difficult for her to understand why Choi Yoori fell for him so deeply. He was dangerous as a King, but a thousand times more dangerous as a man.

"Did you sleep well?" he asked gently, his voice a lullaby against the tranquil backdrop. His dark hair, wet from his swim, was slicked back, bringing attention to his impeccably crafted features and his intense brown eyes. He looked good enough to devour. If Soo Jin were a weaker woman, she was positive she would've thrown herself at him in that very moment.

"Did you come back to tuck me in?"

He grinned at her pointed question. Amusement brightened his voice. "Did you really think I would've let you sleep with your wrist handcuffed to the bed? I promised you an enjoyable week. This means that I have to make sure you get lots of nice rest as well."

"And the windows?"

"My favorite part of the house is my bedroom. There is no better way to sleep than to feel the warm air against your skin and to hear nature in all its glory." He leaned in closer to her. Despite his swim in the lake, there was still the residual scent of cologne on him. He smelled damn good. "Did it work? Did you sleep well?"

Soo Jin shrugged and manufactured nonchalance—both to his enticing scent and how well she slept. "I guess so."

His smile remained before a curious thought entered his mind. "Have you always been a heavy sleeper?"

Soo Jin responded with another shrug. Her eyes traveled downward to admire the sky's reflection on the lake. "Ju Won's rigid training had an unexpected blessing—it taught me to sleep, even in the most dire environment. When he buried me with those corpses, all I had to do was sleep and I would forget about the world around me. Sleeping has always been a great escape."

Tae Hyun nodded, showing open interest in her lips rather than her answer. He was undoubtedly ready to cease the pleasantries and proceed with the flirtation. "As it should be."

She smirked and eyed him from the corner of her eyes. "Did you enjoy your swim?"

"Very much so," he answered in a relaxed manner. He rested his hands behind his back and leaned backward. Tendons of muscles rippled throughout his body at the modified seating position. "I'm enjoying my evening more now that you're awake though."

Soo Jin turned away from the temptation of his body. "What now?"

"What do you want for dinner?"

"Your head on a silver platter."

His chuckle mingled with the rustling of the grass.

"You've used that line already," he retorted lightly.

She finally permitted herself a grin. She did use that line already.

"Everything," Soo Jin said instead. Now that she thought about it, she was pretty hungry.

"Everything?"

"Pasta, spaghetti, noodles, spring rolls, steak, beef . . . everything."

Tae Hyun chuckled again. "You're going to have your hands full in the kitchen then."

Her grin faded. She pinned him with an expression of disbelief. "You're not preparing dinner?"

He tilted his head with a charming smile. "I won the challenge. Apart from servicing you in bed, I do not plan on doing any other form of servicing."

Soo Jin could barely contain her outrage. "You want *me* to cook for you?"

His shoulders lifted in a blithe shrug. "I've missed having a personal assistant. I think it'll be fun to have a Queen as my personal assistant this week."

"You're out of your fucking mind."

"A Queen keeps her word. A girl breaks it," Tae Hyun responded coyly. His eyes challenged her to go back on the agreement she made with him. "Which one are you?"

"Where do you store the rat poison?"

Tae Hyun laughed, utterly unfazed by her growing hostility. "You like me too much to poison me," he stated confidently. He reached out and tucked a loose bang behind her ear. There was no humor behind the action, only adoration. "There are plenty of other things we can do," he provided gently. "Other things that I'd prefer to spoil you with."

"Like what?"

He extended his hand out.

She scrutinized his outstretched hand and then looked at him. "What?"

"I want to hold your hand."

Soo Jin scoffed with contempt. "Are we children?"

"I would like us to be on this trip," he countered without missing a beat. "Let me hold your hand, let me show you a good time, and I'll do all the servicing." His expression was enigmatic, inviting. "What happens here will be between the two of us. No one else will know."

"And if I don't want to hold hands?"

"I wouldn't mind going skinny-dipping with you instead." He grinned at the stupefied look on her face. "What would you prefer, Soo Jin? Holding hands or skinny-dipping with me? I'll tell you that there's one thing I prefer more than the other, but it's up to you what we—"

Soo Jin interrupted his words by placing her hand over his. For the sake of her sanity, she could not go skinny-dipping with Tae Hyun. God help her, at the going rate, she was certain skinny-dipping would be the prelude to something more intimate. She could not have that. Not on this trip—not ever.

Albeit the decision to hold his hand was more innocent, she was slowly realizing that it might have been the more dangerous option. It did not elude her how safe and loved she felt when her hand grazed over his. For a fleeting second, she did not feel like a Queen. She felt entirely human.

Tae Hyun chuckled at her actions and formed a protective grip over her hand. He rose up and pulled her up with him. `

As he began to guide them away from the lake house, Soo Jin gazed at his back and said, "Aren't you going to put on a shirt?"

A smile tugged at his lips when he turned back to her. There was a tantalizing sheen in his eyes that sent an electrical current through her body. "No. I like being half-naked with you. I think I'll stay shirtless for the rest of the night."

Holy shit.

This was definitely not good for her "refute-Tae-Hyun's-charms-at-all-costs" plan.

Soo Jin swallowed with need. She said no more as Tae Hyun began to lead her out of the residential community. With the darkening sunset accompanying their walk, they strode alongside the picturesque lake houses. All the homes stood proud and dominating, shining under the complimentary sky. Not one house looked similar, and Soo Jin liked that. It felt as if every lake house was created to exist in its own world. Soo Jin avoided looking in the direction where she knew the gazebo rested and admired the massively beautiful residences instead.

After navigating through the park and procuring two corn dogs for dinner, Soo Jin found herself staring at a familiar dock. Despite her best efforts to prevent it from coming, a warm, reminiscent sensation rolled over her at the sight of the wooden infrastructure. She did not want to venture onto it because this was one of the few places that truly belonged to her human counterpart. She was not eager to venture anywhere that would awaken the feelings Choi Yoori once had. Regardless of her preference, Soo Jin was aware that what she wanted did not matter. Tonight, she had to simply abide by Tae Hyun's wishes. It was too obvious that this dock had been his destination of choice.

"I believe this is our second date now, Soo Jin," Tae Hyun announced as they walked along the wooden dock.

"So you blackmail girls into going on dates with you?" Soo Jin asked, injecting humor into her voice. She bit into her corn dog with a smirk. Since she couldn't control the events of tonight, she might as well let loose and enjoy it.

"Only Queens," came his amused response. He bit into his own corn dog with a laugh that caused Soo Jin to crack a small smile.

They sat down when they reached the end of the dock and hung their legs over the edge.

Tae Hyun surveyed the darkening sky while he finished the last of his corn dog. The sunset had gradually faded from the world, leaving the beginnings of dusk to take on its reign.

"How are you adjusting to being back?" he inquired, placing his corn dog stick beside him.

Soo Jin looked at him after she swallowed the last of her corn dog. She set aside the corn dog stick and drew in a deep, calming breath. The cool night's air flooded into her lungs, bringing with it the fresh scent of water and tranquility. Soo Jin could feel the intoxication overtake her mind, her very control. She was not drunk on alcohol, but she was drunk on the magic of this place. The reason she feared this lake house community was because it disarmed her. It was too peaceful, too perfect, and too heavenly. She could not help but be open in this environment. It felt too disrespectful to be guarded in such an enchanting place.

"It feels like yesterday that I begged my brother to kill me in the alley," she began openly, surprising herself that she was articulating emotions that she had never shared with anyone. "It feels like yesterday since I left the brothers, Ji Hoon, Ju Won, and everything in the Underworld. It feels like yesterday, but it isn't. I am still the same person, but everyone else has changed. Even Kang Min and Jae Won feel like strangers to me." She swallowed quietly, allowing a moment's pause before she delved into an unfiltered truth. She reluctantly held Tae Hyun's gaze. "The only one who doesn't feel like a stranger is you. You are the only one I feel like I know, even if I only know you through someone else."

Tae Hyun regarded her in an understanding manner that made her feel relief. Even though they were fated to be enemies—to be warring Gods—she still trusted Tae Hyun more than she trusted anyone else.

"You know," he started in a whimsical tone, "when we were younger, I wanted to meet you."

Soo Jin could only smile at that comment. "Did you really?"

He nodded as the cool breeze filtered around them. "I think I was sixteen when I first became curious about you. I was visiting Ju Won at the mansion, and there was a room that I was prohibited from going into."

"*The Throne Room*," Soo Jin thought out loud, knowing exactly which room he referenced. It was the room she trained in—the room where she lost her soul.

"I asked Ju Won what was behind that door."

"What did he say?"

"He said that my future Queen was in there," shared Tae Hyun. "He said that the one who will rival my throne—and the thrones of all the other Underworld Kings—was in there."

"That must have pissed off your sixteen-year-old self when he said that."

Tae Hyun's lips curved into a confirming smile. "It did. I remember telling him that I would love to go in there and challenge you—that I could teach you a few moves." He shook his head. "But he said that our battle would come in due time. There was no glory in two teenagers fighting. Glory only comes when Gods fight—when they battle one another for the supreme throne."

Soo Jin let out a knowing breath. That sounded exactly like Ju Won. He would never allow two teenagers to battle one another, especially when the battle would be more historic if they fought as King and Queen of the Underworld.

"I forgot about you for a while after that, until you made your official debut in the Underworld." A colder, more powerful breeze spread over the dock. "The Queen of the Underworld," he murmured softly, letting the power of the epithet weigh over him. "Overnight, you took this world by storm, and I could not for the life of me understand why we had not crossed paths yet. I wondered if you were as awful as they said, as powerful as they said, and as beautiful as they said. They say that this world loves me, but you fascinate it. Even in death, you held more power than any King in Underworld history."

He let out a long sigh. "I remember being disappointed when I heard you were 'dead'. I didn't want to believe it. It didn't make sense for you to die without us meeting, especially considering how small the Royal circle is."

"It would have only been a matter of time before we met."

"Aren't you surprised that we had never met each other before?" he inquired, gazing into her eyes. "All those parties, and we never crossed paths?"

"We were too busy losing our souls," Soo Jin offered offhandedly.

Another thought invaded his mind after he nodded. "Do you think we would've fallen for each other if we met as the King and Queen of the Underworld?"

Soo Jin did not have to ponder that answer. She shook her head. "I think we would have been too distracted with going to war with one another."

Tae Hyun smiled in concurrence. "I agree. I think we both would've been too distracted with the influence of the Underworld." His warm smile evolved into a playful smirk. "You just had to inject Yoori into our story, didn't you?"

A smirk edged Soo Jin's lips. Unlike Tae Hyun's, her smirk was more bitter. "If I had known that I would've been 'dead' for three years, I would sooner murder Young Jae in his sleep than allow all this nonsense to occur."

Silence descended over them at the acidity of her response.

"Were those three years that bad?" Tae Hyun finally whispered over the wind.

Soo Jin paused as she felt soft sprinkles drizzle over her. She was so riveted with their conversation that she did not even realize a storm had been brewing above them this entire time.

"Those three years complicated things," she clarified, refusing to disrupt this conversation because of a light rain. Their conversation was too interesting. "If not for those three years, we would not be here right now. We would not be entertaining each other."

Tae Hyun nodded, showing no signs of being affected by the light rain. He was also too engrossed in this conversation. "You're right, Soo Jin. If I had met you in your current state as a Queen, it is unlikely that I would have fallen for you. I would have been fascinated by you, I would have been physically attracted to you, but none of those would have stopped me from bringing war upon you."

"But you fell for Choi Yoori."

"The human in me fell for her," he amended swiftly. "The part that I thought died long ago somehow came to life without me knowing it. By the time the King in me realized what was happening, everything was shot to hell."

"But the King in you fell for her too," she supplied, watching as small ripples formed in the dark lake from the droplets of rain.

"Just like the Queen in you fell for Kwon Tae Hyun."

A self-deprecating smile outlined Soo Jin's lips. At this stage of the conversation, it was counterproductive to lie about her true feelings. The Queen in her did fall for Kwon Tae Hyun. She fell for Kwon Tae Hyun, but not for the King of Serpents. Not for the one she was destined to battle.

"The humans in us fucked us over," she stated wearily, truly loathing the chain of events that took place in her life.

If not for Choi Yoori and Kwon Tae Hyun, their lives would be much simpler.

Tae Hyun chuckled. "The ironic thing about all of this is that, as the King and Queen, we are the perfect match."

She agreed with his statement. They understood each other, knew what the other went through, and shared the same status in life. This was why Yoori and Tae Hyun fell in love; this was why the King and Queen had to go to war with one another. In other worlds, they would be considered the perfect match. In the Underworld, they were considered the perfect duel.

Soo Jin gazed at him as a torrent of rain started pouring. Unlike the gentle nuzzling of the drizzle a few breaths ago, this downpour was powerful and unforgiving. It demanded that they seek shelter before it washed them away.

As amusing as this topic had been, she was suspicious of his motives.

"What do you hope to achieve here?" she asked bluntly. She did not find it necessary to beat around the bush. With this storm ravaging them, it was better to get to the point than to linger any longer. She could ignore a small drizzle, but not a torrent of rain.

"I want the Royals in us to get to know each other."

Her laughter became muted under the growing storm. "Haven't we already established that we would go to war with each other?"

"That's only if Yoori and Tae Hyun had never met." Despite the presence of the storm and Soo Jin's critical expression, Tae Hyun did not let this dissuade him from his objective. He was too determined, too hopeful to give up. "Let's face it. No matter how inconvenient it is, we can't deny that they fell for each other." His measuring eyes fixed on hers. After a meaningful pause, he bluntly said, "Are you afraid of falling for me?"

Soo Jin's eyes narrowed at the accusation. "I'm afraid of you distracting me," she corrected tightly.

"I *am* a pretty distracting guy," Tae Hyun proudly concurred. His face brightened with optimism. "You asked me what I hope to achieve. What I want is to woo you, make you fall for me, and have a grand ole' time here."

"Is that the King or the man speaking?"

He flashed her a breathtaking smile that made her heart jump. "Both."

Soo Jin swallowed uneasily. "This will not end well."

"Really?" Tae Hyun humored, never looking more eager to pursue something in his life. "Because I see a very happy ending if it goes according to plan."

Soo Jin swayed an agitated head as rainwater began to drench her clothes. Having enough of this, she rose to her feet and began to walk away.

"Where are you going?" asked Tae Hyun's entertained voice.

"It's raining, and I've had enough of this absurdity for one night. I don't need to get sick before I become the Lord of the Underworld."

His laughter accompanied the pouring rain. Soon after, she felt the wooden dock rumble with footfalls. The rumbling stopped when he reached her.

"The absurdity is just beginning," Tae Hyun assured. He extended his hand out, smiling at her as he said, "I still have a surprise planned tonight."

She glared at the outstretched hand that was moist from the rain. "What?"

"I want to hold your hand," he stated charmingly. He leaned down and playfully nipped his rain-kissed nose with hers. "Or do I need to come up with another excuse to hold your hand?"

Her eyes expanded at the prospect of walking around handcuffed to him. There was no way in hell she would allow that.

Bitterly, she took his hand. She blinked rainwater from her eyelashes and scowled at him. "I will make you pay for this."

Tae Hyun grinned. He gently tugged at her hand and began to pick up the pace. "I'm counting on it."

"Where are we going now?" she asked as they raced from the dock and ran off the commonly traveled path. She looked over her shoulder. They were headed in the opposite direction of Tae Hyun's lake house.

"To find shelter from this rain."

"Your lake house is in the other direction."

"We're not going home yet," he answered, his pace never slowing down.

Soo Jin angled her head down to keep the rain from submerging her eyes. "Where are we going then?"

From the corner of her eyes, she saw him point at something in the distance.

"There."

She lifted her gaze and followed the direction he pointed her in. Through the growing rain, she saw a lighthouse.

"What's there?" she asked.

"The next part of our date."

"Yet every one of us continues to seek that forbidden fruit..."

16: The Lighthouse

The lighthouse resembled a masterpiece from a whimsical painting. It was approximately one-hundred-and-fifty feet tall and made completely of bricks. It was surrounded by tall trees, lush green grass, and a well-manicured garden. Unlike other lighthouses, there was no safety reason involved when the people of this town decided to construct this tower. It was built purely for aesthetic purposes; it was built solely for enjoyment.

"It looks closed," Soo Jin observed when they reached it. The windows at the top of the tower were pitch dark, and there was not a soul in sight. Despite its beauty, it was not a place she wanted to seek shelter in.

"It's open," Tae Hyun easily assured, guiding her to the front steps. He withdrew a set of keys from his pocket and unlocked the door.

A burst of cool air hit Soo Jin when the door opened. It was chillier inside the tower than outside in the rain. Soo Jin assessed the world inside the lighthouse. There was nothing that greeted her on the ground level but spiral stairs leading up to the peak of the tower.

"You own this lighthouse?" Soo Jin asked, still assessing the building from the outside. She was not eager to go in.

"Don't be silly," he said with a laugh. "Everyone who owns a lake house here has a key."

"Do we have to go in?" Soo Jin asked wearily.

Tae Hyun pocketed his keys and gazed at Soo Jin with playful eyes. "Afraid I'm going to lock you up in the tower and never let you go?"

"I'll push you off the tower before you can even try," Soo Jin retorted gravely.

Tae Hyun chuckled. "Then there's nothing to worry about." When he sensed her hesitation, he lightly said, "Remember the third ground rule you agreed upon."

Soo Jin sighed when she recalled that the third ground rule was to keep an open mind. With no more to say, she simply nodded her acquiescence.

Tae Hyun smiled favorably. Holding her hand, he led her up the spiral stairs. After navigating their way through the darkness, they reached the room at the top of the lighthouse. A canvas filled with indiscernible shadows greeted Soo Jin's eyes as they walked into the shadowy room. The darkness dispersed when Tae Hyun lit the various candles throughout the room.

As he brightened the room with more candles, Soo Jin approached the window seat at the north side of the room. She settled on the soft white cushion and stared out the rain-streaked windows. From this angle, she could see the lake and the lake house community. The lake rippled like fabric in the wind as the rain poured over it. The lake houses illumed with bright white hues, indicating that all the residents were safely inside their homes for the night. A tranquil sensation coursed over Soo Jin. The fact that the weather outside looked so uninviting made her feel safer in this lighthouse.

She was initially reticent about entering this building. Now that she was inside, she had to admit that the last thing she wanted to do was leave.

"What do you think?" asked Tae Hyun from behind her.

Soo Jin could not take her eyes off the hypnotizing scene. She always loved the rain. "It's beautiful."

"It's one of my favorite places," Tae Hyun shared.

He took a leisure seat to the right of her and gazed admiringly out the window. After offering his respect to the view, he vested his full attention back on her.

"You must be freezing," he noted, lightly grazing his warm fingers over her cold cheek.

Soo Jin did her best to not appear affected by the sudden attention. She was doing a valiant job—until he started to unzip her leather jacket.

She firmly gripped his offending hand. "What do you think you're doing?" she growled menacingly.

"Your jacket is wet," he pointed out, unfazed by her reaction. "You shouldn't wear it indoors. You might get sick."

"I can take off my own damn jacket."

Tae Hyun chuckled, raising his hands in surrender. "I was just trying to be a gentleman."

"More like a pervert," Soo Jin griped, taking off her jacket. She tossed it to the ground and stared back out the window. Goose bumps formed over her body now that she was only wearing a black tank top. She was tempted to shiver from the cold, but refused, as she did not want to compromise her indomitable façade. Tae Hyun did not need to see how cold she was. She did not need to give him any more ammunition to be a "gentleman".

Tae Hyun kept a pleasant expression and reached down to pull a drawer out from beneath the window seat. He withdrew a purple throw blanket and proceeded to wrap it around Soo Jin like a cloak.

Soo Jin held her breath. She did not know if the newfound warmth she felt came from the blanket or from Tae Hyun's chivalrous gesture. Countless suitors had wooed her numerous times in the past. This type of gesture should not cause her pulse to race, but it did. It evaded her understanding as to why Tae Hyun's simple actions affected her so much. Was it because of the romantic setting? Was it her human counterpart? Or was it truly her who was smitten?

"I have a question for you," she launched, wanting to eradicate the perturbing emotions roiling inside her. The only way to do that was to discuss subjects that a Queen would bring up.

"Shoot."

"Do you ever wonder why Ju Won decided to preside over the 2nd layer as opposed to the 3rd layer?"

Tae Hyun looked at her with piqued interest. He pondered the question before admitting, "I've been curious about that my whole life."

Soo Jin nodded. She, too, had been curious about this her whole life. It seemed only fitting that she discussed this with a fellow Royal. Since they were stuck on the uppermost part of a tower for the night, they might as well discuss topics relating to their Kingdom.

"He had Dong Min and Jung Min by his side," she went on, voicing her train of thoughts. The pitter-pattering of the rain played in the background as she spoke. "They could've formed their own gangs, and in turn, served under him. Ju Won could've easily been the Lord of the Underworld himself."

Tae Hyun leaned his head against the wall behind him. His expression told her that he had also reached this conclusion. "Why do you think he decided to become an Advisor instead?"

Soo Jin tried to conceal her nerdy smile. She had harbored this theory her whole life and was excited to finally verbalize it. "Do you ever think that there's another society that is more secretive than ours?"

She could see that he was trying not to laugh at the earnestness exuding out of her. It was clear he thought her theory was a bit far-fetched. "We're as secretive as they come."

"We are," she agreed. Her voice then became lower, more enigmatic. "But sometimes, I can't help but think that there are more secrets about our world that even we aren't aware of." She measured him with critical eyes. "Why did Ju Won decide all of a sudden that there should be a Lord of the Underworld to preside over all three layers? The Underworld had been ruled over by multiple crime lords for decades. That is what keeps the power balance in check—that is what keeps our world vicious and powerful."

"You think there is another layer to our secret society, like a secret society within a secret society?" Tae Hyun folded his arms and gazed at her in a doting manner. "That is an urban legend, Soo Jin. A story told to young Underworld Royals to keep them in line."

"Maybe," Soo Jin conceded, recalling the stories she heard when she was younger about "Titans" who came before the "Gods" of the Underworld. According to the stories, these Titans controlled the inner workings of their society from the shadows and would not hesitate to take out Gods who were unfit to rule. "But it should not be discounted that we are one of the youngest new societies. There are many others that have existed before ours."

She briefly stared out the window. Her eyes involuntarily charted over the grassland overrun by newly formed mud puddles. "Maybe we have grown into power too fast. Think about how powerful our Underworld is. Think about the Underworld in America, in Japan, and even in Germany." She turned back to him with a dark glint in her eyes. "What if Ju Won is part of that secret society? What if he has been charged to pick the new Lord because this new Lord will be inducted into their society?"

Tae Hyun tilted his head in understanding. "Is that one of the reasons why you want the Underworld throne so badly?"

A ghost of a smile adorned her lips. One shoulder lifted in a coy shrug. "I believe that there is power beyond the Underworld throne. Whether it be entrance to a more powerful society or governance over several Underworlds at once, I do not know. All I know is that I can think of no greater life purpose than to pursue this boundless power."

"If these Titans exist," Tae Hyun began as he shifted closer to her, "do you think they know our story?"

"It is likely," she whispered, wrapping her blanket tighter around her at his growing proximity. "It is likely they are taking bets on who will win the Underworld throne."

Tae Hyun nodded with light amusement. While he did not believe that this secret society existed, he was clever enough to use its possible existence to further his own agenda.

"They will not know the continuation of our story here, not in this part of the world. This part of the story is ours and ours alone."

A genuine smile brightened her lips. It was so genuine, so unexpected that she didn't even think about concealing it. "You are very lucky to have found this place. No one from the Underworld would be able to find you here—at least not for a very long time."

A bittersweet light shrouded his visage. "Unfortunately our time here is limited. It may be difficult for them to find, but as long as it's in this country, they will find it sooner or later."

Soo Jin released a concurring sigh. "I know."

He reached his hand out and gently held her cheek in his palm. His eyes held hers in a hopeful manner. "What do you think would happen if we both disappeared from the Underworld?"

"Disappeared?"

"What if we both left everything behind and started a new life somewhere else?"

Soo Jin smirked to herself. Perhaps being up on this tower was too much of a fairytale experience for her fellow Royal. "No one can get away from the Underworld."

"I can't think of two better people to defy the rules than us."

Her next words burst out before she could stop them. "You were more realistic when someone else begged you to run away with her."

A morose light flickered in his eyes at the mention of this "someone else". When he posed his next question, she knew that her openness had been contagious and transcended onto him as well.

"Can you tell me what she was feeling?"

Soo Jin furrowed her brows as the rain continued to pour outside. "What she was feeling?"

The poignancy in his eyes became more powerful. His next words were not spoken by a King, but by a man who missed the love of his life.

"When did she fall for me?"

An ache surfaced in her heart when she registered what Tae Hyun was asking. He wanted to know what the love of his life was feeling when she fell for him. There was no denying the pain in his voice or the longing in his eyes as he looked at her. Since Yoori no longer existed, all he had to hold on to were her memories. His only connection to his love was Soo Jin.

"When you brought her here," Soo Jin answered. She was surprised herself that she was granting him this allowance. She had spent weeks trying to forget about Choi Yoori and Kwon Tae Hyun. The fact that she was willingly reliving Yoori's memory for Tae Hyun was unbelievable. Yet, she could not refute his earnest need. She did not want to talk about Yoori, but for Tae Hyun, she felt an intrinsic obligation to do so.

"She loved it here," she forged on, meaning every word. Her eyes wandered over the beauty of the lake house community. "Everything was magical. She felt safe. It was the first time she felt like you let your guard down, if only slightly." She peered at him perceptively. "But you know that. That is why you brought me here."

Now that she had given him this boon, it was only right that he gave her something in return.

"You never answered me."

He looked at her in curiosity. The sky above them darkened as little specks of the town's streetlights birthed into life. "Answered what?"

"What made you fall for her?"

Tae Hyun smiled. After quickly admiring the rainy scene, he started to enlighten her.

"When I asked her if she'd tell me what it feels like when she finds Paris." Warmth suffused his eyes as Soo Jin relived this very moment with him. "I had been so consumed with the quest for power that I had forgotten what it felt like to want something other than my throne. I remember being utterly captivated when she spoke of Paris. Despite the fact that I had been raised to never seek 'Paris', I still found myself enticed by it." He let out a weary laugh. "I was so envious of the lucky bastard who would get to take her to Paris. I remember harboring so much resentment for this nonexistent bastard. The fact that he would get the honor of being by her side when she finally found what she was looking for triggered every animosity inside me." He shook his head. "That was when I realized that what I was feeling wasn't simple jealousy, but human emotion. For the first time in my life, I realized that there was something I wanted more than power. Her. I wanted her. I wanted to be the one she found Paris with; I wanted to be the one to show her Paris."

Soo Jin laughed quietly after she digested his answer. She could not help but display her judgmental view on his answer.

"How precious," she remarked sardonically.

He regarded her with soft eyes. He did not take her sarcasm to heart. "I know that you're not her—not exactly. I know that you must think I'm weak to permit myself to be this vulnerable. I know what you're thinking because I used to be just like you. I despised what this world had turned me into, and I used to believe that the only way to make things right was to rule over the world—just like the God they raised me to be." He leaned forward, his eyes never once wavering from hers. "What you should know is that all of this does not make me weak. On the contrary, I am the strongest I've ever been. I no longer fear the repercussions of my choices; I no longer fear turning my back on the throne."

A resentment Soo Jin did not know she harbored burst at that moment. His foolish and idealistic words were too much for her to bear. Considering everything that led up to this moment, he was the last person who should speak so idealistically.

"Do you remember what happened after she revealed to you that she was me?"

Silence claimed his lips.

For this, she became angrier.

"You left her," she reminded. Her voice was a soft lilt that rumbled with fury. "Even when she begged you not to, you left her."

He stayed quiet.

She smirked, becoming more incensed with his mounting silence. The more she relived those memories, the more furious she became. "She was in so much pain. I don't think she had ever felt that much pain in her life."

He gazed at her with pain of his own. Although she was reliving those memories with anger, he was reliving them with agony.

"I was in pain too," he whispered at long last.

"But you were the one who chose to leave," Soo Jin corrected spitefully. Her smirk became colder, more merciless. "I would've never given you a second chance. I would've never forgiven you," she said truthfully. For the first time, she was not resentful of Choi Yoori. She was protective of her—she was angry *for* her. "But she loved you so much, even when she didn't know it."

"What happened during her last moments?" Tae Hyun asked now that they had ventured into Yoori's world. Soo Jin had lifted the veil for him into the inner workings of Yoori's mind. Now he wanted to know what the love of his life went through before she departed from this world.

"She held on to a hoodie that you had given her and embraced it like she was embracing you," Soo Jin shared, staring at him with emotionless eyes. "She apologized that you had to meet her, and she said that she'd make things easier for you. She'd leave." She tilted her head and measured the anguish on his face. Her next words were mocking and spoken with the sole purpose of hurting him. "Are things easier for you?"

He shook his head and verbalized what she knew he was feeling: immense regret.

"She would never know the things she does to me," he whispered, disclosing feelings he had never shared with Yoori. "She would never know that being around her makes me want to be a better man—that being around her makes me want to renounce everything I've been given in this life so I could give her the life she deserves—a safe and happy one. But I am not a better man. I am the bastard this world raised me to be. I should've let her go when we first met. I should've never kept her with me for so long. I should've put her needs before mine, but I was too selfish. I wanted her too much."

Soo Jin did not want to voice her next question, but her masochistic heart beat her to the punch. "You wish she was here now, don't you?"

He nodded as the anguish magnified on his face—as the anguish increased in Soo Jin's heart.

"I wish I could tell her that I never wanted to leave her—that walking away that night was the hardest thing I ever had to do. I wish she was here so I could tell her how much I miss her."

His beautiful eyes held hers, and when he spoke, he was no longer referring to Yoori as a separate person. He was addressing her personally.

"I think about you everyday," he uttered brokenly, holding Soo Jin prisoner to his words. "There is not a moment that passes where you don't consume my mind. I wake up yearning for you, wishing that you were beside me. I go to sleep longing for you because I know that no matter how awful life is to me, you are the only one who could make things right." His aggrieved eyes searched hers. "I miss you, more than you will ever know."

Soo Jin's smirk became venomous. While she could not deny that his words touched her, she also could not deny how much she resented him. She did not hesitate to verbalize this.

"Isn't it funny that you left her because you knew that An Soo Jin would return one day?" She leaned back against the window and laughed mockingly. She assessed him up and down with judgmental eyes. "Now look at you . . . chasing after the Queen of the Underworld like a lovesick puppy. Look at how far you've fallen, King of Serpents."

He offered her an expectant smile. He was unfazed by her cruel words. Resolution teemed in his once aggrieved eyes. "Things are different this time."

"How so?"

"Because of our past."

She was mystified with his answer. "What are you talking about?"

His warm eyes held a secret that he planned to only unveil when the time was right.

"You do not remember me," he began enigmatically, "but I remember you. It was so long ago, but I remember now where it all started. I also know now where I want things to end up."

She continued to stare at him in utter confusion.

"I fucked up with Yoori—I know I did," he continued. Regret vibrated in his quiet voice. "I allowed my upbringing to cloud my relationship with her, but I will not make the same mistake with you, Soo Jin. I will do things right this time."

"What will you do differently?" she asked doubtfully.

"The humans in us fell in love, but not the Royals within us." The familiar expression of a determined King overtook his face. He no longer held the demeanor of a man who had fallen in life. He now possessed the demeanor of a King who would permit no obstacles to keep him from what he wanted. "Like I said, you *will* fall in love with me, Soo Jin. Not as a woman, but as a Queen. After that, I will take you far away from here. I will take you far away from the shadows of the Underworld, and I will give you the life you've always dreamed of. "

"The Underworld is everywhere," Soo Jin stated firmly. Considering the cacophony of emotions that were tormenting her, it was a miracle that she was able to keep her voice so controlled. "You can never escape it. You know better than that."

"There is no Underworld here."

"What do you call us?"

"We are not the Underworld. In this place, we are just humans." He extended his arms out to demonstrate his point. "Look around. No one knows who we are here. We do not have to reside over anyone here. All we have to do is exist; all we have to do is enjoy our lives." He moved closer to her. The heat from his body blocked the night's chills. "I have everything set up. All you have to do is say yes, and we can leave tonight. We'll leave this country and never look back."

Disillusionment threatened to break her tight smile. No matter how pretty his words were, she knew there was no substance to them. They would never hold up to the reality of their world.

"Ho Young gave me amnesia, tucked me away in another city, and I still managed to come back," she reminded him. "Our society spreads far and wide. Wherever we go, we would never be able to escape for long."

Her doubtful words did not rupture his confidence. "You said it yourself. This world loves me. Even when I killed my own brother, it rallied together to protect me." His eyes searched hers. "Can't you trust that I have everything worked out? That if I'm finally asking you to run away with me, it means that I truly believe that the Underworld will never find us?" His gaze implored her to trust him. "I would never ask you to do this unless I know that you will be protected. I would never risk your life."

She shook her head mockingly. The ridiculousness of this conversation was too much. "Don't you think it's comical that you're so confident? Especially given the fact that I'm not even that fond of you?"

His boyish grin told her that he did not believe her last statement. "No, because the first hurdle has already been completed. You already like me."

"Oh, really?"

His broad shoulders lifted in an innocent shrug. "I don't imagine you hold this much patience for anyone else. There must be a reason why I'm so special."

She smirked. He had her there. "I admit that I do have a fondness for you, but that will not cloud my better judgment. Yoori was a fool, but I am not. I will not fall for you. I will never allow that."

And she meant it.

She meant every word.

His visage lit up with elation. This was a challenge he was up for. "Which is why I know this will be a fun trip." He regarded her with a silent promise in his gaze. "A battle of the wills between the King and Queen of the Underworld. I wonder who will come out triumphant in the end." He shrugged playfully. "Whatever the answer may be, I think it's only right that we continue our fun here." A sneaky grin graced his lips. "Kiss me."

Soo Jin did a double take. "Excuse me?"

"It is my will," he answered softly. "It is what I want."

Fire enflamed her cheeks. She was tempted to wrap the blanket around him like a noose. "I didn't think you'd stoop so low."

"I did not think so either," he whispered. "But I can't help it." He touched her hair while staring at her lips. "I can't control myself. When I look at you, all I want to do is kiss you." He slanted his head. "Just once," he negotiated, his voice a melodic lilt against the rain outside. "Just once to sate my need; just once to put me out of my misery—"

Soo Jin kissed him before she could think twice. The effect was instant—electrifying. Once their lips met, a bomb detonated inside her. She should have pulled away, but every time she tried, her yearning lips would lean in for more. Next thing she knew, she was lying across the window seat. Tae Hyun leaned on his arms above her, showering her with kisses that she could not get enough of.

She felt like *she* was being put out of her misery.

Her hands roamed over his bare back. She had wanted to touch him all night and could barely contain herself when she was finally able to do it. It was a good idea to stop, but who the fuck cared about good ideas when you were in paradise?

Boom!

Soo Jin awoke from her stupor when a clap of thunder rang through the night. She could've sworn she felt it shake the lighthouse. Or was that the shaking of her own disbelief?

"You bastard," she voiced breathlessly, abruptly tearing away from their kiss.

"Aw, shit," Tae Hyun groaned. It was clear that he did not get enough of their kiss—not even close.

"You planned for that, didn't you?" she accused pointedly.

"I hoped for it," he admitted sheepishly. He bit his lower lip in need. "I never thought it was possible to want someone as much as I want you right now."

Her face went bright red. It infuriated her that she felt the same way. She could no longer entertain this ridiculousness.

"Keep dreaming, asshole," she growled, pushing him away while throwing the blanket at him. With heat cloaking her cheeks, she propelled from the window seat, grabbed her jacket, and shot down the spiral stairs.

"Where are you going?" Tae Hyun shouted behind her. "It's pouring rain! You're going to get sick."

"I'd rather get sick than be here with you."

He let out a disbelieving laugh and chased her down the stairs.

"It was just a kiss, Soo Jin," he uttered, bursting out into the rain with her. He broke into an easy jog beside her. "We're adults here. We can kiss if we want to."

"It is on my bucket list to kill you," she reminded stiffly, covering her head with her jacket. It was a piss-poor attempt to manufacture an umbrella. The force of the wind was tossing the rainwater every which way. Her jacket helped block the rain, but only slightly.

"You are still allowed to kiss me if you want." He smiled, looking devilishly handsome in the rain. "What are you afraid of?"

"Getting herpes."

Tae Hyun faked an injured hand to his heart. "I would take offense to it, but let's keep in mind that the only one I kissed before you was Yoori. If there's herpes involved, it's from someone else who kissed Lee Ji Hoon when she made her dramatic homecoming."

That witty comeback would have been funny had she not been so pissed at the absurdity of her current state.

"Fuck off," she retorted instead.

His amusement remained. "How can I when you're going the wrong way?"

Soo Jin stared back at the lighthouse like it was her north star. She was indeed going in the opposite direction of the lake house.

"You know what?" she prompted, returning her attention to a smug Tae Hyun.

"What?"

Boom!

She charged at him like a bull and rammed him into the ground. Mud splashed all around them as she wrapped her hands around his neck.

"Still think this is funny?" she snarled, tightening the chokehold she had on him.

"You know . . ." he laughed in between words, "if you slid just a little further south, this would be the perfect position to make my pain go away."

"Ugh!"

Furious that she couldn't scare the shit out of him (and instead unknowingly turned him on), she childishly grabbed a handful of mud and flung it at his face. If she couldn't scare him, she might as well temporarily fuck up his face.

Tae Hyun groaned dramatically. He began to rub his eyes in surprised pain. "You got my eyes!"

"You're lucky I didn't gouge your eyes out," she muttered before getting up and high tailing it out of there like a scared kitten.

"What about the first ground rule?" he bellowed behind her.

When all she did was flip him the middle finger, she heard Tae Hyun utter with a laugh, "Oh, it's on, Princess. It is on."

"Because it's the only thing that makes us human..."

17: Further South

Soo Jin was enraged when she kicked the punching bag the next evening. She had avoided Tae Hyun like the plague the entire day: she hid out in Yoori's old sleeping quarters in the morning, she distracted herself by enjoying a day out on the town during the afternoon, and she only continued to avoid him by barricading herself in the lake house's workout room that evening. If she could not be productive at home, she might as well be productive and train here.

Soo Jin continued to brood as she attacked the punching bag. She did not understand why she was entertaining him. Why the hell was she still here when she could be doing more useful things at her Siberian Tigers' estate?

"Is that punching bag supposed to represent someone?" asked a familiarly infuriating voice.

She turned to see Tae Hyun leaning against the doorframe. He wore an all black attire that made him look more harmless than he was. He was smiling as he gazed at her with doting eyes.

"Your corpse," Soo Jin stated in an annoyed voice.

Like water coursing over steel, Tae Hyun let her hostility roll off of him. He strolled into the room and handed her a water bottle. "Truce?"

She took it without saying anything. Ignoring him, she downed the drink, tossed the water bottle to the side, and continued to hit the punching bag.

Undeterred by her chilly treatment, Tae Hyun persevered with his advancement. He went to the other side of the room and stood across from her. The punching bag was a few feet between them.

"Can I train with you?" he asked innocently.

"I prefer to workout alone."

"Afraid I might show you up?"

Soo Jin ceased her workout and glared at him. "You really want to go there? Especially after what happened last night?"

"When we kissed?" he reminded sheepishly.

"When I rammed you into the ground. I could've choked you to death."

He had a faraway look on his face as he recalled that event.

"I went easy on you," he mused out loud. "Both last night and that homecoming night."

Considering that she didn't strangle him the night before, it was safe to say that she showed him the same courtesy. "As did I."

"If we're going to have our once-in-a-lifetime duel soon, then we might as well see what the big deal is."

Soo Jin paused to consider his words. It intrigued her that he would want this. It *would* be entertaining to get a prelude to what their war would be like.

Her lack of response—and by default, her agreement—triggered Tae Hyun's smile to broaden. When he started to slowly unbutton his shirt, Soo Jin's breath became lodged in her lungs. She did her best to maintain a cool expression as he stripped his shirt off, revealing the muscled body beneath it.

"Were you a stripper in a past life?" she inquired pointedly, getting sick and tired of him disarming her with his provocativeness. It was obvious he was the most handsome bastard in the world. He did not need to use that as his ultimate weapon against her. "Is it that difficult to keep a shirt on?"

His soft chuckle permeated the workout room. "Apparently I'm a stripper in this life too." He winked suggestively at her. "Maybe you should give me a good tip later on."

"I'm out of dollar bills."

"I accept other forms of payments." His eyes did not conceal his carnal need for her. "Especially when it involves stripping for you."

She rolled her eyes.

He released a thoughtful sigh. "But this is not about stripping." He pointed a reproving finger at her to get them back on point. "I'm mad at you."

Now this was a new and interesting development. Curious, Soo Jin folded her arms. She slanted her head and decided to humor him. "Why?"

"You fought dirty last night."

Her lips threatened to edge up in a grin. "You gonna do something about it?"

"Yes," he stated solemnly, his stern voice holding an edge of seduction. "You are going to be punished tonight."

"How?"

"I'm going to do what you hate most: show you up."

With no warning, he took one powerful swing at the punching bag. The bag vibrated from the impact, nearly falling off its hinges.

Soo Jin glowered at him as the punching bag swung like a pendulum between them. "You have some gall to say that."

His lips stretched into a serene smile. He easily retained his charisma while simultaneously pissing her off. "I did not become a King because of my good looks alone."

"I think I just swallowed my own vomit."

Tae Hyun pleasantly shrugged off the acidic remark. "Truth hurts."

Soo Jin tightened her jaw in controlled rage. The constant swaying of the punching bag lured her like a bull to a red cape. It was taking everything she had to not unleash the monster inside her.

"This is a change from your charming personality last night," Soo Jin noted, wondering why he was deliberately pissing her off.

"You're mean to me when I'm charming," he voiced with a slight pout. He shrugged again, his expression becoming more mischievous. "Now I'm mad at you, and I think it's more fun to piss you off."

"You piss me off by existing."

He faked a dagger to the heart. "You have an 'insult-of-the-day' flashcard in your mind or something? You can do better than that."

Soo Jin chewed her lower lip. She had a witty one-liner to say, but given his recent insult, she kept it to herself. She would rather respond by punching his neck.

Tae Hyun laughed as though reading her mind. "Let's train together. I can teach you a few things."

He struck the bag again, and it swung at her like a wrecking ball.

Without hesitation, Soo Jin punched it like a tether ball, and it flew back to him. As his retaliation, Tae Hyun triple-kicked the bag with brute force.

Boom!

The punching bag caught Soo Jin off guard when it slammed into her and caused her to crash to the ground.

What the fuck?

She breathed in disbelief. Did she just let her opponent knock her off her feet, and with a goddamned punching bag, no less? A fiery rage swept through her when she peered up at Tae Hyun.

He offered her an apologetic smile while hugging the punching bag. "Sorry about that."

Soo Jin clenched her fists. She would most certainly make him sorry.

Hungry for his blood, it was Soo Jin's turn to catch him off guard. With an angry growl, she leapt up in the air and kicked the bag with an intensity so brutal that it sent Tae Hyun slamming into the squat rack behind him.

Boom!

Soo Jin feigned an apologetic smile as she watched him tear away from the squat rack.

"Sorry about that," she murmured, mocking his previous words.

"It's alright, baby," he uttered, unexpectedly propelling up and striking the punching bag right into her stomach.

Boom!

Although Soo Jin did not tumble over, the force was enough to knock the wind — and the pride — out of her. She hunched forward and pressed her hands into her stomach to assuage the unanticipated pain.

"I'm the one who should be sorry," he finished with a breathless whisper. He laughed to himself and appraised her injured state. "Is that how easy our historic battle is going to be? Do I have to go extra easy on you?"

"You piece of—!"

Unable to control herself, she rocketed forward, grabbed the punching bag, and then swung it at him. The bag blasted into him like a cannon, whacking him off his feet.

Although he was on the ground, his taunting laughter did not cease. "Someone's mad."

Still pissed off, Soo Jin seized a fifteen-pound dumbbell and chucked it in his direction.

Displaying amazing dexterity, Tae Hyun evaded the flying dumbbell.

Boom!

As the heavy weight crashed into the wall behind him, he rammed into Soo Jin and thrust her onto the floor.

"Bad girl," Tae Hyun crooned, easily pinning her writhing form to the ground. "That dumbbell could have knocked me out cold."

"*I* could knock you out cold," she snarled before head-butting him.

Bam!

"Aw, shit!"

Tae Hyun recoiled from her after their foreheads nearly split open. Blinking to clear his vision, he stumbled off of her and crashed into the weights beside them. Before he could surge to his feet, Soo Jin raced over to him and kneed him in the solar plexus, sending him flying back onto the weights.

Boom!

A long, thunderous crash infused the room. This time the remaining weights on the shelf came crashing down, falling onto his unmoving body with pitiless force.

An unsettling silence spread over the room after the last of the weights hit his body. It was so eerily quiet that chills started to materialize on Soo Jin's body.

"Hey," Soo Jin called, staring at him with apprehensiveness. He was lying face-first on the ground, breathing quietly. "You alright?"

Tae Hyun remained silent. Apart from the slow rising and falling of his back, he did not move an inch.

"Tae Hyun?" she called out with a louder voice. Soo Jin's pulse raced once she realized that he was not moving at all. Shit, did she go too far? "Stop playing and get up."

When he still did not respond, Soo Jin started to panic.

"Shit!" She sped over to Tae Hyun with the intention of helping him up. She was three inches from him when he unexpectedly whirled around, swung his leg, and stole the ground from her feet.

"Ugh!"

As Soo Jin fell towards the floor, Tae Hyun repositioned himself and caught her in time. With a satisfied chuckle, he laid back down on the ground and pulled her with him so that her legs were on either side of his body.

"You have a death wish, don't you?" Soo Jin asked after she registered the precarious position he placed her in. She was sitting on his abs while he was smiling up at her.

"I like you on top," he drawled before repositioning himself so that she was under him. He leaned on his forearms and gazed sensuously down at her. When he voiced his next words, she felt this primal need stir inside her. "But you should know that I can be dominating with my positions as well."

"I should skull-bash you again," she gasped, uncertain of how much longer she could resist him.

"But you were so worried about me," he countered with a knowing laugh.

"Why were you playing dead?"

"Because I wanted to see how worried you would be." He chuckled, leaning down and favoring her with a kiss to the cheek. "Were you worried?"

Heat swarmed her cheeks.

She said nothing.

"I heard it in your voice that you were worried," he insisted, hovering his lips over hers.

She continued to say nothing as she felt his tempting body press closer to hers.

His breath was a hot whisper against her fiery skin. "Should I play dead again?"

His laughter became warmer in her silence.

"Are you playing dead now?" He suspended his lips over hers. "Should I wake you up, baby?" Her silence did not make him relent from his advances. If anything, it only spurred him forward. "Please wake up, baby. You're too pretty to play dead."

What transpired next was a distorted haze to her.

She was ignoring him one second, and before she knew it, she had shoved him off of her, propelled to her feet, and pushed him against the wall. She had every intention of breaking his nose. Yet, all control was lost when he smiled at her and said, "You are the sexiest and most stunning thing when you're mad."

Instead of punching him as she intended, she hurtled herself to him and pressed her lips against his.

When she realized her error and tried to break away, he tugged her closer and deepened their kiss. To her horror, Soo Jin found that she could no longer deny this walking aphrodisiac. He might as well lace his lips with an addictive drug. The more their lips met, the more she wanted him—the more she yearned for him. She was out of her league and had been since she lost the shooting challenge to him. Resigned to the fact that it was fruitless to deny herself this intoxicating moment, Soo Jin did what she had been dying to do: she ran her hands over his statuesque body.

The sensual concession did not sate her needs. If anything, the indulgence only served to worsen it. As she felt his muscles undulate beneath her touch, she became drunker with need. An unstoppable inferno consumed her, and it took all her power to maintain her sanity.

"You have no idea how long I've waited for this."

The very guttural sound in his voice caused an excess of heat to shroud over her. Anymore of this, she was sure she would faint from a lack of oxygen.

"You ready?"

"Ready for what?" she gasped, slowly coming out of her intoxicated state now that he had pulled his lips from hers.

The smile he gave her was pure sex. It was a smile that excited her and scared the living daylights out of her at the same time.

"You're sharing my bed tonight, baby."

"It is the only thing that makes life worth living."

18: Only Yoori

"Perverted lunatic!" Soo Jin shouted, bouncing on Tae Hyun's bed after being pushed onto it.

She cursed to herself. She had really reached a new level of idiocy. How the hell did she manage to go from beating Tae Hyun's ass to being his new sexual plaything?

To make matters worse, she could not blame alcohol for her loss of better judgment. She was sober, completely and utterly sober. She allowed Tae Hyun to disarm her. He utilized his goofball side as a placebo to make her comfortable—to tear away the last of her resistance. In truth, she had no one to blame but herself. She had given into his seduction, and because of this travesty, the gorgeous bastard took it as his open invitation to invite her into his bed.

Soo Jin muttered another expletive. It did not escape her how dangerous this very moment was for her. Kwon Tae Hyun was a master at seduction. He oozed sexual magnetism with little to no effort. The very fact that he was making an effort to get her into his bedroom only meant one thing: he was done with foreplay. He was determined to put their complicated relationship to bed—literally.

"You were the one who kissed me first," Tae Hyun retorted, climbing onto the bed like a tiger on the attack. Tempting muscles corded to life with his every predatory movement. His dark eyes glittered with tantalizing promises of the pleasures to come. "You started this. Why can't I finish it?"

Instinctively, Soo Jin began to back away on the massive bed, using her hands to pull her body away. Unluckily for her, Tae Hyun was mirroring her retreat with his own advancement.

"Finish what?" she asked stupidly.

A lazy and seductive smile embellished his face. He continued to move, his muscles flexing gorgeously. "Seducing my girlfriend."

"Oh God, this is insane," she complained after her back met the cold headboard. "This whole trip has been insane."

"How is it insane?" Tae Hyun murmured after he reached her. He leveled his eyes with hers and rested his big arms on either side of her. The heat from his body stirred over her like an open flame, silently beckoning her to touch him. "You're the one who started this." A smirk perched on the edge of his lips. "You were the one who lost the challenge." He laughed at the reminder of how he had won—how it was a duck that sealed the deal for him. "Embarrassingly so, if I may add."

"You know that wasn't fair," Soo Jin argued in a rough breath. She desperately pressed harder against the headboard. Even though it was against the laws of physics, she was hoping that if she pushed hard enough, she would find a secret tunnel within the headboard to escape into. "You only won because that stupid duck appeared out of nowhere and screwed me up. I demand a rematch."

His laughter intermixed with the soft quacking of the ducks outside.

"Rematch?" He shook his head and rested his hands on the headboard, locking her between his arms. He raised his glorious body up into a sitting position and faced her with a devilish look on his face. "I'm sorry, but I'm not a saint, Princess," he apologized, his smooth voice coursing over her like honey. "I'm simply a guy who's going crazy for his girlfriend right now."

"This is such a ridiculous conflict of interest," Soo Jin vented with exasperation. She maintained control of her hands while the heat from Tae Hyun's body continued to tempt her. "I trained years upon years for you. I fought with everything I had to reach this moment in life. I've given up everything for you, and the epic battle—the epic God—I've been waiting all my life to challenge is seducing me? Oh God, this is irony at its best."

Tae Hyun arched a pleased brow.

"You see me as a God?" he crooned gently, feathering his lips over her red-hot cheek.

When she didn't say anything, he forged on by pressing his scorching body forward. He nipped his nose with hers before leisurely moving his lips to her earlobe. Soo Jin gasped when he skillfully took her earlobe into his mouth and began to nibble on it. "What kind of God, Soo Jin?"

Sex God, she wanted to answer, but kept her mouth firmly sealed. She was afraid if she opened her mouth, nothing but appreciative whimpers would pour out. Her "Sex God" was already driving her crazy with his teasing. She refused to give him more ammunition by letting him know how much she was enjoying his advances.

Tae Hyun grinned at the tense anxiety engulfing Soo Jin. He shifted his lips from her ear and grazed them over the corner of her trembling lips.

"I can't seduce someone who doesn't want to be seduced," he whispered, holding her gaze when their eyes locked. After appraising how much effort she was exerting into not making a sound, the seductive air he emitted thinned marginally. Perplexity troubled his once carnal eyes. "Why do you hate me so much?"

"Because you challenge my existence," Soo Jin answered at long last.

The mystification mounted in his eyes. This was the last answer he had been expecting. "What?"

Soo Jin was initially resolved on not divulging the reason to him. Nevertheless, when she felt the answer bubble in her throat, it felt too much like a burden to not release it.

"I've been conditioned to be the best, and in our world, there is only room for one legend in a generation's lifetime." She looked at him unblinkingly, feeling the heat from their yearning bodies mingle together. "There could only be one champion in our era, and I want to be that once-in-a-lifetime legend in this world. I want to be the first Lord of our society. I want the generations to come to always remember my name, and I want to be alive—even after death." Jealousy began to infuse into her eyes like a virus. "You challenge that very endeavor with your existence. Now I understand why Ji Hoon hates you so much. If you weren't alive, then he would've been the favored one. Although my return demoted him to the third ranking, the simple truth is that this only means that I am just one rank above him—this only means that I'm still second to you." She swallowed convulsively, physically choking down her jealousy. "I hate that—I hate *you*. I hate that you were never trained to be in this layer, yet you hold so much power over everyone. I hate that you're arrogant, and I hate that you have every right to be because you are truly legendary." She appraised him critically. "But what I hate most is that it is your throne to lose. On this stage, I'm merely a contender for the throne—the one fighting for something that has already been primed and ready for you."

"You can have this world," he told her without hesitation. "I don't want the throne."

"And *this* is why I despise you the most," she gritted through her teeth. Fury vibrated in her words. "How dare you throw the throne away like it's yesterday's trash? How dare you belittle something that I've worked my entire life for?"

"Because I want something else more," he told her desperately, genuinely. "I do not want to fight you for it."

"*I* want to fight you for it," she emphasized hatefully. She could feel her heart race in anticipation. "This throne means nothing to me if I don't fight you for it. It means nothing if you simply hand it over to me. I did not train my entire life to win a throne by default. I trained my entire life to conquer another God for it."

He smiled sadly. It was evident that her words were cutting into him like a knife. "You will only be satisfied if you fight me to the death?"

"Yes."

Albeit the anguish in his eyes was undeniable, the enduring love in his warm stare was also difficult to overlook. It was clear to Soo Jin that Tae Hyun could never hate her for anything she wanted to do. This concept flabbergasted her. Her own brother and ex-boyfriend would never be as forgiving. Any other Underworld King would not be as forgiving, and yet, here Kwon Tae Hyun was: staring at her like she was the best thing to ever happen to him. It was disconcerting to say the least.

"What is it about Yoori that has you so hooked?"

The words came out faster than she could have controlled them. She hated Yoori, despised any given moment where she had to be reminded of the girl's existence. Regardless of her hatred, she was fascinated that a simple girl like Choi Yoori could capture the King of Serpent's heart to this degree. He was not only willing to give up his throne for her, but he was also willing to risk his life for her. What was so special about this girl?

Tae Hyun lifted his hand up and began to stroke her face with a light caress. His eyes filled with warmth at the reminder of the love of his life.

"She saved my life," he answered quietly.

Soo Jin laughed at the silly answer. "Oh, you mean at the warehouse with Ji Hoon?"

He shook his head, not in the least bit offended by her laughter. "That's not what I mean."

Soo Jin went quiet as he went on, his eyes growing lost in a reverie.

"Before I met Yoori, I was living a very . . . numb life. I had all the money in the world, I had people who respected me—feared me, I had people ready and willing to bend to my every will, I had women throwing themselves at me, and on top of all of this, I was the King of this Underworld—the one every powerful entity the world was ready to kneel before." He drew in a slow breath. "But there was something about that life that began to bore me. I was becoming more and more numb to everything. I started to realize that I was living too much of a solitary life. People constantly surrounded me, but I always felt alone. That's why I moved out of the Serpents' estate. I couldn't handle sitting in my enormous living room alone, I couldn't handle staring at the fireplace alone, and I couldn't handle being in the big mansion alone. Everything about my estate reminded me of how alone I was—how alone I would always be." He smiled to himself. "I thought things would change when I moved into my own apartment. To my disappointment, life still felt the same. I was still going through the motions, still watching the seconds pass me by. My life no longer felt meaningful. I no longer felt—"

"Alive," Soo Jin mindlessly finished for him.

What he described felt too hauntingly familiar to her.

His bittersweet smile was confirmation that she used the right term. "That was when I realized that this was the debt all 'Gods' must pay. The longer you live your life being above human, the more you become numb to the simple human emotions that make life—*life*. I had a deteriorating soul, and all I had left was my ruthlessness and greed. The only love in my life was power. That was all I woke up for. It was all I lived for."

The melancholic hue in his eyes gradually dissipated. Happiness began to illume in his once dim gaze.

"Then Choi Yoori came and changed everything. Like a fallen angel, she turned my world upside down. In the beginning, she amused me because there was something about her feisty personality that intrigued me. It was fascinating how she always managed to put me in my place—how I always seem to let her. Not long after, she started to make me happy—really happy. She's such a strange and dorky girl, but everything she does has me eating from the palms of her hands. I'd never felt that way about any other woman." He let out a reminiscent sigh. "Then I started to realize that I was smiling more as I went to sleep, smiling more as I woke up, and smiling more because of her simple existence. It wasn't until I brought her to the lake house that I realized how I had changed. It wasn't until I kissed her that night that I truly felt human again."

"You felt alive again," Soo Jin provided instinctively. It was terrifying how much she related to what he was saying.

He smiled, his eyes holding hers.

Seconds later, with no preface to what he was about to do, he snaked an arm around her hip and melded their bodies close together. His eyes searched hers with yearning.

"I can't wait anymore," he told her gently, gazing at her like she was a gift he waited his whole life to unwrap.

The last of his control deteriorated as he held her to him. She could feel the tensing of his muscles and the growing heat from his body. He was ready to take her, to make her his.

Pressing his forehead against hers, Tae Hyun managed to exert one last shred of control before it began to dwindle from him.

"I won't be a mistake on your part." Conviction pulsated in his declaration. "I won't force you to do anything you don't want to do. I won't force myself on you." His gaze never wavered from hers as he spoke, and neither did Soo Jin's. She was mesmerized by him and wanted everything he could offer her. She no longer wanted to be logical. Not right now, not when she wanted him this much.

"So right here, right now, I'm giving you your chance," he said with effort, every part of his body telling her that he didn't want to let her go. "Tell me you don't want this. Tell me to leave you. Tell me you don't want me—that you never want to be with me, and I'll walk away. I will never bring you to my bed, I will never touch you, and I will never chase after you again. Just say the words. Say it and I'll go."

Soo Jin parted her lips to vocalize those damning words. Her mouth was open, but none of those words came out. Instead, she wrapped her arms around his neck and did something she knew she would regret: she kissed him.

She pressed her lips against his and felt the world recede around her. No circumstances mattered but her kiss with him. No problem was big enough that they couldn't overcome. Nothing else mattered but this perfect moment.

She kissed her denial into his gorgeous lips, kissed her heart into his, and kissed what was left of her soul into his.

"I love you."

Her words caused every muscle and nerve in Tae Hyun's body to freeze up. He pulled his lips from hers. Staring at her with shell-shocked eyes, a myriad of pain, love, and desperation clutched him while he touched her face. His eyes lit up with hope as he tried to decipher whether she actually said those three words. When he concluded that she did voice those beautiful words, the hope and joy in his eyes grew brighter.

"Yoori . . ." he whispered.

The world stopped for Soo Jin.

Akin to being splashed with ice-cold water, Soo Jin felt her logicality return. An ache unlike anything she had ever experienced sliced into her heart, slaughtering any trace of ecstasy she felt seconds prior. Devastated, she pulled away from him and physically trembled from the onslaught of sorrow that consumed her.

Yoori.

He was calling her Yoori.

"I'll never love Soo Jin . . ."

His previous words echoed in her mind, stabbing into her like scalding knives. An excruciating truth hit her.

He would *never* love her. He would never love Soo Jin.

It would always be Yoori. It would *only* ever be Yoori.

"Get off me."

Panic enflamed his eyes. He could see that she was putting her walls up again. He knew that this time, if he did not stop her in time, it would be a hundred times harder to break those walls down.

"Yoori," he pleaded. "Please don't leave—"

"Get off me! Get off me!" she bellowed, using all her strength to push him off the bed. Adrenaline and torment pumped through her as she jumped off the mattress, grabbed his car keys, and bolted for the door. Her bare feet ran across the surface of the glass stairs with unmatched speed.

"Yoori!" Tae Hyun shouted, desperately chasing after her.

"Stop calling me that!" she screamed over her shoulder, running so fast that Tae Hyun was unable to catch up. She threw herself into his car and locked it before he was able to open the door. Soo Jin backed out of the driveway while Tae Hyun urgently pounded on the window. As he pleaded for her to stay, she put the car on drive and without another wasted second, drove off into the night.

"Yoori!"

She heard Tae Hyun scream for her, but she did not turn back. She did not so much as look at the rearview mirror because she knew she would see him running after her—or more precisely, running after Yoori. Determined to not allow him to catch up, she floored the gas pedal, and just like that, Soo Jin was gone. She was off in her own world of agony, off in her own world of misery.

Yoori, she thought with immense anguish.

She could not stop thinking about Yoori and Tae Hyun as she drove back home. She could not stop the heartache as she relived her misery.

All he would ever see is Yoori . . .

"Ahhhhhhhh!" she screamed hours later in her living room, destroying everything in sight. An uncontrollable firestorm raged through her, blinding her rationale and rendering her unable to do anything but destroy everything in her path.

Unfortunately for Soo Jin, every decimated object acted as reinforcement to a reality she could no longer deny.

"I love you . . ."

She couldn't deny it any longer.

Yoori and her . . .

Yoori and—*Oh God, no!*

Boom!

Lamps were strewn across the room, sofas were thrown upside down, and chairs were broken apart. Anything and everything that stood in her way was destroyed, yet she felt no satisfaction. She breathed unevenly in the darkness, briefly quelling the monster inside her. As she ran her fingers through her hair, she recalled something that had yet to be destroyed—something that needed to be destroyed.

Her eyes fixated on the hall with a feral light. Resolute on destroying this item, she stormed into her dark bedroom, extracted the black hoodie from the closet drawer, and ran back outside.

No more temptation . . .

Before she could process her decision, she let out another grating scream and hurled the hoodie in the fire.

Whoosh!

The moment the open flame devoured the black fabric, she felt her heart and soul rip apart. Unable to withstand the mind-numbing pain, she collapsed onto her knees and watched the fabric that once held her memories, her tears, and her dreams burn.

She breathed quietly, clenching and unclenching her injured knuckles. They bled from the damage she inflicted onto her estate. As Tae Hyun's jacket burned before her eyes, all she could think about was reaching her hand into the fire. She was tempted to grab hold of the hoodie so she could save it—so she could save her dreams. But she held still, forcing herself to fight the temptation that destroyed Gods, the temptation that enticed her to reach her hand into the fire, the temptation to finally become human and *live* again.

She allowed Tae Hyun's hoodie to burn to ashes, for she had made her final decision. There would be no more temptations for her. There would be no more weakness. There would be no more tempting of the Gods.

There would be no more Kwon Tae Hyun.

"Welcome, Paris . . . to my Underworld."

19: The Temptation of Gods

Numb.

Numbness was all Soo Jin felt for the days following her altercation with Tae Hyun.

She felt numb, but the best part was that she didn't feel the pain. Just like a God, her human emotions were draining out of her and fading from existence.

Grateful for this small mercy (and desperate for some private time to herself), she decided to brave the unforgiving weather and explore the world outside. She smiled to herself as she walked in silence, thinking of the day when she would never feel anything again. She imagined how great that day would be because it would mean that she was finally invincible, that she was finally a God amongst humans.

What a liberating day that would be.

Snow crunched beneath her black boots as she strolled through the snow-covered streets. With her long black trench coat swaying in the wind, Soo Jin did as every Underworld soldier once did whenever they were about to go to war. Twenty-four hours before her life changed, she decided to journey into the world outside her estate to compartmentalize her emotions. She wanted to clear her thoughts and prepare herself for the war to come.

She walked through bustling, congested sidewalks before taking a lesser-used path into a park that was lined with balding winter trees. Although the journey was aimless at best, it offered a serenity that she would have never been able to find at her estate. The unbearable frigid weather demanded that people stayed indoors, thereby meaning that she was gifted with the opportunity to enjoy the world alone.

Her exploration around her beloved city was simply an aimless walk . . . until everything started to look all too familiar to her eyes.

Soo Jin came to a brief pause and surveyed the landscape ahead of her.

How she managed to saunter into the familiar playground and lock her eyes with a swing that was swaying listlessly, she didn't know. How she found herself walking through a row of benches that she once sat on, she wasn't sure.

How she was walking on the familiar trail that breathed dreamlike memories into her, she wasn't certain. All she knew was that it took all her strength to not look at the swings that Yoori once sat on with her boyfriend. It took all her will to not stare at the bench where Yoori stole a kiss from her boyfriend, and it took every ounce of her control to not recall how Yoori was given a piggyback ride by her boyfriend on this very trail.

Soo Jin continued to navigate through the cold, windy night.

She did not miss the trail of footsteps that marked itself into the snow, leading her down a path that was all too memorable to her.

Voices from a distant past infiltrated her reality, and she wondered if she could survive them . . .

"Tae Hyun, this better be good." She ducked her head when she was near a tree branch. "Where are we going?"

"Choi Yoori, can you exercise a little patience?" Tae Hyun whispered before picking up speed. There was no doubt he was excited. "What fun would it be to tell you now?"

A disturbing paranoia invaded her mind when he jumped over a log. "Oh my God, you're not going to kill me for punishing you this week, are you? Is that what you meant by taking my breath away?"

Tae Hyun snorted at her unreasonable question. "Yes. I spent the entire week being obedient, nearly breaking my back to give you your stupid piggyback rides to throw it all away by killing you at the end of the week."

She frowned. "Your sarcasm is not appreciated."

"Nor is your stubborn heart," he whispered, stepping onto broken tree branches.

"And what do you mean nearly breaking your back?" she asked, not hearing what he just whispered. "Are you insinuating that I'm fat?" Before even giving him a chance to answer, Yoori already said, "For your information, I'm not fat. I'm deliciously plump."

"I swear, I'm going to spank some sense into that deliciously plump little butt of yours if you don't stop assuming that I think you're fat."

He held on to her more tightly just when he jumped over a pair of twin bushes.

She gaped. "You wouldn't dare spank me!"

"Dare me to do it. I dare you."

"How dare you dare me to dare you? What kinda assistant are you?"

A smug look embellished his face. "One who, at the stroke of midnight, will turn back into your boss."

Yoori laughed at his clever response. She played along. "Oooh, you're just a modern day fairytale pumpkin, aren't you?"

"A deliciously plump pumpkin," Tae Hyun *corrected lightheartedly. "You got that, my deliciously plump Cinderella?"*

"I prefer Princess," Yoori mischievously corrected . . .

The voices stopped when she entered the secret garden to which Yoori's boyfriend once took her. The exquisiteness of the garden caressed her eyes.

The sight was still so breathtaking.

Blue Christmas lights still embellished every corner of the garden and the Winter Wonderland here glowed just as exquisitely as the night it was first introduced to her. To her pleasant surprise, the white bridge had also been rebuilt during her absence. The bridge hovered above the frozen lake, looking so magical that it caused Soo Jin's heart to skip a beat.

Lost in a dreamlike stupor, she walked onto the bridge, her boots stepping in the snow that adorned the foundation. Her fingers moved over the blue icicle lights that embroidered the bridge, and instinctively, she sat down with her legs suspended off the edge.

An icy breeze tousled her hair about, keeping her company as she quietly stared at the frozen lake. The splendor of the blue decorative lights and the calm snow brought her peace. A multitude of thoughts rushed to get through her mind, creating something alike to a traffic jam. Nothing but jumbled sounds came out from her mind. For this, Soo Jin was relieved because she no longer wanted to be consumed with any thoughts. All she wanted was to be a soul with no emotions—a soul that was better than human. All she wanted was to be a God.

Then, as the tranquility lingered around her, a sound ruptured the silence. *Creak.*

Soo Jin averted her attention to the sound. When she saw who had joined her, she froze in her seat.

A handsome face stared back at her, nearly taking her breath away as he stood in the middle of the falling snow.

Kwon Tae Hyun.

The images of the swing swaying back and forth, the imprint of a body laying across the bench, and the footprints in the snow told her that he was here before her—that he came here long before she did.

She smirked to herself.

Of course the irony of her life would lead him here.

She paused briefly.

Was it irony, or did she subconsciously come here because she knew he would be here? There was no time to get her question answered, as Tae Hyun chose that moment to sit down beside her.

"By the way," he uttered after situating himself in the seat, "I'm not stalking you. I've been here for a while."

Soo Jin nodded, aware that it was a coincidence that they wound up here. She breathed peacefully, too numb to exert any open hatred for him. She no longer felt the need to push him away because she had already made a resolution to herself—she had already promised herself that she would never let him affect her again. Considering that their battle was a mere day away, she was certain she could keep her promise to herself.

"*I love you.*"

The words that she said to him replayed in her mind. It was three simple but powerful words that made her grasp the reality of her situation and made her realize what a fool she had been. Looking back, Soo Jin saw now how careless she was to continuously allow Kwon Tae Hyun to come near her, to continuously allow him to tempt her. She knew all along that he was her epic match. He was the only man who could sway her conviction and the only man who could be her downfall. It was unquestionably reckless of Soo Jin to give him so much power over her, but the mistakes of her past were no longer relevant because she had already made her decision. After she voiced those three words, an inescapable truth presided over her. It was a cold, hard truth that she could no longer avoid. There was nothing more to say, nothing more to prove. She not only knew the truth about herself, but she also knew who she really was. In addition to that, she was also aware of what she had to do twenty-four hours from now. Her decision was set, and nothing could change her mind.

Perhaps it was for poetic reasons, or maybe it was because being around him always had a warming effect on her, but she no longer had a problem with being in his presence. She welcomed his company as they sat there, both quiet, with their legs hanging listlessly off the bridge.

Silence was all that accompanied them until she said, "Being here . . . is really strange for me."

He was quiet for a longer moment before saying, "I've missed you."

Right to the point—that was always Kwon Tae Hyun's style.

Something leapt in her numb heart. She wasn't sure if it was real or if it was purely her imagination. It astounded her that after days of numbness, all it took was a simple statement from him to rouse her senses back to life.

"I need you," he went on, pouring his heart out to her. Anguish pulsed in his quiet voice. His cold hand intertwined with hers. The flash of cold from the touch was gradually replaced with warmth. As he interlaced their fingers together, she finally took her eyes off the lake.

Soo Jin was quiet, attentive as her emotionless face appraised his wounded one. There were dark circles under his eyes that indicated that he had not gotten enough—if any—sleep. He looked pale, like he had the blood drained out of him. He looked like he had lost weight, and most importantly, he looked like he was in tremendous pain. Pity overcame Soo Jin as she examined his current state. She wondered why it was taking so long for him to acknowledge how much better it was to be a God rather than a human in this world.

"I can't be without you any longer," he whispered, tucking her loose bangs behind her ear. He stared into her eyes, his warmth thawing the ice that used to inhabit her gaze. He no longer looked like a King that all men feared. He simply looked like a brokenhearted man that no man ever wanted to be. "Tell me what I need to do, and I'll do it. Just come back to me."

The smart decision would have been to maintain her silence. The strategic choice would have been to walk away right then and there. In spite of all these strategic choices, she no longer felt it was necessary to be reticent with him. They were already at the edge of the end; she might as well put it all out onto the table. What was the harm when they were only hours away from their war?

"Do you remember one of the last things you said to Yoori?" she prompted at long last, staring deep into his eyes. She fought past the agony building up in her chest and forged on. "She said that she was supposed to be worth it, but you said that it was a lie. You told her that you loved her, but you could *never* love Soo Jin. Do you not remember saying that to her? *'I'll never love Soo Jin.'* That was what you said."

"I didn't mean it," he breathed, his voice becoming quieter than a whisper. Despair magnified in his remorseful eyes. "You know I didn't—"

"All you see is your Choi Yoori," she interrupted, shaking her head at him, "and the only person you will ever love is Choi Yoori." She hastened to finish her words when he was about to interject. "All my life, I've been told that I'm better than everyone else. I used to believe this until Yoori came along . . . until you came along. I wondered to myself how this simple girl could cast such a shadow over my life. There was nothing special about this spineless girl. She was so weak, so human, but she had enough power to steal the untouchable one's heart—to steal Kwon Tae Hyun's heart." Her eyes held his with heartbroken realization. "No matter how much I tell myself that I'm better than her, I can't help but envy her because of the love she was able to claim from you."

She exhaled past the rock that had somehow lodged itself in her throat. She did her best to maintain her steady voice, but was slowly failing.

"I know that I can't compare to your Yoori. I can't and never will compare to that innocent Princess who stole your heart. I know that this is your story with her. This is your place with her, not me. This is not my story; it has never been my story." She looked at the beautiful garden that surrounded her. "Everything here was created for Choi Yoori, not An Soo Jin."

Torment teemed in her eyes while immense heartache filled his.

"I know who I am in this relationship," she concluded as the cold chill spread around them. "I'm the one who ruined everything for you and her. I am the one who ruined the dream because I am the nightmare that comes with Choi Yoori—the reality that destroyed the dream you once lived with her." She bit her quivering lips, shivering not from the cold, but from her internal pain. "I know that she loved you, and you love her, but *I* love you too." She drew in a shuddering breath that rocked her very soul. "And I know that doesn't matter. I'll never be able to compete with her because she was the one who stole your stubborn heart, not me."

Sorrow tormented Tae Hyun's face while he listened to her words. With his hand still intertwined with hers, he held on even tighter.

"I thought that if An Soo Jin ever made her return, then I'd be able to kill her with ease because the Yoori I love—the Yoori who stole my heart—wouldn't be here anymore. I thought I would be able to kill you without a second thought, but when I looked into your eyes that night after Ju Won's party, when I held the sword against your throat, I didn't see the heartless Queen who ruined everything. All I saw was Choi Yoori staring back up at me, all I saw was Choi Yoori wearing my hoodie, and all I saw was the girl I fell in love with. All I saw was the dream girl I fell in love with."

He stared down at her with such love that it pained her to keep eye contact.

"I'm sorry," he professed softly. "I'm sorry for saying that I'll never love Soo Jin. I didn't realize then that no matter what name you go by, no matter what memories you have, you will always be the Brat who stole my heart. I'm sorry for leaving you when I should've held on tighter. I'm sorry for saying that it wasn't worth it when it's clear now that you're worth everything to me."

She shook her head, refusing to accept his words as truth. "You're just replacing her with me."

His next words caused her to freeze where she sat. It was spoken with so much heartache, so much conviction that she could no longer deny it as the truth.

"Do you think I can't see the love of my life when I look into her eyes?" he challenged, staring into her eyes as if he was gazing into her soul.

His shaking fingers stroked her face, and from that, she could feel his pain.

Her heart tightened in agony as he went on, shedding the remainder of her denial and her shield.

"*Nemo*," he called quietly, breaking through the exterior she once held with a simple pet name that had always belonged to her—the pet name that touched what was left of her soul. "Stop giving me the silent treatment. You know I hate that. Please come back to me. I know you're in there; I know that you never left. Others may see An Soo Jin and Choi Yoori as two different people, but I know that the two of you are the same. An Soo Jin has always been Choi Yoori, and Choi Yoori has always been An Soo Jin. There has never been a difference, and there will never be a difference. No matter what name you go by, my love for you will never change."

He bit his lips, stroking her face as he revealed his heart and soul to her. It easily shined through the love in his eyes, through the touch that promised her his unconditional love.

"Please come back to me, Brat. I've been looking for you, but I can't find you if you don't come out. Please stop hiding, stop being in denial, and come back to me."

" . . . You said to make it easier for us and leave," she finally whispered, tears clouding her eyes. "So I made it easier, and I left."

"Yoori," Tae Hyun breathed out, tears misting his own eyes after finally hearing her voice—after finally hearing Yoori's voice.

Yoori's lips quivered while snow tumbled all around them. The despondency she felt was becoming unbearable.

"I made it easier, and I left, and I tried not to come back, just like you told me." The tears veiled over her eyes as she stared into his saddened ones. "I made it easier for us, so why are you making this harder?"

"Because I love you," he said simply, sending ripples of anguish through her at the sincerity of his beautiful words. She believed every single word he said. She knew he meant it with all his heart, which was why it was so difficult for her to listen to it.

She shook from where she sat, realizing now that Tae Hyun had always known that she was there. Even when she herself was in denial, he knew that even though An Soo Jin had regained her memories, Choi Yoori never left. She was just lost—lost in a world of pain, denial, and misery of her own.

"I know that the only reason why you allowed your memories to come back was because you wanted to give me a chance to get my revenge. The only reason why you were in denial, why you fought so hard for me to hate you is because going to war in this world is the only way for both of us to live—at least for the time being."

"We're not meant to be," she told him agonizingly, finding it hard to breathe. No one said coming to terms with your reality would be easy, but she just wished it wasn't so excruciating. "The Yoori you love died that night. Her innocence died that night. I wish she hadn't because I was content as that Yoori. Even with amnesia, a part of me knew what was happening, but I was stubborn. I was in denial because I didn't want to remember anything. Even when the shadows of my past started coming back, I still didn't want to accept the truth because I wanted to keep you—I wanted to be with you. I knew that the heartless Soo Jin would never deserve Kwon Tae Hyun, but Yoori did. She deserved you. You belong to her and only her."

She smirked to herself as the snow fell heavily around them.

"This is why I hate it every time you say her name because the Choi Yoori you met was merely a dream. *This* Choi Yoori is the one who killed countless people, *this* Choi Yoori is the one people kneel before in fear, *this* is the Choi Yoori who is the nightmare of the dream. I can't compete with the Yoori you fell in love with, Tae Hyun. I'm too tainted. I am far from the innocent girl you met at the diner."

"I love you," Tae Hyun repeated, agony throbbing in every corner of his voice. "I don't care about your past, I don't care about your demons, and I don't care what anyone says. My life before you was a nightmare, but you had always been the dream. You were the dream when I first met you at the diner, you were the dream when I took you to the lake house, and you're a dream right now. I don't care about anything else. You have and will always be the only one who matters to me."

Tears dripped from Yoori's eyes while she shook her head. She felt every mind-numbing torture from his sweet and genuine words.

"I'm not that naïve girl anymore. I know that a relationship like ours will never last in this world. Nothing but misery and pain awaits us if we continue to go down this road." She inhaled sharply before finally adding, "I don't want to be like your mother."

She pressed her hands into her stomach to mitigate the ache coursing through her. While doing so, she despondently recalled her last encounter with Tae Hyun's mother.

"When I found her that night, I was ready to kill her. Yet, when I saw her in the state she was in, not only did I not kill her, I actually found myself feeling sorry for her. It astounded me as to how she ended up in that state. I didn't understand why she couldn't move on after her husband's death, why she allowed herself to fall in love with someone in this world, and why someone else's life—someone who wasn't even related to her by blood— meant so much to her." She laughed bitterly, nearly choking on her own tears. "She told me that one day, if I choose to accept the gift and the curse, then I would understand it. I would understand why she couldn't live anymore and why she wanted to kill herself. She said I would understand what it meant to love someone more than life itself."

Yoori's eyes grew resolute. Innocence no longer teemed in her gaze.

"I don't want to be like your mother. I don't want to die like her, and I don't want to fall in love with someone to such a degree where if they died, I'd kill myself too. I don't want that. I don't want any of that. I can't handle that much pain. I don't want to be human anymore."

"Yoori, don't do this," Tae Hyun pleaded again, his chest rising and falling with dread. He knew what she was getting ready to do.

"I'm sorry that you haven't realized it by now . . . how hopeless it is," she began, staring into his eyes now as a numb Choi Yoori, "but I pray that you will soon because in twenty-four hours' time, I'm killing you and eradicating any trace of my human side. After that, I'll finally be a God. I will never be tempted with the desire to feel alive again because you'll be gone, and I will be an immortal in this world."

"So this is what you want?" Tae Hyun asked, staring at her with tears glistening in his eyes. "For us to fight each other for the throne? For us to fight each other to the death?"

"Would that not be better than falling in love completely, than giving our hearts to each other completely, and risking someone else take one of us away from the other? You and I both know that we're held to a different standard in this world. The only reason why people supported my relationship with Ji Hoon was because his ruthlessness made me a God. But you and I, our love would only make each other humans." Her eyes grew firm. "You know what they do to fallen Gods in this world."

Yoori pressed a pained hand on his chest, allowing the last of her tears to dry. Her eyes implored his to see reason.

"If you love me, then you'll fight me with everything that you have tomorrow. Give me the war I've been waiting for, give me the battle that will immortalize my name in this world, and just fight me as the Gods we were always meant to be. *This* is our destiny. We were never meant to be humans together. The pain that awaits us is too great, and I'm not strong enough to be human with you. You told me it wasn't going to be easy, and to be frank, I don't think it's worth it anymore."

"Yoori," he whispered, his heart breaking at the resolution in her words.

"You're not worth it, Tae Hyun," Yoori told him with finality. She stood up, never allowing her cold eyes to leave his aggrieved ones. Her tears had dried up and her decision was set. "You were never worth it, and you will never be worth it. And come tomorrow, I'll show you exactly how worthless you are to me."

With that said, she left him, knowing that she had not only ripped out the heart of the love of her life, but also that in twenty-four hours' time, she would be in the battle of her life.

"There will be no more temptation," she whispered to herself as she prepared for the end. "It is no longer worth it, and it will never be worth it."

251

"Thank you for staying despite all the hardships I've caused you."

20: The Battle of Gods

In the Underworld, there were few events that would unite the leaders of the powerful and enigmatic society together. The Royals of the Underworld, as busy and powerful as they were, rarely took a day off with the exception of those few special events that required their attendance. They would only come out for three things: to congregate with other powerful associates, to celebrate a revered crime lord's birthday, or to witness a historical event that was about to take place.

It was a rare occasion for the elites of the Underworld to spare time from their busy schedules, but it was an even rarer occasion for the *entire* Underworld populace—the elite of elites and their soldiers—to assemble in one venue. There was always the matter of confidentiality to protect everyone involved. The last thing the secretive society wanted to do was attract the attention of the police. Albeit they did not harbor fear for the authorities (why should they when they had the power to sway the flow of the media and bend the law as they wished?), any damage control took time and effort, and these were two things the Underworld Royals rarely enjoyed giving away.

Indeed, the Underworld society rarely took the day off, but in the case of the historic battle between a celebrated King and a revered Queen, no one in the Korean Underworld—as well as those from the Western and neighboring Eastern Underworlds—wanted to miss this once-in-a-lifetime event.

Confidentiality no longer mattered to them as they took their seats inside the various high-rise buildings of Seoul. They filled every office in the business district with murmurs of excitement and anticipation. Every floor possessed a 130-inch theater screen TV of its own. Similar to a security footage, there were approximately twenty live streams at once. The stage for this epic battle was big, risky for everyone in attendance, and very expensive. Regardless, it was all worth it because this was *the* fight to remember: two

Gods, two former lovers, two contenders for the throne, and one legend to officially rule over as the first true Lord of the Underworld.

No one was missing this momentous occasion.

Standing in the epicenter of the business district, right on the snow-covered roof of one of the more prominent skyscrapers in the city, the eyes of the Underworld populace were on two individuals as they stood frozen on the roof.

All around the two contenders, the city night speckled with life, illuminating in beauty and grandeur as if bowing down to their presence. Whereas the buildings surrounding them hummed with an air of excitement, the atmosphere on the roof was grim, ominous.

An unforgiving chill moved through the air, swimming over the guns behind their backs and coursing over the swords in each of their hands. As the Underworld populace convened around them, watching like spectators before a sporting event, the King and Queen remained stoic and unmoving. Had it not been for the warm breath that escaped from their lips, no one would know that they were alive.

Dressed in a sleeveless black blouse, jeans, and boots, Yoori's watchful eyes were buried on Tae Hyun. Her gaze roamed over his black dress shirt and dark pants. He had his sleeves rolled up to his forearms, revealing his watch and bringing attention to the sword in his hand. Like Yoori, his eyes were blank and undecipherable of emotion.

He wasn't permitting her to read his thoughts, just as she wasn't allowing him to read hers.

Yoori let out a preparatory breath. It was clear to her that they were both ready to have the fight of their lives.

After she left him at the park, Yoori spent the next twenty-four hours awake, playing out the possible scenarios of what would transpire tonight while concurrently assuring herself that she was doing the right thing.

Nothing matters anymore, she assured herself as she continued to gaze blankly at him, refusing to let her emotions surface. Her heart galloped fiercely as though preparing to take its last beat. She would do what she had to tonight, and it would all be over before she knew it. *It will all end soon.*

"Kwon Tae Hyun," Ju Won's voice suddenly materialized in the night, filtering out of the speakers of a red phone lying on the snow-dusted rooftop. "An Soo Jin."

Yoori could ascertain by the fluctuation of his voice that he was extremely excited. He had trained her for this moment; he had trained her to rival a great King, and there was no greater King than Kwon Tae Hyun.

"We're typically fans of subtleties. We don't like to make a scene. However, the centuries can come and go and we'll likely never hear a story like yours again; we'll probably never see a fight as grand as this again. For such a momentous event, subtleties and bylaws are simply not suitable. As a society, we have decided to forge this stage for you. There are security cameras situated upon every possible angle of the building, allotting us the opportunity to be there with you as you make history. This entire building—from its roof to the ground floor—is your fighting arena. Use it as you please. Use anything within it as you wish, and do not worry about the damages—your epic battle will hold no bars."

A sadistic smile was projected into his voice when he added his next words.

"Given that we have such powerful Gods on stage—and because we know you will be able to withstand anything thrown your way—we decided to add a challenge to the battle. In the buildings surrounding you are some of the Underworld's best snipers. They will join in on your fight and will be firing at both of you without prejudice. If you can figure out a way around it, you are free to utilize their involvement as another form of defense."

A smirk played on the edge of Yoori's mouth. Ju Won was suggesting that they could use each other as shields against the snipers. Of course the old bastard would encourage something so callous.

"With that said," the eldest Advisor concluded, eager to enjoy the show with the rest of the Underworld, "good luck to both of you." There was a brief pause before he wrapped up the call. "And please remember, if you go easy on one another, we will know. We're not interested in being ruled over by two Gods in love. We want one ruthless Lord who will lead as a powerful example in our world. Please fight as you would anyone else and for the one who survives, we all look forward to serving you. Thank you and once again, good luck."

A tense silence presided over the rooftop after Ju Won disconnected the call.

Officially alone, Yoori and Tae Hyun stood like Royals underneath the heavens while towering over the unsuspecting city beneath them.

Once he determined that no one in the Underworld could hear their conversation, Tae Hyun finally parted his lips. "Is this the moment you've been waiting for?"

His face maintained an expression of neutrality. Despite his undecipherable demeanor, it was apparent to Yoori that he hadn't slept since their last encounter. She could not read his face, but she understood his motivations. The only reason why he was here, ready and willing to fight her, was because she wanted him to.

"Yes," she answered coolly. She secretly hoped the indifference in her tone would encourage him to fight with everything he had. She did not plan to go easy on him. With the Underworld watching their every move, she couldn't go easy on him even if she wanted to. "Fighting under the heavens, amongst the Gods. This was exactly how I imagined it."

As a bitter smile bloomed across Tae Hyun's lips, a male heir from the 1st layer stepped onto the rooftop of the building across from theirs. The teenager held a flare gun in his hand, a traditional Underworld tool used to commence historic battles between the Gods.

"We'd better make your dreams come true then," Tae Hyun whispered softly, stoically.

"Fight me with all you have, King of Serpents," she reminded him gravely.

At the neighboring building, the heir raised his arm and pointed the flare gun up to the sky.

"As you wish," Tae Hyun conceded as fresh snow cascaded down from the heavens, "Queen of the Underworld."

Boom!

The red flare shot up into the canvas of the dark sky like a shooting star and exploded in a sea of fire. The fiery blaze soared through the descending snow, signifying the start of a battle unlike any other.

As the red flare disappeared into the night, a myriad of bittersweet, happy, and heavenly memories were placed aside as the war between the former lovers began.

Yoori did not waste another second.

Just as a sniper bullet flew past her ear, she gripped the hilt of her sword and charged at Tae Hyun.

Swish!

Her sword swung at an unstoppable velocity towards his throat, missing by a mere centimeter when he swiftly snapped his head back. Yoori wielded the sword again, intent on taking another swing at his neck. She was sidetracked when another round of bullets came at them.

Bang! Bang! Bang!

As they maneuvered their bodies around the flying bullets, Yoori took a swing for the top of Tae Hyun's head. The sound of metal hitting metal reverberated in the air when Tae Hyun fended off her sword with his own. Undeterred, she continued to charge at Tae Hyun. Bullet after bullet chased them as Tae Hyun and Yoori jumped and ran over the roof, wielding their swords with such strength that sparks flew into the air. Although he was exchanging blows with her, she could feel him holding back. He did not want to hurt her; he did not want to kill her.

An avalanche of rage engulfed her at the realization.

"You can do better than this!" Yoori roared over the next set of bullets that came at them. One nearly submerged itself into her shoulder while another almost went into Tae Hyun's neck. "You can fight better than this!"

Frustrated that the sword fight did not offer her the results she wanted, Yoori let out a loud grunt and kicked him across the jaw. She followed that attack by jumping with both legs in the air and sinking her boots into his stomach. The wind was knocked out of Tae Hyun, causing him to tumble backwards with a string of bullets chasing after his body.

Bang! Bang! Bang!

"Get up!" Yoori shouted, reflexively fending off the bullets with her sword. "If you love me like you say you do, then you'll fight back!" She glared at him with a mixture of hatred and disgust. Her next stream of words thundered over the ice-cold wind. "If you really love me, you'll give me this battle!"

Her angry words acted as a splash of cold water on Tae Hyun. Struck by the fury in her voice, something snapped within him. Despite his preference to go easy on her, he also knew that he could show her no mercy tonight. The conflicted look faded from his eyes. In its place came stern resolution. If Yoori and the rest of his society wanted a battle of the Gods, then he would give it to them.

"Ugh!"

Yoori was in the process of kneeing Tae Hyun across the face when he suddenly swept his leg on the snow-covered roof. As a flurry of snow flew upward, he stole the ground from under her feet and proceeded to kick her hard in the stomach. Akin to being hit by a semi-truck, Yoori shot across the roof, soaring directly into the door that led to the stairwell.

Bam!

A pained gasp tore from her chest when she slammed against the door, jarring it open with a loud crash.

"That's more like it," she approved with an agonized pant.

Her entire body went on full alert once she saw him advance towards the stairwell landing. Satisfied that he was finally playing his part, she gripped her sword. Now that the King of Serpents had joined the battle, it was time for the Queen to play her part as well.

At the same moment Tae Hyun ran towards her, she swung the sword at full force and sliced the blade through his left arm.

"Auugh!"

The razor sharp blade cut through his shirt, grazed his flesh, and claimed his blood.

Tae Hyun clutched his wounded arm and fell back against the wall. Warm blood oozed from his arm, profusely dripping onto the quiet stairwell. He took in a sharp breath and peered up. When he sighted a security camera in the stairwell, a hardened mask encased his face. Pushing himself off the wall, he executed a spin kick on Yoori just as she moved closer to him.

Blindsided from the attack, Yoori staggered back, slamming against the railing before she fell down the flight of stairs. Dark stars exploded in her field of vision as she crashed hard onto the next landing.

"Ugh."

Blood poured from Yoori's moaning mouth as she tried to move. She scarcely moved an inch before an inundation of pain coursed through her, nearly knocking her unconscious with its manifestation. Determined to fight through this, Yoori used all her might to lift herself up. While doing so, it felt like every nerve within her was etched with knives. It was excruciating to breathe, let alone move.

Bang! Bang! Bang!

Yoori barely had time to take another painful breath when the large windows to the stairwell shattered one after another, paving way for an avalanche of bullets. The once quiet stairwell vibrated with the thunderous entrance of the sniper bullets. The bullets stampeded into the stairwell, striking against the railings, puncturing walls, and hammering into the ground.

Yoori and Tae Hyun were not spared from the destruction.

"Ahh!"

"Ahh!

Simultaneous screams emitted from them after the bullets grazed over the top of his shoulder and skimmed over her left leg.

"You've dreamed of this moment?" he asked, looking down at her from the upper landing in disbelief.

The barrage of bullets slowed for a moment before ceasing completely. The only sounds that could be heard in the stairwell were Tae Hyun and Yoori's labored breathing.

Yoori could hardly keep her eyes open. The throbbing within her body was killing her and her ears were ringing from the deluge of bullets. She only regained her bearings when she eyed the security camera. A constant red blink came from the camera hanging over the stairwell, indicating that the Underworld was still watching them. She pushed back the last of her pain and rallied together all the strength she had left. She refused to be viewed as a weak human in front of the Underworld. She was raised to be better than this, to be stronger than all of this.

She gripped the railing of the stairs and pulled herself up. She saw Tae Hyun stagger down the stairs, getting closer to her with every step. He was not paying attention to her, but tending to both the wound from her sword and his new bullet wound. Using his moment of distraction as her opportunity, she jumped in the air and swung across the open space of the stairwell. She used the momentum of her jump to kick Tae Hyun right across the face. Coagulated blood flew from his mouth at the attack.

"Yes," she answered, jumping back onto the stairs, "this entire moment is all that I've dreamed of—all that I've lived for."

Tae Hyun fell forward, his entire body smashing over the concrete stairs several times with bone crushing echoes. He was barely moving when he crashed onto the next landing. Tae Hyun slowly opened his eyes and looked at the second camera in the bloodstained stairwell. A flood of energy poured into him after catching sight of it. As Yoori jumped down to complete her assault, he rocketed up and kicked her in the chest. A loud thud poured into the stairwell when his foot connected with her chest. The force of the impact was so strong that it sent Yoori crashing through the door by the landing. At the same instant, another stampede of bullets entered the stairwell, missing Yoori as she flew into an empty office floor and nipped off pieces of Tae Hyun's shirt as he ran in after her.

Unlike the anarchy in the stairwell, the dark office floor they stumbled into was utterly peaceful. The change in environment was such a breath of relief that for a suspended moment, Tae Hyun and Yoori put fighting one another on the backburner. While Yoori laid on the floor, chest rising and falling in agony, Tae Hyun took a seat against the wall, shaking while clutching his wounded arm.

Their moment of peace was short-lived when a flood of bullets pierced through the enormous windows of the office floor.

Bang! Bang! Bang!

Tae Hyun let out a curse of fury, leapt away from the wall, and dove behind a desk in the center of the room. At the same second, Yoori propelled from the floor and lunged behind the same table as Tae Hyun. They sat close to one another, catching their breaths as a mass of bullets flew over them like a stream of arrows. When they strategically peered over the table to assess where the shots were coming from, they saw two sniper rifles sitting on the office table, illuming under the moonlight like an offering to the Gods. It did not take Yoori long to deduce that these rifles were a gift from Ju Won—they were to either use the rifles to combat with the snipers, or with one another.

"Motherfuckers," Tae Hyun seethed, pissed that he was being shot at while he was trying to concentrate on fighting.

"Pieces of shit," Yoori muttered, furious that her leg hurt like hell from the bullet that had grazed it.

She signed up to fight with a fellow God, not to have faceless snipers shoot at her like it was target practice. The rage inside Yoori mounted. She was not going to allow them to fuck up this historic battle. She would not allow them to fuck with her plans.

"Should we show them who they're fucking with?" Tae Hyun asked, reading her thoughts. He shared her fury. He, too, wanted to kill these faceless assholes for screwing with his battle.

Yoori gave a stiff incline of the head, wordlessly agreeing to a momentary ceasefire in order to teach these bastards a lesson. She would return to fighting him soon enough, but for now, they had a lesson to teach.

They each grabbed a rifle and propped them on the desk. They strategically aimed past the windows and began to fire their rifles with accuracy, successfully shooting through the glass windows and killing several snipers within their vantage point.

Their offense worked in their favor. The instant they shot back, the barrage of bullets ceased. For the time being, it was just Yoori and Tae Hyun.

Now that she was done with the snipers, she had a King to return to.

Fully aware that Ju Won would send in replacements for the dead snipers soon, Yoori did not waste time. She had to end this fight before the next set of snipers joined this battle.

Without warning, she jammed the back of the rifle against Tae Hyun's neck.

Soon, her heart assured as her body ached in torment. *It will all be over soon.*

Tae Hyun staggered back, but not before he used the rifle to perform an uppercut on Yoori. The back of the rifle slammed into her jaw. The impact caused her teeth to clack together. Fresh pain surfaced over her. Yoori doubled over and smashed into a metal computer chair in the process. While unbearable aches engulfed her wounded body, she bit back a scream of agony, grabbed the office chair, and slammed it against Tae Hyun's back.

Bam!

Tae Hyun arched his spine, violently gasping for air. It took Yoori everything she had not to reach out and help him. She empathized with his pain, for she was going through the same thing. Anyone else would've died by this point, but not him and definitely not her. She curbed her impulse to help him. She could not show that she cared for him. Not while the Underworld was watching.

Tae Hyun spit out blood from his mouth and eyed another camera on the floor. Once he drew in a preparatory breath, he speedily jumped on the desk and flew in the air, delivering an air kick so powerful that Yoori went airborne across the room. She crashed on another set of tables with a loud bang. To add insult to injury, her head collided with the corner of a computer monitor that nearly knocked her unconscious.

"Augh . . ."

Refusing to allow the pain to deter her, Yoori jumped back onto her feet. When she stood upright on the desk, she found that Tae Hyun was already standing on an office table that was about five desks away from hers. Like alpha dogs fighting for territory, Yoori and Tae Hyun sped towards each other. Years upon years of training came out in her battle with Tae Hyun after they collided on the center table.

Punch after punch was thrown, block after block held up, kick after kick bestowed, and blood after blood was spat out as they fought across the room like warring tornadoes.

Bang! Bang! Bang!

The snipers reappeared with a vengeance, and no expense was spared. Countless bullets thundered into the room, destroying everything in sight. As this scene of pure pandemonium took place, Yoori and Tae Hyun continued beating the living hell out of each other while simultaneously avoiding all the bullets.

Fuck you, Ju Won, Yoori screamed out in her mind, knowing that he and the rest of the Underworld were enjoying this too much. By now, ninety-nine percent of the people in the world would have died in this situation. Their King and Queen were making them proud.

In spite of the bullets that were increasing with every progressing minute, Yoori and Tae Hyun continued to forge on with their fight.

Yoori glanced over at the security camera just as another bullet missed her head. She executed a flying knee kick and elbow punch combo that knocked Tae Hyun against the wall. Using this moment before he regained his strength, she grabbed the side of his neck and slammed his head against a cubicle wall. She could feel the pain multiply in his body. He was in complete agony—not just physically, but also emotionally—just like her.

Now, her subconscious commanded. *This is the moment. Enough is enough.*

It was time to end the fight.

It was time to crown the Lord of the Underworld.

Yoori took in a preparatory breath to curb her emotions and to prepare her body for what was to come. Then, she punched him. Repeatedly. Mercilessly. She punched him again and again and again, until she realized he wasn't fighting back.

The bullets stopped coming and Tae Hyun stopped fighting.

He merely sat there, motionless as his head rested against the wall. His quiet and tired eyes gazed up at her with soft hope. It was as if he was taking a mental picture of her in his mind before he prepared himself for death.

Torture inundated her at the sight of this. She swallowed past the lump in her throat and fought through her tears.

"Fight me!" she shouted, falling to her knees. She pushed against his chest, urging him to take action. "Fight me back!"

She was ready.

She was ready for him, so why wasn't he fighting back?

"Why aren't you fighting me back?" she cried, hurting more from seeing him in this state than from the pain in her own body.

"I think . . ." he began faintly, hardly moving as he locked eyes with her. "I think by now, they know what a powerful God you are." He swallowed softly, eyeing the camera in the room as he had been doing the entire time. "They know you deserve this throne."

Her stomach coiled in misery when she realized what his plan was all along.

He purposely fought her the way he did because he wanted the Underworld to witness how gruesome this battle was. He wanted them to see how powerful she was; he wanted them to fear her so that they would think twice about betraying her once she sat on the throne. This was why he fought back so mercilessly. It was because he wanted to give her the throne. He wanted to give it to her in such a manner that no one would dare challenge her for it. He wanted to ensure her safety, even after his death.

"You know why they stopped shooting, right?" he asked quietly, staring at her while she felt her own heart clench in unrivaled pain.

She remained quiet as he went on.

"Because they know it's ending. They got the epic fight they wanted, and now they know it's ending. You've won."

He smiled at her, his eyes harboring no hatred or bitterness. There was only love and adoration—the same ones he always held for her.

"When you kill me," he advised, displaying no fear for what was to come, "cut my head off in front of the cameras. Do it so they can clearly see, so they will never forget how powerful you are."

Agony twisted inside her. His words stabbed her like swords.

"You stupid idiot! Why are you giving up already? You're not supposed to give up!" she shouted, shaking him as she ripped a knife from her pocket and held the blade to his windpipe. "Fight me back!"

She trembled while holding the knife underneath his chin. She was infuriated that he was making no movement to defend himself.

"Fight me back!" she commanded, threateningly pressing the blade deeper into his chin. She was one pressure away from cutting into the skin. "Fight me back—"

Yoori stopped yelling when she noticed the necklace he was wearing. She felt her entire world come to a standstill. Her disbelieving eyes ran over the pendant he wore as a necklace—a ring. A silver ring from a past that felt like a lifetime ago.

Tears that she could no longer hold back shrouded her eyes. A distant memory coursed through her mind as she gazed at it, bringing forth emotions that crippled her very being.

"...Gosh, what should I get him?" Yoori asked, running around the mall with Kang Min.

She had been at the mall for a few hours, plowing through all the stores in an effort to find the perfect birthday gift for Tae Hyun. The birthday shopping turned out to be more challenging than Yoori anticipated it to be. There were no potential gifts that spoke to her; no potential gifts that seemed perfect enough. After another half hour of no success, she was ready to call it quits when something in a display window arrested her attention.

Yoori backtracked, nearly crashing into Kang Min as she ran into the jewelry shop with a big smile on her face.

She found it.

Tae Hyun's perfect birthday gift.

Yoori leaned over the glass counter, admiring an identical ring to the one she saw in the display window. An engraving of a serpent ran across the outer surface of the silver ring like a protective guardian. It emanated nothing short of awesomeness, and she knew Tae Hyun would rock it well.

While admiring the serpent on the ring, her eyes traveled to the interior of the ring. A light bulb illuminated in her mind. She had an idea of how to make this gift even more perfect.

"Hey mister!" Yoori shouted ecstatically, scaring both Kang Min and the shop owner behind the counter. She waved him over to her. "Excuse me, but is it possible to engrave something inside a ring like this and have it done by tonight?"

His reluctant expression told her that it was highly improbable given the time limit. "I . . ."

Refusing to accept "no" as an answer, Yoori dramatically slammed her credit card onto the counter. With her personal assistant salary from Tae Hyun, Yoori had more than enough money to spend. She would spare no expense for her BFF's birthday gift.

"Money is no object," she stated firmly, sliding the credit card over to him.

While Kang Min rolled his eyes at her dramatic exaggeration, the chubby shop owner's eyes swelled wide in exhilaration. Even if the timeframe was close to impossible, he made sure with the "money is no object" credit card that anything was possible.

"What do you want to inscribe on the inside?" he asked, handing the ring to her for assessment.

"A trail of duck footprints."

Kang Min and the man stared at her as though she was high on drugs.

"The hell," Kang Min stated dubiously. "What does a trail of duck footprints mean to boss?"

Yoori grinned, handing the ring over to the man so he could finish up Tae Hyun's perfect birthday gift. She knew out of everyone, it only mattered that Tae Hyun understood its significance.

"It means that I really love getting attacked by ducks . . ."

The air escaped Yoori as she stared at the ring, or more specifically, the trail of duck tracks hidden in the interior of the ring. It now rested innocently on his chest, arresting her attention as she held a knife to his throat.

Her heart had never felt heavier.

"Where did you get that?" she breathed out in disbelief.

She was never able to give it to him. She had forgotten it at the diner, tried to get it back, but Chae Young was raped, and Yoori had been through hell since. She hadn't had the time or the recollection to go back to the diner to get it for him. It didn't make sense to her as to how he came into possession of this ring.

"Chae Young gave it to me."

Yoori then sighed knowingly. She recalled Chae Young and Tae Hyun going to the back of the diner several days ago. She was making her getaway from the diner and Chae Young had stopped him from chasing after her, telling him that she wanted to give him something. Chae Young must have given him the ring then.

Do not waste time, a soft voice in the back of her mind urged. The presence of the ring only reminded her of what she needed to do. *Finish this now.*

"Kwon Tae Hyun," she called with a broken voice. Her control was fading. It took everything she had left to maintain her composure. "Stand up and fight me."

He shook his head. "I'm done."

"Fight me back," she ordered through clenched teeth.

This was not how it was supposed to happen.

He was supposed to fight back.

"Kill me now," he urged her weakly. "Do it before they start shooting again. I don't want you to get hurt anymore."

This was when she lost it.

She could no longer camouflage the truth. She could no longer conceal what she had decided to do since she burned his hoodie and met him at the park.

"Fight me back! Why aren't you fighting back?" she shouted, pushing him in frustration. Tears brimmed over her eyes. "Fight me back! I'm giving you this throne! Just fucking kill me now, and they'll kneel before you forever!"

Shock blazed in his eyes. He looked absolutely stunned. "Was this your plan the entire time?"

It was.

After she told him that she loved him at the lake house, Yoori knew there was no going back. Her society revered them, but it was also a sadistic and vicious world. The fact that they pitted her and Tae Hyun against each other spoke volumes about how they viewed the relationship. The Underworld did not want two humans to rule over their world together. They would never allow their first Lord to set such a terrible example to the future heirs of the Underworld.

Although Yoori wanted the throne, she wanted Tae Hyun to be alive more. She wanted him to be a God, and she wanted him to live a long and prosperous life. This was why she wanted to fight him. She wanted to give the Underworld the epic battle it wanted. She wanted them to see what a true God Tae Hyun was; she wanted them to see him kill her, because only in her death would Tae Hyun be back in the good graces of the Underworld. And only in the good grace of the Underworld would he live forever.

"They'll kill you if you don't kill me," she continued, aware of how cruel her world was. "Hurry and kill me! Get it over with, *please*."

"Does it look like I'm capable of killing you?" Tae Hyun asked incredulously. His tormented eyes locked with hers. "It nearly killed me to attack you the way I did for the cameras, so they could see I wasn't going easy on you. I did all that so you would be viewed as a legitimate God in this world, and now you're telling me to kill you? Just like that? Like it's so easy for me to do?"

"Can you imagine what a legendary God you'd be if you killed me?" she whispered, her entire body trembling from pain. "You'll live forever in this world. No one would dare to touch you again."

He laughed self-deprecatingly. "You think I want to live forever knowing that I killed you?"

Yoori bit her lips. Her eyes begged him to be logical. "Please kill me, Tae Hyun. I've been ready to die the moment I allowed all my memories to come back. I was ready to die under your hands when you thought I killed your mother." She placed the knife in his hand. Her tear-filled eyes held his in despair, in utter desperation. There was no other option left but this. "I'm ready. I'm ready to die now—"

"Aw, how sweet." A callous, mocking voice sprang through the room, jarring Yoori and Tae Hyun from their conversation. "I guess the coldblooded bitch of the Underworld has a heart after all."

Yoori jerked her head in the direction of the voice. Her eyes bloomed when she saw Young Jae standing in the corner of the office. He wore a black suit and had on a cruel, venomous smile on his face. As Yoori and Tae Hyun tried to make sense of his sudden appearance, Young Jae wasted no more time.

He raised a black gun and trained it directly on Tae Hyun.

"Your end has come," Young Jae said sadistically. "Welcome to your new war."

He fired the gun at Tae Hyun, effectively ending the battle between the King and Queen, and commencing a war of the Titans.

"Thank you for being with me until the very end."

21: War of the Underworlds

Bang!

"Tae Hyun!"

Yoori rushed to shove Tae Hyun out of the way. She gasped for air when a blast of pain ricocheted through her, searing every nerve in her body. The scorching bullet penetrated her left arm, plunging deep into her flesh. The pain was so potent that she nearly blacked out from it.

"Yoori!"

On instinct, Tae Hyun grabbed her around the waist and protectively pulled her against him. With the swiftest of speed, he pulled out one of his silver guns and shot at Young Jae. Young Jae ducked out of the way, leaping behind a cubicle before another swarm of sniper bullets infiltrated the room. This time the bullets were not aimed with the intent to injure them; they were aimed to kill them. The new sniper shot with such precision that the bullets actually grazed several parts of their bodies. Maneuvering around the bullets while holding onto Yoori, Tae Hyun navigated through the office floor before ducking them behind an empty cubicle.

As they hid in silence, it did not take Yoori long to deduce who had replaced Ju Won's snipers.

"Ji Hoon is back," Yoori whispered, her voice barely audible in the darkness.

Tae Hyun nodded, gently tending to her bullet wound. He had also gathered that Lee Ji Hoon was the new sniper shooting at them. "I know."

"Soo Jin, Tae Hyun . . ." called Young Jae's taunting voice. The distant voice moved around the room, gradually coming closer to them. "I told both of you that I'd bring a war unlike any other, didn't I?" He laughed, his voice circling the area they were in. "You two are disappointing me. The entire Underworld is watching this fight and you hide from me like cowards? You were raised to be stronger than this." His laughing voice came closer to them. "Well then. Since you're hiding like animals, it is only right that I hunt you down like one."

Bang!

A bullet flew through their cubicle, gliding right over their heads and missing them by a mere inch.

Tae Hyun gently unwrapped himself from Yoori and leapt up in the direction the bullet was fired. He shot across the room, aiming at Young Jae who was diving away from the bullet. He crawled on his hands and knees as Tae Hyun's bullets chased after him. Displaying amazing alacrity, Young Jae rocketed upwards and ran into one of the cubicles, concealing himself from sight.

"At this very moment, my Scorpions from Japan and Korea are occupying this building with Ji Hoon's Skulls," his disembodied voice told them loftily. "It's only a matter of time before you find yourselves completely surrounded."

Yoori could no longer suppress her rage. Battling with the love of her life proved to be the most difficult thing she had to endure; the last thing she needed was for her bastard brother to show his face. The fact that he was putting on this show for the entire Underworld was sickening to her. She could tolerate them seeing her weakness with Tae Hyun, but not with Young Jae— not with anyone else. Young Jae was going to pay for everything he had done to her.

She took out her gun and made a move to go after Young Jae. Before she could get up, Tae Hyun was already on the floor with her.

"*Don't,*" he said firmly. "This is what he wants. He's goading you."

"It's working," she said through clenched teeth.

"You can't go out there." His gaze moved over to her bullet wound. "Not like this. Not when you're this hurt."

Yoori pressed her head against the cubicle in frustration. She was prepared to acquiesce with his words before Young Jae demolished the last of her control.

"You two are never leaving this building! By the time we're done with you, you'll be eating bullets as your last meals."

"Shut the fuck up!" Yoori screamed, fed up with this bastard. He killed her father. He convinced her second older brother to help him kill their father and now he was looking to kill her. He was the epitome of everything she hated in a human being. She couldn't sit by and allow him to taunt her anymore. "Just shut the fuck up! I'm tired of listening to you, you piece of shit!"

She whipped one of her gold guns out before Tae Hyun could stop her. She stood up and fired two shots at the cubicle his voice originated from. As she watched Young Jae's silhouette circumvent the bullets, another succession of sniper bullets fired through the glass window, nearly plunging into her head before she dodged them in time.

"Come out here and say that again, lil sis," Young Jae mocked, eager to give Ji Hoon another opportunity to shoot at her.

"Yoori!" Tae Hyun shouted, pulling her back down to the ground. More concerned with getting Yoori to the hospital than killing Young Jae, Tae Hyun wrapped her close to his body as he prepared their exit plan.

"What are you doing?" Yoori moaned, finally feeling the fatigue that came from her fierce battle with Tae Hyun. It did not help that she had lost a substantial amount of blood from her fresh bullet wound. She had always had a high tolerance for pain, but this one was taking the cake for being one of the toughest ailments that she had to endure. "W—we have to fight him!"

"No," Tae Hyun told her quickly. "You're in no condition to fight right now. That's why he's here, because he knows that we've depleted our energy. He knows that now is his best chance of killing us."

"I don't care," she grunted through the pain. "I want to kill him!"

And then, just as more sniper bullets invaded the room, Tae Hyun reached for a stapler on the office desk. He wheeled towards the elevators and threw the stapler at the elevator switch. The stapler collided with the bottom switch button. The switch glowed for a few seconds before the elevator door beside it slid open.

"No!" Yoori screamed. She wanted to stay and battle it out with Young Jae. She wanted to stay to kill him.

Without another word, Tae Hyun wrapped himself around her like a shield, picked her up, and sprinted across the office at lightning speed. While evading bullets that were firing past him, he shot at Young Jae, who was running across the office floor in an effort to get to them. Although Tae Hyun missed, he did succeed in slowing Young Jae down with his gunfire. Once they reached the elevator, Tae Hyun threw Yoori into the metal box and spun around to fire two more shots at Young Jae.

Young Jae easily avoided the two bullets. He let out a laugh as he watched Tae Hyun join Yoori in the elevator.

"There's nowhere to *runnnn*!" he taunted in a singsong voice. The elevator door slid shut while Tae Hyun pressed a random floor for them to descend to. "You're surrounded, and your heads will be mine tonight!"

Immediately after the doors closed and the elevator began to descend, Tae Hyun pushed the emergency button and locked them there momentarily. His frantic eyes swam down to Yoori. Concern blanketed his features once he saw her sitting in the corner, shaking while she held a hand over her gunshot wound. She was doing her best to put pressure on the wound to minimize blood loss.

"God, Yoori," he uttered, ripping his shirt off and revealing his bruised and assaulted body. He bent down and looped the black shirt around her gunshot wound. He tied it tight to slow the flow of blood. "Why'd you have to do that?"

Yoori pressed the back of her head against the wall. Too prideful to be viewed as a weakling, she merely rolled her eyes and answered, "Bad reflexes." She paused to regain her steady breathing state before adding, "And I'm not a damsel in distress. I can take care of myself."

Tae Hyun laughed, looking down at his naked upper body. He briefly glanced at the bruises and large sword wound on his arm. "I'm well aware that you can take care of yourself." He sighed and crouched down before her, trying to get her to see reason. "But we need to get you to a doctor. I don't know about you, but I'm completely fucked up from our fight. I can't imagine that bullet in there is making you feel better." He gestured at the elevator door with his index finger. "Now once we get out there, stay close to me. As the first five floors would more than likely be filled with Scorpions and Skulls, we'll start at the sixth floor. After we reach the sixth floor, we'll use the stairwell to get to the ground floor. By then, our Serpents and Siberian Tigers should be in the lobby fighting them. There's going to be a lot of Underworld soldiers coming after us, so you'll definitely have to take care of yourself."

Yoori smirked and nodded. Kwon Tae Hyun would never cease to amaze her with his quick thinking. If she had to conjure up an escape plan, she would have come up with the same plan as his.

He stood tall and freed the elevator from its "emergency" state. "You ready?"

Adrenaline pumped through her. She held a firm grip on her gun. She was more than ready to show these Underworld soldiers why she was the Queen of their world.

"Yes."

The elevator doors glided open, and the King and Queen came through. Blasting out with Yoori in one arm and his silver gun in the other, Tae Hyun began to fire rounds upon rounds of bullets at the Skulls and Scorpions who had filtered into the sixth floor of the building. He fired with precision and one by one, they began to crumple to the floor as Tae Hyun ran with Yoori in his arms.

Never content with being the dead weight—even though her arm was killing her—Yoori started shooting as well. Every shot she fired met its intended target, leaving behind a trail of bodies as they swept through the floor.

"Oomph!"

"Ahhhh!"

"Ugh!"

Yoori and Tae Hyun raced through the office floor by jumping across walls, punching, kicking, and sending gang member after gang member flying across the room. Many either crashed into the walls or flew out the windows of the high-rise building. Alone they were powerful, but together, they were an unstoppable and untouchable force.

They separated when a big meeting table appeared in their path. A sea of Underworld soldiers swept through the room, heading straight towards them. Displaying amazing dexterity, Yoori easily slid underneath the table. As she slid over the floor, she took out her second weapon and pointed her two gold guns out. Yoori began to shoot at the gang members on either side of the table. While those gang members buckled to the ground with screams of pain, Tae Hyun jumped onto that same table. He ran on it for a fleeting second before launching himself in the air. With his guns outstretched, he began to fire at the sea of Underworld soldiers as well.

Bang! Bang! Bang!

They converged at the same time when he jumped back on the ground and when Yoori slid out from underneath the table. Tae Hyun wasted no time in reaching down to help her up. Once their hands connected, they sprinted towards the stairwell, both dodging and avoiding the bullets that were chasing after them like shadows.

"Nice move," he commented in amusement, referring to her sliding under the table.

"You too," she lied, even though she didn't even see what he did while she was underneath the table.

Although the adrenaline was pumping through her, she could also feel her body throbbing. It was begging her to stop fighting and rest. Never one to give up during a fight, Yoori pushed back that temptation and punched a Scorpion. The sound of his skull cracking resonated in the air as she ran past him with Tae Hyun.

Once they arrived at the entrance of the stairwell, Tae Hyun kicked the door open and inadvertently sent six men plunging to their deaths. Yoori used this moment of distraction to shoot at the rest of the soldiers in the stairwell. The onslaught of bullets jumpstarted a domino effect that sent men upon men tumbling down the stairs.

They used the fallen bodies as doormats, jumping on their chests and running over their faces without any regard to their injured groans. Tae Hyun held on tight to Yoori, who was starting to become woozy. She looked like she was about to pass out at any second.

"Stay with me, Brat," he encouraged, holding her closer against him.

They continued to dash down the stairs, shooting at gang members and skirting around bullets that were flying all around them. To their great fortune, the further down the stairwell they ran, the more the Skulls and Scorpions began to decrease in number. In fact, the more they ran, the more they could feel the presence of Serpents and Siberian Tigers. Yoori and Tae Hyun were no longer the only ones fighting against the Skulls and the Scorpions. The entire Serpents and Siberian Tigers army had united to defend their King and Queen.

This was no longer an ambush.

This was war.

A war of the Underworlds.

The biggest Underworld war in history was currently taking place as Yoori and Tae Hyun sped down the stairwell. Chaotic sounds of gunshots, screams of agony, and the scent of death reverberated across the stairwell, chasing after them as they finally arrived at the first floor lobby. Eager to finally get out of this godforsaken stairwell, Yoori kicked the door open while Tae Hyun killed the men behind him.

"Ugh."

Spots of darkness began to edge Yoori's vision. Pain pulsated throughout her body. The aftermath of being shot at and battling Tae Hyun had finally taken a powerful toll on her. The ground beneath her feet no longer felt solid. She could hardly maintain her equilibrium, let alone see straight.

In the lobby, hundreds of Scorpions and Skulls were going to war against Serpents and Siberian Tigers. Dead bodies dropped down to the floor at an accelerated rate, screams occupied the lobby at its highest octaves while blood smeared every inch of the building. Everywhere Yoori turned, there was blood; everywhere she turned, there was death.

"Bosses!" Jae Won shouted out of habit once he saw Tae Hyun and Yoori emerge from the door. He was fighting with four Skulls, easily overpowering them with bone-cracking punches that left them collapsing to the floor.

Kang Min was in the back, snapping the necks of four Scorpions. Across from him, Mina, Ace, and the rest of Tae Hyun's Cobras were jumping all around the walls, bouncing off desks and pillars while shooting down their adversaries.

Chaos.

Complete chaos gripped the lobby.

It was complete chaos, and all Tae Hyun cared about was getting Yoori, who was getting paler and paler by the second, to a hospital.

Still holding her firm against his body, Tae Hyun leaned down and whispered, "Stay with me, okay, Brat? We're almost out—"

"Boss!" Ace bellowed at the top of his lungs. "Watch out!"

It was too late.

The baseball bat that Young Jae wielded already made contact with the back of Tae Hyun's head.

Bam!

"Augh!"

"Tae Hyun!" Yoori cried, her eyes widening once she heard the sound of metal colliding with the back of his skull.

Pushing her aside so that he wouldn't fall on her, Tae Hyun stumbled to the ground. Young Jae stood behind him with smug pride while Yoori tried to fight past the wooziness that was overtaking her. Keen on capitalizing on Tae Hyun's weakened state, Young Jae jabbed the baseball bat into his stomach and then used the bat to give Tae Hyun an uppercut to the jaw. Blood oozed from Tae Hyun's mouth as he collapsed to the ground beside Yoori.

Though fatigue was riding her, Yoori was too infuriated with Young Jae's cowardly attack on Tae Hyun. It was one thing to go after her, but it was another thing entirely to go after Tae Hyun. She was determined to make him pay for his offense. Without warning, she whipped her leg up and kicked Young Jae in the throat. Young Jae could barely let out a breath as he fell off balance. The baseball bat slipped from his grasp and clinked onto the floor as he attempted to maintain his equilibrium.

His furious eyes sharpened on her once he straightened himself up. A cold smirk crossed his lips.

"You've waited a long time for this moment, haven't you, little sis?" Young Jae accused, spitting out blood from his mouth. He began to circle her slowly, dangerously. "To murder me?"

"You should die for what you did to our father," she spat out, using all the strength she had to keep herself awake, to keep from going unconscious. She could not succumb to weakness at a moment like this. She could not be human when she was in the middle of an Underworld war. At the moment, her biggest enemy was standing in front of her. It would be a cold day in hell before she allowed herself to black out now.

"He deserved to die."

The anger inside her erupted. She had been patient with him long enough. It was time the bastard paid for everything he had done.

"He's our father!" she shrieked, lunging at Young Jae like a bloodthirsty lion.

They went after each other with all the strength they had. She performed a spin kick that left him reeling to the side for a brief second before he punched her across the face. Soon, they were dueling all across the busy lobby, punching and kicking one another without mercy.

"You manipulated Ho Young!" she shouted after she grabbed the back of his head and banged it against a pillar. All the hatred and disappointment she harbored for Young Jae came bursting out. "*My* brother! *Your* brother! You manipulated our brother to help you kill our father! Our family is ruined because of your jealousy!"

"He fucking betrayed me!" he yelled, blocking a punch from her. As if a douse of adrenaline had trickled into his body at the reminder, the bloodlust in Young Jae's eyes increased. He kicked her across the face as though he was kicking his own father.

Blood shot out of Yoori's mouth. Despite the affliction, she continued to pour out her feelings, her resentment.

"He raised you!" she combated. It still amazed her that he felt like he did nothing wrong. It still astounded her that he was playing the victim. In spite of the blood that was coursing from her bullet wound, she fought him harder. "It doesn't matter what he was planning to give me. He still loved you and raised you! Why can't you understand that?!"

Her father wasn't the perfect man, and she knew that. Despite this human flaw, she also knew that he loved his children. He may have been too ambitious with them at times, but he loved them and raised them nonetheless. She would forever be grateful for that. She would forever be in her father's debt for that, and in turn, she would forever hate Young Jae for killing him—just out of pure jealousy.

"That's easy for you to say," Young Jae contested. Misery started to pour out of his voice. "He didn't betray you. He didn't crush your heart."

"But you made sure to crush his," Yoori provided brokenly. "You made sure he would die in the worst way possible: being shot down by his own sons." She laughed to herself. "How would you feel if your own child did that to you, big brother? How would you feel if your own child brought that type of misery upon you?"

Anguish immersed in Young Jae's eyes as he listened to her words. Whether or not he took in what she said, she would never know. Before she could utter another word, Tae Hyun had gotten up and kicked him across the face, thereby ending their conversation.

As she watched Tae Hyun go after Young Jae, Yoori could feel the last of her energy leave her body. Every inch of her body was throbbing and she could no longer feel the strength in her legs. She was close to going limp before a bloodcurdling scream arrested her attention.

"Boss!" Kang Min screamed at the top of his lungs. "Watch out!"

At Kang Min's warning, Yoori ducked when she felt a whiff of air run over her. A sword swiped over the air where her neck would have been. When the sword reverted its aim, she stood upright and punched the attacker across the face. She caught the sword that slipped from his grasp and proceeded to swing the blade forward, slicing his head off as though it was fabric. Warm blood splattered over her face as the severed head fell down beside her feet. Yoori stumbled back while wiping the blood from her face. She could slowly feel her energy deplete. Although she was running on no fuel, she was determined to keep fighting for as long as she could.

Her eyes peered over to Tae Hyun.

There was no missing the fury that poured from Tae Hyun as he bashed Young Jae against the wall. There was no denying the anger as Tae Hyun body-slammed him to the floor, and there was no refuting the hatred as he kicked Young Jae across the lobby. He had not forgotten that Young Jae was the one who took a shot at him, nor had he forgotten that Young Jae was the one who put a bullet in Yoori's arm.

The crowd parted ways for Tae Hyun like he was a living God, giving him free reign to go after Young Jae on an uninterrupted stage. There were a few Scorpions who attempted to intervene to save their King, but Tae Hyun would not tolerate the interruption. As they tried to fight him, Tae Hyun would easily snap their necks and step over their dead bodies in an effort to go after Young Jae with unrelenting determination.

Though he didn't need it, Yoori was ready to go help him in her dazed state. Out of nowhere, someone else stole her attention. On the opposite end of the crowded lobby, she sighted Anna next to a pillar. Yoori's blood boiled while her feral eyes raked over Anna. The wooziness she experienced vacated, leaving behind a conflagration of rage that she could no longer contain.

The one who betrayed her was right there, right in front of her.

She wished that she had left Anna to die all those years ago, but now, fate had connected them together once more. Only this time, she would not be a God and save Anna's life. Today, she would be the Queen she was raised to be and take Anna's life. Anna had failed to repay her debt to Yoori and as such, it was only right that she gave Anna the ultimate punishment for this failure.

Her resolve set, Yoori clenched her fists in anticipation and took slow, predatory steps towards Anna.

Unaware that her former Queen was stalking after her, Anna's eyes roamed the lobby in sheer panic. Her eyes enlarged when she found the person she was looking for. Horror consumed her when she observed that Young Jae was fighting with Tae Hyun and that he was surely losing. Desperate to help her husband, Anna reached behind the pillar and yanked someone out.

Yoori's blood went cold after Anna pulled Hae Jin out by the collar of her neck. Blood poured from Hae Jin's mouth while a big swelling covered her left eye.

"Hae Jin," Yoori whispered, stunned to see her in this state.

"Hae Jin!" Kang Min shouted the instant he saw what Anna had done to her.

He ran forward, intent on saving her. He stopped in his tracks when Anna went behind Hae Jin and looped her arm around Hae Jin's neck. Anna held Hae Jin in a headlock while she pressed a black gun to the bottom of her chin.

"Kwon Tae Hyun!" Anna screeched from the top of her lungs, her eyes unblinking with rage and desperation. She could not take her eyes off her husband, who was barely conscious as Tae Hyun continued to beat him half to death. She tightened her grip around Hae Jin's neck. "Let Young Jae go or I'm blowing her brains out!"

Tae Hyun could not hear her. Her voice was lost under the roar of flying bullets, murderous screams, and sounds of skulls and bones cracking. Tae Hyun continued to fight Young Jae, unaware that Anna was holding his sister hostage.

"Anna, don't!" Jae Won screamed. Desperate to appeal to her humane side, he revealed, "She's pregnant!"

Anna either didn't listen or didn't care. Her frantic eyes were solely on her husband. He was all that mattered to her.

Kang Min, on the other hand, was rocked by this revelation.

"Hae Jin!" Kang Min screamed, all rationale escaping him. All he had left was instinct, all he had left was desperation. He tried to run to her, to perhaps knock Anna down before she could do anything to Hae Jin. He was several feet from Anna when three Skulls appeared out of nowhere and attacked him. They got close to knifing him before he blew up in rage. He grabbed the knife from the one closest to him and went berserk, cutting into their faces and necks without discrimination. He was covered in blood when they all crumpled to the ground. "Hae Jin!"

As Kang Min's manic screams tore through Tae Hyun's ears, he stopped dead in his tracks. Tae Hyun whipped around. The blood drained from his face when he saw that his little sister was held hostage with a gun to her chin. She was struggling to breathe with the grip Anna held around her neck.

"Hae Jin!" he called, abandoning Young Jae like he was a day's old trash. He plowed through the crowd, running to his sister at full speed.

Thrilled that Tae Hyun was finally away from her husband and right where she needed him to be, Anna forcefully tossed Hae Jin to the side, nearly causing Hae Jin to slam face-first into the ground. Fortunately, Kang Min caught Hae Jin in time. While Kang Min hugged Hae Jin and pulled her away from Anna, Anna raised her gun and aimed it at Tae Hyun, who was still running towards Hae Jin.

It happened in a split second. It happened on impulse.

A fear unlike any other spread throughout Yoori. Without even thinking about her actions, she sped towards Anna with the velocity of a predatory cheetah. She bent her knees and rolled on the ground with her sword in hand. Before Anna could pull the trigger, Yoori rolled up in a half-crouch, gripped the sword with both of her hands, and plunged it backwards, piercing the blade through Anna's stomach.

Swish!

"Augh . . ."

Clack!

Anna's gun dropped.

"Anna!"

Shocked silence poured through the lobby after Young Jae's bloodcurdling scream shook the building.

Yoori turned. She watched in silence as tears filled Anna's eyes when she realized that she had been stabbed through the stomach. Shaking while her eyes grew wide with tears, Anna slipped out of the sword's grip. A trail of blood dripped from the blade before she stumbled to the floor. Gasping for air, she laid in a fetal position, cradling her stomach as blood pooled around her.

A horrific realization cascaded over Yoori as she watched Anna cradle her stomach, as she watched Young Jae run towards his wife with tears clouding his eyes. Anna was not cradling her stomach because of the pain; she was cradling her stomach because of what was growing inside it.

Yoori's world tilted on its axis.

Anna was pregnant.

Anna was pregnant with her brother's child.

She just killed her brother's wife . . . and his unborn child.

The torrent of guilt that engulfed her was crippling, blinding. She fell to the ground, dropping the bloody sword while staring at her brother and his now dying wife in shock. What had she done?

"Anna, why the hell did you come?! I told you not to come!" Young Jae cried, holding his wife in his arms. A stream of tears poured from his agonized eyes. "Anna . . . Please, baby. Please stay with me."

"Young—Young Jae," she whispered in broken gasps. Her voice became softer, the light slowly dimming from her tear-cloaked eyes. "Young Jae . . . I—lo—love . . ."

"No, no! Please stay with me, baby!" Young Jae begged, kissing his wife's hand. He tried to stop the flow of blood from her stomach. "Please don't leave me! Please don't leave me!"

"I love you," Anna breathed out brokenly. As though feeling her own child die with her, she gently cradled her stomach and stared at her husband one last time. "*We* love you," she emphasized quietly.

And then, after exhaling her final breath, she closed her eyes. As Anna's lifeless body laid in his arms, all that could be heard was Young Jae's screams of agony. It saturated the room, moving all those present and crushing Yoori's heart.

"Boss! We have to go!" P.C. shouted, running in from the side. He grabbed Young Jae, who was still holding onto his dead wife.

Young Jae was sobbing uncontrollably. In that suspended second, Young Jae was no longer a King. He was simply a man who lost his wife; he was simply a father who lost his child.

Yoori stood paralyzed, utterly horrified with what she had done. She never wanted this for him. She never wanted to hurt him like this. She could feel Tae Hyun stand beside her, his eyes tormented as he stared at the scene before him in desolation.

Welcome to the Underworld, a voice in her mind whispered as tears rippled in her own eyes. *This is what happens in our world. Love doesn't exist in our world. If it does, it will only be a matter of time before it dies. Would you be able to handle that? Would you be able to hold Tae Hyun in your arms and watch him die?*

This was exactly why Yoori did not want to be with Tae Hyun.

This very moment was exactly why she could never be human with him.

"Boss!" P.C. continued to scream out, using all his strength to pry Young Jae away from Anna's dead body. "Things are happening in Japan! We have to go!"

At long last, P.C. was able to rip Young Jae away from a lifeless Anna. In the same second, sounds of sirens pouring in from the streets echoed into the lobby, triggering the remaining Skulls and Scorpions to disperse from the building like scared rats.

The sound of his pregnant wife's dead body hitting the floor pierced into the air after P.C. picked Young Jae up. P.C. tugged at his dazed King's arm and began to herd him out of the building. As he ran out with the crowd, Young Jae's eyes gazed at his wife for one last time before his heated eyes locked with Yoori's.

Yoori felt the breath still in her lungs.

If there was any chance of her brother and her ever reconciling in the future, then all of that was shot to hell the instant she killed his wife and unborn child.

Hatred. Nothing but hatred encased his dark eyes.

His glare said it all: retribution.

"You're going to pay," she heard him whisper—heard him promise—before he disappeared out of the building. "You're going to pay for everything."

Yoori remained rooted in her position, for she was disgusted with herself.

This was her world, and what a disgusting world it was.

Anna betrayed her; she deserved to die, but the unborn baby didn't deserve to die. The child that would have been her niece or nephew didn't deserve to die, and that was what was killing her. Although she was furious with her, Yoori now wished that she didn't have to kill Anna. Killing Anna brought her no satisfaction. If anything, it only served to bring her more misery. She could not deny how excruciating it was to watch her own brother cry as the love of his life left him. It was unbearable for her to realize that he would never meet his own child because of her.

"Yoori."

Tae Hyun wrapped his arms around her. He pulled her against him and held her to his chest. His touch brought her comfort, but it did not conceal the agony she experienced. She could feel the pain run up and down her body. The mind-numbing heartache haunted her as she stared at her brother's dead wife.

"We can't be here anymore," Tae Hyun announced, his voice barely discernible over the sirens. "We have to leave now."

Yoori nodded numbly. They could no longer loiter within this building, not when the authorities were going to find this place—and the carnage within it—soon. Knowing that there was nothing more for them here, Yoori took one last look at Anna before walking out of the lobby with Tae Hyun.

She could feel eyes on her once they stepped out of the building. She instinctively peered up at the building across the street. Chills trickled down her spine when she saw what stood above them.

High up in that building, she could see Ju Won standing in front of a glass window with ten other Underworld elders by his side. Each and every one of them were staring down at her and Tae Hyun with rage in their cold eyes.

Tae Hyun's phone rang and instantly, she and Tae Hyun knew who it was.

While holding her close and staring at Ju Won, who also had a phone to his ear, Tae Hyun picked up.

"Forty-eight hours," Ju Won's livid voice filtered through succinctly, sending more chills to cover their bodies. There was no more diplomacy, no more bullshit. "Forty-eight hours to correct the mess you've made, the embarrassment you've brought to our world. Forty-eight hours for you to get your rationale back, and forty-eight hours for one of you to kill the other. If you don't correct your mistakes after forty-eight hours, then the entire Underworld will have both of your heads. Think about it."

"Looks like you've already made your decision."

22: Royals Without a Throne

Tae Hyun and Yoori were quiet for a long moment after spending the majority of the day in the hospital. Jae Won and Kang Min had rushed them to the hospital and sought the aid of Tae Hyun's private physician—Dr. Han—and Yoori's private surgeon—Dr. Kim. While Yoori spent hours in the surgery room getting the bullet out, Dr. Han stitched up Tae Hyun's cuts and bandaged his wounds. It was hours later, when Yoori was out of surgery and Tae Hyun was done with his meeting with Dr. Han, that they found themselves on a bench within the empty hospital corridor.

Yoori felt lost as she stared out the window. The hospital's courtyard was covered in blinding white snow. The rampant wind was thrashing the snow every which way. There did not appear to be an end in sight for the blizzard. It mirrored the storm ravaging her life.

Everything that transpired today had gone horribly wrong, and now, they had not only made enemies out of her brother and Ji Hoon, but also the entire Underworld society. This was not what she had planned for; this was not how she wanted to protect Tae Hyun. She was supposed to leave him with a throne, not a coffin.

Beside her, Tae Hyun remained quiet. He, too, was staring numbly at the storm ravaging the world outside. Although he did not speak, she knew very well that his mind was processing the same thoughts as hers. This death sentence was not what he planned for; this was not what he wanted for them.

The sound of footsteps moving across the corridor roused them from their daze. They relinquished their focus from the storm and averted their attention to the new Royal in their presence.

Yoori straightened her spine when she observed that Choi Min Hyuk—arguably the most powerful crime lord in the 1st layer—was approaching them. He wore a black suit with a long, dark trench coat that nearly touched the floor as he walked. His expression was grim and completely free of emotions. If he were wearing a hooded cloak, she would daresay that he'd make an excellent Grim Reaper.

Yoori smiled to herself. Perhaps that was what he was. Perhaps the Underworld had decided to kill them right then and there. He was coming to collect their souls—or what was left of their souls.

"Did you enjoy the show?" Yoori asked coolly, watching him like a hawk.

Min Hyuk took a seat on the bench opposite from them. Once situated, he released a breath of annoyance. "I would have enjoyed it more if there was actually an ending."

"There would have been an ending had we not been interrupted," Yoori responded with the same tone of annoyance. She tilted her head critically. "Did you know Young Jae and Ji Hoon were planning to ambush us?"

The line of Min Hyuk's mouth hardened. "I did not know," he answered bluntly. A tinge of reproaching fire blazed in his eyes. "But I will give Ji Hoon credit for fighting for the throne. It is something the ones in front of me should be doing."

"What are you doing here, uncle?" Tae Hyun asked quietly, staring at Min Hyuk with tired eyes. If it had been another crime lord, Yoori knew that Tae Hyun would manufacture a fearless expression. Given that Min Hyuk was one of his most trusted mentors, he did not feel it was necessary to put on a mask.

"Our layer asked me to come," Min Hyuk replied, his grim expression thawing when he finally laid his focus on Tae Hyun. "They requested that I come reason with you before the end comes."

Hope surged through Yoori when she realized that Min Hyuk was not there to collect their souls; he was there to save them—or more specifically, save Tae Hyun. The crime lords of the 1st layer rarely involved themselves in the happenings of the 3rd layer, much less inject themselves into something as controversial as her situation with Tae Hyun. The only time in history this type of intervention occurred was when Tae Hyun killed Ho Young. The 1st layer rallied together to not only protect him from the bylaws of the Underworld, but also crown him as a King in the 3rd layer. This very moment was proving to be the second historic moment for the 1st layer. The only difference was that they were not uniting to protect Tae Hyun from the Underworld; they were uniting to protect Tae Hyun from himself.

"I no longer want the throne," Tae Hyun stated without hesitation.

"It no longer matters what you want," Min Hyuk said patiently. "As of this moment, you are no longer a King. You forfeited that privilege the moment you decided to choose 'love' over your throne."

Tae Hyun humored Min Hyuk's statement. "What am I now?"

"You are an example," Min Hyuk responded in a low, controlled voice. "A tale that will be told as a lesson to the future Kings and Queens of the

Underworld. Fortunately for you, how this story will be told is still entirely up to you. Will you be the King who rose to power after sacrificing the love of his life . . . or will you be the King who died pathetically for a woman?"

"I am not just a 'woman'," Yoori corrected firmly. She did not want Tae Hyun to die for her, but it should not be mistaken that she was any less worthy. "I am a Queen. There is no greater honor than to die for me."

"Then why did you not give Tae Hyun the honor today?" Min Hyuk inquired in a dismissive voice.

"Because I want to reserve the honor for someone else," she said fearlessly, not liking his tone with her. She felt the Queen in her rouse to life. She appraised him with the hunger of a bloodthirsty lioness. "Perhaps I should give you the honor."

"Yoori," Tae Hyun called softly. Even though his voice was barely above a whisper, there was no denying the steel behind it. He did not want her to fight with someone he harbored so much respect for. "Despite his words, he is on our side."

Yoori fell silent. He was right. She should not allow her ego to take precedence tonight. The most important goal was to save Tae Hyun's life. Since Min Hyuk's very reason for being there was to do this, the last thing Yoori needed to do was treat him like an enemy.

"Why must we choose one or the other?" Tae Hyun asked when an unspoken truce was given between Yoori and Min Hyuk. "If we were in any other world, they would jump for joy at the thought of being ruled over by a King and Queen like us."

"Our world is different from the rest," Min Hyuk said solemnly, voicing what Yoori had grown up hearing her entire life. "For a title as powerful as the 'Lord' of the Underworld, the recipient must possess every trait worthy of this epithet."

"Because the Korean Underworld is the first Underworld to crown a Lord, the rest of the Underworlds are watching," Yoori provided, knowing exactly why Tae Hyun and her could not rule this society together. "Our society will not allow this historic battle to end in a 'happily ever after'. They cannot set the precedence with the rest of the crownings if this first one does not set the bar high. The first Lord must represent everything the Underworld is: they must be cruel, they must be powerful, and they must love power above all else. They must be willing to sacrifice everything for their throne."

Min Hyuk nodded. At long last, a sliver of emotion entered his eyes as he quietly said, "If it was up to me, I would crown you both as our Lords because as we all know in the business world, an organization becomes unstoppable when a union—a merger—is formed. Your combined stature will catapult this society to unmatched heights, and your reign will be legendary. If it were up to me, I would have spun your story a different way. I would have made sure it worked out in your favor."

"But?" Yoori prompted, knowing there was something powerful keeping this from ever coming to fruition.

"But there are other"—he paused to utilize the right word—"*forces* that do not want such a union to occur."

"Ju Won?" Tae Hyun supplied hatefully.

Min Hyuk smiled to himself. "Despite what Ju Won likes to make others believe, he is not the be all, end all of the Underworld. His opposition to your union may be the most outspoken one, but he is not the only one who feels this way."

"What are you alluding to?" Yoori breathed out. "What 'other forces' are so influential that even the Gods of the Underworld have to bend to their will?"

"The answer does not matter," Min Hyuk dismissed gently. "The only thing that matters is the outcome of what you will need to do next."

"I will not choose a throne over her," Tae Hyun professed with finality. "I can live without the throne; I can't say the same if I lose her."

"That is where you're wrong," Min Hyuk countered at once. "You cannot live without the throne—not in this society. A King without his throne is simply a man. You have made too many enemies to simply be a man in this world, Tae Hyun. You will not survive without your throne, and you will lose her either way." He looked between the two of them. "You two will never win; you will never be together because your story has already been written. One of you will die for the other, and if you do not play your parts, then both of you will die." He swallowed tightly before announcing something that caused Yoori and Tae Hyun to stop breathing. "Your armies have been immobilized."

Yoori and Tae Hyun stiffened in their seats.

"What?" they asked at the same time.

"The Serpents and the Siberian Tigers are no more," he clarified solemnly. "At least for the time being."

By now, Tae Hyun was beginning to breathe harshly. Anger twisted on his face. "Who has the authority to take our own soldiers from us?"

"You gave the Advisors that authority when you reneged on your agreement to battle one another."

Tae Hyun smirked, clearly recalling the Underworld war that transpired a few hours prior. "If I call for them, my Serpents will come for me. They will not abandon me."

"But you will not do such a thing," Min Hyuk corrected knowingly. "You will not put them in harm's way, especially not when it involves the

Underworld elders. You may be more than happy to relinquish your throne, but not your duties as their King." He turned to Yoori. "Or their Queen."

He stood up as silence descended upon Tae Hyun and Yoori. Despite their fury with the Underworld immobilizing their gangs, the last thing they would do was put their Underworld soldiers in harm's way. They had already failed as their Gods. They could not fail as their King and Queen.

"This immobilization is temporary," Min Hyuk went on. "It will end as soon as you see your battle through. Once one of you conquers the other, your armies will not only be returned to you, but you will also have the Underworld at your feet as well. Until then, please use your forty-eight hours wisely."

When it looked like he was about to leave, Min Hyuk temporarily stopped. With gentle eyes, he placed a fatherly hand on Tae Hyun's shoulder.

"Whatever your decision," he advised faintly, staring down at Tae Hyun with melancholy in his eyes, "once you make it, do not turn back. Never turn back again."

Yoori did not know what Min Hyuk meant with that, but she was too troubled to care. His appearance only reminded her of how hopeless their predicament was. It only served to reinforce the fact that Tae Hyun was truly living on borrowed time—that *they* were living on borrowed time.

"You should have killed me when I told you to," she finally whispered when Min Hyuk left them. She turned to face Tae Hyun with anger on her face. "Look at what has happened. This is not what I wanted for you."

"What about what I want for you?" he countered, gazing at her with the same anguish. "What I want for us?"

"There is no 'us'!" she snapped piercingly. Was he not part of the same conversation? "Don't you get it by now? Haven't they made it clear? In this world, there is no 'us'. It is you *or* me. One of us has to kill the other to survive. One of us has to die for the other to live!"

"Then leave the country with me," he uttered, shocking Yoori with his proposal.

"What?" she asked disbelievingly.

"Leave the country with me," he repeated, his sincere brown eyes gazing into hers.

An exasperated laugh escaped her. After all that went down, what made him think that they could actually be together and have a happily ever after? The absurdity of this suggestion was too foolish for her.

"Run?" Another withering laugh poured from her. "You think we can run? You know we won't get anywhere running. Our people are all over the world."

"I don't care anymore," he retorted. It was clear that he had been set on this decision since their conversation with Ju Won. Min Hyuk's appearance only served to further strengthen his decision. "They can hunt us down and we'll run. We'll keep running. As long as I'm with you, I don't care about anything else."

She swayed her head in agitation. He truly did not see the complexity—or the flaw—in his "simple" plan.

"I can't kill you, but that doesn't mean you're worth enough for me to invest my heart into you, Tae Hyun." Her heart ached at the thought of losing him. "I'd rather die alone than fall like your mother."

He closed his eyes in exasperation. "Yoo—"

"Did you not see how Young Jae looked at Anna when she died?" she cried at once. "Do you want that type of hell for either of us?"

She shook her head again. She was unwilling to put herself in a situation where she would experience even half of what Young Jae went through. A part of him died with his wife. A part of him died, and Yoori did not want a part of her to die if anything were to happen to Tae Hyun. If she completely gave her heart to Tae Hyun, then this tragedy was possible. And she wasn't strong enough for it. She was not strong enough to withstand such a cruel fate.

Yoori stared at him with tormented eyes. "I told you that I wasn't strong enough to be human with you. I told you—that even as Yoori—I did not want to be with you because I knew it wasn't going to be easy. It's not worth it, and I'm not risking a lifetime of misery for a few stolen moments with you. I can't do that. I'm *not* doing that!"

She knew how cowardly she sounded, but being fearless was her last priority. This was about self-preservation. There was too high of a chance that only misery would await them if they stayed together. Yoori could not endure that type of aftermath. She'd rather die than be forced to bear it alone.

For a long lingering minute, all Tae Hyun did was hold her pained gaze in his eyes. When she tried to turn away, his hand caught her chin.

He gently guided her gaze back to him.

"Nemo," he whispered, easily holding her prisoner to his words. "I saw how Young Jae looked at Anna when she died. I saw the hell he went through. That's why I'm here right now, that's why I want to run away with you. There's no guarantee that we'll survive past the forty-eight hours mark. The only guarantee we have right now is a choice to ignore all of our fears and allow ourselves to be swept into something we've been yearning our entire lives for. I could spend an eternity in hell if I could have five more minutes with you. I would happily endure any hell if I could be with you—alone, together, and completely in love. I'd rather do this than spend a lifetime of misery alone, wishing I had you by my side."

His finger grazed her cheek.

"This will be worth it," he promised her earnestly. "I promise that this time, it will all be worth it."

Yoori's heart expanded as she processed his words—his promises. She wished that she were strong enough to accept it; she wished she were strong enough to believe it. But she was no longer the fool that Yoori once was. The coward in her would not allow her to risk what was left of her heart.

Tae Hyun smiled sadly at her silence. Instead of resenting her for her cowardice, he nodded understandably.

"Think about it. Just think about it," he told her before walking away to give her time to think—to deliberate everything before making her final decision. "When you're ready, you know where to find me."

"Is Kwon Tae Hyun worth it?"

23: Every Stubborn Inch of It

Fear.

Nothing but fear and apprehension accompanied Yoori during her aimless walk in the hospital corridors. The pain assaulting her body was no match for the heartache she was experiencing. The events of the day replayed like a vivid film in her mind: her failed plan to give Tae Hyun the Underworld throne, Anna's death, the hatred in her brother's eyes, their meeting with Min Hyuk, and the most prominent of her memories—her recent conversation with Tae Hyun.

Her congested mind churned at a relentless speed.

If she chose not to run away with him, then she would never know the type of hell her brother and Tae Hyun's mother experienced when the love of their lives were taken from them. Tae Hyun was the only person on earth who could carry her to the highest of highs and bring her to the lowest of lows. What would become of her if she gave up everything and ran off with him? What would happen if she gave him her entire heart and he was taken from her? Her heart ached at the very thought. She would happily die for him to live, but she did not think she could survive if he was taken from her, if she had to watch him die.

Don't go with him, a fearful voice in her mind pleaded. *Please don't be human with him. Humans die, humans feel pain, humans go through hell, but Gods don't. Gods are numb, Gods are stoic, and Gods will never go through hell.*

Yoori took in a deep breath, looking upward to prevent the tears from overtaking her eyes. She was so incredibly overwhelmed. If only it was easier to make this decision. She would give anything for her life to be much simpler.

As she took in another shaky breath, her eyes involuntarily strayed into a hospital bedroom. She came to a halt when she spotted someone she recognized. The Queen within her prohibited Yoori from walking into the hospital room. It warned her to not seek any interaction with this person. Her human side, on the other hand, had no such reservation. It wanted to speak to

286

this person, to see how this person was doing. Given that she was the very reason why this girl was at the hospital, Yoori concluded that it was only right that she went in to see her. The girl would be a good distraction to her congested mind.

"Jin Ae," Yoori called, walking into the room.

Jin Ae, who was resting on the bed and staring out the window, turned her head. Her eyes enlarged after she observed that it was Yoori who called out her name. She rocketed up into a sitting position.

"What the fuck are you doing here?" Jin Ae spat out, making no effort to conceal her animosity towards Yoori. Her cold eyes watched as Yoori approached her bed. "Came to finish the job?"

Yoori curiously appraised Jin Ae. Albeit her face appeared to be healing, Jin Ae's arm was still shielded with a cast. Despite her aversion for Jin Ae, she could not deny how awful she felt to see Jin Ae in this predicament.

Ji Hoon had orchestrated Chae Young's rape and framed the entire thing on Jin Ae. Like a fool, Yoori fell for the ploy and went after Jin Ae like a bloodthirsty animal. She not only beat the girl senseless, but she was also one step away from ending Jin Ae's life. Fortunately, Tae Hyun pulled her away in time. He saved Jin Ae's life, and he saved Yoori from killing the wrong person. Because of this transgression, Yoori had already decided to let bygones be bygones with Jin Ae. They were more than even.

"If I wanted to finish the job," Yoori began patiently, "I would've snapped your neck apart before greeting you." She uncomfortably gave off a shrug. She did not know how to tell Jin Ae that she simply wanted to make sure she was recovering well. After a pregnant pause, she decided to just come out with it. "How are you?"

Jin Ae squared her shoulders. It was clear in her eyes that she harbored a large amount of resentment for Yoori. She did not believe Yoori's intentions were as diplomatic as she was making them out to be. "How do you think I am, *Soo Jin*?"

The emphasis on her birth name triggered a smile to grace Yoori's lips. Although Jin Ae was condemned to this hospital bed, she was still up to date in the happenings of their society. "I see you've been apprised of all Underworld business."

"I was hoping you'd die in the battle with Tae Hyun."

Straight and to the point. Jin Ae definitely had all the qualities of an Underworld citizen.

Yoori flashed Jin Ae a mocking grin. "Sorry to disappoint you."

"Well . . ." Jin Ae swallowed tightly at the reminder of Tae Hyun. Her lower lip quivered in dread. "Did you kill him?"

287

The concern in Jin Ae's voice stupefied her. Yoori slanted her head with curiosity. "After everything that happened, you're still infatuated with Tae Hyun?"

"He's the love of my life," Jin Ae stated simply.

There came another statement that evaded her understanding. Yoori arched a brow of inquiry. She was not sure that Jin Ae understood the gravity behind her own words.

"If he's the love of your life, why did you cheat on him with Ji Hoon?"

"Because I didn't want him to get bored and leave me," Jin Ae responded, cringing at her own immature answer. Given that she had time to grow up and reflect, it was evident that she saw how foolish her logic was. Jin Ae smirked to herself. "I wanted to make him jealous. Little did I know, he would leave me regardless because he found you instead." Her eyes teemed with contempt for Yoori. To this day, she still resented Yoori for stealing "the love of her life" from her. "And Ji Hoon, Ji Hoon was just a nice distraction. I actually thought he was nicer, but when that fucker framed me for what happened to your friend, the entire 'nice guy' persona went down the toilet. Considering I got the shit beat out of me because of him, it's safe to say I hate that fucking bastard."

A wider smile curved on Yoori's lips. Anyone who detested Ji Hoon was a friend in her book. Now that the ice had been broken between them, she decided that there was no harm in staying with Jin Ae for a few moments longer. Tae Hyun had left her with the decision of a lifetime, and she did not mind the distraction from Jin Ae.

She moved from the other side of the room to sit on the foot of Jin Ae's bed.

"Why aren't you apologizing to me for the unnecessary beating?" Jin Ae asked as she watched Yoori with weary eyes.

Yoori was sitting with her hands on her knees. She stared out the large hospital window. Outside, the snowstorm was still going strong.

"You deserved the beating," Yoori stated coolly, maintaining her gaze on the falling snow. "If not for that crime, then your crimes in the past. I haven't forgotten how you treated me when I was just an innocent and unsuspecting girl. No girl should ever be put through the hell of being raped, but you sent your men to attack me like I was a piece of shit." She turned to face Jin Ae with stern eyes. "Are you not embarrassed as a woman to do that to another woman?"

Jin Ae's bruised face was void of remorse. She tilted her chin up in a defiant manner. "I don't give a flying fuck."

Yoori regulated the fury that set a fire in her blood. The temptation to punch some sense in Jin Ae tingled in her clenched fist. She took a deep breath to curb her temper. She had already beaten the shit out of the girl. As far as she was concerned, Jin Ae had met her quota with Yoori. She was not allowed to punch Jin Ae anymore in this lifetime, especially not for a reason as silly as being an annoyance to her.

Calmed by her own reasoning, she exercised further patience by asking, "Have you ever had your men rape anyone? Have you ever actually killed anyone?"

A long silence suspended over Jin Ae. It took a few breaths before she honestly answered, "No."

Yoori nodded expectantly. She understood now why this stupid little girl was acting so high and mighty. The truth was: Jin Ae was all bark and no bite. She never had to get her hands dirty because she never had to kill anyone. She was essentially an untainted Royal who still had her soul.

"I thought your uncle would've trained you," Yoori murmured more to herself than to Jin Ae.

"I've had my men beat people up, but I'm not very good with training. I came to my uncle when I was fifteen, right after my parents died," Jin Ae told Yoori, affirming her suspicions that she was a late bloomer.

The majority of the Underworld heirs received their training at a young age. They were to start losing their souls by the age of ten, become monsters by fifteen, and turn into Gods by the age of eighteen. The fact that Jin Ae came to Ju Won at fifteen meant that he had never anticipated this life for her. She was given enough training to survive in this world, not to rule over it.

"Apparently I didn't start young enough." There was bitterness in Jin Ae's voice as she looked at Yoori. "I've always wished that I started at ten."

The thought sickened Yoori.

"You wish to train with rapists and killers?" she asked critically, surprised by the gravity of her own voice. She gazed at Jin Ae with hardened eyes. If Jin Ae knew what hell she had been put through, the last thing she would ask for was her upbringing. No ten-year-old should ever endure what she had to endure. "You wish to be beaten to near death for crying? You wish to sleep in a coffin with the decapitated body parts of the people you've killed?"

Horror filled Jin Ae's broadened eyes. "I—I didn't know that you had to sleep with amputated body parts," she stuttered quietly, staring at Yoori in a whole new light. She swallowed convulsively. "I just thought that you kill them, and you become desensitized that way. You know, clean and easy, and then you become famous in our world . . ."

Yoori softened her stare on Jin Ae. It dawned on her why she felt such a need to come and talk to Jin Ae. Now that they had the opportunity to interact in a more civilized manner, it occurred to her that Jin Ae was almost the exact replica of her when she was younger. She was too prideful for her own good, too impulsive, and too dependent upon the Underworld for happiness and satisfaction in life. The only true difference was that Jin Ae had yet to kill someone. For this, Yoori also found herself staring at Jin Ae in a brand new light. Perhaps this girl wasn't as monstrous as she led others to believe. Perhaps in this fleeting moment, she could be a friend to Yoori in her time of need.

"I didn't kill him," Yoori finally revealed, earning a shocked reaction from Jin Ae. "I didn't kill Tae Hyun."

It took Jin Ae a few seconds to digest this information.

"My uncle said that this was a battle to the death," she breathed out, relief hovering in her voice. "How can you both be alive? What happened?"

"Young Jae and Ji Hoon intervened. During the battle, they intervened and ambushed us. Instead of fighting each other, we united and fought against their army instead."

The shock had yet to leave Jin Ae. She still looked mystified. Out of all people, she knew how crucial this battle was for her uncle, for the whole Underworld. She was aware that nothing good would come out of a crownless battle.

"Who would have won had there not been an intervention?"

"We fought each other," Yoori whispered brokenly, unable to directly answer the question. "For a very long time we fought with each other. We showed no mercy to one another until the very end, when I wanted it all to end . . . when I didn't want to hurt him any further."

Jin Ae appraised Yoori's fragmented state. She did not look like a Queen who had won a battle; she looked like a Queen who was still at war with herself.

"You never planned on coming out of the battle alive, did you?" Jin Ae deduced shrewdly. When Yoori said nothing, she continued to reach for answers. "Why didn't you kill him?"

Yoori pondered the question with a deep inhalation. She considered lying, but decided against it. Without filter, she said, "Because I want him to live forever."

"If that's the case," Jin Ae began slowly, looking at the door as if expecting to see Tae Hyun there, "why aren't you with him right now?"

Yoori looked down at the tiles. Her grief-stricken heart clenched at the recollection of their last conversation. "Because we're not meant to be."

A smile touched Jin Ae's face. For the first time, some attributes of kindness marked Jin Ae's eyes towards Yoori. She reached a hesitant hand out and placed it on Yoori's shoulder.

A companionable air floated between them, making the room feel warmer and safer as the seconds ticked by.

"The two of you gave up the throne for each other, you risked your lives to keep each other alive, and now you say you're not meant to be?" She laughed, looking at Yoori like she was the dumbest girl in the world. "You know, if I were you, and if Kwon Tae Hyun loved me like that, I'd risk everything to be with him."

A nerve tugged at Yoori's heart.

She looked at Jin Ae, alarmed by how much her simple statement rattled her. In the past, it had always been Tae Hyun who argued for their relationship. He had always been her opponent, the very conflicting force in all her decision making. It was one thing to hear him argue for their relationship, but it was something else entirely to get advice from his ex-girlfriend. It was no secret that Jin Ae disliked her. The fact that she was saying these words was not only disconcerting to her, but it was also jarring. Jin Ae had nothing to gain from convincing Yoori to be with Tae Hyun. Because of this, Yoori could not help but be attentive as she spoke to Jin Ae.

"You would risk everything for him," Yoori clarified slowly, "even if it means you would be miserable for the years to come if he leaves you?

"Wouldn't you be miserable if you never went back to him?" Jin Ae shrugged, amazed herself that she was encouraging this relationship. "I'm no expert in love, but I think there are three different types of loves in this world: the ones you give up on, the ones you hold onto forever, and the rare ones that go beyond love, the kind where you find something else—something better than love."

"*Once-in-a-lifetime love*," Yoori mindlessly finished for Jin Ae.

In that dreamlike instant, it felt as if dawn had spread over her dark world, illuming over the shadows that once filled her mind with abject misery. She could feel the emotions within her spark up into life, blossoming with renewed hope.

"You would have to be human to get once-in-a-lifetime love," Yoori mused to herself. Knowing what she had to do to make her final decision, she turned to Jin Ae with keenness. "Every gang member is given a lecture on 'love' when they enter the Underworld. I know your uncle must've given it to you because he hates anyone who falls in love in this world. Do you mind repeating it to me? So I can be reminded why all of this is a bad idea?"

When Jin Ae gave her a strange look, Yoori said, "Please?"

Despite being slightly perturbed by Yoori's strange request, Jin Ae conceded.

While she spoke, Yoori was reminded of that one special memory she had with Tae Hyun, where she gave him pearls of wisdom of her own. Like an epic duel, the notions clashed with one another, battling with each other to win what was left of Yoori's soul.

"Our world isn't a society where love conquers all."

Paris is the city of love . . .

"It is a cruel world where the heartless and vengeful are revered like Kings and Queens—and the weak, the distracted are punished without mercy."

You can't go to Paris unless you're madly in love with the person who is taking you.

"May the Kings and Queens who had fallen before you be your examples, may their demise dictate your choices in life. You may have been born human, but you are raised to be a God. You are raised to rule over this world, not succumb to its weaknesses."

And not just the type of love where you tell one another that you can't live without each other.

"If you are weak, then you are not fit to be a Royal. And if you are not fit to be a Royal, then you are no longer a God. We have no room for humans in our society, for we are plagued with the never-ending pursuit of power—morals cease to exist here."

No . . . not that type of love . . .

"When you become human, then you have become a parasite. In our society, parasites must be punished—they must be exterminated. Remember that the next time you become tempted, remember the stories you've heard of all the legends that fell from grace. If you go against our bylaws, you will never be the exception. You will be made an example of, you will be punished, and you will regret ever being born. This is a world where Gods walk amongst humans—"

"—Once you're in, the only exit is death," Yoori finished for Jin Ae. "You can run, you can hide, and you can fight all you want, but the inescapable truth is that your blood belongs to this world. No matter where you go, we will find you. No matter where you hide, we will drag you back. No matter who protects you, we will annihilate them. You were born into this world, you lost your soul in this world, you became a God in this world—it is only fitting that you see your end in it," Yoori concluded, feeling no more hesitation as her own words filtered in and out of her mind.

The prospect of death could never compare to that once-in-a-lifetime moment when you are given the gift of falling in love with someone who loves you unconditionally. Yoori realized this all but too clearly as she placed aside the horrors of the Underworld and focused on her relationship with Tae Hyun.

"Love is every God's worst nightmare," Jin Ae continued, "every God's death sentence."

But the type of love that is unconditional—the type that is undying.

"It is the one human aspect that is strong enough to break Gods—and make them human again."

You know . . . the type that can withstand anything . . .

"Yet every one of us continues to seek that forbidden fruit . . ."

One of those once-in-a-lifetime love . . .

"Because it's the only thing that makes us human—it is the only thing that makes life worth living."

Yoori's heart expanded. She had never seen things more clearly. She had never felt braver as she stared out that snow-streaked window.

Her decision had been set.

Her lips quivering, she felt the hope grow stronger in her once embittered soul. She no longer cared about the dark possibilities. All she cared about was her timeless distraction. All she cared about was her once-in-a-lifetime love.

Welcome, Paris . . . to my Underworld, she thought breathlessly, thinking of Tae Hyun. *Thank you for staying despite all the hardships I've caused you. Thank you for being with me until the very end.*

Nothing mattered anymore. The impossible didn't matter anymore. Revenge on her brother didn't matter anymore. Revenge on Ji Hoon didn't matter anymore. The threat of the Underworld didn't matter anymore.

Nothing mattered more than loving him and being with *him*.

Nothing mattered but Kwon Tae Hyun.

Jin Ae smiled favorably, noting the new glow that took over Yoori's face. She illumed in a way that only a person in love could when they gave their entire heart to someone.

"Looks like you've already made your decision," Jin Ae observed warmly, ending the last encounter the girls would have with one another. "Is Kwon Tae Hyun worth it?"

"Every stubborn inch of it."

"You'll tell me what it feels like, right?"

24: Welcome to My Underworld

He was quiet as he stood there, his eyes running over the snow that cascaded from the dark sky. Beside the peaceful lake, the white gazebo glowed like a beacon in the snow-covered night. Icicle lights twirled all around the pillars of the infrastructure, converging together with the green leaves and snow.

Standing in the center of this picturesque scene was Kwon Tae Hyun.

He wore a black hoodie and blue plaid pajama pants, simple clothes that did little to help ward off the winter chills. Although his face was pale, he did not allow the unforgiving weather to deter him from his purpose. As though expecting someone special to join him at any moment, he continued to stare straight ahead at a dark pathway, his eyes teeming with hope. Not once did he budge from his position.

During his wait, several elderly couples stopped by to ask whom he was waiting for. Always the gentleman, he smiled and told them he had just gotten into a fight with his girlfriend and that he was waiting for her to come back to him.

"You're sure she's coming in this weather?" they asked, staring at him with pity in their eyes. It was palpable that he knew what they were thinking. He was aware that they wanted to tell him: "*If she hasn't arrived by now, then she's not coming.*"

Paying no mind to what they were thinking, he merely nodded and said, "She's coming."

And with that, he continued to wait as the minutes passed him by.

One hour turned into two hours and six minutes.

Two hours and six minutes turned into three hours and fifty-eight minutes.

Three hours and fifty-eight minutes turned into six hours and forty-three minutes . . .

At six hours and forty-three minutes, he remained where he was, his pale face as determined and hopeful as when he first stepped foot into the gazebo.

The winds of the snowstorm picked up in acceleration, bringing a stampede of snow into the gazebo. Even though it felt like everything around him was conspiring in forcing him to leave, he easily ignored all these distractions.

To him, nothing mattered more than waiting for the one he loved.

Then, as another cold breeze tumbled into the gazebo, warmth presided over him once he felt a pair of arms wrap itself around his stomach.

An elated smile appeared on his face when she rested her head against his back.

He closed his eyes, never looking happier as he reveled in her company.

"I just wanted you to know," Yoori began softly, tears filling her eyes as she held the love of her life close to her, never again wanting to let him go, "that no matter where life takes me, no matter the distance, no matter the length of time, no matter the obstacles—I'll *always* come back to you. Even if I, myself, am not sure if I'll come back—in the end I'll *always* come back. 'Cause that's the thing about boomerangs, right? They come back even if they feel they shouldn't, they come back even if the world tries to stop them, they come back because they ultimately know *where* they belong . . . and *who* they belong to."

At her words, he expelled a joyful breath.

Tae Hyun turned to face her. Warmth and love emanated from him while he cupped his hands over her cheeks. He stared deep into her eyes, his emotions overfilling him, just as they were overfilling her.

"It feels like it's been a lifetime," he said quietly. "Welcome back, boomerang."

She smiled meekly, holding back the tears to keep from crying in joy. It had been a very long journey. She was relieved to finally return to where it all started for them. This gazebo was where they had their first real kiss. It was only fitting that they put all the shadows of their past behind them and return to this very special spot.

"Thanks, boomerang. Long trip."

He grinned, his eyes rippling with affection before he playfully added, "Yeah, took you long enough. My ass is freezing . . . and I have to pee."

"Shut up, jerk-face," Yoori snapped, choking back laughter. "I was making life-changing decisions, and I got lost on the way here. It didn't help that the first time I came, I was sleeping on the ride here."

A big, genuine laugh poured from him. Given all that had transpired in the past twenty-four hours, it was an understatement to say that Tae Hyun was thankful that they had finally reached this moment in time.

"Still a brat I see," he murmured adoringly.

Yoori beamed up at him, knowing she made the right decision. This was it. This was the once-in-a-lifetime love she had been dreaming about all her life.

"Still a snob I see."

Tae Hyun gently pulled her closer to him. "You're not afraid of anything that may happen in the future?"

"I don't care anymore," she told him genuinely. She had never felt braver as she stood in his company—as she stood in the presence of the one person who not only made her human, but also made her the happiest person on earth. "I'd rather spend a lifetime in misery after completely giving myself to you than spend another second without you."

Tae Hyun nodded, his eyes telling her that he'd prefer the same.

"So," he began warmly, "what do we do now?"

She wrapped her arms around him and brought his head down so that their foreheads were touching, so she could stare into his eyes with pure hope.

"My Illusionist, will you take me into a world filled with timeless magic?"

He smiled, grazing his hand over her face. "Are you willing to disappear?"

"Will you disappear with me?"

His smile grew wider as he nodded and then pressed his soft lips against hers. With no more inhibitions, he kissed her like a man possessed—like a man who had finally found true paradise.

He, like Yoori, no longer cared about anything else.

They no longer cared about the Underworld or what was in store for them in the future.

All that mattered to them was the here and now.

All that mattered to them was their timeless distraction.

"Let's disappear, Princess."

"When you find Paris?"

25: Perfection

There are moments in life when you feel nothing but a sense of perfection.

The stars have aligned, time has stood still, the storms are at bay, the cruelty of the world has receded, and you have been given one of those few perfect moments in life where everything makes sense, where everything is beautiful, where everything—*even for a brief moment*—is perfect.

For Choi Yoori, or An Soo Jin, or whatever name you want to call her (though she'd prefer Choi Yoori as it was the only name that made her feel human—made her feel *alive*), that perfect moment in her life emerged as she walked barefoot on the grass lawn just outside of Tae Hyun's lake house.

Several days had passed since their reunion at the gazebo, and her life had never felt more magical.

Wearing a simple white dress with a soft smile sprinkled across her lips, Yoori locked eyes with Tae Hyun. He was standing atop a white wooden boat, his outstretched hand beckoning for hers. He favored her with a smile that rivaled the illumination of the moon and stars. It was enough to intensify the beating of Yoori's already smitten heart and enough to send all her feminine sensibilities over the edge.

Damn sexy bastard, she thought breathlessly.

Biting her lower lip to keep her soft smile from morphing into an uncontrollable grin, Yoori took his hand. She tightened her stomach to subdue the butterflies that were beginning to frolic in her tummy and happily climbed onto the boat with him.

Before they permanently left the country—destination still unknown, as the contact Tae Hyun used was still drawing up plans to safely send them out of the country—Yoori and Tae Hyun wanted to temporarily disappear to the place where all this magic started for them: the lake house.

During the course of their stay, Tae Hyun, being the multitalented heartthrob and charmer that he was, spoiled Yoori rotten by making her breakfast in bed, lunch in bed, and dinner in bed while they disappeared into their own private world. Each delicious meal came with amorous kisses that he showered over the column of her neck and bare shoulder. With his knees propped up, he held her safe between them as he embraced her from behind. While doing so, Yoori, who would have a mouth full of scrumptious food, would lift food over her shoulder and dotingly feed him as well.

They wore matching black and blue plaid pajama pants and couldn't have looked more like the perfect couple as the ducks and geese celebrated the first day of spring in the wide open lake adjacent to their master bedroom. It was a blissful and heavenly state. Yet, as with any situation that came with being in the company of Kwon Tae Hyun and Choi Yoori, no matter how in love, their fiery and combative personalities would never fail to make their long awaited appearances during their stay at the lake house.

"You dumb Snob!" Yoori yelled several days prior, holding up a DVD box. She was in disbelief of Tae Hyun's idiocy when it came to pop culture. "How the hell did you mistake a Nemo DVD with *Jaws*?"

"You little Brat!" Tae Hyun would scream the day after, his face marred with annoyance. "Are you trying to kill me? Why do we have to watch Twilight every second of every goddamn day?"

"Oh my God!" Yoori would cry out in hysteria, walking into the living room a few hours later only to find him crouching in front of the fireplace. He was holding what suspiciously looked like her most favorite set of books in the world over the raging fire. "Are you burning my romance books?!"

Finally, there was the dramatic instance where Tae Hyun and Yoori were playing with a boomerang in the park beside the lake house.

"What the hell is wrong with you? How can you throw a boomerang, of all things, *wrong*?"

Standing beside one another on the grass lawn, Yoori couldn't help but scrunch up her face in bitterness at the fact that, even after twenty-one consecutive attempts, she still couldn't get that stupid flying object to come flying back to her.

While at the store, Yoori had spotted some cool boomerangs. She was eager to buy one so they could actually play with the one object they had been using to define their love story. Both Yoori and Tae Hyun were initially excited. Lo and behold, after the lameness Yoori displayed, both were getting pretty damn impatient with her consistent failure.

Yoori felt embarrassed, not only because Tae Hyun was getting annoyed with her and her lack of skills, but also because she had a small crowd of viewers who were watching her every move.

In addition to the opinionated spectator that was Tae Hyun, six little kids—three young girls and three young boys—were sitting on the space of grass behind them. They were watching her and Tae Hyun with unwavering fascination. Whatever their purpose for observing her and Tae Hyun so keenly,

Yoori didn't care, nor did she deign to think much of it. The only thing she cared about was to impress them—or in this particular case, failing to impress them.

The heat of mortification crept up Yoori's cheeks. She resented that she could not show off in front of the little kiddies. What kind of role model was she if she couldn't even successfully throw a boomerang and get it to come back to her? Although she was being hard on herself, her self-criticism could never match that of Tae Hyun's.

She already knew the hot jerk-face was a straight shooter, but she didn't think the guy would be that blunt until he carelessly added, "How much can you fail at life?"

Yoori was close to exploding at Tae Hyun for the digs he was giving to her. She demonstrated impressive control by curbing her anger. Under normal circumstances, she would have handed Tae Hyun's ass to him. Given that they had a susceptible young audience behind them, Yoori did well to censor her temper by staying calm, composed, and demure. There was no way in hell she was going to be a bad influence on the cute, chubby little kiddies.

"Life isn't measured by the success rate of throwing boomerangs," she diplomatically stated, trying to save face in front of the children, "it is measured by the moments that take your breath away."

Tae Hyun furrowed his brows at the irrelevancy of what she just said. He gaped at her with a blank face while glancing at the children behind them.

"You just made no sense and now you've made yourself look like a fool in front of the cute, chubby kiddies behind us. Good example that you're setting for future generations, smart one."

Yoori scoffed defensively. Though she agreed with him in terms of the idiocy of what was just said (it sounded much better in her mind), the jerk didn't have to continue to provoke her.

She folded her arms to keep from punching him and sourly said, "What's the big deal anyway? Why are you getting offended? Why does it matter to you if I successfully throw a boomerang or not?

Heated offense touched Tae Hyun's eyes. He stared at her like she just did the unthinkable and cursed in church.

"Are you serious?"

Yoori shrugged again, not knowing what answer to give him. Of course she was serious. What was he getting all butt-hurt for?

Taking one step closer to her, his tall and powerful body overshadowing hers with seriousness, Tae Hyun did well to enlighten Yoori as to *why* he was offended. He also did well to enunciate with extreme fervor exactly why she should feel guilty for offending him.

"You're the one who started this weird boomerang shit with all the talk about 'you will always come back to me.' Now our love story is defined by it.

Hell, even I got into it. I made a heartfelt speech relating our love to it and this is what you do? You can't even effectively get the instrument our big speech is based upon to come back to you?" An accusing frown morphed on his handsome face. "*Really*, Brat? Are you *really* going to butcher our love story like that?"

Leave it to Kwon Tae Hyun to be the only one who could successfully guilt trip Choi Yoori into embarrassment.

"You're so overdramatic," Yoori grumbled under her breath.

She outwardly feigned nonchalance to his words. Internally, she was embarrassed because what he said was true. That big, monumental speech they used as their way of "making up" was forever engraved in their love story. How much could she fail at life if she couldn't even get the damn instrument itself to come flying back to her?

"Here!" she prompted heatedly, snatching the boomerang out of his grasp. She was determined to get this right. She was the Queen of the Underworld for Christ's sake. She could shoot bullets with accuracy, she could wield swords with ease, and she could kick ass without breaking a sweat. Hell would freeze over before she allowed this innocuous flying object to bury her. "Let me try again."

"Don't put too much pressure on it," Tae Hyun instructed, proud that she was giving it another shot. He looked determined to help her get this right. "Just let it glide out of your hand, and it will do everything by itself."

Yoori vehemently nodded at Tae Hyun's instructions. She sucked in a hopeful breath and angled the boomerang with her hand. Then, with pure anticipation, she tossed it . . . only to find herself groaning dejectedly when the supposed "flying object" crashed to the ground in yet another display of failure.

Tae Hyun shook his head, his face blank.

He was out of words.

"You can kick ducks and send them flying like soccer balls, yet you can't even toss a boomerang," he murmured critically, breathing in disbelief. "Wow. You really suck at life."

This was when an already hotheaded Yoori lost it.

"Then you do it! You do it!" she snarled, picking the fallen boomerang off the grass and shoving it into Tae Hyun's hand, wishing with all of her heart that he'd fail at throwing it as well.

He released a dramatic sigh and spared a glance at the kids. He tilted his head as if to say, *"I'll be a good example to you, little ones,"* and with the ease of a warrior tossing a knife, Tae Hyun raised the boomerang up and hurled it into the air. Then, magic happened.

Astonishment stole the expressions of Yoori and the children as they watched the flying instrument defy gravity. It glided through the air, twirling beautifully in the sky. It nearly disappeared into the sunny horizon before it obediently came flying back towards Tae Hyun, landing submissively in his hand like it knew where it belonged . . . and to whom it belonged to.

"This can't be happening," Yoori whispered miserably, taking a moment to eye the little kiddies.

The little girls were staring at Tae Hyun with stars in their big brown eyes, sighing as if they had never seen a man as perfect as he. On the opposite end of the spectrum, the little boys were scrunching their faces in bitterness, not believing that anyone could be impressed with a show-off like Tae Hyun. Needless to say, in this particular instance, Yoori related to the little boys more than she did the little girls.

"You think you're hot stuff just because you can toss a boomerang, huh, Kwon?" she prompted jealously. "You think you can do no wrong and that you're super perfect?"

He gave her one of those perfect, charming smiles. Though Yoori did well to not sigh dreamily at the sight, the future of her fellow female species did not show the same strength. Giggling while the stars in their eyes shined brighter for Tae Hyun, the little girls fanned themselves while the boys irritably rolled their eyes.

Undeterred by her hostility, Tae Hyun laughed, doing well to strategically use his charms on Yoori to counteract her anger—something he always did to drive her crazy. Wrapping one arm around her hip, he pulled her closer to him. After making sure that she was tucked safely beside his body, he tilted his head down to her ears and allowed his tempting breath to tickle her skin. His actions spoke of adoration for her. His words, however, throbbed with competitive playfulness.

"I'd rather be super perfect than suck at life by failing to get a boomerang to come back to me."

A vein in Yoori's body twitched.

"You know what?" she incited impatiently, pushing herself away from him.

Tae Hyun slanted his head, the attractive yet annoying smile still embellished across his kissable lips. "What?"

Then, Yoori did the unthinkable.

Abandoning all the bullshit about being a good example for the cute kids, she relinquished all self-control and snatched the boomerang from Tae Hyun's grasp. She slammed it brutally against his chest. The impact stunned Tae Hyun, leaving him to unexpectedly gasp for air just as the boomerang-turned-weapon fell back into her hands.

"What was that for?" Tae Hyun breathed out, outraged by her violent outburst. The reaction on his face mirrored that of an innocent kid who didn't understand why he was being punished.

"There!" she said petulantly, throwing the boomerang on the ground. "It came back to me!"

Angrily huffing to herself, Yoori fixed her hair, gave a still stupefied Tae Hyun a murderous look, and then proceeded to stomp away, setting the stage for the bigger theatrics to come.

Akin to little poachers who finally saw the opportunity to capture their prized treasure, the children's eyes lit up at the sight of Yoori walking away from Tae Hyun.

"Yay!" they all cheered shamelessly, getting up from their seats with the happiest of joy.

Like excited ducklings, the three chubby boys waddled after a fuming Yoori in exhilaration.

"Miss, miss! Can you be my girlfriend now?" they shouted, thinking that Yoori and Tae Hyun had broken up. "I'll treat you better than that jerk!"

Adjacent to them, the three chubby little girls ran over to Tae Hyun in glee. "Mister! Mister! Can you be my boyfriend now? We've been waiting for you guys to break up!"

Hour after hour, they would argue, and hour after hour, they could be found hiding in corners of the lake house, making out like no tomorrow. She would be standing on her tiptoes while his arms wrapped around her waist. He would kiss her with such love that she would wonder if there ever was a more perfect man in the world for her.

"Have you ever thought about being a pop star?" she asked mindlessly earlier that day, her arms encircled around his neck. She appreciatively played with the short strands of his hair, admiring how striking he looked wearing nothing but white pajama pants. She felt fortunate to be able to gawk, touch, and molest that gorgeous body as she pleased.

A bewildered expression flashed across his face. Dry amusement filtered from his lips. "I'm standing here half-naked and yours for the taking . . . and you're asking me if I've ever considered being a pop star?"

"A singer," she clarified, grinning at his perplexed reaction. "I think you have a lot of charisma. You'd blow any other artists off the charts with just a smile."

He laughed, nipping his nose with hers. His smile was lazy, soft, and completely sexy.

"Is this your strange way of complimenting and seducing me?" he inquired before playing along and adding, "Should I join a boy band? Is that what it'll take to get me some action tonight?"

Yoori laughed as he raised her chin up and took it upon himself to shower her with loving kisses over her jaw. He sensuously trailed his lips down to her neck and nipped at the skin there.

"Like DBSK or Big Bang?" she murmured playfully.

"I have no idea who those kids are," he began with a disbelieving chuckle, "but I'll have to crush your dreams right there, *Choi*, because I can't sing. I'm a businessman through and through. My talents don't extend further than meeting rooms . . ." A naughty glint caught his eyes before he pulled her tighter against him. He placed his lips on the sensitive skin of her earlobe and started to skillfully nibble on it. The act caused her legs to give out. Luckily, he was able to hold her steady in his strong arms. When she was able to regain her breath, he teasingly added, "*Or bedrooms . . .*"

She nodded stupidly at the last bit. She fought back an avalanche of whimpers while he continued to drive her crazy with his supple mouth. She couldn't have agreed more. If Kwon Tae Hyun were to ever gift pop culture with his existence, he'd blow those idol kids out of the water by simply being the sexiest man to ever grace the soils of the earth. Men like Kwon Tae Hyun were a rarity in life, and she had no problem keeping him to herself. She did not want to share him with the whole world anyway. While contemplating this, Yoori smiled to herself as she thought about the irony of her life.

Even though the entire Underworld was after them, instead of worrying about her future, she was stupidly arguing about the awesomeness of her favorite books, the absurdity of not being able to correctly throw a boomerang (while being hit on by some adorable kids), and the randomness of having a silly conversation about him becoming a pop star. All of these things that had occurred within the solace of their own world felt so safe and lighthearted. Given the dangerous life that Yoori had led, she would not have it any other way. It felt like it had been a lifetime since she had the opportunity to hold him and love him like this. It felt like a lifetime since she had been this *human*. She wasn't going to let this wonderful moment pass her by worrying about a future she couldn't control. All that mattered to her was the gift of the present. All that mattered to her was the world they had disappeared into. All that mattered to her was her timeless distraction. All that truly mattered to Yoori was Kwon Tae Hyun.

The scent of lake water filled their lungs as they rested side by side on the wooden boat. With their hands on their stomachs, their eyes grew lost in the plasma of stars swimming above them. The soft melody of crickets, ducks, and geese played all around the serene lake, harmonizing with the beating of Yoori's relaxed heart.

"How long do you think it'll take before the ducks realize who we are and attack us again?" Tae Hyun voiced with a lighthearted smile.

Yoori laughed, her heart lifting at Tae Hyun's mischievous inquiry. After the phone conversation they had with their friends, she was beginning to feel a bit down. She appreciated any effort employed to make her smile.

Only moments prior, they had a three-way phone conversation with Hae Jin and Kang Min, as well as Jae Won and Chae Young. It was an emotional call that weighed heavily in Yoori's heart. Kang Min and Hae Jin shared their plans of running away to Sydney, Australia to raise their child there. They had hoped to return to Seoul once things were calmer. As for Jae Won and Chae Young, they had recently come clean to Mr. Lee about Jae Won's status as a gang member. They couldn't toy with the idea of running away without bringing Chae Young's only family member, a man whom Jae Won had come to view as his own father, with them. Because of this, they knew that they could no longer keep Mr. Lee in the dark. At the offset, Mr. Lee had been stunned and hurt with this revelation. However, because he had come to love Jae Won like the son he never had, Mr. Lee did something uncharacteristic: he agreed. Much to the elation of Chae Young and Jae Won, Mr. Lee agreed to follow them wherever they needed to go because all that mattered to him was his family.

Prior to all this talk about running away, Jae Won and Kang Min were initially reticent with leaving the gang they grew up in. Or more precisely, they were reticent with leaving the one who saved their lives and literally raised them. They were so troubled that they promised Yoori they would return once things were calmer. It wasn't until Yoori broke through their unease with her own plans did they find liberation. She essentially told them that she and Tae Hyun were done.

They were done being the King and Queen.

They were done with the Underworld.

And then, with her heart growing heavier with the passing seconds, Yoori did one of the hardest things she ever had to do in her life: she finally parted ways with the best friends she grew up with.

"Thank you for everything that you've done for me," she whispered over the phone, wishing that she could see them again before she left for good. "You've been more like brothers to me than my own flesh and blood. I couldn't feel more blessed and honored to have both of you by my side. Please take care of yourselves, and if anything happens to either of you or the girls, I'll kill you both in your next lifetimes. Do you hear me?" A short bout of forced laughter filled the other line before Yoori added, "Chae Young and Hae Jin, I love you both so much. I will miss you. Please be safe until we meet again."

It was an emotional call that needed to be made for their very survival. It was no longer safe for the three couples to be together. This case was especially true for Yoori and Tae Hyun, both of whom knew that the Underworld were going to be after them when news broke that they had forfeited their thrones and chose to be together instead.

The Underworld rewarded only the most ruthless of people. Yoori and Tae Hyun couldn't have embodied the very opposite of the persona. Their ruthless society was not going to let them off easy, and there was no way in hell they were going to involve Hae Jin, Kang Min, Chae Young, or Jae Won into their quandary. It was simply too dangerous.

"When things are calmer, we'll have another dinner get-together soon," Tae Hyun assured, trying to ease the solemn mood.

At the thought of something so bright in their future, everyone laughed through their tears. They recalled how wonderful their last dinner together was and agreed vehemently that once things were more settled, they'd meet again. With whispers of their final goodbyes, they hung up, each starting a new road to their lives.

Their hearts may have been heavy with grief, but Yoori knew that everyone shared the same excitement for the journey ahead of them. After being consumed by the darkness within the Underworld for so long, it was a godsend to be blessed with an opportunity to escape from it and finally start brand new lives as ordinary humans.

While inhaling the fresh crisp air circulating around the boat, Yoori's eyes landed on a couple of ducks swimming beside them. The ducks were waddling peacefully, completely oblivious to their presence.

"Maybe if we don't argue or bicker, they won't notice us and they'll leave us alone," she responded to the question Tae Hyun posed about the ducks recognizing them.

He smirked at this. "Try holding your breath. Let me know how that goes, and I'll let you know how easy it is for the two of us to spend time together and not argue or bicker." A chuckle escaped him before he expelled a relaxed sigh. "We'll try it your way for a while though."

"Okay," Yoori uttered, never feeling more relaxed as they allowed the serenity of life to wash over them. She was grateful for the moment she was sharing with Tae Hyun. There was nowhere else she'd rather be than there with him.

"Hae Jin's pregnant," Yoori breathed out after a stretch of silence. She turned to Tae Hyun with a wide smile. "Kang Min and Hae Jin are going to have a *baby*."

Tae Hyun's lips lifted into an astounded smile.

"My baby sister is pregnant," he repeated, sharing in the amazement. He swayed his head from side to side, taking a second to absorb the enormity of his words. "Kang Min knocked up my baby sister," he reiterated to himself, closing his eyes disbelievingly. He shook his head again, groaning to himself at the ludicrousness of that piece of information. "If this was any other situation, I would've already skinned his ass alive."

Yoori giggle, trusting that Tae Hyun would. The only other person in the world for whom Tae Hyun would give up his life was his baby sister. She didn't imagine that big brother was ecstatic to hear that his baby sister had been knocked up by one of his underbosses. Though Kang Min was one of the greatest guys in existence, in the protective eyes of Tae Hyun, Kang Min and the rest of the guys in the world would never be good enough for his precious baby sister. It wasn't personal; it was just an older brother thing.

"I think they're going to have a baby girl," she casually shared, changing the topic while her face glowed with warmth. She could already envision how cute and pretty this baby was going to be.

Tae Hyun glanced at her in interest. He readjusted his body so that he was completely facing her. The boat creaked softly when he did this. "How do you know?"

"I just know," she stated confidently.

She readjusted her sleeping position to intimately face him as well. "And you're going to spoil her rotten. You're going to give her all the best toys you could find, you're going to feed her and keep feeding her until she's plump and round . . ."

Her words died in her throat when another train of thoughts came into the horizon. The warmness she felt was eclipsed by the awfulness that shrouded over her. The happy glow faded away when she was reminded about the niece or nephew she would never meet.

"You're going to be the best uncle ever," she finished optimistically, going to great lengths to keep the artificial smile on her face. She did not want to worry Tae Hyun. Alas, her efforts proved to be futile when a knowing light flashed in Tae Hyun's eyes.

Sensing her despondency, Tae Hyun lifted his hand and delicately stroked his fingers over her cheek.

"What happened with Anna," he began consolingly, his eyes gentle and comforting, "wasn't your fault."

"I killed my brother's wife and his unborn baby," she replied dejectedly, the hollow part in her stomach becoming bigger with each progressive breath. "How is it not my fault?"

"You didn't know she was pregnant."

Yoori smiled self-loathingly. She appreciated his efforts to appease her guilt. It was a kind thing for him to do, but it would never be enough to assuage the remorse she felt.

"You know just as well as I that the equation is irrelevant. It's the end result that matters." She breathed shakily, her fingers mindlessly playing with

Tae Hyun's. "It's funny. When I regained all my memories, I couldn't wait to bring war upon him. I couldn't wait to make him suffer for what he did to our father—to kill him for betraying our family. But nothing is as black and white as I want it to be. When I actually made him suffer for what he did, I felt myself suffering with him. I felt and still feel myself suffering too because no matter what he did, I will always remember the older brother I grew up with—the one who always protected me and the one I'll always love." She smiled resentfully to herself before adding, "Do you know what's fucked up?"

"What?" asked Tae Hyun, giving her the opportunity to ease her congested mind.

"I know that he still loves me," she breathed out painfully, "that he cares for me. But the thing about love is that it doesn't venture far in this world. We can never go back to the way we used to be. This world has corrupted us to the point of no return. I will never forgive what he did to our father. In the same token, he will never forgive the sole fact that I killed his wife and his unborn child. We may have ties by blood, but our ties by heart have been severed beyond repair." She exhaled sharply, taking her eyes off Tae Hyun for a fleeting second. In that moment, another daunting reflection came to her mind. "I can't help but think that he got what was coming to him. The most horrible thing that could happen to a human being happened to him, and I can't help but think that he deserved it."

The nerves in her body tightened. Fear inhabited her eyes while she applied the logic to her own life.

"Sometimes . . . I can't help but think that it will only be a matter of time before I get what's coming to me." She swallowed agonizingly. "My brother will never forgive me for what I took from him. I know him—I grew up with him. If you're true to him, then he'll protect you until the end. But if you cross him, he would go to any lengths to destroy you." Yoori could feel dread surge through her like a vicious fire. The idea of having someone as vengeful as her brother coming after her terrified her. "He will search all ends of the earth to find me. He will make me pay for everything I took from him."

A cool breeze swept through the boat again. Though it was strong enough to ruffle her hair, it wasn't strong enough to distract Yoori from her thoughts. Staring deeply into Tae Hyun's eyes, she asked him something she had wanted to ask him since they reunited at the gazebo.

"You're really not afraid of being with me? Of what's to come?"

"Young Jae does not evoke any fear from me, neither does the Underworld," Tae Hyun replied reassuringly, tucking the bangs that had blown astray back behind Yoori's ear. His calm voice pulsed with steel-like confidence. He truly wasn't afraid of anyone. "The only thing I'm afraid of is losing you. I don't ever want to lose you again."

Yoori blinked in concurrence. She shared the same sentiments about him. She did not fear what Young Jae or the Underworld might do to her. She only feared what they would do to Tae Hyun, and in turn, what *that* would do to her.

Another sequence of thoughts then appeared in her mind, veering her off course and taking their topic of conversation onto another road.

"They don't look alike though," she launched quizzically. "Ho Young and Young Jae . . . they do not resemble one another. If I had seen a resemblance, then I might've had an idea about the possible relation. However, they do not resemble each other at all. I know they're not identical twins, but the sole fact that they're fraternal twins must mean that they would look alike in some way, right?"

"If you were your father and you hid a son in an enemy family, wouldn't you go to lengths to change everything about the son being raised by you?" Tae Hyun reasoned, enlightening Yoori with his logic. She could see in Tae Hyun's eyes that talking about a "brother" he had so much history with was a painful topic for him. For her, he kept his composure. Now that Ho Young was dead, he had already made his peace. "There must be a catalyst as to why Young Jae even found out that Ho Young was his fraternal twin. Was there ever a point during your childhood where you started to realize that your brother was looking . . . different?"

Yoori pondered his question. "Young Jae grew up and was trained in Japan. There were periods of time during his teens where he would train for years without coming back. When he did come home, I would notice subtle differences in his face. Because we were so young, I thought it was a natural change because he was growing up. Now that I think about it, I wouldn't be surprised if my father started to give my brother subtle facial surgeries then and gradually worked on that as he grew up."

She recalled during their childhood when a thirteen-year-old Young Jae told her that their father had "accidentally" broken Young Jae's nose when he was training. She winced and shook her head at the thought.

"I think my father may have used training as an excuse to injure him. I think that may be how Young Jae was tipped off, but who knows what he did and how he truly found out." She laughed self-mockingly. The soap opera story-like plotline that came out of her mouth was incredulous, even to her. "What a screwed up life we lead, right? I not only killed one of my brothers' wife and unborn child, but I also helped kill the other brother I didn't know existed. I spread information I knew would have you running back from America to kill him."

She stared into his eyes when this damning thought slammed into her like a jet plane, reminding her of how fucked up her family was. No matter how anyone cut it, it was all too apparent what terrible people her family members were. As the apple that came from that same tree, she couldn't help but take responsibility for the horrors they inflicted upon Tae Hyun and his family.

"I'm sorry for everything that my family has done to your family," she told him sorrowfully, thinking about how her father killed his actual brother to hide Ho Young within his family, how Ho Young raped his baby sister, and how Young Jae was taking part in helping to ruin everything else.

"It's fine," he assured her, his finger stroking over her cheek. "Yoori, it's fine. Whatever happened, it's all in the past. You're not perfect, none of us are. We do the best we can, learn from the things we can learn from, and live the best way we can. The past is the past. All that matters is the here and now, and the person that you currently are."

Yoori smiled gratefully before asking something that lightened the mood and brought silly smiles to their faces.

"So, what was the first thought in your mind when I came in that night during Ju Won's birthday party? Don't lie! I know it must not have been a pleasant one."

"My first thought?" Tae Hyun laughed. He feigned a dramatic sigh as he recalled what was playing in his mind at that particular moment. "Well, I wasn't really paying attention to what was going on that night. I just sat on the throne and brooded. I was lost in my own world until I heard the doors slam open and everyone gasping and stuff. My first thought was, '*What the hell? Why is everyone all shocked all of a sudden? Who the fuck just walked in?*'"

Yoori laughed at his ridiculous answer. She playfully pushed at his chest. "You did *not* think that!"

He nodded. "Yeah, I did."

Although she rolled her eyes and accepted his answer, she wasn't done with her curiosity pertaining to his first thoughts about her as An Soo Jin. "What did you think after that then?"

"That you were acting like a bigger brat than I remembered," he answered bluntly, hiding back a smile. "Still the same spoiled brat, but the more arrogant version."

"Do you miss the old Yoori?" she asked suddenly, her voice barely above a whisper. It was a dumb question to ask, but since she was being dumb and talking about all the random things on her mind, she might as well ask that as well. "The one who was more innocent? Less tainted?"

"Why would I miss someone who's here in front of me?" he replied instead, his eyes warm while gazing into hers. "I told you once already that it doesn't matter what name you go by or what memories you have. I fell in love with you. An Soo Jin, Choi Yoori, or whatever other name you want to go by—it doesn't matter to me." He grinned teasingly, pressing his forehead against hers with fondness. "You're stuck with me no matter what, Princess."

She blushed, her heart jumping at the feeling of them being so close. God help her that she would love a guy this much that just the feel of his warm body next to hers was enough to drive her hormones over the edge. Their chemistry was undeniable, but the thing that was still a question mark to her was his determination and his unwavering certainty about that chemistry.

"Why were you so sure that we belong together, Tae Hyun?" she prompted softly, running her fingers over his cheek. "I gave you such a hard time. How the hell did you put up with all of it? What was it about us that gave you so much strength to keep pursuing me?"

He went quiet for a fraction of a second. His warm brown eyes stared at her as if deliberating whether or not he should enlighten her with his answer. After another second, he parted his lips.

"Do you remember when we first met?"

"Yes," Yoori responded tentatively, taken aback with the strange query. Why was he bringing this up? What did this have to do with anything? "At the diner."

He shook his head, and that ignited every combative nerve in her body.

She stared at him blankly, unimpressed with his lack of skill in the memory department. She knew it felt like a lifetime ago since they had met, but it wasn't like they had a boring meeting. How could he forget?

"You're disagreeing with how we met?" She laughed incredulously. "Do you not remember me spilling coffee on you and you blackmailing me, buddy? Remember our 'boss-and-assistant' days?"

He chuckled, knowing that they were definitely not on the same page. He posed another question in an effort to get her on the same page as him. "How did you come up with the idea to mix the tea together?"

"I mixed it together for fun," she answered carefully, wondering what Tae Hyun ate for dinner. The hottie was acting especially strange tonight. Why was he being so random?

"No," he continued. "Where did you get the inspiration?"

Albeit she thought his method of answering her first question was strange, Yoori went along with it. If there was anything she knew about Tae Hyun, it was that he had a reason for doing everything.

"It just came to me," she responded slowly. She pilfered through the distant memories of her childhood. At long last, she was able to latch onto a distinct memory: the image of her younger self rifling through the drawers in Ju Won's kitchen. "I vaguely remember that Ju Won had all these teas in his kitchen. I had a day off from training, and I was really tired and sad one night. I wanted something nice and warm to drink, and I didn't like how any of those teas tasted. So I just started mixing teas together. It was like I was looking for a particular taste or something. After going through multiple trials and errors, I finally had the heavenly tea in front of me." She raised a questioning brow at him. "What does this have to do with our first meeting?"

A coy grin edged his lips. It was apparent that he had already decided he wasn't going to make it easier for her by enlightening her further.

Tae Hyun may have been resigned to not tell her, but Yoori didn't share in the same sentiment.

"Tell me," she coaxed, playfully running her finger down his chest to seduce him into telling her.

When he feigned a hurt expression and pretended to turn away from her, she continued with her efforts to cajole him into telling her.

"Tell me."

He kept his mouth shut.

"Tell me."

He continued to remain silent.

"Tell me—"

"Maybe one of these days I will tell you," he finally appeased.

"Tell me now," she commanded, unwilling to let this go. She wanted to find out what the hell he was trying to insinuate to her.

He grinned at her insistence. As if he had it planned out all along, he casually pulled out a boomerang that was hidden in the corner of the boat and held it up in front of her.

"Throw it right, get it to come back to you, and I'll consider telling you."

Her face turned stoic. She stared at the boomerang like it was an object infected with the bubonic plague. "You're serious?"

"Get it to come back to you," he repeated. He gave her one of those encouraging, breathtaking smiles of his. It was his subtle way of convincing her to see things his way. Then, he hummed softly, his fingers finding a comfortable hold on her hip while he pushed himself closer to her. He made sure she felt the heat of his body while the boat rocked slightly at his movements. "Perhaps I'll reward you with something nice if it actually comes back to you."

Feeling her perverted ovaries cheer at the proximity of his hard body, she breathlessly asked, "What are you going to reward me with?"

His smile remained, yet he didn't say anything. He merely held the boomerang up higher for her to take from him.

Curious as to what Tae Hyun might "reward" her with, Yoori reached for the boomerang and slowly stood up.

Placing his hand on her hip to make sure she was balanced while standing on the boat, Tae Hyun slowly sat upright and watched as she attempted to redeem herself.

At least if I fail, it'll plunge into the water, and I'll never have to deal with it again, she consoled herself, running over the scenario of what would occur if she failed again.

She hesitantly looked down at Tae Hyun, who was smiling at her with encouraging eyes, and swallowed uncomfortably. After a preparatory breath, she whispered a prayer as she felt the weight of the boomerang anchor down her hand. Then, with the lowest self-confidence anyone could have, she threw the boomerang.

She gasped as she watched the flying object . . . actually fly.

Twirling beautifully into the air, the boomerang swam across the expanse of the star-reflected lake. It became one with the wind and disappeared in the distance. Shortly after, the boomerang came gliding back, landing submissively into Yoori's outstretched and shocked hands.

"Ahhhhhhhh!" Yoori cheered excitedly, spooking all the ducks and geese around her. She unknowingly jumped up and down, dangerously rocking the boat from side to side in her bout of pure exhilaration. Her happy voice barreled through the tranquility of the night, completely lifting up the mood. "It came back to me! It came back to meeee!"

"Holy crap!" Tae Hyun blurted out, sharing her astonishment. "It actually came back!"

Drunk with happiness, Yoori jumped down and embraced Tae Hyun, showing an uncharacteristically girly side. She stared up at him with unadulterated excitement. She was so happy and proud of herself. "Are you proud of me?"

He laughed, enjoying the cuddly version of Yoori. "You know I am," he cooed to her. He carefully deposited her back against the boat and repositioned himself on top of her. His eyes gleamed with adoration while she lay underneath the length of his body. "You deserve a prize for that."

"Yeah?" Yoori murmured stupidly, still on a high from her successful boomerang tossing.

"Yeah," he confirmed, brushing his lips against hers and attracting her lips like a magnet.

Unable to resist, she instinctively raised herself up and wrapped her arms tightly around him. She was about to kiss him when—

Crrrr—crrrrack!

The side of the boat suddenly burst open, allowing water to torrent into the boat. A tsunami of water attacked Yoori and Tae Hyun just as their lips were about to unite.

Instead of feeling Tae Hyun's supple lips on her mouth, Yoori felt the force of the lake water deluge into her ear, saturate all over her face, and the most horrifying invasion of all: escape into her mouth.

"Ahhhh!"

"Holy shit!"

Whimpering at the unexpected attack from nature, Yoori had her eyes and face covered the whole time as she propelled upright, bashing into Tae Hyun's head along the way.

Bonk!

"Ah!"

"Argh!"

Yoori could swear she saw stars twinkling in her eyes at the force of the impact.

The fury of a thousand suns materialized in her body as she rubbed her forehead. She knew who was to blame for this travesty.

"You dumb, Snob!" she growled, watching Tae Hyun rub his head in pain. Water clung to him like crystals, drenching him from head to toe. The sight of Tae Hyun in this state was tempting at best for a still horny Yoori, but it wasn't enough to placate the bratty Yoori within her. Why the hell was she sitting in another faulty boat? Why was she going through this embarrassment *again*?

She glared at him.

His stupidity must be brought to light!

"Is this the same boat as last time?" she shrieked accusingly.

"What the hell?" Tae Hyun shouted, just as outraged as Yoori. He moved to the drier edge of the boat. Fury swarmed into his eyes. He gazed at the faulty area of the boat that still had water coming in. "Did the bastard at the boat shop sell me the same boat I threw away last time?!"

"Ugh! Only you," she murmured bitterly, moving away from the line of fire. "Only you would bring all this ridiculous bad luck to me."

"Oh, here we go again from the drama queen," Tae Hyun groaned miserably, looking like he'd rather drown in the water than hear Yoori chastise him.

"It's true, isn't it?" she muttered, hitting one side of her head to pop the air bubbles in her ear. Her face was completely drenched.

"Whose idea was it to take a romantic late-night boat ride around the lake?" he countered, not believing that he was getting blamed for this again.

"How was I supposed to know that your smart ass would buy the same faulty boat that ruined us last time?" When she said this, she felt the taste of the lake water that was still present in her mouth. Yoori scrunched up her face and spat it out with disgust.

"*Ewww*," she complained while Tae Hyun watched her sympathetically. He did not envy her lake breath.

"Yuck!" she breathed out, sourly wiping her mouth with the back of her hand. "Water where those ugly, chubby ducks do the dirty-dirty."

All of a sudden, the high she experienced from successfully tossing her first boomerang was overshadowed by another failed romantic boat ride around the lake.

Hanging out above large bodies of water . . . why did they even bother? She scowled at him again. "I hate you."

Tae Hyun looked at her in outrage. He was about to give her a piece of his mind when his eyes suddenly landed on the drenched, white dress she was wearing. In an instant, all trace of anger obliterated from his visage. The emotion was replaced with a different type of fire—one that had Yoori feeling like she was some succulent dessert being offered to him. Her once hot-tempered attitude chilled like ice.

"W-what?" she stuttered, feeling self-conscious. Why was he looking at her like he was about to pounce on her?

A slow smile framed his delectable lips. In a low and teasing voice, he murmured, "You have a thing with wearing white while on a boat, don't you?"

Before even giving Yoori a chance to gaze down onto her chest, Tae Hyun abruptly stood up, slightly rocking the boat with his abrupt movement and rocking Yoori out of her thoughts.

"You know what? I'm done with this boat thing. I have other things planned for tonight anyway."

"What do you mean?"

The question was irrelevant at best. If her heated body meant anything, then she definitely knew what he meant.

He gazed at her quietly, the passion in his eyes seemingly increasing. With a stoic and matter-of-fact voice, he said, "I mean what I mean."

"What—what does *that* mean?" Yoori asked nervously, though internally, she was secretly screaming: *This is it! This is it!*

"You can stay out here and argue about the faulty boat by yourself. However, if you want to . . ." His eyes measured her up and down, reveling in the sight of her drenched from head to toe. Forbidden carnality glowed in his eyes, causing Yoori's feminine whims to go into overdrive. ". . . have some other type of fun tonight, then I suggest you follow me back inside."

"Tae Hyun?" she began fretfully, wanting to make sure what she was thinking was correct. She felt slightly sheepish for being so nervous all of a sudden. "What do you have planned?"

He favored her with a suggestive and sexy smile that basically said: "You *know* what I have planned," and then with the grace of an Olympic diver, he dove into the water, disappearing within the confines of the lake for several seconds before resurfacing. He flashed her with another dreamy grin. With feigned innocence like he wasn't trying to seduce her, he swam back to shore.

The whole time as he did this, Yoori watched unblinkingly, shamelessly mesmerized.

She was rapt as he swam with grace through the lake, his strong arms rising in and out of the water like he was born to swim. When he reached the embankment, he rose from the glistening lake like a water god. Droplets of liquid streamed down his statuesque body; the water lovingly clung itself to his taut muscles like it had a yearning mind of its own.

Holy hell . . .

Yoori could feel herself—and all the ducks around her—hold their breaths as they watched him stand tall on the grass, breathing softly to catch his breath from the little swim he had just had. Then, with a sultry look that nearly had her fainting into the water, Tae Hyun's lips drew up into a slow, sexy smile. His fingers reached up, easily finding the buttons of his black shirt. Little by little, he began to release the buttons from their moorings, gradually revealing his chiseled chest and washboard abs under the admiring moonlight.

Tossing his shirt aside ever so slowly, his seductive eyes met hers. An air of grace accompanied his smile as he sensually inclined his head towards the house, openly inviting her in for some playtime.

Yoori took in a lungful of air, watching unblinkingly as he turned away from her. He ventured back into the direction of the lake house, sweeping past their glimmering gazebo, which seemed to pale in comparison in the company of someone as enchanting as Tae Hyun.

Her heart raced beyond its limit while her eyes followed his every move. Tae Hyun made her hot all over with his little nighttime swim, but when she saw him reach for the button of his black pants, she felt an inferno of desire explode within her.

She gasped, her eyes expanding like golf balls.

Just as he turned the corner and went out of sight, Yoori could've sworn she saw him pull his pants down, revealing a blur of something so amazingly *toned* and defined that she, along with the ducks around her, couldn't help but gasp out in perverted shock.

Did the enchanting scene just take place?

Did she really just see Kwon Tae Hyun's naked booty?!

She continued to gape at the area where he disappeared. The grass there was dancing in the wind, waving at her as if beckoning her to come to shore.

This is unreal, she thought to herself.

At that amazingly dreamlike instant, while lake water continued to burst into the boat, a distracted Yoori contemplated grabbing the necks of the two nearest ducks so they could quickly herd her back to shore. Surely their assistance would afford her the opportunity to shamelessly throw herself into naked Kwon Tae Hyun's arms and beg him to have his way with her. She wanted to do this (and was *seriously* considering it while eyeing two unsuspecting ducks). She immediately vetoed that idea when she rationalized that such tactics only worked with dolphins. If she attempted such a method with ducks, she would surely drown with them rather than make it safely back to shore. And what a shame it would be to die before seeing Tae Hyun naked.

Blushing while still sitting on the sinking boat, Yoori cleared her throat, trying to act as though the sight of Tae Hyun all glorious and naked didn't turn her on. Very calmly, she unhurriedly grabbed a paddle and began to stroke the sinking boat back to shore. When the boat hit dry land, she demurely stepped onto the grass with all the womanly grace in the world and took the time to patiently twist the water out of her hair.

But then, just as five ducks started to waddle back to the lake house as if hoping to catch sight of Tae Hyun in all his naked glory, Yoori abandoned all poise. She excitedly sprinted off, kicking a couple of perverted ducks out of the way before running into the lake house to officially claim what belonged to her.

Mine. All mine.

"I know you're not seeking Paris..."

26: I found Paris

Yoori shyly poked her head from around the corner and carefully walked into the hall with a white towel wrapped securely around her chest.

For the past three minutes, as she wandered around the lake house in search of Tae Hyun, Yoori could not help but feel slightly disappointed that he was nowhere to be found. Her initial plan was to "bump" into him while conveniently wearing a towel. She didn't want to sound perverted by shouting: *I'm only wearing a towel! Come get me!* As such, she decided it was better to walk down the hall all seductive and seduce him right then and there. Yoori could swear that she could hear her perverted ovaries giggle with each other, clapping in glee that she was finally ready to take the next step with him.

Unfortunately for Yoori's ovaries, her plan was dutifully foiled when the BFF she needed for the mating dance was nowhere in sight.

"Where the hell are you?" she muttered to herself, bitterly clutching onto her towel.

After three more sexually frustrating minutes of peeking into various rooms, Yoori bit back a curse when chills started to course down her body. Her hair was still drenched with lake water, and she felt as if she was about to catch a cold from walking around under-clothed. One could only be sexily dressed in a towel for so long before they succumbed to the unforgiving cold temperature, and Yoori was no exception.

Cold and disappointed that she didn't know where stupid Tae Hyun was hiding, she gave up on her efforts to find him. She might as well take a shower by herself like a loser. She sluggishly kicked a random bathroom door and walked in, unaware that her sexy counterpart was already inside.

"Took you long enough to come in here, Nemo."

Yoori straightened at the sound of his sultry voice. She looked up, her eyes widening at the sight before her.

There her partner in crime was, with his arms crossed and back leaning against the wall beside the bathroom door. Tall and dominating, he only wore the silver ring necklace around his neck and a white towel around his hips. The onslaught of sexual heat that poured out from him was so extreme that it had every hormone in her body kneeling in absolute awe. Yoori had already deduced that she was in trouble as soon as she heard his voice, and now, after seeing him, she knew her last vestige of control was fading fast.

The bathroom they were in was unlit, completely void of any artificial light; it was solely illuminated by moon rays. In the backdrop, the glass roof gave a clear view of the star-embroidered sky. Underneath, the floor-to-ceiling windows hugged the room, holding the splendor of the iridescent lake in its grasp. To add to the ambiance, several ducks and geese flew over the glass roof, emitting a feeling of such peace that Yoori felt like she had just disappeared into a magical new world with Tae Hyun. The beauty of this scene was only perfected by the view of the picturesque gazebo in the distance.

Nevertheless, no matter how breathtaking every inch of her world appeared to be, none of it held a candle to the extravagance that was Kwon Tae Hyun. The bathroom they were in was gargantuan, at the least mirroring the size of a master bedroom. Ironically, at that particular instant, it couldn't have appeared daintier as Tae Hyun saturated the room with his powerful presence.

"What are *you* doing here?" Yoori asked, attempting to sound scandalized while hiding her cheeky grin. She did her best to keep from gawking at the tight abs she loved so much. Although she was internally excited to see him, she refused to outwardly show it.

Tae Hyun merely smiled at her query. He pushed himself away from the wall in a fluid motion, the muscles within his body rippling teasingly.

"Waiting for you," he answered delicately, walking over to the bathroom door. He wrapped his hand around the gold knob and lightly pushed it shut. The soft click of the door filtered into the room.

Though Yoori didn't verbally admit that the mere sight of Tae Hyun scantily dressed was a turn on for her, her body's reaction was a telltale sign as to what her mind was thinking. Her face was flushed, and her lips were somehow becoming a bit more swollen from the sheer exhilaration of seeing him. The very thought of that flaming hot body being covered up with nothing but a measly towel was driving her over the edge.

Freaking irresistible bastard, she thought caustically, resenting that he had such power over her body. It took all her self-control to not throw him against the wall, rip off his towel, and take him right then and there.

She continued with her efforts to control her hormones by briefly averting her eyes from him.

"Did you shower already?" she asked nervously, though she already knew the answer to that.

"No," he replied, his voice low and hypnotic.

Purposeful footsteps echoed in the bathroom as he moved away from the door. Maintaining his appreciative gaze on her, he walked past her, casually pulling open one of the glass doors to the enormous shower stall. He leisurely stepped in and pulled the lever, releasing a stream of fresh clean water from the showerhead.

"Like I said," he said, stepping out of the shower stall. He left the shower door ajar as the water poured out. He leisurely drew closer to her and began to circle her with deliberate slowness. Though it was clear that he wanted nothing more than to claim his prize and devour her as a predator would his prey, Tae Hyun maintained commendable control. This was foreplay, and he was just beginning to tease her. "I was waiting for you."

"Excuse you?" Yoori said pretentiously, keeping her eyes on Tae Hyun. He continued to walk in a slow and deliberate circle around her, making her feel more and more like prey. She protectively clutched onto the knot that held up her towel, still pretending that she wasn't a willing participant in this raunchy little bit of foreplay. "What would make you think I'd want to shower with *you*?"

Tae Hyun laughed, the muscles on his bare upper body rippling gorgeously for her.

"Oh, I'm sorry, Princess," he began blithely, manufacturing confusion. "Was that a duck with a towel I heard walking around the house for five minutes looking for me? With all your muttering, I could've sworn it was you."

"I . . . I . . ."

Yoori blushed, clamping her mouth shut. She did not know how to respond to the more-than-on-point accusation. She had been caught, and for the first time in her life, she had no witty reply to give in an attempt to save face. Fortunately for her, a reply wasn't needed on her part.

"Do you have any idea," he launched, suddenly closing in on the space separating them. With his arms securely wrapped around her hips, he pulled her close to his powerfully built body. "How long I've waited for this moment?"

"H-how long?" she stammered, caught off guard when she felt the heat of his body rolling off him and onto hers. It was a miracle she did not melt in that instant.

"A little over an eternity," he answered lazily, a hand stroking over her hair in appreciation. There was a wickedly sexual glint in his eyes when he said this.

Yoori smirked playfully at the reply. Still managing to hold onto some semblance of her wits, she said, "That doesn't seem very long . . ."

A dark, sensual smile kissed his lips. "I don't intend on waiting anymore."

He was about to lean in to shower her bare shoulder with all the kisses he could give her when, in a swift and unexpected motion, Yoori extracted herself from his hold and ran to the opposite side of the bathroom.

Making sure the towel was still wrapped around her body, she turned back to a stupefied Tae Hyun. He looked confused with her behavior, and if the lust and desire building in his wickedly sexy gaze was any indication, his sexual prowess was at an all-time high.

"Do you really think you could outrun me?" he asked carefully, surveying her with acute interest.

A teasing look played on Yoori's face.

"As far as I'm concerned," she answered coyly, her hands holding her towel safely—almost mockingly, "you're not the only predator in the room."

Although Yoori wanted nothing more than to throw herself at Tae Hyun, she was also adamant about inviting the sex God to come out and play. Tae Hyun, in this gentlemanly state, was seductive as hell, but she also knew that he was holding back. After months of denying them this very experience, Yoori wasn't going to settle for anything less than a passionate, uninhibited Kwon Tae Hyun. Being graced with the primal desires of Tae Hyun's aside, Yoori was also feeling a bit naughty. Foreplay was always fun.

Strained muscles adorned his arms, indicating that he was using every modicum of strength to keep from freeing the beast within him.

"You're really going to tease me like this?" An amused chuckle graced the room while competitive fire burned in his coffee brown eyes. He resumed his predatory gait around her. His eyes on her were voracious and utterly rapt. He was regarding her as though she was a decadent treat that had been kept out of his desperate reach.

Yoori lifted her shoulders into a playful shrug. "I just want to play a game."

Laughter rolled throughout the room, warming all the places in Yoori's body and heart.

"You suck at games, baby," he purred with affectionate amusement. "You always lose when it comes to me."

Yoori felt her hormone level increase ten-fold at his strategic usage of the term "baby". He was a master at the game of seduction. He knew better than anyone else that using that particular word always turned Yoori on.

Proud of himself, and convinced that he had just won this courting game, Tae Hyun moved to reach out for her. He was determined to end this game and catch her once and for all.

"We'll see who the loser in this game is," she replied swiftly, evading his capture by bolting for the door.

"Oh, you're definitely getting spanked for this," he murmured, skillfully catching her just before she could reach the door. He embraced her from behind and began to herd her back to the center of the bathroom. "Uh-uh," he disapproved, smiling as he held her in his grasp.

Yoori laughed, faking a defeated posture. She purposely fell limp in his arms. At the signal of her compliance, Tae Hyun let his guard down by loosening his hold on her.

"No running in towels," he whispered into her ear, unbeknownst to him what she was planning to do once he had "caught" her.

In an unanticipated move, Yoori's fingers strategically latched onto a healthy amount of fabric that was his towel. Mischief twinkling in her eyes, she looked up at him and teasingly said, "For the record, you didn't catch me. I *let* you catch me."

And then, while holding her breath, she did the impossible.

Whoosh!

Unable to deny her desires any longer, and too damn perverted for her own piece of mind, she swiftly ripped his towel off. Magic spread over her world at this action. The innocuous white cloth that had been the bane of her existence submissively came off, clinging to the tips of her fingers before falling listlessly to the ground. Oxygen immediately dissipated from her stunned world. Yoori could scarcely breathe as she stared at the result of her handiwork. A surge of heat electrocuted through her, energizing points of her body that she did not know could be charged. While she struggled to keep from fainting, the desire she possessed for Tae Hyun rose above its capacity and shot through the roof.

Holy moly . . .

God of all Sex Gods.

Perfection.

Kwon Tae Hyun was nothing short of a breathtaking and sexual perfection, the very embodiment of sex come to life. She could hear her perverted ovaries giggle, cheer, and applaud in joy that he belonged to them and only them.

Yaaaaaay! Score! Score! Score!

"Oh . . . oh . . . oh my . . ." she uttered breathlessly, melting like butter on toast. Her eyes feasted on the mouthwatering sight before her. She had died. She had definitely died and gone to heaven. "You . . . you look good."

"For the record," he began, his voice a velvety smooth melody. He stood before her in all his naked glory, proudly noting how much her big brown eyes were enjoying what they were seeing. "I *let* you rip the towel off."

By now, Yoori was past listening. She was too lost in the best view any woman could ever dream of having. In a move she didn't even realize she was commencing, Yoori began to retreat backwards, her heart hammering feverishly against her chest. She couldn't take her eyes off him. The way the soft hues of the moon illuminated on his striking body was too much for her to bear. He was perfect—inside and out.

He looks good enough to eat, she thought perversely.

"There are several things you should know about me," he prompted professionally, strategically stalking her across the grand bathroom.

His advancing legs mirrored her every retreating movement while his warm laughter reverberated throughout the room, further weakening any little strength she had left to "play hard to get". His gait was graceful and confident. He wasn't the least bit self-conscious about his body, and why would he be? He very well knew that he possessed the body that even Gods would envy and had absolutely no problem in exploiting this God-given gift when it came to her.

"Yeah?" Yoori asked stupidly, still admiring the stunning view before her. The strength in her legs waned the more she retreated from him. She clutched onto her towel. It was terribly embarrassing how willing and ready her body was for Tae Hyun. She was eager to give up on the foreplay and throw herself at his mercy, especially now that he had started to use his full sexual ammunition on her.

"I'm a demanding lover," he drawled out, moving in a fluid motion that had him filling in the gap between them faster than a distracted Yoori had anticipated.

His masculine and tall frame towered over her, reminding her how small she was compared to him and how much she wanted him. It was an overpowering feeling, but then again, everything that radiated off Tae Hyun was simply overpowering.

Nothing was left to the imagination when he pulled her against him. It was all too clear how much he wanted her.

"I'm arrogant, insatiable, dominant, and possessive in every sense of the word. Once I have you, I'll probably never get enough. I'll keep you in bed for as long as I can, probably until the end of our lifetimes. I'll want to kiss every inch of that body of yours, and by the time I'm done, there will be no more questions about whether or not I've claimed every part of you—that you're mine and only mine." He smirked, staring down at her. "Can you handle that type of man? Can you handle me regardless of all those bad traits?"

"Those seem to be overbearing traits," she murmured dazedly, staggering back at his sudden proximity. She had never felt more like a mindless fangirl, and they hadn't even done *it* yet!

"Very overbearing," he agreed delicately, taking note of how infatuated she was. They were still retreating backwards, him holding her while they moved closer and closer to the shower stall. "And to add to all that, I'm also poor now."

Yoori laughed at the unexpected addition to his list of bad traits. "You're poor now?"

He nodded, joining in her laughter. Even in the face of unimaginable sexual tension, they would never fail to find something random to laugh about.

"I gave up my job promotion for a certain someone. I've also been disowned by the world I grew up in. Unfortunately, this means that my bank accounts are now under surveillance. I can't touch any of it ever again."

Yoori feigned a pout. "So, you're really poor now?"

"I'm broke," he confirmed, feigning a pout of his own. "I'm completely broke now. All I have to offer is my body."

Another string of unfiltered laughter escaped from Yoori's lips. She shook her head, pretending to give him a scolding stare.

"Slut," she teased.

Her feet drifted over the tiles that were wet from its proximity to the running shower. Before she could help it, she was falling backwards and becoming one with gravity.

"Ah!"

The ground giving way from under her feet, Yoori tumbled backwards. She nearly slammed her head against the opened shower door when Tae Hyun looped an arm around her waist and pulled her up against him.

Sensuous eyes stared down at her while gorgeous lips lifted into a seductive smile.

"Falling for me already?" he inquired mischievously, allowing a free hand to trace the silk of her long black hair.

Nothing but desire teemed in her eyes as she gazed up at him. Resolution thundered inside her. She could no longer handle this teasing and she did not want to play around anymore. She wanted him and she wanted him now.

"You're not going to seduce or tease me anymore?" he cajoled, smiling down at her. "I thought you'd hold out for a bit longer than that, Nemo."

Yoori just smiled dumbly, not even knowing what to say. She was too shell-shocked. What could you say after seeing God's gift to women in all his glory and being mindlessly seduced by him?

"For what it's worth," he began gently, moving them closer to the shower stall where the gentle sprinkles of water were splashing onto them, "you didn't have to try to seduce me, Princess. You could be wearing a hoodie and simple pajama pants, and you'd still have me in the palm of your hand."

Yoori returned the smile. Her emotions were seemingly rising to her throat as she watched his appreciative eyes run over her bare shoulders before landing on the towel that covered her. Then, she was unable to breathe when she felt his fingertips graze her cheek. His fingers trailed down the column of her neck, caressed the skin of her shoulder, and slowly rested on the little knot on her towel. His desire-filled eyes touched hers, and in that suspended moment, as if they could read each other's thoughts, a silent understanding was shared between Choi Yoori and Kwon Tae Hyun.

After months of waiting for that perfect moment, it had finally arrived.

An onslaught of affection filled her as she stared at the one she loved. She wanted to do this; she wanted to experience this with Tae Hyun. There were no more ifs, ands, or buts. She wanted this with him—only him.

With his breath seemingly caught in his chest, a dazed Tae Hyun turned his attention to the innocuous fabric. He moved his eyes to her. "Can I?"

Even under the indomitable reign of his raging testosterone, Tae Hyun was still the gentleman. No matter what, he always put her needs before his.

With her heart beating out of her chest, Yoori could only nod in confirmation.

Exhilaration lit up in his eyes. With nothing more holding him back, he gripped the knot on Yoori's towel. As though he was unwrapping a long-awaited birthday present, Tae Hyun slowly loosened the knot. Yoori's breath, along with his sanity, was lost when the towel came flowing down and landed on the tiles, resting just above his feet.

"Lord have mercy," came the guttural sound of his voice.

He exhaled a sharp breath that ran over every excited nerve in her body. He looked at her like she was a gift from God; he looked at her just as how she looked at him, like he had finally found heaven on earth. The way he looked at her made Yoori feel like the most powerful woman in the world.

What happened after that became an exquisite blur to Yoori.

For the first time in his life, Kwon Tae Hyun was an inarticulate idiot. He stupidly mumbled something along the lines of how gorgeous she was, how perfect she was, and added to that by passionately stating that he was the luckiest fucking bastard in the whole world.

Possessed with passion, he wrapped his arms around her and covered her with the heat from his body. He savagely threw her into the shower stall, his hands catching her back before she made contact with the hard exterior of the marble wall. With deliberate care, he positioned her against the wall, his body protecting her from the wrath of the water. Even under the pretense of uninhibited desires, Tae Hyun continued to subconsciously take care of Yoori. The bandage wrap that covered over her bullet wound was still present on her left arm, and he was still careful to protect it.

Taking care of her was his first priority, but kissing her was his second and most prevailing priority.

The kiss was done without thought.

Mindlessly, mind-numbingly, and mind-blowingly, he kissed her. The kiss reminded her of how much they had been through, how far they had come, and how much she loved him. In the past, she had never understood why her body told her to wait for this moment—that when the right time came, she would know. She had never understood why . . . until now.

As she stared up at Tae Hyun, Yoori felt grateful that she listened to her own intuition and waited for the right man she wanted to give this intimate part of herself to.

"It took us," he breathed out, pressing his forehead against hers, "a while to get here."

Yoori happily nodded as water splashed across his back. The world around them silenced as they stood in the darkness.

"Can you believe we spent these past few days arguing about Nemo DVDs, stupid pre-teen books, faulty boats, and boomerangs?" There was awe in her voice when she recalled the day where they fought in the business district like Gods. It was surreal how things went from something so horrible and menacing to something so ordinary and simple.

Warmth rippled in his eyes while he reflected the same train of thoughts. "We bicker about the most stupid things."

She nodded again, thinking about everything they had been through. They had been through a world of hell as Gods; it was truly a blessing to finally be standing together as humans.

"Thank you for waiting for me," she murmured, touching him while the showerhead sprayed in the back, dimming in presence as they stared at one another.

She felt her heart swell at the enormity of all her thoughts. The events of her life replayed like a movie in her mind. She was still in disbelief that, after everything that came between them, they had finally made it here.

"I wouldn't give up these moments with you for anything," she whispered, meaning it with all her heart. "If I had to go through everything I did just to get here again, I would do it."

Tae Hyun appreciatively stroked her face. "Thank you for coming back, baby," he whispered, cradling her cheek in his hand. His tone of voice was humble, grateful. "Thank you for being here with me—for giving me these moments. I wouldn't want these moments with anyone else but you."

Yoori swallowed past the suffusion of emotions that were fighting to escape from her eyes.

As she did this, another smile of amazement crossed his face.

"Do you know what's crazy?" he inquired softly. He reached behind his neck to unclasp the necklace that held the ring she had given him for his birthday. Once off his neck, he held each of the clasps in between his fingers, allowing the necklace to briefly hang in the air before he brushed it over the skin of her neck. He clasped the necklace around her and allowed their ring to swim atop her chest. The silver ring glinted in the soft darkness while water sprayed in the background.

"What?" she asked quietly, feeling white-hot heat wash over her at the intimacy they shared. The weight of their ring pulled gently on her neck, reminding her of the moment she bought this for him and the moment she first saw him wear it. How far they had come . . .

"Do you realize that our whole lives, every decision we've made, all the roads we've chosen—good, bad, big, and small—everything has led us to this very moment in time?"

Yoori smiled in nostalgia, remembering that they had this conversation when they first visited the lake house. Not understanding why he was bringing this up, but humoring him anyway, she merely replied, "What a crazy thought."

It was only after she said that while gazing into Tae Hyun's eyes, and while feeling the weight of their ring weigh above her chest, did another realization dawn upon her. At long last, she was finally enlightened with a reality that seemed like a lifetime ago—a reality that had somehow come full circle in her life and found its way back to her.

Soft voices entered her mind as various images drifted from her memory. She didn't know how it all fell into place for her.

It was possibly because of the hints Tae Hyun gave her or possibly because of the plethora of emotions that were making their way through her body, but for reasons unknown to her, a door that she never knew existed opened in the depths of her mind. From behind it, the memory from a lifetime ago came to her, finally bringing everything full circle for Yoori.

Her eyes lit up as she saw his face, as she saw them underneath that table, and as she saw them sadly walk away from each other when their borrowed time was up . . .

"The boy with the teacup," she finally whispered, causing Tae Hyun's eyes to light up.

Tears glistened in Yoori's eyes while the distant memory resurfaced in her mind, making her realize how small her world was and how simple it became as the contents of how she actually met Tae Hyun came into her mind. *That* was how the tea was created, that was how it all began, and that was where it had all started—the first real beginning for them.

He favored her with a smile, relieved that she finally remembered their first true meeting.

"Hi Princess," he said to her, that nickname meaning more to her now than it ever did. "It's been a while, hasn't it?"

"How . . . how long have you known?" she asked incredulously, staring at him like he was a dream. Emotions overwhelmed her; she couldn't believe that, after all these years, somehow, they had found their way back to one another.

"When you spoke about Paris on the dock, I was reminded of that little girl, but I wasn't sure. But when we were sitting in the park the other night playing drinking games, and you accused me of stealing the tea mix that you created, I knew then that it was you—that you were that bratty girl I met at the masquerade party, the one who took part in creating that tea." He laughed, his demeanor still amazed as well. "That was how I knew we belonged together, that you had always been mine and that you will always be mine."

Yoori genuinely smiled at the sheer astonishment of what she felt.

"Fourteen years later, and you're still a Snob," she murmured in awe.

He nodded, exhibiting the same awestruck daze. "Fourteen years later, and you're still a Brat."

"It took us . . . a while to get here," she repeated again, not knowing before how long it actually took for them.

It had been a lifetime for them. It literally had.

"It has always been you," she uttered, astounded with the enormity of the type of love she had with him. They had always been meant for each other. They were always meant to be.

. . . There are moments in life where you feel nothing but a sense of perfection.

The stars have aligned, time has stood still, the storms are at bay, the cruelty of the world has receded, and you are given one of those few perfect moments in life where everything makes sense, where everything is beautiful, where everything—*even for a brief moment*—is perfect.

For Choi Yoori, that beautiful and perfect moment in her life emerged as she stood there with Tae Hyun, the sudden epiphany swimming through her, filling her with amazement.

It has always been him.

Stroking his face, unable to control herself anymore, she raised herself on her tiptoes and kissed him passionately, tears of comprehension gliding down her cheeks as something extraordinary happened. As she pressed her lips against his, she could feel her entire body illume into life. The very fibers and senses that made up her very existence came into play and made themselves known—it was though for the first time in their lives, they were actually living and breathing for the first time.

The vision of color in her eyes had suddenly gotten more vibrant—as if it, too, was excited for a future it saw with Tae Hyun.

Her lips ached as they struggled to find his—their yearning pout also longing for the feel of Tae Hyun's lips brushing against them.

Her skin sighed against Tae Hyun's touch—the fibers within it begging for more attention as it pulled itself closer to his loving hands.

And finally, her heart—the one entity in her body that Tae Hyun left the biggest impression on. Pumping furiously and relentlessly, it attacked her chest, never in its life loving someone as much as it loved Tae Hyun.

It was a simple, yet complex, set of emotions that shook Yoori to the very core of her existence.

Yoori didn't need Tae Hyun to live—she very well knew that.

She didn't need him to survive—she knew that too.

She knew all of that.

She knew all of that as she tightened her embrace around him, her tears flowing freely for him while she basked in his hold.

She didn't need Tae Hyun to survive; she just yearned for him.

She yearned for him to make her life complete. She yearned for the happiness, the beauty, and the timelessness of loving him. How would she ever go back to having a lifeless mind, body, and soul without him? How would she ever go back to living the same life she did when she finally saw the magic of life when she was with him? How would she continue to breathe without him by her side to make her feel alive, to make her feel human, to take her breath away?

Her heart twisted in agonizing knots at the thought.

I could never go back to that life, Yoori concluded easily.

She could very well live without him, but without him, life just wasn't worth it.

"I love you," he breathed out, his hands raising and cradling her cheeks. His loving fingers caressed her skin with unparalleled adoration. There was no uncertainty within his voice. It was delivered with a vow that had Yoori's heart expanding. "I will *always* love you."

It was the single most extraordinary and amazing sensation she had ever experienced in her life—to know that standing before her, the man who had stolen every inch of her stubborn heart was feeling the exact same sensation as her. He loved her more than he loved himself, more than life itself, and he would continue to love her past his own lifetime.

It was a silent understanding on each of their parts, but she knew at that exact second, Tae Hyun was experiencing the same type of epiphany. The way his fingers stroked over her, the way his body leaned into hers, the way she felt his heart pound away, and the way he looked at her . . . She knew that he felt everything she was feeling: awe, disbelief, gratefulness, amazement, and finally happiness. Pure, unadulterated happiness.

They had finally found *it*.

They had finally found the city they were looking for.

". . . Paris is the city of love . . ." Her own dreamy and hopeful voice whispered into her subconscious, acting as a lullaby to her ears. *"You can't go to Paris unless you're madly in love with the person who is taking you. And not just the type of love where you tell one another that you can't live without each other. No . . . not that type of love. But the type of love that is unconditional—the type that is undying. You know . . . the type that can withstand anything . . . one of those once—"*

Then—

"You'll tell me what it feels like, right?" Yoori breathed out quietly, never feeling more blessed in her entire life. "When you find Paris?"

Smiling lightly, Tae Hyun's fingers continued to trace its affection over the skin of her cheeks. He stared deeply into her tear-misted eyes with glistening eyes of his own. Without another second wasted, the once seemingly impossible occurred.

"Choi Yoori . . ." Tae Hyun whispered, his voice filled with awe that he had finally reached this moment in his life—that what he wished for had come to fruition.

He pressed his forehead against hers, allowing their hot breaths to mingle together while his lips brushed over her yearning ones. With the world seemingly quieting itself in awe, the water from the showerhead deluging down as if in celebration, and the steam arising from the warm water as if hiding them in their own magical world, all that was left in Yoori's world was Tae Hyun.

All that was left in her world were the most beautiful set of words that she would ever hear in her lifetime. The melodic words streamed from his lips, sending her into a world filled with nothing but timeless magic.

"I found Paris," he began softly, pressing a world of emotions into those three simple words. "It's a thousand times more beautiful than I could've ever dreamed it to be. So, you know what that means, right?"

Standing there, with everything in her world never having felt more perfect than before, Yoori continued to listen to him as he spoke, while happy tears cloaked her eyes.

With his eyes locked on hers, he parted his lips and told her exactly what it meant. He told her how everything that led to that moment made him feel, he told her how it felt right then and there to be standing there with her, and he told her what that all meant to him, and the sobs escaped Yoori's chest.

She nodded and held him close to her, her heart expanding as she agreed with everything he said. She did not know it was possible to love someone so much until that very moment, as she realized how much he meant to her and how much he would always mean to her.

". . . Until it fades," he assured her again, his eyes promising that this was a vow he would never break to her.

"Until it fades," she agreed with him vehemently, knowing in her heart that such magic would never fade. It would live on and on, past a lifetime and past all the lifetimes to come.

"My dad said that Paris is the city of love. If you want to win a woman's heart, then you have to take her to Paris—you have to *show* her Paris," Tae Hyun said moments later, his smile widening as he thought about the distant past in which he first said all of this. Yoori couldn't help but smile as she listened to him go on. "When I was younger, I told myself that I'd go there when I was older, when I have a girl I want to take."

He let out a long breath, getting intimately closer to her while placing his hand on the shower wall behind her. He leaned in to give Yoori an up-close view of all the perfect features of his gorgeous face.

His voice soft, he quietly said, "Is it a no-brainer to tell you that we're leaving for Paris tomorrow?"

"I would've punched you if you told me you were taking me anywhere else," Yoori replied, laughing through her tears.

Paris.

They were finally freaking going to Paris!

He laughed, the dark sexy gaze returning to him while he took a moment to gaze appreciatively at her body.

"Punch me, right?"

His amused expression was inviting and challenging. Being poetic and romantic aside, Tae Hyun's raging hormones had yet to be quelled, and after finally finding what they were looking for, he was more than ready to celebrate the finding with the love of his life. He planned to not only take her to Paris tomorrow, but also showing her Paris tonight.

"Do your worst," he challenged. A mischievous glint then caught his eyes. He easily feigned disappointment by then adding, "But to be perfectly honest, you seem to be the fragile little doll type . . . too controlled and prudish. I like my woman uncontrolled, wildly demanding in my bed, and I don't think you're wild enough to take me on."

"Oh, really?" Yoori inquired humorously, placing her hands on her hips like she was extremely offended.

He nodded, his eyes continuously challenging her to prove him wrong. Another appreciative gaze swept across her petite body before he added, "You're free to try and prove me wrong if you want."

Yoori grinned, accepting the challenge. "You're going down, you shameless womanizer."

His face completely illuminated with excitement. "Yeah?"

Lifting her hands from her hips while her own sensuous eyes were still on him, she moved her fingers up to his chest. She felt the scintillating muscles ripple at her simple touch. Her eyes pulsing with suggestive desire, she lightly pressed the palm of her hands into his chest, feeling the heat of his body and the beating of his heart. She positioned him right underneath the raining water and watched as the rivulets of water ran down his body, kissing every inch of that perfect physique with adoration.

No more waiting.

She was done waiting.

Seeing that the moment was perfect as Tae Hyun once promised, she now wanted him to show her why every splendid, euphoric, and magical moment of what would come next, would be *worth it*.

"Welcome to Paris, Boomerang," Yoori whispered thoughtlessly.

She beamed uncontrollably, her body waiting in anticipation for the magic to come.

After twenty-four years of waiting for the perfect man to give this moment to, she finally found the most perfect one of all: her once-in-a-lifetime love.

It has always been Kwon Tae Hyun, and it will only be Kwon Tae Hyun.

"Welcome to Paris, Boomerang," Tae Hyun whispered back, a wickedly seductive smile holding onto his lips. It was a smile that promised her nothing but perfection for what was to come.

With a relieved laugh, knowing that he could finally free himself from sexual frustration hell, an insatiable and ravenous Tae Hyun swiftly draped his arms around her waist like his life depended on it and pulled her to his chest. He brought her through the cloud of steam, and when his delicious lips found hers, he wrapped her against the length of his powerful body.

Exhibiting ardent care that was coupled with primal animal needs, he finally quelled all the sexual frustrations that had been the bane of their existence by finally making love to her, by finally giving her the perfection he had always promised her, and by finally bringing down the stars, the moon, and the city she had wanted all her life.

"But things might change in the future..."

27: Wherever You Go, I'll Follow

He wasn't there when she woke up.

Subconsciously seeking his warmth in her sleep, a once slumberous Yoori woke up when she was met with a vacant space in bed. Curiosity veiling her newly opened eyes, she instinctively touched the empty spot. The coldness of the bed chilled her, resulting in a dreaded chasm that materialized in the core of her stomach. The coldness signified to the observational Queen within her that Tae Hyun hadn't been in bed for a while.

"Tae Hyun?" her hoarse morning voice whispered.

When she received no response, Yoori turned her attention to the entirety of their enormous bedroom. Her eyes drifted past the floor-to-ceiling windows, which revealed the picturesque view of the quiet lake under the dark morning sky, and swam across the dim room. Her gaze was expectant, hopeful that she would find Tae Hyun popping his head out from the bathroom. That hopefulness was eclipsed by the persevering silence.

Tae Hyun was nowhere in sight.

The beating of her heart grew in franticness and the silence within the room was becoming deafening. An unfounded fear she didn't comprehend began to grip her mind, making her uneasy in ways that terrified her to her very soul. Under any other circumstances, Yoori would not have found herself so worked up over the fact that Tae Hyun wasn't in bed. Yet, for some odd and unexplainable reason, she felt differently today.

She wanted him by her side today; she didn't want him to go missing.

Not today.

"Tae Hyun," she called anxiously, "where are you?"

Never one to sit around and hope for an answer, Yoori threw off the comforter and jumped out of bed. She made a beeline for the black hoodie closest to her and rapidly threw it over her naked body. Tae Hyun's black hoodie draped over her upper body and rested just above her thighs. Yoori hurried towards the door, but abruptly stopped when her eyes caught sight of the bedside drawer that was slightly pulled opened. It was the drawer that held their guns.

The drumming of her heart escalated at the sight.

Approaching the innocuous-looking drawer, Yoori's hand trembled as she pulled the wooden handle and slid the top drawer further out. All the air escaped from her lungs when all that she found were her gold guns.

Tae Hyun's silver guns . . . they were missing.

A sprout of paranoia ignited in her chest. Anxiety spread like a wildfire through her body. Where was he? Where was Tae Hyun, and why were his guns missing?

Yoori frantically grabbed her guns. In a matter of seconds, she was out of the room and searching for him.

"Tae Hyun?" she called softly, running down the stairs barefooted. Shivering from the morning cold, she hoped to hear his voice in the house. When she didn't, she felt the fear within her soar even higher.

A million different questions tore through her mind—all of them pertaining to the Underworld. Had the Underworld found them? Did they come after them? Did Tae Hyun go to fend them off? Another thought troubled her mind. Tae Hyun didn't do anything stupid, did he? He didn't go back to the Underworld to fight them by himself, did he? There were countless questions that circulated in her frightened mind, and she knew the only way to get them all answered—to silence them all—was to find Tae Hyun as soon as possible.

A blast of morning breeze skidded across her skin as she ran outside. Undeterred by the cold, Yoori's frantic eyes continued to search for Tae Hyun. The silence, though deafening to her within the barriers of the house, was a song of relief in this setting.

There were no gunshots out here.

There was no Underworld out here.

Slightly comforted by this fact, but only slightly, as she still had no idea where the hell Tae Hyun was, Yoori ran to the front yard. Her relief was heightened when she found that their cars were still in the driveway. A grateful exhalation emanated from her chest. Tae Hyun couldn't have physically left the lake house if his Jaguar was still here. Her anxiety subsiding by the second, Yoori continued to look around, softly calling out his name so that she wouldn't wake their neighbors. She circled around the lake house, her bare feet stepping over the newly watered grass lawn.

Reprieve cascaded over her when she finally saw Tae Hyun.

He was standing in front of the colossal lake with his two silver guns in hand. Shirtless and wearing only his black and blue pajama pants, he stared quietly at the lake. The wind grazed over his still body before drifting through his hair and tousling the fabric of his pants. He looked calm, collected, and at peace while his eyes admired the expanse of the landscape before him.

The fact that he was safe and unharmed was all that she needed to see; it was all that she needed to bring order to her once anarchic world.

Yoori smiled self-mockingly to herself.

She understood now why the Underworld forbade them to fall in love. It was an understatement to say that Yoori couldn't have felt more vulnerable. In a society ruled over by selfish entities, the last thing they wanted was for their leaders to be co-dependent upon someone else. She understood all too well why the Underworld looked down upon love, but now, as emotions that she had never once felt invaded her, she understood all too clearly why it was such a dangerous emotion for the Gods of the Underworld to fall victim to.

Love was the most powerful feeling humans could ever dream to experience. In that same regard, it was the most weakening and the most debilitating emotion that humans could ever realistically live with. With it, you would never feel more powerful, like you were an invincible entity protected by the heavens. Without it, you would never feel more weak and broken, like you were an insignificant creature who'd fallen from grace. Love was an antidote and a poison, the former or latter being solely dependent on the one you gave your heart to.

Yoori briefly closed her eyes and permitted the magnitude of her feelings to rain down upon her.

Everyday, she was learning something new with this emotion, and everyday, it surprised her more and more with how powerful this emotion was. It was incredible how it was capable of making a fool out of a woman like her. God help her that she could love someone so much that the thought of him missing was enough to drive her insane, and the sight of him without maladies eased all her fears. God help her that it was humanly possible to love someone more than life itself. God help her if she should ever lose him. It was a thought that Yoori couldn't bear and a thought that she didn't know if she could live with if it ever came to fruition.

Luckily for Yoori, these morbid thoughts did not progress any further. Before she could focus any more energy on it, she became sublimely sidetracked with the more timeless distractions of life.

As if feeling her presence, Tae Hyun averted his eyes from the lake and turned them curiously in her direction. Upon seeing her, he graced her with a smile that had every cell in her body awake and lively. In that dreamlike moment of seeing that gorgeous smile of his, everything was all right in her world again.

"Hey," he greeted warmly, turning his entire body around to face her. Though it was evident in his gaze that he was curious as to why she was awake and outside, he didn't voice it. He merely smiled at her, not caring about her reasons. He only cared that she was with him.

Already putting the small bout of fear she felt in the backburner, Yoori allowed a warm smile to touch her face. She approached him in eagerness.

"Hi," she replied quietly, her voice cracking slightly as she stopped in front of him.

Tae Hyun laughed, tilting his head after hearing the hoarseness in her voice. Guns still in hand, he gently wrapped his arms around her hips. He lovingly pulled her close to him.

"What happened to your voice, Princess?" he asked, playfully nipping his nose with hers.

Yoori clamped her mouth shut, blushing slightly when she recalled why her voice was so hoarse. She shook her head at him, wordlessly telling him that she wasn't planning on answering that question.

His persevering smile ensured her that he was not about to let this go. He then posed another question to push her into a corner where she would have no choice but to answer him.

"How was your night last night?"

Yoori blushed harder, remembering all too clearly how her night was. Throughout the entirety of the evening, as they fell into their own world of bliss, Tae Hyun and Yoori, after months upon excruciating months of teasing and sexual frustration, spent the entire night into the late morning making love. She recalled the euphoric state she was in while she was with him, the King who conquered all the cities last night while he drove her crazy with ecstasy at the same time.

He was animalistic in bed, yet gentle. He made her scream while simultaneously whimpering in satisfaction. He was insatiable, yet attentive. He possessed her, but he made love to her. He was a contradiction in every way possible, and he was simply perfect in every way possible.

Needless to say, on Yoori's very satisfied part, Kwon Tae Hyun was a Sex God in every sense of the word. He more than proved it as he gave her countless moons, stars, and cities the night prior. He worshipped her body as he promised he would, and she enjoyed every moment of it. Screw Prince Charming when you had an Illusionist who could produce the type of timeless magic Kwon Tae Hyun evoked for her last night.

"I was with my Illusionist last night," Yoori teased, humoring the one who had not only stolen her heart, but also every inch of her body and soul.

"Oh, really?" he inquired, fighting hard to keep his smile from morphing into a huge, prideful grin.

She nodded, hiding her silly grin as well. "I think he used magic and made my voice disappear."

She screamed, she was screaming so much from the extravagance of being with him. Goddamn her. Yoori didn't know why she was such a prude and waited this long to have one of the most magical nights of her life.

Better late than never, she mused bitterly.

"Yes, I do recall you screaming, biting, clawing your nails into my skin, and telling me how wonderful I was last night," he murmured, subtly bringing her attention to the bite marks she left on his shoulders. Pride undulated in his voice as he pulled her just a bit closer to him. He reminded her of how much fun they had by pressing his warm body against hers. "I've been keeping that pretty little body of yours busy, haven't I?" A wickedly prideful grin curved his lips. "Didn't you pass out quite a few times?"

"I did *not* pass out," she defended weakly. Yoori felt like a fool as she felt her body lean into his involuntarily. It was like the fibers in her body were now conditioned to want to be touched by him. Even if she had some semblance of control, it was all shot to hell with her treacherous body continuously seeking him out. "I was just closing my eyes."

"No," he helped amend, "you just took a cat nap."

"You're enjoying this 'morning-after' moment, aren't you?" she accused sourly.

"Very much so," he admitted shamelessly. He nipped his nose with hers again. "For what it's worth, I would've passed out too if I wasn't so greedy and wanted more of you." A playful grin appeared on his handsome face before he abruptly added, "You know what this makes us, right?"

Yoori curiously tilted her head at the odd question.

"Lovers?" she answered uncertainly.

He shook his head, his lips twitching as if fighting to keep from laughing.

Doing well to keep his face free of emotions, he nonchalantly said, "Friends with benefits."

Yoori giggled girlishly, unable to help it. "You're my booty call?"

"I'm your booty call," Tae Hyun concurred disbelievingly, laughing with her.

"Was the wait worth it, my Illusionist?" Yoori prompted seconds later, curious to know how last night panned out for him.

He did not disappoint with his answer.

"Every splendid, euphoric, and magical moment of it."

They smiled again, unable to help but stupidly grin at the moment they were having—the wondrous moment every human being spent a lifetime waiting for and a lifetime missing when it disappeared.

"Why aren't you sleeping?" Tae Hyun then asked. "I know you didn't get much sleep last night, if any at all."

"Why aren't you?" she challenged. "As I recall, it was the King who conquered all the cities last night." It was only after asking something as playful as this did her rationale return. She lowered her eyes and appraised the guns in his hands. The humor from her face subdued faintly. "What are you doing out here anyway?"

"I wanted to see the sunrise," he told her thoughtfully. He turned back into the direction of the lake and the dark morning sky. "Do you realize that for as long as we've known each other, we've never watched the sunrise together?"

Yoori thought back to all the sunsets and stargazing she had seen with him. She, too, recalled that never once during their time together did they ever sit down to enjoy the most peaceful time of day with each other: the dawning of a new day—a new beginning.

"The Underworld is active in the latter part of the day," she said distractedly, her eyes lost in the skies above. "We stay up late and usually sleep in when the sun rises."

His eyes wandered over the vastness of the scene before him.

"I don't know why, but when I woke up this morning, I really wanted to see the sunrise." He looked at her with warm eyes. "I was hoping I'd get to see it with you, but I didn't want to wake you." He laughed at the irony in that. "So much for that, huh?"

At that second, Yoori considered telling him how worried she felt when she woke up and discovered he wasn't by her side. She contemplated telling him how afraid she was when she realized that his guns were missing. She wanted to tell him that the fear was unlike anything she had ever experienced, but she chose not to. She reasoned that Tae Hyun didn't need to listen to her unfounded fears. Her paranoia was simply a result of residing within the Underworld for so many years. The last thing she wanted was for him to worry as well.

"What are you doing out here with your guns?" she managed to whisper out. She didn't plan on discussing her paranoid wakeup call, but she was still curious as to why he had his beloved weapons with him.

His eyes still set on the twilight sky, he said, "Saying goodbye to a life I grew up in."

Yoori paused. It finally registered to her what Tae Hyun was doing, why he was standing in front of their lake with his guns in hand.

He wasn't going to take his guns with him to Paris.

He was going to leave it all behind—his power, his throne, and his Underworld—by getting rid of his father's gift to him. The two silver guns were the last remaining symbols of his bloodline and his prestige in this powerful and volatile world. By discarding his beloved guns, he was finally

337

solidifying that he was done with the Underworld, that he was never going back to his old life. He was after something else. He wanted a new beginning.

"Can you really leave this world without seeking your revenge on Ji Hoon?" she inquired when the gravity of what was taking place wrapped itself around her mind.

The perfection of this little escapism of a world was intoxicating, but she also knew how difficult it was to actually leave something like the Underworld behind. It was akin to being addicted to drugs. The user was aware of how bad it was for them. Despite this knowledge, they would continue to seek it because of the high it gave them. The Underworld was just like that. No matter how cruel it was, the power that came with it was an addicting feeling. It was a dangerous and toxic addiction, but an addiction nonetheless.

"Can you really leave this world without avenging your father? You're at the very top of this society—a position that humans could only dream of being in. Can you really leave all that power behind?"

"I have two choices in life," he answered thoughtfully, undeterred by her playing devil's advocate. "I can either spend the rest of my life consumed by the shadows of the Underworld, or I can spend it breathing in the same air as you." He smiled, turning back to her. His eyes were as gentle and as loving as ever. "I don't want to be anywhere but with you."

"Why are you so sure, Tae Hyun?"

"This time yesterday, I wasn't sure if I was making the right decision," he shared honestly. "I knew that I wanted to be with you, I knew that I would kill anyone who dared to hurt you, and I knew that I could never live without you . . . but there was still a part of me that lingered for the Underworld, for the life I led there. I wanted you, but I wasn't sure I could leave all that I'd worked for—everything that I gave up my life for—behind. I didn't know if I could leave my greed and my insatiable need for power behind to be something that I hadn't been for fourteen years: human."

He smiled at her while Yoori felt her heart warm.

"But when I held you last night, never feeling more human or more alive in my life, I knew there was no contest. Being a King—a God in this world— could never compare to being human with you. It would never measure up to having these moments with you, being distracted by you. I know without a doubt in my mind now that I've made the right decision. I would never regret choosing you over the world."

He tilted his head at her, ready to pose the same question to her. "A million people would kill to have the status you have in life. You don't regret giving up the throne and being with me instead?"

For the first time since their meeting, Yoori saw humbleness in Tae Hyun's eyes. From that, she felt her own humbleness shine through.

"In my twenty-four years of existence," she began truthfully, "I've seen more in my short life than a twenty-four-year-old girl should ever see in her lifetime. I've seen every cruelty there is to see, I've met all the awful human beings who exist in this world, and I've made every deal there is to be made with the devil."

She inhaled shakily, recalling the faces of all the people she had killed, all the ones who had to die in order for her to become a "Queen" amongst heartless killers. If there was a balance of justice in this world, then that balance was surely faulty because she was undeserving of a wonderful man like Tae Hyun after all she had done.

"I . . . I don't know how it's possible for someone like me to find the type of love that even Gods envy. I don't know how it's possible for a monster like me to be so blessed when there are countless people out there—good people who would never torture or kill anyone—who would never know what it feels like to find this type of love. I don't know how, through all the darkness in the Underworld, you came to me and found me." Conviction illumed in her eyes as she stared up at him. "But know that I will never regret meeting you, I will never regret being with you, and I will never regret choosing you over the throne. I could have a million Royals kneeling before me and none of that would equate to being here with you—to being human with you."

He gave her a grateful smile before his eyes glanced down at the guns in her hands. "You're still uncertain though, like you expect something terrible to happen right now that would ruin everything."

She nodded, biting her lips to keep her emotions from getting the best of her. Leave it to Tae Hyun to figure out her fears, even when she did not want to voice them.

"Sometimes . . . I can't help but think that the only way to keep you alive is to hold onto my old life, the life that's so revered that people wouldn't dare come after us." She breathed in deeply, staring at his guns before honestly sharing what was on her mind. "If you get rid of those, then the last remaining symbol of your prestige in this world will die with them. You will be powerless when they come after us, and we both know they will come after us." Her stomach coiled in unbearable knots at the knowledge of this. "The world we disappeared into last night is fleeting. They will never let us live in peace, they will always come after us, and we will always be on the run. Can you honestly live like that after being so revered in this world? Can you really become human like that?" She sighed, her voice quieter than she had ever heard it when she added, "Am I really worth all of that?"

His smile was soft when he gently reached for her necklace and pulled it out, revealing the ring that she had given him. The engraving of a serpent curling around the outer exterior of the ring came into view, as well as a circular sequence of duck footprints following after one another in the interior of the ring.

To anyone else, Yoori knew that they would never think twice—or understand—why she had the ring engraved in that manner, why she had the serpent and the duck footprints follow one another in the same direction. She knew that no one else could figure out why she did what she did. The only exception was the one she gave this ring to, the one she wordlessly gave her vow to.

"Wherever you go . . ." he started, confirming to her that he understood the meaning, as well as the promise, behind the ring.

"I'll follow," Yoori finished for him. She felt her guns grow heavy in her grasp as soon as she vocalized this.

"No regrets, Nemo," he promised her. "Our past may be the most fucked up past one could ask for and our ending is as dark as the night is long, but I wouldn't change a thing about it if it meant that there was a possibility that I wouldn't have you by my side right now, standing here in my black hoodie after the magical night we had." He stroked her hair, his eyes filled with love. "Whatever may come from this, know that I would gladly burn in an eternity of hell for these few stolen moments of heaven with you."

Yoori nodded, wordlessly telling him that she felt the same way.

With that, Tae Hyun took one final glance at his silver guns, a final homage to the life he led and the life he was leaving behind.

Then, with no more reservations, he threw the guns, one by one, into the far distance of the lake.

The guns glided into the far depths of the lake, twinkling under the rays of the wakening sunrise. The sound of splashing echoed through the tranquil lake as the guns made contact with the surface of the water. Ripples ignited through the water from the impact. The discarded guns floated above the surface of the water for a few seconds before submerging into the depths of the lake, finally disappearing from sight.

Following suit with no hesitation, Yoori threw her left hand back and tossed her gun into the same direction. Her gold gun flew in the same manner as his and died in the same manner as his. Although throwing the first gun was easy, she couldn't say the same for her second one.

Yoori felt nothing but confliction as she held the last remaining gun in her hand. With a heavy heart, she stared at the treasured gift from her father—the last lifeline, the last official string to the Underworld, and her last official symbol of status as the Queen of the Underworld.

Her greed and fear assailed her mind, begging her to not throw it away. *What about the throne? What about Tae Hyun? How will you keep him alive without this? How will you instill fear into anyone's hearts if you throw away the last remaining shred of your bloodline? How will you keep this dream alive without this?* One by one, she could feel her coldblooded greed and her fears of losing Tae Hyun blind her logicality, urging her to hold onto a life she knew was poison to the future she wanted.

Her mind felt so congested.

She felt conflicted, until she raised her eyes to stare into Tae Hyun's eyes. Everything fell silent the moment she grew lost in his gaze. His understanding eyes silently assured her that whatever decision she made, he would go along with it. He said nothing, and this said everything to her.

Being afraid of what was to come was overshadowed by her timeless distraction. She could feel the love he had for her and the love she had for him. As a result, any hardship that came with throwing the gun away ceased to exist. There were no more uncertainties, no more doubts, and no more fear.

For the first time in her life, Choi Yoori—and An Soo Jin—felt inarguably human.

She was irrevocably human again, and now, as the sunrise illuminated over them, she not only accepted her fate, but also embraced it.

Lifting her hand up, she kept her gaze on him as she threw the gun into the far distance. The sunrise appeared, spreading over the world around them and marking their new life together. Whatever may come from this moment, they had finally accepted their fates. They accepted that they were at the mercy of the world and that they were no longer Gods. They were merely human beings doing the best they could with the fate that they had been given.

The moment was perfect, absolutely beautiful. It was a perfect, blissful, and life-changing moment until—

Thump!

"Quaaaaaack!"

Yoori's and Tae Hyun's eyes widened at the ear-screeching sound.

Once they jerked their attention back to the lake, Yoori's eyes bulged open even further. She covered her mouth in absolute shock. In the distance, she could see the dent the gun made into the newly lit golden water. And much to her own horror and disbelief, she could also see a white chubby duck floating on top of that golden lake, completely and utterly unconscious.

She had just smacked a duck with the gun!

"You just knocked a duck out with your gun!" Tae Hyun shouted, horrified.

"Holy shit!" Yoori cried into the hands covering her mouth. She was still staring wide-eyed at the floating duck and the ripples of water surrounding it.

"Can't you go one damn day without hurting a duck?!" Tae Hyun blurted out, still in disbelief.

"Did it look like I had malicious intentions when I tossed the gun?" she shouted back. She couldn't believe that an unconscious duck had just eclipsed one of the most monumental moments of her life. A duck so stupid that it didn't have enough survival instinct to make any attempts to evade a flying object.

The once romantic and life-changing interchange they shared was outshined by the absurdity of the scene before them.

"That stupid duck shouldn't have gotten in the way of a flying gun," she growled, trying to take the accountability off of her. How the hell was she supposed to anticipate a suicidal duck getting hit by her gun? She bit her lips and stupidly added, "The other ducks should've warned him."

"By saying what?" Tae Hyun asked incredulously, still gaping at the knocked out duck. "'Hey fellow duck! There's a flying gold gun coming at you! *Duck!*'"

Yoori was now beside herself. She had no more mechanisms for defending herself other than resorting to being angry with Tae Hyun. He always chose those feathery animals over her.

"You always side with those ducks," she stated bitterly.

"You're not the one knocked out cold in the lake right now, *Choi*."

"Maybe I should knock you out and have you join your buddies, *Kwon*."

"You always ruin the mood," he retorted, amusement overfilling his voice. It was apparent that although Tae Hyun loved this species of animals dearly, he couldn't deny that the situation they found themselves in was just ridiculous and utterly hilarious. His lips twitched to keep from bursting out into laughter. "Anytime we do anything and get romantic, you always manage to find a way to kill the mood."

Yoori kept quiet because she knew it was true.

In her defense, who could have anticipated this? Tae Hyun had tossed his guns without trouble, and he had touched her heart and soul when he did that. Yet, when she tossed her guns after much contemplation, instead of securing herself a way in touching Tae Hyun's heart, she wound up touching a funny bone in his body instead. The absurdity of life was too funny to her. If this didn't make them human, she did not know what would.

"It's not like I meant to do it," Yoori grumbled under her breath.

As a response, Tae Hyun could only nod while both of them, with much curiosity, folded their arms and stood closely together. Their eyes were still locked on the poor floating duck. At that moment, there were other ducks quacking around it, poking at it with their beaks as if to say, *"Dude! Wake up, you're going to drown soon if you don't!"*

"This is our life," Tae Hyun breathed out in amazement long seconds later. Above them, the morning sun continued to bloom over the land.

"This is our life," Yoori repeated, sharing the same amazement. Their past and future were not ideal, but their present was just too wonderful to not be in awe of. "This is *our* silly life."

No more guns, no more blood, and no more darkness—just ducks, boomerangs, and Paris.

Done with giving his attention to the duck, Tae Hyun turned away from the lake and rested his eyes on Yoori. A mischievous sensuality cloaked his eyes. It was a sensuality that had her entire body coming alive in wonder. Playful and pensive Tae Hyun had left the building while irresistible, charming, and seductive Tae Hyun was out of his cage and ready to play.

"For ruining the mood of our otherwise monumental and life-changing moment," he began in a business-like tone, his eyes still dark with desire, "I want seven babies."

Tires screeched to a halt in her head. "Uh . . . *what?*"

"Seven kids," he repeated, capitalizing on the fact that she was more than freaked out with his proposition. Leave it to Tae Hyun to mess with Yoori in a way that no one else could. "I want seven chubby little kids," he continued as her eyes grew wider and wider from shock, "snobs and brats alike, running around the place, driving me crazy."

He laughed, humorously wrapping his arms around her. He pulled her into his warm, hard body before seductively nipping her lips.

"You know what that means, right?" he prompted, his lips moving from her lips to her jaw, her chin, and then her neck. The trail of his kiss nearly drove her insane. She fought to maintain her equilibrium when all she wanted to do was succumb to the weakening of her legs and allow Tae Hyun to have his way with her. "It means that I'm going to keep you round and deliciously plump with our babies."

Enjoying euphoric pleasures aside, Yoori couldn't help but get alarmed at the thought of herself being "deliciously plump" with seven babies.

"Seven kids?" Yoori choked out, her eyes wide like golf-balls. She knew he was joking, but goddamn, seven kids? She laughed to herself, shaking her head as she jokingly pulled herself out of his grasp. "Well, it seems you're gonna have to find yourself a mistress, buddy, because I'm not a bunny making machine."

"We'll give each of the kids a duck as their pet as well," he continued to tease, biting his lips to keep from laughing at the ridiculousness of what he was saying.

Joke or not, Yoori was appalled. "A— a duck?!"

He was going to gift their nonexistent, hypothetical chubby kids with her archenemies? If that wasn't a recipe for disaster, then she didn't know what was.

343

"Well, not Korean ducks because they hate us here," he corrected as if reading her mind. "But we can give them French ducks. We haven't pissed off that country's ducks yet."

"Don't birds migrate?" she asked gravely, her eyes shifting uncomfortably to the ducks in the lake behind them.

Tae Hyun was quiet as well, his face shrouded with uncertainty. After an ominous breath, he slowly said, "You think the Korean ducks will follow us?"

They took a minute to stare at each other in a stupefied silence. Then, they just burst out laughing at the absurdity of their conversation.

"Peace out, Korean ducks!" Yoori shouted joyfully, raising both her hands at the lake.

"It's been a good run!" Tae Hyun added, raising one hand to wave at them while his other arm was still wrapped around Yoori's waist. Together, they waved and walked backwards, treading further and further away from the lake and closer and closer to their new life together. "Thanks for putting up with this duck-hater! We shall let her be the misery of the French ducks now!"

Yoori was laughing as she ran back to the lake house.

"Hey Snob! We have half a day left before our flight to Paris. What should we do with our time?"

He grinned, running towards her with the speed of a bull and picking her up with ease. "I have something fun in mind," he proposed. His hot breath glided over her skin as Yoori instinctively wrapped her legs around his hips and circled her arms around his neck. His body was hot, hard, and welcoming, just like how she blissfully remembered it from the night before. "It involves you screaming my name the entire time from sheer euphoria. You know . . . something like last night."

"Uh-uh," she joked, moving her index finger from side to side. "Just because we're friends with benefits now doesn't mean that you get guaranteed, *you-knowing*, like last night, Kwon." She wrapped herself tighter around him. The same desire that teemed in his eyes rippled in hers. "You have to work for it."

"Oh, I plan on it, Princess," he whispered, already lost in the yearning he had for her. He sighed before staring at the outfit she had on. A sultry and suggestive voice filled her ears when he said his next words. "I love seeing you wear nothing but my hoodie, but I love seeing you naked even more."

"Funny," Yoori mused, nibbling on his ear with her tongue. "I was about to say the same thing about you."

"Yeah?" Tae Hyun asked, holding her as he treaded back inside their lake house.

Yoori grinned sheepishly. "Yeah."

He chuckled at this, kicking the doors down as they barreled inside, completely and utterly lost in their desires for one another. "Let's give each other what we want then."

They barely made it up the stairs before their impatience took over and they took each other right then and there on the steps of their lake house. The glorious sunrise flooded around them, shielding them and giving them another stolen moment of paradise.

Another stolen moment of heaven . . . before hell came back to claim them.

"And you might happen upon it without having to look for it."

28: Two Steps from the Underworld

"Paris . . . I can't believe I'm finally going to Paris!"

Sweeping through the busy airport terminal, where they received giggles of approval and murmurs of jealousy as no one glowed brighter than the beautiful couple, Tae Hyun and Yoori were locked hand in hand as they walked towards their plane to finally prepare for boarding. They were both dressed in all black. Yoori was wearing his black hoodie with the hood resting on top of her head and a comfortable pair of pants, while Tae Hyun wore black pants, a leather jacket, and a hat to shield the upper features of his face with its shadow.

"I can't wait to see the Eiffel Tower," Yoori whispered, tightening her hold on his hand.

She thought about all the romantic things they'd do there, and she couldn't help but be gleeful. Although she was certain that the Underworld had already begun to send people after them, she was also positive that it would probably take her vengeful society a while to track them down. Tae Hyun was very careful in not using any of his personal funds to finance this trip, only enlisting the help of those that he trusted from his college years and were outside of the Underworld circle. This was why this trip to Paris took a couple of days to plan. His contacts were being very careful to ensure that nothing leaked out to reveal where Tae Hyun and Yoori were going. However intimidating it was that the entire Underworld was after them, Yoori still wouldn't change anything about her situation. She would gladly live life on the run as long as she was with her own Paris.

"I want to dance underneath the Eiffel Tower," Yoori continued, "and then I want to kiss you underneath it."

Tae Hyun looked down at her with a smile. His eyes gleamed with excitement. "Far be it from me to complain about you wanting to kiss me underneath it."

"If you dare say my lips are salty again, I'll bash you with a Parisian umbrella and run off with some French guy," she warned, being reminded of his bleak observation about her lips when he first stole her kiss.

"Well, aren't you the little romantic minx?" he said dryly. He then smirked. "I'd like to see you attempt to run off with some French guy though." His tone of voice was aloof, like he didn't think she would do it.

"What?" Yoori asked, catching on to his sarcasm. "You think I'm not capable of being shady?"

"No," he appeased. "I think you're very capable of being very shady, but I'm not worried. To be shady in another country, one would have to speak the language." He grinned at her. "Do you even know how to speak French?"

"Of course I do," she lied. She didn't know left from right about anything French, other than the fries.

As a test to verify her answer, Tae Hyun started mumbling something in French, and Yoori's eyes bloomed in awe.

"What did you just say?" she asked wondrously, giving away that she had obviously lied about knowing how to speak French.

A slow, sexy smile met his lips. "What I'd like to do to you in bed with the Eiffel tower in the background."

"You know," Yoori prompted, very turned on with her multilingual "friend with benefits". "You could easily say, '*Your ass is fat*', and I wouldn't know better and still think it was sexy."

He nodded mischievously, laughing as he raised their interlocked hands and planted a kiss behind the back of hers. "This is why I love having the language advantage. I could get away with saying anything."

Yoori rolled her eyes with a playful snort. They continued to laugh, walking for several more minutes before their gate was finally in sight. Tae Hyun pulled out their tickets, smiling at Yoori as they continued to walk closer to their new beginning.

Yoori felt her heart race in anticipatory excitement. They took the first step by choosing one another. The second and final step was the one she was most excited about. She had never been more hopeful and eager to board a plane in her life.

Paris.

After so many hardships, so many obstacles, and so many tears, they were *finally* going to Paris.

They were near the gate, just a couple of steps left towards their new life together, when Tae Hyun's phone started to ring.

"Who is it?" Yoori asked just as they got in line to board the plane. While still holding her hand, Tae Hyun pulled his phone out. He glimpsed at the Caller ID and smiled in perplexity.

"Hae Jin," he told her.

Yoori's smile grew wide. "Yeah?"

Excited to talk to Hae Jin, and perhaps Kang Min, before they boarded the plane, Tae Hyun and Yoori excused themselves from the line and went to a private area in the terminal to speak. Standing beside several large plants with the night view of the stationary airplanes in the background, Tae Hyun placed the phone on speaker.

"Hae Jin," Tae Hyun greeted warmly, holding the phone up between himself and Yoori. There was a big smile on his face. It was evident that Tae Hyun had missed his baby sister dearly. He was ecstatic to be able to talk to her before their flight. "What's going on? Are you already in Sydney?"

"Now that would be the convenient alternative, wouldn't it?"

The colors that once illuminated their faces were drained of vitality. The instant Yoori and Tae Hyun heard the familiar voice of Lee Ji Hoon stream through the speaker, Yoori could feel herself spiral down. Her brief moment in heaven was over and her descent back into the depths of Hell—or in this particular case, the Underworld—had just begun.

The breath left her body as she watched a once carefree Tae Hyun close his eyes in agony. His face contorted in misery when it became clear to him that they were going to get dragged back into the hell of the Underworld much sooner than they had anticipated.

As she watched the wretchedness take over his visage, Yoori could feel her own body tremble. The happiness that once inhabited her body dispersed, leaving her to feel only dread and misery when she concluded the inescapable truth: Ji Hoon had them.

Ji Hoon had Hae Jin and Kang Min.

In that precise instant, all her dreams of ever making it to Paris with Tae Hyun were destroyed with a simple phone call. Letting out a pained exhalation, she hopelessly fell back against the sky-high window. She gazed dejectedly at Tae Hyun. All she could do was helplessly listen to the phone conversation that would change the course of their lives forever.

"Lee Ji Hoon," Tae Hyun spoke gravely into the phone. His voice was filled with business-like composure, yet the undercurrent beneath it coursed with steel. An unforgiving fire burned in his gaze when he opened his eyes. He was momentarily perturbed, yes, but due to his years of training as a King of the Underworld, Tae Hyun was also skilled at keeping his composure—no matter how worried and angry he may be. Swallowing tightly, his grip on the phone grew stronger. While a muscle leapt in his strong jaw, he solemnly added, "Where is my sister?"

Ji Hoon's cruel laughter transmitted through the phone.

"You know, it's a funny story," he launched lightheartedly, the absurdly big smile on his face pouring out of his voice. "I actually ran into her when she was in the car with Kang Min. I think both were getting ready to leave the country." He paused as if to look at something. "Oh yes, Sydney. They were looking to head out to Sydney when I ran into them." His lighthearted tone of voice evolved into a darker tone with his next statement. "They're a bit tied up right now, which is why I'm calling you, Tae Hyun."

"What do you want?" Tae Hyun demanded through clenched teeth. The composure he once held was fading fast. He was trained to be better than this, but when faced with the possibility of his loved ones being hurt, no amount of training would prepare him for this.

"You know what I want," Ji Hoon responded at once. There was no more amusement in his voice. He, like Tae Hyun, was ready to get down to business.

"I've already given up the throne." The fury multiplied on Tae Hyun's face. "I've cut all ties with the Underworld, and I'm no longer going after you, you piece of shit. None of this could have worked out better for you. Why the fuck are you doing this?"

"Because your very existence aggravates me," Ji Hoon retorted emotionlessly. "You've been the bane of my existence since your appearance in my layer, and you've been nothing but a nuisance to me. I'm sick of how much this world reveres you over me, and I'm sick of everyone falling to their knees for you. I want to put you in your place."

"Then come after me," Tae Hyun said calmly. "Let my sister and Kang Min go. They have nothing to do with us."

An exasperated sigh emitted from Ji Hoon's lips. "I don't think you seem to understand the dire predicament that you've found yourself in, Tae Hyun. You are in no position to offer up suggestions as to what I should do." A slight pause occurred as Ji Hoon seemed to have taken a moment to look at something. After a second of tense silence, his cold voice added, "Perhaps your baby sister will do a better job of imparting to you the severity of this situation."

A transitory silence came over the line.

Then—

A hard slap rang into the phone.

"Ahhh!"

Hae Jin's screams came out through the receiver, breaking Yoori and Tae Hyun's hearts as her labored breathing filtered through the speaker.

"Don't you fucking touch her!" They heard Kang Min's voice just before the sound of someone hitting him stole his breath.

"Noooo! Kang Min! Don't hurt him. Pleas—ah!"

Another thundering slap filled the receiver, silencing Hae Jin once more.

On the other line, Tae Hyun and Yoori felt themselves unraveling. Any shred of composure they had dissipated with Hae Jin's screams. For a King and Queen who were accustomed to protecting the ones they loved, the fact that they could not help Hae Jin and Kang Min was soul-wrenching.

With his eyes closed in anguish, Tae Hyun slammed his forehead against the window. His free hand clenched into a frustrated fist while Yoori inhaled shakily, her agonized hands running through her hair in misery. She felt her heart and soul break at the sounds of Hae Jin and Kang Min being beaten by Ji Hoon.

Unable to regulate his anger, a furious Tae Hyun roared, "Ji Hoon! Don't you dare lay another hand on—!"

Another ear-splitting slap thundered through the speaker.

Hae Jin's scream after the third slap was what caused Tae Hyun to contort his face in torture. Afraid that his screams would antagonize Ji Hoon and give him more fuel to hurt Hae Jin, Tae Hyun stopped midway in his sentence and winced in misery. It was torture for Tae Hyun. For the first time in his life, he was absolutely helpless.

"What," he enunciated in controlled anger. "Do. You. Want?"

Pleased with receiving the response that he wanted, Ji Hoon's voice came over the line. The sounds of Hae Jin's soft cries and Kang Min's angry voice became dimmer and dimmer in the background.

"Come meet me, Tae Hyun, and I'll let them go."

"No! Oppa, don't come!" the distant voice shouted in horror.

"Don't come! Don't come!" Kang Min's voice yelled desperately. He could scarcely get another word out before the sound of fists hitting flesh came over the line. Then, with the sound of a heavy door closing, their voices ceased to exist.

Though silence had presided over the line, the volcanic eruption within Yoori was uncontainable when she grabbed the phone from Tae Hyun.

"Lee Ji Hoon!" she roared. The monster in her was hungry for his blood. She could no longer tolerate listening to this. She wanted nothing more than to rip this fucker to pieces. "If you fucking lay another hand on them—"

"Ah, there you are, baby," Ji Hoon interjected, his voice lighting up after hearing her voice. There was a mixture of adoration and amusement in his tone. He knew that she had been listening in on the call. It delighted him that she finally made herself known. "I've missed the sound of your voice. How are you?"

Nausea plagued her with how this scumbag was speaking to her.

"Leave them out of this," she growled instead, ignoring his attempt at exchanging pleasantries with her. "We've already given up the throne. You can have it—everything. The Underworld is yours. We're no longer after you, we're no longer a threat to you. Take advantage of that, let them go, and leave us alone."

A mocking laughter came through the receiver. "As much as I love the thought of my ex-girlfriend running off with the one bastard I hate the most in this world, I'll have to insist on seeing you both tonight, just to settle some things and give our lives some closure."

"You won't be seeing her," Tae Hyun snapped, snatching the phone from Yoori.

"Tae Hyun," Yoori snapped just as angrily. "I'm coming—"

"She's not coming, do you hear me?" Tae Hyun's voice was ice cold. He turned away from Yoori and spoke into the phone himself. "This is about you and me, and we'll keep it that way. You're not pulling her into this."

"Again, Tae Hyun, you do not seem to understand your place in this conversation." Ji Hoon paused before he used an anchor that thrashed any further arguments that Tae Hyun could give out. "Your sister is pregnant, isn't she?"

"Ji Hoon!" Tae Hyun snarled at the thought of Ji Hoon even knowing that his sister was carrying a child. "Don't you dare hurt her or the baby!"

"Then I take it that the King of Serpents and the Queen of the Underworld will come and save them?" There was a smile in Ji Hoon's voice while he lightheartedly added, "2:00 A.M. at *The Stadium*. Both of you, be there, or I'm cutting Kang Min and Hae Jin into a million pieces, and I'll send you their body parts as souvenirs."

When it appeared as though Ji Hoon was ready to end the call, Tae Hyun's cryptic voice stopped him in his tracks.

"Ji Hoon," Tae Hyun warned dangerously, rage emitting from every inch of his powerful body. "If you truly insist on doing this, then know that tonight will be your final night on earth. If you don't let them go right now, then I will show you no mercy and I *will* kill you. I *will* make you pay for everything, and you will *never* see the light of day again."

There was a suspended moment of silence before Ji Hoon's fearless voice came on.

"We'll see if you can hold up that promise. See you soon."
Click.

The phone call disconnected, and all that was left after the destructive earthquake they experienced were its heart-wrenching aftershocks.

"God damn it," Tae Hyun cursed, the bones in his knuckles cracking as he delivered an unrestrained punch to the glass. The otherwise enormous and powerful sky-high window trembled in weakness at the impact.

Tae Hyun closed his eyes and when he opened them, a quiet Yoori could see his focus land on the plane in front of them, the plane that was their ticket to Paris—a world that was their beacon of heaven when compared to their vicious Underworld. Yoori could see the pain immerse his eyes as he stared quietly at the innocuous plane.

With a heavy heart, she allowed her eyes to rest on it as well. She felt the breath leave her when she drank in the sight before her. The plane couldn't have looked more majestic, its body promising them a world filled with dreams as it sat in the darkness of the night, beckoning them to board it. As she stood in the tunnel between heaven and hell, Yoori had never sought heaven more as she felt the fires of hell chase after her, just waiting . . . just waiting to consume her.

"Get on the flight."

Yoori averted her eyes from the plane and gaped at him in disbelief. "What?"

"You're not coming," he said sternly, turning away from the plane and settling his eyes on her. From within those brown eyes, she could only see remorse and pain. "I'm going alone."

Yoori's blood boiled. "You expect me to be a coward and run off when Ji Hoon has your sister and Kang Min?"

"Young Jae and Ji Hoon are working together," Tae Hyun reminded her, concern plaguing his now dim eyes. "Are you naïve enough to believe that Young Jae won't be there, waiting for you? Are you naïve enough to think that he won't be waiting to kill you after what happened to his wife?" His tortured eyes went over the bruises on her face and landed on the arm that had been shot—the arm that was still healing and no way near healed. "I can't let you go, Yoori. You're in no condition to fight anyone right now, much less Ji Hoon or Young Jae."

"And you're in the condition to fight?" she countered, stepping closer to him. She knew that Young Jae would be there. She wasn't a fool to think otherwise. Regardless of her knowledge, she didn't care.

Her eyes traced the healing bruises on his face. The mental picture of all the scars and bruises on his body came into her mind. He didn't show it too often, but Yoori knew that Tae Hyun, like herself, was severely injured from their battle. He, just like her, was in no condition to fight anyone, especially Ji Hoon and Young Jae.

"I will manage," he stated inflexibly, his mind still set on going alone.

Yoori wanted to cuss him out for being stubborn and stupid. She wanted to beat the hell out of him for even entertaining the idea that she would leave him to fend for himself while their loved ones were in trouble. She wanted to do all of this, but couldn't bring herself to do any of it. She knew too well how tortured Tae Hyun was. His outward demeanor was strong, but inside, it was clear that he hated this situation more than anyone. Even if it meant something happening to him, he would always put her, his sister, and his loved ones above his own safety, above his own life. This was a trait that Yoori admired and hated about him. This was a trait that they both shared and despised about one another.

Yoori took in a painful breath and placed her hands on Tae Hyun's chest. She moved closer to him, her soft eyes imploring him to see reason.

"We can help each other," she told him, her voice soft yet stern. "I'm not leaving you, Tae Hyun, and I'm not leaving the two people who are like my little brother and sister. We're in this together. I'm not abandoning you. I don't care about my brother. He can try to kill me for what happened with Anna, but I won't let him get at me easily." She held his hand, feeling the necklace she was wearing burn into her skin. "We're in this together, right? Just like we said to each other this morning when we threw our guns into the lake?"

"You have to leave first," he told her stubbornly, pain growing exponentially in his eyes. He placed on an artificial smile as a means to assure her that he would be okay. "I will be fine by myself. I'll go, I'll get Hae Jin and Kang Min back, and then I'll meet you in Paris. It'll all work out, but you have to go first. You can't be here to distract me. You can't be here and put yourself in harm's way."

"I told you already that I'm not getting on that plane." Her calm voice grew unyielding. "Did what happened this morning mean nothing to you?"

She could see the hurt in his eyes when she mentioned this. She capitalized on it by stroking her finger over his cheek to further implore him to see where she was coming from and why she wasn't going to leave him.

"'Wherever you go, I'll follow.' That wasn't just a promise from me, Tae Hyun. That was my vow to you. I'm not leaving you behind. Wherever you're going, I'm coming with you. I will stay by your side until the end." A hopeful smile lit up her lips. She hoped that he would stop being stubborn and allow her to keep her vow to him. She did not want him to brush her off so that he could protect her. She wanted to stay so she could protect him. "We're in this together, right?"

He looked conflicted as he stared down at her, still unable to say anything.

"Tae Hyun?" she voiced again. "We're in this together, *right*?"

"Yes," he, at long last, confirmed with the weight of the world anchoring down his voice. His eyes were cloaked with a storm of emotions that she could no longer decipher. "We're in this together."

Yoori smiled, nodding approvingly as he kissed the back of her hand.

"We're in this together," he said again, this time his voice truly meaning it.

Gazing at one another, they could hear an announcement that the flight to Paris was having their last call for boarding.

Against her better rationale, Yoori's eyes strayed back onto the airplane before them. Misery overfilled her heavy heart. Doing the same, Tae Hyun turned his attention to the plane, the glow that once shined from him at the prospect of finally taking Yoori to Paris fading under the shadows of the Underworld.

It was like they were mourning a memory that would never be. It was like they were mourning a Paris that they would never see.

After a long lingering second, as if to prepare their heavy hearts for the reality of what was to come, they reluctantly pulled their eyes away from the plane and intertwined their hands with one another's.

With much effort, they wheeled around and began to walk out of the airport terminal, their eyes staring straight ahead. They never turned back to stare at the memories they could've had, they never turned back to lust after a dream they could've lived in, and they never turned back to bid goodbye to the magical and timeless life they could've had.

"Are you ready for what's to come?" Tae Hyun asked as they walked out of the airport and into the parking garage.

Their once troubled faces were replaced with the expression of warriors going into a battle of a lifetime. They had bid goodbye to the lives they could've led as ordinary humans and were now, once again, desperate Gods under the mercy of their cruel and sadistic Underworld.

Yoori nodded, feigning composure and fearlessness.

She parted her lips and gave an easy lie that contradicted every trembling and fearful nerve within her body. She didn't know what to expect and she didn't know how everything was going to play out. The only thing the deep subconscious part of her knew was that she wasn't ready.

She would *never* be ready for what was to come.

"Yes . . . I'm ready."

"How about we both make a pact..."

29: The Stadium

The atmosphere surrounding them was quiet, morose.

After they departed from the airport, Yoori and Tae Hyun drove back to Tae Hyun's apartment to retrieve their backup guns and any other weapons they might need. Under normal circumstances, Yoori and Tae Hyun would not have been too concerned with packing up weapons. But this occasion was different. Their injured bodies were not up to par to fight in a strenuous battle. They would be fools to not acknowledge and correct this disadvantage.

Packing weapons proved to be the easy part as it was the mental battle that Yoori was falling victim to. She would be lying if she said she was not fearful of what Ji Hoon had in store for them. She wasn't afraid for herself, but afraid for the ones she loved: Hae Jin, Kang Min, and Tae Hyun.

The memory of what happened that morning replayed in her mind, reminding her of the sudden paranoia she experienced when she discovered that Tae Hyun wasn't by her side. She remembered the unexplainable fear that assailed her when she realized that there was a chance he could be hurt. She understood now why she reacted the way she did. She had anticipated this moment. No matter how far off or improbable it appeared, she foresaw this very moment. The only small mercy of this tragedy was that he was still by her side; she could still protect him every step of the way.

After spending several hours in Tae Hyun's apartment—basically awaiting judgment day—Tae Hyun and Yoori were anything but conversational with one another. The only thing they spoke about (and agreed upon) was keeping all of this from Jae Won and Chae Young. They wanted their participation in all of this to be kept at a minimum for their own safety.

The rest of the time was spent together, but also apart. While Yoori was sitting outside in the living room, replenishing the bullets into the two black guns that she borrowed from Tae Hyun, Tae Hyun was in their bedroom, speaking on the phone with one of his contacts. He instructed them to delay the funds to Paris, that he and Yoori had postponed the trip because they had some unfinished business to take care of first.

355

It was a heart wrenching conversation that Yoori wished she hadn't heard. Regardless, she understood it was something she had to hear. She had to hear it to help mentally prepare herself for everything. The vacation she took from the Underworld—no matter how brief—was a detrimental one in terms of bringing her mind back into the mode of things. She needed to discard her mindset as an ordinary human girl and return to being the most feared Queen in the Underworld. With that thought in mind, she got into the car with Tae Hyun and left for *The Stadium*.

The humming of the wind blew against Tae Hyun's Jaguar as they drove down the quiet road. As silence suspended over them, Yoori and Tae Hyun grew lost in their own worlds, which were intertwined with the same pain and misery. Both were worried about the two people they loved and were concurrently heartbroken with their impending return to the Underworld.

How could one go back to the darkness when they had seen the light? How could one go back into the cave of hell when they had already found their Eden?

Thoughts and regrets like this cycled through Yoori's mind as she thought about who they were going up against.

When she was An Soo Jin, there was a lot about Ji Hoon that she didn't understand and a lot about him that he never showed her. From the point they met up until the night of her "suicide", he had always been the actor—and a most talented actor at that. Lee Ji Hoon, in comparison to herself and Tae Hyun, was always seen as being in third place. Though some people may have underestimated him after what took place at Ju Won's party, Soo Jin knew that in the Underworld, people like Ji Hoon were the most hazardous and calculating ones. Their jealousy gets the best of them, and in turn, they are willing to do anything to get what they want. These people, in any type of world, are always the most dangerous ones.

At least with Young Jae, she could understand how his mind worked because she had the luxury of growing up with him. However, not even that small solace made her feel better. Sadness weighed in her heart at the thought of him, Anna, and their unborn child. As terrible as she felt, she knew Young Jae was a lost cause at this point. They would never reconcile. She knew her brother too well. He would make sure she died the most terrible of deaths before he gave up.

It didn't make Yoori feel better to think about this as they drove in the dark.

Desperate to distract herself, she turned to Tae Hyun.

The light from the dashboard glowed on Tae Hyun's face, showing the pensive expression he had on.

Yoori pressed her hands into her stomach to quell the pain curling within her gut. She hated that just the night before, they were having the night of their lives. In a cruel twist of fate, they were now on their way to meet two coldhearted people who would stop at nothing until they were both dead. She once thought that her epic battle with Tae Hyun was a difficult night to bear, but this night was proving to be even grimmer. At least with that battle, she went in thinking that she had everything planned out nicely. It didn't work out the way she wanted it to, but at least she went into it with some peace of mind. With this new and unexpected battle, she had absolutely no idea what to expect, and this scared every inch of her soul.

Unable to help herself, though she knew it was probably best not to distract Tae Hyun from his concentration, she reached her left hand out. Her face contorted in slight pain when the bullet wound acted up. Releasing a sharp breath, she allowed her trembling fingers to slowly touch his hand while he drove.

Tae Hyun expelled a lungful of air when she did this. Curiously enough, it was as though he had decided on something as soon as she touched him.

"Where is *The Stadium?*" she asked, yearning to hear his voice. No matter how daunting all of this was, all she needed was his voice and she would be brought back to earth. For a short moment, she would at least be fine again.

It was one in the morning and they were the only ones driving on the dark road. There were no other cars or living entities in sight.

"Just up the corner," he told her quietly, driving a little bit further up before bearing right. At this new turn, she could see the reflection of the sea in the close distance. "It's a big warehouse seaport. Very secluded and rarely anyone comes around this area."

Yoori smirked as the road became more gravelly. The thrashing of the wind picked up against the car. "How convenient for gang fights," she mused to herself.

He laughed, sending a sprout of warmness into Yoori's heart. "Yeah."

His laughter wouldn't mean much to anyone else, but it meant the world to Yoori.

"Remember to stick by my side," he instructed just as they went over a small speed bump.

"You forget that I can take care of myself now." Even though she said this in a lighthearted manner, she truly meant it. She did not want him to be distracted with her. She could fend for herself.

He smiled, turning to her. "Queen of the Underworld or not, martial art skills that could rival Gods or not, when you're with me you're under my protection. My woman, mine to protect. No one will hurt you if I can help it."

"I know," Yoori responded. She knew that it didn't matter if she was a helpless damsel in distress or a revered Queen who could kill men without blinking an eye. In the eyes of Tae Hyun, she would always be the one who he would give everything to protect. "No one will hurt you if I can help it either."

Tae Hyun smiled at this. With his eyes back on the road, he sighed and finally announced, "We're here."

Yoori released a sharp exhale and nodded. She was ready, at least somewhat mentally, for what was to come.

The car slowed down as they made a right turn into an empty parking lot. The tires moved over the loose gravel before coming to a complete stop at the center of the parking lot. Turning off the engine, Yoori and Tae Hyun stepped out into the cold night. The icy wind from the sea sent chills up their spines while they closed their doors, walked over to one another, held hands, and began towards the area of the seaport where the railings were.

It happened in an instant. As Yoori breathed in the cold sea air, she could feel her gut twist in uneasiness.

Something wasn't right.

Thinking that she was being too paranoid (and not wanting to prematurely alert Tae Hyun of the uneasiness she was feeling just yet), Yoori allowed the cold breeze to drift through her hair as she surveyed the immediate vicinity. The building beside them seemed vacant, the parking lot was empty, and the area around them was quiet—too quiet.

Something was off about this place.

Once they approached the railing in front of the sea, Yoori couldn't help but vocalize her unsettling nerves to Tae Hyun.

"Tae Hyun, there's something off about this place," she whispered, squeezing his hand to get his attention.

Tae Hyun turned to her, his eyes gazing at her with uneasy curiosity. He subtly picked up the pace, bringing them closer to the railing. "What do you mean?"

"There's no one here," she said, looking around the abandoned and eerily quiet seaport. "If Ji Hoon had set this up, then there would be at least some activity going on here. This place is just dead. It feels like no one has been here for days—"

Click.

Yoori ceased midway in her sentence when she felt something cold encircle her wrist.

Her insides went cold instantly. Snapping her head back around, her eyes enlarged in shock when she lowered her gaze and realized that Tae Hyun had just handcuffed her to the railing.

Stunned with confusion, Yoori stared up at Tae Hyun. "Tae Hyun, what are you—?"

"I can't let you go, Yoori," he interrupted, his eyes gazing into hers with agonized pain. Anguish cloaked his face when he said this. His jaw clenched tight, he moved his hands behind her back and pulled out her guns and the knives hidden within every pocket of the outfit she wore. "I can't risk letting you go."

"What are you talking about?" she breathed out, trembling where she stood. The weight of the handcuff anchored down her wrist, worsening her bewilderment. Her breathing became shallow and rapid. She watched with horror as he hurled the guns and knives into the far distance of the parking lot. Her mind still reeling, she turned back to him with perplexed and accusing eyes. "But we agreed—"

"I can't risk you getting hurt," he told her excruciatingly, bringing a hand up while his palm touched her cheek. Even his touch was filled with confliction; it was like he was wordlessly apologizing for what he was doing to her. "I can't risk *anything* happening to you."

Yoori's throat grew dry. This was his plan all along. He was never going to allow her to meet Ji Hoon. He intentionally took her to the wrong place so that she wouldn't walk into the lion's den. He took it upon himself to be the one who gave her protection, to be the one who had the last say in whether or not she could risk her life.

"Tae Hyun," she called brokenly. The thought of him facing Ji Hoon and Young Jae alone was torment for her mental state. All the fear she felt this morning manifested in her soul again. Only this time, it was a million times worse because it was actually happening. "Tae Hyun . . . why are you doing this?" she went on with a trembling voice. Her eyes begged him to set her free. "I can do this with you. I can help you. I'm no longer the old Yoori. I know how to fight; I know how to take care of myself now. You don't have to worry."

"You're in no condition to fight," he told her again. His fingers caressed over the bruises that had yet to heal on her face. He then grazed the bandage covering her bullet wound, looking more saddened as he did this.

Yoori glanced at the bruises on his face. "And you are?"

"I have not been recently shot." His voice was gentle, yet inflexible. After taking a moment to breathe quietly, he finally enlightened her as to why he was so adamant about her staying here and why she was never going to change his mind. "I can't have you go, Yoori. Not when Ji Hoon is there, not when Young Jae is there, and especially not when the entire Underworld is there."

Her eyes grew wide at the last statement. "Why would the entire Underworld be there?"

The muscles in his jaw clenched. It was clear he did not want to share this information with her. Though he didn't want to, he shared it regardless.

"After your 'death' three years ago, shortly after I was crowned the King of Serpents, *The Stadium* was built to house the entire Underworld for their summits—for their meeting grounds."

"That was *The Pyramid*," Yoori voiced, recalling the very meeting ground where the entire Underworld layers convened and where historic Underworld events occurred. They would attend a big gathering outside of the city. This arena was built in a secluded area to give them privacy while they performed monumental ceremonies and events that included, but were not limited to, the appointing of new Advisors, the crowning of new Kings, and the punishments of Gods whom had fallen from grace.

"A new meeting place was built shortly after your death. It was built for me when I was crowned the new King of Serpents." Tae Hyun's face turned conflicted while a cold breeze skittered past them, sending goose bumps to materialize on the entirety of Yoori's body. "That new arena is *The Stadium*. The entire Underworld is going to be there. I can only imagine how Ji Hoon must've gotten back into their good graces because of our departure—"

He paused momentarily.

It looked for a split second that he didn't want to finish that sentence, but when Yoori told him to go on with her eyes, he did as she asked.

As his next words came over her, Yoori's world collapsed.

" . . . And because of Young Jae's new status in the Underworld."

Her heart stopped beating while her eyes grew wide in vigilance.

"*What* new status?" she asked slowly, fearing the answer.

"Young Jae was crowned as the Lord of Japan's Underworld last night."

Yoori felt her whole world tilt on its axis as the enormity of this information came over her, pummeled her, and left her reeling from its unforgiving destruction. She could no longer breathe. Gasping for air, she stumbled back against the railing.

"The first Lord of all the Underworlds," she breathed out disbelievingly.

She returned her eyes to Tae Hyun and looked at him in sheer disbelief. She didn't want to believe this; she didn't want to believe her brother had *this* much power. Her mind spun with questions. *How*? How did he acquire so much power in such a short period of time? How was any of this possible?

"But the Korean Underworld was scheduled to have the first Lord," she uttered, still unable to grasp the reality of her new world. "How is it possible that Japan acquired the first date?"

"Japan moved theirs up," answered Tae Hyun. "That was why Young Jae disappeared to Japan so much . . . because he had killed every other potential

Lord. That night in the business district when he left with P.C., he went back to Tokyo and killed the final King standing in his way."

Yoori ran through the last memory of her brother and recalled that exact moment when this occurred:

"Boss!" P.C. continued to scream out, using all his strength to pry Young Jae away from Anna's dead body. "Things are happening in Japan! We have to go!"

"My brother," Yoori said in breathless stupefaction, "is the first Lord."

"He has used his power as the Japanese Underworld's newly crowned Lord to get Ji Hoon back into the good graces of the Korean Underworld," Tae Hyun went on with difficulty. "Ji Hoon is now the elected Lord of the Underworld for Korea, and because you and I have forfeited our positions, he is the *only* elected candidate. The title is guaranteed to him. Ji Hoon's only task is to punish and execute me in front of the entire Underworld, and then serve my head on a platter to them. After which, he would officially be the new Lord." His tortured eyes searched Yoori's. "Because he is in Young Jae's favor, it is in his best interest to lure you out. He plans to give you to Young Jae so that Young Jae can exact his revenge on you and execute you the way he sees fit."

Yoori trembled when she recalled earlier in the night, when Tae Hyun was speaking softly on the phone. She didn't initially think much of it. It occurred to her now that sometime during his conversation about postponing the trip to Paris, he must have called his Underworld contacts and gotten a briefing about everything that was going on in the Underworld—everything that he knew he had to keep Yoori away from.

Overwhelmed by the heaviness of her congested mind, Yoori briefly closed her eyes and absorbed all the new information. The most predominant thought on her mind was Young Jae and his part in all of this. After what transpired during Ju Won's party, it was an impossibility for Ji Hoon to get back into their good graces. However, if he had the support of the first Lord of all the Underworlds, then there was no question that he would get back the position he once renounced. Her next crippling thought in this maelstrom of pandemonium was that *everything* that had taken place tonight was the result of Young Jae becoming the first Lord. This ultimately meant that everything that happened tonight—the misery that awaited them—was the result of Yoori preventing Tae Hyun from killing Young Jae when they had the chance.

I should've never let him go, Yoori thought regrettably, reflecting back to the moment when Tae Hyun was ready to kill her brother and she stopped him. She had never regretted anything more than saving her own brother's life. *None of this would be happening if I hadn't let him go . . .*

Overwhelmed by the sheer extent of everything finally hitting her at once, Yoori broke out of her reverie. She stared at Tae Hyun in pure horror.

"You know that the entire Underworld is going to be there and you still want to go alone?"

Yoori felt her heart pound, never hating it more that he loved her so much that he wouldn't let her help him with this. If the entire Underworld turns against you, you don't walk into it alone—*you just don't*.

"Tae Hyun," she begged as a million different scenarios of what could happen ran through her mind, crippling her. All these horrific scenarios started with Tae Hyun in danger and ended with him not being able to make it out alive. "We can take them. We can fight them all together."

Tears welled up in her eyes when she saw that Tae Hyun was no closer to un-cuffing her. The knowledge was agonizing for her.

"Please don't go alone. Let me go with you," she pleaded, grabbing his hand and gripping it tightly. "Let me *follow* you. We made a pact, Tae Hyun," she added desperately, wishing he could just take out the keys and un-cuff her. "We made a pact to be together, to be by each other's side no matter what."

He smiled sadly and touched her face. "I know that we made a pact," he told her delicately, his voice shaking faintly. "And I didn't want to break it. I didn't want to break it, but I can't risk you going, Yoori. I saw how Young Jae looked at you; I *know* that he will be waiting for you there." He inhaled painfully, thinking of an entity that was crueler than Young Jae could ever hope to be. "And I know how vicious our world can be when it punishes someone. I can't risk you going. I can handle it all by myself, but I won't be able to handle it if even an inch of you gets hurt." He breathed in softly. "I can't protect you there, so I'll protect you here."

"Please, Tae Hyun! Don't—don't!" she cried, becoming hysterical.

He closed his eyes in grief at the sight of her like this. His body trembled faintly as he pulled her to him and kissed her forehead.

"I'm going to call Chae Young when I leave," he went on slowly, his conviction set when he made a move to walk away. "When she comes, promise me you'll leave Seoul. Don't come looking for me. Just leave, just go to Paris first, and I'll follow you after I save Hae Jin and Kang Min. I'll meet you there."

It was a lie.

She knew it was a lie.

She could tell by his eyes that even he was unsure of his own words, that he was only saying it in hopes of assuaging her hysteria and her tears.

"Tae Hyun, please. Please let me go with you," she pleaded brokenly, frantically holding onto him with her free hand. "Oh God, what if something happens to you?"

"Yoori, don't be like this," he begged, his voice breaking as he cupped her face in agony. "*Please*. Don't be like this, Brat."

She could see that he was tortured, especially when his anguished lips sought hers. She knew he was tortured, which was why she snapped her head back, not wanting to give him the kiss he was seeking. Kissing him like this only meant that it would be the end; it would only mean that he would never come back to her. And for that, she wasn't going to give him that kiss; she wasn't going to let it be the end.

"Please don't leave me," she implored instead. Her heart twisted in sorrow as she stared at the one she loved more than life itself. "Un-cuff me right now. Let me go with you. We made a pact. We made a pact!"

"I'm sorry," he uttered, swallowing past the tears that were beginning to well up in his own eyes. "I'm sorry."

Without another word, he made an effort to walk away. A panic-stricken Yoori caught him in time by pulling the sleeve of his jacket, desperately tugging him back to her.

"Please let me go with you," she pleaded, repeating the same mantra she had been vocalizing all day. It was repetitive, yet each time she said it, she felt her desperation for it grow. Then, she simply lost it. "You can't go into this alone! You can't leave me like this and go there alone!"

Tae Hyun closed his eyes as if to prep himself for what he had to do. Shortly after, with pained reluctance, he pulled out of her grasp, leaving Yoori to stumble forward and fall to the ground, the cuffed wrist catching her fall as she landed on her knees.

"I'm sorry," he repeated again, his face twisting in agony. This was not what he wanted. This was the last thing he wanted for them.

He took the key to the handcuff out of his pocket and bent his knees. He crouched down and placed it on the floor, close enough to her, but also far enough so that she couldn't reach out for it and un-cuff herself. He was leaving it out for Chae Young, not for her.

Standing up, he gazed at her one last time.

He drank in the sight of her, taking a final mental picture of her to catalog in his memories before he turned away from her and voluntarily walked into the depths of hell by himself.

"TAEEEEEEEE HYUUUUUUUN!" Yoori shouted at the top of her lungs, horrified to see him walking away.

She could see his muscles bunch underneath his clothes at the sound of her tortured voice. She could see his body stiffen up, its reaction wanting nothing more than to come back to her and wipe her tears away. Yet, against his needs, he continued to walk straight ahead, never allowing himself to turn around to face her again.

Panic set within Yoori.

She started tugging at the handcuffs, blood flowing from her left wrist while she tried to fight the impossible and run after him. The flesh on her wrist started to chafe from the impact, the fibers on her skin ripping slowly. Despite this injury, she continued to struggle to pull herself free.

Her heart was breaking; it was killing her.

Every ache and pain she once felt worsened as tears streamed down her eyes.

"TAEEEEEEEEEEEE HYUUUUUUUUUUUN!" she cried past the sobs in her chest. Her entire upper body collapsed to the cold floor in exhaustion. The flesh on her left wrist bled as she fought against the handcuffs. "Please come back! Please don't leave!"

It was the sound of his car driving away that broke her. It was the sound of his car making a turn out of the parking lot that left her in a world of hell, and it was the sound of complete silence that tore up her heart and reminded her of why she was so afraid of giving herself completely to him.

All of *this*.

This was the reason why she was afraid of becoming human for him.

"No," she whispered once she found herself completely and utterly alone. "No . . ."

Exhaustion riding the last of her remaining strength, Yoori allowed her tears to drip onto the cement. All the while as she cried, she tried to stretch her right hand out to grab the key. Blood started to seep out of her bullet wound. The strain she was putting on it aggravated it immensely. She could feel her body break apart as unfathomable pain ripped through her. Alas, all of that couldn't hold a candle to the pain ripping through her very soul.

Tae Hyun . . . Oh God, Tae Hyun . . .

She tried to tug harder at the cuff. She was determined to rip it out of her entire wrist if she had to. Her efforts proved futile. Nothing was working. She couldn't reach for that unobtainable key, and she couldn't bring herself closer to going after Tae Hyun.

"No . . . Oh God, no . . ."

Realizing that she wasn't getting anywhere, realizing that he was getting closer and closer to meeting an entire Underworld that was waiting to kill him, and realizing that she couldn't do anything to help him, Yoori let out an anguished sob from the depths of her constricted chest.

She cried to herself while she helplessly pressed her forehead onto the floor. She sobbed at the pitiable state she was in. The love of her life, the one who meant the world to her, was on his way to fighting an unbeatable battle alone. All the while she was there . . . sitting there crying and unable to do anything.

"Tae Hyun," she called through her pained sobs. "Come back. Please come back to me . . ."

Then, out of the silence, came familiar voices.

"Yoori?! Oh my God, Yoori!"

"Shit! Boss!"

Like a lost sailor spotting a beacon in the darkness, Yoori's eyes blossomed once she heard the two voices scream out her name. She lifted her gaze up. A tsunami of hope surged into her when she saw Chae Young and Jae Won run towards her.

"Yoori! Oh God, what happened, Yoori?" Chae Young shouted in horror, sprinting quickly to her.

She helped Yoori up while Jae Won swiftly grabbed the key Tae Hyun left for them. He ran to the railing to un-cuff her.

"Tae Hyun!" Yoori breathed out, never more thankful to see two people in her life. "I need to go after Tae Hyun!"

"Boss! Boss, calm down," Jae Won told her, his face worried at the hysterical state Yoori was in. He injected the key into the handcuffs and unlocked her. "What happened? Boss Kwon called Chae Young and told her that you needed to meet her somewhere, that you wanted to give her something. We were in the area and came right away. What happened? Where the hell is he, and why are you handcuffed like this?"

They were in the area. Thank God, thank God they were in the area, she thought with gratefulness. There was a flaw in Tae Hyun's plan to keep Yoori away. He couldn't have anticipated Jae Won and Chae Young being out of the city and close to this place. In turn, this was the opening opportunity that Yoori needed to get to him in time.

Refusing to waste time, Yoori abandoned all reservations and told them everything that happened. They *deserved* to know everything.

"Ji Hoon has Hae Jin and Kang Min," Yoori urgently told them as the cuffs fell free from the railing. "He's working with my brother and he's setting a trap for Tae Hyun. The entire Underworld is at *The Stadium* right now, and Tae Hyun's going to face them alone!" She pulled her wrist away, struggling to get up, not even bothering to have Jae Won remove the cuff still on her left wrist. They didn't have any more time to spare. "I need to get to him. I need to be there with him. He can't do this alone!"

As Chae Young smothered her cries of shock in response to everything Yoori unloaded onto them, Jae Won's eyes enlarged at the fact that his brother and his brother's pregnant girlfriend had been kidnapped. It did not help that his King was not only going after them alone, but that he was also in morbid danger.

"I know where *The Stadium* is," he told Yoori. He and Chae Young helped her up. "Let's go," he urged as they helped steer Yoori to their car. "We have to go now."

After Chae Young joined Yoori in the backseat to help nurse her wounds and unfasten the handcuffs hanging on her wrist, Jae Won stepped on the gas of the car. The tires accelerated beyond warning. With a single jerk, the car took off and became one with the wind.

Yoori's frantic mind was running while she sat in the back.

We need help, she concluded urgently.

The war they were in was too calamitous to fight alone. She needed someone else. Even if they couldn't do much damage, they could act as a distraction to help disrupt the event. At this rate, Yoori was willing to utilize anything to secure the chance of Hae Jin, Kang Min, and Tae Hyun making it out of *The Stadium* alive.

"Call the cops," she instructed Chae Young, whose eyes broadened at Yoori's command.

"W-what?"

"Call the cops," Yoori repeated again to her best friend. "Tell them that the ones behind the massacres these past few weeks are gathering at one location. Tell them that tonight is their one and only chance to catch these murderers before they lose them forever."

"Can they really do anything against the Underworld, Yoori?" Chae Young asked quietly, already seeking the purse that held her phone.

"I don't know," Yoori said honestly. There was not much hope in her response, but at this point, even a little hope was better than none. "But we're out of options. If they can at least distract the Underworld by coming in while everything is still in session, then there might be a chance that we can all make it out alive."

Nodding, Chae Young dialed the police and spoke to the operator.

The rest became a big blur to Yoori when she closed her eyes. The only thing on her troubled mind as she used her last vestige of strength was Tae Hyun. She was in no condition to fight. Regardless, when faced with the prospect of losing the person you love with all your heart, your limitations in life take a backseat.

Every part of her better rationale was telling her that she didn't stand a chance against what was to come. Despite the odds, her instincts ignored such logicality. The only thing that made sense to her was Tae Hyun. The only thing that made sense to her was doing everything in her power to protect the one she loved—even if that meant giving up her life to save his.

Tae Hyun, I'm coming . . . I'm coming.

"... To let the other know when Paris has been found?"

30: Kingdom of the Fallen Gods

The Stadium was an elliptical amphitheater inspired by the Colosseum in Rome. Built on top of the green mountains with an unobstructed view of the god-like skies above its grand infrastructure, *The Stadium* was located in a secluded terrain that humans could only dream of seeing and Gods could only hold their breaths in anticipation of one day residing within. It was enormous, it was majestic, and it was all too divine.

The magnificence of this imperial amphitheater was further accessorized by the massive, royal-gold onyx tiles that swept over the arena, acting as the center point of attention in this grand venue. This towering stadium was further complemented by the tiered seating arrangement that embraced the entirety of the arena. In a perfect and sequential order, the ascending stair of seats rose from the ground floor and swung up towards the star-canopied skies where the cold wind, the fresh cool air, and the touch of the heavens could be felt with ease.

The arena was grand and powerful enough to rival the Colosseum, which was exactly what it did as every plush and expensively constructed seat was occupied by close to 17,500 Underworld Royals and soldiers. The only uninhabited seats were the ones at the further end of the amphitheater, opposite from where the King of Skulls sat. Only one throne sat in that area while the ten seats behind it were also unoccupied. They were reserved for the group of people who had yet to make their appearance.

Yes, the presence of the Underworld in distributed numbers was powerful, but the presence of the Underworld in a gathered and united number was simply divine power at its most potent.

Due to the fact that it was the official meeting facility for the entire population of the Korean Underworld, it was rarely opened for anything. There were only two exceptions: the crowning of a new King in the Underworld, and the trials and punishments of Underworld leaders. In essence, it was an arena built to honor the Gods who have risen to power as well as an arena built to punish the Gods who have fallen from grace. It was a stage constructed to either shower the rewards of heaven or to execute the punishments of hell. The latter was what drove the silent anticipation as the gathered society sat there and waited for judgment day to come.

All eyes were rested on the ground floor where the notorious King of Skulls sat on a gold throne. Adjacent to him were four people: a pregnant Kwon Hae Jin, her boyfriend Kang Min, and two guards.

Hae Jin and Kang Min were both dressed in comfortable jeans and hoodies, like they were prepared to go on a long flight as opposed to being kidnapped. They were sitting on the floor, tied up with sturdy ropes. Behind them, two Skulls—Ji Hoon's most trusted soldiers—Yen and Ash held guns to their heads. Hae Jin and Kang Min's eyes were wide and their faces were pale. It was blatant in the fear within their gazes that they were praying that a certain couple *wouldn't* show up to save them, for they knew the fate of anyone who dared to walk into this arena.

Whilst they sat there completely powerless, the cold, dark eyes of the infamous Lee Ji Hoon were dead set on the entrance in which one could enter onto the stage of the arena. There was a lingering look of satisfaction marked on his handsome face. Dressed in black from head to toe, his ankle was propped over a knee while his arms rested on the armchairs of his throne like the King he was.

All around him on the first ascension of seats, which rose up six feet with a black marble wall acting as a divider around the enormous arena, sat all the Royals in the Underworld. They sat in thrones of their own. These powerful individuals consisted of the influential Kings and Queens in the different layers, the influential elders who have become legends in this world, and the various Royals who were visiting from all the other countries' Underworlds. In that circular and powerful row also sat the three elder Advisors, all of whom were sitting far enough from each other in an effort to bond with the rest of the Royals in attendance.

Shin Jung Min had a proud smirk on his face while he chatted with his fellow Advisors. Shin Dong Min had a despondent expression on his face as he spoke to some of the 1ˢᵗ layer Royals. Finally, Seo Ju Won wore a dissatisfied and very angry expression on his face as he stared unblinkingly at the entrance.

Ju Won was known as the creator of legends, and he could not have been more embarrassed by what transpired during the battle of what was supposed to be the most epic battle in history. The King and Queen he invested so much pride and hope in gave up a throne that countless others would give their lives for. And for what?

Love?

The one human emotion that had been drilled into their brains that they shouldn't fall victim to?

The thought disgusted him on all levels. He did not bother to hide this displeasure from his face, and he didn't hide it when he met with Young Jae and Ji Hoon.

After calling a meeting with him, they had essentially told Ju Won that with or without his support, Ji Hoon was going to become the new Lord of the Korean Underworld. The end was guaranteed, but they offered him a token of peace to placate all that had taken place.

Before his official crowning, Ji Hoon promised Ju Won, as well as the entire Underworld—all of whom were in an uproar over the failure of their King and Queen—that his main priority was punishing Kwon Tae Hyun and his second priority was punishing An Soo Jin. *This* was when the once stubborn eyes of Ju Won, as he was still on bad terms with Ji Hoon and Young Jae, grew with malice while the rest of the Underworld elders listened in interest. They all wanted the fallen Gods to be punished, and they were more than willing to support Ji Hoon so he could bring that punishment to fruition.

Calling a summit, the Underworld elders amended the conditions of what Ji Hoon needed to do to regain their support. They were not a society that would give handouts so easily, and they voiced this to Ji Hoon by telling him that he would work for his throne, just like any other Royal. They went on to decree that his first priority was to get Kwon Tae Hyun and An Soo Jin onto that onyx stage. Once they were there, the rest of the conditions set forth would commence. The former King and Queen of the Underworld had to be shown the error of their ways—they had to be punished.

Indeed, the anticipation was high as the entire Underworld awaited the ones they were all ready to kneel before at one point—the ones they once looked at as the most powerful King and Queen to ever set foot in the Underworld, the ones who disappointed and angered them beyond all levels of tolerance, and the ones who would be the pendulums that would set this eventful night into motion.

The silence mounted.

And then at last, when the clock struck 2:00 A.M., sounds of footsteps emerged from the entrance of the amphitheater. All eyes of the Underworld landed onto the opulent arena. They watched quietly as one of the fallen Gods—the once great and revered King—finally appeared.

Kwon Tae Hyun.

Dressed in all black with an air of superiority radiating from him, the fallen God marched onto the intimidating and hushed arena with fearlessness. His head was held high, his unyielding eyes refusing to allow even one shred of trepidation to shine through.

369

At the sight of him, sounds of shuffling and whispering swept through the once quiet and orderly arena. Though the majority of the Underworld was poised with keeping their excitement intact, resigning to staring with quiet anticipation, as soon as they saw the fallen King, many of the younger soldiers and 1st layer heirs were filled with excitement. The younger crowd came to life in the upper echelons of the arena. Below them, their more powerful elders maintained their composure by merely staring down at the fallen King with reserved amusement.

Poised or not, the consensus was the same: the arena had come to life, for they knew the entrance of the King only meant that the night they had been waiting for was about to start.

Tae Hyun stopped at the center of the arena and faced the ocean of spectators around him. His eyes perused over the colossal arena while all 17,500 pairs of eyes rested upon him.

Three years ago, when he was crowned the new King of Serpents in this very same venue, he sat on a throne like a God. Now, after his display of humanity and weakness by being unable to kill the Queen of the Underworld, Kwon Tae Hyun no longer stood before them as a God. He stood before them as a once legendary King who gave up everything to merely be a fallen God— to be a simple man.

"Boss, no," Kang Min whispered after his swollen eyes fixed on Tae Hyun. Panic clawed him while hysteria plagued Hae Jin.

"Oppa! Why are you here, oppa?" Hae Jin sobbed, tears rippling in her eyes. There were traces of dried blood around her lips and bruises on her skin: all signs indicative of being beaten recently. She was in no condition to be worrying about anyone else. Despite being held hostage by Ji Hoon, Hae Jin was more worried for her brother's life than her own safety. She began to shake, her eyes urging him to leave while he still had a chance. "Just leave! They're going to kill yo—!"

Hae Jin and Kang Min were abruptly silenced when Yen and Ash tied black cloths around their mouths, effectively gagging them. Soft moans and groans could be heard as they tried to fight the bounds that held them. Their eyes gazed at Tae Hyun. Though neutralized, they were still silently telling him to leave them and escape while he still had the opportunity.

A fleeting flicker of emotion leapt in his eyes. He stared at them, registering all of their wordless admonishments with a stoic and emotionless face. After this short-lived emotion passed from his eyes, he regained the entirety of his composure, gave them a stern look that pretty much said, *"I'm not leaving the two of you,"* and then veered his attention back to the arena before him—back to the crowd that resembled nothing short of an imperial council.

The soldiers that he used to rule over stared down at him, disappointed with his decision to abandon his legacy, and in turn, abandon them. His mentors, his supporters, and his Advisor fixed their gazes on him, anguish teeming in their eyes with the fact that the protégé they loved so much had given up everything to merely be a man standing amongst Gods. The powerful Underworld that he used to preside over gazed down at him with a mixture of pity, excitement, disgust, and curiosity that someone this great could make such horrible choices and fall so far down from grace. And finally, the group with the most power tonight and the ones who would ultimately decide his fate—Ji Hoon, Jung Min, Ju Won, and the majority of their supporters—could only stare down at him with arrogance and bloodlust in their eyes.

It was an understatement to say that the Underworld had divided feelings towards the former King of Serpents. Some wanted to give him another chance while others wanted to execute him for his actions. However at odds the Underworld was in terms of wanting Kwon Tae Hyun to be set free or to be punished, the end result was the same: the law only existed with the King who sat in the stage of that arena.

No friends, no mentors, and no supporters could leave their seats and run onto the ground floor to save Tae Hyun. If they even attempted to do so, it was in the unwritten bylaws of the Underworld that they could and *would* be executed for disrupting the stage that was only meant to be governed by the chosen King or a chosen elder crime lord of that country's Underworld. This was the precise reason why Tae Hyun's closest friends from the 1st layer— Choi Hyun Woo and Daniel Lee—were strictly prohibited from coming to the summit tonight in fear of them doing anything impulsive. It didn't matter how divided the powerful society was because the majority was still out for blood. Fortunately for them, Ji Hoon was also out for blood.

The law was him, and the law from the King of Skulls mandated that tonight, there would be hell to pay.

"It feels like it's been a lifetime since I've been here, standing before you like this," Tae Hyun began diplomatically, behaving in the manner that he was always trained to be—a King amongst Gods. Stripped of his title or not, Tae Hyun still knew how to behave in front of his Underworld. He knew the things to say to show them that even without a throne and an army to command, he was not an individual who would be easily intimidated by them.

An expression of neutrality solidified on his face, his eyes drifted through the entire arena. His body spun in a slow circle while he stared back at the close to 17,500 people in the vicinity. He briefly dropped his gaze to Ji Hoon, who was still sitting comfortably on his throne. His silence persevered while he stared at Tae Hyun in amusement.

"Things," Tae Hyun continued, unimpressed with the sight of Ji Hoon being the only King on the stage, "have definitely changed since three years ago."

"You have disappointed us, Tae Hyun," came Ju Won's icy voice. In the first ascension of seats, Ju Won's arms were rested on his own throne while his critical gaze burned through Tae Hyun's from the distance. Tae Hyun reminding him of how much things have changed became the catalyst he needed to break out of his silence. "Years upon years were invested in you to become a King. Countless upon countless Underworld soldiers have died to get you to the precipice of your career and in a matter of days, you have not only managed to insult all our teachings, but you have also managed to spit on everything we've done for you. We spoiled you, we gave you everything, and this is what you ultimately choose?" There was revulsion in his voice when he added, "What do you have to say for yourself?"

Tae Hyun regarded Ju Won with no fear or apology. His head held high, he said, "I don't regret anything. If given the opportunity, I'd repeat everything in a heartbeat."

Ju Won smirked dryly. Behind him, the majority of the Underworld reprovingly shook their heads. Tae Hyun's indifference was insulting to them.

"Never the one to be smart and see the error of your ways, are you, Tae Hyun?" Jung Min inquired, voicing everything the majority was thinking. His voice vibrated with vile distaste. He looked at Tae Hyun like he was the worthless disappointment he had always suspected him to be.

Instead of responding to the Advisor, and no longer feeling the need to prolong this superfluous chat, Tae Hyun got right back into the business of why he came. He averted his attention to Ji Hoon, who was still seated quietly—and quite smugly—on his throne.

"Let them go," Tae Hyun said tightly, finally addressing the one who orchestrated everything and brought him here in the first place.

A smile curved on Ji Hoon's face. He leaned forward, making no effort to command for Hae Jin and Kang Min to be released.

"Do you know why you're here, Tae Hyun?" he asked casually.

"Let my sister and Kang Min go," Tae Hyun repeated again, this time more severely. "You wanted me. Now I'm here to take their place. You don't need them anymore. Leave them out of this mess and take me instead."

"On the contrary, Tae Hyun," Jung Min launched ominously from above, "there is someone else we want just as much as you." His face turned cold. "If not more than you."

An amused stream of laughter escaped from Ji Hoon's mouth. He nodded, agreeing to what was stated.

"Where's the Queen of the Underworld, Tae Hyun?" Ji Hoon inquired in an airy tone. "As I recall, I remember asking for her to come as well."

"She won't be coming," Tae Hyun dismissed sharply. His impatience showing, he firmly said, "Now let them go."

The amused expression on Ji Hoon's face dimmed. Tae Hyun's dismissive tone did not sit well with him. Though he had yet to lose his mocking demeanor, his expression did get more foreboding. "I really wanted her to be here."

"Why?" Tae Hyun's caustic voice left nothing to the imagination. "So you could show her how much you love her by screwing up her life some more?"

Ji Hoon laughed boisterously. "An Soo Jin, no matter the circumstances, will always be the woman who stole my heart. Granted, there's not much of a heart for her to have, she has it regardless. I don't fare well with the woman who claimed my heart to give herself to someone else—especially to a bastard I hate." He smirked, comfortably readjusting himself in his throne. He kept a gaze of mocking pity on Tae Hyun. "Your mistake was loving her more than the throne, Tae Hyun. If you had done things right and kept her as your second priority, then you would've been able to have both." His eyes darkened at this rationale. "Which is what *I* plan on having tonight when I finish you off and try to slap some sense into her."

Tae Hyun's eyes glanced at the thousands upon thousands in attendance. He found hilarity in Ji Hoon's illogical train of thoughts. He did not bother to hide it. "You think they would be open to you having her?"

Ji Hoon was unfazed by the question. "I am the sole elected Lord of the Underworld. My whims, as long as they don't interfere with my performance, will be met. The Queen of the Underworld is still the Queen of the Underworld. She is still the pride of this world and still the trophy I want. Even if I have to beat some sense into her to get her to see things clearly again, I'll do it."

"You won't be going near her, you piece of shit," Tae Hyun snapped, finally losing control when it involved Yoori. With anything else, it would take the sun and the moon to ruffle his feathers. When it came to Yoori, all it took was the mere mention of her name and the wrath of a thousand suns was unleashed, burning anyone who dared to incite his rage.

A frown shadowed Ji Hoon's face. "Such prideful language from a bastard who is about to die," he remarked dryly, the veins on his temple visibly throbbing in irritation. He attempted to act as if he had control of his emotions, but the small nuances within his demeanor were telltale signs that he wasn't doing such a good job with that.

Tae Hyun smirked at this, capitalizing on the anger radiating from Ji Hoon.

"It must be so satisfying to know that the only reason why you're sitting on that throne is because I didn't want it," he instigated tauntingly, showing everyone how he became such a powerful King in the 3rd layer. Few men could back up their arrogance; Tae Hyun was one of the few men in the world who had every credential and ability to back up his confidence. "How does it feel, Ji Hoon? To sit there as the second-tier God the Underworld chose by default while you are in the presence of the one they've chosen time and time again over you?"

"You are no longer a King in this layer, Tae Hyun." Jung Min's voice permeated through the arena. No matter how factual Tae Hyun's words, Jung Min did not plan on allowing him to blemish Ji Hoon's new status as the sole King, especially with the entire Underworld as an audience. "It would be in your best interest to speak to Ji Hoon with more respect. He is the sole King of this layer now, and as I recall, the one who gets to decide your fate tonight."

"I don't see a King," Tae Hyun replied acidly, smirking at Jung Min, "just a parasite licking up the throne that I threw away." At that instance, realization flashed in his eyes once he stated this. Something clicked for him when he turned back to Ji Hoon. His shrewd eyes scrutinized Ji Hoon. "This was your plan all along, wasn't it? How you got the throne, the things that you allowed to happen . . . you planned this moment all along, didn't you?"

A slow, dark smile touched Ji Hoon's lips. With an arrogance that would be unmatched by any other in his society, he got up from his seat and approached Tae Hyun.

"It is ironic that out of everyone in this world, the only one who truly knows me and the ways of my nature is you. An Soo Jin never saw through me, Choi Yoori never saw through me, my alliances never saw through me — hell, the world I grew up in never saw through me. People assumed that I was a King in love, and for this, they looked down upon me. They underestimated my true strength, thereby meaning that I'm given the freedom of doing everything I could possibly do to fool everyone and rise to the top." He laughed, still taking careful steps towards Tae Hyun. "To be perfectly honest, I didn't think it would be that easy when Soo Jin came back into the Underworld. As soon as she came back, I knew that I was going to get pushed back for her. The throne was yours to lose and it was hers to fight for. There was no place for me in this equation."

Tae Hyun scoffed in disbelief. "This was why you so eagerly agreed to allow her into the game, wasn't it?"

"Every instinct in my body was against it, but I knew all too well how our world works. Even if I didn't agree, I knew the Underworld would have her regardless. So why not agree to the terms to further exemplify the 'heartbroken-King-in-love' persona and to get back in her good graces?"

Bitterness encased his eyes. "I'll admit that I really couldn't have anticipated being dumped immediately afterwards, but everything that took place following that night became my opening."

"What about that tantrum you threw at the party?"

"Something done to throw the entire Underworld off and take myself out of the running while the two of you—my main competitors—were left to battle amongst yourselves." He laughed at the genius of his plan. "In all honesty, I didn't think it would be that easy for my two competitors to battle it out with one another, weaken each other, and in the process, show the Underworld how weak they truly are." He pointed a disbelieving finger at Tae Hyun. "But you just made it so easy for me to go to the elder Advisors later, to tell them that it was simply a calculated move on my part to 'throw a tantrum' and assure them that instead of seeing two Gods fight, they would ultimately see two Gods fall from grace and become human right before their very eyes." He sighed. "I told them that I was the only one who deserved the throne and that everything I predicted will come into play. I proposed to them to be the one to take the both of you out if you were to do what I predicted: give up the throne while becoming human for one another."

"And what better way is it for a King to become a Lord than to have his two biggest opponents fight and become weakened by one another?" Tae Hyun added caustically, his voice also filled with disgust. "Especially when that would make it easier for you to get rid of them once it was time to steal the throne."

Ji Hoon grinned shamelessly. "It helps to have a calculating mind, especially one that people underestimate. There are no limits to the things that you can do and what you can take advantage of."

"Why didn't you just finish us off at the business district? You could've ended it right then and there."

"The agreement was that I would have license to kill you, but I didn't want to kill you right then and there. I didn't want to kill you that night, but Young Jae insisted on seeking revenge on his sister. As my token of gratitude for his help with my endeavors, I allowed him his fight." His grin turned malicious. "I did not want to shoot you and grant you an easy death that night, Tae Hyun." He looked around the amphitheater and gestured his hands out. "I wanted you to die here, right in front of the Underworld, kneeling before me as a man taking his last breath."

Returning his eyes to Tae Hyun, Ji Hoon regarded him with full, unfiltered hatred, silently despising him for all that he represented. After swallowing tightly, the veins in his temples became more visible.

At long last, Ji Hoon revealed the type of King that he was: a jealous and embittered one.

"What do you have that I don't have?" Ji Hoon incited hatefully. "What's so special about you that hypnotizes our world so much? What's so special about you that gives you so much influence in our Underworld pyramid? What's so special about you that people were already prepared to kneel before you as the new Lord when you were only crowned the King of Serpents three years ago? *Especially* when you're nothing but a spoiled bastard who was merely trained for the 1st layer?" His face rippled with rage at his next thoughts. "What's so special about you that made her give up the throne—everything she has wanted all her life—for you? What the fuck do you have that I don't?"

The stream of anger that emitted from Ji Hoon was potent and unrestrained. His hatred for Tae Hyun was undeniable. He loathed him, and tonight, he was dead set on making Tae Hyun pay for merely existing in his world.

The dimness in his eyes blackened further.

"Where is Soo Jin?" Ji Hoon prompted coolly. Tae Hyun may know the right things to say to get under Ji Hoon's skin, but in that same token, Ji Hoon also knew the right things to say to get under Tae Hyun's skin. "I specifically asked for Soo Jin as well."

The muscles on Tae Hyun's face strained at the mention of Yoori. "She isn't here, and she won't be coming tonight."

Ji Hoon grinned callously at Tae Hyun's reply. He then spared a glance towards Hae Jin and Kang Min, both of whom were still staring at Tae Hyun with dread in their eyes.

"If you want them," Ji Hoon began nonchalantly, "then make the choice. Contact An Soo Jin, get her to come here, and I'll release them both." He stared at him with amused curiosity. "Who will it be, Tae Hyun? Who do you love more? Your baby sister and Kang Min, or An Soo Jin?"

"She's already left the country. She knows what's in store for her here. She won't be coming back," Tae Hyun lied easily, feigning disappointment in Yoori as a means to get Ji Hoon to back off. "I can't make someone who has already left come back, especially to this place—especially when she already knows what's in store for her here."

"An Soo Jin—or Choi Yoori—is capable of many things . . ." A voice emerged from the further end of the arena, stealing everyone's attention with his simple presence.

Wheeling around, Tae Hyun's eyes settled on the former King of Scorpions, who was now the first official Lord of Japan and the first official Lord of all the Underworlds.

Young Jae surfaced from the first ascension of rows into the arena. He walked slowly around the top row. His eyes were on Tae Hyun's as he approached his awaiting throne at the adjacent side of the room. As he did this, several of his higher-level Scorpions walked down into the awaiting seats from the opposite side of the arena. They took their seats behind the unoccupied throne—Young Jae's unoccupied throne.

"But the very last thing someone would call her is a coward. She would be smart enough to leave, but our survival instincts take a backseat for the ones we love, don't they?" Young Jae forged on, still walking and still staring into Tae Hyun's eyes. "She would never leave you, Tae Hyun. She has already given up her throne for you, just as you've already given up your throne for her. She won't leave you, but on the flip side, you won't let her come to this place, will you? Especially knowing what will await her?"

Tae Hyun's face tautened dangerously. Young Jae's correct assumptions about Yoori lit the fury inside him.

"She's your *sister*," Tae Hyun breathed out, not believing that an older brother could be this cruel to his own sister. It astounded him that Young Jae could conspire to have her come into a summit filled with people who wanted nothing more than to see her punished.

"Only through blood," Young Jae reasoned guiltlessly. "She has severed every emotional tie there is and is nothing but the bane of my existence now." His eyes turned cold and unforgiving. "I haven't forgotten what she had done to me, and I will make sure she pays for everything." His anger quelled briefly while he gazed at Tae Hyun in pity. "But that doesn't mean you or your family has to suffer with her." His eyes landed on Kang Min and Hae Jin. "She is not worth protecting, Tae Hyun. She isn't worth your sister's, Kang Min's, and their baby's life." He continued to coax Tae Hyun, knowing just the right words to say. "One life for three lives. Is that not the better deal? Just call her, get her to come here, and the conditions will be met. Hae Jin, Kang Min, and their unborn child will be set free. Will that not be worth her sacrifice?"

"She will not be coming," Tae Hyun replied inflexibly, knowing that Young Jae couldn't care less about his sister, Kang Min, or their unborn baby. He saw right through it. All Young Jae was after was his revenge.

Young Jae's face morphed into a savage expression. The muscles in his jaw leapt in anger. Tae Hyun's dismissal did not sit well with him.

Breathing deeply, as though to rally together his composure, Tae Hyun turned back to Ji Hoon and made him a proposition that Ji Hoon couldn't refuse.

"Just let them go, Ji Hoon," Tae Hyun said tactfully. There was no more mockery or smugness in his voice. He was genuinely there to help his sister and Kang Min while keeping Yoori safe. Upsetting Ji Hoon would only harm his efforts. He could no longer behave like a protective man; he had to behave like a reasonable businessman. "No matter what has happened, the truth is . . . you got the one thing you've always wanted: me at your mercy. You hate me, and I hate you more than I've ever hated anyone in my life. Under any other circumstances, you know that I'm not the type who will voluntarily fall unto anyone's mercy. However, if you let them go right now, I will let you impart whatever hell you want to bestow on me."

Ji Hoon's eyes lit up in interest as Tae Hyun went on.

"You can beat me, spit on me, and bruise any pride there is for me to have. In turn, I will not do a thing about it. I will not fight you back." He looked at him challengingly. "Will you really forgo this opportunity—something this enticing as to having the chance to amply embarrass me in front of our world—just because you want Yoori here as well? If she comes, then you know we both will fight to the death. However, if you agree to this, then I will forfeit any fight within me and you will get what you've always wanted: the chance to show the Underworld why you are better than me."

Ji Hoon's mouth drew up into a slow, calculating smile. He loved the contents of this proposition.

"Well, that changes the conditions, doesn't it?" he mused carelessly, his mood brightening at the prospect of such an enticing proposal. His decision made, his eyes temporarily found Young Jae's, whose arms were folded in front of his chest. He regarded Ji Hoon with a critical stare. It seemed that even Young Jae knew that this proposal was something Ji Hoon was going to agree to, no matter how much he wanted him to turn his back against it.

"Please take a seat, Young Jae," Ji Hoon said diplomatically, his focus returning to Tae Hyun. "There has been a slight change in the conditions. This is an opportunity I can't pass up. I want to see if Kwon Tae Hyun is truly the heroic King he appears to be."

Young Jae took a moment to stare at Tae Hyun as if to say, *"You've just made the biggest mistake."* Then, with his head held high, he sat down on his throne, his emotionless eyes also interested in what was about to transpire before them.

"If you can last for a sizeable amount of time, then I'll *consider* letting them go," Ji Hoon prompted, cracking the bones within his hands and neck in anticipation. He stared directly at a valiant Tae Hyun. With vindictive malice pouring from his face, Ji Hoon callously added, "I will enjoy every second of this."

Then—

Bam!

The destructive sound of bone hitting flesh vibrated into the arena. It was shortly followed by shuffling and shocked whispers from the audience. They were astonished to witness the once mighty King of Serpents take Ji Hoon's assault. They were more bewildered to see Tae Hyun continue to take the assault as Ji Hoon went after him without mercy.

Bam!

As he assaulted Tae Hyun, Ji Hoon didn't let this historic moment pass him by. Glorifying in this very occasion, he used it as an opportunity to show the Underworld audience why they should've revered him over Tae Hyun, and why he was a better King than Tae Hyun.

"This is your King!" Ji Hoon stated to the hundreds upon hundreds of Serpents sitting in the arena, all of whom were watching in disbelief. They couldn't believe their once mighty God had fallen so far from grace.

The entirety of the Serpents gang, as well as some Siberian Tigers, were quiet with astonishment. The only gangs who seemed to be enjoying this were the Skulls and Scorpions sitting in the crowd. They cheered Ji Hoon on with their laughter and roars of approval.

"He renounced you when you gave him your allegiance!"

Bam!

"He deserted you when you needed him most!"

Bam!

"And he abandoned you when you risked your lives for him!"

Every sentence was enunciated with a punch that left Tae Hyun reeling to one side. Impressively, regardless of how often he was hit, Tae Hyun would never stay down. He would always get back up. He did not fight back, but he also did not just lie down and play dead. He persevered, no matter how tied his hands were and no matter how demeaning the entire thing was.

"You gave up everything for him, and what does he do in return?" Ji Hoon continued to address the crowd, punching Tae Hyun across the skull. The attack left him to tumble down momentarily. "He spits on your faces, giving all of you up to be the one thing we were all trained never to be"—a gasp spurted from Tae Hyun after Ji Hoon kneed him across the stomach. Ji Hoon further exacerbated that attack by elbowing him across the face, triggering blood to seep out from his lips— "weak and distracted."

Ji Hoon laughed maliciously, walking after Tae Hyun after he crashed to the floor.

Tae Hyun's breathing was an uneven hoarse. In the background, the muffled tears and screams from Hae Jin and Kang Min could be faintly heard. While the majority of the Underworld watched in excitement, all Hae Jin and Kang Min could do was watch helplessly as Tae Hyun took all of this embarrassment and pain for them.

"He gave up all the glory that has been given to him, and for what? For *my* second helpings? For a worthless whor—*ugh!*"

Ji Hoon never got to finish his sentence when Tae Hyun's foot flew across his cheek, battering him across the side of his face and causing his bones to vibrate.

With a growl to rival the most ferocious beast in the wild, Tae Hyun delivered a second kick that was dispensed with so much force and anger that once the sole of his shoe landed on Ji Hoon's chest, the ground abandoned his feet and Ji Hoon was sent flying across the arena. He flew like a skipping rock, his body tumbling violently onto the golden onyx floor.

The Underworld reacted in uproar.

Some were shaking their heads smugly, knowing that a prideful King like Tae Hyun would never be able to sit back and not fight Ji Hoon back, while others were outraged to see their sole King be beaten down so fast.

Tae Hyun was breathing hard, his eyes dangerous and scorching with fury.

He was able to withstand any physical assault that Ji Hoon wanted to bestow upon him. The only thing that he could not stand—the only thing that his instinctive reflexes could not tolerate—was someone speaking so crassly about Yoori.

Tae Hyun was angry.

For a moment, he forgot why he was accepting all of this embarrassment in the first place. His emotions getting the better of him, he charged towards Ji Hoon, intent on further making him pay for his insolence. He stopped short when the sound of a vicious kick echoed throughout the arena, reminding him of the mistake he made by hitting Ji Hoon back and reminding him of the conditions he agreed to with Ji Hoon just moments prior.

Tae Hyun's eyes enlarged when he saw blood spurting out from Hae Jin's nostrils, signifying to him that after seeing him attack Ji Hoon back, Yen had taken it upon herself to punish Hae Jin in the same violent manner.

Though she was gagged, the bloodcurdling groan that emitted from Hae Jin did nothing to hide the excruciating pain she was in. One could see how hard she was fighting to not show that she was in pain. She did not want her brother and her boyfriend to worry about her. Sadly, all of that determination took a backseat to the instinctive nerves of her body, which were crying in the purest of misery.

Looking as if someone had just slammed a sledgehammer into his stomach, Tae Hyun's face grimaced in torture. It was clear he blamed himself. Hae Jin was being tortured because of his rash actions. The anguish in his eyes only grew worse when he heard Ji Hoon laughing.

Ji Hoon stood up from behind him and wiped the small bout of blood from the side of his lips. He smiled in satisfaction. He knew the outburst by Tae Hyun was a one-off. He still had him right where he wanted him.

Extending a hand out to the right side of the arena, a kendo stick flew in from one of his Skulls in the crowd. The weapon landed obediently in Ji Hoon's hand. With the new weapon in his possession, Ji Hoon sauntered back to Tae Hyun with a malicious smirk. He was very aware that after seeing the punishment his baby sister had to endure, Tae Hyun would do well to control his instincts. This time around, it was guaranteed that Tae Hyun wasn't going to fight back. Tae Hyun was going to take every abuse he wanted to give, and Ji Hoon loved every moment of this power he had.

Swoosh!

Eager to further torture Tae Hyun, he raised the stick and delivered a slash across Tae Hyun's back. Half a second later, he circled around Tae Hyun and jabbed the stick into his hard stomach, finishing the triple attack by swiping the powerful weapon across Tae Hyun's face.

Tae Hyun spit out blood from the brutal attack. In the face of this abuse, he tried to maintain his equilibrium—his composure.

"You got anymore of that, Tae Hyun?" Ji Hoon laughed out haughtily. He enjoyed that Tae Hyun was simply standing there, not saying anything and not making a move to attack him.

It was clear in Tae Hyun's pained expression that he had learned his lesson in this game. Every time he fought back, Hae Jin would pay for his lack of self-control. This was something that he wasn't going to let happen again.

"You're not going to fight back?" Ji Hoon taunted before whipping the stick in the air and jabbing it into Tae Hyun's stomach again. He finished the assault by hitting him across the face with the bamboo stick, causing Tae Hyun to topple to the side. "You're not going to show me why you're better than me?"

With his kendo stick firmly held in his hand, Ji Hoon began to mercilessly beat Tae Hyun with it.

The sound of bamboo hitting flesh and bones rumbled throughout the enormous amphitheater. During the course of this, Tae Hyun took every hit, every attack, and every embarrassment with self-restrained misery and control.

"Who do you think you are?" Ji Hoon jeered, continuously hitting Tae Hyun with the vicious stick. "You think you're being so noble. The truth is: you're nothing but a pathetic piece of shit right now." He cruelly laughed at Tae Hyun's lack of reply towards these insults. "This is the life you wanted, Tae Hyun? A life without power? A life where you're at the mercy of Gods like me?" His laughter grew after he kneed Tae Hyun across the face for trying to get back up. Ji Hoon lifted his stick, prepared to hit Tae Hyun several more times with it. "Is she really worth all of this? Is the Queen really worth all of thi—?"

A collective gasp filled the amphitheater as Ji Hoon delivered another attack to Tae Hyun.

The velocity of the flying kendo stick was quick with speed, but not powerful enough by nature to be able to withstand the hand that appeared out of nowhere. At the same second Ji Hoon's arm went down for the attack, it was abruptly stopped midway when a powerful hand gripped his forearm.

"What the fuck?" Ji Hoon whispered, stunned as to who had the audacity to stop him. He turned around, intent on beating the fuck out of the person who intervened.

His angry eyes morphed into shock when there she stood before him—the Queen of the Underworld—staring at him with unforgiving fire.

"Get," Yoori incited angrily, sending chills throughout the arena with the fury in her voice, "the *fuck* away from my boyfriend."

A muscle cracked within Ji Hoon's arm when she mercilessly twisted it back. As a result, the kendo stick flew free from his grasp and fell into her hand. She did not waste this weapon of opportunity.

Swoosh!

"Umph!"

With the velocity of an expert fighter, Yoori wielded the stick in the air and bequeathed Ji Hoon with the same assault he had been bestowing upon Tae Hyun. The kendo stick struck his face, triggering him to tumble to the side. Right before his knees hit the floor, she performed an uppercut using the blunt head of the stick against his jaw. For good measure, she added in a powerful sidekick that had Ji Hoon falling to the floor with a loud *thud!*

Adrenaline pumped within her as she tightened her grip on the kendo stick. She breathed irately, furious to walk into this arena to find Ji Hoon beating Tae Hyun. It did not take her long to figure out the deal Tae Hyun tried to make—the deal for him to not fight back if Ji Hoon pardoned Yoori and allowed Hae Jin and Kang Min to go free. This admirable action aside, Yoori couldn't stomach how stupid Tae Hyun's decision was. There was little chance that Ji Hoon would keep his words, and she knew that Tae Hyun was aware of this. The fact that Tae Hyun would rather get beaten (with no guarantee of Ji Hoon keeping his word) than risk getting Yoori involved was infuriating to her. She did not conceal her fury when she finally rested her eyes on him.

Yoori's blood boiled when she was faced with a furious Tae Hyun.

He wore a look of disbelief and rage in his eyes. He was physically hurt, yes, but at that moment, nothing hurt and angered him more than seeing Yoori in the very arena he did everything in his power to keep her away from.

"What the fuck are you doing here?!" he raged, standing up and towering over Yoori. "Did it look like I wanted you to fucking come here?!"

"Shut the fuck up!" Yoori fiercely shouted back, looking up at him without fear or apology. She furiously tossed the kendo stick to the floor.

In moments like these, where his temper got the best of him and the true power of his aura came out, Tae Hyun may intimidate ninety-percent of the other human beings in the world, but he evoked no such fear from Yoori. She had spent her life as a Queen amongst monsters. At this very second, it was Tae Hyun who should fear her wrath.

"Get it through your fucking thick head!" she roared at the top of her lungs. "You don't tell me what to do and you don't control what I do! Does it look like I give a fuck about whether or not you wanted me to come here?"

"You think this is a joke?" he growled. The muscles straining beneath his hard body became visible, even beneath his clothes. Though his words and tone of voice were angry, Yoori could still see the worry in his eyes. He wanted her safe somewhere else; he didn't want her here, and he sure as hell wasn't grateful that she came to "save" him. "I did everything in my power to keep you away from this place, and you still have the audacity to show up, be stupid, and play hero, even when I don't need you? The last thing I need is your help!"

"Yes," Yoori remarked sarcastically, "you seemed to be doing so well a second ago."

"I *let* him hit me," he snarled back swiftly. A dangerous muscle leapt in his tight, strong jaw. "If I wanted to fight back, then the bastard would have no chance against me."

Yoori knew that this was true. If Tae Hyun wanted to fight back, there was little chance that Ji Hoon would be able to withstand his wrath.

"So you were planning on just letting him have his way with you, hope that the bastard will keep his word, and let your sister and Kang Min go without having me come into the mix?"

She didn't attempt to hide the critical tone in her voice—the tone that indicated what a stupid idea that was.

"The slight chance given to this situation was worth it to me," he defended, not regretting his choice.

"The slight chance wouldn't have worked out and you know it," she countered at once.

His nose flared while his jaw clenched again, the muscle beneath it tightening very severely. "I had it handled."

Yoori shook her head reproachfully. This conversation with Tae Hyun was becoming more redundant than beneficial. It was time to end their squabble. They had more important things to deal with, more important battles to fight. They could not be opposing forces in this arena. They had to be a united front. If they wanted to make it out of this amphitheater alive, they had to show this world what a powerful King and Queen they were.

"It doesn't matter what you had handled anymore, does it?" she dismissed curtly, promptly ending their argument. "Because I'm here now, and I'm not leaving you."

Leaving Tae Hyun to mutter a curse behind her at her hardheadedness, she finally turned around to face the arena that had been awaiting her entrance.

"It's nice to see you again too, baby," Ji Hoon greeted casually. He cracked his neck as though he was only warming up by beating the hell out of Tae Hyun (and that he wasn't affected by Yoori's beating). Very much satisfied with her long-awaited appearance, he stood up, dusted his shirt, and ventured back to his throne. "Took you long enough to come here. I was wondering how much longer it would take for Tae Hyun to show his true colors and fight me like the selfish bastard he is. I knew he couldn't last long playing the heroic King."

He took a seat on the throne with a big smile on his face. He enjoyed the extracurricular activity that came with taking advantage of Tae Hyun's desperation to save his sister, but he heavily enjoyed that the Queen was standing there amongst them more.

Yoori made a point to ignore him. Speaking to him would serve to do nothing but boil her blood. In her eyes, he was a disgusting parasite. She would give him what was coming to him soon enough, but for now, she had bigger fishes to fry.

Her stern eyes skimmed over the eyes of the 17,500 people in attendance. Even under the cloak of an ominous omen about this place, Yoori could still feel her eyes light up in awe at the majestic amphitheater before her. She could see how this arena was inspired by the Colosseum. The sheer size of this society's gathering was a thing of divine decadence. When one stands on this very onyx podium, you are left feeling one of two things: a God in a world so powerful or a simple human in a world so powerful. Regrettably for Yoori, although she and Tae Hyun still possessed the qualities that made them "better than the rest", at that very moment, they were merely seen as humans. And by being human in this arena—the lowest life form to this elite world—their lifespan would be slim to none.

It was an intimidating realization to have as she regarded the arena with feigned valor.

As a God without anyone to anchor her human emotions down, she had nothing to lose. Conversely, as a human blessed with loved ones, it terrified her that she had everything to lose. Bottling up this fear, she went to great lengths to regain her composure. She could not show weakness, not now, and especially not in this godforsaken place—

Her survey of the arena stopped cold when she spotted Young Jae sitting in a row above the entrance in which she walked in. He was staring solemnly at her, his eyes unblinking. Her stomach twisted in knots at the sight of him. Yoori hadn't seen him when she walked in because she was too engrossed with saving Tae Hyun from Ji Hoon. It occurred to her that he was probably the first one to see her walk in. From the excited and sadistic expression on his face, it was clear that he wanted to be the reason why she didn't walk out of this amphitheater tonight—or ever.

Refusing to allow him to ruin her focus, she put her thoughts about her brother aside. Her survey continued all throughout the arena. She had too many other things to address, and the highest priority on this list was the society surrounding her.

"You wanted me," she declared loudly and clearly, her brown eyes dark with confidence. "Now I'm here."

She regarded Tae Hyun, who was standing beside her. His face did not hide that he hated everything about this moment. To her pleasant surprise, she also found that she was not the only one who was putting her A-game on tonight.

She appraised Tae Hyun in awe.

There were no more remnants of blood around his lips, as he had dried them off himself. Despite being beaten ruthlessly, Tae Hyun showed no weakness as he stood tall and proud. Had it not been for the dirt on his clothes and the minor wounds on his face, one could not surmise that he had recently been attacked. He couldn't have looked more like the King that commanded reverence from such a powerful world, and for this, she was proud of him. Yoori had always considered herself an expert at hiding her weakness, but Tae Hyun was no doubt the master at that. There was no one better to have her back.

"We're *both* here for them—just as you wanted." Her eyes narrowed onto Hae Jin and Kang Min. She had avoided looking in their direction as soon as she came in. Once she saw how beaten they were, she remembered why she did so. She felt her heart tear apart. It took everything within her to control the quivering of her lips because she loved them so much and never wanted anyone to hurt them. Swallowing past the despair, she removed them from her line of sight. She turned back around and stared specifically at Ju Won. Her eyes throbbed with severity. "Just let them go and we can go from there."

"You make a lot of demands for a bitch who no longer has any power," said one of the young Royals from the upper echelons. His chin was held high. He couldn't stomach that someone as "lowly" as her was addressing them in the bold manner that she was.

"Get your ass down here and call her a 'bitch' again," Tae Hyun confronted gravely. His expression was deadly and intolerant while he stood protectively beside Yoori. He was still pissed at her, but he wasn't going to allow some lowly bastard to talk to her like that.

The young Royal immediately cowered away, growing quiet as he avoided eye contact with Tae Hyun. It was obvious that even as a "fallen God", Tae Hyun continued to evoke fear from those who crossed him.

"Even without your title, you are still every bit of the King we know and revere," Ju Won voiced from above. There was a mixture of veneration and frustration in his voice. He shook his head, disappointed that Tae Hyun squandered all of his potential. He shifted his attention to Yoori. He held the same disappointment for her in his eyes. "You both still embody the characteristics of Royals that we all hold dear. It is unfortunate that you no longer share the beliefs of our world and its bylaws."

No amount of poise and diplomatic speeches could conceal the ire that poured from his very being. If Ju Won was not bound by the bylaws of the society, there was no doubt he would have shot them right then and there.

Taking a deep breath to center himself, Ju Won snapped his fingers.

A commotion soon followed from the entryway before impending footsteps reverberated throughout the arena.

An onslaught of distress assailed Yoori and Tae Hyun when three huge men wearing dark business suits suddenly pushed Chae Young and Jae Won into the arena.

No, Yoori thought, watching them with tortured eyes.

Chae Young and Jae Won were gagged with black cloths while their wrists were bound together. The three men kicked the back of their legs, forcefully making them kneel on the tiles. Three feet away, Kang Min and Hae Jin gaped at this scene in horror. The pain magnified in their eyes at the sight of Jae Won and Chae Young in the same arena as them—taken hostage as well.

Yoori could feel the misery envelope Tae Hyun. The awful realization that two more of their loved ones were trapped in this same arena hit him like a ton of bricks. She could feel her own stomach coil about in despair. After much arguing with Jae Won, Yoori was able to convince him that it was safer for Chae Young to be sent home rather than for her to be anywhere near this arena. It was a ploy Yoori used to hopefully stall for their safety. She had hoped that she would be able to save Tae Hyun, Hae Jin, and Kang Min before any harm could come to her other friends. However, as she drank in the sight of them in this state, she felt all hope evaporate before her eyes. Now they didn't just have Kang Min and Hae Jin to worry about. They also had the lives of Chae Young and Jae Won (as well as their own lives) to be concerned about.

Yoori shook her head internally. The maladies on her body became more noticeable after realizing that this night was going to be a thousand times more difficult—both physically and psychologically—than she could ever truly anticipate. Everyone she cared about in this world was here and they were all in danger. The worst part was that she no longer had any power to protect them. She was simply a shadow of her former self: a fallen God. Desperation gnawed at her very soul. She had never felt more helpless—more human—than at this very instant.

"The truth is," Ju Won went on, earning back Yoori and Tae Hyun's attention, "myself and the rest of the Underworld have been revolted with the way that things have been ran. As mentors, we took both of you under our wings. We gave both of you the best advisement anyone could dream of having; we offered you our undying support, and this is what you do in return?"

Mounting anger pulsed in his voice. "You created anarchy. As the most powerful Royals in our Underworld pyramid, you've created absolute anarchy with everything you exhibited at the business district." His face morphed into an icy mask. "You've spat in our faces and renounced the very throne we bestowed to you on a silver platter. You've spat on the teachings of our world and sought to be the one thing we've drilled into your heads that you should never be" —his glare landed specifically on Yoori, indicating subtly that she was his biggest disappointment of all—"*weak and distracted.*" His eyes swiveled back to Tae Hyun. "This is the legacy you've written for yourselves. This is the forbidden road that you've chosen when you showcased your entire weakness to the ones you were supposed to set an example for."

He shook his head, conviction set in his gaze. "Kwon Tae Hyun, An Soo Jin . . . tonight, in this very summit with the Underworld as your witness, you will be shown the consequences of your mistakes. You will be shown the consequences of allowing your humanity to poison you."

The entire Underworld shifted in their seats at his words, silently preparing for the show ahead of them.

"You do not abandon your throne, you do not spit on the faces of the ones who catapulted you into your position as Gods, and you do *not* choose each other over the bylaws of this society. All of that is simply . . . unacceptable. It is unacceptable, and it will be corrected." He regarded the quiet and anticipatory crowd. "You will be made into an example tonight, my children." Then, an expression in his face changed while his voice grew lower, softer. "But there *can* be some kindness displayed if you cooperate with what we want."

When Yoori and Tae Hyun's eyes turned inquisitive at his last sentence, Ju Won went on amiably.

"We're not entirely cold-hearted." He looked over at their loved ones. "As a token of our residual feelings for you—and a last favor as a courtesy for once being like children to us—we're going to let your friends go." He faced Ji Hoon, his eyes stoic. "That is . . . if the King concurs with this."

Ji Hoon smiled politely and nodded cordially at Ju Won. "Whatever the entire society wants, I will be more than happy to sign off on." He sharpened his eyes onto Yoori and Tae Hyun before inflexibly adding, "The only thing that cannot be wavered is that I will be the one to show these two the consequences of their transgressions."

"What type of mercy will be shown to them, Ju Won?" Yoori asked slowly, unaffected by the wickedness in Ji Hoon's eyes.

She cared more about her loved ones. She knew the Advisor all too well. Whatever "mercy" he was talking about, it sounded too good to be true. However, whether or not she trusted the validity of what was being offered, she was in no position to barter. The only priority was making sure they left this building alive.

"They will be set free," Ju Won said carefully. A hint of stiffness inhabited his voice, indicating that he did not like that she referred to him as "Ju Won" instead of "Uncle". Albeit her lack of respect displeased him, he continued to speak as if it never bothered him. "And they will receive full immunity from our world."

Yoori and Tae Hyun's eyes bloomed at this once-in-a-lifetime deal.

Her heart hammered at the possibility that her loved ones could be free from the wrath of the Underworld—forever. She could feel every cell within her body rise up with hope. Unfortunately for Yoori, her happiness was short-lived with Ju Won's next words.

"If you agree to our next terms, that is."

Yoori could barely conceal her smirk. She already suspected her Advisor would never be this "kind" unless there was some malice attached to the arrangement. The devil was making his deal, and Yoori knew it would be a gut-wrenching one.

"If you agree to our next terms, then we will not only let them go, but we will also promise that they will never be pursued again. They can go about their lives as they wish." He eyed Jae Won and Chae Young. "They can start a new life together without fear." He swiveled his eyes to Kang Min and Hae Jin. "And they can start a family without having to look behind their backs all the time. They will be given one of the few mercies this society will ever show, and they will be truly free from the wrath of our world."

"And what are the terms?" Tae Hyun asked critically. There was apprehension in his voice, like he knew this condition wouldn't be a favorable one for them. Things already weren't favorable, but from the tone of his voice, he clearly feared the worst.

"That will be discussed when your friends are safely out of the arena," Dong Min finally voiced out from several seats away from Ju Won.

Surprised to hear from his Advisor, Tae Hyun redirected his attention to him.

Up above, Dong Min sat on his throne and stared down at his fallen advisee. Although he wore a disappointed expression, his kind eyes silently assured Tae Hyun that no matter his mistakes, he still considered him to be the son he never had.

"You grew up in this world. You know that every agreement is binding once made in front of the entirety of the Underworld, especially in this type of capacity," continued Dong Min, his voice moving over the arena. "There are strings attached to the conditions to come, yes, but this offer will truly set your loved ones free. This is a gift that doesn't need to be given to you, but is presented anyway. No one in our Underworld will dare go after them. All that said, do yourselves—and the four of them—a favor and stop prolonging the inevitable. We all know your answer will be yes. So stop wasting time and get on with your farewells."

Adhering to the words of Dong Min, for she trusted that he would always look out for Tae Hyun's best interest, Yoori didn't hesitate to agree. Whatever the terms to come, the only thought in her (as well as Tae Hyun's) mind was that they wanted their loved ones to vacate the premises as quickly as possible. They wanted their brothers and sisters to leave so that they could become less human, so that they could force themselves to be Gods in the face of the hell to come.

"I want the Cobras to be the ones who escort them out," Tae Hyun then whispered, not yet agreeing with the terms. He eyed Ace, Mina, and the rest of the Cobras sitting high above in the crowd, their expressions still inflexible— still loyal to him. "I want them to be the ones who administer this release. Allow them to do this, and I will agree."

Yoori understood what Tae Hyun was doing. He trusted his Advisor immensely, but he did not trust the rest of the Underworld. If anyone else administered the release, then Yoori and Tae Hyun would never have peace of mind that their loved ones were actually safe. On the other hand, with Tae Hyun's very skilled and very loyal Cobras, there would be no doubt that their loved ones would truly and inarguably be safe.

"Very well," Ju Won agreed promptly, clearly wanting to get the night over with. "Now get on with your goodbyes. You still have much ahead of you tonight."

"Sounds like a plan."

31: The Darkest Hour

The sound of ropes being cut was heard as Hae Jin, Kang Min, Chae Young, and Jae Won were finally released. While this took place, Tae Hyun and Yoori remained rooted in their positions. Their eyes were focused on Tae Hyun's Cobras. They watched as the Cobras rose up from their seats in the upper quarter. Descending footsteps poured through the arena when they raced down the stairs and jumped onto the landing of the six-foot high marble wall. Once all nine leapt down the wall and landed on the onyx stage with enviable agility, they fell on one knee and showed their respect to Tae Hyun.

"You know that you don't need to do that anymore," Tae Hyun voiced softly, uneasy with their insistence with revering him like a King. Given his new status in life, any further kneeling was not only considered inappropriate, but also blasphemous. If the Underworld saw fit to it, the Cobras' transgression would be punishable by death.

"No matter what you choose, you will always be the one who took us in and saved our lives. We will always be in your debt, and we will always do this," Ace answered for the rest of his Cobras, touching both Yoori and Tae Hyun's hearts.

With a wave of a hand for them to rise, Tae Hyun looked at each of them for reassurance. His eyes glanced briefly to his loved ones before he turned back to the Cobras. "Can you watch over them for me? Can you protect them for me?"

"With our lives, sir," they all answered without hesitation, without fear.

Tae Hyun smiled, giving them a nod of appreciation. With his Cobras following closely behind him, he walked beside Yoori and finally went over to their loved ones to bid their farewells.

"No!" Hae Jin screamed as soon as Yoori and Tae Hyun reached them. "You guys can't do this!"

They were all standing in the corridor that acted as the entrance and exit way of the arena. The door to the world outside was opened, allowing the cool breeze of the night to filter through. The limited lighting in this space gave them the privacy to say their goodbyes without filter, without having to make a conscious effort to appear emotionless in front of the Underworld.

"There has to be another way," Chae Young breathed out, holding back tears when she realized that Yoori and Tae Hyun were going to be left in this amphitheater alone.

"There is no other way," Tae Hyun answered quietly.

"They will kill all of us regardless," Yoori added gently, knowing that this was a difficult farewell for everyone involved. "At least with this, *you're* all guaranteed safety while Tae Hyun and I can fight without fearing that they'd hurt you."

"We'll stay. We'll fight with you," Jae Won and Kang Min said in unison. Their eyes pulsed with valor and determination. They weren't afraid of fighting beside them in this battle.

"And you will risk *their* lives?" Yoori inquired pointedly, gesturing at Hae Jin and Chae Young.

She expelled a weary sigh. She had no doubt that the brothers would fight to the death with her, and this was her fear because they were no longer her soldiers. They had their own loved ones now. She would not allow them to behave so foolishly. They were not going to stay—she was going to make sure of that.

The brothers fell silent when Hae Jin and Chae Young's safety was brought up. Confliction and anguish undulated in their eyes. They were torn between protecting the love of their lives and protecting their King and Queen.

"You know that if you stay, then the deal will be voided and no one will receive immunity," Tae Hyun added solemnly, looking at the brothers. "They will kill all four of you." His eyes became more critical. "What do you think that would do to us? Do you think we can fight for our lives while being consumed with the guilt of watching them kill you?"

Yoori knew that she and Tae Hyun got to the brothers when they said all this. No matter how painful it was to hear, the inexplicable truth was that this was their reality. Without the extra burden of worrying about their friends, Tae Hyun and Yoori would be able to become "Gods" in this world once more. That in turn would give them a better fighting chance to actually make it out alive. The only person they would have to look out for was the other, and even that alone was already going to be a difficult task.

Though conflicted with emotions, their loved ones fell silent because they saw Tae Hyun and Yoori's point. They miserably acknowledged that their presence would do more harm than good. If they wanted to help Tae Hyun and Yoori, then they had to leave immediately.

Desperate to get his loved ones out of this building before the Underworld reneged on its deal, Tae Hyun exhaled slowly and approached Hae Jin and Kang Min with a heavy heart. He stopped in front of Kang Min, and from man to man, he did something that was difficult for every older brother to do: he bequeathed another man with the responsibility of keeping his younger sister safe.

"I leave her with you now," he declared, emotions overfilling his firm voice. "Please . . . take care of my sister. If there's anyone in this world that I would trust to take care of Hae Jin and to love her, it would be you."

Tears brimmed in Kang Min's eyes as he accepted this responsibility. He shook his head in shame while looking into the arena behind them. From his vantage point, the bright lights from the onyx stage looked like the fires of hell. It was a fire that he did not want Tae Hyun and Yoori to return to.

"I'm sorry I didn't do a better job this time," Kang Min uttered, remorse crippling his voice.

Tae Hyun gave him a reassuring smile. "This was beyond your control." He turned to Yoori, his eyes making brief contact with her. "Sometimes even when you give everything to protect the one you love, you fail. That's how life works." Something in Yoori's gut coiled at what Tae Hyun said. Before she could further process it, he turned back to Kang Min, leaving Yoori to revert her focus back to the farewell rather than what he had just said. "You will do well."

After patting Kang Min on the shoulder, he pivoted his attention to his baby sister. Giving her a farewell hug that only siblings could give to one another, Tae Hyun bestowed her with an emotional embrace that left Hae Jin to sob into his arms.

"I know this . . ." Hae Jin cried between her words. The agonizing guilt in her crying voice brought tears to Yoori's eyes. "This is all my fault."

Yoori took in a breath to quell her tears. She hated seeing Hae Jin cry. It evoked all the older sister instincts within her and tore her up inside. If she could, she would give Hae Jin the world for her not to cry.

"It's not your fault," Tae Hyun assured, his voice truly meaning it.

"You wouldn't be here if you didn't want to save me," she went on painfully, the tears freefalling down her cheeks. "You would've left already, and you would've been safe. You wouldn't be standing here in this goddamn place right now."

"It's not your fault," Tae Hyun stated again. He hugged Hae Jin tightly, not wanting to let her go. It was clear that he feared this would be the last time he would hug his sister. "None of this is your fault. It's mine. They wanted me, and they used the people they knew would have me running back. I got you involved in this, but I'm getting you out now."

Upon being reminded of what she needed to do, Yoori glanced over to her best friend and the brothers. Then, she abandoned all composure and ran to Chae Young. She embraced her like there was no tomorrow.

"Thank you for everything, buddy," Yoori whispered, her heart racing at the knowledge that there was a strong chance she would never see her best friend again. "Thank you for befriending that new girl who came in looking for a job, and thank you for being there with me since."

"I love you, Yoori," Chae Young replied, unable to control her own sobs as she hugged her best friend. "Please come back. You have to come back."

Afraid to answer that plea with a verbal response, as Yoori herself wasn't sure about the chance of her survival tonight, Yoori gave a half-hearted nod as a means to calm Chae Young's nerves. She disengaged from the embrace and immediately went into the arms of the two brothers. She embraced Kang Min and Jae Won together, never in her life imagining how difficult it was to finally say goodbye to the ones she grew up with.

"Thank you." The statement was simple, but after all that they had done for her, it couldn't have been more meaningful. "Thank you for everything that you've done for me. I love you—I love both of you so much. More than you'll ever know."

"We love you, boss," they responded, tears bubbling in their eyes as they held her. Ten years. After ten years of growing up together, the trio couldn't believe they had to say goodbye like this.

Soon after, as the tension within the arena became somber, Tae Hyun brought everything to an end. With conviction set on his face, he finally pulled out of the embrace with his sister and ended the group's farewell.

"Leave now," he said to all of them, wanting to waste no more time, "before they change their minds."

"No! Oppa, there has to be another way!" Hae Jin cried hysterically, reaching out for him when the reality of what was happening finally hit her. He was leaving; her brother was actually leaving now. She tried to reach for him, but Tae Hyun moved his arm away from her in time.

He began to walk out, his eyes on his Cobras and his muscles tense from what he was doing to his sister. He knew he could no longer allow all these human emotions to filter into him. He still had an Underworld to face; he wasn't going to permit himself to get further entrenched in this.

"Secure a plane for them and make sure they leave the country tonight— right now," he told Mina and Ace. "Do not take them anywhere else but the airport. Do not listen to them if they beg you to keep them here, and do not let them out of your sights. Watch over them as I would and protect them as I would."

"We will, boss," all nine Cobras assured him, bowing their heads as a sign of their understanding and future adherence of his orders.

"Thank you," he said to them with genuine appreciation. "Thank you for everything you've done, and thank you for everything you will do."

With that, Tae Hyun, without giving one last glance at his loved ones, regained his composure and walked back towards the arena where the Gods of the Underworld awaited him. He stopped just halfway at the entrance hall, several feet from the light of the arena. He waited for Yoori, who knew it was finally her time to join him.

"Yoori," Hae Jin called softly, trying to appeal to Yoori when she realized her brother had already made his decision. "Please . . . don't do this. There has to be another way. Just come with us right now. Just leave and run right now."

Knowing that the clock was ticking, Yoori pulled Hae Jin into an embrace and kissed her on the forehead. She cupped Hae Jin's tear-filled face with adoration and forced a smile to come upon her face.

"You will be such a great mother," she merely whispered, regretful that she would likely never see Hae Jin's child. Her own conviction set, she finally turned away from them. "Please take care of yourselves."

Yoori sped away, the commotion behind her triggering her heart to rip into pieces. She could hear Hae Jin clamoring to get to her, crying for her to not go. She could hear Chae Young holding her back, crying tears of her own. With her misery worsening from hearing their hopeless sobs, she continued to walk straight ahead, nodding at the Cobras to take them away now.

Yoori took a moment to regain her bearings and approached Tae Hyun in the darkness. When she stopped in front of him, the very last thing she heard was Hae Jin and Chae Young crying before the big doors slammed closed, officially freeing their loved ones, and officially entrapping Yoori and Tae Hyun at the mercy of the Underworld—officially telling Yoori that the end was near.

It was finally just them.

It was finally just her and Tae Hyun.

Yoori looked up at Tae Hyun while the beckoning mouth of hell awaited their return.

Yoori could feel her fears come into play when their eyes met. Their gazes mirrored each other. They were both scared, both deathly afraid.

"I wish . . . that you hadn't come," Tae Hyun told her regrettably, finally giving away the fear that he had been concealing from their loved ones.

"I wish you hadn't come either," she whispered, feeling the same regret. An unrivaled fear wrapped through her while they took another minute to bask in each other's presence. Given the chaos that was about to take place, this stolen moment of reprieve was a gift before their descent back to hell.

No matter how much they embodied it, Yoori knew, just as Tae Hyun knew, that they were no longer Gods. They were merely humans now. Humans who knew that they were facing wrathful Gods, and humans who did not fear for the safety of their own lives, but the safety of the one they loved more than anything in the world.

Yoori was so afraid, but what could she do now?

All she could do was fight past her fears and hope against hope that they could make it through this seemingly impossible night.

God help us. Her desperate mind prayed to a being she had never once prayed to. *Please help us.*

At long last, with a silent nod to one another, they inhaled deeply and put on their masks of fearlessness. With their hands intertwined, they marched back into the entrance of hell and faced the very society that threatened to rip them apart.

Pushing her fears aside, Yoori used all her strength to summon the Queen from within her—the Queen who would do things that her human counterpart could never do.

Ju Won and the rest of the Underworld watched Tae Hyun and Yoori approach the center of the onyx stage with their heads held high.

"I trust you're satisfied with how smoothly that farewell went?" Ju Won asked expectantly, sitting comfortably on his chair.

"Cut the political bullshit, and let's get to the point," Tae Hyun dismissed, taking the words right out of Yoori's mouth. Now that his loved ones were no longer hostages, he showed no more inhibitions to his true nature as a King. He looked angry and unforgiving—just as Yoori did.

"What do you intend to put us through tonight?" Yoori asked in the same firm voice.

"You've caused quite a ruckus in our world. This is unacceptable for two individuals as influential as the two of you," started Ju Won.

Around him, the majority of the Underworld murmured in agreement. They narrowed their critical eyes onto their former King and Queen, listening as Ju Won elaborated further.

"I had such high hopes." Ju Won eyed Yoori. "I raised you." He then turned to Tae Hyun. "And I spoiled you. I gave you every possible chance a King could have because I believed in your greatness." He smiled bitterly, swaying his agitated head from side to side. "Mistake after mistake, I looked the other way for you. I, along with the ones who supported you, persuaded the Underworld society to forgive you for your momentary lapse in judgment. We assured them that once you had seen the errors of your ways and realized what was at stake, you would use that forty-eight hour period to make the right decision." He looked at both of them. "I think we can see now that rationality has not returned to either of you. This is something we want to drill into you tonight."

He faced Yoori again, addressing her and only her.

"Before you came here, you had Chae Young call the authorities, telling them enough of what they needed to hear for them to come here and 'capture' us."

While Tae Hyun's eyes enlarged at this revelation, Yoori maintained her cool façade. She was aware of how connected the Underworld was to the authorities, but she didn't anticipate that they would be privy to this information so soon. She took a tremendous risk in involving the legal authorities. Nevertheless, it was the only option she saw left in someone saving them—or at least distracting her world enough so that she and Tae Hyun could make their escape. She saw now how futile everything was. No one would come save them in time. The only ones they could count on were themselves.

"But you should also know that our 1st layer is very close with those who sit in the government chairs. Even if they are coming, it will be slow, and it will be difficult for them to find this exact location. You will be executed before they arrive." Ju Won's lips edged up in a grin. "But it doesn't have to boil down to this."

The suggestive tone in his voice earned the undivided attention of Yoori and Tae Hyun. Their ears perked up in interest at the possible meaning behind his words.

"If you agree to our next terms, then there is a chance the both of you can walk out of here *safely*."

Tae Hyun stepped forward. He did not believe what he was hearing. "What do you mean?"

"You have turned this world upside down with your choices in life, and in turn, I, along with our Underworld and our brothers from several other Underworlds, have grown curious." An amused chuckle emitted from him. "Does 'love' really conquer all? Are the teachings of the Underworld just guidelines that can be ignored? Can Gods who have turned human really win over the wrath of the Gods they betrayed? It's an interesting philosophical question that we would like to get an answer for."

"What are the terms?" Yoori asked solemnly, eager to finally learn what they had in store for them tonight.

"You will get rid of all your weapons," Ju Won instructed, looking from one to the other. A dark, measured stipulation poured from his lips. "Injured or not, when those guns are in your hands, the two of you will always be unstoppable—*untouchable*. But if you voluntarily give it up and adhere to the rules of combat we have set forth for you tonight, then we will not only give you a chance to be set free, but we'll also give you the same immunity your loved ones received." Tae Hyun and Yoori's eyes grew wide at this, and Ju Won smiled at their expected reactions. He capitalized on the amazement in their gazes. "This is a once-in-a-lifetime offer. With your guns, you will be able to fight nearly everyone off, but do you think you could endure such a battle with your injuries?"

Yoori felt herself and Tae Hyun stiffen once Ju Won mentioned their injuries. She could see the eyes of the Underworld crowd light up in curiosity too. They hadn't forgotten that Yoori and Tae Hyun were not the Gods they could be. They had been weakened, severely so. Without their guns in their possession, anything tonight would be fair game.

"At least with this agreement," Ju Won continued, trying to reason with them, "there would be a *chance* that you will finally be out of all of this. You could finally be free from the Underworld."

"What," Yoori demanded quietly, "are the rules?"

The condition of this deal was a death sentence, but the end reward was too valuable. An immunity from the Underworld—what a great reward that would be. They would finally be free from this affliction. They could finally be happy.

"An initiation takes five minutes," Jung Min answered. "For our former King and Queen, we'll give you an hour to make your exit from our world. An hour to beat anything and everything thrown your way, and an hour to still keep breathing. If you make it through this hour, then you'll have all of our words that no one in the Underworld will come after you. You will be able to disappear, and you will be able to live the life you gave up your thrones for."

"Why such leniency?" Tae Hyun inquired, voicing the question that was circulating in Yoori's mind.

Considering that the Underworld could easily execute them at the drop of a hat, it was bewildering to be given this once-in-a-lifetime deal.

"The Underworld has become very divided because of the two of you," Dong Min answered from the other side of the amphitheater. "There are some who are disappointed, but will always have a soft spot for you. There are some who still feel loyalty towards you, there are some who want you to be punished severely, and some so apathetic that they do not care what happens. They simply want to be entertained."

Ju Won smiled and took over Dong Min's monologue. "In the interest of perpetuating civility amongst the divided society, we have come up with a more entertaining compromise for everyone involved."

"You want a show," Tae Hyun and Yoori said knowledgeably, comprehending now why Ju Won, Ji Hoon, Young Jae, and the majority of the Underworld agreed to this one-hour term.

They wanted to be entertained.

Setting this "compromise" up was a way to appease those who didn't want to punish Yoori and Tae Hyun. It was also employed as a way for Ji Hoon and the rest of the Underworld to be entertained. As for Ju Won, Yoori

397

was certain he wanted all the younger generations of Underworld Royals to learn from the "mistakes" of Yoori and Tae Hyun. What better way to drill the importance of not falling victim to love than to punish the ones who fell so far from grace? Theoretically, it was a win-win compromise for everyone involved.

"A way to keep the peace, right?" Yoori couldn't help but state caustically. "And a great way to be entertained while two fallen Gods fight for their lives and fight for the slim chance of making it through the hour."

Ju Won merely smiled at her words. In lieu of directly responding, he said, "The terms have been set. Do you agree or disagree?"

Sarcasm streamed from Tae Hyun's dry expression. "Do we really have a choice?"

"Not in so many words." Ju Won admitted. He grinned pleasantly. "You may not have much of a choice, but you do stand a chance to make it out of this. You may question our intentions for setting this up, but even you have to admit that this offer is something that has never been presented in our world. It is likely that it will never be offered again. An opportunity like this should not be discounted; it should be taken advantage of—it should be seized."

Yoori agreed with everything he stated. This chance of freedom was an offer that had never been given in their world. They could not allow this moment to pass them by. They had to take the chance. It was the only chance they had left.

Showing no more hesitation, Yoori and Tae Hyun gave a wordless nod to one another. Soon after, they began to toss their guns and knives onto the tiles of the arena. As soon as the weapons touched the ground, two Underworld soldiers immediately swept them up and vacated the arena with the weapons in tow.

Weaponless, Yoori and Tae Hyun stared at the crowd without a shred of fear.

"What will this hour consist of?" they asked simultaneously.

"That," Ju Won said impassively, returning his attention to the one who would control the remainder of the night, "will be at the will of the King."

Above them, the two glass ceilings of the amphitheater slowly raised up, mechanically closing out the world above. An ominous rumble reverberated through the arena when the two glass dome ceilings met in the middle, officially starting off the event of the night.

Ice-cold chills pulsed in Yoori's veins. She understood all too clearly now why Ji Hoon was sitting so comfortably the entire time.

He knew.

This entire time, he knew that their lives would literally be in the palm of his hand. He allowed Ju Won some semblance of control because he knew that the rest of the night would be spent under his governance—under his will.

Yoori glanced at Tae Hyun.

It was clear that he shared the same thought: an hour under the wrath of the Underworld was already considered hell on earth. An hour under the wrath of Lee Ji Hoon was going to be hell of the most apocalyptic proportions.

This wasn't going to be easy.

It was going to be agonizingly hard and painfully unimaginable.

"You're sleepy already?"

32: The End of Gods

The atmosphere of the Underworld was an anticipatory one.

Sitting eagerly in their seats, all eyes of the Underworld populace were focused on the King sitting comfortably in his throne. His back was pushed contentedly against the cushion of the chair, his elbow rested on an armrest, and an ankle was propped onto his knee.

Ji Hoon gazed at the two people whose fates were held within the palm of his hand. His lips were curled up into a vindictive smile.

"Isn't it funny how life works out?" he asked them offhandedly, leaning forward in his seat. "That after all we've been through, the moment would come where you would be at my mercy like this?"

"It must be nice," Yoori launched curtly, unknowingly critiquing Ji Hoon in the same manner Tae Hyun had earlier in the night, "to know that the only reason why you're sitting there is because Tae Hyun and I threw away that throne. How nice it must feel to know that you're only a second-tier choice compared to us."

Yoori reveled in the subtle anger that surfaced on Ji Hoon's face. She despised the bastard. It infuriated her that their lives were in his hands. She wasn't afraid of him, and she wasn't afraid of what he might do. The only thing she feared was the unexpected, the unimaginable, and the inevitability that came with tempting the wrath of anyone in the Underworld. It had been mere days since Tae Hyun and Yoori battled one another. They had done a number on each other. They did not need a doctor to tell them that they were going into battle with an extreme disadvantage.

One minute at a time, Yoori coached herself to further get her mind back in the game. One minute at a time. If they did things right, then they might have a chance of surviving this night.

"I will enjoy every bit of this," Ji Hoon murmured to them instead. He did not appreciate their assaults earlier in the night, and he most certainly did not appreciate Yoori's recent insult. If the cruel expression on his face was any indication, then he was ready to make them pay for their offenses with blood.

Eliciting a breathy sigh to prepare himself for the fun he was about to have, he motioned a "down" prompt with his index finger.

In that instant, twenty men and women, all of whom were covered from head to toe in black, propelled down the newly closed ceilings with harnesses. With their faces covered with ski masks, they jumped out of their harnesses a few inches from the onyx tiles and swiftly landed on their knees. They created a circular formation around Tae Hyun and Yoori, trapping them in while kneeling before Ji Hoon. With their heads hung low, they awaited his further command.

Ji Hoon grinned, dividing his attention between Tae Hyun and Yoori.

"Let's warm you up, shall we?" He waved an index finger at the two, like one would to trouble-making children. "Remember that you are not allowed guns or swords for this particular battle. It would be an unfair advantage given your . . . skill level." And then, with a fleeting silence to mark the beginning of what was to come, his eyes darkened. He rested his cruel gaze on his assassins, and with a simple command of "Commence", the beginnings of hell began.

Twenty glinting swords emerged in their hands. Sparing no more precious time, they stampeded towards Yoori and Tae Hyun without fear.

"You got my back?" Tae Hyun asked lightheartedly, trying to quell any fear that may have risen within Yoori. With that prompt, he was also subtly letting her know that there were snipers all around the arena. The snipers were getting into position to shoot at them as well.

Yoori smiled, grateful for this heads up. With their backs to one another, Yoori kept her eyes on the assassins who were charging towards them.

She let out a small laugh and just as lightheartedly replied, "As long as you got mine."

Twenty assassins and several unidentified snipers fighting a former King and Queen—even for two people trained to be better than the rest, they knew that without their guns, the next best weapon they had to overcome the odds was to fight together—to fight in synchronization.

Without another wasted second, as she felt herself and Tae Hyun pull away from each other, a string of sniper bullets flew at them, commencing the beginning of their organized defense.

Bang! Bang! Bang! Bang!

Tae Hyun and Yoori fought in a coordinated motion and ducked at the same time. Each grabbed hold of the kendo stick left adrift on the tiles. With their hands holding the opposite ends of the bamboo stick, they raised it over their heads. In that same moment, multiple swords came down upon them. The blades struck the protective shield of the kendo stick, their sharp tongues hungry for a taste of flesh.

Yoori glanced at Tae Hyun. Though no words were exchanged, they knew exactly how to fight together. After a nod of confirmation, Yoori took full estate of the bamboo sword. She jabbed it upwards, breaking through the maze of swords up above and weakening the attackers with her skillful wielding.

Just as this happened, Tae Hyun used the opportunity to kick various assailants across their stomachs. The attack triggered a tide of assassins to tumble onto one another. In this spell of chaos, he seized a lone assailant from the tide and grabbed hold of his arms. Tae Hyun became the puppet master of the night when he held up the arms of his captive and fought the other assassins with him. While directing his captive's sword grasping hand, he began to wield the weapon as though it was in his own hand.

Swish!

The sword whipped through the night, slicing through flesh and injuring a myriad of assailants.

Bang!

Anticipating the next wave of attack, Tae Hyun used the captive assassin as a shield for the chain of bullets that came flying in his direction. Multiple bullets plunged into his captive, prompting blood to pour profusely from the masked man's wounds. While his captive took his last breath, Tae Hyun proceeded to kick another lone assassin over to Yoori, who effectively used the masked soldier to block another thread of bullets that came for her.

Bang! Bang! Bang!

As this shield assassin died for her, Yoori was still fighting her own set of attackers with the kendo stick. Displaying enviable skills, she whipped the bamboo stick with a force so strong that it left multiple opponents to go airborne across the room. Despite how difficult it was to concentrate in this massive arena, Yoori was careful to use her heightened hearing as she fought. Whenever she sensed the bullets coming for her, she would use the assassins around her as living shields.

Bang! Bang! Bang!

Strangely enough, the longer she fought, the more taken aback she became. It occurred to Yoori that she actually recognized some of the moves being used against her. To her horror, she then realized that those moves were the ones she taught—those moves were the ones Tae Hyun taught. Her stunned eyes raked over the masked men and women in a brand new light. They were not fighting unknown assassins. They were fighting their own people.

Her Siberian Tigers and his Serpents: their own people were being used against them now.

"It is ironic, isn't it?" Ji Hoon stated offhandedly, reading the shocked reaction of not only Yoori's, but also Tae Hyun's. "Fighting against the ones you trained, the ones who once revered you?"

Although this discovery hurt them, they did not allow it to cripple them. If they were attacking her and Tae Hyun, they were enemies—it was as simple as that. In an arena where they were fighting for their lives, they could not allow things to become complicated. Putting that knowledge aside, Tae Hyun and Yoori used all the power they had left to fight their ten remaining adversaries.

Bang! Bang! Bang!

In a harmonized motion, Tae Hyun and Yoori leapt onto the harnesses that were still hanging from the ceiling. They swung their bodies into the air and used their controlled momentum to kick several assassins at once. Up above, the snipers shot away, the bullets grazing over Tae Hyun and Yoori, but fully lodging themselves into their opponents.

Even though she was able to hold her own, the various maladies plaguing Yoori's body were beginning to take a toll. The bullet wound on her arm was acting up after she used the last of her strength to swing on the harnesses. And then, just as she grabbed another harness, the wound became her undoing. An excruciating ache surged up and down her arm, momentary blinding her with pain.

Tae Hyun, who was unaware of the pain Yoori was experiencing, jumped in the air and spin-kicked several assassins at once, leaving a wave of black figures to plummet brutally to the floor.

Bang! Bang! Bang!

Swish!

"Augh!"

Distracted by the pain weaving through her deteriorating body, Yoori was unable to defend herself when one of the attackers sliced his sword over her left arm, cutting through her stitches and opening up her bullet wound. A rush of blood flowed from her wound as she fell from the harness and crashed to the ground.

Bang! Bang! Bang!

Applying pressure to her wound, Yoori dodged around the bullets and ripped out the bottom hem of her shirt. She tied a knot around her newly opened wound and secured the knot by using her teeth to pull at one side of the fabric. After taking care of her injury, she angrily went after the assassin that attacked her. Then, just as countless bullets overflowed the stage, just as Tae Hyun killed the five assassins he was fighting against, and just as Yoori snapped the head of the bastard who attacked her, the sound of another pair of feet dropping onto the floor pulsated through the amphitheater, signifying the beginning of the *real* battle to come.

"Vacate," said the authoritative voice of An Young Jae.

His demand was instantly met.

On direct cue, the fighting ceased and the bullets stopped. With a groan of agony from the four surviving assassins, all of whom were bleeding nonstop from battling against their former King and Queen, they struggled to bow to both Ji Hoon and Young Jae. As commanded, they vacated the onyx arena, leaving the blood-covered stage to the Kings and Queen.

Tae Hyun and Yoori breathed in vigilance. They stood in the center of the arena, watching with unblinking eyes as Young Jae stepped over the fresh corpses from the carnage that had taken place. He began to make his way over to Ji Hoon. On the other side, Ji Hoon rose from his throne and made his way over to Young Jae. They convened in the center of the arena where they stood parallel to Yoori and Tae Hyun.

Yoori regarded them with disgust. She should have known that Ji Hoon and Young Jae would only administer the full duration of their "punishment" after they had been brutally weakened by their former soldiers. Others might view their strategy as ingenious. She simply saw it as cowardice.

"You didn't think your one hour would be that easy, did you?" Ji Hoon asked nonchalantly, rolling up the sleeves of his dress shirt to prepare for battle.

Tae Hyun smirked. Even after the attack, he still looked unscathed. The only difference in his appearance was the splatters of blood that belonged to those who were foolish enough to fight him.

Yoori, on the other hand, was feeling the excruciating after-effects of the "warm-up" battle.

"It would make sense that you'd be cowardly enough to wait until others had fought and weakened us before you were brave enough to come down yourself," Tae Hyun remarked dryly, unaware of how weak Yoori was becoming.

In spite of her mounting pain, Yoori maintained her mask of composure. She refused to distract Tae Hyun by bringing attention to her injury. In this type of capacity where they were fighting for their lives, it was better to keep these useless, demoralizing facts to herself.

Young Jae smiled as he picked up a sword and tossed it to Ji Hoon.

"It was entertaining to watch you fight the ones who once loved and respected you so much." Young Jae laid his cruel eyes on Yoori while reaching down to grab hold of his own sword. "But there's a reason why I came here, a reason why the entire Underworld is here, and a reason why the two of you are here." He smirked at Yoori and motioned his head to a fallen soldier. His eyes sharpened onto the sword that was in the dead soldier's hand. "Pick up the sword, little one. You weren't allowed to use those as weapons in the warm-up round, but in this round with me, seeing as our skill levels are highly comparable, I want you to have every advantage there is before I give you what you deserve."

Unnerved that he used the nickname he had given her when they were children, Yoori did her best to stow the once pleasant memories of him aside. She bent down as he suggested and picked up a sword of her own. She knew all too well how this fight between the Gods would be split up. It would be Yoori versus Young Jae, and Tae Hyun versus Ji Hoon.

Yoori felt the anticipation rise up in the amphitheater. The Underworld was on its hands and knees at the prospect of watching two Gods battle one another when it came to Yoori and Tae Hyun. But this very moment was different. The enormity of this entire scenario was too perfect for her sadistic society. The four Gods that stood across from each other had so much history with one another, so much individual reverence, so much power, and so much desire to kill one another. The battle between Yoori and Tae Hyun may be considered the epic fight of the century, but this . . . this fight would be infamous and legendary, and it would live on for the ages to come. It was truly the battle of a lifetime, and it was truly a battle fit for the Underworld.

"We have been waiting a while for this battle, haven't we, Tae Hyun?" Ji Hoon asked coolly, kicking a sword-holding cadaver over to Tae Hyun. It was his wordless prompt to Tae Hyun to pick up the sword.

"I've been waiting for this day for five years now," Tae Hyun answered, ripping the sword from the corpse's hand. "I can't wait to finish you tonight."

A smirk edged Ji Hoon's lips.

"Funny," he murmured, expertly twirling his sword in his hand. "I was thinking the same thing about you."

Tae Hyun smirked. Whereas Ji Hoon's smirk was calculating and mocking, Tae Hyun's was filled with deadly promise.

"When I kill you, I will make sure to line this floor with your blood while your head falls beside my feet. We'll see then if you still have your sense of humor."

Fury morphed onto Ji Hoon's visage. He tightened his grip on his sword and looked at Tae Hyun with fire in his eyes. "Let's see what you've got."

Clank!

Akin to two bulls finally being released from captivity, Ji Hoon and Tae Hyun charged at one another at full force. Their swords clanged together, causing sparks to fly in the air as the fight between them commenced.

As this occurred, Yoori and Young Jae were still circling one another.

Young Jae's eyes were filled with bloodlust while Yoori's eyes rippled with regret for the situation they found themselves in. She knew that he had been waiting for this moment with great anticipation—the moment to finally bring his revenge to fruition. For Yoori, this moment could not be more heart-wrenching. Despite how much guilt she harbored for killing his wife and unborn child—and despite how much love she still had for him—in the end, she saw the unforgiving truth behind their story. She was not a fool. There was no chance for reconciliation. Not after everything they had been through and especially not after everything they had done to each other. Although every part of her agreed that his thirst for her blood was justified, in the same token, every selfish cell within her body found this justification to be inconsequential. She would not give him an easy fight; she refused to die by his hands tonight. She had too much to live for to die without a fight. It was inevitable that one had to kill the other to make it out alive, and for her own survival—and more importantly for Tae Hyun's survival—Yoori hoped that she would be the sibling who came out alive before the hour was up.

"The first Lord of all the Underworlds," she began, still circling him with her sword held high in her hand. She was ready to battle him within a moment's notice. "Your dream has come true."

"A bittersweet dream to the nightmare you bequeathed to me," he replied coldly. Hatred bled through his stare. "You should've listened to your boyfriend and stayed away." A cruel smile outlined his lips. "But I'm glad that you came. I would've never been able to live with myself if I did not make you pay for what you did."

A bloodthirsty mask crept onto his face at this very statement. As though this was the very catalyst he needed to summon all his strength to destroy her, he did not delay the inevitable any longer.

Swish!

Young Jae initiated the battle by swinging his sword in the air. The metal blade sped for Yoori's neck. It was an inch away from connecting with her flesh before Yoori proficiently blocked the attack with her own sword. A loud clang surfaced over the arena as Yoori used her sword to wield his away. Once their swords parted ways, she maneuvered her weapon around his. There was no longer any hesitancy weighing her down. He was not going to go easy on her, and she planned on doing the same. Family no longer existed in this arena. All that existed was survival.

Rallying together all her strength, Yoori swung the sword across his chest. Her blade cut through the fabric of his suit jacket and would have sliced into his skin had Young Jae not back-pedaled in time.

Bang! Bang! Bang!

Her plan to spur forward to wield another attack came to a standstill when she heard the bullets come her way. Her instincts taking over, she spun the sword around her. Her talented hands dexterously manipulated the weapon to serve as her shield. She threw the sword behind her to cover her back from flying bullets and then flipped it forward to veil her face. As another wave of bullets came storming into the onyx stage, she threw the sword in mid-air to block a bullet that was coming for her neck. In the same moment, she also performed a quadruple backflip to evade ten consecutive bullets that chased after her like shadows.

Gasps flooded the amphitheater. Yoori's effortless demonstration of her God-like skills held the Underworld audience in absolute awe.

Excited whispers poured from the upper levels of the arena.

"Holy shit, that was a bomb-ass move!"

"No wonder she's the Queen, right?"

"What a fucking great show."

Yoori landed on her feet, grabbed a sword, and quickly looked up once the snipers momentarily ceased with their shooting. Above in the highest echelon of the arena, where the 1st layer heirs and heiresses sat, she could see their eyes glow with amazement. They were in awe of the unparalleled skills she displayed in protecting herself with a simple sword. In that instant, everyone in the arena was reminded of why she would always be the Queen of legends in their world.

Yoori took her eyes off the 1st layer Royals when she felt seething eyes lay upon her. Her eyes rested on her brother, who was watching her with composed rage. There was fury in his eyes because she had gotten the better of him in front of their society. This was a travesty that he would not permit again.

Yoori gazed at the bullets that rested beneath her feet and examined the spotless ground around Young Jae's feet. There were no bullets surrounding his immediate proximity. Sans the piece of his jacket that she cut through, Young Jae had no other maladies on him. A slow realization dawned in her eyes. This time, unlike the previous bullets that hit everything that moved, the last bullets fired were not shot without discrimination. It was fired with extreme prejudice.

She smirked to herself, knowing how this game would be played now.

The bullets were only deployed when it looked like Young Jae or Ji Hoon were about to lose their fight and needed assistance. It was used as a surefire way to ensure that the show would go on until the hour was up. More importantly, it was used to keep Yoori and Tae Hyun from defeating Young Jae and Ji Hoon.

Cowards, she thought disgustedly. Only in the Underworld would this callous technique be looked upon as entertainment rather than a cowardly act.

"You ungrateful bitch," Young Jae growled, breaking her out of her reverie. The composure he held melted away from the heat of his anger. He was not happy that she nearly sliced his chest open. If looks could kill, Yoori would be dead with her heart ripped out of her chest.

Yoori held the sword tight in her grasp, ready for round two with her brother.

With an inferno blazing in his eyes, Young Jae did not disappoint her anticipation. He spurred forward and charged at her, expertly swinging his sword in the air. This time, he was ready to give her the fight of her life.

Yoori met his sword with hers and poured her own anger into their fight.

Battling one another with unmatched rage, they simultaneously jumped in the air, punched one another, kicked one another with bone-crushing force, and nearly destroyed one another while their swords violently clanged together.

"Spoken by the ungrateful bastard who killed his own father," Yoori spat out moments later, responding to his earlier remark. She bequeathed him with an uppercut to the chin that nearly took his head off. Unfortunately for Yoori, Young Jae was quick to recover.

Speeding back to her, he bestowed her with a powerful punch across the face. The force of the punch weakened her legs and caused her to fall on one knee. Darkness edged her vision as she tried to see past the pain. All the injuries she incurred while fighting with Tae Hyun in the business district sprouted to life, reminding the nerves of her once healing body that the same treatment was coming again. Her body begged Yoori to remove herself from this situation, warning her that it wasn't physically strong enough to go on.

She heard all of this, but chose to ignore it. Instead, she chose to listen to her heart. She would not leave Tae Hyun here. She would stay with him until the very end.

Not long after this resolution, Yoori felt her instincts spark to life when she heard the snipers rustle up above. *They're getting ready to shoot again!* Placing her pain on the backburner, Yoori blindly groped for something to aid her while the darkness dissipated from her vision. Her hands grazed over the harnesses in the arena and she gratefully clung to the one closest to her. With an impromptu plan in mind, she propelled herself up onto that harness and speedily removed herself from the incoming gunfire. In that same second, seven sequential bullets came at her while she hung in mid-air, nearly causing her to crash to the ground. Refusing to fall, she tightened her grip around the harness and swung her sword about, shielding herself from the random bullets that were still coming after her.

"Ah!"

Yoori screamed when her grip nearly failed her. Aware that it was physically impossible for her to hang onto the harness any longer, especially given her injuries, Yoori changed her tactics. Using her body as the catalyst to move the harness further along, she swung like a pendulum. Giving herself one powerful push with her swinging body, she finally let go of the harness. With wind running through her hair, Yoori soared through the air with the grace of a bird. She braced herself, easily landing in a crouching position on the foundation of the six-foot-marble wall that embraced the arena.

Yoori caught her breath. She slowly realized that by landing on this marble ledge, she had not only given herself a moment of reprieve, but she had also inadvertently given herself a close-up view of the international Royals visiting from other countries' Underworld. From what she could see in her immediate vantage point, these Underworld Royals descended from countries such as Italy, Russia, and the United States.

Sitting regally in their thrones on the first ascension of rows behind the marble wall, the various international Kings, Queens, and future heirs all had smiles on their faces. Many had crossed continents to witness the legendary King and Queen of the Korean Underworld fight for their lives. From the impressiveness in their eyes while they gazed at her and Tae Hyun, who was still fighting Ji Hoon in the opposite end of the arena, Yoori knew that they were not disappointed in the fighting abilities displayed. The four Underworld Royals on the onyx stage had far exceeded the reputations that surrounded them. The very battle that was occurring right now made their trip well worth it.

Behind their impressed gazes, Yoori could also see disappointment. Disappointment for her that she wasted her gift and disappointment that it was likely her legendary status would die with her tonight.

"Such a waste of a powerful God," she heard one say. Concurring voices streamed through the row of thrones before someone glanced at Tae Hyun and said, "What a waste of *two* powerful Gods."

Done with her momentary assessment of them, Yoori gave no more attention to the spectators behind her. She had someone more important to look after. Using the international Royals' proximity to her advantage, as she was certain no sniper would dare fire a bullet in fear of hitting a protected Royal, she stood atop the ledge of the marble wall and freely looked ahead. Her eyes landed on Tae Hyun and Ji Hoon, both of whom were battling one another in the distance.

They were on the marble ledge as well, jumping and twisting themselves in the air while doing such groundbreaking and out-of-this-world moves that she knew they fascinated the world on that end of the arena just as she had. A relieved breath escaped from her when she could see that although Ji Hoon was one of the best fighters in the Underworld, Tae Hyun was slowly but surely overpowering him.

Kick his ass, she silently encouraged Tae Hyun, feeling energized from seeing that he was winning his battle. It only served to remind her how crucial it was that she did her part as well.

For them to survive this night, she had to win her own battle too.

Empowered by witnessing Tae Hyun's fight, she tightened her grip on her sword and returned her attention to the world below her. Young Jae was now making his move to follow her up the ledge of the marble wall. With his predatory eyes on her, he grabbed a nearby harness and easily propelled himself up by walking his legs up the marble wall. Within a moment's notice, he was on the ledge with her. His dark expression was hungry for retribution.

"After all I've done for you, you little bitch," he went on, the bitterness still present within his voice. He wasted no time going after her as he went on with his words—as they alternated between wielding their swords and maintaining their equilibrium on the marble ledge. "After all I've given you. After giving you the leading position in the gang, after taking care of you, and after spoiling the hell out of you . . . you do this to me? You betrayed me, and if that's not enough, you decided to take it upon yourself to destroy everything I love?!"

"I didn't know she was pregnant!" Yoori finally shouted as she twisted herself in the air and successfully slashed him across the arm.

She thought about his betrayal, about how he had ruined everything. Then, when she thought about him and what he was going to do to her and Tae Hyun, she lost it. She didn't want to apologize because in the end, Young Jae would always be the origin that started everything.

"*You* jumpstarted *every* decision I've made," Yoori seethed furiously. She loved him, but she could never forgive him for ruining her life. "With your greed, with your love for power, and with your need to rule over the Underworld. You murdered your own father and fucked up everyone's lives in the process!" Her lips began to quiver as her emotions overtook her. "I feel guilty for killing your wife and your unborn child. I wish I could take it back, but I can't. But the difference between us is that I actually feel guilt. I haven't lost my soul like you think I have, Young Jae." She stopped fighting and simply looked at him with tears rippling in her eyes. "But what about you? Do you even feel anything? Do you even feel guilt anymore? It's been five years since you've killed our father. Five years since you colluded with our brother to end his life and tore this family apart. Do you even feel guilt for that?"

He ceased with his attacks and stared at her with unreadable eyes.

After a long pause, he finally said, "No, I don't."

It was a simple and honest answer. He had no guilt for what he did to their father, and he had no guilt for using Ho Young to kill him. This was the final nail on the coffin for Yoori. It was no longer possible for her to contain her rage.

"Do you not think that you deserve this fate?!" she launched heatedly, well aware that she would incur his wrath by stating this. "Do you think all the good you did in the past for me will excuse your actions now? Look at what you've become! You're not even human anymore."

Fuming and no longer wanting to stand here and discuss this—to further distend a pain that both of them would never be able to reconcile—a now agonized Yoori used this opportunity to attack him. She speedily swept her leg over the five-inch wide marble ledge and stole the air from beneath Young Jae's feet. Gravity tried to claim him, but he was resourceful enough to deny its call. With one hand stretched out, he caught himself on the ledge before he fell down. Displaying the strength of the undefeatable God that he was, he easily lifted himself back onto the marble wall.

"You're right," Young Jae casually concurred as he stood peacefully on that ledge. He nodded with a smirk. "You're right. I have jumpstarted every decision that you've made. I've pushed you to your breaking point, and I deserve every bit of the misery you've afflicted onto me." Yoori wondered what he was getting at until his cruel eyes strayed across the arena. His gaze settled on Tae Hyun as he fought Ji Hoon. "I deserve every bit of the misery you've inflicted on me, so in turn, because you've now pushed me to *my* breaking point, it is only right that you jumpstart all the decisions that I'm about to make." He returned his focus to her, his eyes swelling with unforgiving fire. His next declaration was a vicious promise that chilled every inch of Yoori's soul. "You will lose *everything* tonight, little one. You will pay for everything that you've done, and I will return the misery that you've given me tenfold."

"You will not touch him!" she breathed tightly, panicked at the thought of him doing anything to Tae Hyun.

"After you lose him," Young Jae persevered cruelly, "I want to see what you become. Will you be human . . . or will you be a monster like me?"

The last vestige of her control dispersed into oblivion. Fiery indignation began to engulf her very being. With her protective instincts for Tae Hyun blinding her, she let out a growl and abruptly charged at Young Jae.

She swept her leg on the ledge again, knocking him off his feet. Only this time, she did not allow him to be at the mercy of gravity. She wanted him to be at *her* mercy. On the heels of her first attack, she suddenly extended both her legs up and locked them around his neck as he was about to fall. Forming an iron grip around his neck, she hoisted Young Jae down with the force of a bulldozer. The assault sent him flying down onto the onyx floor. He tumbled over several dead bodies like a skipping rock and came to a violent stop at the center of the arena.

Determined to put an end to this fight, Yoori seized the opportunity to finish him off while he was still discombobulated. She jumped back onto the onyx floor and ran after his immobile body with her sword in hand. She raised her sword when she was near him, and without any hesitation, she stabbed the sword into the ground where his body laid. Regrettably for Yoori, finishing her brother off was not as easy as she anticipated. The sword that was supposed to impale him missed by a mere inch when several bullets came down upon her, sidetracking her while giving Young Jae the opening to gather his strength and use her momentary distraction against her.

Young Jae soared into the air and extended his right leg out, giving her a triple spin kick that literally left the bones within her body to vibrate in pain. The force of this attack blinded her temporarily, leaving her unable to shield herself. Despite the fact that she could hear the bullets coming, there was little Yoori could do when a bullet flew past her, searing off a good amount of skin off her right shoulder. Hot flashes of pain assailed her, nearly knocking her out.

"How about you protect yourself first?" Young Jae murmured haughtily, kicking her so hard in the stomach that she could feel her intestines contract in pain. There was no moment of reprieve when he delivered a second kick that sent her soaring through the air. Just like Young Jae's previous fall, her body tumbled and bounced mercilessly against the floor, exponentially increasing the pain that spread like cancer inside her body. Yoori expelled a sharp breath when Young Jae grabbed the back of her neck. Tipping her head back so that she was forced to stare up at him, he ruthlessly said, "How about we put you through your punishment before we talk more about Tae Hyun?"

Bam!

There was no time for Yoori to digest his words. In that same second, Young Jae grabbed a chunk of her hair and slammed her head against the marble wall. The force was so brutally hard that Yoori's entire body trembled from the excruciating throbbing. As Yoori struggled to breathe, Young Jae allowed her severely injured body to fall to the floor beside his feet.

He gripped his sword, staring down at her with malice in his eyes.

"You took it all from me. So now," he began, getting ready to raise his sword, "I'm going to take it all from you."

All the while as this occurred, moments before Yoori laid helpless beside Young Jae's feet, another battle raged on—a battle between old rivals who were finally getting a taste of war.

"You have no idea how long I've waited for this moment," Tae Hyun said angrily, staring down at a newly fallen Ji Hoon from the marble wall. Various parts of Tae Hyun's body were now covered with sword wounds that infiltrated his clothes and skin. However hurt he was, it did not compare to Ji Hoon's current condition.

With blood seeping profusely from the areas of his body that Tae Hyun was able to successfully cut, along with the areas of his body that had skin seared off because Tae Hyun used him as a shield to protect against incoming bullets, it was an understatement to say that Ji Hoon was in worse shape than Tae Hyun.

Regardless of his physical injuries, Ji Hoon's arrogance did not cease. "Yes, the death of daddy dearest is probably still with you, isn't it?" he provoked derisively, laughing even as blood was dripping relentlessly from his arm. Standing up from the fall he just took, Ji Hoon comfortably cracked his neck as if the fall meant nothing to him. He turned back around and stared up at Tae Hyun with mocking eyes. "Is this the best you can do?"

"You should have listened to my warning over the phone, Ji Hoon," Tae Hyun reminded, jumping down from the marble wall with ease. His sword outstretched, he swung it again, this time cutting Ji Hoon two more times before he performed an axe kick that sent Ji Hoon crashing against the marble wall behind him. "I would've left you alone. I would've swept everything under a rug and forgotten about you."

Ji Hoon smirked mockingly. He couldn't care less of what Tae Hyun warned him. All he cared about was his hatred for Tae Hyun and his need to hurt him.

Without uttering a response, he simply charged at Tae Hyun again, fighting with all the skills that made them renowned Kings of the Underworld. Though they appeared evenly matched in strength, the one with the most skills—Tae Hyun—was proving to be the better opponent. He jumped against the marble wall, used it as a prop to propel himself in the air, and proceeded to deliver a spin kick once against Ji Hoon's face, another when Ji Hoon was in the process of collapsing onto the floor, and a final spin kick that knocked Ji Hoon to the floor.

Tae Hyun breathed angrily, finally preparing for his final attack. He was sick and tired of Ji Hoon and was ready to end him once and for all. Just as Ji Hoon was about to meet the ground, Tae Hyun seized the kendo sword that was lying on the floor. He positioned the butt of the stick to meet Ji Hoon's chin when he fell and performed an uppercut that had his head twisting back up. As his finale, Tae Hyun twirled the bamboo sword with unmatched velocity and slammed it like a baseball bat against Ji Hoon's neck. The stick cracked in half when this occurred, and Ji Hoon was left rocketing backwards onto the floor.

Tae Hyun watched him with pity.

"You should've backed off while you had the chance to live," Tae Hyun said coldly, bloodlust present in his eyes. From his demeanor and the way he approached Ji Hoon, it was apparent that Tae Hyun was no longer interested in allowing Ji Hoon to breathe any longer.

"What fun . . . would that be?" Ji Hoon coughed, resting his head against the marble wall. His breathing was rapid and shallow. Even though he was at

Tae Hyun's mercy, Ji Hoon was anything but humble. "*Especially* when I wanted to be the one who took everything away from you tonight."

"It's over, Ji Hoon," Tae Hyun replied, picking up the sword from the ground. "It's over for you."

Ji Hoon smiled before eyeing the scene on the opposite end of the arena. "Maybe you should see how your little Yoori is doing before you focus too much on my death."

Perturbed by this unusual prompt, a newly distracted Tae Hyun veered his attention to the other side of the arena. Alarm entered his eyes. Instead of seeing Yoori hold her own as he obviously expected, he was horrified to find that she was actually struggling while fighting with Young Jae. Even through her thick black hoodie, he could see that blood was dripping freely from her left arm. She was hurt and was also about to be finished off by Young Jae.

The sight of Yoori in this treacherous state rocked Tae Hyun's sensibilities. Abandoning all focus on Ji Hoon, he took off for the other side of the arena—for Yoori.

"Yoori," he whispered. The soles of his shoes sped over the tiles as he flew towards her.

Yoori was lying face down on the ground, her breathing raspy. She did her best to fight through the throbbing of her newly assaulted head and the pain shooting throughout her body. Although she managed to keep herself from blacking out, she could not find the strength to get up and fight. She was too monopolized by the pain—too crippled to save herself when Young Jae emerged from behind her and raised his sword . . .

Swish!

Speeding up just as Young Jae was about to cut into Yoori's back with his sword, Tae Hyun lunged towards him. He grabbed onto a harness in front of him and swung forward, viciously kicking Young Jae across the face.

Young Jae screamed a curse before dropping his sword and collapsing to the ground.

Tae Hyun landed easily onto the balls of his feet and grabbed two corpses as he did so. He transported his lifeless cargo over to the marble wall where Yoori laid. Without missing a beat, he set up the corpses as shields around them. Half a second later, a stream of bullets came for them, burying into the lifeless bodies as Tae Hyun tended to Yoori.

Bang! Bang! Bang!

"Hey," he called to her after the gunfire came and went. He gently placed his hand on the back of her head and helped her sit up. "Hey, how you doing?" he continued, making conversation to keep her awake, to keep her from blacking out. This arena wasn't the place for her to pass out.

As Yoori fluttered in and out of consciousness, Tae Hyun took inventory of her left arm. He carefully touched the blood that formed around the fresh sword wound of the jacket. Anger poured into his eyes when he noted that the bullet wound that was once healing had been re-aggravated. His eyes shifted along her slow breathing body, and he could see the maladies plaguing her. The swollenness of her face, the various cuts on her body, and the newly seared flesh on her right shoulder caused more fury to seep into his observant eyes.

"I'm okay," Yoori whispered after regaining her full consciousness. She hissed in pain as she sat straighter, relieved that Tae Hyun was sitting beside her. All she needed was a moment away from Young Jae, a moment to breathe and work through her pain. After being given that grace period by Tae Hyun, she was feeling slightly better already.

"You really shouldn't have done that, Tae Hyun," came Young Jae's icy voice from behind them.

Tae Hyun wheeled around to find Young Jae standing three feet away from him, brandishing a sword in his hand. Young Jae's face did an excellent job of conveying his dissatisfaction in Tae Hyun's intervention.

Alerted and in combat mode again, Tae Hyun held his sword and stood back up. He pushed the dead bodies off of him and faced Young Jae. He strategically stood between Young Jae and Yoori. His protective stance said it all: Tae Hyun would not prohibit Young Jae to get near Yoori again.

"Stay the fuck away from her, Young Jae," Tae Hyun warned, his steel voice unforgiving.

Young Jae smirked before raising his sword. He harbored no qualms about battling Tae Hyun to get to his sister. Challenge throbbed in his composed voice as he got into his fighting stance.

"Try and stop me then."

Like a lion on the attack, he charged at Tae Hyun and jumped into the air. Wielding the sword over his head, he swung the blade down with the intention of burying the sword into Tae Hyun's skull. His attack was thwarted when Tae Hyun lifted his own sword up and blocked it just over his head.

Once Tae Hyun was able to deflect this attack, he maneuvered the sword onto his opposite hand and swung the weapon from side to side, effectively slicing into Young Jae's shoulders.

"Ahh!"

Young Jae let out a scream and tumbled backwards, clutching onto the blood that was beginning to seep from the new flesh wounds.

As Yoori watched this, she felt vigilance consume her when she saw Ji Hoon running in from the side, ready to take advantage of Tae Hyun in his distracted state with Young Jae. Having regained much of her energy, Yoori reflexively lifted the female corpse that lay beside her and threw the corpse at him with both hands. The lifeless body hit him like a cannon ball, stopping him in his tracks while giving her a split second opportunity to charge for him. Utilizing her speed as her momentum, she slid on the tiles using the side of her body. Once she reached him, she spun herself up in a diagonal motion. With her right leg extended out, she kicked him clear across the jaw in mid-air. As she landed gracefully onto the balls of her feet, she jabbed a hard elbow across his face. Far from done with her assault, she used the heel of her palm to strike his nose. A loud crack rung through the arena, indicating that she had successfully broken his nose. Her adrenaline still pumping through her at lightning speed, she swept the floor with her left leg. While he fell toward the floor, she used her full body weight and kicked him across the stomach with both her feet.

Boom!

The attack left Ji Hoon to hurtle across the tiles, crashing into dead bodies while slicing his own skin with the rogue swords that were still lying on the floor.

Breathing heavily, Yoori stood several feet from Ji Hoon's fallen body. Although she conquered him in this fight, it was clear that she was not ready to give him such a merciful end. For the moment, the Queen was back in action, and she wanted Ji Hoon's head on a stake.

"It doesn't have to be like this, Tae Hyun," Young Jae breathed out from the opposite end of the arena. He straightened his back and stood upright, his energy regained. His expression implored Tae Hyun to be practical. "This doesn't have to play out like this."

"You going after the woman I love will *always* result in this," Tae Hyun retorted sternly. His furious eyes fastened on Young Jae as he walked in a predatory circle around him.

Bang!

Tae Hyun's trail around Young Jae came to an abrupt halt when a bullet shot down, hitting Tae Hyun's sword and landing so close to his hand that the heat seared the tip of his skin off. Tae Hyun released a pained hiss and inadvertently dropped his sword, allotting Young Jae the chance to take advantage of a now weaponless Tae Hyun.

Meanwhile, on the opposite point of the arena, the fight between Ji Hoon and Yoori was just getting started.

Ji Hoon smiled as he raised himself up after her sudden attack.

"Let's not do this," Ji Hoon whispered. He began towards her as though she hadn't just physically assaulted him. "I don't want to fight you."

"Really?" Yoori asked critically, clenching her fists together. She was eager to beat his ass down again. "Because I can't wait to fight you."

An agonized expression morphed on his face. He continued to walk with his hands clutching his injured hip. "I don't want to hurt you, baby," he assured through a pained breath. "I never want to hurt you."

His words were sweet like honey, but his actions embodied spinelessness when he suddenly grabbed a sword from the ground, ran to her, and swung it in the air. Though Yoori was quick enough to evade the attack to her shoulder, she wasn't quick enough to avoid the sidekick that followed. He propelled his foot right into the problem area of her left arm, leaving her to topple to the side and sink to the ground.

"I loved you. God, did I love you," he lamented, staring at her with manufactured pity. He perched his foot on her neck, displaying no reluctance to hurt her as he applied pressure on it. Her chest constricted as her flow of oxygen instantly halted. Violent heaves raked through her body as she struggled for air. He pressed down, deepening the pressure. His next words were spoken with pure bitterness. "I was ready to give you the world, but you just had to choose Tae Hyun over me, didn't you?"

Yoori did not bother to say anything. She simply closed her eyes and struggled to free herself from his clutches. Although this silence infuriated Ji Hoon, it did not dissuade him from trying to get her back on his side.

"It's not too late, Soo Jin," he provided. His voice was gentle as he stared down at her in remorse. "I still want you more than anything; I'm willing to forgive you for all the mistakes of your past."

Queasiness infiltrated her stomach. His bullshit words were the last straw for her. Fed up with listening to his voice and keen to kick his ass again, Yoori summoned all the energy at her disposal. As she felt the last of her strength rally together for her, she flipped herself out of his hold. And then, with the utmost untrained, but highly useful, tactic to use against a guy twice one's size, Yoori stood up and kicked him hard in the balls.

"Augh!"

While a scream poured from Ji Hoon as he doubled over to the floor and pathetically tended to his wound, the battle on the opposite side of the arena was still going strong.

"I do not want to kill you, Tae Hyun," Young Jae expressed, his voice sincere. Though Tae Hyun was weaponless, Young Jae did not use the allotted opportunity to attack him. Instead, he used it to try and reason with him. "It's Soo Jin that I want; she's the only one I want."

Tae Hyun clenched his fists in preparation for any sudden attack from Young Jae. Even without a weapon in hand, he did not plan on backing down. He would kill Young Jae with his bare hands if he had to.

"What difference does it make if you kill me or not?" Tae Hyun inquired suspiciously.

"You must think I'm heartless," Young Jae went on, flickering his focus to Yoori, who was preparing for another round of battle with an embittered Ji Hoon, "that I'm inhuman for harboring this much hatred for my own sister, but you must remember what she ultimately did to me and what she took from me." He turned back to Tae Hyun with genuine respect in his eyes. "I'm not irrational. I don't go after people who haven't done anything to me, Tae Hyun. I try to avoid that as much as I can in my career."

Boredom mounted on Tae Hyun's face. He had never been the one who enjoyed listening to roundabout points. "What does that have to do with you not wanting to kill me?" he asked, swiftly picking up a sword from the ground.

"Ji Hoon and I are working together, but he does not have my respect," Young Jae shared. "You have no idea how far people's reverence of you extends, Tae Hyun. *You* are the God this Underworld wants. You are the God I want to stand beside when we take our respective Underworlds to new heights, and you are the God that every other future Lord wants to stand beside when we change this world." With a smile gracing his face, he finally enlightened Tae Hyun on a secret that was only reserved for the few top elites of the Underworld. "We're Gods in our respective countries, but we can become Titans in this world."

Tae Hyun furrowed his brows, puzzled with what Young Jae was implying. "What are you talking about?"

Young Jae's voice became softer. He only wanted Tae Hyun to hear this secret, not the rest of the Underworld. "I've seen it, Tae Hyun—another society that is bigger than ours, older than ours, and more powerful than ours; a society that would unite all the future Underworld Lords together. And in this grand order, the individuals within it want you to be the Lord of Korea's Underworld. Some of the members, they know you, Tae Hyun. They've heard great things about you and they want you to be a part of this grand order. We want you there . . . to be a part of something bigger. *That's* the prize that's worth fighting for. You're not only getting the Underworld throne, but also a piece of the world." He tilted his head, his expression urging Tae Hyun to stop adhering to the foolish desires of his emotions. "Work with me, Tae Hyun. Work with me, and I will kill Ji Hoon right now. I could end his life this instant, and you will be able to regain your rightful throne again. You can lead the life you were always meant to lead—a great, historic, and legendary one."

"And in exchange for all this greatness, all I have to do is sit back and allow you to kill Yoori?"

Young Jae was quiet, and that was confirmation enough for Tae Hyun. Albeit he showed curiosity in this "other society" that Young Jae was speaking so cryptically about, he displayed no further interest in seeking out that type of power, especially not when it involved hurting Yoori.

He pointed the sword at Young Jae. "You're not touching her, Young Jae," he stated decisively. "I'm not turning my back on her."

Disappointment cloaked Young Jae's eyes. His grip on his sword tightened and he slowly raised it. He was not happy with Tae Hyun's answer, and he intended on letting Tae Hyun know that.

"I'm sorry to hear that."

Harboring no further inhibition, he lunged forward with his sword outstretched. Bloodlust was present in his eyes as he went after Tae Hyun, intent on making him regret his decision.

While Tae Hyun defended himself against Young Jae, Yoori wasn't having any luck as she continued to fight with Ji Hoon. The pain rummaging through her battered body wore her down as their swords ate away at each other. It was taking everything she had to lift that sword to simply defend herself. Under any other circumstances, it would be a simple task for Yoori to hold her own against Ji Hoon. However, as the weight of her mounting injuries congregated in her body, she slowly found that her strength was dwindling by the second. Instead of feeling like a revered Queen who was fighting a rival King, she simply felt like a defenseless woman fighting a man twice her size. It was a hard fought battle that she was afraid she was losing.

"You're not going to make it out of here," Ji Hoon sneered after he blocked her incoming sword. He looked down at her, urging her to be rational. "Come to my side. Stop this foolishness, and I'll take care of everything for you. I'll get rid of Young Jae for you."

Yoori smirked, elbowing him across the face.

"You really have no loyalties, do you?" she asked critically, unsurprised that Ji Hoon was more than willing to betray his biggest "ally".

"My loyalties are flexible," he replied shamelessly, temporarily placing pressure on his newly assaulted jaw. He issued a careless shrug. "I do what's best for me, which is something you should endeavor to do as well." He gazed at her intently. "What do you say? Come back to me, get rid of Tae Hyun, and you will be well on your way to getting the power you've always wanted."

Yoori manufactured a fake smile that would do stage performers proud. "I'd rather die than go back to being with you, you disgusting pig."

"You shouldn't be so rash," he cautioned, his face tightening in annoyance. His growing impatience signaled that he was at his last straw with her. "Such rashness will be the death of you."

Eager to teach her a lesson, Ji Hoon abruptly pulled out of the scuffle with Yoori. He lifted his sword up and strategically angled the metal blade towards the lights hanging above them. When the right angle of light landed upon it, the reflected light danced in a blinding motion—a silent cue to those up above to commence chaos in the amphitheater.

In a synchronized sequence, a multitude of blaring drums swarmed the arena, compromising Yoori's senses. The deafening sounds penetrated her ears, leaving her discombobulated. She tried to command her hearing sense to be mindful of incoming bullets. Unfortunately, she heard nothing under the distracting sounds. Next thing she knew, bullets were firing every which way, and before she could even attempt to hide behind a shield, a bullet got to her.

Bang!

"Augh!"

A tortured gasp ripped from her when the bullet plunged into her right shoulder. A conflagration of heated pain coursed through her already battered body, nearly putting her into shock. It was so agonizing that tears actually formed in her eyes as she struggled for breath. Unable to withstand the shock, she collapsed onto the floor. While shudders overtook her weakened body, several pairs of feet hit the floor right after she fell down.

It was clear that another stage of this one-hour battle had started, and it was even clearer that this third round would not only include Ji Hoon and Young Jae, but also their people.

The remaining assassins had been on standby for the grand finale this whole time.

Like sharks, six brand new masked assassins formed a circular formation around her. They reveled in her fallen state before they participated in this battle of the Gods.

Yoori had anticipated the attack, but there was little she could do when Ji Hoon kicked her body, his shoe puncturing mercilessly into her flesh. A teardrop slipped from her eyes when she squeezed them shut in agony. A fear that she had not felt in years came rushing back to her, paralyzing her even further—fear of losing a battle; fear of an inevitable death. She had not felt such terror since she was a teenager. To be wrought with this type of horror now was crippling to her sensibilities. She was not accustomed to being in this pathetic state, to lying at her enemy's feet and being at their mercy.

Get up, her desperate mind screamed through her pain. *Get up!*

The order fell on deaf ears. She could hardly move a muscle without convulsing in pain. Her body was officially broken. There was nothing she could do but lay there and endure Ji Hoon's punishment. It was a punishment that she knew he would give without mercy, and it was a punishment that was about to become even more intolerable.

Ji Hoon motioned a hand over to his assassins for them to come forward.

"Show her how you treat a fallen Queen in this world," Ji Hoon said simply, amusement dancing in his voice.

That was the only cue they needed to partake in this beating. With sounds of grunts and laughter emanating from them, they kicked her across the face, nearly causing her neck to snap. They moved on to her chest, kicking it so hard that Yoori had to bury her face into the ground to mute her screams. What occurred next was a kaleidoscope of pure torture. They simultaneously kicked her spine, her skull, her legs—essentially every inch of her body—so hard that it made her feel like she was falling down an endless tunnel filled with jagged rocks.

She couldn't breathe.

It hurt to breathe.

Throughout the duration of this assault, all she could do was attempt to open her eyes. Through the storm of pain ravaging her, she laid her eyes on Tae Hyun as he fought with Young Jae in the distance. He was unaware that Yoori had lost her fight and that she was simply waiting for death to take her.

Don't look at me, Yoori pleaded in her mind. She did not want Tae Hyun to run over to her to save her. She did not want to endanger him.

She bit her lips to prevent herself from crying as the beating became more unbearable. The beating she was enduring was unlike anything she had ever experienced. She had trained her entire life—had been in countless fights—yet it felt like those years did not amount to a fraction of the agony she was in right now.

Yoori buried her face further into the tiles, muffling her growing screams. She hated herself for not being strong enough to fight through the pain, for being weakened by her own debilitating body. Most of all, she hated that she knew as soon as Tae Hyun saw her in this state, he would abandon all rationale. He would be distracted, he would run to her, and in doing so, these barbaric bastards would bring him down as well.

Please don't let him look at me, her tortured self begged the heavens. *Please don't let him see me like this . . .*

"Augh!"

Yoori's heart briefly stopped beating when one of the assailants kicked her beneath her stomach, shifting her so that she was flipped onto her back. Once this occurred and once she felt the steel-like feet jab into her ribs, she felt herself fading. It would only be a matter of time before this was over for her; it would only be a matter of time before she took her last breath . . .

"It seems," Young Jae prompted tauntingly, looking over Tae Hyun's shoulder, "that even *you* can't control the inevitable."

Staggered by this prompt, Tae Hyun turned around mid-fight. His eyes enlarged when he saw Yoori across the arena with blood sprouting out of her body. She lay under the mercy of Ji Hoon and the masked assassins' assault. She was being assaulted in every direction, and it was clear that she could not withstand it any longer.

"Yoori," Tae Hyun breathed in pain.

Young Jae was no longer his priority. His only priority was saving Yoori.

421

Turning his back on Young Jae, he ran to the other side of the arena.

"Lee Ji Hoon!" he roared at the top of his lungs, his voice eclipsing over the drums and the cheers from the crowd. "Get the fuck away from her!"

Yoori lifted her head up when she heard his scream. An onslaught of fear enveloped her when she saw what was happening behind him.

"Tae Hyun!" Yoori screamed after Young Jae appeared behind him. He was getting ready to raise his sword, his aim on Tae Hyun's back. "Behind you!"

Before Tae Hyun could come any closer to Yoori, Young Jae used his moment of distraction against him. Rolling forward and moving his sword left to right, he sliced into the skin of Tae Hyun's back and outer thighs. The ambush crippled Tae Hyun, leaving him to crash to the ground right before he reached Yoori.

Bang!

Shortly after, a bullet sprung from the ceiling and buried itself into Tae Hyun's thigh, further incapacitating him.

"Tae Hyun!" Yoori cried miserably, wishing with all her might that she could rally her strength together to save him.

To her horror, she could only helplessly watch as several more assassins entered the arena. She could only helplessly watch as the same type of beating she was receiving was bequeathed onto Tae Hyun, whose blood was beginning to mar the onyx floor underneath him, just like her own blood was polluting the tiles.

"Ahhh!"

Screams emitted from Yoori when someone grabbed the locks of her hair. They yanked her head up and viciously slammed it against the bloodstained floor.

Bam!

An explosion of pain rocked her world, hurtling her into a hell she had never experienced. Watching the love of her life fight for breath whilst his attackers bestowed their fury onto him was torture, and being unable to help him—for she was too crippled by her own pain—was excruciating for Yoori. Darkness blackened Yoori's vision as her head throbbed excruciatingly. She was certain that her nose was bleeding, but she could not see it through her momentary blindness. The pain inside her multiplied; she could no longer breathe.

Once the darkness lifted from her eyes, the first thing she did was lay her sights on Tae Hyun.

She expected to see Young Jae administer the attacks on Tae Hyun. She was stunned when she discovered that it was Ji Hoon who was administering the assault.

Her eyes bloomed in shock.

If Ji Hoon was there, then that only meant—

"Ah!"

Her pulse jolted to a stop when someone wrapped their hand into the locks of her hair and brutally heaved her head and upper body up. She looked up, and sure enough, there Young Jae was, crouching beside her.

A cold smile adorned his lips. Cruel, taunting words began to filter from his mouth. "Did you really think Ji Hoon and I would allow you to make it through your hour without taking extra precautions? Were you really that stupid to think that you'd ever make it out of here alive? This isn't a battle, little sister. This is your death trap. This is where your story will end."

Laughter poured from him when he eyed Tae Hyun, who was now being beaten ruthlessly by Ji Hoon and five other masked assassins. While he was getting beaten, Yoori could see Tae Hyun open his eyes. Fear filled the brown eyes she loved so much when he saw that Young Jae was crouching beside Yoori. It was evident in Tae Hyun's gaze that he wasn't afraid for himself. He was afraid for her.

"This is the perfect view for the two of you, isn't it?" Young Jae voiced heartlessly. "The perfect view for the two of you to see how the other is doing—how the other is suffering."

Yoori silently cried to herself, seeing now that this was what the Underworld had planned for them all along.

They were *never* meant to win.

They were only meant to be given false hope, they were only meant to be entertainment for their cruel society, and they were only meant to lose as they watched the other get annihilated. They were only meant to be an example to the younger generations that love would *never* conquer all in the Underworld.

This entire hour . . . had been useless.

They had given everything for it . . . all the energy they could give . . . all the strength they could give. They gave everything, but it all amounted to nothing. All they had to show for it were two humans who realized that there was no more hope for them.

And now, as they lay in the trap that had been set for them since the beginning of the night, this world was going to show them the consequences of becoming human in this world—of choosing love over power.

"Enjoy the show, little one," Young Jae instructed. "And enjoy the show I'm going to make out of you for him."

Bam!

An explosive fire raked her nerves when Young Jae slammed her head against the floor three times, causing blood to start free flowing from her mouth.

"Yoori . . ."

Even through the sound of drums monopolizing the senses in her ears—and even with the chaos of everything occurring around her—Yoori could hear Tae Hyun's voice.

When she looked past the blood streaming down her swollen eyes, she could see him with blood seeping from his own mouth. They were still beating him without mercy; they were still torturing him without an end in sight. And throughout his ordeal, Tae Hyun kept his pain-filled eyes on her.

There were tears in his eyes. Tears that Yoori knew he wasn't shedding for himself, but for her. For the pain she was going through. As a result, she felt the tears bubble in her own eyes. She began to cry for him.

"Tae Hyun . . ." she whispered brokenly, slipping over her own blood as she tried to crawl to him.

She no longer cared about fighting.

All she wanted was to be with him during their last moments, before this world killed them.

She just wanted to be with him again.

Using all the strength she had, Yoori crawled on her elbows, ignoring the pain shooting through her body every time she used her aching muscles. No longer caring about anything but sliding herself across the tiles and moving herself closer to Tae Hyun, she fought through the pain while her eyes rested on his.

"Ah!"

She had scarcely made it a foot away before a soldier grabbed her by the locks of her hair and tugged her back, dragging her inside the angry mob again. Once she returned to the center of their brutality, the mobs' beating became more violent, more unforgiving.

"Yoori!"

Tae Hyun jolted upward to run to her. He was promptly immobilized when a smirking Ji Hoon ripped a harness hanging from the ceiling. He haughtily strode over to Tae Hyun and proceeded to loop it around Tae Hyun's neck. Ji Hoon jerked the harness back with an entertained bout of laughter, tugging Tae Hyun back to him like he was an animal.

"Your end has come," he told Tae Hyun, pulling him backwards and throwing him right into the center of the murderous mob. "You are never walking out of here."

At the same moment, Young Jae leaned down towards Yoori, whose heart was breaking at the sight of Tae Hyun in this state.

Young Jae's voice was dark and calculating when he announced, "Now I will show you the very consequences of going against me."

The next series of events were an agonized blur to Yoori. There were no martial arts and there was no hand-to-hand warrior combat involved. There was nothing. It was just the simple beating of two fallen Gods. It was just the simple beating of two dishonored Royals, and it was just the simple beating of two human beings who were considered to be worthless.

They had lost.

They had *lost*.

Yoori could feel it in her dying body. She could feel it as the blood cloaked over her eyes, as her tears began to swim free, and as her eyes tried to glance at Tae Hyun for one last time. She could feel her body worsen as she watched Tae Hyun endure the wrath of Ji Hoon—as the mob brutally pulled on the noose around his neck . . . torturing him, stepping over his wounds, and beating him senseless. She could feel herself dying as Young Jae and his people did the exact same thing to her, as they beat her to death.

Agony tore through her when she was able to lock eyes with Tae Hyun's broken ones amidst the chaos. Their hearts continued to yearn for the other and their bodies continued to work every last bit of its strength to keep them alive for each other.

The pain . . . it was excruciating.

It was unbearable, and it was everything that embodied hell.

At long last, as she inhaled softly and felt her deteriorating body start to shut down from all the beating . . . the anarchy stopped.

The pounding of the drums ceased, the mass beating stopped, and the world around her grew quiet.

Slowly, while being able to breathe now that her body had been given time to rest, she opened her eyes.

Confusion crossed her face after she looked up.

Ji Hoon was standing above her, his expression filled with pity for her. What was more shocking was the person that was standing across from him.

Ju Won.

It stunned her to discover that Ju Won was standing on the opposite side of her. He stared down at her like a towering statue, sharing the pity that existed in Ji Hoon's eyes.

Yoori closed her eyes in dread.

She did not have enough strength to go over the possibilities of what they were planning to do.

All she knew was that if Ju Won was here, it only meant that while her physical agony may have been over, her mental agony was about to begin.

"No ... I'm just resting my eyes ..."

33: You're Worth All of It

Lethargy weighed on Yoori's eyes as her battered body collapsed into a numb state.

She was tired.

She was so tired . . .

"Look at how far you've fallen from the very throne you spent your entire life fighting for, my child," Ju Won stated beside her. His disappointed voice brought her out of her dazed and lethargic state.

When Yoori opened her eyes, she could see that Ju Won and Ji Hoon were now crouched down on either side of her.

Her weary eyes fixed on Ju Won. She remained quiet as he continued to speak to her in a gentle voice.

"This is the fate I tried to dissuade you from. This is the life of a God turned human. There is no happy ending for you on this road. Only death awaits you." He paused meaningfully. "Unless you use your last remaining breath to see the errors of your way now."

"Let me save you," Ji Hoon insisted from the right side of her. He skimmed his fingers over her bloodstained face, behaving as though he wasn't the one who inflicted all this misery upon her. "Tae Hyun isn't worth it. He isn't worth any of this. You made the wrong decision by becoming human for him, but you can still correct it." He picked up a sword and rested it beside her hand. "Make things right, Soo Jin. Get rid of your distraction."

In that moment, she realized what was happening.

This was their plan all along.

The Underworld had not given up on the battle between Yoori and Tae Hyun. This entire thing was a ploy used to force their hands—to make Yoori and Tae Hyun so desperate to survive that when the end came, one of them would finally succumb to the darkness and kill the other.

That was why the Underworld showed leniency to their loved ones. It was because they still wanted one of them to be a God and because they wanted to appease whichever God returned to power.

This was the deal that Ji Hoon ultimately received. He had to bring Yoori and Tae Hyun back here, he had to make them go through all this hell, and in the end, he had to successfully break one of them. He had to get one of the fallen Gods to kill the other so that they could compete with him for the throne—a throne that the Underworld refused to give to him by default.

His motives finally made sense now. He was intent on persuading Yoori to come to his side because he'd rather fight her for the throne, not Tae Hyun.

Yoori shook internally. She could not believe that she had not foreseen any of this.

Tae Hyun and her were never meant to survive this hour. There was only one who could survive—one who had to kill the other to survive.

A fist clamped Yoori's broken heart.

It was hopeless.

It had been hopeless since the beginning—since they walked in, since they gave up the thrones, and since they fell for each other.

It had always been hopeless.

Just as Yoori stared at the sword beside her and just as she came to this conclusion, from the corner of her eyes, she saw someone approaching Tae Hyun.

"Kwon Tae Hyun."

And there he was. Young Jae stood beside Tae Hyun, who was lying on the floor, his back to the ground and face to the ceiling. He only stirred from his numbness when Young Jae called out to him.

"Look at how you've fallen," Young Jae began as Tae Hyun slowly opened his eyes. Anger was still present in Tae Hyun's dimmed gaze when he stared at Young Jae. "Weeks ago you were on top of the world. Now look at you. You're nothing but a dying man fighting to live." He took out his sword and placed it on the floor beside Tae Hyun, just like Ji Hoon had done with Yoori. "But you can still save yourself. Look around," he prompted while a weakened Tae Hyun did just that. "This Underworld still loves you; it still reveres you. No matter how much you've disappointed them. Your soldiers, your mentors, your supporters—*everyone* is still rooting for you. *Everyone* still wants you as their God—their Lord." Young Jae smiled pitifully at Tae Hyun. "What are you fighting for Tae Hyun? For An Soo Jin? For *Yoori*?" Young Jae peered across the arena to where Yoori resided. "Is she really worth all of this?"

"Do the right thing, Soo Jin," Ji Hoon persuaded in her ear, staring at Young Jae and Tae Hyun from across the arena. "You and I both know that a desperate man is willing to do anything to survive. When Tae Hyun promised himself to you, he wasn't a desperate man. He was on top of the world. But look at him. He's desperate now; we both know he'll kill you."

427

Upon being reminded of Tae Hyun, Yoori slowly rolled to the side to sit up. She wanted to see him while she was sitting. She didn't want to lay down and feel broken any longer.

"You will never know how much it pains me to see you like this," Ju Won said beside her ear, watching as she sat like a child and kept her lifeless gaze on Tae Hyun. "I was the one who raised you, and I wanted you to avoid all of this. Tae Hyun is beyond salvation now. He is too stuck in his ways, and this world will kill him for it. But you . . ." He smiled genially. "You can still return to your station in life. You are different from everyone in this world. You are the Queen amongst Kings, the Queen amongst Gods. Tae Hyun may be one of the most respected and beloved Kings in the Underworld, but you will always be the eternal Queen of this world, in *all* of the Underworlds." He pushed the sword closer to her grasp, his eyes growing stern. "'To get into a position of power, some actions are unavoidable.' You remember those words from your father, don't you?" Ju Won asked after Yoori stiffened up at the familiar words. He immediately capitalized on this reaction. "The time has come: do the unavoidable. Make the tough call, and your position of power and prestige will come back."

"You've done all that you can for her," she could hear Young Jae say to Tae Hyun while Ju Won's words swam in her mind. "Do you not wonder why Ju Won is there with her instead of with you?"

Something changed in Tae Hyun's dazed eyes when Young Jae said this. Awareness returning to him upon the constant mention of Yoori, he slowly rolled over to his side. He sat himself up with gradual strength and rested his attention on her.

As he kept his lifeless eyes locked on Yoori, Young Jae continued to plant more seeds of doubt and paranoia into Tae Hyun's mind.

"Because, out of the two of you, the one that he trusts would break first is her. And even if she doesn't break first, she is as good as dead right now. We both know that. You've done all that you can do for her. Now allow her the honor of doing all that she can do for you." Young Jae narrowed his eyes and shifted the sword closer to Tae Hyun's unmoving hand. His next words pulsated with urgency. "Finish her off and rule over this world once more. I promise you the life you had as a King is nothing compared to the life you would have as the Lord. You will be one of the most powerful men in this world. You will *literally* own the world."

Tae Hyun remained quiet, his eyes still on Yoori when Young Jae added, "There are only five minutes left, Tae Hyun. You know that she isn't walking out of this arena alive. Not when this entire Underworld is furious with her for pulling you down from grace and certainly not when I want her to suffer for what she did. She will die tonight anyway, so do yourself a favor and have her death be your saving grace." His eyes returned to the sword. "Grab the sword and do what needs to be done. Make the right decision."

"Do the right thing, Soo Jin," Ji Hoon said into Yoori's ear again. This time his plea was more urgent. "Grab the sword and finish him off. There are only five minutes left, and by the time there are thirty seconds left, both of you will die. Both of you will die anyway if you don't kill him. So save yourself now and just do it."

Yoori was still brokenly staring in Tae Hyun's direction, just as he was staring at her. There was no movement between them, no uttering of words. All they did was drink in the sight of one another.

Then, as the seconds of life ticked away, a spark of realization ignited in Tae Hyun's eyes. For the first time, his eyes displayed the unequivocal truth of what he accepted to be his reality.

He had *lost*.

There was no more hope. There were no other choices left for him.

He slowly broke eye contact with Yoori and surveyed the world around him. He took inventory of everyone in attendance and how quiet they had become. And then, with a pained breath, his eyes came down to the sword sitting beside him—the one thing that could be his salvation, the one thing that could save his life.

He stared at it, his expression becoming unreadable.

Then slowly . . . *very slowly* . . . just as a cold chill spread through the quiet amphitheater, his shaking hand extended out. His fingers wrapped around the sword before he eventually picked it off the ground. He gazed up, gradually locking eyes with Yoori as he raised himself from the ground.

There was no more love in his hollow eyes, just brokenness and desperation.

After rising to his full height, he began to approach her. Never once did his dimmed eyes waver from hers.

"Welcome back, my King," Young Jae said proudly, stepping to the side for Tae Hyun. His expression beamed of satisfaction with Tae Hyun's decision.

Young Jae motioned a wave with his hand, and by then even Ji Hoon and Ju Won had left Yoori's side. They stood far behind her and left her to sit there while she watched Tae Hyun approach her.

Yoori's grief-stricken heart clenched as she watched his every advancing move. Anticipation mounted inside her. She had thought Tae Hyun would use the opportunity to turn around and attack Young Jae—or anyone for that matter—but he did no such thing.

He merely kept walking, his focus solely on her.

Not making a move to retrieve her sword, Yoori simply sat there, waiting for him to reach her. Her heart drummed feverishly as it waited for the love of its life to come closer—even if it knew how broken he was, how desperate he was, and how likely it was that he was going to use the sword in his hand to kill it. Despite recognizing this, Yoori's foolish heart—just like her—continued to wait for their Tae Hyun to come to them.

A sense of serenity flowed over Yoori.

She was already resolved to do everything in her power to keep him alive. Now that she was given the chance, she was ready to do whatever it took to guarantee his survival.

Dying for him would be worth it; dying to keep him alive would be completely worth it.

"Why did you come?" Tae Hyun finally uttered to her. His voice throbbed with despair as it moved throughout the arena. He was still approaching her slowly, his once hollow eyes now glazed with internal conflict. "You knew this was going to happen. You knew we weren't going to win this war."

Yoori didn't say anything. She merely stared at him as he continued to approach her.

It's better not to say anything, she reasoned to herself. *It would be easier for him if I didn't say anything.*

"I told you not to come," Tae Hyun went on, pain emitting from his tortured voice. He clutched onto the sword, more anguish slipping into his eyes when she said nothing back to him. "Not because I didn't want you to get hurt, but because of the things I'm afraid I'd be willing to do when pushed past my limits . . ."

"Tae Hyun, it's okay," Yoori finally assured when she heard the grief in his voice. She did not want him to be broken over this. She hoped her assurance would make this easier for him. "I'm not mad at you."

She *wanted* him to do this.

If her dying meant that he could live, then she would gladly do this for him. The only thing that ever mattered to her was him.

"I didn't want you to see me like this," he continued agonizingly. Guilt plagued his features as he watched her sit there, waiting for him. Never once did her hand make an effort to grab the sword beside her. "I didn't want you to see me fall like this."

Yoori nodded, never blaming Tae Hyun for any of this.

She wasn't worth it.

She wasn't worth any of this for him.

He did all that he could for her. He protected her more than anyone should; he loved her more than anyone else in this world should ever love her, and this was enough for her. It was enough to calm her, to prepare her body for the mortal ending that awaited it.

"I thought I was stronger than this . . . that I could overcome this." The regret in his voice magnified the closer he got to her. "I thought I was strong enough to give all of this power up, but I realize now that I can't—I can't go like this. I can't die like this. I can't die a fallen God. I can't die like any other human."

"I know . . ." Yoori nodded again, assuring him that she understood his dilemma and that she *wanted* him to do this.

At long last, he finally reached her. He fell to his knees in front of her. The sword was still gripped tightly in his hand while the pain grew prominent in his gaze. Tears welled in his eyes, showing her the conflict within him, showing her how much he hated this moment in his life, and silently telling her that he wished he had another choice.

"It's okay, Tae Hyun," Yoori murmured, having to exert control to keep from touching him. Tears built up in her own eyes. "I'm ready. I'm ready for this."

He inhaled deeply, swallowing past his own tears. His eyes searched through hers while he tightened his grip on the sword.

"Will you forgive me for what I have to do?" he asked softly, brokenly.

She nodded. Albeit tears were dripping down from her eyes, she felt her body grow warm at his proximity. She was grateful to be this close to him, to be near him once more before the end. There was no question. She would forgive him for anything he had to do to her.

He exhaled laboriously, nodding as he slowly raised the sword up.

"I'm sorry," he whispered, lifting his free hand to touch her tearstained cheek. He agonizingly added, "I never wanted to leave you again . . ."

Swish!

Without another word, he spun his sword in the air.

Yoori could feel the wind glide over her head. Yet, instead of killing her, Tae Hyun abruptly stood up. Much to the surprise of everyone who thought he had been broken, he began to slash the throats of all those who stood near them, never giving any of them an opportunity to defend themselves.

As the last of the assassins closest to him collapsed to their deaths, Tae Hyun rested his enraged eyes on Ji Hoon.

Stunned with Tae Hyun's unexpected actions, Ji Hoon backtracked and was about to run off. Unfortunately for him, Tae Hyun would no longer permit him the ability to escape.

With his eyes set on Ji Hoon like a hawk, Tae Hyun ran after him and rolled on the floor for added acceleration. When he jumped back onto the balls of his feet, Tae Hyun was half a foot away from Ji Hoon. Crouching down with his back turned to Ji Hoon, he aimed his sword behind him.

Ji Hoon did not see the attack until it was too late.

"Ugh!"

Tae Hyun gripped tightly onto the sword and with all the force he had in his body, pushed it back powerfully, stabbing through the flesh of Ji Hoon's stomach. A gasp of shock and pain escaped from Ji Hoon as he stared down at the sword that punctured through him. An endless stream of blood poured from the stomach wound, telling him that he only had seconds to live.

Yoori could only gasp to herself while she watched this.

He had planned this; Tae Hyun had planned this all along.

He knew all along that he could never get to her if he didn't pretend to be desperate and pretend to want to kill her. He couldn't protect Yoori and kill all the threats around her unless he tricked the entirety of the Underworld into believing that he had turned on her.

"I told you that tonight will be your last night," Tae Hyun stated gravely, raising himself from the ground. Never once did his eyes waver from Ji Hoon's dying ones. Then, with satisfaction on his face, Tae Hyun swiftly ripped the sword from Ji Hoon's stomach.

"Augggh!"

Another gasp of agony came from Ji Hoon before he fell to his knees in front of Tae Hyun.

"Your end has come," Tae Hyun stated emotionlessly, raising his bloodied sword up one more time. He was ready to make do on his promise of killing Ji Hoon off before the night was over. "Enjoy your death."

"No—!"

Ji Hoon never got a chance to finish his words when Tae Hyun swung the sword with unparalleled velocity. The metal blade ran across his throat, slicing the flesh open like fabric. Blood spurted from Ji Hoon's open wound before the life dimmed from his eyes.

Thud.

Soon after, all that could be heard was the sound of Ji Hoon's lifeless body hitting the floor. Once the shock of what had just transpired passed, gasps began to swarm the arena. The entirety of the Underworld society gaped down at their motionless King, not believing their eyes.

Lee Ji Hoon . . . was finally dead.

Clank!

Tae Hyun tossed the sword after the havoc he wreaked and whipped back around. He ran over to a bewildered Yoori, who was still in disbelief after what she just witnessed, and gently picked her up. He protectively held her against his body. With the swiftness that surpassed the speed of light, he carried her to the further end of the arena where he used the marble wall as one side of a shield for her. Before Yoori could process what he was doing, Tae Hyun threw himself over her, pinned her against the wall, and then covered the entire length of his body over hers.

On the heels of his actions was a sea of footsteps that stampeded towards them in merciless fury.

Tae Hyun took a deep breath, held her tight against him, and braced himself for the hell to come.

"Kill them!" Ju Won shouted murderously, crouching above Ji Hoon's lifeless body.

Young Jae came to stand behind the furious Advisor. His shocked eyes took in the sight of Tae Hyun covering his body over Yoori. Just like the rest of the unnerved Underworld, he couldn't believe what was happening before his eyes.

"Kill them before the hour ends!" Ju Won continued to scream throughout the arena. "Kill them *now*!"

If Tae Hyun heard Ju Won's words, then he ignored them because all his attention was focused on Yoori. She was staring up at him quizzically, her mind still fragmented with everything that was happening at once.

"What are you doing?" Yoori asked, not understanding why he was covering himself over her.

Though it was evident that he was in extreme pain from his injuries, he gave her a reassuring smile. Very quietly, he said, "I told you that I would protect you, didn't I?"

Yoori could hear the impending footsteps rush over to them. Her eyes searched through Tae Hyun's while the footfalls came closer. In that hectic moment, his response evaded her understanding. She didn't understand his motives until a dozen masked assassins towered over them.

"Augh!"

When Tae Hyun groaned in agony at the first kick that connected with his spine, Yoori felt tears burn her eyes. Everything clicked together. She finally realized what he was doing. There were less than five minutes left, and because of this, Tae Hyun was going to make sure that she made it out unscathed.

He was going to make sure she made it out of this arena alive.

No . . .

Torturous screams poured from her chest when the chaos began—when the sound of boots kicking Tae Hyun's already assaulted body penetrated her eardrums. The sound of fists punching his skull and the sound of Tae Hyun breathing in anguish became murder to her soul. Yoori trembled underneath him, feeling every inch of the attack that was bestowed to Tae Hyun by the sounds of his groans—the sounds of his pain. Every inch of her soul started to rip apart at the sight of Tae Hyun leaning over her, his body accepting every blow and every attack for her.

"Tae Hyun?" she whispered, feeling the sobs escape from her chest as his blood, his pain, and his agony washed over hers.

"No," she tried to whisper past her sobs. "G-get off! Get off!"

She didn't want him to do this.

He was supposed to kill her and make it out alive; he wasn't supposed to sacrifice himself for her!

Squirming beneath him, Yoori tried to get herself out from his grasp so she could help accept a portion of the attack for him. Once Tae Hyun felt her do this, he strengthened his embrace around her. He used the last of his dwindling energy and pushed her further to the ground to anchor her down. Breathing brokenly, he continued to lay over her, acting as her protective shield.

All the while as he protected her, the assassins tried to go after Yoori, to kill her before the hour was up. Their attempts were futile. Tae Hyun would not even give them an inch. He did not allow them to touch her.

"No!" Yoori continued to sob. She could feel the pained quivers raking over his body, telling her how much he was suffering for her. "You're not supposed to do this! You're not supposed to do this!" she continued to scream, pleading for Tae Hyun to get off her so that he could save himself. "Stop! *Stop!*"

She begged him to stop, but Tae Hyun remained where he was. His embrace on her was as tight as ever.

His physical response said it all: he *wanted* to do this for her.

He could no longer protect her with his strength, so he did the only thing he could do—he protected her with his life; he protected her with his last remaining breath.

Every ambush that was meant to pull him away from her—to leave her exposed for their attacks—was deterred when Tae Hyun held on tighter, not permitting anyone to pull him away from Yoori. Every time they tried to tear him away, he would pin her across the marble wall and intensify his hold around her. His throbbing body quaked the entire time he kept himself as her armor.

"Please don't cry," he whispered painfully into her ear. Down to the last sliver of energy, he rested his chin above her head. Tears dripped from his eyes and landed on her hair as he tried to breathe through the insufferable pain. Even when he was suffering, Tae Hyun did all that he could to calm her, to keep her from crying. It was clear that he experienced more pain from seeing her cry than from being physically attacked. "It's almost over. It's almost over."

He buried his face in her hair and kissed the top of her head. Then, he continued to lie there, never giving the attackers any opportunity to get to her, no matter how much his own body was dying from it.

Below him, Yoori felt herself dying as well.

The sound of fists hitting the back of his head, the sound of kicks stabbing into his bloody flesh, and the sound of metal instruments making dents in his back acted as a knife that skewered her heart and soul to shreds.

Desperate, she peered out into the arena. Red-hot tears bubbled within her gaze while her eyes ran over the individuals sitting up there watching them.

"*Please*," she pleaded to them, her cries growing stronger. "Please stop this."

She knew that they could hear her. Some stared down at her in pity as a response, others stared down at her with a disgusted look on their faces, while others stared down at her with indifference. Surprisingly, there were also others who were staring down in a manner that she did not anticipate. The more she begged for their help, the more potent the reactions became. For the few who sat in the audience, she could see them gaze at her with horror. They were stunned, utterly taken aback that their human emotions were coming into play as tears rippled in their eyes. It was as though in that moment, they could feel her heartache.

Many of the younger generation of 1st layer Royals and soldiers averted their eyes, no longer finding entertainment in an event that they were once so excited to witness. However much they empathized with her pain, she knew by the conflict in their eyes that none of them could help her. They were all bound by the bylaws of the Underworld. *None* of them could come down to help her unless they had a death wish.

Overwhelmed with the devastating truth that they could be of no help to her, she returned her attention to Tae Hyun. The desperation inside her mounted when she could still feel Tae Hyun's throbbing body. His breathing became raspy as he buried his face on the top of her head to protect every inch of her. Her distressed, tear-shrouded eyes shifted to the ground floor where through the gaps of legs kicking at them, she spotted Ju Won and Young Jae standing together, their arms crossed while they stared quietly at the scene in front of them.

"Uncle . . ." Her eyes became pleading when she locked eyes with her Advisor. *"Please."*

She had hoped that he would remember all those years when he raised her and that he would show her mercy. His cold gaze told her a different story. His dark and utterly unforgiving eyes illustrated to her what a truly spiteful man he was. She had failed him, and in turn, he would make her pay for her failure.

This was her punishment.

This was his last lesson for her.

As a last resort—as she would do anything to save Tae Hyun—her gaze swept to her brother's.

435

"Oppa," she begged brokenly, seeing that—to her own shock—tears were dripping down from his eyes. He stared at her in a way that only an older brother would when his baby sister was in pain. Nevertheless, it was the anger in his eyes that told her that even though he may still love her, he would never forgive her for what she took from him. He was still set on vengeance, no matter how much it saddened him to witness it.

"Stop!" Yoori cried at the top of her lungs to anyone who would listen. It tortured her to realize that no one would lift a hand to help her stop this. Her screams grew louder. Never in her life had she felt as human—as helpless—as she did now. All she wanted to do was save Tae Hyun. All she wanted to do was save the love of her life. "Please! Oh God, please stop this!"

"Yoori, it's okay." The hoarse whisper from Tae Hyun coursed over her. His injured eyes stared down at her to assure her that everything was going to be okay. "It's almost over—*Augh!*"

Tae Hyun did not get to finish his sentence when someone kicked him at the back of his neck.

His breathless groan tore at her, making her feel as though someone was stabbing her relentlessly with a million different knives. She shook with violent sobs as she watched the life fade out of Tae Hyun's eyes.

Hysteria came over her.

"Stop it! Stop it!"

But no one stopped.

No one stopped hurting him. No one stopped hitting him. And no one stopped tearing her heart apart.

The entire time as they hit him, he stared down at her, his eyes holding so much love even when pain plagued his face.

"*I love you,*" he breathed out, his voice barely above a whisper. He hardly had the energy to breathe, let alone talk.

Those three words were what caused her soul to rip apart.

Bam!

"Augh!"

And then, when Tae Hyun took that one last, *painful* gasp that people exerted when their body was ready to give up on them, Yoori lost it.

Her right hand reached out blindly, desperate to find something around them to end all of this. A tsunami of relief bathed over her when her hand found a dead body. In the pant pocket of that dead body was a gun.

She ripped the gun from the dead body and positioned her finger on the trigger. With a wrath that could rival a thousand suns, she lifted the gun in the air and allowed her rage to consume her.

She was going to make them pay for this.

They were all going to pay.

"YOU MOTHERFUCKERS!" she shouted at the top of her lungs.

Her wrathful eyes aimed on the bastards standing above them, the bastards who were still assaulting Tae Hyun.

As she felt Tae Hyun's embrace on her loosen from the enormous bout of pain rippling through his body, she lifted herself up. An unstoppable rage blinded her and she began to pull the trigger, unleashing her own hell on earth.

Bang! Bang! Bang!

One by one, bullets swam through the foreheads of the bastards standing above them, and one by one, they all fell lifelessly to the floor with a loud thud. Their bodies landed at the feet of the enraged Queen who now had bloodlust in her eyes. She gently pushed her fallen King off of her and locked eyes with the two bastards she wanted to kill the most.

Ji Hoon was already dead, courtesy of Tae Hyun.

She was hell-bent on giving Young Jae and Ju Won the very same ending.

The first one to know her wrath—the first one she wanted to kill—was her brother.

Bang!

Young Jae wasn't able to react fast enough when the hungry bullet dashed towards him, its ravenous jaws lodging itself above his chest. He screamed out in pain after he plummeted backwards from the sheer force of the hot bullet. He did not get to stay down long when he realized that Yoori wasn't done with him. Her gun aimed at his heart, Yoori pulled the trigger without any hesitation.

Bang!

Just as a cowardly Ju Won was preparing to run in the opposite direction to save himself from Yoori's wrath, an opportunistic Young Jae saw his ticket for survival. Clutching onto the bullet wound in his chest, Young Jae propelled to his feet and grabbed the collar of Ju Won's neck. With quick reflexes, he hoisted Ju Won in front of him like a shield, allowing the bullet that was meant for him to plunge into Ju Won's heart instead.

Gasps of outraged fury dispensed throughout the amphitheater.

They could not believe what had occurred before them. They could not believe that Young Jae had used their eldest Advisor as a shield for himself.

Fury burning a blazing trail through her soul, Yoori continued to shoot in Young Jae's direction, watching as he stumbled to the floor. He dragged Ju Won's dying body with him and made sure that the old man's body took every hungry bullet that was meant for him. Ju Won coughed out blood and gasped for air as his blood stained the arena floor.

It was a despicable sight to watch her brother drag Ju Won like he was a worthless piece of meat, but it was a tactic that worked for Young Jae as he was able to make it to the exit. Safe from Yoori's gunfire, Young Jae abandoned Ju Won's body and ran to the exit hall of the arena. When his eyes met Yoori's, a satisfied expression danced in his gaze.

It was at that moment, as she scrutinized the look in his eyes, that Yoori realized it was never in Young Jae's plans to kill her tonight.

He had something else in mind for her, something more cruel and more painful. He wanted her to feel the *exact* pain he felt. He wanted her to live the rest of her life remembering how it felt to have the love of her life die in her arms. He wanted to bequeath her with the same misery that he had to live with for the rest of his life.

With that satiated expression marked on his face, he silently told her that he was done with her. He no longer cared about killing her. There was no need because he got the exact revenge he wanted to inflict upon her.

He killed her in a way that was even more unbearable for Yoori.

Wanting nothing more than to see him die for merely existing, for being so cruel, Yoori aimed the gun at him one final time. She pulled the trigger just as he was about to disappear. However—

Click.

Click.

Panic rocked her when Yoori discovered that she had no more bullets to shoot. She had no more bullets to kill Young Jae with, to make him pay for everything he had put them through.

Alas, killing Young Jae proved to be the least of her worries when a red laser light suddenly flashed before her.

Her eyes raked over her chest and her entire body. A circular formation of red lasers marred her black hoodie, aiming directly at her heart. The now chaotic and wrathful Underworld finally had enough of her. They were determined to execute her once and for all.

And just as the snipers were about to pull their triggers to take her life—

Beep. Beep.

The beeping sound of an alarm went off, indicating to the amphitheater that the most eventful hour they had ever witnessed had finally passed.

Yoori and Tae Hyun had done the impossible.

They had won.

They had made it out of this battle alive.

The red laser lights on Yoori dispersed into oblivion at the knowledge that the hour was up. All around her, a sweeping silence came over the 17,500 people in attendance. They could not believe what had taken place—what had just transpired.

Their eyes roamed over Ji Hoon's dead body, Ju Won's dead body, and then ran over the countless Underworld soldiers who had been slain during the one-hour battle. Then, their disbelieving eyes rested on their former King and Queen.

Yoori dropped the gun when she realized that their hour was finally up and crawled back to Tae Hyun. She kneeled beside him, no longer caring what the Underworld wanted to do with her. The only one she cared about was Tae Hyun.

"Tae Hyun?" she called. She gently touched his face while he rested his head against the marble wall. His forehead pressed into the cold wall as he tried to keep himself awake.

"Sir," one of the subordinates spoke to Min Hyuk, who was now the interim commander of the Underworld after the deaths of Ji Hoon and Ju Won. In the background, the whole Underworld listened in on the conversation as the subordinate announced, "The police are close. We have to leave now."

Although the authorities were harmless to the Royals of the Underworld, they were considered to be a nuisance nonetheless. The last thing the Underworld wanted was to waste their time and effort with the legal "authorities". Rather than waiting at the arena like sitting ducks, it made more business sense to vacate the premises and get on with their busy lives. The show was over. There was nothing left to keep them here.

"Very well," Min Hyuk replied. He rose from his throne and enacted the orders to end the summit. "Commence the evacuation plan."

"What about An Soo Jin and Kwon Tae Hyun?" Jung Min questioned angrily, getting up from his throne.

"Leave them," Dong Min chimed in, painfully gazing at them from afar. His tight voice did its best to conceal his emotions. "They have already received their punishments."

"I've seen enough," another female Royal stated. Her face was disgusted by the weakness exhibited by Yoori and Tae Hyun. Considering that they were supposedly such great legends, she expected more from them.

"The children have been entertaining enough," another elder nonchalantly dismissed. He got up from his seat in weariness and put on a black coat. "Give them a bone."

"They've been through their hour," Min Hyuk stated, showing no hint to the fact that he had been one of the Royals who locked eyes with Yoori during the final minutes of the hour—that he was one of the people who shed tears for them.

As the rest of the Underworld surged to their feet, Min Hyuk continued to stare down at them with pity in his eyes. He took one last glimpse at Yoori and Tae Hyun before giving his mandate to the entire Underworld.

"The agreement given to them is binding for everyone in this world. They made it through their hour. In turn, they will receive full immunity as part of the agreement. Anyone from this world who breaks this agreement will be executed without exception." He expelled a breath as everyone rose up from their seats and began to evacuate the premises. "Now let's leave before we have to waste our time dealing with cops who think they have the power to incarcerate us. The summit ends now. Vacate."

Buttoning his jacket, Min Hyuk turned away from Yoori and Tae Hyun and began to descend out of the arena with the rest of the Underworld in tow. The amphitheater that was once filled with life and divine power was becoming more and more hushed.

Soon, all that remained were the two humans below.

As the seconds passed and as the chaotic world around them receded, all that was left in the amphitheater were dead bodies . . . and Tae Hyun and Yoori.

"Tae Hyun," Yoori whispered, gently stroking over his face. Her once heavy heart expanded as she smiled with relief. "We made it through. We're done. We're done. They're leaving us alone."

"Yoori . . ." Tae Hyun whispered slowly, his voice barely audible. Even in this type of condition, Tae Hyun still exhibited more strength than she could see any one person have. Instead of lying limply on the floor, he remained in a sitting position. The side of his body was now resting beside the marble wall. He continued to breathe softly, his eyes opening and closing slowly for a few moments before Yoori called out to him again.

"Tae Hyun . . ."

His once heavy eyelids opened at the call of her voice. His tired eyes looked at her as though she was his anchor for staying awake. Yoori paused when she saw how much pain he was still in. Her smile of relief vacated. In its place came mounting concern.

"Tae Hyun?" she called brokenly, terrified at how weak Tae Hyun was becoming.

Tae Hyun briefly closed his eyes to subdue the pain with his labored breathing. When he opened them again, his eyes were filled with worry and concern. He knew why the Underworld was leaving, and he wanted her to leave for the same reason. He didn't want her to get arrested by the police.

"D-don't . . . don't stay," he breathed out painfully. It was clear that it was taking everything he had to speak, to protect her as much as he could. "Go . . . go now. Just . . . leave me."

Yoori shook her head, refusing to leave his side.

She *wanted* the cops to come. She wanted them to distract the Underworld, and in the end, she wanted them to take them to the hospital and save Tae Hyun—save them both. It was a plan that was a long shot, but a shot of a chance nonetheless. It was a plan that she hoped would work as she sat there with him, trying to keep Tae Hyun talking and awake before they arrived. However, sitting there and talking to him was proving to be more difficult than she could ever anticipate.

It was so hard for her to see him like this.

Sitting parallel to him, Yoori took in the sight of his bloodied and completely broken state. Fresh tears bubbled in her eyes. She prayed to the fates to have the cops come faster, so that they could save him from the pain he was experiencing. She wanted them to save her from the pain she felt as she sat there helpless, wishing she had the ability to heal him instead of just watching the blood drip from his assaulted body.

"I'm not leaving you," she assured, agonizingly wiping the blood from his face. She struggled to not sob uncontrollably and struggled to not accept the reality of what was occurring before her very eyes. "I'm *never* leaving you."

He swallowed tightly. Pain immersed his eyes as he drank in the very vision of her. He appraised the sword cuts on her skin, the bullet wounds on her body, and the bruises and blood covering her from head to toe. Summoning all the strength he had, which seemed to be diminishing with every progressing second, he slowly lifted up his hand and began to wipe away the blood and tears from her face.

"I'm sorry . . . I didn't do a better job protecting you," he whispered achingly, his hand trembling as he strained to touch her, to still take care of her.

"No, no. You did great," she assured him quickly. Her lower lip quivered when she brought a hand up to place over his hand, to help keep it on her cheek. "You did so great."

Though she tried to stop it, she couldn't control the tears that fell, the tears that glided down from her eyes and touched his hand. She could not control the tears that caused Tae Hyun to gaze at her regrettably.

"Tae Hyun," Yoori whispered. The hopelessness in his expression was killing her. "It's okay. You're going to be okay."

"I didn't want you . . . to be here," he said quietly. Then, unable to hold in his desire to be near her warmth, he forced his body to move closer to her. With his hand still on her cheek, he pressed his forehead against hers. While his slow breath intermingled with hers, she felt his body tremble even more. It was as though it was beginning to lose all of its strength to go on. Agony and regret throbbed in his shaky voice when he painfully added, "I didn't want you . . . here. I didn't want you . . . to see me like this . . ."

Yoori began to choke on her own tears. She shook her head, her soul twisting in excruciating knots when she grasped the reality of her life.

Tae Hyun . . . Tae Hyun was dying.

Her Snob . . . was *dying*.

"I'm sorry, Brat." His face contorted in torture while they shook where they sat, their hearts and souls never hurting more. "I didn't want you to see me like this."

This was when Yoori lost it.

"Tae Hyun, please," she begged from the depths of her breaking heart. A shattered plea poured from her quivering voice. "Please stop leaving me."

His eyes glistened at her words. His hand not only shook from his deteriorating strength, but also from the despair that had plagued him.

"I'm sorry. I'm so sorry." There was so much pain in his voice that she could hear his heart bleeding at the sight of her crying like this. "I never wanted to leave you. I . . . I never wanted to make you cry again."

The tears that he held in began to bubble relentlessly in his eyes when another realization washed upon him.

Regret rippled in his gaze.

"I wanted to take you to Paris," he breathed out remorsefully, knowing that he would never have the chance to do this now. "I wanted to *show* you Paris."

These statements alone were the breaking point for her.

The sobs wouldn't stop ripping out of her chest. Her heart galloped against her ribcage, begging to jump out so it could hold onto Tae Hyun one last time.

"Please don't go," Yoori begged as she trembled uncontrollably. Hot tears glided down her cheeks. Hopelessness filled her hollow and aching heart. "You know I can't do this without you. You know that I can't live without you." She bit her lips at the thought of something so unimaginable. "I *can't* be without you."

Misery filled his eyes as he shook his head at what she said.

"Don't follow me," he told her painfully. His tormented eyes implored her to listen to him, to never do something so foolish. He did not want her to do what his mother had done. He did not want her to take her own life to follow him. "Don't follow me. I don't want you . . . to follow me."

Yoori was past listening.

"Tae Hyun, please," she whispered desperately, her mind completely unraveling. Her eyes begged him to stay even though she knew that if he really had the choice, then he wouldn't do this to her.

He would never make her cry; he would *never* leave her.

Yet, even when she knew this, she couldn't stop herself from begging him not to leave her.

"Please stay with me," she cried past her sobs. "Please don't leave. Please stop leaving me."

An endless stream of tears dripped from his eyes. The truth of what was happening was hitting them. They knew the end was near and that the inevitable was coming.

He stared at her, and at that moment, she could see his life flash through the souls of his eyes.

"You're worth all of it," he told her, the truth of his words coming from the depths of his soul. Gazing at her, his tears fell and mixed with hers as they dripped onto the ground. "You've been nothing but worth it."

Dying to be close to her, he leaned in and brushed his soft lips against hers. Their quivering and heartbroken lips kissed one another desperately. Tears continued to shed from their eyes as they kissed like lovers once separated, as they kissed like lovers about to be separated.

Neither wanted to let the other go. Both wanted to prolong this moment for the eternities to come . . .

"I love you," Yoori finally uttered, unable to control the desperation ravaging her very being.

She hugged him tightly and sobbed into their embrace. She thought about all that they had been through. She thought about everything they had shared together. And finally, she thought about how much she loved him with all her dying soul.

Burying her face into his shoulder, she allowed her body to shake as every inch of her struggled to touch Tae Hyun, as every inch of her being tried to remember the feeling of his warmth one final time.

"I love you," he told her, his tears dripping relentlessly. He rested his chin on the top of her head before he buried his face into her hair. He wanted to remember her warmth, her scent, and her essence before the end came for him. He kissed the back of her head and moved his lips close to her ear. His next words were spoken with desperation, with undying promise. "I will *always* love you."

And then, with one final kiss to her cheek, Tae Hyun allowed the last of his tears to fall as he tightened his embrace on her, allowing the cells on his skin to cherish the feel of her for the final time. He nuzzled his face into the side of her neck and just breathed slowly. He swallowed past the pain and agony and slowly . . . very slowly . . . closed his eyes. The last of his tears dripped onto her neck before a hushed silence suddenly came over him.

"Tae Hyun?" Yoori softly prompted when she felt him go still.

She raised her gaze. Her shaking hand grazed his cheek, trying to get him to open his eyes.

"Tae Hyun?" She touched his face, feeling her fingers tremble as she lightly shook him, the breath within her stalling in her pained chest.

"Tae Hyun?" she called out again, her body quivering as she stared up at his pale and sleeping face.

"*Snob?*" she uttered breathlessly, desperately shaking him again and again to wake him up.

She did not believe that he was gone.

She was convinced he would come back, that was why she sat there for thirty seconds, her eyes never leaving his face.

Tae Hyun's coming back, she told herself. *I just know he is.*

Thirty seconds then became forty-eight seconds.

Forty-eight seconds became one minute.

One minute then became one minute and thirty seconds.

It was after two minutes did Yoori stop counting.

It was after two minutes and nine seconds did Yoori's eyes blur beyond recognition with red-hot tears.

It was after two minutes and twenty seconds did Yoori feel her world disintegrate as she covered her hands over her mouth in agony.

It was after two minutes and twenty-nine seconds did tear after tear escape from her eyes as she sobbed quietly to herself.

It was after two minutes and fifty-nine seconds, where she continued to sob there, staring at his lifeless body, did Yoori finally admit to herself that Tae Hyun wasn't coming back.

He wasn't coming back for her.

He left her . . .

. . . and he was *never* coming back.

A voiceless sob escaped her tormented chest as the force of a volcano erupted from her once peaceful state. She shook and shook for a moment. An ocean of tears gathered in her eyes before the wall broke, the flood came in, and the destruction began . . .

"Taeeeeee Hyuunnn! Oh God, no! Taeeeee Hyunnnnnnnn! Please wake up! Please don't leave me!"

She was dying.

Every part of her heart, her body, and her entire soul was dying.

Cops, who somehow appeared without her noticing, made themselves known when they surrounded her and did their best to calmly pull her from Tae Hyun. They tried to separate her from Tae Hyun, but Yoori wouldn't have any of it.

"Taeee Hyunnn!" she sobbed uncontrollably. Her voice and body trembled as she crawled back to him, wrapped herself around him, and hugged his body with all the strength she had.

Every time they tried to pull her away, she would push them off of her and tighten her grasp on him. Desperate to feel his warmth before they took him from her, she greedily held onto him and cried her sorrow into his chest.

"Tae Hyun . . . Tae Hyun . . ." she sobbed in pure agony, wrapping herself tighter around him.

She buried her tears into his chest. Her body shook from the pain of being so badly injured from the battle and from the unequivocal pain of losing Tae Hyun.

As Yoori trembled and cried harder than she had ever cried in her life, she felt herself dying. She felt her vision dim, her lips grow dry, her skin rip apart, and her entire being go numb as it strained to hold onto the one person who made it feel so alive.

"Tae Hyun, please come back," she pleaded into his chest, hugging him one last time before her own body gave up on her, before her own tears blinded her eyes, before her own broken heart weakened, and before her world blackened in despair. "Please come back to me. Please come back to me," she begged softly. Her quiet pleas echoed throughout the amphitheater. "Please come back to me. Please come back to me . . ."

As her words swam around the last of his warmth, Yoori felt her entire world darken as one last thought invaded her mind, bringing to light that one final, *agonizing* and heart-wrenching truth that she could no longer deny.

Gone.

Her once-in-a-lifetime love was gone.

"What's your one wish tonight, Yoori?"

Epilogue: Until Paris Fades

The country of South Korea was in disarray the days following Tae Hyun's death.

Tae Hyun, Ji Hoon, Ju Won, and a score of other Underworld soldiers were all pronounced dead at the amphitheater upon the arrival of the police officers. The announcement of their deaths—and where and how they died—sent shockwaves throughout the country that such horrific and ghastly murders could take place.

In this state of disorder, the Underworld found itself in pandemonium as it tried to absorb the enormity of what took place.

An Young Jae, though critically injured, had flown back to Japan to answer to the "inconvenience" he had caused in the Korean Underworld. The elders and Royals in Japan were already questioning their decision in making him the Lord of their Underworld. The fact that he caused such a big catastrophe by using an Advisor in the Korean Underworld as his human shield was infuriating to them. The Underworld's most important relationships were those with their allies. Now that the new Lord had just effectively caused a rift between the two Underworlds, it was an understatement to say that this important relationship had been severed, so much so that the extremists within the Korean Underworld wanted to go to war with Japan to make Young Jae pay for his offenses.

In adjunction to this, as the world began to question the existence of an underground society powerful enough to perpetuate a crime on such a grand scale, the Korean Underworld was facing more pandemonium than any other entity.

Once considered the most powerful Underworld in the world, Korea's Underworld had found itself divided after the death of two Kings and an exiled Queen. The 3rd layer was without a monarch. Ultimately, with no King or Queen to govern the biggest layer in the Underworld pyramid, the Korean Underworld had now found itself at an impasse. It was completely unsure of its standing for the future as it attempted to ride out its anarchy.

As this pandemonium took place, Hae Jin, Kang Min, Jae Won, Chae Young, and Chae Young's father were all safely out of the country. Unfathomable grief plagued them the moment they found out about Tae Hyun's death and about Yoori's condition in the hospital. Helpless as they couldn't attend Tae Hyun's funeral and powerless as they didn't know where Yoori was, all they could do was cry to themselves as they sat by the phone, praying for a phone call from the lone survivor found at the scene of the unspeakable crime—the lone survivor who was rushed to the hospital and was waiting to be taken into custody.

"I need to question her," the investigator announced to the doctor standing outside her hospital ward. He stood tall in his black suit, his dark eyes challenging the doctor to stand in his way.

"I'm sorry, sir," the meek doctor replied. Dressed in a white overcoat over his black suit, there was pity in his voice as he went on. "Her body had been badly assaulted, and she's been through a substantial amount of emotional stress. She's in no condition to speak to anyone."

"She's the primary, sole, and key witness in giving us information about a secret underground society that had been the cause of massacres that have taken place all over our country," the investigator said impatiently. "It doesn't matter if she's in no condition to speak to anyone," he went on, brushing past the doctor. He walked into the high-security hospital ward of the young, unidentified woman. "It's been two and a half weeks. I need to talk to her, and I need to talk to her *now*—"

The investigator was abruptly silenced when he laid eyes on the room before him. His breath caught in his throat. His dark eyes widened as he stared at the empty bed and the opened hospital window. He moved to assess the white drapes that were dancing in the wind. A look of doom overcame his face. Realization hit him that his key witness—his only witness—had escaped from custody. And if the simple fact that she was able to escape from a high-security hospital wasn't enough, the fact that she was also able to escape without so much as alerting an officer was astounding.

The investigator let out a curse.

He knew all too well how skillful she must be to be able to escape with such ease, even in spite of her extensive injuries. Another curse escaped from him. Although he radioed for back up to find her, he knew in the back of his mind that if she was gone, then much like the wind, she was never going to be found again.

■ ■ ■

The world was quiet when the soles of her boots met the wooden structure of the dock.

Stepping forward while the dark lake glittered under the glow of the full moon, all that she could hear was the sound of wind blowing in the cool night. Its calm chill swept over the slumberous lake, the sleeping grass, and the soothing world around her.

As her emotionless eyes stared into a space of nothingness, she continued to tread down the creaking dock. Her fatigued face grew paler and paler as the seconds ticked away. Though she was quiet as could be, the device pressed against her ear was overflowing with frantic worry.

"Boss?" Jae Won's concerned voice came over the line, streaming out of the cellphone. "Boss, please tell us where you are. We'll come get you. We'll come get you, then we'll all leave together again."

"I can't leave him," she breathed out, her voice barely audible over the wind. Undeterred by their imploring voices, she continued to walk down the dock. Her dazed eyes continued to gaze at the dark lake while wind streamed through her hair.

"Yoori!" She could hear Chae Young's desperate cries after she grabbed the phone from Jae Won. "Yoori, please! Tell us where you are!"

"Boss, please," came Kang Min's pleading voice.

In the background, soft sobs emanated from Hae Jin. "Yoori, please," Hae Jin begged. "Don't do this!"

The worry in Hae Jin's voice—in all their voices—was a pain that she could not bear, especially given that she couldn't give them what they wanted. Their presence, their worry, and their love—they only served to remind her of the one who was no longer there . . .

"Please just tell us where you are," Kang Min implored, concern undulating in his voice. "Jae Won and I will come for you. We'll bring you back here so that you can be with us."

"It is safer for all of you to no longer be around me," she told them, knowing very well about all the events that were transpiring in the Underworld. "The chaos I created isn't forgotten, nor will it be forgiven. Some gave their words that they won't come after me, but others will come looking for me. They will not give up until they find me."

She knew her Underworld far too well. Albeit there was a high probability that the majority would keep their words, all it took was one individual to break the agreement. And because of this small chance alone, she could never go back to her loved ones. She would never risk the lives of the people she loved again—she would never let anyone die for her again.

"Boss—"

"Please don't come looking for me," she said with finality, her decision set. "Just stay out of the country and be safe." She briefly closed her eyes to prepare for the despair in her next words. "Just forget about me."

"Yoori, what are you doing?" Hae Jin whispered, horrified. "Why are you talking like that?" Pained emotions swelled in Hae Jin's voice as she desperately went on. "Please just tell us where you are. I want you here with us. Please be here with us."

"I can't leave him," Yoori said again, her voice completely broken as she reached the end of the dock. "I can't leave him. I'm sorry. I'm so sorry."

She bit her lips to keep the tears from inundating her voice. She had to save her composure to bid her final goodbye to them. That was the only reason why she called them. She wanted to hear their voices for the very last time.

"I love you, all of you," she whispered before finally ending the call, before finally taking her cursed self out of their lives. "Please . . . be safe."

"No! Don't—!"

Yoori closed her eyes in agony and allowed her cellphone to slip from her grasp, and along with it, the life with the loved ones she would never put in danger again. The phone pierced the air and plunged into the lake with a soft splash, silencing the voice of her friends, while inviting the company of silence to drown out her ears and bring peace to her mind.

Silence.

Finally silence.

Standing at the edge of that dock, she held the black hoodie that she wore during the arena battle—the hoodie that belonged to the person she loved most in this world. With her hand clutching tightly onto the fabric, she allowed her quiet eyes to take in the horizon that stretched ahead of her.

She gazed at the glorious moon, the stars that bejeweled the night's sky, the twinkling crystals reflecting atop the tranquil lake, and the vast world in the distance. While she did this, birds flew overhead, giving out an ambiance of unpolluted peace.

How odd it felt for Yoori. It felt odd to watch as this world continued to revolve so beautifully, so lightheartedly. Such peace made her wonder how the world around her could be so calm and beautiful when she was so tired, so broken. How could this part of the world still feel so magical . . . when nothing but darkness had spread over her life?

Yoori remained stoic until a sudden breeze swept past her, running over the bandaged bare arms that couldn't be covered by the black blouse she was wearing. Shivers raked her body, reminding her with simple realization that she was alive, that she didn't die at the arena like she thought she would. The simple shiver painfully reminded her that the one who always kept her warm was no longer with her.

He would no longer be able to keep her warm again; she would no longer feel his warmth—never again.

She was alive . . . and *he wasn't*.

Then, without any warning, as the magnitude of this realization fell upon her, her knees buckled, triggering her to fall to the ground. Her legs collapsed into a kneeling position with a loud crash. While pain shot up and down her legs, tear after tear flowed out as she was reminded of all the pain she felt—all the agony that would never leave her for as long as she lived.

Tae Hyun.

Her Tae Hyun, her Snob . . . was no longer alive.

He left her.

He left her, and he was never coming back to her.

". . . Tae Hyun," she sobbed brokenly. Tears dripped into the lake as she pleaded for him to come back for her, to take her away from this place and save her from the misery of being without him. The necklace she wore hung from her neck, the silver ring crying with her as her tears kissed over it.

"Please," she pleaded agonizingly. Her hand rose to the moon in longing, in desperation. She reached out to it as though she was reaching out to her beloved. "*Please take me with you* . . ." She shook and shook, despair washing over her and drowning her in her own ocean of tears. "Please let me be with you . . ." she continued past the sobs in her pained chest.

Crippled with heartache, she pressed her forehead against the dock and cried her sorrow into the wooden foundation. She was unable to do anything but cry for the love of her life.

The pain she felt was unbearable, unimaginable.

It hurt to breathe.

It hurt to live.

It hurt to *exist* . . .

Lifting her head up, she leaned over the dock to lifelessly stare at the lake. Her glistening eyes numbly followed the trail of her trickling tears. Envy ensued within her once she saw her tears drown into the mercy of the lake beneath her.

She felt envy for the tears that were shed; she felt envy for how easily they disappeared unto the clemency of the lake, unto the leniency of oblivion where they didn't have to feel pain ever again—*where they could be with Tae Hyun again.*

A powerful gust of wind came over the world, whipping her hair and clothes about. With a sense of clarity filling her eyes, she numbly pressed her hands on the ground and pushed herself up. She stood unsteadily at the end of the creaking dock, her anguished eyes gazing at the peaceful lake like it was a salvation, like it held the key to freeing her from all this torture.

She wasn't strong enough for this. She wasn't strong enough to live like this, to spend every second of forever missing Tae Hyun. She wasn't strong enough for the pain. She wanted it to end. She just wanted it all to end so she could be with him again.

I want to be with you again . . .

With broken-hearted tears still slipping from her eyes, Yoori lifted her left foot up. She was ready to allow the wind to carry her into the dark lake when another violent breeze whipped over her, causing the hoodie to slam into the pocket of her jeans. The wind hit it with such impact that it was able to free something that was stuck to the top edge of her pocket. Freed from its captivity was a rolled up piece of paper that fell onto the wooden dock.

Distracted momentarily, her eyes followed the descent of the innocuous object. Yoori stared at it numbly, watching as the small object hid in the nook of the dock to keep itself from being blown away. Unable to help herself, as something deep within her was urging her to inspect it, she crouched down. She retrieved the rolled up paper from the ground and unraveled it to appraise its contents.

Her eyes widened.

Yoori felt her heart expand after she read the contents and realized what this piece of paper was.

A mentor is in town.
I'll be out all day.
You probably didn't remember and
I didn't want to wake you
but have fun on your day off.
Don't do anything I would do.
--TH

It was the note that Tae Hyun wrote to her during their "boss-and-assistant" days.

Overcome with its sudden appearance, Yoori covered her mouth in disbelief. Warmth suspended over her as she held onto a note that Tae Hyun wrote to her so long ago. She held his note in her hand like it was a priceless artifact. Tears bubbled in her eyes as she greedily soaked in his writing. The note only served to remind her of how far they had come and how much she loved him.

She loved him so much.

So much so that even a simple note from him from months ago could make her feel warm inside and quell the storm brewing within her, if only for a fleeting moment. She cried softly, her tears trickling onto the piece of paper. As her tears moistened the note, it revealed a shadow of something on the back of the letter.

Holding her breath, she flipped the note over.

Yoori felt her world stop in its revolution when she read what was written on the back. It was a piece of writing so small that she had never noticed it before. She desperately read the contents of the words. Her heart rate accelerated while she read a message that was meant to pertain to him and Yoori separating that day when she took her day off.

P.S.
Don't miss me too much, Brat.

Below it, in a smudged up area that appeared to have been erased by Tae Hyun, she could read the additional message he left her a lifetime ago. It affected her more today than it could ever affect her months back.

P.P.S.
I'll miss you.

As soon as she read this, Yoori then remembered one of his last words to her before he left her. Words that haunted her—words that would prevent her from doing what she wanted to do to escape from the misery of missing him every second of every day.

"... Please don't go," Yoori begged as she trembled uncontrollably. Hot tears glided down her cheeks. Hopelessness filled her hollow and aching heart. "You know I can't do this without you. You know that I can't live without you." She bit her lips at the thought of something so unimaginable. "I can't be without you."

Misery filled his eyes as he shook his head at what she said.

"Don't follow me," he told her painfully. His tormented eyes implored her to listen to him, to never do something so foolish. He did not want her to do what his mother had done. He did not want her to take her own life to follow him. "Don't follow me. I don't want you ... to follow me."

Expelling a hardened and pained breath, Yoori felt the tides change within her. She painfully abandoned all thoughts about jumping into the lake. Instead, she allowed her body to fall back to the foundation of the dock.

Tears shed from her eyes when she realized she wasn't going to do it.

Yoori held the note close to her chest while she sat at the edge of the dock. She rested her hands just above their necklace and closed her eyes in resolve.

She wasn't going to do it.

It did not matter how much she wanted to free herself from the pain. She couldn't disappoint Tae Hyun like this.

He died to keep her safe—to keep her alive.

He died for her, and now . . . she had to live for him.

No matter how much pain there was to come, no matter how unbearable those lonely nights would be, no matter how agonizing the years to come would be, she was resigned to endure this simply because she loved Tae Hyun more than she loved herself. Simply because whatever he wanted, she wanted to give to him.

Looking out into the lake as she held all the worldly possessions that belonged to her and Tae Hyun beside her, she forced a smile to appear on her lips. She grew lost in the horizon that she once gazed into when they first sat on this dock. She gradually allowed herself to breathe again, to take things one second at a time—to slowly breathe and live again.

"You're worth it," she whispered long seconds later, still feeling all the pain there was to feel. Only this time, she was determined to endure it—all of it.

He was the only one she would do this for; he was the only one she loved more than her own life.

"You're worth all of it."

Laying her body across the wooden dock—while hugging the hoodie close to her and allowing her tears to drip into the fabric—she fixed her gaze on the breathtaking horizon and made preparations to close her eyes so she could dream about him and a love she would never forget.

How she would go on after this, she still wasn't sure. How long before the Underworld would find her, or if they would even care to find her, she was uncertain. How agonizing and heart-wrenching the pain to come was a thing she couldn't estimate. How she would continue to live and breathe without the love of her life by her side was something that still eluded and terrified Yoori. The only thing she knew with certainty was that she would continue to breathe for him, to live for him—just like he wanted her to.

All that she knew was that she wanted to lie there and stay there for as long as she could, perhaps until the end of her lifetime. All she wanted to do was stay at the place where the magic began for them—the place where the magic of his existence would always be her comfort, her guiding light, and her source of strength in her times of frailty.

She wasn't going to leave the lake house; she wasn't going to leave him.

"I love you," her soft voice promised before the weight of sleep fell onto her, claimed her, and took her away with its magic. "I will *always* love you."

As the wind graced her face and as the last of her tears dried from the kiss of the breeze, Yoori allowed the sweet lullaby of the lake to enrapture her senses and lull her into a peaceful slumber.

The last thing she heard before she fell asleep was *his* voice.

His voice when the magic began—when they first came to this dock. His voice to lead her through the darkness, his voice to give her strength, and his voice to keep with her through all the days of her life . . .

■ ■ ■

". . . What's your one wish tonight, Yoori?" he whispered softly, purposely keeping his voice low so she didn't wake up entirely.

Yoori was silent for a while, still registering the question as she fought to stay awake. She was slowly losing.

"I want us to both find Paris," she answered slowly and thoughtlessly, drifting further and further into a deep slumber.

"What would be your one wish?" she managed to mutter out before she finally drifted into the land of no return.

Tae Hyun appraised her. Hilarity suffused his eyes as he watched his precious assistant fall unto the mercy of her own slumber.

"It would make sense that you'd fall asleep as soon as it was my turn to answer," he muttered with bitter amusement. He shook his head at her and the predictability that came with the spoiled one's behavior. She got away with too much when it came to him. Unfortunately, he seemed to always be the stupid one who ended up spoiling her rotten by *always* allowing her to get away with anything she wanted. "Damn little Brat . . ."

He watched as a cold breeze flew through them, causing her to shiver from the cold.

Unable to help himself, he stood up and gave her full estate of the purple blanket by covering his portion over hers. Then, after sitting back down on the dock—before he could consider his own actions—he bent his knees up and carefully positioned her small body between his legs. Mindful to not wake her up, he became her source of warmth by gently embracing her from behind.

The shuddering of her body instantly ceased while her petite figure instinctively relaxed under his hold.

At the sight of this, Tae Hyun couldn't help but allow a smile to grace his lips. How strange it was for him to feel so protective over a girl. He didn't understand his own set of emotions when it came to her. There was something about Choi Yoori that softened areas of him that he once thought were ice-cold. There was something about her that brought out emotions he thought had left him after being immersed in the darkness of the Underworld for so long.

He sighed internally, determined to keep himself from venturing into an area of thoughts that he should never privy himself to. To further help his cause, Tae Hyun briefly tore his gaze from her sleeping face, silently begrudging the effect this strange and energetic girl had on him.

454

While keeping his eyes on the vast expanse of the shimmering lake, the question she posed before she fell asleep came floating back into his mind. It veered his peaceful state off course as he considered the question again.

"What would be your one wish?"

Double-checking to make sure she was asleep before he went on—his heart never weighing more than it did as he spoke with nothing but emotions and instincts—he took the opportunity to answer her.

"I think," he began, his eyes never leaving her sleeping ones. His warm breath caressed her cheek. "I think it would be nice if I became human again and fell for you."

Before he could sift rationale into this illogical train of thoughts, the depths of his heart and what was left of his soul continued to carry the words out.

"I imagine it would be nice if I could love you unconditionally with no guilt or qualms," he mused to himself. For the first time in his life, he was speaking without filter, without thought, and without care. "It would be nice if I could make you unreservedly happy as we fade into the enchantment of our own world and have that undying, once-in-a-lifetime love that the world dreams about. The type that would be worth living for—*the type that would be worth dying for*."

He laughed self-mockingly while taking a second to stare at her sleeping face.

What an odd thing for a King who had everything to desire, but Tae Hyun couldn't control his yearnings. Something about how Yoori spoke about finding her once-in-a-lifetime love, and giving the guy the honor of taking her to Paris, made him jealous beyond all measure. He was jealous because in the deepest core of him, he wanted to be the one who gave her that type of magic.

He wanted to be the one who gave her the city she wanted all her life.

Tae Hyun smiled bitterly, knowing that a King as ruthless and power-hungry as him would never have the opportunity to do any of this.

Perhaps in another lifetime, he would be the guy who would possess the strength and willpower to not only stop his own greed from taking over his soul, but also be strong enough for her. Perhaps in another lifetime—even through the dark shadows of his own life—he'd emerge from the unforgiving darkness and find the mercy of being able to welcome Paris to the Underworld—to his own personal Underworld. Regardless of the impossibilities that something like this would ever come to fruition, it did not stop Tae Hyun from voicing out the remainder of a wish he never knew he wanted.

"I think it would be worth it to wish that I get"—he inhaled deeply before allowing the unspeakable words to come out of his lips—"to be the one who disappears with you and shows you the magic of Paris." He smiled, easing her bangs away from her sleeping face. "And if the impossible occurs, then I'll whisper in your ears:

"*Choi Yoori . . . I found Paris. It's a thousand times more beautiful than I could have ever dreamed it to be. So, you know what that means, right?* It means that anything and everything that has led to this moment has been worth it to me because it means that I've found you—I've finally found my Paris. Philosophers spend their entire lives trying to find the meaning of life and they never find it. But right here, right now . . . being with you, being human with you, being unconditionally in love with you—*this* is heaven, *this* is the meaning of life, *this* is what makes life worth living."

He quietly laughed to himself and stroked her sleeping face, his heart never in its wildest dreams imagining that his thoughtless wish would one day come true—that he would look into her eyes and say this to her months later in the privacy of their lake house, right before he gifted her with the city she had wanted all her life.

"It means that from this moment forth, I am unconditionally and eternally yours."

No longer able to resist the temptation, he allowed his lips to brush against her cheek in the faintest of whispers. Then, knowing that it was time to take his assistant home before the spoiled one caught a cold, he picked her off the wooden foundation. He walked down the dock with her in his arms, listening as she murmured sweet nothings while comfortably nuzzling herself into his chest.

Both of them did not realize then how their wishes would come true, and how that night would change the course of their young lives forever.

"Death will never part us. I'll love you until the last breath of forever; I'll love you until Paris fades . . ."

The End

ABOUT THE AUTHOR

Con Template currently resides in California. When she is not outside with her DSLR capturing reality, you can find her in between realities when she is writing about the Underworld, the Anointed Stars, the Omegas, the Ancients, and the Covenant.

She is introducing a new series, An Eternity of Eclipse. The first book in the series is scheduled to be release in the Summer of 2015.

You can follow her at *contemplate13.wordpress.com* or *twitter.com/contemplate13*.

"Something big is coming ..."

An Eternity of Eclipse

Coming July 2015

■■

Breaking News:

6-Year-Old Slays Entire Family

December 26th, 1996

At midnight, police officers responded to numerous calls from residents in Serenity, a prosperous gated community in the heart of the country. Neighbors reported hearing numerous gunshots from the Hwang home, a wealthy family known for their endless fortune that derived from owning some of the best-known luxury hotels in the world. When police officers arrived at the estate, they were greeted with a horrific scene fit for a scary movie.

"It was terrible," Officer Joo stated as his men carried out four body bags from the home. "As soon as we walked in, the smell of death just permeated the room."

Mr. Hwang, Mrs. Hwang, and both of their older children (15-year-old daughter and 13-year-old son) were all shot and stabbed to death. The only survivor was their youngest, a 6-year-old daughter. Found covered in blood with a gun and knife in hand, officers were horrified to find that the sole survivor was also a likely suspect in the murders of the Hwang family. The child was taken into custody for psychological evaluations and a full investigation is underway.

Brought to you by **THE-SERENITY-CHRONICLES**

■■

Made in the USA
Lexington, KY
23 April 2015